I0743738

# THE IKIRI DUOLOGY

## KEPT FROM CAGES
## GIVEN TO DARKNESS

## PHIL WILLIAMS

## MMXXIII

Copyright © 2023 by Phil Williams

The moral right of Phil Williams to be identified as the author of this work has been asserted by him in accordance with the Copyright, Designs and Patents Act 1988.
All the characters in this book are fictitious, and any resemblance to actual persons living or dead is purely coincidental.
Warning: delving into the secrets of Ikiri and attempting any of the activities presented in this book may prove dangerous. The Legion are watching.
*Kept From Cages* first printed by Rumian Publishing 2020.
*Given to Darkness* first printed by Rumian Publishing 2021.

All rights reserved.

This book or any portion thereof may not be reproduced or used in any manner whatsoever without the express written permission of the publisher except for the use of brief quotations in a book review.

ISBN-13: 978-1-913468-20-0

Cover design by P. Williams

Published by Rumian Publishing

Visit **www.phil-williams.co.uk** online for more information and regular news from Phil Williams. Join the newsletter to be the first to hear about new projects.

# Contents

Kept From Cages ... 1
Given To Darkness ... 193

# KEPT FROM CAGES

# 1

"Don't blame yourself," Reece said, hefting Stomatt's unconscious bulk up the dirt track. "None of us guessed he lost that much blood."

"Even still," Caleb replied, stooping to help. "Shoulda been me behind the wheel. Always shoulda been me behind the wheel."

"He insisted, didn't he? What were you gonna do, two maniacs shooting at us?"

"Insist back!" Caleb's eyes shone in the dark. "Coulda said, 'No, listen, Sto, I'm driving.' Coulda got us clear with no hassle."

"We *got* clear, and you did *good*." Reece grinned. A grin that could charm the devil's horns off his head, Leigh-Ann liked to say. Even in a thick boiler suit, torn and dirtied from a day's fighting and fleeing, his hair dyed a murky green. They might be filthy and stinking and hurt in places they were yet to check, stranded on some unlit path to the middle of nowhere, but they were damn alive after taking on a billion-dollar company of thugs. Yeah, their car had flipped and they were still a long way from the safety of Stilt Town, let alone home, and Stomatt might be seriously injured – but they'd done what Reece said they would do and *won*. That's what the smile said, and Caleb smiled back.

"Sure," he said. "But we maybe shoulda switched driver. Made for the main roads after all?"

Reece checked the wood-panel house ahead again. A little further and they'd hit its two-step porch, knock and see who, exactly, lived in the empty fields halfway between Waco and Shreveport. Only an occasional tree on the black horizon told them they were anything short of stumbling through limbo itself. But lights shone yellow in the cross-barred windows, behind curtains – beacons to salvation.

"Reckon they cannibals?" Caleb said.

Reece traded his it's-all-good smile for his that'd-be-a-laugh one. Even if this wasn't the home of good honest farmhands, there wasn't much the Cutjaw Kids couldn't handle. They dragged Stomatt across a shingle drive, the scrape of boots on stone announcing their approach. Caleb grumbled, "Don't like leaving Leigh-Ann alone back there neither."

"She's better than fine," Reece said. "You wanna worry? Worry about how we're gonna spend all that money once we get back to Cutjaw."

The floorboards creaked as they climbed the steps. The only sound besides them breathing. All those lights on and nothing happening inside: no talking, no TV, no movement.

"Think they're not in?" Caleb said.

"Find out, won't we? Lower him here, easy."

With Stomatt propped against the wall, Reece straightened out the boiler suit and patted down his legs, then twisted his gun belt round so the pistol was hidden to his rear. Caleb caught his eye like he wanted to suggest something worrisome, and Reece smiled it off before it was said. Because everyone liked Reece once he got talking. He rapped a knuckle on the door. "Excuse me, good people! I know it's late but we're in bad need of assistance." No reply. "Had ourselves an accident back up the road. Damnedest thing, you wouldn't believe – car on its roof, and we got a man down."

Nothing. Caleb worried, "Think they heard us coming, hid away?"

"Why'd anyone hide from a couple harmless musicians?" Reece said. Caleb's eye tracked down to the gun belt. Reece curled his nose: even if they did see La Belle Riposte holstered there, it was an instrument as exquisite as his trumpet. And they were in Texas – who *didn't* have a gun? He knocked again. "Hate to be a burden, but my friend here lost a lot of blood – can't even stand right now." Still nothing. "We're decent people, like yourselves – just trying to get back home."

Caleb shifted. "We could try another one?"

"Another house?" Reece raised an eyebrow to indicate the hundred miles of nothing surrounding them. He called out, "We don't need to stay long, just got to patch up my friend – get him some water, fresh bandages. I gotta insist on that much at least." One last pause. "We'll make our own entrance if we have to."

"Better y'all go on your way!" a gruff voice finally answered – a big man.

"Gladly, with the barest assistance!" Reece answered amiably.

"Get on! What you're looking for's not here."

"All the same, if you could open up, it'd save –"

The door swung in on a man with a double-barrelled shotgun. "I said –"

Reece spoke over him fast: "No need for that, sir, we didn't come looking for trouble. Name's Reece Coburn, horn-maestro, as reviewed in *Two Shoots Magazine*, and this here's my associate Caleb 'Low Bone' Gray – heard of him?"

The man's mouth hung open in surprise, his threat trapped there. He was large with over-indulgence, someone that could knock you down with a swat if it didn't give him a heart attack. His ruddy face was partly hidden by a tangled beard, and he had on a faded check shirt, leather suspenders clipped to mud-caked jeans. Over his shoulder, in a doorway down the hall, was another man, as lean as the first was wide, snub-nosed, warty-faced, with shirt and jeans as tatty as a scarecrow's. Unarmed and nervous.

"What?" The shotgun farmer recovered slowly from Reece's friendliness, eyes darting to the green hair and back. "No, listen here – get on back down that road or I'll –"

"We would *kindly* get on," Reece said, "but see, Caleb and me with our tender frames, we're not up to carrying this burden far." Reece scuffed a foot to draw attention to Stomatt. The farmer looked at the bleached-blond oaf splattered black with dry blood.

"The hell –"

Reece stepped into the kitchen, pushed the shotgun down with one hand and drew his pistol with the other. Stunned the farmer with his speed, as his companion exclaimed, "Jesus!"

"Stay put, friend, and relax," Reece said, grip tight on the shotgun. "I got no intention of hurting you, I mean it. Water, medicine, shelter, that's all we want. Our priority's keeping him alive. Anything else is a bonus we won't assume." Moving around the farmer, Reece sped on, "You *can't* have heard of us – two parts of the Cutjaw Kids – otherwise you'd know we're decent people, only ever hurt them that deserve it." The slim man threw an instinctive glance back, into the next room. Blocking that doorway for a reason. Reece slowed down. "We interrupt something?"

The farmer went rigid on his shotgun, for a second seeming like he might pull the trigger just to shake Reece off. Reece warned him against it with a casual wave of the pistol.

"Caleb, you haul Sto in here?"

"I'll try," Caleb answered honestly, and gave the farmer an apologetic look as he started to manoeuvre Stomatt's bulk through the doorway.

"Listen," Reece said. "We got problems enough of our own not to interfere with yours. But I think you oughta let go of this gun now."

The farmer didn't shift. Caleb huffed upright from struggling with Stomatt. "Want I should cover him, Reece?"

"Wish you didn't have to."

"Go to hell," the farmer said.

"That'll be a yes."

Caleb drew a pistol from inside his boiler suit. "Got him."

The farmer gave him a sceptical glance. People tended to go one of two ways with Caleb; kind-faced, softly-spoken, hunched with self-consciousness, he struck people as either slow enough to take advantage of or too quietly calm to trust. After a moment, the farmer settled on the latter, and finally loosened his grip on the shotgun. Reece took it. "Now what's the fuss?"

The slim one straightened up. "You ain't coming through here, no way –"

The man flattened himself against a wall as Reece pushed past into the next room. The farmer called out, an explanation or a dismissal. Reece didn't hear it. A woman on the far side of the room gasped, but she wasn't his concern. Dead centre, with the other furniture cleared to the sides, was a girl no older than seven, sat on a wooden chair. Her arms, legs and chest were bound by thick leather belts. Her black hair hung in locks over hazel skin, the white of her eyes haloing big dark irises that fixed on Reece.

Reece glanced at the woman for an explanation; young but built big, in the same farming slacks as the men. Likely the farmer's daughter. She cringed at the pistol, too scared to speak. Reece turned back to Slim, who raised his hands.

"Ain't what it looks like! She's the devil, I swear!"

"What is it, Reece?" Caleb asked.

"Like y'all ain't involved?" the farmer snarled.

"What in hell kind of –" Reece spun back to the girl. "They hurt you? Jesus – what'd they do –"

He crouched, about to grab her bindings, when Slim pleaded, "No, don't!" He flinched at Reece's pistol but continued, "Look at her eyes!"

Holding his gun steady, Reece checked the girl again. Her gently dark skin was marred around the extremities: grubby at her neck, dark under the eyes and nose, scratched. She had on a white t-shirt and denim dungarees, all stained – fallen in mud a few times. Her gaze hadn't left him since he entered. Eyes massive in her face. The irises, now he looked, were red as blood.

"You see it, don't you?" Slim said.

"Don't bother, Donny," the farmer growled from the hallway. "Think they come rolling in here by chance? With all that thing's been saying?"

"Dammit," Caleb said, "let's see."

Reece frowned as Caleb pushed the farmer into the room. "That *thing*?"

"Ho-*ly* hell," Caleb gasped, over the farmer's shoulder.

"She ain't right." The farmer's daughter found her voice, a squeak. Terrified as slim Donny, getting busted like this.

"We wanted to *help* her, man!" Donny insisted. "But she says things –"

"Get yourself up against that wall," Reece said. "The pair of you. And you" – to the woman – "untie this goddamn child."

"I ain't staying." Donny made a move. "Not if she's loose."

"Please," the girl said, weakly. Donny winced. "Help me …"

Reece said, "None of y'all are leaving. Didn't I ask you to untie her?"

"Don't you dare," the farmer rumbled, before his daughter could budge.

"You miss the part where we got guns on you?" Caleb asked. "Shit, I'll do it –" He stepped forward and the farmer lunged for the gun. The pair of them twisted over it, the farmer's weight bearing them to the ground. Donny sprang for the door and tripped, the stumble making Reece's shot hit the wall where his head should've been. The farmer shouted murderously, grappling with Caleb, and the daughter screamed, as Donny dived out the room and Reece's second shot hit the doorframe.

A third shot sounded, muffled by Caleb's scuffle. The farmer's angry shout spiked and Caleb yelled, "Get this fat bastard off me!" But Reece was running through the hallway, as Donny sprawled spider-like out across the drive. Reece aimed as he reached the door, but hit a patch of Stomatt's blood and slid, landing on his rear. He scrambled upright and saw a last slither of Donny's angular joints slipping into shadow. Man moved like a damn greyhound.

Caleb grunted around the farmer's bulk and the daughter's screams turned to fierce curses. Caleb insisted, "Ma'am, you saw him attack me! Woulda killed me!"

Reece trotted back to the living room to find the farmer inert on the carpet, blood pooling under his chest. His daughter was shuddering in a crouch as Caleb stood over her, gun at his side. "Stop screaming, please – I didn't want to have to do it!"

And in the middle of the chaos sat the red-eyed girl, eyes locked on Reece again. Afraid. Reece holstered his gun and took a knee. "It's gonna be alright, cher. We've got you." The farmer's daughter kept whimpering, *no no no*.

Rapid footsteps came over the entrance boards and both Reece and Caleb spun with pistols raised. It was Leigh-Ann, running in with a MAC-10 submachine gun and a deadly look on her face. Reece yelled, "Dammit Leigh there's a kid in here!"

She shouted, "What in hell are y'all doing?"

The shrieked question stilled the room, even the farmer's daughter going quiet. The trio of gun-toting criminals looked at each other, the dead farmer and tied-up girl. Reece stood, in silent admission that this had got well out of hand.

Leigh-Ann laughed. "Shit, boys, this your idea of getting help?"

# 2

The closer he got, the more Agent Sean Tasker, Ministry of Environmental Energy, hoped something was actually wrong in the fishing village of Laukstad. He'd been sceptical flying from Tokyo to Norway, and for the three-hour drive from Tromsø, and occupied his mind trying to focus on the snow-blanketed mountains that he could describe to his daughter Rebecca, rather than consider how he was travelling especially far for this latest dead-end lead. His driver and escort, Police Inspector Akre, refused to believe there was anything worth investigating. Red-faced and cheery, he had explained that Laukstad had sporadic phone connections at the best of times, so two days without hearing from the village was nothing. Three days, by the time Tasker arrived, was slightly unusual, but not enough to raise alarm. Snowstorms might have cut them off, but the villagers would be taking care of themselves.

Tasker imagined some slick-suited bastards in corporate offices laughing at him, redirecting MEE resources to the strangest possible places, to find nothing amiss. This "lead" had come from Duvcorp, after all, a corporation known for making their own rules. Some bored Duvcorp researcher had told a newbie MEE director that they'd picked up unusual energy readings out here, so why not have an agent travel all the way from Japan to check it out? Well. It was about time he came home to debrief anyway, and he hadn't seen Helen and Rebecca in three months, but even so – the deputy director had lapped it up, insisting this contact was going behind Duvcorp's back, giving the Ministry a unique chance to subvert them. Tasker knew better than to trust that crap. Most likely, it was revenge for him hounding Duvcorp's mates in Tokyo, Mogami Industries. Some vindictive Duvcorp strategist figured exactly how to position this so that it'd be him making this hopeless journey.

But as Tasker watched the roads getting narrower, winding and remote, he found *some* hope creeping in that this might be an exception, at last, and he could actually take one of these companies down a peg and make a difference.

Duvcorp had exploded into the American automobile industry in the late 1970s and reinvested huge profits into electronics, to become world-leaders in computing technology in the '90s. Their components quickly became ubiquitous: whether you settled on a Mac or a PC, you still got a Duvcorp sticker somewhere. Making all the right connections in business and government, they soon became one of a handful of corporations who wielded as much power as the governments who might hold them accountable. And, somewhere along the way, they got wind of the technology the Ministry tried to keep out of the public eye. Unexplained phenomena, dangerous curiosities. It was simple enough to keep a lid on individuals and smaller entities, but

Duvcorp were too powerful to regulate. Putting untold lives at risk.

Every four or five months, Tasker found some way to humble a big corporation, when their latest (classified) technology was revealed to be dangerously esoteric. Ferociously catastrophic events were averted and mid-level fall-guys were imprisoned (or conveniently disappeared), and Tasker could go back to his wife and daughter proud that he was Making a Difference. He had to be, to justify staying away from home for so long, missing Rebecca growing up, leaving Helen alone, even if she always managed words of support when they spoke. He wanted to be with them both, badly, but more than that he wanted to come home knowing it was safe. These corporations were stretching their grubby claws into every corner of the world; it was only a matter of time before one of them accidentally unleashed some unholy force in their own backyard.

He'd travelled to Tokyo for that; seeing that Mogami now had connections in Ordshaw, UK, he needed to know exactly what they were up to. But Mogami's Japanese prosthetics project had been swept under the rug before Tasker had uncovered exactly what untold horrors they'd been experimenting with. They'd probably resurface in two years, building clones or engineering war spiders or something.

Everything about Laukstad felt like an opportunity to double his losses. The snow cover was thick on the roads, no one had been in or out of this area in days – all he was going to find was a town whose phone-lines had gone down. They probably had Duvcorp hardware up here, that was how the informer had known . . .

After a final turn, the village sat ominously below, at the bottom of a steep slope, by the harshly churning sea, in the eerie mid-afternoon dark. Akre grunted at the wheel to say he felt something was off. Tasker felt it too, tensing at the too-quiet scene.

They drove closer and the officer slowed right down. He whispered a Norwegian curse. Tasker leant into the windscreen to see why. Laukstad was a tiny community, not more than a dozen timber houses, a jetty and swaying boats. All unlit. Its single road was scattered with bumps of snow, like a mess of randomly placed speed bumps. The length and height of prone bodies. The closest one had a smaller bump out to the side – like an outstretched arm. Bodies was right, buried under snow.

Akre stopped, cursing again in whole sentences Tasker didn't need to translate to understand. Disbelief and fear and outrage. The officer turned a questioning face to Tasker, like he would know what was going on here. Tasker did not, but the Duvcorp lead had contacted his Ministry for a reason. Whatever this was – and it *looked* like a lot of people dead – then it must border on the unnatural. A test gone wrong, a substance spilt, or worse? A creature set loose?

"Have your gun ready," Tasker advised, drawing his own pistol from under the heavy winter coat. Akre nodded, doing the same but clutching his weapon tightly. They hopefully wouldn't need them. Whatever happened here happened days ago. When Duvcorp's leak said so.

They each took a torch and exited the 4x4 into a biting gust of wind. It passed in a second, having taken the top dusting off one of the nearest mounds, revealing boots underneath. Akre rushed ahead to brush handfuls of snow away, uncovering a man with taut clutching fingers, eyes open under a shimmer of ice, blood frozen around his neck and chest and mouth. His throat had been torn out as though by a wild animal or a jagged tool. Fishing hook or wolves, who could tell the difference now? Tasker's gut hinted worse. What lurked in the Arctic circle? The ice jackals of Archangel had been culled years ago, but it wasn't unthinkable.

Akre shook all over with horror, so Tasker patted his shoulder to indicate they move on.

There wasn't enough left of the next body's smashed face to preserve the pain and terror.

Tasker stepped away as Akre radioed back to Tromsø in stuttering starts. He noticed other mounds in the snow, now – smaller ones. Bits of debris and household items partly covered. A long pole stuck out of one buried body like a grave marker. Harpoon? Windows in the buildings were shattered. A door rocked against its hinges. Another had been broken off entirely, jammed across its entrance. Walking between the bodies, looking into the dark recesses of the houses, Tasker saw how the people had fallen, chased out of their own homes? There was blood around a door jamb. Smashed crockery in one entrance. He moved closer. Another body in there, feet pointing out, opposite direction to those that died fleeing. He crouched and gasped at the likeness. It could easily be Rebecca – a girl no older than ten with frozen blonde hair, stubby nose, and a death-mask of terror, neck raked by four claw marks and a chunk bitten from her cheek. How could this happen – what manner of monster left marks like this, a bite that size and shape? He moved from the girl to the next nearest body, a woman fallen while fleeing from the building. A horrible gash ripped from her throat. He brushed the snow away from her hand, revealing nails cracked and bloody. Whatever this was, these people had fought against it, coming and going.

"What happened?" Akre demanded, torch-hand shaking. "I don't see any animal tracks."

Tasker cleared his throat, swallowed, making like he was giving the massacred village another careful look while trying to stop his voice coming out in a frightened squeak. He tried not to picture the worst, that this was Rebecca and Helen, that this was so close to home. "Cut off out here, four hours of sunlight a day, must've been people not right in the head. Junkies on a spiked batch of drugs or outsiders with a bad religion?"

Akre wore a horrified expression Tasker was all too familiar with. The policeman could scarcely believe such a thing possible, *knowing* things like this didn't just happen, but forcing himself to take this mysterious expert's explanation seriously. Akre couldn't know there was only one reason for the Ministry to have been alerted to this. This wasn't a random attack. Someone or something had made this happen, with means that would be anything but natural.

*

"No weapons used that weren't the basic tools they had lying around," Tasker confirmed to Caffery, his handler, over the phone. "Teeth marks, clawing from fingernails, lot of blunt force, but no signs of unusual tracks in or out of the village."

"Not ice jackals, then," Caffery said.

"My instinct says there's a human element, or something close to it," Tasker admitted. Were there reports of yeti in Norway? He doubted it; this felt messier. "There was a fight, or at least the start of one. These people *thought* they could defend themselves. But so far they've not identified anyone who shouldn't have been there, and it doesn't look like anything was taken. It's like some gang of killers swept in from the mountains or off the sea and disappeared in the mist."

"A cult?" Caffery replied hopefully. "Or a particularly effective mass-murderer. Unthinkable, sure, but perfectly human."

"Except someone in Duvcorp knew it was happening."

A couple of hours of surveying with extra hands flown in from Tromsø turned up little more they could go on. Back in the main station, the officers milled about in stages between vengefully angry and utterly devastated. They insisted it never happened – people were *used* to these conditions – but he insisted back, it *could* happen. A mass psychosis brought on by isolation and dark. There was one glaring discrepancy, though: how had an Englishman happened to check on it?

For the locals' sake, Tasker settled on his usual ground somewhere between the truth and a cover. He explained that they monitored for unusual energy readings, this one being a particularly dramatic change in atmospheric pressure. Something *like* atmospheric pressure, he corrected – in case their meteorological offices disagreed. Chances were the weather had been affected by whatever Duvcorp picked up on, anyway. Could this anomaly have driven a group of people to brutal murder for no good reason? Sure, possibly.

Besides the chill mystery of exactly what had happened – and how the killers had left no traces of their retreat – Tasker found himself most concerned with what in hell it had to do with Duvcorp. Their mole must have been aware that something was going down. Concerned to the degree that they would go behind their employer's back. Tasker told Caffery, "I recommend sending a Support team up, take energy readings on the ground, see if anything unusual was left on the bodies."

"Done," Caffery replied. "You staying on the ground to ease them in?"

"I've seen all I need to," Tasker said. "I want to talk to the mole myself, as soon as possible. It was the Ordshaw Ministry that put us onto this, right? Have them pick him up."

"I can put in a request to Duvcorp's management –"

"Pick him up, Caffery, as soon as possible."

Caffery went quiet. He was technically Tasker's superior, but as Tasker was the one physically wading through these messes, it was rare that London didn't accede to his demands. "The Commission won't have us provoking a company like Duvcorp."

"Yeah, not without an airtight case, which we won't get without provocation."

"What *case*, Tasker? Duvcorp picked up on this, but it doesn't mean they're involved."

"Please, everything that company touches stinks. You don't want to pick up their mole, at least put a man on him until I get there. Which will be how long?"

Caffery sighed deeply, like Tasker was the bane of his existence. Eighteen people dead, and he had the gall to sound put out by Tasker's travel demands and willingness to cross a big company. "I'll look into it. Meantime, you keep a lid on things there."

"Already done," Tasker said. Unlike some people, he didn't need telling to do his job. But saying that, he saw more looks coming his way across the station. Upset cops, wanting to blame him, suspecting he knew more than he was letting on. Well, it couldn't be a rabid doppler; they stayed mostly hidden, and the massacre clearly wasn't the work of one creature. The venom of the *tremer vesper* might induce madness, if Duvcorp had poured that into the village's water supply. But why would they? And if they had done this deliberately, where was the clear-up? The only thing he did know was that the answers weren't here in Norway.

# 3

"Here, rest here, cher," Reece said, lowering the girl onto a squeaky bed. She weighed nothing but he had to prise her fingers off him. Her unusual eyes glowed with desperation. *Don't let go.* "Sorry you had to see that, but you're safe now, understand? How you end up here – with them?"

Her lower lip trembled.

"You're *safe* – it's over." Reece stepped back and smiled to show it, triggering tears. She pressed her face into her small hands. He glanced to the empty doorway, half-expecting Stomatt to jump in laughing at her for crying. But Stomatt was unconscious downstairs, with Leigh-Ann tending to him, while Caleb hunted after Donny. The kid was Reece's responsibility alone.

She whimpered, almost too quiet to hear, "I want to go home."

"Sure," Reece said. "Where's home, cher? How you get here?"

Sniffing in her last sobs, the girl knotted her brow against the question.

"How about a name? I'm Reece" – he put a hand on his chest – "and you?"

She braced herself, then said, "Zip."

"Your name's Zip?"

She nodded.

"Weird, but I *like* it." He wore a goofy grin. Zip watched his teeth suspiciously. "Zip's a real pretty name. These people, Zip, they take you from your family? Your school?" She shook her head. "So where you live? My friends and me, we come outta Cutjaw, Louisiana – you ever heard of a place like that?"

Another head shake, getting curious.

"Long way from here, right now. Cutjaw's like nowhere you've been, we got swamp and a river nearby, every family a different trailer. You ever slept in a trailer? No? Well, we live in them. People in Cutjaw work wood, mechanics, all good with our hands – decent, family folk."

Zip watched him warily, and her eyes ran up to the green hair.

Reece ran a hand through it, laughing. Seemed a good idea at the time – confuse anyone looking for him once he washed it back to black. "Ah, this – *not* my natural colour. Part of this shabby costume, see." He picked at the boiler suit. "We do *not* normally look like this. The Cutjaw Kids are usually the most best dressed crewe you ever saw. That's *crewe* with an *e* – making us like family. I got no brothers but Caleb and Sto are my kin. Leigh's got no dad but mine treats her like a daughter, see? You got brothers, sisters? Mama, a daddy?"

Zip considered it carefully. "Dad."

"Just a dad?"

She nodded apologetically.

"Well, stick with us and we'll be your family. Cutjaw moms raise us to take care of strangers. Talk proper round kids and ladies. Respect elders and all that. We even came into Texas to do some good." Reece pointed vaguely, probably in the direction they'd come. Maybe not. "Working with Caleb's uncle, against people that would take advantage of us in Cutjaw or elsewhere. We're good people, see?"

"You've got guns," Zip whispered.

Reece paused, then twisted his gun belt forward. "This? This isn't any old *gun*. You looking at La Belle Riposte. A work of art. Wanna hold it?"

Zip blinked disbelief. Yes, he was offering a child a gun.

"Maybe later, huh? We armed because of people like them downstairs, Zip. We been into Waco to tell some bad men *No*. Same as we told them *no* downstairs, understand?" She didn't entirely. But the kid didn't need all the details of how Steer Trust had been forcibly expanding their "Gold Star" network into Louisiana. How the gang had valiantly combined sending a message that Louisiana didn't want them with stealing a lot of money. He diverted: "Speak funny, don't I? That's Cutjaw – ain't no one talk like us, no one play music like us, no one play *cards* like us. Like that where you're from? Your home special?"

Zip remained silent. She did *not* want to talk about home.

"You local, at least? Don't look like a Texan."

Her face crumpled guiltily. "No."

Reece laughed, lightly. "Then how you get all the way out here? Cher, please. Tell me something, I'm dying here."

"I . . ." Zip searched the carpet for an answer. "I wanted to help. My daddy. He didn't know – he never let me – said I *always* should stay home –" Speaking quicker, upset. "Never follow, never talk to strangers, never *think* about it –"

"Slow down," Reece said. "Your daddy ain't gonna blame you, okay?" Her accent was a clue, at least. Cracked from dryness and crying, but refined, almost British. Fancy folk in country estates adopted accents like that. "You got a big house?"

She shook her head, then stopped rigid, realising she was giving something away.

"All right. I'll have to earn that trust, won't I? So you were supposed to stay home but followed your daddy to work, that's how it went? But these folk picked you up along the way?"

Zip swallowed, then nodded.

"So forget home a second – where might Daddy be?"

She considered this carefully. "There was a big river. A blue pyramid. Grithin."

"A griffin?"

"Gri*th*in," Zip accentuated the sound, tongue against her teeth. Definitely moneyed.

"Forgive my ignorance. Gri*th*in it is. Well I don't know that for dirt, nor a blue pyramid, but I know rivers. Gushing like the Mississippi or piddling like a creek?"

"Mississippi." Zip liked that word. "Mississippi. Yes. Mississippi. That's a very big river?"

"The biggest. But that's three hundred miles away."

She went quiet again, like she'd done something wrong.

"Hey, I'm not saying that's not it," Reece said. "Only that's a long way for a kid. Your daddy had business there, did he?"

Her lip trembled again, eyes worried. Tired, stressed.

"Tell you what, let's have a break. Important thing is we're friends now, ain't we? I'll get you a hot drink. Have Caleb put on a Cutjaw stew. You talk when you're ready, doesn't have to be a second before."

He moved towards the door and fear at being left crept into those big eyes. She voiced it in a simple, bleated word: "Reece?"

Reece grinned back in at her. "We'll take care of you. That's a promise."


Leigh-Ann perched on the chair-back with a foot where the girl had been bound, staring hard, wondering what the fuck these yokels were up to. The living room was heady with the stench of stale blood and sweat. The farmer lay against one wall, rolled in a rug, and Stomatt was hanging half off the three-seat sofa. He was even paler than usual, and his bleached-blond hair was patterned like a hyena's hide with blood and dirt. Leigh-Ann had removed his jacket and wound a clean bandage round his neck, while the farmer's daughter cowered in an armchair.

Mostly, Leigh-Ann was marvelling at how they'd managed to make a shitty day this much worse. The gunshots from the farmhouse had come right when her nerves were finally calming from the car crash, and the crash had come only when her nerves started to calm after escaping Waco. They'd started the day prepared for a fight but hoping there wouldn't be one. Only Stomatt had been overjoyed at finding more Steers in the warehouse than they expected. Now at least three of Dustin Fallon's men were injured or dead and Stomatt was shot. Leigh-Ann didn't think she'd hit anyone herself, laying down covering fire, but who knew? And now they'd offed a random farmer and had a distraught daughter hostage – a woman even younger than them.

Leigh-Ann moved to a counter and found some mail. Mr Hexley, that'd be the farmer. One addressed to Ms N. She asked, "That you? *N*?"

The daughter didn't look up.

"*N* Hexley. What were you up to here, *N*? Why you couldn't leave that kid alone? *N*, you gonna talk to me?" Leigh-Ann tapped the MAC-10 against her thigh. The daughter saw that. "Come on, *N*."

"Nina," the woman said. "My name's *Nina*."

"There's a girl. And why's *Nina* Hexley kidnapping kids?"

Nina stared back boiling hatred.

Leigh-Ann smiled. Reece entered to interrupt their clash of intellects, so she fixed on him instead. "Here's a quote, Reece Coburn, circa eighteen minutes ago: 'What's the worst that can happen?' Didn't I warn you never say shit like that? And another one, 'They're probably decent folk.'"

"I'll admit on this occasion I was wrong," Reece said, scanning Stomatt.

"Don't he look peaceful? Not running his filthy mouth nor snoring up a storm. Oughta get shot in the throat more often."

"He gonna be okay?" Reece asked. "He said it only clipped him."

"He also claims he met Kid Ory – you believed that, too?" Leigh-Ann blew air out her teeth. "Bullet took a chunk of flesh with it, but he's okay. Just bled more than a little. He'll get back to pissing us all off once he wakes, mark my words. More than can be said for some." She nodded to the farmer's body.

Caleb came in the other door, grumbling. "Had no choice. You saw, didn't you Reece? He went for my gun. He woulda shot *me*."

"No sign of our friend Donny?" Reece asked.

Caleb shook his head. "Got as far as the fence and lost his tracks. Figure he cut across a field on foot, but there's no houses for miles. His truck's out front, I reckon – three vehicles, total. I took out the spark plug cables. Can we get going, Reece? This place gives me the creeps."

There was a question. Half-hour ago they were making good time, now they had a kidnapped child and a house of horrors to deal with. Leigh-Ann said, "That kid okay?"

"Near as I can see," Reece said. "She's not saying much. But I figure she's an awful long way from wherever she's supposed to be."

"So are we."

"We got time. Donny's not going to the cops, is he? Worst case, he comes back with some friends, and if they're involved in this I'd happily give them a piece of my mind. But my bet is he's halfway to Alaska." He indicated the daughter. "She spoken?"

"Name's *Nina*," Leigh-Ann said. "That's as far as we got."

"Nina?" Reece echoed. There were those hate-eyes again. "We're all sorry about your old man. Even if maybe we shouldn't be. Wanna explain your side?"

"Go to hell," Nina said. "Murderers – animals, bastard pigs –"

Leigh-Ann snorted laughter and clapped a hand over her mouth. "Sorry – this bitch is moralising at us? Like, we're gonna be judged by child molesters?"

"Cut it out, Leigh." Reece said. "She mightn't have had a choice. Did you?"

Nina had another insult waiting, but held it in.

"Not so sure it was molesting anyway," Reece said. "That kid's well-spoken. Dirty but not hurt. Maybe your old man wanted to lean on her rich parents, Nina?"

"He was a good man!" Nina spat at him. "You came in with guns!"

"What choice we have?" Caleb said, too loudly. "Answered that door with a shotgun, he did. Then snatches at my weapon? A guy tying up *kids*? I'm putting that bastard down eight days in a week."

"She needed binding!" Nina's voice rose too, veins popping up on her neck. "Promising we're all gonna die! Screaming murder in her sleep! She's got a devil in her, look in her damn eyes!" She went to stand, but Leigh-Ann took a step towards her and she dropped back.

"Nina," Reece said, "you gotta do better than that. Where the kid come from?"

"You tell me!" Nina snorted. "You're the ones came for her, exactly as promised!"

The gang exchanged looks. No one could've been expecting them – only got into Texas last night, hit the Steers dressed in masks, switched cars, and only diverted up these lanes on Reece's snap decision. Shit, they'd even left their phones back in Stilt Town so no one could ever track them.

"Nothing to do with us," Reece said. "We're here by happy chance. Lucky for her."

"Plenty places we'd rather be," Leigh-Ann added.

Nina faltered, but shook her head. "No. You're the same wickedness. Why else you come and kill – kill –" She choked on the word. Tears in her eyes. "That kid turned up on *our* land. We tried to *help*. Spiteful little monster. She came in making threats – said trouble was coming."

"She's out of her mind," Leigh-Ann decided, then told Nina, "If any of that's true, this *ain't* a rational way to deal with a kid making threats."

"And she sure didn't summon us," Caleb said.

"Then who in hell are you?" Nina snapped. "How *dare* you! You animals! Get out of my house! Get out!" She sprang up and shoved Reece with both hands. He took a step and pushed back on instinct, sending Nina over the armchair. She fell near her dead dad and froze on her hands and knees; the sight of him rolled up in carpet made her slide lower, blubbering, the fight all knocked out of her.

Caleb took a step forward to pick her up, comfort her, but Leigh-Ann caught his arm. He shook her off with annoyance, but stopped where he was.

"Caleb," Reece said, a little strained for once, "do me good and take Nina here to her room? Secure her. We'll have a chat once she's calmed down."

"What –" The woman turned with panic.

Caleb closed on her quickly, showing his pistol but saying politely, "If you'd be so kind. I don't want to do nothing we'll all regret."

"And you come with me, Leigh. Let's get our shit out the car."

Leigh-Ann held down the urge to resist for the hell of it, didn't need telling what to do now. But with Nina bucking against Caleb she figured she had the better job.

She headed outside, scuffing her boots, Reece just behind her. Back down the long dirt road to their overturned car, both of them watching shadows along the way, in case Donny was waiting after all. They reached the car and admired Stomatt's handiwork – the thing lying dead and crumpled on its roof. A miracle they all made it out unscathed. Together, they squeezed the big black duffel bags out past bent metal and broken glass. Damn heavy; one filled with guns and the other stuffed with more cash than any of them had ever seen. Leigh-Ann unzipped it just to look at it. Reece grinned, too.

The gang were now richer in their twenties than most Cutjaw trash got their whole lives. Alban Gray in Stilt Town still had to clean the cash, but they were as good as free. Reece had delivered exactly as he said he would. His easy smile as they hefted the bags up promised he'd figure this latest setback out, too. Leigh-Ann's bag clanked as they walked; somehow she'd ended up with the one full of guns. Definitely the heavier of the two.

"Prefer to swap?" Reece offered.

Leigh-Ann kept on walking. "I'd prefer you found us a place where the locals welcomed us with apple pie. Didn't think we'd have to kill anyone else today."

"Well," Reece said. "Imagine if we didn't come out here when we did. That kid."

"Yeah," Leigh-Ann said. "Assuming we're any better for her than them. It wasn't all good, what we did today, Reece."

"No." He didn't deny it. Didn't remind her everyone on Fallon's payroll knew who they were working for. Steers had gone into gas stops busting up displays, broken a guy's wrist near Shreveport. Spread slander online about anyone not paying premiums to join their loyalty network. That didn't exactly forgive killing them, so all Reece said was, "Saving a child's a step in the right direction, though."

"What're we gonna do with her? Stilt Town's no place for kids."

"They got families there."

"You know what I mean."

Reece hummed concession.

Yeah. They needed Stilt Town for shelter, to process the cash they'd stolen, and all of that, but Alban Gray and his progeny were not Leigh-Ann's favourite commune of God-bothering loons. She pointed out, "They think I'm unholy for being Black with tits – what's a kid with red eyes to them? Might find they agree with Nina."

"They think you're unholy for living a life of vice," Reece reminded her. "Gray's not gonna have a problem with her. Trust me, Leigh. It's a *good* thing we found her. We get to be heroes twice in one day."

She could believe he'd convinced himself of that already. The world didn't hold Reece Coburn back. "Only you could come out of a shitty day smellin' of roses."

But he smiled again and it was infectious.

"So we taking one of their rides, then? It's late as hell."

"No," Reece said. "The kid's shook up, Sto's down and we got no idea where we are. It's time for a break, I say. Food, sleep, get out of here come dawn. No one's finding us here, are they?"

Leigh-Ann wanted to argue. Sensible thing was to plough right on. Like any of them had the momentum to keep going all night long. But hell, the invitation was there now and she wasn't batting it away. She wasn't ever turning down food and sleep. They came back into the farmhouse and she tossed the bag down in the kitchen, calling out to Caleb to rustle up dinner. Meantime, she prowled back through the house looking for the master bedroom. A big room upstairs, where a couple photos of the dead farmer and his presumably gone wife scowled at the bed. This would do. And damn if she didn't need to get out of this boiler suit. Made her look even more like an overgrown Popsicle than usual, with her skinny neck and massive ball of hair sticking out the top of formless drab blue. She wrestled at it, got it down to her ankles when Caleb entered. He recoiled – spent their whole lives together and the idiot still got bashful at a bit of flesh. Leigh-Ann breezed over it. "Food ready?"

Caleb nodded, lingering in the door. "But first we gonna move the . . . out to the barn." Didn't wanna call a corpse a corpse. The guilt hunched his shoulders up. And it left him falling back on old instincts, gravitating her way for comfort. Never mind Leigh-Ann wasn't ever thinking of him as more than a brother.

With the day they'd had, she threw him a bone. "When we're done, you crash here with me. Plenty room in the fat man's bed. You keep your hands to yourself."

His face screwed up – not expecting that. "There's floorspace in the office, or I could be watching over Sto." Yet he lingered.

Leigh-Ann put her hands on her hips. He wanted to talk, or for her to talk to him, to let him know he was still good people, the way Reece did for her. But she wasn't Reece and didn't want to be. She said, "If you're gonna sleep on any floor, might as well be here so you can keep watch over me. Now show me what the hell you cooked up."

# 4

"Agent Tasker?" As he left the arrivals terminal, a woman in a dark suit approached. Short and mousy with the uncertainty of an intern. "Deputy Director Ward. Is that all your baggage?"

Tasker stopped. He was aware that Ordshaw's new deputy director was young, but at least expected a go-getter arranging power meetings in central offices, not someone who'd pick up subordinates from the airport herself. How understaffed were they? She was keenly waiting for a response, making him look at the bag. "Yeah. I don't need much more than a spare suit and toiletries."

"Then we can get moving. I thought it best I come personally. I've got some bad news." She turned her back on him and started marching before he could confront that bombshell. Ward led Tasker through scattered crowds and out into a car park, with occasional tosses of small talk: how was your flight? How was Tokyo? Did you have any problems with the Norwegian police? He dismissed it all with growing irritation that she had let him stew on the *bad news*.

"We've put you up in the Grand Hotel, in Central, I hope you'll like it," Ward said. Then added, a little graver, "The least we can do."

He slowed down, now they were alone in a quiet alley of parked cars. "What's happened?"

Ward scanned their surroundings, no one around. Over her shoulder, through the gap between floors, was the steel sky of cloudy England. Drab, disappointing England. She said, "Someone reached Parris before us."

"Piss and hell," Tasker huffed, looking away from her disappointed face. She didn't comment, so he went on: "I've just come from a damn open graveyard. We had one lead. One *pissing* lead." He took a breath, closed his eyes, and remembered this was *not* just another hapless escort. Even if she was ten or fifteen years younger than him. "Apologies, Deputy Director, I mean no disrespect."

"I'm the one who should apologise, Agent Tasker. I sent an agent as soon as I got word from London, but it was already too late."

"How bad?"

"Bad," Ward admitted, then continued towards a little Honda Civic. Not a director's car. "I've got a file for you."

Tasker got in and checked the glove box as Ward started the engine. He took out a manila folder which would no doubt contain details of the featureless, traceless death of a corporation target. Duvcorp and the like were rumoured to have "fixers" on their payrolls, so good at hiding their crimes you'd never know they were there. It was why Tasker spent half his life checking surfaces for poisons and worrying about unattended vehicles, and he'd had more than a few arguments with Helen by shifting those fears onto her. But the photos inside were not what he expected.

Duvcorp's researcher, Simon Parris, was captured slumped in a bathtub, one jaggedly cut arm hanging over the edge. Blood all around him, across the porcelain, sprayed up his face and across the tile floor. Tasker turned over one photo then another while Ward, eyes averted, started the car and pulled them out. As staged suicides went, it was crude.

"Don't suppose he left a note?" Tasker asked dryly.

Wards took it seriously. "No. And it's stranger than it looks."

"He was pregnant?" That got a frown. "Sorry, gallows humour."

Ward hummed, preferring to brood on it. Hell, they just lost a crucial contact, wasn't he allowed some deflection. As Ward studied the traffic with exaggerated care, Tasker sat back and mused, "Someone got to him after he leaked information. Suggesting he wasn't on their radar before he talked to us."

That got an even more uncomfortable look from Ward. She put it off a second, pulling out into the flow of the motorway, and finally said, "I've considered that. The information passed through a lot of hands between me, you and Norway. There was discussion in London about it. Half a dozen people with all their assistants could've tipped someone off."

"Great," Tasker said. He tapped the folder. "So how'd this go down?"

"Our agent was the first on the scene," Ward said. "He found the door open, with signs of a struggle in the living room. Take a look."

The next photos showed a modern lounge, a blood smear by one door, a smashed glass. Parris had been forced into the bath but the attacker had fled without clearing up. "They leave anything to go on?"

"The security feed for the building was cut," Ward said. "The neighbours haven't reported anyone coming or going, but one heard shouts, something smashing. She thought it was the TV, at the time."

"Of course she did."

"We found fingerprints in the blood. No matches in the database. The police are taking over now, treating it as a home invasion."

Tasker found a picture of a fingerprint. Part of a handprint, in the blood smear on the wall. If there were no matches, it was either someone with zero record or someone who'd been erased from the system. The former unlikely to be trusted with something like this, the latter unlikely to leave traces. What was the third option? "They sent in a pro to arrange a suicide, but they got interrupted."

"Or wanted to send a message?" Ward suggested. "To show they didn't care enough to pretend it wasn't murder?"

Tasker gave her a look. "How's your relationship with Duvcorp in Ordshaw?"

"Tenuous," Ward admitted. "As far as rank and file are concerned, it doesn't exist. But we're on sharing terms in a needs-must situation. This isn't the first time Simon Parris has been in touch, and last time it happened, Tycho Duvalier himself tried to have strong words with me."

Tasker appreciated her use of *tried to*, imagining this small woman standing up to one of the world's most powerful moguls. "What happened?"

"We borrowed some measuring equipment. Parris wanted to help, being ex-Ministry. You were aware of that? And of how their research intersects with ours?"

"Yeah." It wasn't commonly known, but Duvcorp's studies into a life energy the Ministry called novisan were always troubling Tasker. They had their own scanners and were definitely researching ways to exploit it. Possibly to weaponise it. He wasn't aware it was being done right here in Ordshaw, but he could've assumed. With Rebecca just two hours down the road. "And Parris just handed over their tech?"

"Under some pressure," Ward admitted. "This might have been his attempt to call in the favour. But all he sent me was the suggestion that was forwarded to you. 'Investigate Laukstad.' No explanation, no extra details. And the reality is, if they were sending a message, it's received. My people aren't used to tackling corporations, Agent Tasker."

Tasker nodded, no surprise. Most local Ministry offices were in place to contain what trouble already existed. State secrets. Monsters. They weren't homicide detectives, and hadn't signed on to tackle mass murderers or corrupt companies. Likewise, they weren't necessarily the most professional or trustworthy colleagues he could hope for. Not everyone had the training and experience of an international agent, that was simple fact.

Tasker checked the photos again. He realised none of the pictures of Parris showed any injury beside that wrecked arm and the splattered blood. In fact, going by Parris's pose, and the shower curtain hanging neat, it didn't look like he had struggled. Might've been drugged. No, the method and the mess didn't add up to a message. Tasker said, "Let's assume the attacker was interrupted. But not by someone looking to help Parris. Was anything taken?"

"Apparently not," Ward said. "His laptop was left behind, his phone too. Duvcorp's lawyers are already on us to hand them over. It's all strange, isn't it?"

Her tone was hopeful, because *strange* might mean the big bad corporation *weren't* in control. Yet.

As for Parris's devices, well. Tasker had got his hands on electronic devices that promised untold secrets before. Between corporate encryptions, lawyers and Ministry bureaucracy, there was often nothing to be gained from them. Still, he said, "You have the devices, but haven't accessed the laptop?"

"We'd risk a lawsuit."

"If Duvcorp found out about it."

Ward cleared her throat uncomfortably, but without looking at him gave a slight nod. Enough to say yes, they might sneak a peek. Good, she got it. Considering how dirty this whole situation was, they'd get nowhere playing by the rules. An entire village wiped out, a man with some clue as to why, and his killer driven off by an unfriendly third party. He couldn't let the Ministry itself get in the way. Tasker said, "Presumably you have some idea of how I can be of use?"

"Right now, I thought you'd appreciate the chance to freshen up in the hotel, get some rest," Ward said. "But I've set up a meeting with Parris's manager for this afternoon."

Tasker nodded appreciation. She got it alright. Thrown into a situation like this, you brought in a man like him and let him do what was necessary, even if it was just grilling office workers. He'd at least help her look tough while Duvcorp flat denied everything.

The motorway slanted up, to a raised ring-road that gave a view towards Ordshaw Central's skyline. An expanding, prosperous city a world apart from the isolated hovel of death Tasker had visited last night. Exactly the sort of place to harbour people who could get away with the murder of distant foreigners. At the least, Tasker could look them in the eye.


Left alone in his room, Tasker took a long, hot shower, trying to ignore reality whispering at him that this was already over. The more time he took, the more doubts crept back in. He'd posture and make them look good, sure, but Ward's meeting would be a bust and might mark them as future targets themselves. Duvcorp's connections to something terrible would go unproved, and next time it might be Ordshaw with a score of savage murders. Hell, why not Bracknell. Helen would be expecting a call later, and what would he say? *Hey, I've made it back to the UK, but guess what? I failed to stop these bastards, so keep the doors locked.*

Or. Or he could end the Duvcorp meeting with his gun. Storm the offices, up to the top floor where he'd take Hank Duvalier by the lapels, fuck the rules and evidence, throw him off the roof. His son, too, if Tycho was around. Two lives for eighteen fishermen, that was a start. Assuming Duvalier himself ever touched this city with a barge pole. He was off on some American ranch or in a New York penthouse, wasn't he?

Tasker came out the shower and stared at himself in the mirror, plush white towel around his waist, darkness dragging his eyes down and a taint of grey misery misting his chest. He had time to hit the hotel gym before the meeting. That was something he *could* control. He put his glasses back on and scratched his stubble, knowing he would be neither shooting up offices nor relaxing on beaches. He'd do everything he could for Ward and Laukstad over two or three days, finally return to Bracknell and spend three days off unable to explain to Helen exactly what he was worried about, then take guidance from London as to what pointless stepping stone to take next. Smugglers dealing in monster parts in rainy Eastern Europe or weird lights in the sky outside a sewage plant or something.

He exited the bathroom with a gust of steam and stiffened. His eyes shot from his pistol, holstered on the desk, back to the woman standing in front of it.

"I ordered room service," she said, brightly. "You want something for yourself?"

She had a gun of her own, and blood all over her clothes and face.

# 5

*Bare feet padded against hard-packed ground, a warning beat as she reached the village. "Help! Someone!" Charlene shouted outside her neighbours' huts. Why weren't they answering? They couldn't have all disappeared too . . .*

*A door opened – Ade! Big-chested, bearded Ade, strongest in Igota. He wore the same confusion at the stillness, and her shouts further flustered him. Charlene told him, "Quick, Ade – to the crossing – I was walking with Marie –"*

*"Slow down," Ade said, moving into the open, watching the other huts. As troubled by the quiet as by Charlene's fear. Where were the boys? The talking, the laughter? Had more people disappeared? "What's happened?"*

*"Here?" Charlene swallowed.*

*The outsiders were responsible. It had all begun the night before they arrived. Men missing in the night, and now this. Everyone else. She listened, and finally heard goats, braying fearfully. Snapped out of it, she locked on Ade again. "Marie – she's been attacked. Richard – I don't know what came over him. Please hurry!"*

*She started away, but after a few steps skidded to a stop. Ade almost bumped into her. Both looked to the side, between shacks. There were the children. Ade said, loudly, "What are you doing, boys? You didn't answer this woman shouting!"*

*They said nothing.*

*Charlene moved closer to Ade. He stepped towards the skinny boys, half-naked in the afternoon sun. They stood still as stalks. "This is some kind of game? Ezra, come here right now!"*

*"Ade –" Charlene warned. He was a stride away, already, and the children pounced. Their shrill cries were met by noises from every hut.*

Reece imagined a composition. It started super simple, two perfect D fifths an octave apart – maybe two octaves – and a five-step descent. Repeat. Again. You keep doing it, until you break free and go wild – chase the sound up, weave around inside the fifth . . . but keep coming back to that bold refrain. It wasn't jazz, he had a sense of that. A march? Another new Cutjaw sound. Creeping in his mind – he couldn't wait to test it out in Stilt Town, where the instruments were stashed. But this wasn't trumpet material. Wanted a piano at least. Might work on their little pipe organ, if Gray's people let him touch it.

Either way it had him happy. Had to keep happy, not thinking about all them people they hurt. Remember what it was for. Freedom of expression, freedom from oppression. That's what the tunes would speak of, without words.

Different ways to get themselves heard and seen. He ran a hand through his hair, rocking on a little wooden chair on the porch while the others slept. That was another way to be seen, damn smeared green hair that hadn't come out in a wash like he intended. Then, they should've been back in Stilt Town already, where he had other dyes or bleach to deal with it. Instead of here, where none of them had imagined sleeping, as much Reece's fault as Stomatt's. The back roads seemed a good idea at the time – it was a wild ride that'd brought them here.

A squeaking floorboard made him sit up in the chair. Light footsteps on the porch. His hand slipped to his pistol but it was only Zip, looking worried out the door. Reece rubbed his eyes and said, "Come see, cher. You sleep well?"

Zip considered the question carefully. Her skin and clothes looked grubbier in the low light of dawn, from tiny mud-caked tennis shoes up to hair hanging in disarray over her shoulders, but there was class and intelligence in those eyes, same as he'd heard in her voice. She said, "I had a funny dream."

"Make you laugh?" Reece suggested.

Her expression suggested no. "There were poor people, far away. Goats crying."

"Ah. Just a dream, huh? No goats here. The others up?"

Zip must've passed Stomatt on the sofa to get here, but she ignored the question. "They died. The goats knew, but they weren't ready. *Igota*." She lowered her voice, experimenting with her dream memories. "A village in the rainforest."

Morbid, but her dreams could've been plenty worse after what she'd been through. Now she'd rested, her voice was even clearer – might actually be British. A bright foreign kid dreaming of exotic places. Reece said, "You been to a rainforest before?"

She shook her head, then her attention lingered on his pistol. Reece took it out and her worry shifted to wonder. The sun peeked between the clouds to catch its mirrored shine.

"I told you this was art," Reece said, and spun the gun round his finger. He turned it back and forth at speed. "Platinum and gold plated, etchings designed by Blanc Tweedman himself. Le Belle Riposte is the finest sidearm in the States, count on it."

Zip's nose wrinkled. "How did you get it?"

"I wouldn't settle for anything less, that's how." Reece stood. He stretched and fought down a yawn, scanning the horizon. Open corn fields, dotted with trees. To the right, beyond the parked trucks and farm machinery, was the wooden barn where they'd stowed the farmer's body. Need to bury him before they go. And then there was the daughter . . . Reece smiled at the kid. "We're artists, Zip. Try to be in all we do, but we especially like making music. Me on the horn, Caleb's on the bass, Sto on the drums. You bring us anything that can make music, we'll give it life." He held up the gun again. "This another instrument I try to play my best."

Zip looked sceptical. "You can't play a *horn*."

"Trumpet," he explained. "And you better believe I play. No one expects it, bunch of white boys outta trailers with some kinda swamp jazz. But we live our best lives. They played us on the radio, you know? Whispers Phan, he called us *revolutionary*. You like jazz?"

Her scepticism shifted to positively pitying, as though his entire life philosophy, laid out before her, was misguided. Reece laughed. "Right. You don't play music where you from?"

Zip considered it carefully. "We have a piano. But I don't know if it works. Daddy doesn't like me to touch it."

"That's sour," Reece said. "He play himself?"

"No," Zip said, then focused on the gun. "He has a sword hand."

"That so?" Reece said. "And what's he need a sword hand for?"

"Killing monsters." She turned thoughtfully, towards the barn, like she knew the body was there. Serious enough to make Reece pause.

"What kind of monsters?" he said. "Big old bears? Criminals, maybe – the police? In England? You don't have guns so he has to use a sword?"

"A sword *hand*," Zip said, but he'd made her smile, like he was teasing. "Because guns aren't enough. And because he has to *always* be ready. The monsters used to be people – he gets them before they can get us."

Well hell. It sounded like she was being literal, and her father genuinely had a blade instead of a hand or something. Which didn't gel; a kid this well-spoken coming from some mutilated sword-fighter? Must've been some tale he told her, or she told herself, to make sense of something else. Reece asked, "Was that what he was doing on the Mississippi? Hunting monsters?"

She nodded. "Just one. Grithin. *Slippery scum.*" She accented it like quoting a rough-talking thug. So yeah, she might be cut from different cloth to Dad. "He was looking for Grithin for *years*. And he was worried. That's why I followed. I wanted to help. I didn't mean to . . ." She trailed off.

Reece cocked his head to one side. "This Grithin dangerous?"

"Yes," Zip whispered. "But my dad's not scared of anyone. Only, I . . . I got a bad feeling. I told Daddy not to go and he told me off. Because I was listening to my feelings. I'm never supposed to listen to those feelings." She picked up speed, as Reece floundered on that messed-up detail. "I followed him – I even got on a plane – so busy and noisy and long, but I came here – not here – the river – and it *was* bad, but not because of Grithin – a real monster, one Daddy never stopped – two monsters – coming for *me* –"

"Hey, *hey*." Reece crouched. "Those men are gone, hear me? You don't got to worry about it, not now you're with us. We'll get you home, sure enough. Meantime, we're headed to the safest place in all Louisiana. Ever heard of Stilt Town?"

Zip shook her head.

"Caleb in there – you like Caleb? He's nice, isn't he? – his uncle owns this place, Stilt Town. Grew up in Cutjaw himself but left to start a church, and that church became a whole town, but not like any town you've seen. Because Alban Gray – that's Caleb's uncle – he still got some Cutjaw in him. Never lived in brick houses with concrete streets and that. *He* made houses all lifted up in the air. A church, a school, floating so you can run underneath. High enough that no flood can take them. And they got animals – you like animals? Pigs, cows, chickens."

"Rabbits?"

"Yeah, they got rabbits. You like rabbits?"

She jumped forward and wrapped her arms tight around Reece's neck. He went rigid with surprise before relaxing. He patted her head and she whispered, "Thank you, Reece." Then she pushed back. "Can we go there now?"

"Soon. Once we're all up and figured out what to –"

"We should go now," she said, seriously. "Before they find us."

"Who?" Reece frowned. She didn't get to answer, as a yell shook the farmhouse and Zip jumped with surprise. "What in *damn* hell is going on here?"

Reece stood, putting a hand on her shoulder. "Sto! Get your ass out here!"

"Reece!" Stomatt shouted. He sounded like a bull charging through the house. "Where the fuck are we? You motherfu –" Stomatt skidded to a halt on seeing Zip. Her eyes screwed shut in fear. The big guy's face went from angry confusion to delight. "Did we take hostages?"

"It's okay, cher, he's one of us," Reece assured. "For what it's worth."

Stomatt was bigger than most, thick around the middle, and not a handsome man. His top lip and nose curled slightly up and his mouth was always open, like he was forever mildly perturbed. He looked especially unhinged this morning with the bandage loose round his neck and his tatty, unbuttoned boiler suit all covered in blood. He looked up from Zip. "We make Louisiana, Reece? Don't look like Stilt Town."

"You don't remember? We weren't halfway there when you passed out."

"Passed out –"

"At the *wheel*. You flipped the damn car. Fortunately we –"

"Because you took us on this fuc –" Stomatt caught himself, eyes on the kid. "On this *frigging* detour, didn't you? Unlit damn dirt roads."

"Just as well you crashed out here, with no one to notice the wreckage."

"That don't look like no one."

Before Reece could fill him in, Leigh-Ann burst out onto the porch. "Stomatt you motherfu –" she spotted Zip and expertly redirected "– ungus. You're up and uglying up the place!" Dressed in just an enormous (stolen) flannel shirt, with her big ball of curly hair a tangle, she cut a balance between sultry and dishevelled.

"Woke on a damn sofa by some leather straps like some kinda bondage chamber," Stomatt said, moving off the porch to check the view. He noted the house's second storey. "Took all the beds for yourselves, huh?"

"You want hauling upstairs next time you get shot," Leigh-Ann said, "*weigh less.*"

"Hey fu – urget you." Stomatt stumbled over the words, frowning at Zip again. He gave up on minding his language: "Why the shit is there a kid out here, Reece, come on!"

"Things got strange," Reece said.

"Sicko farmers had her tied up," Leigh-Ann said. "Now she's our new lucky charm."

"You want to take a *kid* –" Stomatt started, but Caleb lumbered outside to interrupt.

"Sto, you're loud enough to wake a rock."

"Interrupt your beauty sleep?" Stomatt only got louder as he plodded on the shingle. "Someone fill me in! Did we or did we not hand it to those shitbergs yesterday, and are we or are we not now rich and clear?"

"Rich but we ain't clear," Leigh-Ann said. "Not by a few hundred miles yet."

"Then why the hell we stop?"

"Because you wrecked our car!" Caleb cried. "And then – this!" He gestured wildly to Zip, who cringed closer to Reece. Their volumes had escalated loud enough to hit bursting point, but they all quietened on seeing how Reece watched them.

"So where we at?" Stomatt asked.

"Ready to keep going," Reece said. "Soon as someone gets a grill on. Barring one loose end here – got a girl upstairs."

"Another girl?" Stomatt cocked an eyebrow. "She older?"

"She's a *pederast,*" Leigh-Ann said. "Or at least mixed up with them."

"So she needs taking care of," Stomatt said. "Yes?"

"Ain't no *way* you leave it to him," Caleb said.

They all went quiet again, looking to Reece. He'd been telling himself they could just up and leave Nina. She wouldn't want the police out here, so what was the harm? But however seedy those men might have been, it was hard to accept that young lady's involvement. Was that him being hopeful, naive, sexist or what? He looked at Zip. "Cher, that woman? She as bad as the men?"

Zip hesitated under the attention. "She didn't touch me. She didn't want to come close."

Everyone kept waiting for Reece's guidance. He said, "I'll talk with her while y'all get ready to go. Zip, Leigh'll take good care of you. Once she gets some pants on."

Neither Zip nor Leigh-Ann looked happy about this, and Stomatt made it worse by whispering, really loud, "And just what the hell is *up* with her eyes?"

But Reece winked off the worry. "It's gonna be a good day, guys, wait and see."

Leigh-Ann could've thrown something at him, plain enough. Damn if she didn't hate optimism.


There was a scuffle of movement when Reece entered the bedroom, as Nina kicked up over the bed and against the wall. As far as she could manage with one wrist cuffed to the metal frame. Sat on the pillow, she stared fire and held her free hand up taut like she might gouge his eyes out if he came close enough. Reece stayed in the doorway.

"You've rubbed your wrist raw," he said. There was also a boot on the desk and another near the door, evidently tossed to help her escape. He couldn't guess how.

"I gotta pee," she said with her mouth closed.

"All right." Reece held the key up. "I'm trusting you're smarter than to try anything. Right?"

That wasn't getting an answer, but he approached anyway. She breathed heavier and recoiled when he unlocked the cuff. Quickly nursing her wrist. He stepped back to give her space and she slunk into the hall, never taking her eyes off him. Over to the john where he waited outside trying not to listen. After the flush, she stayed inside. The gang were arguing below.

"You never do it right, that's not enough mayo," Stomatt was complaining.

"You want a sandwich or a soup?" Leigh-Ann snapped.

The restroom door opened and Nina looked out with a resigned huff. Admitting that whatever new escape plan she had concocted had come up bunk. Reece flashed her a smile and gestured back to the bedroom. She considered making a break for it and he let her think it through, as Leigh-Ann's voice bounced up the stairs, "I swear to God you're the only man I know asshole enough to be able to sleep off a damn gunshot so he can irritate the hell out of everyone!"

Realising there were more people here than she could outrun, Nina moved back into the bedroom. Reece followed and closed the door behind them. He said, "Now we're rested, why don't I start? We've got a kid taken from her family, tied up and –"

"Eyes red as the devil," Nina said viciously.

"Lemme finish," Reece told her. "We've got a guy drew a gun to hide her away; would've shot us rather than let us get near her. His pal, I guess, was helping, and here's you – young, frightened? Forced into your old man's sick hobby? I pray that's true – it'd mean we did you a favour. The alternative, though . . . you your dad's daughter or what?"

"My *dad* was a good man – you have no idea."

"So fill me in."

Nina crossed her arms tight. "I told all. That little bitch showed up on our doorstep and we took her in. Fed her. She was mute as a plank except she started raving and screaming when she went to bed. Freaking the hell out. Talking prophecy of doom shit."

"A scared kid starts talking and you tie her up?"

"Wasn't just talk! There's more'n red in her eyes! It's a demon in her! Donny almost chopped a finger off under her witch words!"

"She distracted him from cutting carrots?"

"Cursed him, more like! She was talking ghosts and – and apes! Coming for her, here, gonna kill us all." Nina snorted. "And look what happened. You blame my dad? The kid *warned* us you was coming – he was defending his home."

"Forgive me," Reece said, "but tying her up and waving guns about still ain't a reasonable response to an upset child, even if she did get lucky predicting someone might come save her. Someone ties you up, you're not gonna make threats?"

Nina's eyes bored into him, not caring to hear his reason. "You gonna kill me, too?"

Reece saw fear, more than anything, gripping her. He said, "I guess we've –"
A noise tore through the farm like the low war cry of some nightmarish animal.

The windows shuddered as Reece froze. Nina's terrified eyes went to the window.

Reece asked, "What the fuck was that?"

As if in answer, Zip shrieked from below, "They're here!"

# 6

Tasker sat on the hotel bed as the woman ran her free hand over his gun holster on the desk. His was government issue, modern, sleek; her gun was faded around the edges like something salvaged from a grandparent's loft. It fit her vagrant look: medium height with a brown leather jacket worn bald, loose jeans ripped not by design and once-white trainers breaking at the seams. Bloodspray patterned her shaved head and face like warpaint. The door was closed, but the lock-chain lay on the floor amid shards of snapped wood. The fact that he hadn't heard her kicking her way in warned him she was likely more capable than she looked.

Why hadn't he taken the gun into the shower room?

Her eyes probed the armchair, heavy green curtains, bed and mirror. When she spotted her reflection, her cracked lips stretched to a grin. "This place is too fancy for me." The accent was a breezy Eastern European. "You do not say much. What's your name? I'm Katryzna."

Matching her conversational tone, Tasker said, "You broke in and don't know who I am?"

"I know *what* you are. Government spook. Yes?"

"Sure. If that's me, then what are you – a corporate contractor?"

"Can you imagine? I could have business cards. What was your interest in Parry?"

"Parris?" Tasker corrected.

"Potato potato." She pronounced both words the same. "You are some kind of specialist, isn't it? They paused everything to pick you up from the airport, I was watching. What's your name?"

When he didn't answer straight away, she frowned at her left shoulder.

"I didn't kill him. The opposite." Her eyes rolled up. "No, I didn't give birth. Or keep him alive. Yes, some of this *is* his blood. What's your name? Are the UK government investigating Duvcorp?"

Tasker stared, a little stunned at her random chatter.

"Please." Katryzna sniffed hard. "I can practically smell government on you. What's your *name*?" She glared and waited this time.

"Agent Sean Tasker."

"Working for?"

"The Ministry of Environmental Energy." Tasker nodded to his wallet, near the gun. "ID's in there."

Katryzna rummaged through the cards – not just his warrant card but the bank issues and Frequent Flyer memberships. She cooed at the Platinum. "This is to use those fancy lounges?"

"Some."

"Your Ministry treats you well. Putting you up in a place like this. And you travel with your gun? I like that. You were already on the way when Parry died? I guess they wanted him dead because of you? Why did he call you? What does your Ministry *do*?"

Tasker gave the flurry of questions a moment, before answering the final one, by rote: "The Ministry are concerned with environmental concerns. Those outside typically human factors. Parris suspected Duvcorp were involved in something that might interest us. We didn't get to ask him what. Now maybe you can explain your part in this?"

Katryzna stepped closer to him. Her clothing smelt of decay. "Sean. I'm likely to do bad things –" She twitched and hissed something foreign. Polish? Was it some kind of tick? She put on a friendly face again. "You obviously know something, otherwise why fly you in? We can be friends, but if you are sneaky around me, you might get hurt."

Tasker gave her a flat smile. "Friends don't point guns at each other."

"I am not *pointing* it at you. It's just ready in case I need to shoot you." Katryzna looked sharply aside again. She had to be hearing voices. "That's not the point. But okay." She placed the gun on the desk, within reach. Her jacket fell open to reveal the hilt of a large Bowie knife sheathed at her hip. "Now. You may continue."

Tasker quickly made assessments. She was part of their system – one of the corporate hired guns, even if she didn't look the part. But not Duvcorp's hire; she was suggesting she was the one who interrupted the murder. If she was lying about that, he was dead anyway, so he might as well make the most of this. He said, "You're not familiar with the Ministry?" She shook her head. "We monitor unusual energy patterns, amongst other things. Parris was ex-Ministry himself, and went on to do similar work for Duvcorp. He tipped us off to something their research picked up in Norway, four days ago. A lot of people dead. For some reason, Duvcorp didn't want anything to do with it themselves."

"Four days ago," Katryzna echoed, a little disappointed. "I got a call *yesterday*."

"Sorry," Tasker said. "Parris called you himself?"

"Oh no." Katryzna took an old Nokia handset out of a pocket. The sort only good for calls and texts. "He tried to message a friend of mine. What kind of *unusual* energy readings do you chase? Are you ghost hunters? Is your UK government that advanced?" Her expression became eager like a child's.

Tasker said, "You think that's likely?"

"What did I say about being sneaky? I want –" A knock on the door interrupted her. She narrowed her eyes. "Who's that?"

"Room service," a young man called.

In a flash, Katryzna had both her pistol and Tasker's in hand. "If you used some kind of alarm –"

"You said you ordered food," he reminded her.

The knock came again, and Katryzna said, with a testiness that didn't seem directed at him, "I *know* – I appreciate that *now*." She gestured. "Open the door."

Tasker tightened his towel and did as she said. He blocked the busboy from seeing into the room while he accepted the covered plastic tray, and the moment the door clicked shut Katryzna tore it from Tasker's hands. She piled an entire limp burger into her mouth. Both pistols were back on the desk. Tasker made no move, aware of how fast she had snatched them up before. She paused, cheeks bulging, and spoke messily around the mouthful, "Wampth thome?"

"No," Tasker said.

"Fine. Talk. Whaph waph Parrith doing?"

"Didn't say. There must have been an unnatural force involved in these deaths in Norway. Duvcorp either recorded it and didn't want anyone to know they could – or they caused it themselves. You weren't sent to silence him?"

She shook her head as she struggled to work her jaw around the burger.

"But you met the killer?"

Katryzna nodded as she swallowed with a series of impossible gulps that could've been retches.

"My word, woman," Tasker said, "were you raised by pelicans?"

She raised a finger for silence, finished swallowing, then said, "I was not. But you will want to have my babies. I have your *unnatural*. This message from Parry was my first clue in forever for what happened to Eyes. He was *swimming* in unnatural."

"Eyes?" Tasker questioned carefully.

Katryzna nodded, starting to shovel greasy chips into her mouth. "My only friend I ever had." A pause to chew, giving Tasker a moment to unwrap her diction. "He disappeared. Or died. Eight years ago?" More chips. "Eyes was Duvcorp's best secret weapon. He made things seem like they didn't happen." She finished her rapid feast and choked back a small belch. Tasker could barely focus on her words. "I have meant to kill Hank Duvalier for a long time. He never appreciated Eyes enough. Definitely to blame for whatever happened to him."

"Forgive me for being slow," Tasker said, "but what was the unnatural element?"

"Oh," Katryzna said. "Hank had Eyes chasing ghosts and ghouls and silly legends. He complained about it all the time, how ridiculous it was. Except the last assignment, that worried him. We met just before he left – he helped me chop up a Libyan." Her eyes glazed over as she sank into the grim memory. "He didn't need to come, he just wanted to see me, and turned up uninvited, smoking against a wall like I should expect him. He asked to talk. Sure, I said, once we kill Fahid – *and* feed him to crocodiles. But no, he said, talk and work, and started to explain while we dragged the body off a balcony. It landed on a car." This didn't sound like the high-grade contract killing Tasker had assumed the big corporations capable of, and his expression must have showed it, because she quickly added, "It made Eyes laugh until he coughed and almost fell over. He never let things like that happen, he was always so *specific* – he only laughed around me. But what were we talking about?"

Tasker gave a shrug, letting her flow.

"Ah. So he reminded me about these ghost stories. He said this one felt different and he gave me his phone, in case things went wrong. I never got a call and he never came back, so, great plan, Eyes. No contacts or anything on the phone. All I knew was that he flew to Africa."

"But you were already in Libya?"

"We killed the Libyan in Madrid, try to keep up, Sean. Do your Ministry know anything about Africa?"

Considering it was a whole continent of activity, yes, Tasker could imagine there were a thousand cases of note to the Ministry across Africa. But the woolliness aside, she was talking about Duvcorp setting contractors onto investigating the supernatural. The origins of the company crossing over into Ministry territory. He said, "Was Parris involved this Africa trip?"

Katryzna shrugged. "Eyes wouldn't give that number to just anyone, so *probably*. Duvalier had him looking into strange things. Bigfoot and haunted houses. So." She took a step forward and prodded a finger into Tasker's chest. "Does that fit your idea of unnatural?"

Her poke left a chip-grease sheen on his clean flesh. He said, "We might, conceivably, investigate haunted houses. To disprove them."

Katryzna backed off with a smile. "Then you will want to work together with me. Take Duvcorp down." She punched her opposite palm.

Tasker paused, unsure of what she even was, let alone what aligning himself with her meant. But here was a promise of results, nonetheless. He said, "Are you alone?"

"Well. I am with you? And –" She pointed to her left shoulder, which had distracted her before. Indicating an earpiece he couldn't see? "There's Rurik? Listen, Eyes was the only person that ever treated me right –" Her mouth tightened with irritation, then she spoke sideways. "You do *not*, you do nothing but *annoy*." No, there was no earpiece, just voices in her head. She collected herself. "We have the same interests, isn't it?"

"Maybe," Tasker replied slowly. "But I don't take partners outside the Ministry."

"That's good," Katryzna only smiled wider. Strangely healthy teeth. If you ignored the food stuck between them. "Me neither. You can help us move around. Legally, so I don't have to keep leaving weapons behind. Less people get hurt this way, that should make you happy." A bitter twist towards her shoulder suggested that wasn't meant for him. She smiled again. "Sean. I see you're overthinking this. I am here to help. You are making a face – be honest, remember?"

"I make a career of discretion," Tasker said. "You look like roadkill."

Katryzna put her hands on her hips. "And I got into your super-cool hotel without any alarm going off, yes? You want to cross Duvcorp, you need me. Stuffy suits and government regulations don't work against them."

Well, that was true. Tasker could see himself wrapped up in the same red tape and complications that surrounded Parris's electronics. Conversations that amounted to no more than warnings to back off. Questions unanswered, guilty forever free. With eighteen senselessly dead – probably more to come. That poor girl, a Norwegian Rebecca, her face ripped apart. Tasker said, "I'm interested, but you need to give me more than that. Your friend died eight years ago? What've you learnt since then?"

"Ah." Her face went blank a second. "I thought you might ask. Now, when I say we were friends – we did not see each other often – and, life is hard – actually Eyes used to get me out of trouble, a bit, so without him around –" She stopped herself, took a collecting breath and rushed out the explanation. "Long story short, I was out of circulation and a bad friend but I am compensating now."

Tasker eyed her. He could believe this erratic, unwashed woman could be the sort to leave the disappearance of her friend unanswered for years. "But you are connected to these people," he said, "the corporations and the –"

"I work occasionally." She rolled a dismissive hand. "Not right now. This is personal. Lucky I was nearby when I got this message." She clicked her fingers, then took up the phone again, thumbing through. "Just yesterday."

Tasker read off the two-tone screen: *It's Parris. Not sure you remember me. You said contact you if things got bad. Please come to Ordshaw ASAP.*

They had a past agreement Parris was cashing in on from eight years ago?

"I had people trace the message," Katryzna said, "and found this guy who was all muscle bending over Parris in the bath. Not perfect timing. I cracked his skull with my gun, so I could question him, but he didn't stop. He made a lucky punch and ran, while Parry was gargling his last words."

"You got a good look at the killer?"

"For what's it's worth. Big, like a thug, with a tattoo" – she gestured vaguely around her neck – "military insignia? Short dark hair, flat nose. Stupid eyes. Average ex-army goon. Ring any bells?"

It was about as useless as descriptions of thugs went. Tasker said, "I'll run it by my people. What'd Parris say to you?"

"Well, he spat two names. *Ikiri* and *Miguel Lopaz*. From how his face looked, they're *really* important. That's where I need you. With all your Ministry resources, with those two names, you can tell me where in Africa we need to go, isn't it? More importantly, you can get us there. With our guns." What she lacked in a plan, she made up for in enthusiasm.

"I'm visiting Duvcorp," said Tasker, evading the point. "I'll ask them about it, shall I?"

Katryzna raised an eyebrow. "If you want them to kill you? I'd better come with you."

"Absolutely not. If you knew this Eyes, I assume they know you?" She didn't deny it. "I'll get my people on this. You can . . . lay low here for now."

"I relax while you do the boring work?" Her face shone at the offer, and she took in the room anew. Her hand was suddenly in front of Tasker, dirty skin cracked. "Deal."

"I just washed," he reminded her.

Katryzna wiped the hand quickly on her jacket and held it out again. Possibly dirtier. But it was earnest enough. Tasker shook and she squeezed hard before backing off with a wink. "Great, this is going to be *fun*."

It would be something, he was sure enough of that. His best bet was probably to get a couple of local agents to watch her in the meantime, run background –

"Oh!" She raised a finger. "Don't tell anyone you met me. Even your friends. *Especially* your friends. That's for your safety, more than mine."

# 7

When she was done needling Stomatt, Leigh-Ann moved from the kitchen to crouch in front of Zip, whose little legs dangled over the edge of a stool. "Well, little miss, how you hanging in here?"

"I'm fine," Zip said, going still at Leigh-Ann's proximity.

"You don't gotta be scared, okay? Get past Sto's loudness and everything else about us is pure charm. I, for one, am glad to have another woman on the team."

"Are you Reece's girlfriend?" Zip asked, so blunt it made Leigh-Ann back off and laugh. The kid looked hurt, not sure what was funny.

"No, nope, never," Leigh-Ann said, summarising a complicated relationship in three simple words. Not all true; they'd had a fling when they were, what, fourteen? Awkward, fumbling shit – on account of they knew each other too well. All the girls loved Reece, but it didn't click for either of them – and that was the start of Leigh-Ann having all sorts of Doubts she wasn't entirely resolved on yet. But she gave Zip the simplest explanation: "We like family, okay? All of us. Now, do I hear a tinge of the English in that accent? I've got some British in me – *Leigh's* spelt all funny with the *g* and the *h* – my dad wanted me to have an old country name."

"It's pretty," Zip replied. "Zip's from the Bible. Zipporah."

Leigh-Ann snickered. "Wow. And your God-loving sadistic-child-naming mommy, where's she right now?"

That flummoxed the poor kid.

"Your mom, Zip? She home with Daddy?"

Zip chewed her lower lip.

"Don't you wanna go home?" The child nodded vigorously. "Then what's this hang-up? You can trust us, we're your *crewe* now. Even though Sto smells like garbage and Caleb would give up a kidney for magic beans, we stick tog –"

A roar shook the room and Leigh-Ann shot upright. A great raw sound, not machinery but something alive, something massive. Zip's eyes got bigger as Stomatt stumbled in – then the kid shrieked, so loud Leigh-Ann had to cover her ears: "They're here!"

"Damn hell!" Stomatt shouted, and the noise outside came again.

Leigh-Ann turned towards it, about to run for the door, but Zip latched onto her, crying, "Don't let him get me don't let him get me!"

"What in hell, kid?" Leigh-Ann barked, pushing back at her. "What is that?"

"Who's coming?" Stomatt demanded, as though they'd been keeping something from him. "Sounds like a damn dragon!"

"Please please please!"

Leigh-Ann struggled to disentangle Zip's clawing grip. Every time she got a couple fingers free the others snapped back into place. The roar came again, closer, a battle cry. Leigh-Ann shoved, hard, and Zip stumbled with a gasp.

"Leigh!" Reece's voice cut through the room. Suddenly staring from the door. Hell of a time to walk in.

"She wouldn't let go!" Leigh-Ann snapped, not about to apologise with some devil beast out there. She followed Stomatt's example, going for the weapons bag, and pulled the big guy out of the way. He dragged his stumpy shotgun with him as Leigh-Ann got a hand on the old familiar MAC-10.

"What is it?" Reece said. "Anyone see –"

"It's them, Reece, it's them!" Zip said, running terrified to embrace him.

"What's she talking about *them*?" Stomatt yelled. "That's something inhuman!"

"Something in the field!" Caleb skidded into the room. "Think it's Steers? Sto?"

Stomatt ran out the door, pounding for the back porch. Slipping free of Zip, Reece moved right behind him, pistol twirling out the holster. Leigh-Ann and Caleb exchanged a dumb look – the child trembled worriedly in the middle of the room. Leigh-Ann said, "You got those trucks going?"

"Was just –"

The roar came again, undulating as whatever made the sound moved up and down, quickly approaching. Stomatt shouted back at it, loud and harsh and without meaning. Leigh-Ann said, "Fuck it, load up! Grab the kid!"

Caleb swooped to lift Zip, as Leigh-Ann hoisted the weapons duffel over a shoulder and snatched the other bag. Weighed down like her knees might buckle, she charged through the living room away from that awful sound.

A gunshot boomed, Stomatt's shotgun shaking the windows.

"Go go go!" Leigh-Ann screamed and Caleb raced ahead. She burst into daylight and skidded over the porch, twisting to see Stomatt and Reece running to the side of the building. "What in damn hell is it?"

"Damned if I know!" Reece shouted. "Ran right past – quick as a snake, big as a bull!"

"I'm getting it!" Stomatt disappeared around the corner. He fired again.

"We're leaving!" Leigh-Ann shouted, and Reece backed up, nodding. Caleb was already halfway to the trucks. Leigh-Ann moved on, throwing a look back at the door as Nina emerged, pale and uncomprehending. "What kind of animals you got on this fucked-up farm?"

Nina's mouth moved wordlessly, shocked as the rest of them.

"More messed up by the second," Leigh-Ann muttered, then shouted to Reece's back, "What's the worst that can happen! What's the worst, he says!"

A huge crash of metal and snapping wood came on the other side of the farmhouse, spurring them all to move faster. Caleb threw the first truck's door open and gently, for all the urgency, lifted Zip in.

"Whoa!" Reece warned and Leigh-Ann twisted to see the beast tear into view, breaking through the far corner of the house and ripping chunks of wall with it.

"Holy hell," Caleb gasped, stepping back from the truck.

"The fuck . . ." Leigh-Ann added.

It was a creature of size and ferocity to match the noise that carried it here. Its skin was black as pitch where it wasn't patterned by clumps of grey fur, and its eyes shone mad, murky yellow, within a flat face of wrinkled flesh and bared fangs. Though hunched, with its hind legs doubled and back arched, its shoulders stood tall as the truck and the front-arms that supported it were wide as pillars, ripped with muscle and jointed in more places than looked natural. Breath came out its big nostrils in steam as it reared up.

In hushed, fear-filled awe, Zip gave it a name: "Giza."

Leigh-Ann swung her gun round, pulling the trigger before she'd got close to aiming. The gun bucked and bullets spat all over the ground in a stream up to the monster, giving it enough time to lurch sideways before her spray rioted past it. In one great stride it closed half the distance to them, dipping around the vehicle so Reece couldn't get a clear shot past Caleb. Its second stride brought it up in the air, knuckles punching the ground away, and both fists windmilled above it – cut off mid-jump by a booming shot to the side. It twisted with a high roar, both arms flapping as its momentum carried it on into the truck. Caleb pulled Zip clear with a split-second to spare, the beast smacking the windscreen with such force it folded the roof in.

Stomatt ran into the open, pumping the shotgun, yelling incoherently. Reece and Caleb dived for cover as he fired again, shot sparking off the closest truck chassis. The beast rolled off the other side, the vehicle banking under its weight.

"Other truck, other truck!" Reece pushed Caleb and Zip ahead of him. Leigh-Ann hiked up the duffel bags to follow. Stomatt pumped and fired, bullets pinging off the crumpled truck, and the shadow of animal mass rolled out of view. Onto the ground and then suddenly away. Off the lot with unbelievable speed, out through the fence and into the long grass, before disappearing around the barn.

Stomatt chased after it, passing the wrecked vehicle.

Reece shouted: "Here, Sto! In! Leigh!"

Leigh-Ann nodded, breathlessly following under the bags' weight. Caleb dropped behind the wheel of the next pick-up, Zip in the back, as Reece waited by an open door.

"I hurt it!" Stomatt backed towards the truck. "Didn't you see I –"

Another gunshot cut him off, bullets pinging into the vehicles around Stomatt as he dropped for cover. Leigh-Ann's gaze darted from him back to the farmhouse, to the porch where Nina stood with her father's double-barrelled shotgun in shaking hands, swinging it from their direction to out over the field, then back again. Torn between protecting the farm from that creature and revenging herself on them. The gun fixed on Leigh-Ann, the girl making a decision, and Leigh-Ann froze. There was another shape moving beyond Nina, a shadow stalking up through the fields. Smaller than the monster.

"Behind you," Leigh-Ann uttered, unable to say it louder. "Behind you."

Nina stepped out off the porch. Wanting to look Leigh-Ann in the eye.

"Leigh, move!" Reece shouted, from behind the truck.

The huge beast roared on the other side of the barn, no quieter for having been shot. Leigh-Ann held up a defensive hand. "Sweetie – I swear –"

Nina made a noise little more human than the monster attacking them, taking another step closer. Reece peeked up again, and, seeing the situation, raised his pistol. "Nina you drop that now!"

A loud scrape on the shingle announced Stomatt stumbling, trying to get up but slipping, and Nina threw the gun his way and fired on nerves. Leigh-Ann flinched her eyes shut and needed a second to check she was still there. A hand locked on her arm and dragged her back. One of the bags was lifted off her shoulder and Reece shouted by her ear, "She's empty, move!"

But Leigh-Ann was looking back as she stumbled after him, trying to spot that shape she'd seen before. Nina fumbled in a pocket for another shell, breaking open the gun. "Reece –"

He wasn't listening, dragging her to the truck. Stomatt moved parallel in a crouch as Caleb got the engine going, calling, "Come on guys!"

"You bastards!" Nina screamed, jamming the barrel flush again. "You –"

Leigh-Ann snapped a look back just before Reece bowled her into the truck, seeing the shadow reappear behind the farmer's daughter. A man, dark as a silhouette, so quick he barely seemed to move. Metal glinted in the sunlight and Nina's expression flicked with surprise – on to off in a second. The girl split into two parts as she fell to the ground. Leigh-Ann shrieked, "Reece!"

Zip shrieked louder, "Giza!"

With another tremendous roar, the first beast tore out the front of the barn, beating its huge chest. Half in the truck, Reece slapped the truck roof for Caleb to drive, then straightened his pistol-arm over the roof and fired three times. Leigh-Ann rolled over the back seat, watching through the windscreen as the beast fell back into the barn wall, arms smashing through the wood. The truck wheels spun and the tail swung out as Caleb hit the accelerator. With a massive eruption of dirt and shingle they sheared forward. Reece was thrown to the side, almost falling out, and Leigh-Ann caught him by the belt. She tugged him in, down on top of her, and they both fell onto the scrambling kid.

In the bed out back, Stomatt rose and slammed his beefy hands into the rear window, laughing madly. "Did it! We fucking did it!"

Leigh-Ann struggled upright to look back. The creature was out of sight, but the other figure was calmly walking through the dust cloud. A short, slender man, with a sword down at his side. She whispered, "What in hell just happened?" She turned the question to Reece. He wasn't looking back, but down, at Zip, like she was the one to ask.

The child was curled up against the far door, head buried in her arms, making little sobs.

"Reece," Leigh-Ann said, because damned if she was going to ask that child. "What in hell just happened?"

# 8

Leaving Katryzna to enjoy the shower, Tasker met Ward outside the hotel. He didn't mention his bloody guest as Ward drove through the city, instead silently ruminating on what she had told him. He wasn't sure if it was a threat or simple fact that mentioning Katryzna's name was dangerous: he suspected both. After all, if she had stumbled upon Parris's murder, someone was likely to be out to silence her next. Provided, of course, everything she'd told Tasker was true. A quick online search had turned up a small mountain in the heart of the Democratic Republic of the Congo called Ikiri, but identifying Miguel Lopaz required more nuance than Google could offer – a job he delegated to Caffery with a brief call. The only thing he could really be sure of was that Katryzna had *some* connection to the dark side of the big companies, and if the Ministry found that out, they would want to Do the Right Thing and capture her. Interrogate her. At the very least hire her.

He should probably want to Do the Right Thing, himself, but was hesitant. She was youthful, vibrant in her own degenerate way. Repellent but also fascinating – she kept her weapons close and heard voices, and was likely highly dangerous. He couldn't help wondering what if . . . . What if this potentially weaponised woman really was looking to turn against Duvcorp? It was a different kind of insurance, a promise of meeting these people on their own terms for once, instead of with the limp impotence mandated by the Ministry's restrictions. The image of the dead child in Laukstad came back to him, her blonde hair stiff and brittle in the ice. Didn't she deserve that justice?

Ward took Tasker's silent contemplation as an invitation to fill him in on her own developments. They could all but confirm Parris showed no signs of struggle – something about his posture or the blood splatter indicated he had been calm when the wounds were inflicted. And the blood in the living room did not belong to him. Ward said, "Looks like your theory was right. But were there two intruders there separately, or did two hitmen disagree in the middle of a job?"

Tasker leant heavily towards the former. Somehow, he believed Katryzna's claim that she worked alone.

Ward also explained, quietly, that her people had scanned Parris's laptop for the most recently accessed files. One file stood out for its ambiguity: a spreadsheet of thousands of rows containing five columns of numbers that seemed to show energy readings with dates, co-ordinates and what appeared to be angles, with numbers ranging from 1 to 360. They were already trying to see if any of the co-ordinates pointed towards Laukstad. Meanwhile, Ministry people testing on the ground there were reporting novisan fluctuations standard for a coastal village. Reports that were useless: they needed readings from four days ago, but Norway didn't have their own MEE, so no one was watching then. Except, apparently, Duvcorp.

Tasker's initial perception was so far validated, though; the investigators had turned up a variety of wounds on the bodies, caused by knives or blunt instruments, but the claw and bite marks could well have been from human teeth and nails. Ward went on to say her Support team had run historical checks, for similar unexplained mass murders, with no apparent motive or specific suspect. There was a village in Estonia, Silna, in 2009. Sixteen people killed in some kind of mob attack. It was during a heatwave and got passed off as caused by unusual atmospheric gas – one of the Ministry's favourite fallbacks. There was also an unresolved group murder in the Brixton riots, in the early '80s, and an Arctic expedition who all died violently in the '60s. Nothing flagged more recently, not concerning the Ministry. But then, they might not have flagged Laukstad without being tipped off to it.

They took a great stone bridge across Ordshaw's river and the skyline opened up to the right of the car. Duvcorp's HQ stood out: a trio of cylindrical towers at staggered heights, reflecting light even on this dull day. The opposite of subtle.

"The lady we're meeting," Ward said, "is Ms Marge Cosgrove. Head of their Renewable Energy European division. In company structure, she's not far below the upper executives. London advise that we don't bring up their novisan research, though."

"I'm sure they do," Tasker murmured. There wasn't much they could discuss, was there? This was just an opportunity for Duvcorp to confess, if they'd be so kind.

Ward parked in a large drop-off zone and a stiff-legged man led them through a cathedral-scale lobby to a gilded lift. That took them onto an expansive roof terrace, atop one of the building's lesser towers. A dozen tables sat opposite a café bar, overlooking an expansive view of Ordshaw's South Bank. Marge Cosgrove was the café's sole occupant, waiting in a crisp grey suit. She had the hard-lined face and straight posture of someone who strategised her life down to the most efficient way to breathe. She put on a welcoming smile, about as genuine as the ones Tasker used.

Cosgrove invited them to sit and said, "Naturally, we were all devastated to hear about Simon." You could almost believe it. "It's shocking anyone would want to hurt him. He was quiet, kept to himself. Hard working. But I expect you know all that, given his history with the Ministry."

Ward gave Tasker a deferring look and he started, "He fit in at work?"

"I never saw a problem," Cosgrove said. "He was a senior researcher, promoted multiple times. Simon was pioneering new solar energy solutions."

"Did it somehow concern activity in Norway?" Tasker dived straight in.

The smile tightened, the rest of Cosgrove's body motionless. "Why do you ask?"

"Parris specifically requested me," Tasker lied. "That is, an agent based in Norway. Did your work involve surveying irregular energy readings?"

She looked at Ward as though asking if such topics were really fair game, and

Ward didn't meet her eye. Cosgrove said, "In Norway? Do they even have sunlight at this time of year?"

Tasker waited for a proper answer.

Cosgrove calculated him carefully. "Agent Tasker, we have no concerns in Norway. If you're alluding to that tragic village massacre, I can emphatically insist there is no connection. But . . . Simon brought such concerns to you? He had ideas of his own, separate to his research here. Perhaps he couldn't leave his Ministry work behind? When we have access to his computer again, we might check exactly what he was up to."

Sure – check, delete and/or replace.

"He didn't bring any concerns to you?" Ward proffered. "Before he came to us?"

Cosgrove put on the act of trying to recall. Then evaded the question. "He was a private man, he didn't like to cause a fuss or draw attention."

"Well he got someone's attention, didn't he?" Tasker bristled.

"After talking to your people, you mean?"

"Do you mind me asking," Tasker moved straight on, "where Parris's work *was* concentrated? Geographically. Do you have overseas production centres? Research labs? Elsewhere in Scandinavia, or Europe? Maybe south, to study solar energy research – Africa? I don't know – the Congo?"

For a second, Cosgrove was surprised. Then the wall returned. "I don't follow."

"No? Parris never got assigned work in Africa, I suppose? What about his coworkers? A Miguel Lopaz, for example?"

Cosgrove's mouth twitched, just a little. "Agent Tasker, I have no idea what you're referring to." Ward frowned, looking more confused than their host.

Tasker said, "Just a name we've an interest in."

"One he told you?" Cosgrove said, making a show of checking her watch. "Something to do with the Congo?"

Tasker held her eyes, waiting for more, and her mouth curled tightly.

"Very well, let's be frank – from one illicit research body to another. Yes, Simon was involved in research that might overlap your own. No, it had nothing to do with anywhere in Africa, nor Norway. That he spoke to you about it, and not me, suggests a throwback to a project from his past which he clearly never let go. I couldn't begin to suggest why he would do that, unless . . ." She indicated Ward with a knowing look.

Ward frowned. "He wasn't working for us."

"Interesting." Snideness crept into Cosgrove's tone. "It would seem he wasn't entirely working for *us* either." She stood. "Now, without meaning to be rude, if it's only a name you have to ask about, I'll have someone from HR talk to you."

"Wait." Ward rose, too. "We'd like to discuss Parris's job –"

"Ha" – Cosgrove dropped the friendly act – "but you are clearly better informed than me, Ms Ward. And I'm sure you're well enough informed to know how complicated pushing your point could make things, for everyone. Good day to you both."

Ward looked to Tasker, chilled by the audacity of that tone. He gave her the slightest shake of his head and Cosgrove indicated for their stiff-legged escort to take them away. They rode the lift in silence and were taken back to the lobby, where Tasker noticed two burly men emerge from some double doors, looking their way with all the appearance of nightclub bouncers. Tasker couldn't make out a neck tattoo.

Ward asked, "Who's Miguel Lopaz?"

"I don't know," Tasker admitted. "And I'm not sure she did, either."

"And *Africa*?" Ward prompted. "Where'd you get these ideas?"

"We should get moving." As they walked, heading down wide steps towards the car, he said, "I've got a contact. Someone who spoke to Parris."

"You've –" Ward started incredulously.

"I'm sorry, but considering his fate I'm being cautious about who I share with. Those details in there probably marked us already, but I'll go through my handler to follow up, keep it out of your office. You should make a show of releasing Parris's case to the police."

"Releasing the case? Hold on –"

"You said there's nothing left to involve us in Laukstad," Tasker said. "Better they believe there's nothing tying us to Parris, either. I'll leave town, continue alone."

"Tasker," Ward said firmly. "The MEE is not afraid of corporations like Duvcorp."

"We don't know who we're supposed to be afraid of yet," Tasker replied. "Right now, the best thing we can do is get to Lopaz before they do, and I can do that best without people thinking it's what I'm doing."

Ward didn't like it, but left it at that. They got back in the car and as she drove he called Caffery again. Yes, Duvcorp had an office in the Democratic Republic of the Congo's capital city, Kinshasa, and there was a Miguel Lopaz who worked there. Their own contact out there was Special Intelligence Service, not someone to be trusted with Ministry business. But the way Cosgrove had given them the brush-off was enough to convince Tasker that Katryzna was on the money, so he had a new destination. He could do with the African sun. He immediately demanded a flight out there – with two seat bookings, the second anonymous, to protect his contact – but Caffery postured and complained and said it was a big ask with or without a travelling companion. The DRC was a war zone and they couldn't even be sure this was a Ministry case.

Wait and see, the bastard said. Enjoy the hotel, check in with your family.

It caught him off guard for a second. Helen and Rebecca were almost close enough to touch, but to let them know that he was here and leaving again would be crueller than them not knowing at all. He curtly ended the call, asking that Caffery merely do as he was asked.

Ward said, "Time's a factor, isn't it?"

"Yeah," Tasker said.

"My people could help," Ward continued, carefully.

Tasker raised an eyebrow.

"Agent Tasker. It's my job to enable people like you to do yours; that can include expedited travel arrangements. I'm not . . . always convinced

Management run things smoothly out of London. We can have you on a plane in a couple of hours, I'm sure."

A manager offering him the support he actually needed? Here was a marvel. "I'd appreciate that."

"And I'd like to drive you to the airport myself, to be safe."

Ah. There was the choice – between introducing Ward to Katryzna and waiting on damn Caffery. Well, it was her funeral. He said, "All right. But fair warning, I just met this woman and I'm not sure how safe she is."

Ward looked happy enough just to be trusted, though, and after they pulled up to the hotel he left her waiting by the car to go get his errant guest.

Katryzna greeted him, gun in hand. She had changed into fresh clothes sent up by the hotel lobby, and looked almost presentable in too-big khaki trousers and a pale blouse – more like she had escaped from a penal colony than just murdered someone. Though she had failed to get her shaved head completely clean, and her knife-belt remained strapped around her waist. Tasker pointed to her neck, still flecked with blood. "You missed a spot."

She stuck out her tongue to show how little she cared. As he gathered his things, and packed away her weapons, he explained about the meeting and the next step taking him to Africa. Katryzna smiled at his drive and said she knew he'd deliver – eager to keep moving herself, right away.

Despite her shower and new clothes, Katryzna's appearance at the car still startled Ward. Katryzna gave her name then jumped forward for a hug. She aborted at the last second and backed off, abashed. Ward did a bad job of hiding her confusion. Tasker settled into the passenger seat and watched Katryzna in the mirror. She flashed him a cheeky smile but kept quiet as they started driving.

Ward confirmed she'd arranged things in the time it had taken Tasker to round up his vagrant travelling companion. Then she put her effort into avoiding the urge to stare, while Katryzna flicked little looks at her. Studying her body as well as her face. Tasker wondered if she might bite out Ward's throat mid-journey, and his concerns mounted when Katryzna snapped little whispers at her invisible companion. Ward shot Tasker a sideways look.

"Do you get cute little assistants everywhere you go?" Katryzna asked Tasker, face suddenly appearing between the seats. Ward almost swerved into the next lane.

"This is the Deputy Director of Ordshaw's MEE offices," Tasker told her, levelly, and Katryzna fell back with an impressed whistle.

"You're important, Sean. Can we take her with us?"

"I'm sorry," Ward said. "Who exactly *is* she, Agent Tasker?"

"I kill people."

The car got a few degrees colder as Katryzna's grin stretched wider. Tasker could hear Ward's cogs turning. "What's your connection to Parris?"

"Eyes," Katryzna answered with a cheery shrug. Ward mouthed it back.

"A friend of hers," Tasker explained. "He worked for Duvcorp. Parris tried to contact him, same as us, and got her instead."

"I bit his *face*."

Tasker didn't have a response for that, and Ward's frown intensified.

Katryzna continued, "First time I met Eyes. Near London, actually. He was sent to kill me and I bit him to get away. A few months later, we met in Budapest. Bucharest? I get them confused. Anyway, we had dinner in Belarus when he helped me out of prison." Her jumbled thoughts got more tangled. "You didn't fear Eyes, because if he was out to get you, you were already dead. Well, except me. Because I'm *me*."

"Sounds . . . romantic," Ward commented weakly.

Katryzna bolted forward again. "Oh, it wasn't like that. Men? Yuck." Her hand was on Ward's shoulder and the deputy director looked very afraid. When Katryzna looked to Tasker to press her point, he nodded for her to back off. Her brow creased and she carried on. "He was sad, *never* stopped smoking. He only wanted someone to talk to – about how bored he was, unfulfilled. People like talking to me, I'm a good listener."

Hard to believe. She sat back, at last. Ward checked where she'd touched her shoulder like it might catch fire.

"We worked together sometimes, and met up when we were nearby. It's important to keep social. And he *needed* to vent about the ghosts and things Hank Duvalier made him hunt. He hated not knowing things, and he couldn't find explanations for everything. He described something to me once that sounded" – she barked a laugh – "like a floating woman, half-invisible. Dead. He did not understand it at all, so he blamed himself. Overtired, low on oxygen, whatever. Eyes was so *dry*, he saw everything as a logic problem, and this one did not add up. I told him he should pack it in. Retire. Except to retire from our work, usually someone retires *you*. He should have killed them first." Katryzna scowled at her shoulder again and hissed something Polish, then said, "Yes I did. How would you know?" Ward's expression got more concerned and Katryzna smiled like a kid caught misbehaving. "Sorry. My conscience."

Tasker came in to clear that up: "Rurik?"

"Don't worry." Katryzna patted Ward's arm again, more interested in convincing her than him. "You can't see Rurik. He is no problem. Though . . ." She considered something carefully. "I shouldn't have told you *my* name, isn't it? Forget it, okay?"

Ward gave a very uncomfortable nod. When they reached the airport, she shook hands and wished Tasker good luck, keeping her distance from Katryzna, who looked like she might try that hug again. Rurik apparently advised her against it and she stalked aside, snarling at him. Ward gave Tasker a parting look that said now she'd met the contact she was happy to keep clear of this. Rather him than her. Story of his damn career.

# 9

Reece revisited the action at the farm in drumbeats, trumpet blasts. The gunshots and shouts were punctuation in a score. A powerful piece, full of force, fear, triumph. He tapped his fingers against the pistol on his lap, picking out the sound. That's how you made sense of it. Because it made shit-all sense otherwise.

"Almost outta gas," Caleb said quietly, drawing him back into the moment.

"How's that?" Reece said. He was sat in back with Zip huddled down between him and Leigh-Ann. Caleb and Stomatt were in front, both staring ahead like they each had something they were burning to say, not sure it was wise to say it.

"Why I chose that other truck," Caleb muttered. "Had more gas. This one's dry."

"You're telling us now?" Leigh-Ann said, hotly, and Reece gave her a look. They were all on edge. Not a time to take it out on each other. She thumped back into her seat.

"Haven't seen a stop since the farm," Caleb continued. He'd hoped a solution would turn up along the way. But they must've done an hour now, without a break nor barely a word shared between them. It was a bad way to break the silence. Hitting this long, empty highway had been a mixed blessing, a straight line to Louisiana but one likely to be patrolled. Stopping for gas was a sure way to get back on the Steer Trust's radar. The rest stations, the stores along the roads, even some of the roads themselves were their domain.

That's why it made sense to get off the beaten track, Reece recalled now. Why they'd deviated and ended up on that farm. Because he had that feeling they were gonna run into trouble. Same feeling he got now.

"How far till the state line?" Reece asked.

"Not far," Caleb said. "I wanna say twenty minutes?"

"Got enough to last us that long?"

Caleb didn't answer, rather than lie or offer news none of them wanted to hear. The Steers had had time, now, to lock down the state. They were a glorified protection racket, for Christ's sake, they'd be keeping an eye on anyplace Caleb might pull up, and probably had all sorts of people set to inform on a likely crew of miscreants racing by.

"Keep going, it's all we can do," Reece said, because they needed to hear him calm, even if he hardly felt it. "Get as far as we can, then we take it from there."

Caleb nodded, rolling his shoulders with relief at getting his bombshell out the way. But now it was Stomatt's turn, the little bit of chat triggering him into twisting in his seat. The big guy was grinning in an unfriendly way, focused on

Zip. He said, "What do you think, that gorilla knew which vehicle to trash? Make sure we didn't get away." He moved restlessly. "It was a gorilla, right? Big, ugly, hard to put down, but a gorilla all the same. You got it between the eyes, right, Reece?"

"Looked like," Reece said. "But I wouldn't like to go back and check."

"I didn't like leaving her there with it," Caleb said uneasily. "That farm girl –"

"Took a fucking shot at me! Psycho!" Stomatt half laughed. "What was it – what are we into here? This kid? That thing?"

Reece shifted an arm over Zip's shoulders, seeing her tensing. "Calm it, Sto. Kid's got more poise than you right now."

"More poise, more fu–" Stomatt almost stood out his seat. His bandages had come loose in the fight, fresh blood had dried on his shirt and coveralls. "I ran that thing off. You wake me up in some land of dead farmers and freaky kids and mutant gorillas, and you're talking about my *poise*?"

"*You* trapped us out there, dammit," Leigh-Ann snapped, her own bottled feelings at breaking point. "We'd be in Louisiana already if you'd given over the wheel!"

"I was good for it till Reece directed us to the ass-crack of nowhere –"

"And what'd become of her?" Reece said. "Might've been a mistake heading out there – definitely a mistake letting you drive – but if it hadn't gone down like that, no one else was rescuing Zip. She'd be living them horrors alone."

"Last I checked," Stomatt said, "we set out to make money, not run a fu" – he leered, under Leigh-Ann's scolding look – "a *frigging* charity."

"Last I checked we were musicians holding them Steer bastards to account," Reece shot back. "Not cold-as-coal assholes. You can take your share and hike – any one of you can – but I'm not leaving a *child* behind."

"Yeah me either," Caleb grumbled. Leigh-Ann let her expression say the same.

Stomatt looked from one to the other, his mocking grin returning. Pissed off and refusing to admit it. "Think I'm some kind of lunatic?" he laughed. "Of course we're not leaving her. But maybe – here's a thought – maybe *she* can tell us what kind of mess she got us into? What do you say, princess? Time to share that with us, now?"

Zip cowered, tiny in the middle of the seat, and looked up pleadingly to Reece.

"She can talk when she's ready," he said.

"That before or after we're all dead?"

"Sto –"

"I'm sorry," Zip interrupted quietly. "I'm sorry."

"You got nothing to apologise for, sugar –" Leigh-Ann started.

"They came for me," she said. "They came for me before and they'll keep coming. It's why – it's why I didn't get to Daddy. They couldn't find me at home, but I left the safety and now, they'll keep coming, they'll find me *anywhere*."

Stomatt gave that a beat before demanding, "The hell's she talking about? Kid, what are you on?"

Before Reece could tell him to pack it in again, Leigh-Ann came in with a softer question. "You named it. That gorilla? You knew it from somewhere?"

Zip bit her lip. "Giza. I didn't know it before, no, I ..."

"The hell does that mean?" Stomatt started up again. "How the –"

"I felt it," Zip rushed out. "Sometimes I feel things. Feelings. Names. I know I'm not supposed – it's not allowed – it's dangerous, but I can't help it!" She stared at the big guy imploringly, full of apology. That confused him enough to stay quiet for a second.

"You felt that gorilla's name?" Reece clarified, gently, and Zip nodded guiltily. "And that's something you're . . . not allowed to do?"

"That's why they're *here*," Zip said.

"You told me your daddy hunts monsters . . ."

Zip confirmed it with a serious look, and the group were quiet. Even Stomatt kept it down, now he saw Reece was getting onto it. He asked, quietly, "How'd you get here, cher?"

Zip swallowed. "Followed Daddy. On the plane. And when he took a car, I got a bus. I walked. And . . . I couldn't find him so I looked . . . in here." She tapped her head, eyes full of apology. "I looked in here. And I was trying to catch up when they came. So I ran. I found a train – I ran more – until – until those men at the farm found me."

"How long you been at this?"

"*Days*," Zip insisted, "at least four – five days." Like that was the worst thing about it, like it was all the time in the world and not even stranger that she could've made those crazy journeys so quickly. Her eyes swelled with tears. "And I tried to warn them. I *told* them they would come."

But the farmer didn't want to hear it, and figured she was possessed. Thinking something like that monster was after her, and was probably gonna kill them all. Reece imagined her freaking out, making them freak out in turn. They might've been innocent after all.

"Who *are* they?" Leigh-Ann asked. "That gorilla and – the other one? With a sword?"

"Vile," Zip said, with a focus that said it just occurred to her. "He's called Vile."

Stomatt boomed, "*Vile* ain't a name. She's talking shit, guys, why you listening to this? Kiddy fantasies. Runaway from home on planes and trains, as if. Making up names –"

"You're Stomatt. Max Stomatt, but everyone calls you Sto," Zip interrupted, with new firmness now he was pushing her. That got his attention, but she kept going. "You're angry about your mum. I mean, not right now, but actually kind of. Under the other anger. I get angry about my mum, too. The same way. But I don't remember her, not like you remember yours."

Stomatt froze solid and Caleb stiffened on the wheel. Zip looked to Reece, questioning eyes asking if she was right. He stared back. Damn hell she had Stomatt's measure. His drunk mom had beaten her husband, a thick-skulled brute himself, and Stomatt was the only soul in Cutjaw that regretted her leaving without a word. He got especially belligerent during family holidays.

Stomatt said, "You bastards put her up to this?"

"There's power in all of us, my daddy says," Zip said. "Only *he* knows how to control it. Anyone else would be dangerous with it. That's why he has to track the others down. And why I'm not allowed. I . . ." She threw Reece an apologetic look. "I didn't mean to just now. Or before, to get the monsters' names, but it just –"

"Easy," Reece said, and added, "You done nothing wrong." Less sure of that by the second.

"What *is* this?" Stomatt demanded. "Genetic experiments all out the same lab? Red-eyed psychic kids? Damn gorillas with metal skin, freaks with sword fetishes?"

Zip was afraid to answer, or didn't have one, and suddenly everyone was looking to Reece like he was somehow gonna explain this. He didn't have a clue. She looked like any other kid, if a bit grubby and weird about the eyes. But her sensing that thing was after her, reading emotions out the air, what could he make of that? He said, "Where you come from, Zip? You gotta tell us about your home."

"I . . ." She hesitated. "Daddy said it isn't safe. He said don't even *think* about it. They'd find us."

"But we need to know, to help."

Zip swallowed. "It's just where we live, though. The really dangerous place – that's what you want to know. Where the power is?"

Reece frowned. A lab or something, like Stomatt was suggesting?

"I call it the Eye Key." Zip said. "I don't remember it. But I know I was there. It kind of . . . *hurts*? To think about it. I can't ever go back there. *No one can.*"

"Sounds like Sto's trailer," Leigh-Ann tried to joke, but it came out flat.

"Daddy gets upset about it," Zip continued, voice almost a whisper. "It makes monsters, he says. And now I've made things worse." She sniffed, hard. "I should've stayed home."

"Hey, if your daddy kept things from you," Reece told her, "how can it be your fault? Way I see it, Zip, probably he thought you weren't ready for all this yet. Look at us, Zip – people call *us* dangerous, being that we know how to shoot guns. But we use them right – ain't *never* hurt someone that didn't deserve it. Your gifts ain't dangerous, it's how you use them." She gave him a flash of hope and he smiled.

Caleb hit the brakes hard. They all flew forward in their seats, Reece shooting a hand out to hold Zip back, and Stomatt cursed Caleb before the driver hissed, "Company, up ahead!"

The road had curved to look onto a stretch that ran past a gas station, where a burgundy Cadillac was parked blocking both lanes. Close enough to see it was flying the Steers' eagle-skull flag – two little ones, in fact, one above each headlamp – as if that needed signalling. A tall guy in a ten-gallon hat leant against the hood while another with a bolo tie and panelled jeans loitered near the rest stop entrance. Both had pistols in shoulder-holsters out on display over their check shirts.

Ten-gallon stood up straighter, looking their way. Fifty, a hundred yards off, and they'd skidded to a conspicuous halt. Stomatt rumbled, "I can take them down."

"We ain't out looking for a trail of blood," Reece hissed, but his fingers were closed tight on his own gun. "We can pull back, find a side road, find some place to syphon gas."

"I didn't see no side roads, Reece," Caleb warned.

"He's already seen us," Leigh-Ann said. "How far we gonna get if word gets out about our route?"

"I can help," Zip said quietly.

"You all stay put, keep your heads down," Reece decided. "I'll handle it." The gang went quiet. The Steer by the car moved to the side, calling at his friend, so they were both looking up the road. Gripping the door handle, Reece took a breath. He'd talk to them, that was all. Charm the horns off the devil.

Zip watched him with fear. Her eyes went to the gun in his hand. He smiled, like this was nothing, and winked, then opened the door and stepped out. Bolo tie had moved to linger near the driver's seat as Hat stepped away, hand ready to draw. In the truck, Zip whispered something and Leigh-Ann whispered back assurances.

With the door for cover, gun down behind it, Reece called out, "Excuse me, boys, but you appear to be –"

Zip jumped out of the truck as Leigh-Ann grabbed at her. Too fast to stop, she was on the asphalt in an instant, running towards the men. Reece came out of cover after her, shouting, "Zip!"

Hat fumbled at his shoulder holster, flustered at seeing the threat was a waist-high child. Bolo stiffened with confusion. Reece brought his own pistol up. "You boys even think of moving, I'll –"

"Stop!" Zip shouted and Reece skidded to a halt himself. She had both hands up like a preacher as she came in front of the Steers, and the men stared at her raptly. Her voice was different somehow, bigger, impossible to ignore. "We don't want trouble."

# 10

Tasker and Katryzna were picked up at the airport by a uniformed man with a luxurious van, who drove them wordlessly through the dusty, plaster-cracked streets of Kinshasa. Hotel Memling was a welcome oasis against the hot, arid and deafeningly busy outdoors; the sort of opulent satellite haven Tasker was accustomed to the world over. Katryzna had been subdued since the flight, but entering Le Cockpit Bar, a classy room of distressed brown leather sofas and high stools, she whooped and commented, "Colonialism's still going strong, I see."

There was a lot Tasker had wanted to ask her about Duvcorp and their cohorts' shady dealings but she had been oddly quiet on the way, glued to in-flight movies. He instead drafted messages for Helen, explaining the diversion from Japan had been extended, and that he would call later. He loved them, he missed them. He couldn't stop picturing that dead girl's face. When he tried to sleep, the memory was more vivid than ever, and he had finally ordered rounds of whisky to help. Entering the hotel bar, he could happily resume that drinking.

Charles Smail, the Secret Intelligence Service representative for the Democratic Republic of the Congo left his table with a beer in hand to greet them. He was tall, at just over six foot, but gravity pooled his weight around his waist, his tucked-in linen shirt drawing attention to that uneven body shape. He had on brown shorts, sandals, and a too-small sun hat that barely concealed his tangle of straw-like hair. Smail had clearly given up professional appearances long ago. He cheerily invited them to join him, offering local beers. Tasker suggested that whisky, but Katryzna merely requested water. Smail swayed to the bar like a bowling pin ready to topple.

"He's a British spy?" Katryzna asked.

"I guess so."

"Not exactly James Bond."

"Part of the disguise, I suppose," Tasker said.

Smail was posing as a mining official – who was to say what passed for smart when studying holes in the ground amid oppressive heat. He returned with loud comments about the weather, pumping his shirt to fan himself. Never mind the room was air-conditioned. He slid onto his stool and assessed the pair anew. His eyes lingered particularly on Katryzna. "So, all this way to meet our man Lopaz? I must admit I'm keen to exchange notes on him. The chap is shifty as they come, which is saying something in this city. Is he really still with Duvcorp?"

"He give an impression he's not?" Tasker asked.

Smail laughed. "Well, he's been here as long as me, but never talks shop.

Never seems to do any work for them. They have no actual interests in this part of the country – Duvcorp's mining reps are in Kananga. I always pegged their office here down to administrative error. Set a man up on some idle idea they never followed through, but forgot to cancel his pay cheque. Have a seat, won't you?"

Katryzna did so reluctantly, watching him.

"My personal profile?" Smail continued. "Lopaz is ex-military, from a long time ago. He dabbles in underground fighting and tries to stay off the grid. Left whatever his old life was far behind, or at least wants to. I've put word out that you're after setting up a meet, under the guise of investors, but doubt he'll have much interest in it."

"Can we go to him?" Tasker asked.

"Yes." Smail nodded. "He'll be around Club Clash. You know what Clash is?" He turned the question to Katryzna, to include her.

She told him matter-of-factly, "I do not even know what *you* are."

Smail tapped the side of his nose in appreciation of her discretion, not admitting confusion. "Clash is a gym. Some of us keep sane with chess and reading classics by the river; Lopaz manages fighters. Bets big on them. He hangs out at the fight bars, too. Misses the machismo from whatever military he served in, would be my guess."

"Club Clash it is, then," Tasker said.

Smail took a long swig of beer, noting the cabin bag by their feet. "You don't want to check in first? Wait long enough and Lopaz will surface here. All the expats do, eventually."

"I'd rather not wait," Tasker said. "People have a habit of disappearing on me."

"Or dying," Katryzna added helpfully. If it surprised Smail, he didn't let it show.

"Well, so you know, Lopaz won't take kindly to strangers turning up at Clash."

"I don't care what he might take kindly to," Tasker said. "I've spent the better part of three days on planes chasing people that were dead before I got there. I'd rather not add his name to that list."

Smail took that down without critique, clearly assessing the nature of the visit. Katryzna gave Tasker a pleased look, appreciating that irritable, get-things-done edge. The spy nodded and stood. "Okay then. I'll drive. Are you armed? Best leave your gun here. This city is really rather safe, compared to the rest of the country, and it's best we not send the wrong message."

"Are you not taking us into a literal fight club?" Tasker said.

"Trust me, we'll be fine talking, if you let me lead."

"And I will have my knife," Katryzna said.

"What? No. That's worse than a gun. There won't be any trouble, don't worry."

Katryzna's eyes met Tasker's, not convinced, but he said, "All right, no weapons."

Katryzna snorted disgust, but rather than complain she made a sharp comment to her invisible conscience, in Polish. Then she rolled her eyes, presumably at Rurik encouraging caution. She threw up her hands in concession.

They squeezed into Smail's cheap Citroen and drove with the windows down to circulate smoggy air. After twenty minutes bumping over hole-riddled roads, Tasker was starting to feel queasy. Smail's commentary of landmarks provided only scant distraction, as did his breezy account of how the Congo civil war was raging in the eastern reaches of the country. Smail rattled off names of militias and generals that meant nothing to Tasker, movements that had developed over the past months or years that the spy clearly enjoyed discussing but had no one to share the news with. More interesting here – Smail changed tack – was that an election was due but not yet scheduled and people were getting uneasy.

Before they could delve into that, they came upon Club Clash. It sat in a lower-lying district of Kinshasa, surrounded by desolate blocks. A two-storey windowless structure with an external iron stair going to the first-floor entrance. The name was painted above in block capitals, and alongside the door was a black-and-white decal of a man about to smash a guitar – the figure out of proportion.

"Paul Simonon," Smail said. "*London Calling*, you know? Not a bad likeness."

"The Clash?" Tasker raised an eyebrow. The last place he expected to see a reference to an English rock band.

"Used to be a music venue, way back when. I guess there was better money in fights. Now, can I suggest you let me make an introduction?"

Smail led them up the stairs to the entrance. He gave them one last warning with a smile, then entered. Inside was a wide room littered with training equipment, tinted green by filthy skylights and scented with sweat and old metal. The room encircled a central square cage, which cut through down to the ground floor – this area doubling as a viewing platform for a fighting ring on the ground floor. Electronic music blared from numerous speakers as one Congolese man heaved on a weights machine and another whipped large ropes off the floor. Both were hugely muscular, accompanied by similar big spotters, and once they completed a few final reps all four stopped to stare at the newcomers. The closest one addressed Smail in French, a threatening greeting. Smail responded chirpily and, after a second's consideration, the man shouted, "Monsieur Lopaz! Visitors."

Various shouts in French came from below, one voice rising above the others. Their host nodded to an opening, a spiral staircase going down, and Smail thanked him before continuing. Tasker followed with Katryzna, down the rickety stairs, as the men above converged on the stairwell too. On the ground floor, another half-dozen brutes had gathered, all ripped with muscle, every contour visible even under vests and sweatshirts, eyes following the newcomers. Amid the Black locals one man stood out: though not quite white, with leathery skin a shade of cork, Miguel Lopaz was patently not African. He was older and smaller, despite thickset limbs, with mean sunken eyes, thinning black hair and a tatty linen shirt.

Smail spread his arms in friendly greeting as Tasker kept an eye on the decidedly unfriendly men surrounding them. Katryzna shifted close, shoulder brushing his. Not for security, but to confide in a thrilled whisper, "You wish I had my knife now?"

"Lopaz!" Smail said, cheerily. "My friend here just got into town, hoping for an introduction. I left messages for you?"

Lopaz's expression was hostile as he wobbled slightly aside from the group, right leg unsteady. "Friend out of England?" His voice was thickly Latino, and his sneer revealed a gold tooth. "Don't belong here, does he?"

"No, sir, I expect not," Smail said lightly. "Could we step outside? I'll spot you a beer. They've travelled a long way to meet you."

Lopaz's eyes worked over to Katryzna in a way Tasker already knew meant trouble. "No way she's your friend, too."

Katryzna didn't speak, but returned the look with worrying enthusiasm.

One of the tallest men shifted close to Lopaz, leaner than the others, with a thin moustache and a thoughtful expression. He muttered in French, and Lopaz answered in a grave tone, using the man's name, Henri. Tasker's French wasn't up to much, but he got that Lopaz made particular reference to Katryzna as someone they had discussed before. *I told you, didn't I?* Henri regarded her carefully, then chuckled. The others joined in, before he spoke loudly in English, "Excuse me, but Miguel here thinks –"

"I *know*," Lopaz spat. "I know who *she* is." He said it with such venom that the audience went quiet again, though Henri wore his scepticism on his face.

Smail happily continued with no regard for the tension. "So what do you say to a private chat out back?"

"I say no," Lopaz answered. "I say you better walk out of here now and take her with you – *if* you can control her."

Smail turned an uncertain look back to Tasker and Katryzna; she still wasn't talking, eyes shimmering with anticipation. Tasker said, "Whoever you're expecting, we're not them. I'm from the Ministry of Environmental Energy. You've heard of us?"

"Yeah," Lopaz replied flatly. He spoke in French, too quick for Tasker to catch, but with an irritable *I-told-you-so* quality. His companions weren't joking, now – eyes going to the nearest weights and tools, expecting trouble.

"We're just here to talk," Tasker said. "A guy called Simon Parris sent us."

Lopaz's lips tightened, confirming the connection.

"You spoken to him recently?" Tasker asked.

"Why would I have spoken to him," Lopaz said, "recently or not?"

"He died before he could explain that part," Katryzna said helpfully.

Lopaz glared at her. "You've brought wolves to our door, Charles. But I'm ready, aren't I? These boys are ready."

"Great." Katryzna stepped around Tasker, but paused. A glance to her shoulder. "No, they had their chance." Another pause, spreading her hands to reason with her conscience. "It's *boring* and he is *asking* for it." The crowd of men were momentarily thrown. Tasker wondered if it was a trick of hers, like his arsenal of smiles – the imaginary conscience wrong-footing her enemies. She said, "Bla, bla bla, no one cares!"

"*Elle folle?*" Henri wondered aloud, calling her crazy.

"Katryzna –" Tasker said. She gave him a wicked look.

Lopaz stepped back, speaking harshly. "Yes, *Katryzna*. Who else. Charles, you –"

"Ah ah!" Katryzna waved a finger. "He asked you nicely. Sean did too. Now, it's my turn." She paused and swiped an irritated hand over her shoulder, making the nearest two men flinch. She shouted to where Rurik was flung: "You watch me!"

"Stop her," Lopaz instructed, quickly back-stepping. "Before she kills us all."

He turned away. Henri asked if he was serious, on the verge of laughter at the fear this woman inspired, and Katryzna jumped two feet off the ground, her right elbow cocked sharply ahead of her. Henri's head snapped back with a crack and Katryzna rolled off him to clamp both hands onto the next man's face. She slammed her head into his before breaking through the circle, after Lopaz.

Tasker moved after her but a heavy grip landed on his upper arm. He twisted the hand around and caught a wrist, pivoting to use the attacker's own weight to trip him – but another guy slammed into him from the side. He tripped on the first man and pulled his attacker down, all three tangling in grappling limbs. A blow glanced off Tasker's head and his glasses went flying. He got an arm up to protect himself, as Lopaz lunged for a kit-bag across the room. Katryzna was right behind him, another fighter just behind her. Smail shouted, hustled back by two others, as someone swept in to kick Tasker.

Struck again, Tasker writhed, trying to get clear, but they were pressing on him and he reached ahead in vain. Between lashing legs he saw Lopaz reach his bag, but Katryzna dived ahead of him. She pulled back with a bounce in her step, holding his gun. She turned and fired a single shot, clipping the leg of the man bearing down on her. As he crumpled with a cry and everyone froze around Tasker, Katryzna grinned. "Shall we start again?"

# 11

Zip stopped before the cowboy, arms at her sides. The man stood away from his vehicle, regarding her with a strangely distant look. He teased his hat with one hand, the other loose, gun forgotten. Reece crept up behind, his own pistol held behind his back. Something about the stillness of the encounter warned him against any sudden moves. The guy with the bolo tie was sat in the car, now, focusing hard on the dashboard like he was trying to remember something. Reece shot a look back to the truck; Stomatt was standing out the passenger side, his shotgun down out of view. Caleb and Leigh-Ann were all but leaning into the windscreen to watch.

Hat turned to the car, then back to Zip, and between the two showed no interest at all in Reece behind her, much less the truck. He scratched his chin and looked up at the sky. Zip could've been a statue, now, merely watching him. It was all Reece could do not to say something – come in with friendly banter now everyone was quiet. But the cowboy laughed heartily, a smile filling his face, then he turned away. He drew out a cigarette and lit it. The guy in the car reclined in his seat, turning his head to the roof like he was planning to get in a quick nap. Hat sauntered off the road, smoking. Not looking back.

It was like they were both brainwashed, lost in their thoughts and oblivious to the child and her criminal escort right before their eyes. Reece mouthed disbelief. "What in hell?"

Zip looked over her shoulder to him, a doll returned to life. She gave a little thumbs up and whispered, "I think it's okay now?" Not sounding sure herself what was going on.

Reece didn't need telling twice, though: whatever shade of weird this was, it was an opening. He spun to the truck and gave a quick wolf-whistle, gesturing to the gas stop. It took Caleb a second to get in gear. As the truck pulled over the verge to pass the Cadillac, Reece watched the guy in the car, still the least interested in the world beyond his quiet little space. Keeping his voice in a low hiss, Reece instructed, "Fill up before the wind changes. Quick as you can."

Caleb swung in quickly and Reece patted Zip to direct her towards the pumps. She trotted ahead as he threw the Steers one last look. Eerily damn disengaged. The moment the truck stopped, Stomatt was out, pump in hand and feeding the tank.

"What the hell you say to them?" Leigh-Ann asked, opening a rear door to invite Zip in. The child clambered in with her help, and answered happily.

"I didn't *say* it, exactly. But suggested they wouldn't notice us."

"This is freaky," Caleb said.

Reece moved round the front of the truck, looking in the shop. A man stood behind the counter, pole stiff and looking straight forward, hypnotised like the other two. Moving back to cover the Cadillac, Reece said, "Someone get in there and pay real fast – don't need them reporting gas theft."

"With him standing there?" Leigh-Ann exclaimed. "Ain't we already pushing –"

"Dammit Leigh move your ass!"

Grumbling, Leigh-Ann hustled over to the shop. This slight woman with crazy frizzy hair in her over-sized shirt and farmer's slacks, looking around every which way like she might get attacked by bees, it was sure to raise the clerk's eyebrows. She slowed at the door, braced herself then pushed on in, and all the while neither the Steers nor the clerk reacted in the slightest. Leigh-Ann went straight for the counter and reached it as the pump pinged, full.

"He ain't moved a muscle," Caleb commented, not sounding too happy about it.

"You a secret Voodoo queen, girl?" Stomatt said.

The clerk did move, though, engaging distantly with Leigh-Ann as she smiled her way through paying, making quick small talk before leaving. Not looking back. She bared her teeth at Reece as she passed him. "Next time you're braving the zombie."

Reece didn't reply, instead watching the motionless Steer in the car. He gave one more look over to the absent cowboy, now equally still, cigarette hanging down by his side. Zombie was right; this was some hoodoo shit. They all climbed back in and he bid Caleb go, no one else daring a word in case the spell was broken. In a minute, they were well down the road, Cadillac a distant silhouette, and still no sign that the Steers had moved. Finally, Stomatt roared with laughter. "That was some Grade A *freakshow* shit."

Zip smiled proudly in the middle seat, but the others weren't joining in. Caleb was tense at the wheel and Leigh-Ann gave Reece a dirty look. Reece kept an eye behind them, waiting for the moment the Steers realised what'd gone down. He said, "When's it gonna wear off?" Zip's smile disappeared. "*Is* it gonna wear off?"

"I – I don't know," she admitted.

"How'd you do that, Zip?" Reece asked. "Put an actual gris-gris on them."

"Um." She had that guilty face again, the one that said Daddy would be mad. "I'm not sure. I just knew I could. And that – that – no one would get hurt?"

"You never done that before?" Leigh-Ann said.

"I had to!" Zip insisted, like she'd just been caught lying. "To get on the plane – and – and – I was only trying to find my daddy – and they wouldn't have let us past, would they?"

"It's okay," Reece said. "Nothing to be sorry about. That was impressive, Zip – if we're quiet it's because we ain't never seen anything like it. Think your daddy might have been holding out on you."

"I'm telling you she's straight out a lab," Stomatt laughed again, not so bothered about the idea now. "We got some kinda experimental human weapon on our hands. Kid, *welcome* to the gang. But don't you ever try that shit on me." At Leigh-Ann's look, he corrected, "Sheep. Don't ever try that sheep on me."

"You try that on him all you like," Leigh-Ann said, signalling her own softening. "I'd give an arm to make men pay me no mind like that."

Caleb alone remained stiff up front, silent. Reece said, "Caleb? We good now, right?"

"We got gas," Caleb said, implying that, at least, wasn't a worry.

Reece and Leigh-Ann huddled by Zip and eased back into the journey. He let himself wonder, now, what all this was about – and more important where it might lead them. The job on the Steer Trust had set them up, but a kid who could do things like that? Forget a reward from a rich father, they could walk right into a bank. Hell, could get music critics singing their praises!

It was smooth sailing for a couple of quiet, empty miles, before the signs started showing: state line. Welcome to Louisiana. They cheered crossing over and even Caleb finally split a smile.

"Not two hours out of Stilt Town, now," Reece said. Hell, only that long until they were clear. Fallon wouldn't chase them into Arcadia; his Steers didn't have enough sway to pick up their scent here. Plenty bent cops, but not bent his way. Reece drummed a quick beat on Stomatt's headrest. "*Damn,* I can't wait to get back on the horn. Zip, you're gonna hear us *play*. We got magic, too, you wait and see."

It cheered Zip, he could see; them relaxing around her, letting her in. And she turned to Leigh-Ann, thoughtfully, to ask, "What do you play, Leigh?"

"Didn't I say?" Reece laughed. "*She* has the voice of an angel."

"Yeah, Lucifer," Stomatt joked.

"Fuck your eye!" Leigh-Ann snapped, and shot a hand over her mouth. "Shit, kid, I mean –"

"My daddy swears," Zip said. Then she added, "I don't give a fuck."

It took a second of disbelieving silence before they all erupted in laughter. Reece ruffled Zip's hair. "You're gonna fit right in. Start you on a tambourine. We could go far together."

She knotted her brow. "What's a tambourine?"

"A tambourine, sweetie," Leigh-Ann fielded this, quick, "is a lot like Sto there. You gotta beat it hard to make it work, and the harder you work it the more noise it makes."

As Stomatt hooted protest, Zip giggled without quite knowing why, and Caleb turned them down an avenue of Southern oaks. The landscape wasn't all that different from one mile to the next, but this was their territory now. Reece hummed a scatty little tune of triumph. Caleb came over it, improvising a baritone, "Oh take me back – take me down deep – deep *deeper* down – show me Stilt Town!"

Stomatt thumped a paradiddle on the dash, and Reece nodded along.

"Oh I said take me – take me down –"

The truck jolted and the drumming abruptly stopped as Caleb took a better grip on the wheel, a moment's panic. "Ah hell." His eyes were fixed on the rear-view. They all twisted round and saw a shape way up the road behind them. Gaining fast.

"Is that –" Leigh-Ann didn't bother finishing. They all knew what it was.

Zip gave Reece one of her apologetic looks and he quickly shook his head to tell her it wasn't her fault. None of them understood what she'd done back there, so no way she could be accountable for the Steers coming out of their trance.

"Sons of bitches got their guns out," Leigh-Ann said.

"Down, stay down!" Reece ordered. "Get us gone, Caleb!"

Caleb slammed his foot down and they lurched as the truck lumbered on. Weighed down with five bodies, this old farm-tech was already pushing the limits of its speed.

"Shift, shift," Reece told Leigh-Ann, keeping his eyes on the car as he climbed over her. She fumbled under him and came out the other side whispering at Zip not to worry. Reece drew his pistol. The car was tearing ferociously up to them, and behind the windscreen the cowboy driver was grimacing determination, the passenger itching to move in his seat, checking the ammo in a big revolver.

"Coming up on your side!" Stomatt warned, watching in the mirror. He held up his shotgun. "You want the Tonnerre?"

"Keep cool," Reece told him. "Hold us steady, Caleb."

The Cadillac swung out suddenly, over the centre of the road, and shot forward with a new burst of speed to get alongside them. The passenger was pulling himself up out the window, revolver first. Reece whipped up his own gun and fired into the Cadillac door. Enough to rattle the driver and make the passenger fumble, but the guy didn't drop his gun and the car kept coming.

Zip screamed.

"Hands on your ears, like this!" Leigh-Ann said.

The Cadillac pulled up again, the passenger yelling curses. He popped a shot that glanced the truck roof, making Reece duck. Stomatt bucked in his seat with shouts of his own, wanting to shoot over all of them. Reece rested in cover for a moment, steadying his breathing. More shots followed, slamming into the side of the truck and making Zip scream again.

"Reece!" Caleb shouted, warning that one came too close for comfort.

One more steadying breath and Reece rose, angled his arm and fired. Two shots – the first hit home and the Cadillac veered so suddenly the second shot hit the asphalt. He twisted out the window, keeping aim, but the car bounced as its front wheel burst to shreds. The passenger was thrown down in the window, doubled over the door, but somehow kept clinging to that gun. The wheel scraped sparks off the road over him, and the driver swung from side to side trying to keep control. They were losing speed rapidly, no matter what.

"Hell yeah!" Leigh-Ann cried, taking Zip in a tight embrace. "What'd I tell you!"

Reece slipped back down as the others cheered. It was a damn good shot, and they'd surely make Stilt Town now, but the damage was done. It'd been an idiot dream hoping they'd make it there unseen. Sure, Gray could still offer shelter and protection, but it made life more complicated for everyone, having Fallon able to figure out who hit him. Especially with this damn green hair – how hard was that gonna be to follow? No way those Steers hadn't already figured it, chasing the gang out here.

As the others calmed, Caleb picked up on that vibe first. Gray being his uncle and all, he'd always been most wary of taking trouble back there. Talking over

Stomatt's happy comments, he said, "You think they know where we're going, Reece?"

It wouldn't take a genius. A gang of thieves cutting right towards Fallon's most outspoken critic in Louisiana. But rather than admit it fully, Reece said, "I guess we'll see."

 

# 12

"I didn't agree to this," Smail hissed, as Tasker finished tying off the last of the men's hands, all of them now bound to a pipe, sat shoulder-to-shoulder on the floor. "I thought she was your assistant or something."

"Respectfully," Tasker told him, "that was your assumption to make."

He hadn't agreed to this, either, though. Lopaz's fears about Katryzna were clearly justified. But Tasker found there was something refreshing in seeing his "assistant" punch Lopaz to the floor with his own gun. And she'd shown restraint, the moment everything was under control – it's not like she'd gone on a rampage. Lopaz, who doubtless would've otherwise evaded answers or run, at best, was now cowed on a small wooden chair, the opposite side of the room to everyone else, while Katryzna tapped the pistol contemplatively against her chin.

"She's lucky she didn't kill him," Smail said, indicating the younger man who she had shot. Tasker gave the wound a lazy look – a clean shot that missed the bone, now bandaged. The victim had cried up a storm about never fighting again, but it wasn't much more than a flesh wound, and as Tasker's head and most of his torso was throbbing, he was okay with it. Thank Christ his glasses hadn't been smashed. Smail continued, "We're not in the war zone, Tasker – there are rules in Kinshasa. And Duvcorp take care of their own, you know? They've got as much power as a nation state!"

"Relax," Katryzna said. "Lopey will not talk about this, or us, to anyone."

Lopaz looked his age, frail on his chair with all his energy channelled into a hateful stare. She had left him unbound. From the way he regarded her, he wasn't going to try anything else.

"Miguel," Smail said, "understand that I had no idea the MEE would condone this behaviour."

Lopaz's face told him to stop embarrassing himself.

"Notice he does not beg or bargain or threaten?" Katryzna said. It was true – Lopaz had known how dangerous she was, the moment he saw her. The assumption was they were here to kill him. Smail went quiet as he finally accepted that himself.

Tasker pushed his glasses up his nose and said, "We're here to talk."

"Obviously," Lopaz snorted. "*They* wouldn't let me live this long."

"*They* being Duvcorp? Your own people want to silence you like they did Parris?"

Lopaz regarded him carefully, then checked his gym friends before looking back to Katryzna. "You came here with this wrecking ball, why don't *you* explain?"

Katryzna shifted closer to Tasker and whispered loudly, "I don't think he likes me."

"No one likes you!" Lopaz snapped. "Should've been food for worms right out of puberty!"

"Worms don't have puberty," she deliberately misinterpreted. Then asked Smail, "Do they?"

"Mr Lopaz," Tasker continued calmly, as Smail flustered at the attention. "This isn't what you think. Parris was murdered, but not by us. He tipped us off to a massacre in Norway. No explanations, no other clues but your name. And 'Ikiri'. Something Duvcorp definitely didn't want to discuss. So how about we start with exactly who you think would want you dead?"

Lopaz had gone still at the name Ikiri, and it took him a second to regroup. "If you're not here to kill me, you've given them a reason to. Get the hell out of here."

"Oh I do *not* have patience for this," Katryzna announced and walked away. The bound men stirred as she approached them, pistol raised. "Six men. You have six chances to talk." Smail looked to Tasker, but both waited to see where this was going. Katryzna raised her voice: "Three seconds, tick tock!" She pressed the gun to Henri's blood-smeared head. He froze as the others shouted and tugged at their restraints. "Three, two —"

"Stop, goddammit, stop!" Lopaz roared, out of the chair with his hands raised. He was shaking, looking at terrified Henri. "I'm sorry boys, I'm so sorry —"

"Talk!" Katryzna screamed with such ferocity that Tasker almost ducked himself. "You were part of it! What did Eyes die for? Talk!"

"Okay, okay!" Lopaz raised his hands higher, keeping his eyes on Henri. "Don't hurt them, for Christ's sake — whatever I deserve, these are good kids."

Nothing in Katryzna's expression said she cared. Her finger rested heavy on the trigger. Tasker said, "You've got our word, *no one* gets hurt if you talk."

"Your word's not what I need."

"Now, Miguel," Smail chipped in, "our friend from the British government here —"

Lopaz cut him off with pitying laughter. "Charles, you are *in* intelligence, aren't you? And you let Katryzna Tkacz into this city?"

Smail frowned, then studied Katryzna anew. She shrugged with a smile, light and merry again. He echoed, "Tkacz?"

"Autographs later," Katryzna said. "Talk, Lopey."

"Promise you won't hurt them."

"I promise I *will* if you test me —"

"All right, stop!" Lopaz said. "What do you want to know?" He looked to Tasker. "She, I understand. What's drawn the Ministry into this? You've finally discovered the Source?"

"The what?" Tasker asked.

Lopaz paused. "No?" He gave Katryzna another look and his face twisted to an ugly smile. "Oh. Katryzna, is this all you? Did you trick the Ministry into coming here so they'd pay for your airfare?"

"You think this is funny?" She stepped towards him. Tasker put a hand on her chest to stop her. Her eyes widened and nostrils flared, fingers tight on the pistol, as her anger shifted to Tasker.

"No, it's not funny," Lopaz said. "Tragic, is what it is. Charles? I am so sorry you're mixed up in this. And you, if you really are Ministry. She's a lovesick child, still, isn't she? Coming for long overdue revenge for Eyes. Why *now*, Katryzna?"

"I did not –" Katryzna rose on her toes as Tasker held her in place. She slapped his hand away and snarled, "Touch me again and I will end you."

"Eyes was the best," Lopaz said quickly. "The best I've ever seen, maybe the best the world's ever seen – until he met her. She made him sloppy. Sentimental." She shifted around Tasker but Lopaz threw up his hands. "Hold on, I'm talking! It doesn't matter now – they will come, for whatever reason she put this in motion. Eyes came here, yes. Him and thirty of the hardest bastards I've ever put together. They went out into the jungle never to return. That trail ends here." He addressed Tasker and Smail. "And it's got nothing to do with *Norway*."

Katryzna took long enough to process this for Tasker to say, "Not good enough. These were Parris's dying words. How was he connected?"

"You're sure about that?" Lopaz said. "You heard him say that yourself?"

"I'm no *liar*," Katryzna spat, stepping closer as Lopaz took a frightened step back. "You think I invented your name and some African mountain?"

"You might've beaten information out of Parris – that doesn't mean it had anything to do with why he contacted the Ministry." He paused, reconsidering the man in question. "I remember now, Simon Parris – that snotty brat was MEE once, wasn't he? Jesus. He could've had any number of historical ties to you guys, couldn't he?"

Tasker hesitated. True enough, he'd taken details for granted here. But Parris had flagged Katryzna through this long-dormant Eyes connection. Tasker said, "Are you saying Parris wasn't connected to you? And this place?"

"Oh no, he was involved. Part of the research team back in London."

"Not Ordshaw?"

"Whatever. Honestly I'm surprised he was still alive. Everyone else involved must be dead by now. Or 'missing'. But that was eight years ago, and like I said, the trail ended here."

"If it ended then why are you still here?" Katryzna demanded.

"I was their handler," Lopaz said. "After Eyes and the rest of them went into the jungle and their comms went down, I was told to hang tight in case anyone returned. I've been hanging tight ever since. Expecting someone to tie up loose ends. But Hank Duvalier went off on some other tangent while heads rolled for the failure. The head of the project killed himself two weeks before it was cancelled, one of the lead techs was found *headless* in a river. Superstitious types wanted someone left out here in case it wasn't coincidence. As if those thirty lost souls were coming back for revenge. My assumption was that Duvcorp were tidying up after themselves. I guess Parris wasn't important enough to be considered a threat. Like me."

Tasker said, "What needed tidying up? Why not send everyone home with a severance package? You suggested the Ministry might have discovered this ourselves."

"Ah." Lopaz weighed it up for a second. "Those mercenaries made a hell of a mess getting to Ikiri. I don't even know how many they killed on the way." He sent a subtle, guilty look Henri's way. Some connection there. "We didn't get full reports, but after they went missing rumours came back of all sorts. Not just that they had abused people along the way, but that they left such a mess out there. The region was unsettled for a year or more before a militia took over, and people still talk about it like it's cursed. To go there is to die and die badly. That was *our* legacy – we sent in a small army who slaughtered locals for Duvcorp's gain, what do you think the bosses would do to keep a story like that quiet? They might've killed hundreds. Unchecked atrocities that tell you nothing had changed since the Belgians came."

"But what *for*?" Tasker pressed. "That couldn't have all been on them – the stories that continued after they disappeared? What's at Ikiri that was worth so much?"

Lopaz nodded along. "Yeah, that. Probably nothing. If there was any truth in what they were looking for, someone like the MEE or the American government would've come to find it, too. The researchers made jokes, when setting this thing up. Laughing as they promised, 'We're going to find the Source.'" A worried expression crossed his face as the word slipped out. Like he'd not dared say it in years. Then he smiled in sick satisfaction at how it sounded. "That's what it was they were after. The Source."

"Of the river?" Smail probed weakly. "A mineral deposit?"

"No," Lopaz said. "The source of *life*. All life. Everything."

"What are you talking about?" Katryzna said. "Make sense!"

"Eyes must've blabbed to you about the shit Hank Duvalier had him doing. Investigating supposedly haunted locations, anyone claiming to have paranormal connections. He travelled the world looking for proof of the supernatural, and something in all that pointed them out here. Duvalier was hoping to find some clue to ever-lasting life, what else?"

No one answered, waiting for a punchline. But Tasker saw Katryzna putting those pieces together. There was truth in the stories Eyes had told her; Duvcorp really did have him chasing ghosts, and the trail led him here. Their goal was to find evidence of the afterlife? He'd never heard the Ministry give anything like that credence. But he could imagine the justification, as they delved into a study of novisan. It was an energy little understood even by the Ministry, particularly notable around the many unnatural creatures and phenomenon they sought to conceal. It was measurable, fluctuating in line with connections to living creatures, human and monster – but he'd never heard it associated with the afterlife. Or any source. Though with Duvcorp's resources, who knew what they might turn up? Tasker asked, "So what exactly led them to Mount Ikiri?"

"Energy scans," Lopaz said. "They faffed about with big electronic boxes that turned up all sorts of numbers supposedly showing patterns in the air. One of them tried to explain it to me once – sounded like magic nonsense. Chinese medicine shit. They recognised a *pull*, in a lot of places they were scanning, pointing here. To Ikiri."

"Their scans pointed . . ." Tasker didn't finish the thought. It meant Duvcorp were capable of monitoring novisan patterns over massive distances, where the Ministry only ever picked up things locally. Parris might have picked up on something in Norway without having direct interests there – it could be part of the same monitoring. An ability to flag whatever monstrous force had killed those people.

"They never reported what they found," Lopaz continued. "A handful of researchers, twenty-eight mercenaries and your friend Eyes, and all they achieved was a lot of bloodshed. Of course they didn't report *that*, either – those stories came down the river later. Insane, entitled white maniacs freaking out on their way towards Ikiri. They were cut off right before reaching the mountain. Chances are one of the militias got the better of them. It put the Ikiri region into turmoil, with small bands of soldiers fighting over the scraps, and it wasn't until a year or so later that General Solomon, from out east, took charge of the region for himself. Nothing and no one goes in or out now. Duvcorp had given up on it by then anyway. Probably accepted that it was a fairy tale that needn't have got so many people killed."

"So no one actually knows what they found?" Katryzna said. "I guess we need to see for ourselves." Tasker turned with alarm. "There's *obviously* something there, isn't there?"

Lopaz barked a laugh. "This is the DRC. It's not a walk in the woods."

"I didn't ask your opinion."

Tasker locked gazes with Smail, his own uncertainty mirrored there. It was an unthinkable extra step. Lopaz continued, "Maybe you should, you fool. You aren't listening. The Congo alone is dangerous, but Ikiri is beyond reproach. Thirty well-armed men never returned – people continue to die there. Horror stories float down the river. Henri, tell them."

"Ikiri is cursed," Henri agreed, muffled by his bloody nose. "The creatures are wrong."

"The creatures are wrong?" Tasker said. "What does that mean?"

"They aren't normal. Their unnatural cries stop people going close. No one has seen them to say what they are – not seen them and lived. But bits of people have been found. They are horror stories, as Miguel says. Whole villages of people have disappeared – women, children, all gone. Each year, maybe, another village lost. No one knows why, but it is expanding. Those that dare go –"

"Do not come back, yes," Katryzna said. "We got that."

"The point," Lopaz said, "is that whatever our idiot men did, they made it a place best forgotten. The problem is still out here, and you want no part of it."

Tasker met Katryzna's eye. She was beaming, as though her claims had been confirmed. With what they were saying, Tasker didn't doubt a connection to Laukstad, now. Whole villages, Henri said. Dead children in Laukstad, dead children out here. He had to go out there, to know what ungodly force Duvcorp had unleashed. To stop it happening again.

*

A few minutes into the journey back to the hotel, Smail said, "This isn't what you came out here for, is it, Tasker?" He avoided looking in the mirror, as though ignoring Katryzna's presence in the back would make her less threatening. She was quiet, watching for Tasker's take.

He said, "Parris had a reason to connect Ikiri to the Laukstad massacre. Entire villages dead or missing seems close enough to me."

"Except that out here," Smail said, "millions have died without being accounted for. I could give you a hundred village massacres here that would look similar to your Norwegian town. Scores, *thousands* dead. You're aware the civil war is the second most deadly conflict in history? Globally?"

"If it was that simple, why wouldn't they connect that to Ikiri?" Tasker said. "Did that sound like men accounting for war atrocities? Creatures no one's seen, a region no one comes back from? Is that how people usually explain the war zone? Mount Ikiri isn't even *in* the war zone, is it?"

Smail went quiet, confirming Tasker's suspicion. This was different.

"Duvcorp traced something from halfway across the world," Tasker continued. "It frightened them enough to leave someone behind to make sure it was contained. Trust me, Agent Smail, this is precisely my area."

"Being from the Ministry," Smail clarified, in a tone that said the rest of the intelligence community had a few choice thoughts about the MEE. Somewhere between sceptical and distrusting. "Answer me this, then – if it's that unusual, why did Duvcorp give up on it?"

"Presumably," Tasker drew out the answer, not liking its implications, "it was deemed too dangerous to pursue. Which would be precisely why we have to pursue it."

"And will London put up an expedition for you?"

Tasker hummed. The Ministry were tight-fisted at the best of times, requiring a thousand forms before you could so much as requisition toilet paper, but if Caffery could run that gamut he might get some funding for transport and a guide. Little beyond that. He certainly wasn't getting support from Ward's people this time. But it jogged his mind back to Ordshaw and the numbers Ward had turned up. One of the columns appearing to indicate 360 degrees, a direction. He took out his phone and put through a call. Not to Caffery but to Ward. She answered prim and polite, and after quick pleasantries he got straight to the point: "Those numbers off Parris's laptop, have you got anywhere with them?"

"Yes," she said, lowering her voice to a whisper. "Actually. The third column *are* co-ordinates. We've found Laukstad on there. Five rows relate to it, with marginally different co-ordinates and the final column all quite similar numbers."

"Have you tested them on a map yet? As angles?"

"As if the energy reading pointed somewhere else?" Ward skipped a beat. "What have you found out there? Did you speak to Miguel Lopaz?"

"Better we keep it quiet for now," Tasker advised. "Can you just do me a favour and look into that?"

Ward paused again, wanting to know exactly what was going on, but restraining herself. She said, "I'll see what we can do."

Tasker put the phone away, confident even without results that he now understood what Parris had been up to. The research that had pointed Duvcorp out here might have ended or not, but Parris had kept monitoring the patterns that guided them, either way. He had spotted something in those readings that raised alarms over Laukstad, and if the expedition out here wasn't somehow responsible, it at least contained answers.

"You are genuinely thinking to go out there?" Smail said uneasily.

"Relax," Katryzna said, with a laugh. "Me and Sean will be fine."

Tasker went quiet again, her cheery tone drawing another concern to mind. He was riding with a human onion; beneath her layer of dirt and grime sat a disarming liveliness, and that in turn hid a savage, dangerous nature. She might have killed in there. Lopaz, the others, even him. Out of convenience.

Tasker checked himself. He'd been so quick to join with her, and he realised even now it was her infectious, unflinching energy pushing him forwards. It wasn't an attraction; Tasker didn't get attracted to people often. With Helen at home, why would he? She was all he'd ever needed, and they shared a low-burning libido energy that needed satisfying only a few times a year. She didn't ever suspect him of cheating on his long trips away; she knew him too well. No. As always, there was logic in his interest in this young woman. Someone as volatile as Katryzna could be a key to progress, willing to do what he himself could not . . .

At the hotel, he walked her up to her rooms, offering noncommittal responses to her remarks about the hotel awnings and light fixtures and whatever else impressed her. Thankfully, she seemed to be delving into her own thoughts, her enthusiasm gone. Tiring, at last.

They stopped at her door and there he paused to clear his throat. She cracked a weak smile and gave his shoulder a light push. "Save your breath, Sean. I've already had it from Rurik. People like Lopaz are *slime*."

Tasker forced a smile but said, "Parris, the attack –"

"I would *never* lie to you," Katryzna said. "We are friends, aren't we?"

He hesitated and saw some of the liveliness fading in her eyes.

"Right. I'm not what he said, okay?" she went on. "I came from a slum, my uncle was a gangster, I stabbed a policeman through the throat when I was twelve years old – I was *raised* bad. And I've done plenty of bad things since. But I'm honest. *Always*. This does affect us both, it's not just about Eyes. You believe me?"

"Yeah," Tasker replied slowly. "I believe you. We'll talk later. Get some rest."

Katryzna nodded but looked worried. He gave her one more limp smile before turning away.

# 13

Caleb barely let his foot off the gas for the final leg of the journey to Stilt Town. He was driving so fast they almost missed the turn – a gap in trees that flanked the main road, with a mud-track winding into shadow. A wooden board with a painted name read: *Graystown*. Everyone shifted to look back out the windows, scarcely believing they had made it this far without the Steers catching up again. Then it was all eyes forward, passing through the thicket of trees to reach the perimeter wall. Twenty feet of old steel rose in either direction, with a truck-sized gap in the middle blocked by a huge metal grid, where another name sign hung. Through the bars sat an open plain of long grass with buildings beyond.

Leaning way forward in her seat, Zip cooed. What Arlo Gray had built in this small patch of swampland *was* impressive. Wood and metal huts of various sizes stood two metres or more above the ground, supported by thick pillars. From here they could see the long hall, a glass-topped grow-house and a couple of smaller units, raised even higher, connected by swing bridges, all made up of scrap salvaged from shipwrecks and derelict buildings. A scattering of concrete pillboxes were just visible in the field, behind sandbags. On the other side of the gate, a man in jeans, a dark t-shirt and a bandanna ran up, an M16 rifle slung across his waist.

"What is this place?" Zip asked with awe.

"Stilt Town," Leigh-Ann said. "Paranoia capital of the US of A, and a rodeo of truly special people to boot."

"Behave," Caleb said. "They're gonna keep us alive, after all."

Reece leant out the window, waving to the guard. "Teddy? It is Teddy, right? Open up, would you?"

"Was expecting you last night," the guard replied. "Where you been?"

"Open on up and we'll spill all." Reece hid his urgency behind a friendly smile.

"Drive straight through, Caleb," Stomatt suggested. "This thing can handle it."

"Not sure it could," Caleb answered. "And then we'd have no gate to hold off the Steers, wouldn't we?"

Teddy took out his radio, relaying instructions; beyond him, people were stirring from the stilted huts, coming onto balconies to watch. "You got the money, Reece?"

"Yes we got the damn money!" Stomatt shouted. "The hell you think we are, bunch of amateurs?"

"Sto," Reece said. "Yes, Teddy, but we mightn't have shaken the Steers yet."

"You haven't –" Teddy fumbled at his radio again and told someone to hurry up. With a big whir and great squeaking gears, the gate slowly screeched open. Teddy skipped aside, watching through the bars as if to spot their pursuers. "Go on to the guard house, boys, Mr Gray himself will be there."

Caleb drove through the moment there was enough space, and took them over uneven ground around the building cluster, aiming for a space on the near edge. Zip made more appreciative noises as the rest of the township was revealed: the guard house was a squat structure with barred windows and a watch-nest up top; behind that was a tower with a clock on one side and windmill sails rotating on the another. And in the middle of the community of raised buildings stood a huge marble cross, on a stone mound a metre high. Beyond the buildings, the metal walls surrounded the clearing in a vast circle that encompassed large patches of land dotted with fenced animals and crops. People in the fields were pausing their work to watch the newcomers, while three more men with guns hurried over to join Teddy in looking out after their entrance.

"You see," Leigh-Ann whispered an explanation, "Caleb's uncle, he got messages from God, so he thinks, to build this place where his people could be free from the tyranny of men and the rising waters. A flood gonna come, he says – wipe out all the sinners. But not Stilt Town – *Graystown* as they call it – because they ready. Ready to fight off the sinners *and* the flood. Only problem is, they done penned themselves in with a whole community of crazy. Looks nice, though, don't it?"

Zip nodded appreciatively, and asked, "What's a tyranny?"

"There they are, there they are!" a shaky voice called from the guard house as they pulled up. Leigh-Ann winked to let Zip know it was time to keep quiet. The gang got out the truck, looking up at Alban Gray, a bottom-heavy older man leaning heavily on a brass cane. He was dressed in suit trousers and a straw hat, with a mane of white hair and a big, ruddy nose. He came down a short flight of steps, every movement making his body shudder. "Dear Caleb, Reece – you're well! God clearly rode with you. But Maximilian – your neck –"

"Ain't nothing, Alban," Stomatt scoffed at the wound.

Reece got a jab in his ribs and turned to Leigh-Ann's scolding face. He'd noticed the old man leave her out, too. Never mind they were practically family, literally in Caleb's case; Gray's sympathies didn't stretch too far when it came to women in general, and cussing unwed women in particular. Wasn't that she was Black, he kept telling her – Stilt Town had its share of Black folk. Not a debate for this minute, anyway. Reece said, "Got some worrying news, Mr Gray – some Steers picked up our scent crossing the state line –"

"And who's *this*, my dear, what an angel," Gray said, ignoring him to hobble closer to Zip. He came up short, seeing her eyes. She offered a sweet curtsy and a how'd-ye-do. Gray forced his smile again – "Yes, yes" – but looked to Reece for an explanation.

"This is Zip, we came upon her in need of assistance," Reece said. "But that's another thing –"

"How much you get?" a rough voice interrupted him. Noah, Alban's strapping, moustached eldest son, marched around the guard house stilts, in a too-tight t-shirt with a pistol swinging at his hip.

"Got it all, cousin," Caleb told him. "Though not without a fight."

"All of it?" Noah demanded confirmation from Reece. Unlike his father, he was wildly sceptical of the gang's ability to achieve anything, considering their demonstrable lack of faith.

"Take a look for yourself" – Reece gestured to the truck – "but we got company. We shot up a Steer car a ways back on the highway."

"You're safe here," Gray said lightly, as Noah approached the truck. He leant over the bed and rifled through the bags, before nodding reluctant confirmation to his dad. Gray slapped his hands together. "Splendid! Now you must be exhausted –"

The growl of rapidly approaching engines got his attention where Reece's warnings hadn't, with multiple vehicles coming up the path. Hell, they must've been right behind. Probably holding back to be sure the gang came into Stilt Town.

Teddy shouted useless warnings that someone was coming, and a young man popped his head out the guard house to confirm it. Three cars on their way. Noah glared accusation at Reece and went into action-mode, drawing his gun and shouting orders. In seconds, the people in windows or on balconies disappeared inside, and those in the fields came running in. The guards by the gate moved into the cover of the walls and gun barrels appeared from the pillboxes.

"Up here, up here." Gray led the way unsteadily up the steps into the guard house. The gang hustled after him. Tyres screeched near the entrance as Gray ushered them through and shut the door. In the guard house, they were greeted with a wall of monitors, some showing the compound itself, others incongruous blocks of trees, and two showing the entrance: a pair of Cadillacs and a dark Hummer parked outside, with half a dozen Steers piling out, carrying rifles and shotguns.

Noah stepped into view, reaching the gate and shouting almost loud enough to be heard in the guard house. The Steers shouted back.

"Jesus," Leigh-Ann muttered. "This gonna get bloody."

It got her the first look of recognition from Gray, a deeply judgemental one nicely framed by a big cross on the wall behind him. Reece moved in front of Leigh-Ann and said, "Sorry about this, Mr Gray, but it was always a possibility they'd know it was us."

"A slim one, didn't you say?" Gray said. The bumbling friendly act was gone, now that they'd brought actual trouble. "Dressed up in that getup with masks and all, *two* getaway rides, wasn't the point that this wouldn't happen?"

Reece didn't have an answer, so Caleb came in: "Uncle, we've got the goods, all the same."

Gray snorted dissatisfaction and approached the monitoring desk, where a freestanding steel microphone sat. He pressed a button and said, "Teddy, hand me to Noah." They watched Noah take the guard's radio on the monitor. "What're they saying?"

"You might guess, Pa," Noah answered. "Say to hand them over or there'll be trouble."

"Can't the kid make them forget they saw anything?" Stomatt asked, in what passed for a whisper from him. Zip cuddled closer to Reece, and he sensed that no, this was outside her remit.

On screen, one of the Steers broke from the crowd, taking out a phone.

"Jam them," Gray instructed, and their operator threw switches. "Remind them our property extends to the road, Noah, and they're trespassing. Count them down from five."

The Steer making a call looked irritated, clearly not getting through, and he demanded someone else's phone. Noah relayed Gray's message and started counting.

"Get in cover, boy," Gray advised, and Noah did so, ducking around the wall and raising his voice for *three*. The Steers moved closer, flustering at the countdown, their shouts coming through the radio.

"– break your goddamned doors in!"

"– know who the fuck you messing with!"

"Two!" Noah shouted louder.

The Steer on the phone gave up calling to assess the situation. Likely their leader, from the way he carried himself. A big round jaw, eyes close together, a flat-top, black hat.

"One!"

The Steer pushed forward, waving at his men to stand down and yelling loud enough to be heard through the radio: "Big mistake, Gray. We know who y'all are – all y'all – and when we come back it won't be to talk!"

"Time's up," Gray decided and pressed another button. "Tower, put one in a windscreen for me."

A gunshot sounded like thunder in the sky, making Zip jump, and on screen the Hummer's windscreen shattered as though hit by an enormous hammer. The Steers dived for cover, yelling and holding guns above their heads.

"Tell them get back in the cars, Noah," Gray instructed calmly, and Noah relayed the order. "Leave now or next shot's taking a head."

As Noah shouted, the black-hat Steer instructed his men to pile back in, all of them keeping low and watching the gates. He lingered himself, the last to get in, and the radio picked up his shouts again: "Tell your pop he'll be hearing from Dustin Fallon himself – we'll have that green-haired freak's head!"

With that, the Steers retreated, wheels throwing up mud as they disappeared through the trees. They appeared again on another monitor, down the path, then were gone.

"Whatever you're toting up in that tower," Stomatt said, "I *want* it." Reece shot him a warning look and Gray gave one much nastier. But both glares only egged him on. "Seriously, Alban, I'll climb up that tower and take a watch myself. Free. Of. Charge."

"That's enough, Maximilian," Gray told him icily, and turned on Reece. "Get the cash in here. We'll talk over lunch."

# 14

Tasker drank stiff drinks at the bar while waiting for Caffery to get back to him. His handler had said a flight into the Congolese interior was unlikely: only two planes a week connected Kinshasa to Kisangani, and the latter city wasn't much closer to Ikiri, anyway. Together with the civil war out there, and the need to use airports where Lopaz's mystery assassins might spot Tasker, Caffery was veering towards this trip being too dangerous to pursue a dead case that the Ministry didn't necessarily have a stake in. Never mind Tasker's insistence that people were most definitely *dying*, that things were most definitely *fucked up* out here. Along with the initial arguments about their flights, Caffery was being particularly obstructive, and Tasker's mind couldn't help but go back to Parris. Killed after he contacted the Ministry. They were thoughts he almost didn't dare think, let alone speak, but given Duvcorp's reach, could this be big enough that someone on his own team was trying to block him from going further? Tasker sat hoping to pitch the idea to Katryzna, but two hours after they checked in she had not come down.

"Do you mind?" Smail announced his presence. The spy looked no less harassed than in Club Clash, checking over his shoulder. "She's not here?"

"In her room, freshening up," Tasker said, unsure if Katryzna could get "fresh".

Smail looked relieved. He took the stool next to Tasker and gestured to the barman for a beer. "I've been on the phone. Are you blown?"

"Huh?"

"You're not here on strictly Ministry business. You can't have told your people everything, I'm sure. You are aware of who she is?"

Tasker paused, Smail confirming his instinct that the MEE wouldn't have handled Katryzna's overt involvement well. He said, "I've got an impression."

"Do you? Because we have a file on Tkacz thick as six eggs, back in Vauxhall. An awful lot that *looks* like her doing, little proved. Chaotic, unaccountable cases of violence – victims relating to the Russian mafia or the same corporations you're chasing."

"You're not surprising me yet."

"And that troubles me," Smail said. "You must be aware of the possibility that she killed Simon Parris herself? And rather than bring her in, you got her a hotel room in the DRC and want to travel into the rainforest together?"

Tasker looked into his whisky and realised his mind was already made up on this. Katryzna was bold, direct and unafraid. He couldn't see her as a liar, and said, "That's my plan, yes."

"Tell me you know what you're looking for, at least," Smail implored.

"I couldn't say, that's the point. My gut – and a dead man who predicted a *massacre* – says it's worth finding out."

"Well I can't speak for the dead man," Smail moved closer, expression hardening. Tasker could imagine him wielding a knife in a windowless room. "But your *gut* needs educating. No one gets this close to Tkacz and lives, Tasker. She is legend. Charmed, somehow – the things she's said to have got away with. Your energy would be better spent taking her down."

It only made Tasker dig in his heels. "That sounds like your job, not mine. I'm not here for her."

"And what does your Ministry think about you going upriver?"

Tasker said nothing.

"Yeah, I didn't think so. But you intend to do it anyway." Smail took a big breath. "You need to rethink your friendships, at the very least."

"Did you come here to put me down, or do you have some other proposal?" Tasker prompted.

Smail paused. Yes, this was all a preamble to his own ploy; else he would've done as he suggested and gone after Katryzna himself. "As it happens, I do. So long as you know where you stand with her." A pause, pure theatre: he knew exactly where he was going. "I have eyes all over Kinshasa, all the way along the river. Mount Ikiri, however, sits in a region we're not well-informed on. Perhaps I was a little misleading before. I believe Lopaz when he says there are people that would kill to protect the area, and considering it's a long way from the fighting or any resources we know of, these are not atrocities we'd associate with the war, as you rightly assumed. I don't think it's safe, or that you should go, but if you insist, I wouldn't mind knowing what's going on. There's a barge, I can get you passage on it. It's slower than a private hire, but safer. I can get you kit, a guide, whatever you need. But you'll report back to me when you return. If you return."

"And?" Tasker said.

"And as you're fool enough to go with her, I'll turn a blind eye to Tkacz until you get back. If anyone can survive out there, she's likely to, after all. But you'll bring her to me, afterwards, of course. *If* you get back."

"Ah. We get you the dirt on Duvcorp and Ikiri and you also bag a notorious assassin? Earn yourself a promotion and finally get to go home?"

Smail wore a faint smile. "Promotion, perhaps. As for home, like Lopaz, I'm quite happy here. I could take a step back from fieldwork, though."

Tasker's first instinct was to tell Smail and SIS to jog off a cliff. But if Katryzna's reputation was enough to get him moving, he could address the consequences later. In the meantime, whoever Lopaz was afraid of might get wise to their plans any day, so once again, Caffery's resistance was pushing him. With Smail all but confirming Ikiri was a force that warranted investigation, what choice did he have? He said, "You help me get to the bottom of what Duvcorp were up to, and you'll be the first to know about it. But you'll leave Katryzna to me, one way or another."

Smail backed off, studying his face. "We can work with that."

*

"You saw the way he was looking at you," Rurik goaded from the balcony table. Gripping the banister tightly, Katryzna tried to breathe in fresh air but got nothing but humid yuk. It wasn't peaceful here, with car horns honking and the loud discussion of street vendors and revellers audible, what, five storeys below? "You showed your true colours and now he's scared, like everyone else."

"He is not scared," Katryzna muttered. "He would do something if he was."

"He probably has. Phoned his bosses, asked for backup, ready to trap you. He's not just going to come and cut your throat – that's *your* style."

"I have cut no one's throat," she hissed. "I'm doing good."

"Yeah?" her conscience laughed, nastily. "Then why am I here?"

She screwed her eyes closed. She could feel it creeping over her. A dread shadow. Her skin tightening. Mind racing with a thousand unresolved thoughts. He hates you. They all hate you. You killed him, betrayed him – *distracted*, Lopaz said – oh! Eyes talked about you? Mocked you, probably. Or worse, believed in you – got sloppy. He could survive anything. What was a forest? What did she do to him? Why was she *she*?

Katryzna gritted her teeth. Remember one happy moment, one real memory. Eyes sitting on a rock by a lake after they left that Belorussian prison. Smoking, like always, staring into the water. He interrupted her teasing to say, "This is good."

*This* meant the calm – their companionship, their moment.

Those shark-dead eyes – like he had seen too much for anything to interest him again – they had a little light looking at her. Hope. Real emotion. Same when she bit his face, the first time they met, when Eyes was meant to kill her. This ancient source of unlimited cool had discovered he *could* still be surprised.

"You're thinking of when you savaged him," Rurik guessed. "That's your happy thought?"

Katryzna turned on him, looming over the table. But her conscience hadn't flinched from her since she was a teenager, and he didn't now. She deflated again. Had Eyes died distracted by this lunatic girl he had vaguely taken under his wing? Ah. The dread crept up through her veins. Sean *should* fear you. She fell onto the chair and said, "I need food."

"Indeed, why not go downstairs and ruin someone else's night," Rurik said.

She had no energy to argue. He was right. Better not to move or be seen – she'd been visible enough on the way. Prancing about the airport, letting herself *enjoy* it. No. Stay in the shadows – turn out the lights for a week. A year. Disappear into this feeling.

A knock at the door drew her back. She frowned at Rurik.

"Probably come to ask you to leave," her conscience said.

Katryzna dragged herself inside, lazily taking the old Hungarian pistol from the bed.

"Leave the gun!" Rurik shouted. "Listen!"

"I'm mad with listening!" Katryzna spat back. "I've been told! Told and told, how terrible I am!" In her anger she swept the door open. "What!"

Sean stood frozen for a moment, then raised his eyebrows. Katryzna bit her tension down and showed him her teeth. Not really a smile. He returned an empty one of his own. Pitying. "Everything okay, Katryzna?" Whisky on his breath. "I thought you'd come downstairs."

Oh. A little alcohol had made him bold, and ding ding! Activate creep mode. Katryzna rolled her eyes. "Not interested."

"I hoped you'd come down to *talk*." Swinging back to serious, *did* he want to scold her?

Katryzna took a step back. "Not now, okay?" He looked over her shoulder. She mumbled an explanation for the crumpled sheets: "I jumped on the bed." Another stupid thing. As if hurting people wasn't bad enough, she was idiot enough to –

"My people in London aren't happy with where this has gone," Tasker said.

Great. Boo hoo and damn. "Because you think I made it all up?"

"No." He looked even more serious. "They just don't see it the same way I do. But I think you and I are on the same side in uncovering this. Even if our methods differ."

"Okay. Thanks." Katryzna started closing the door. He put himself in the way.

"Without their help," Tasker quickly went on, "it'll take a few days to arrange passage. Can you wait? You'll have access to the full facilities here."

She put a hand over her face, massaging both temples. "Yes, I can wait."

"He's trying to connect," Rurik shouted. "Give him something."

"I will give *you* something in a minute," Katryzna snarled, half-spun towards the balcony. She turned very slowly back to Sean. The man hid his alarm well. Stupid Rurik's stupid idea spiralled behind her eyes. They always wanted to connect, then they got hurt. She said, "Eyes believed in me. I was bad for him. Lopaz was right about that."

"Forgive me," Tasker replied, oozing horrible calm, "but from what I've heard, I don't see that you were the most dangerous thing in Eyes' life."

Katryzna glowered. This was worse than his dislike: pity. "What do you know?"

"Come down for a drink –"

"I don't *drink*, Sean," she said, raising her voice. Then slumped again, suddenly spent. "I cannot. I'm about to get low. Just make your plans and leave me with your" – she flapped a hand – "full facilities. Don't *worry* about me, don't think we have . . . something."

He nodded carefully. "Yeah. So you know, I've got a wife and daughter back home." A brief pause. "They're everything to me, they're why I do this. When I saw those dead in Laukstad – they were the *same* – I couldn't let this go. I'd do anything for them."

Katryzna gave him a well-earned look of disgust. "Then why are you going after *me*?"

"What? I am *not*." A fluster in his cool – how could she *possibly* think that? Ha. "I'm –" He looked into the room, reassessing. "I'm only trying to make sure you're okay. Are you?"

"Always," Katryzna sighed, closing the door without a farewell. "And never."


"I'm not sure when I'll be back," Tasker told Helen, finally calling after breakfast. Even having slept off a long day and a lot of whisky, he was sure he sounded haggard, forlorn. "But once this is through, I'll be home first thing, no compromises."

"You're staying safe, aren't you?" Helen asked. She wouldn't ask why he was delayed or what exactly he was doing, but she did insist: "Just make sure you do *come* back."

That was always the bottom line: guarantee there was a return journey and a chance to reset. She had held him when he came home haunted by the memory of parasitic worms in Kuala Lumpur. She'd made him a hot drink and run him a bath after he'd tracked a blood drinker in Berlin. Then a week or more's respite, which he could dedicate fully to her and Rebecca. Tasker never told Helen exactly what he'd seen or why he woke up in terrified sweats, and she never asked. She knew how important the Ministry's work was, and how important *he* was to them. She was an expert at focusing on the positives, letting go of the negatives.

His silence stretched out, as he thought of home comforts. He could picture Helen leaning against the kitchen counter, talking while putting away dishes. Then he imagined their French windows shattering, smashed from the outside. An invasion of feral people clawing at his family. Suits like Marge Cosgrove would shrug it off and say *oh well*, as they did for Laukstad and had done for the villages of Ikiri for so many years. He imagined taking Katryzna into Duvcorp's palatial offices, unleashed as she'd been in Club Clash –

"Hold up," Helen said. "Here she is."

Rebecca's cheery voice came on: "Daddy? Did Mummy tell you about rehearsals?"

Tasker smiled. Of course, the school was preparing a Christmas play, more than a month in advance. Rebecca had a lead role and quickly rattled out a short account of how hard she was working and how she hadn't made nearly as many mistakes as *Robert*, who didn't even have many lines. Tasker said, "Our little superstar. I promise I'll be back for the performance."

"You will?" Rebecca cried, and bounced away from the phone, relaying that to Helen.

Helen warned, without malice, "Don't if you can't."

Rebecca's delighted squeal made Tasker wince. A flash of that body in Laukstad. He said, "I'll take care of this fast. I have to. I've even got a partner to help."

"Oh my days." Helen's tone lightened. "Agent Tasker with a partner? He must be very impressive."

Of the words he might use to describe Katryzna, Tasker was not sure *impressive* was one of them. Considering their uneven conversation last night, he might go towards confusing, unstable – mysterious if he was generous. He said, "Effective. I'm confident *she* will be effective."

"She'd better be," Helen said. "We can't wait for you to get back."

"Likewise."

Tasker made his farewells, and paused for only a second to switch from home-life back to work mode. He called Ward and immediately said, "I'm confident there's something out here. Tell me you can support that?"

"Yes," she replied, almost excitedly. "We absolutely can."

She confirmed what he expected: Parris's files showed Laukstad's energy pointed in this directions. Other co-ordinates on the list followed the pattern – locations on different continents, roughly pointing to central Africa. He was exactly where he needed to be. Ward said, "This is big. Support might find a dozen applications for a way to trace such large-scale novisan patterns."

"I'm not sure we want to dive into that yet," Tasker said. "This got Parris killed."

It gave her pause, but Ward said, "It's not something we can ignore, is it? We have to analyse the rest of this information, see what else he was onto. If I make the importance of this clear to London, we'll have all the support we need."

"Slow down," Tasker said, recalling the ill-feeling Caffery's reluctance had given him. "Deputy Director. I'm hesitant over who exactly we involve in this. Can you give me some time before passing this up the ladder? And whatever you do, make sure you do it quietly."

Though a little deflated, she agreed to his terms.

While Smail started making preparations for their trip, Tasker took advantage of the lull to rest, drinking in Le Cockpit Bar again. Katryzna had not emerged all day, and he was considering going to her when Lopaz's man, Henri, entered the bar. His nose had been stitched since Katryzna's attack, and he wore the wound well; it somehow matched his moustache. He was beaming – something to offer. "I come to make amends."

"For Katryzna breaking your nose?" Tasker said.

"Not broken, just split," Henri corrected. "And yes, for putting you in that position. Miguel's always been –" He mugged a face to mimic "not-quite-there". "He's like a crazy uncle, always worrying about who's out to get him. We mostly take it lightly. But seeing you come in? We only wanted to protect him."

"All right," Tasker replied, noting he was surprisingly well-spoken, that chiselled body now businesslike in a linen shirt and shorts.

Henri pulled up the adjacent stool, settling in for a heart-to-heart. "You really are planning on going up the river, to Ikiri? I thought you'd be going home by now."

"Unlike Lopaz, I tend to believe in confronting our fears."

"Ha, very good." Henri signalled for a beer, checking to Tasker in case he wanted one. Apparently they were drinking buddies now. "Well. He's gone into hiding again, we might not see him for months. But me, I want to go with you."

Tasker frowned. It was an about-turn after Henri's previous talk of jungle horrors.

"You don't know who I am, do you?" Henri asked. "My sister was Sara Ngoi."

"Yeah. I don't know who she is, either."

Henri's smile stretched, pleased to make the reveal. "She's how I met Miguel. We grew up in Binga, north of the river from Ikiri. We came to the city together, my big sister and me, seeking our fortune. Working in translation, tours, education. This white man, he brought the biggest opportunity. Help organise this trip, guide them out there, come back rich. Sara, she could speak a dozen languages, and she was so smart, so beautiful. Exactly who they needed."

Tasker noted that past tense *was*. "Your sister joined the Duvcorp expedition?"

"She was their guide – their translator. Made bookings on the boats, led the way."

"Never came back."

Henri's smile fell. "I wanted to go, too, but I was young. Miguel said no. I was only good for odd jobs here, not meant for their work out there. The men they gathered, you should have seen them. I've faced many militias, but never men quite as scary as them."

Tasker took a drink. This, he could use. "Did you meet this guy Eyes?"

"I'm sure I did," Henri said. "Most of the crew used made-up names, animals or activities. Moose. Bruiser. I remember the leader – they called him *Boss* – he looked like he'd never laughed a day in his life. Even the nastiest ones were scared of him. There was also a tall, thin white guy who watched over the scientists. He wore a long dark coat, even here, and smoked like an exhaust pipe. My sister, she joked that he was too spooky to die, so she'd stick close to him."

That sounded like Eyes, all right. Shame Sara's plan hadn't worked out.

Henri continued, "I kept working with Miguel, waiting for them to come back. Instead – well, he gave you the idea. You know, a hundred years ago, King Leopold's men hacked off hands for rubber, controlling the Congo with weapons we could not fight against. These people were the same. They had scanners to see rebels coming, guns that kill dozens in seconds, from a mile away. Unstoppable. They left rebel heads on spikes – then dismembered farmers and fishermen, for reasons we don't know. Maybe just because they could. I was terrified for what had become of my sister in their company. And then" – he made a *poof!* gesture – "they were gone. A plague that vanished after running its course. They're spoken of like a myth, up the river. Maybe they became the monsters people are afraid of. Maybe they angered the nature spirits enough to release something worse than them?

"When no one came back, and Duvcorp sent no one else, Miguel insisted it was something to be forgotten – perhaps even by force. I got other work while he got paranoid, but we stuck together, he with his guilt and fear, me with my regrets for Sara."

"So what do you think happened?"

"*No one* knows. Everyone in this country has lost people without knowing how or why. But this time, there *is* something to be done. If you'll have me, I will come to learn the truth. You'll need a guide and a translator. A *bodyguard*, even." This tickled him to laughter, lightening again. "Well, your friend might be able to take care of herself. But I can help with navigating the land; I know you're no better informed than Lopaz was, back then. You think it's a mountain you're looking for?"

Tasker gave him a look. "Kind of implied in the name?"

"We do not call it Mount Ikiri," Henri replied with amusement. "Ikiri sits in the Central Lowlands, there are no true mountains. It's tall, yes, but a range of hills at best."

"You've been there?"

Henri shrugged. "I know of it. An unremarkable area in the heart of dense forest. But I know how to survive the forest. How to avoid men like General Solomon."

Tasker hummed. If anyone was alive in the Ikiri region, they were under Solomon's command. Smail had given Tasker a brief introduction to the general and his Popular Liberation Union. Otherwise known as the Cursed Union. He had been murdering Rwandans in the eastern conflict before he migrated to fill the power vacuum Duvcorp's advance created, and he butchered all who crossed his territory. Tasker said, "You think he can be reasoned with?"

"Ah, no," Henri said. "I think he can be *avoided*. Some believe General Solomon to be a spirit himself, taking orders from the dead, commanding the *zimwi*, monsters that feed on human flesh. But I am a good Christian. I am not afraid of zimwi."

"That's not what you were saying yesterday," Tasker said, warily. "What is it, are there monsters out there or not?"

Henri eyed him with interest, impressed that Tasker took the stories seriously. "There are terrible rumours and things to be afraid of, perhaps. But I believe another reason no one sees Solomon and his beasts is because the Cursed Union is very small. Their brutality is to give them a bigger image. We can hide with just three people. I can find the paths we need."

Tasker sipped his drink, eyeing Henri over that presumptive *we*.

"Do we have a deal, Mr Tasker? Or do you prefer to trust only in Ms Tkacz?" Henri laughed. "Miguel says she is terrifying. He says ask her about Istanbul. And Croatia. And Vultuk, in Kazakhstan – he says that was the worst. Be *scared*. Of someone that looks like her?" He sounded a little too happy about all that, especially considering she'd already floored him. But clearly he had already expressed fondness to Lopaz about Katryzna. A seasoned fighter fascinated by the grubby little lunatic that felled him with one blow. Sure enough, he continued, "Is she coming down? I would like to buy her a drink."

If this journey was going to happen, Tasker had to dampen *that* affection. He said, "We might work together, but don't get any ideas. She doesn't drink. And I'm pretty sure she's gay."

Henri startled, but the surprise passed quickly. "We might work together?"

*

Katryzna hopped out of bed, stretched, threw open the balcony door and breathed in thick, hot air. Ugh. Whatever – to food! She bounced down to the restaurant to be told breakfast stopped half an hour ago, but they could send something to her by the pool. She wandered out into scorching sunlight. In the pool was a broad, muscular man who spent a lot of time in gyms, swimming to the edge with dignified grace that *screamed* Sean. He slowed into her shadow and looked up. Expression souring as he noticed her new shirt and trousers were frayed and stained. Well, she had spent three days in a stuffy room with no change of clothes.

"About time you got some vitamin D," Tasker said. He went to push himself up from the pool, but she placed a shoe on his shoulder. The tatty white trainer also displeased him. "We really need to take you shopping."

Katryzna pushed him back into the water and Tasker took a step back to avoid stumbling. She smiled cheekily, to stay his irritation.

"Good to see your humour's back. Everything's under control, so you know. We've got a guide and we're almost ready to go."

"Did you whisper that through my door last night?"

"It wasn't a whisper. Are you feeling better now?"

"Rested like a baby." Katryzna stretched her arms up with a yawn. She surveyed the pool area, with its sun loungers and one other guest, an older lady with sun-leathered skin. "We can go as soon as you finish floating like a duck."

"That look on his face," Rurik advised, "is because you've been lazing about while he's done all this work. It's been days, Katryzna –"

"I *know*," Katryzna said. "I told him I was taking a break, what's the problem?"

As Rurik cited a half-dozen problems, Tasker said, "We've got the public barge leaving tomorrow. On a schedule, so we can't leave any sooner than that. Enjoy one more night here – you can eat in the restaurant for once. If you tidy up."

"A barge? Not a plane or a helicopter?"

"We need to go unnoticed," Tasker said.

"Please," Rurik groaned, "he's obviously done what he can."

"I'll *try*," Katryzna said, feeling generous. She scratched her nose, looking across to the dormant sunbather, then crouched and gestured for Tasker to come closer. He stayed where he was. "I want to talk privately." He still didn't move. She rolled her eyes. "Okay. I expect Charlie wanted you to turn me in? From him and Lopaz, you must know I am a monster now? Did they talk about Kazakhstan? They always complain about that, but only because there were children involved. It wasn't the *worst*; I completed the job they wanted. Five kids dead instead of two, that's not exactly a massacre."

"That is a massacre," Tasker said, "exactly."

It made Katryzna smile. He spoke frankly, not with Rurik's snideness. He probably killed people for work, too. She said, "No, I suppose it *was* a massacre. But it would have happened anyway, is my point – it only went a little wrong. And Gomer – my handler – he deserved to die. *He* is why people like Lopaz get so upset about that case."

That got Tasker's attention better than the murder of children. Ah, he had a useless handler, too – he was definitely jealous. This was bonding.

"So that's out there," Katryzna continued. "I just want to say, I know I'm not always . . . good for people. And I can go on alone if you want. However crap your life is, I will make it worse."

"This isn't all about you," Tasker said. "And I can happily return the offer. You don't have to come, if you'd rather wait here."

Katryzna stood, squinting at him. "Well that's definitely not happening. Great. Good. We are on the same page, then – if you need me, I will be *gorging*." She turned, waving a hand behind her. "And cover yourself up. No one's impressed."

# 15

*Antonio stumbled drunkenly off the pavement, hand against a cool earth bank to support himself. Piss powerful as a hose and a loud, satisfied groan. Answered by the frightened bray of a donkey. He turned, spraying urine across the road, and looked up the hill, past Raúl's half-finished house. Pockets of darkness between tatty brick, support planks sticking out here and there. Daft donkey got loose out someone's lot, trapped itself?*

*It brayed again, afraid.*

*Antonio grunted and shouted at it, be quiet, coming, coming, struggling with his fly. He tripped on rubble, steadied himself on a pile of bricks. Hooves scuffed back in the shadows, the animal kicking up a fuss. Antonio's buzz was fading as he absorbed the animal's fear. He slowed down, feeling his way through the building site. "Where you at, dumb mule?"*

*The braying got worse, the creature about screaming itself to death.*

*A disruption of rubble just behind made Antonio spring. A guy was standing there, silhouetted against the road behind. Antonio lurched, slurring a comment and pointing through the building site. Got a stuck donkey back there, hear it? The guy didn't move. Upset, maybe angry?*

*"Not trespassing or nothing," Antonio said. "Trying to help. Raúl? Is you, right? Say something."*

*The donkey stomped up a fury like Santa Muerte herself had come calling, and Antonio twisted to the sound, sobering fast. His back to the man, Antonio heard Raúl jump – and added his screams to the donkey's.*

Leigh-Ann stepped out the steaming shower a new woman, clean and free of the smell of cordite; ready to suit up in defiance of the drab dresses of Gray's women. She padded out into the dorm in just a towel, leaving wet footprints between the coarse-linen bunks and their footlockers. Past Zip, curled on her side on a cot, twitching against a bad dream, to her own bed where her suit lay on the mattress. Amazing they hadn't replaced it with a nun's frock or something while the gang were away. She lifted the indigo jacket, tapered about the hip, black patches over the shoulders. Damn sight better than the potato sack of a dress the commune provided Zip. And the first step in getting back to *normal*. Dress to impress, Reece always said.

Zip made a little whimpering noise. Leigh-Ann set the jacket aside to perch on the bunk next to her and gingerly stroked her arm. "Just a dream, sweetie."

"Madero," Zip uttered. "The donkey . . . they're gone."

"Dreaming of donkeys doesn't sound so bad," Leigh-Ann said.

"All dead." Zip sat up suddenly, frightened red eyes seeing something else. "Villa Madero – all dead."

"A dream," Leigh-Ann reminded her, slower now, with how serious the kid took it. Zip calmed with big breaths. "We ain't nowhere as fancy as a villa. But I saw a couple boys playing on a jungle gym outside – you wanna put the bad dream to bed, go have some fun?"

Zip's face twisted with confusion. Not letting go yet. "Something bad happened."

"It was a dream, that's all."

"But . . . I'm scared Leigh. I get them a lot now. It *feels* real."

Leigh-Ann wondered at the best response. Did you invite a traumatised kid to share and relive their imagined shit, or just dismiss it? A sharp knock saved her deciding – Reece followed right on into the room. "How my amazing ladies doing?"

"Jesus, Reece," Leigh-Ann snapped, tightening her towel, "you can't come storming in the ladies' dorm, they'll cut off your damn balls."

"Forgive me, I got bored waiting all day." Reece bowed low, extravagantly, grinning. Asshole. He was dressed already in the same style suit as Leigh-Ann's. The Crewe's tailored uniform, handmade by Brittany back in Cutjaw, each perfect fitting with little flourishes to make them unique. His had lapels that curved out with a little kink halfway up; Leigh-Ann's had a double-stripe of black piping. All deep indigo, worn with crisp black shirts and shining shoes. With his trumpet in hand, as elegant as the pistol at his hip, he could've belonged to some kind of prince's guard, if not for that greenish hair. Some was back to his usual brown, but damn there was a lot he couldn't wash out.

Leigh-Ann informed him, "Your hair looks like clown vomit."

"Yeah." He ran an awkward hand through it but kept up his smile. "New style, here to stay, I guess?"

"I saw something bad," Zip interrupted worriedly.

"In a dream," Leigh-Ann clarified. "She was napping."

"Don't sweat it sweetie, Leigh here's a *lioness*, she'll protect you." Reece winked. "And we're just across the way."

"But why can't we all stay *together*?" Zip asked innocently.

"Because Alban Gray is a cu –" Leigh-Ann stopped herself with a cough. "Are we agreed that the kid's cool now – can we swear?"

"Between you and your God, you wanna live with that," Reece said. "Now there's fierce scents coming from the mess hall, if you would *kindly* join me."

"Look remotely ready to you yet?" Leigh-Ann sneered jokingly.

"Sorry." Reece lifted his trumpet. "You must be waiting on your fanfare." He played a little trill, short and sharp, surprising Zip. She laughed. "Nah, that's not it – here, something I been working on." He played again, a heavy sound followed by quick descending notes, then another bold toot. Zip giggled again. He gave her a cock-eyed look. "Not quite there, is it?" Reece checked with Leigh-Ann. "Not sure this one's for the horn."

"Again!" Zip demanded, then remembered her manners. "Please."

Reece drew it out, then nodded. "Okay." He repeated the same little riff and added a flourish. Pulled his head back to make a show of it. Zip clapped, forgetting the nightmare at last. "Now hold on. I'm getting irresponsible, putting music in a kid when she ain't ready."

"I'm ready!" Zip turned a worried look to Leigh-Ann. "Tell him, Leigh!"

"Sure?" Reece said. "Because I had an inkling we might need your daddy's permission, before we do something like make music. And how we gonna ask him, not knowing where he is?"

Oh, he was smooth. Leigh-Ann imagined him sitting back in his bunk plotting a way to get the kid to talk without pressing her. But Zip's eyes narrowed, recognising a ploy. She said, "He's not here. I can listen to music."

"He might get wind of it, though," Reece said. "Especially if we're close to this river with a pyramid. This Grithin guy? Think they might be nearby, now?"

Zip considered it. "Closer."

She sounded a little too sure, making Leigh-Ann shift. The playfulness was leaving Reece's expression. Hell. Zip had hypnotised those Steers, why shouldn't she have psychic tracking skills. Reece said, "You see him in your head? Know where –"

"No!" Zip suddenly winced, screwing her eyes closed. "I *can't*. It's not safe!"

"Jesus if someone didn't do a number on her," Leigh-Ann muttered. "Sweetie, thinking about a thing ain't gonna do no harm."

Zip considered it carefully, at length, and looked genuinely unsure. Leigh-Ann wasn't so sure herself, now.

"Cher," Reece said, "I got another proposal, for me to think on while you get ready for more music and the *best* food. Can you tell us your daddy's name, at least?"

Another pause, but she accepted this one: "We're Masons. Seph Mason, that's my daddy . . . but they call him something else. Not nice."

"I been called plenty not nice things myself," Leigh-Ann said, imaging the racial shit this half-Black kid might've endured. The slurs might point them in the direction of her father's ethnicity, at least. But Zip's answer caught her breath.

"Headhunter. They call him Headhunter."

Leigh-Ann exchanged a look with Reece, acknowledging the same thing. This was getting more fucked by the moment. She clarified, quietly, "On account of him hunting them monsters?"

Zip nodded, then brightly changed the subject: "Can you play another tune? Please."

"For sure, cher," Reece said. "But after you get some food. If Leigh has the decency to put on some clothes."


In the mess hall, busy with Gray's people eating at long tables, the counter was spread with thick gumbo, spiced rice and beans, crispy bacon and butter-soaked baked potatoes. Reece and Caleb filled their plates while Reece made small talk as scant distraction for his concerns over that kid and the Steers. Gray was right that it *shouldn't* have been like this – he'd planned things carefully, used disguises, found camera blind spots. But the delay, and that gas stop encounter, had cost them all that grace.

The head chef asked Reece, "Y'all dressed for a parade? After missing the welcome dinner last night?"

At Reece's side, Caleb squirmed, resenting the attention garnered by their fine suits. But Reece replied warmly, "My apologies, Chef, you know we wouldn't have missed it but for the gravest circumstances. Sto's still being stitched up as we speak. Though this looks mighty fine – can't imagine how you topped it for last night."

He smiled all the way, no one knowing he was aching with concern underneath.

When they reached a table separate from the crowd, Caleb said, "Don't all seem too happy to have us here, do they? Probably have some idea the people we hurt – they got *thou shalt not kill* engraved big somewhere round here."

"Quoting scripture now?" Reece said. "They all knew there might be casualties."

Caleb tried to keep his next complaint down, but couldn't. "And the kid. Pretty sure they know, Reece. I seen them looking at her."

"Know what? That she's lost and afraid and we're all she's got? Till she's safe, she's part of the Crewe. That sit okay with you?"

Caleb's pause said no, not really, but he said, "Course it do."

"You're more hero than any of us, know that, Caleb? But now's time to quit worrying and start planning how to spend our rewards."

It tweaked a smile. "Not too early to jinx it?"

"Leave worrying about that shit to Leigh. Come on, impress me."

"Figure I might get a ring."

Reece cocked an eyebrow. "You ain't worn jewellery since you gave up that cross your momma gave you. Remember that thing? Heavy enough to bend a horse's neck."

Caleb shook his head. "Nah, not for me. Thought maybe I'd try something – big gesture style. You know? Gotta spend four figures, to make it worth it, I read that online. I found a shop in Lake Charles, they do them special to order."

"Special . . ." Reece should've seen this coming: the consequences of making his boys rich. Wouldn't all be touring the States drinking, playing nightclubs and sprucing up their trailers. But marriage? When Caleb wasn't even *dating*? He had to mean Leigh-Ann, one hundred fifty per cent not interested, which was the epitome of how fools got parted from their money.

Reece smiled uncomfortably, looking for the right way to tell Caleb to absolutely not do that, but Gray entered before he found it. The upset was written on Gray's face and in the postures of the three men behind him. Noah and two Stilt Town soldiers. Gray hobbled up to the table, cane tapping all the way. He pulled a leg over Reece's bench to sit next to him and Noah took the opposite seat, while the soldiers stood, stony-faced.

"Let me guess," Reece said, "you got riled up counting that cash, not knowing where you'd store it all?"

"The money's good, Reece," Gray admitted. "No complaints there."

"How much we talking? With all that escaping we never got a chance to count."

"Money can wait," Noah said. "You said it'd come without strings. Practically guaranteed. Weren't those your words? Practically guarantee the Steer Trust won't know who hit them."

Reece dug a fork into his rice and took a small mouthful. Chewed contemplatively, then said, "Does sound like something I would say. But there was always the possibility you'd need to do more than simply wash that cash for us."

Gray exhaled through his teeth. "Dustin Fallon done wrong, and they've been deserving of righteous punishment – and your contribution to Stilt Town and the church is greatly appreciated." His pale eyes listed to the side.

"But?" Reece prompted.

"But, Reece," Gray said. "You gotta tell me what happened on that farm."

"What –" Reece began, but Gray held up a shaking hand.

"I know you boys," he said. "Basically good, deep down in there. Better than most that come outta Cutjaw, and I oughta know. The memory of those evils I saw growing up out there, they're the mortar that makes our church *strong*. And Caleb – when you reached out, after all them years with your mother twisting in the wind, that gave me so much hope. But it's hard, it is, purging ourselves of the poison Cutjaw sows."

"Mr Gray..." Reece interrupted the trip down memory lane. Another minute and they'd get a lecture on how each of their families wronged the righteous Grays a hundred years ago. "How'd you know about the farm? It make the news?"

"You were there, then?"

"We came upon a place looking for help. Found a girl bound to a chair. Things got out of hand and people got hurt, but it was all in protecting Zip."

Gray's expression shifted. "They had that little girl bound up?"

"You know I was gonna tell you all about it, right now. Your people pick it up on the police scanner?"

"Not my people," Gray said. "Fallon."

Reece straightened up. "You spoken to him?"

"Think I shouldn't have? He's got three cars outside camp and another two in a motel up on the 28. Gearing up for a fight. He reached out, Reece, and I didn't like what he had to say."

"Showed us some things we didn't like," Noah added.

"You can't trust a damn word –" Reece started.

Gray held up a hand. "I know. That one's more snake than man. So let's hear your side of things. You found this girl on a farm, broke her free, carried on your way?"

"A man got shot," Reece said. "And we got attacked on the way out. There was an animal. Tore up a truck, the farmer's daughter. I was gonna ask your boys to help explain it."

"How about this?" Noah placed his phone on the table, showing a photo. Caleb jumped up with a curse. Reece swallowed. "You explain this, at least?"

The face on the screen was contorted and drooping in waxy horror, skin pale and eyes vaguely empty. Donny. His severed head on a wooden pole.

"How did – no way – not –" Caleb paced away, then back.

Donny hadn't made it, after all, cut down by the same guy that got Nina. Vile? With dark echoes of that other name Zip used. Headhunter. Reece said, "Fallon sent you this?"

"You recognise him," Noah said.

"Yes I fucking recognise him," Reece bit back. "He ran out on us and we never found him. You seriously think we could do a thing like that?"

"No," Gray said, eyeing Noah to be clear on his stance. "We do not. Fallon said his people found the man like that. Found your car. You know what he said? Keep the money, for all he cares, he only wants the monsters capable of this brought to justice. No harm to Stilt Town if he gets *your* head." Reece watched the old man's face. No way he would do it, with Caleb being family and the Steer Trust being their sworn enemies. But Gray's expression was severe – at least believing Fallon's suggestion that this wasn't the work of the Steers. He continued, "I reminded him that for your imperfections you've got the Lord's light in you. That he ought to worry about his own judgement before the Lord. And if he outstays his welcome in Louisiana, that'll come sooner than later. But I need to know, Reece. You boys ain't all of the same cloth. And with the woman you travel with –"

"We did not do that," Reece said firmly. "Don't ask me again."

Noah got hot at his tone, but Gray held Reece's gaze steadily. It was all Reece could do not to slam a plate in his face for suggesting such a thing. Gray tilted his head. "We to believe the Steers set you up? Like this?"

"No. We just might have an enemy beside them, right now. Telling you, someone wanted that girl. A guy in black with some kinda gorilla."

Gray glowered hard enough that Noah stifled an instinctive insult. "A gorilla? This a game to you, Reece?"

"I ain't laughing, am I? It was a creature big as a truck. And it don't make any more sense to us than it does to you, but we're working on it, Alban. Trust me on that, and don't for a minute take to Fallon's thinking."

Noah snorted. "Listen to them talking mystery men and gorillas, you gonna allow this, Pop?"

His son's aggravation only worked to make Gray take it more coolly, though. He stood, nodding. He put a fatherly hand on Reece's shoulder. "Frankly, I pray whatever evil you touched out there *does* find itself here. Anyone that could do a thing like that – they will face the Lord's judgement." There was an edge of threat to his voice; still considering one of Reece's friends responsible. With that, he ambled away towards the counter. Noah lingered, to let his hostility be known, then fell into line behind his dad.

Caleb deflated onto the bench, gasping, "Holy hell, Reece. I mean, holy hell. That thing – these monsters – what is this?"

"I don't rightly know," Reece admitted. "But it don't exactly feel like we're safe yet."

# 16

The Congo River barge was a vast platform with multiple staged tiers at its front, crowded with people. Right from when they arrived at the ramp, up onto the boat, everyone was suspiciously friendly, with smiles and handshakes too enthusiastic to be genuine. Strangers wanted to know where Katryzna was from, who she knew *out there*, what she did. She answered with curt snarls and they laughed. Presumably, the locals regarded crazy white tourists as an amusing oddity rather than threatening. It reminded her of Eyes' disarming responses: their second meeting, when she tried to kick his groin and he merely stepped out of the way, showed her his gun and said, cool as a cucumber, "I don't want to use this. I just want to talk."

And they had talked. He asked about her upbringing, listened to her stories of moving to grotty Rostov without judgement or calling her a liar. When she told him how her night-club-owning uncle had first given her a break, a courier job that turned bad, Eyes smiled like it was no surprise. When she explained that she'd finally had to kill poor Uncle Nikodem himself – that creep – Eyes nodded and said he'd been there, too. He never explained that. But more often than sympathising, he looked amused by her. The same way these Congolese were – not afraid. They didn't know they should be.

On board the boat, traders ran small market stalls and the people packed shoulder-to-shoulder were scrambling to get higher up, to where the living conditions were less reminiscent of a landfill. Henri pushed a path through to the highest passenger tier, just one ledge down from the captain's cabin. He offered Katryzna a hand with a leery smile. She sneered. This guy was too eager to please and all – probably wanted her guard down so he could stab her in her sleep for being shamed in the fight club. What was Tasker thinking?

Even on the desirable upper level, there was barely room to move, and the wooden floor was wet with excrement. A caged alligator snapped furiously at its bars on the edge of the deck. Henri muscled on to the small interior, where a handful of rooms lined a narrow corridor. The best rooms the barge could offer were little more than sheds, containing soiled mattresses and buckets for toilets. Katryzna was almost too hot to complain, but managed: "I've stayed in better prison cells."

"I've slept on better streets," Tasker replied, flatly. Joke or fact?

But Henri said, "You prefer to sleep on the lower decks?"

Katryzna threw her heavy canvas bag down with a bang, surprised it didn't go straight through the floorboards. As the men went to their rooms, she tossed through the spare clothing and supplies Tasker had found her, to focus on her fancy new rifle. Yes. He had delivered guns, at least – this and an upgraded pistol. With the barge packed as it was, she could kill a hundred people in a matter of seconds. Her smile returned.

Rurik complained, questioning the judgement of someone who'd give her any weapon at all, and she said, "In a fight, we all know who's going to be saving who." Pause. "Whom?"

There was a knock at the door and she answered, "Go away."

A white man poked his head in: fat, chinless, red from the heat and wearing a vast floral shirt. He spoke in a cheery American Midwestern accent: "Well met young lady. Howard, that's me – bunking down the end of the row and I must say it's a pleasure to make –"

"My God, why are you talking?" Katryzna cut in. "This is a private room."

Fat Howard stood stricken, struggling to maintain a crooked-toothed smile.

Katryzna pulled the pistol from her bag and laid it on the mattress. "Go. Away."

He left, face slack and pale. As Rurik piped up, Henri appeared with a sickly amused smile on his face. "These walls are thin, Ms Tkacz. You might get used to the idea there's not much privacy on this barge. And that" – he nodded to the gun – "won't make you special here."

"It's not what made me special in your gym, either. You want to keep the peace, keep all these idiots away from me." Henri lingered, waiting for more. Katryzna rolled her eyes. "Want me to break your nose back the other way?"

"We dance again, I'll be ready to show you some of *my* moves."

"Your *moves* will involve flying off this boat," Katryzna shot back. Rurik perked up with irritated shouts, and she said, "Seriously? You are defending this sleaze?"

"Hey, not me!" Henri raised his hands innocently, and backed off, grinning. "I'm here to help. You want me gone, I go. You want me to come, I come. Welcome to the barge, Ms Tkacz."

He slunk away and started up another conversation in French. Rurik said, "It wouldn't hurt to make more friends. Especially one willing to forgive you threatening to kill him."

Katryzna didn't answer, glaring at the open doorway, expecting some other irritation to creep in. Sean should be saying she needed to keep calm. But he didn't appear. Good. She wouldn't want to hurt him.


Waiting for her irritability to settle, Tasker kept his distance from Katryzna, difficult as the overcrowding made it. He set Henri to warning others to keep their distance. She prowled the floating market, where excitable men approached her to offer fetishes and bowls of indiscernible food, and the novelty kept her amiable until dusk, when she punched a vendor who stood too close. The press of the crowd kept the fight tight and Henri intervened fast. She restrained herself, to stalk off to her room.

On the second day, Katryzna hung her legs over the edge of the barge as they drifted in and out of ramshackle ports, while Tasker got the measure of the other foreign passengers: a pair of mining consultants, a retired Swedish couple on an adventure, a weaselly French arms dealer and a teacher. All quickly took his hints not to ask about him.

At twilight, Katryzna came to Tasker as he sipped a noxious homemade spirit on the upper deck. She had an armful of skewered meats and offered him one. When he declined she shoved them messily into her mouth. Henri remained in the middle of the lower deck, chatting with one of the captain's lieutenants, one eye on Katryzna. He winked Tasker's way, and by way of dismissing him Tasker turned full on to Katryzna and offered up his bottle.

She suppressed a momentary look of irritation, working through a full mouth, to say, "I was told, Sean, that the mind is a terrible thing to waste."

That made him smirk. "You do hurt people for a living, don't you? I'm not mistaken about that."

"And? I protect *my* mind." She tapped her temple. "My life. Other people's are their own problem. Do you actually know what you are drinking?"

Tasker looked at the unmarked bottle. It smelt like an acid that had been strained through old socks. But it had taken some of the edge off, and he'd seen a bunch of the locals swilling it before accepting any himself. He shrugged and Katryzna rolled her eyes with exaggerated disappointment.

"Well, rot your senses if you want, but do not suggest *I* do so, okay?" She turned away, looking down at the bustle. "I guess you need it, doing this sort of thing all the time. Is your job always this *weird*?"

"It varies," he said, happy to move on. "I once visited a mountaintop village where they wove feathers into their flesh and communicated in bird trills. I was following rumours of vampires. That was nonsense, but the village was strange as hell."

Katryzna's full mouth was partly open. She tried to speak, spitting food.

Tasker grimaced. "Finish chewing, for God's sake."

She winked and swallowed. "Think we're chasing rumours, now?"

"No. I've got a pretty awful feeling about this, actually. If you'd seen the state of that village in Norway, you would too. Women, children, torn apart, no sign of exactly how or why." He trailed off, mind going back to that girl. Rebecca. He took a breath. "Everything about this – with Parris's numbers pointing here, these fears of the monsters in the jungle – this is Ministry material and it's bad. Really bad."

Katryzna eyed him like she was trying to weigh up exactly how serious he was. "Eyes would say do not believe it until you see it yourself. Even then he might not be sure."

"I'm guessing Eyes didn't have quite the same background as me," Tasker said. Screw it, with what they might be up against, she needed to hear it. "Monsters exist, Katryzna. I've seen creatures that can drain people dry, animals that leave you paralysed while they peel off your skin. Things too terrible to reveal to the general public. I don't know what's in Ikiri, but I believe it's something up there with those horrors. The difference being, whatever's going on out here somehow managed to affect people in the Arctic Circle. And if it can reach Norway, it can reach anywhere, including my own home."

She paused. "You're actually serious?"

Tasker nodded.

"Sounds like you should have got us more support, Sean." Katryzna gave a light laugh, betraying just a tiny hint of concern. "Well, supernatural or not, I'm good at making things stop."

"Never said anything about supernatural," Tasker said. "We have people researching these anomalies, explaining them. They're often wholly natural, just better off unknown. But by all means, I look forward to seeing how you destroy whatever this is."

"*Now* you sound like Eyes," Katryzna replied fondly. "He said I could break anything. Often without trying."

"Did he try to get you to wash and eat with your mouth closed, too?"

"He actually did!" Katryzna pushed him playfully. "But he could defend himself against me. You have a death wish."

Tasker smirked, knowing it was the opposite, befriending one dark force to stop another.

"So, Sean. Can your Ministry explain this?" Katryzna pointed at the railing. Tasker frowned, not following, and she picked something out of the air. In her mind, holding up her conscience between thumb and forefinger. "You know how big a headache this guy gives me? And I have to put up with it *alone*."

Voices and imaginary companions weren't something new to Tasker or the Ministry. He answered honestly, "We've come across certain things. Dreavers plant ideas in people's minds. Whisper Casts take over part of the brain, and manifest in split personalities. But they're insidious parasites, they don't directly communicate with the host. The mundane truth, true of most of what I pursue, is that it's likely your own mind's responsible."

"I'm imagining it, right," Katryzna said, placing the conscience back down. "Created my own miniature enemy, always nagging." The miniature was an interesting detail; he might believe she'd encountered a Fae, if she wasn't so clearly indicating an empty space. She frowned as her invisible companion said something disagreeable. "Want me to feed you to a crocodile?"

"You ever seen anyone about it?" Tasker asked.

"Like a doctor? Take pills?" Katryzna twirled a hand around her temple. "This is delicate enough already. And he has his uses. Sees round corners I can't. Pushed a box under my feet when I was strung up by my neck, once."

Tasker looked at the empty space where Rurik supposedly was. The Fae certainly could pull tricks like that, but his instinct said no, the voice was in her mind, and to his knowledge, the Ministry had encountered no proven cases of the ability to move things with the mind. Most likely she imagined those results, too. All sparked by some long-buried trauma. He said, "You remember when you started seeing him?"

"When I was a kid," Katryzna said. "Maybe as a teenager. He's got worse. Back before, he didn't just appear wherever, whenever." Her face clouded over, remembering, considering, but she didn't share, only sighed to let it go.

"I can ask my people to investigate it," Tasker said. "If you like."

"Eh" – Katryzna flapped a hand – "forget it." He followed her gaze down into the sprawl of the noisy barge, adrift in murky waters between the jungle thicket, lanterns glowing yellow. "Kind of romantic, isn't it?"

A group of men were wrestling another alligator into a cage, with onlookers yelling advice or waving sticks. Katryzna edged slightly closer and Tasker's body tensed. She said, "You're really not planning to make a move on me, are you?"

He looked down at the top of her scraggily shaved head. "I've got a wife."

"Not what I asked."

"No," Tasker answered honestly, leaning on the railing, letting it out. "That kind of affection doesn't come easy to me, and definitely not for a girl that can't even keep herself clean." Her eyes danced happily at the blunt assessment. He added, "You've got me curious, that's all. I like knowing things. It's how I protect people."

"Makes you feel important? Behaving like a dad to all the mixed-up girls out there."

He stalled. No, it wasn't *that*. But she smiled crookedly, childlike again, and he thought of home, and Rebecca, and he wondered if maybe it was.


Katryzna accepted an invitation to the captain's dinner on Tasker's insistence that it would be a banquet. A table was decked with steaming plates of meat and vegetables, with all the barge's foreign guests present, but Henri was not invited. The captain sat in the middle, a large man with an old cloth draped over one eye; a temporary eye-patch that had become permanent. He spoke of the area south of Bokema, where they would be alighting.

"People's Free Resistance territory," he said. "Not a good place to be, unless you are hunting Jean-Baptiste Matka. Even then, it is not a good place to be."

"We hear the mountains are nice," Katryzna said. "Mount Ikiri, especially."

The captain's face got more severe. "You plan to cross the Cursed Union?"

"We don't intend to cross anyone," Tasker said.

The French arms dealer said, "They say those that travel to Ikiri never come back."

Howard scoffed. "They say that of most of the interior. Often truthfully."

"General Solomon's head would make you a lot of money," the captain noted.

Katryzna pricked up her ears. "Who's paying?"

"Matka would, I am sure – their territories border. The government might, too. Take enough body parts and you could get paid many times." The captain's shoulders shook with flat laughter.

"Maybe I will," Katryzna responded brightly. They took it as a joke.

Once dinner was over and they moved into relative privacy outside their rooms with Henri, Tasker said, "You know we're planning to lie low, not join in their war?"

"So?" Katryzna leant against the flimsy wall. "We can get paid."

"What's this?" Henri asked carefully.

"Hell," Tasker huffed, his fears that she was serious confirmed. "They were putting ideas in her head about going after Solomon himself."

Henri's face fell. "Why would you do that?"

"I thought you would be pleased," Katryzna snorted. "Didn't men like this get your sister? The rest of your family?" Henri looked shocked – probably as surprised that she'd paid attention as at her plain speaking. "Don't *worry*, claiming bounties on untouchable people is how I maintain this luxury lifestyle."

"No." Tasker's hand was suddenly on her elbow, his face next to hers. Her eyes burned back at him. "Our intention is to avoid them. Henri's here to guide us through without incident. That's the plan."

"*Your* plan." Katryzna placed her other hand on top of his, gently. "Plans go wrong. I improvise." Her fingers tightened and she twisted suddenly, too quick for him to react before his face was pressed into wood, the wall squeaking like it might break. His wrist was pinned between his shoulders, and when he moved his other hand she slammed it against the wall. Henri made the slightest move but her eyes burned a warning at him to freeze. Her lips were at Tasker's ear, body pressed into his back. "You've been doing well, Sean, but you are *not* my dad, understand?"

She backed off abruptly and gave him a companionable slap on the back. He straightened out his glasses, turning slowly back to her. Rurik kicked up a storm on her shoulder, snapping about what the hell had she done – apologise, for God's sake apologise – but she held his eyes. Tasker stared for what felt like a very long time, and, at last, Katryzna couldn't suppress an uncomfortable smile. She glanced at Henri, still watching in mute alarm, and said, "You can plot my murder together, now."

Henri's shock became confusion and Tasker's eyes softened. He said, "We're not going to do that, Katryzna. And neither of us want to be *anything* to you. We'd just like to survive."

She watched him for a lie. Watched Henri, too, and found him nodding insistently. She said, "Then follow my lead. Surviving is what I do best." A light wink and she turned away, problem solved.

# 17

At the centre of Stilt Town sat a three-tier communications hub packed with radio equipment and snaking cables. On the peaked roof was a score of satellite dishes, transmitters and masts to ensure Gray could send and receive broadcasts all over the world. Mostly, he preached messages of the impending flood, and scoured the internet for signs of the coming apocalypse. Occasionally his people could be put to more specific uses, such as searching for Zip's father.

The gang waited for Reece in the widest tier of the hub, a storage space for old electronics, where Zip touched a hand to the old machines with wonder, like she'd never seen radios before. Leigh-Ann kept everyone distracted with made-up shit: "First wired radio in Beauregard came courtesy of this man Arthur McGee, flew cabling over hills, spooling it out like a crop duster – those old cable planes, they were marvels."

Zip's delight was too bright to be real, watching Leigh-Ann's eyes.

"Think my grandpa used to fly one of them," Stomatt said, probably serious.

"We got something," Reece interrupted, returning down the creaking stairs. "Any of you know there was a giant blue pyramid by the Memphis harbour?"

"Oh yeah, right across from their acropolis?" Leigh-Ann whipped back.

"They got an acropolis too?" Caleb fell for it. "What for?"

"You even know what one of them is, Leigh?" Reece said. "Don't answer. But this pyramid *does* exist, in Memphis, and as it happens there was some trouble there not two days ago. Dockworker out with his pals got set upon by some maniac with a sword, hid up his sleeve. But the guy fought back, somehow – got hold of a rebar to fight him off."

"How you hide a sword up a sleeve?" Leigh-Ann asked, and Reece watched Zip like she oughta know. The child shifted uncomfortably, and he continued.

"We can get back to that. So, they chased one another off into the shadows, to God-knows-where. Two friends on the scene said they didn't know what it was about but haven't seen their pal since – stood 6'5", bald, went by *Gus*. Been working the docks two months and no one knew much else about him. Except he had one eye. News article appealed for anyone to share more if they knew it."

"One eye?" Stomatt said. "How in hell this guy fight off someone with a sword?"

"Your guess as good as mine," Reece said. "But it sounds like a lead. Right, Zip?"

The child nodded. "Grithin. He has one eye, no hair. And Daddy . . ."

"He's got a sword hand," Reece said. Zip nodded again, another guilty admission.

"The hell's a sword hand?" Stomatt demanded.

"It extends," Zip said, voice only getting quieter.

"Right," Caleb spoke up. "I'll say it if none of y'all will. This is giving me the damn creeps – heads on poles and sword hands and monsters. We done wrong back in Waco – we done wrong and none of y'all can tell me this don't sound like judgement."

"The crosses round here got you thinking messy, Caleb," Leigh-Ann said. "Nothing religious about us tripping up on some wackos attacking one another."

"We find this Grithin," Reece said, "assuming he survived, we might get some better answers. If not find Zip's father himself. Gray's boys will keep looking long as we're here."

"How long will it take?" Zip said, voice pitching a little high. "We shouldn't stay."

"This place stinks but it's safe, sweetie," Leigh-Ann said. "Those Steers ain't getting in. Even your gorilla would have a hard time with those walls."

"It's *not* safe," Zip insisted. "They'll come for me."

"Ah, let them come," Stomatt said. "Gray's boys up the tower could tear them in two with that elephant rifle."

"Please," Zip said, "Vile is different. We need my daddy, we shouldn't stop."

"I'm in broad agreement, actually," Reece said, turning his gaze to Caleb now. "Makes me a little uncomfortable relying on Alban right now, given he's already got his doubts about all this. Maybe should've kept some of that cash back for ourselves."

"So we could ditch this place?" Leigh-Ann said. "For where?"

"I dunno, I'm spitballing. Not to her dad yet, at least. Gray's people found no word of any Seph Mason, anywhere to do with Memphis nor nearby, and these guys" – he screwed a thumb towards the ceiling – "are scary with what they can turn up. Your daddy got another name, Zip?"

"Other than Headhunter," Leigh-Ann added.

Zip shook her head. "Mostly, he doesn't use a name."

"When he took that flight? Books in a hotel? What's he tell them?"

She shook her head again, as though he didn't give names ever. It recalled the weird trance of the Steers at the gas stop. Leigh-Ann said, "You guys travelling hypnotists or something?"

"Mortal enemies with a one-eyed bandit and a mutant gorilla," Stomatt said.

"It's the power," Zip said uncomfortably.

"These other bastards got this weird power too?" Stomatt asked.

"It's not *weird*," Zip replied defensively. "It's *dangerous*."

"All right," Reece asked. "I gotta ask, Zip. You ready yet to tell us where's home?"

Zip's expression got stonier. Still a no.

"You sure we even want to be taking her back?" Caleb said. "Her dad don't sound like good people, I'm gonna say it. It ain't normal hiding away from the world, having her scared of her own feelings."

"Not exactly our place to say," Reece said, holding Zip's eyes, "but Caleb's right, cher. Some of the things your daddy's told you, I wouldn't necessarily trust them. Specially when he's saying trust no one else. We're here for you, see? You can talk to us."

Zip stared, locked in conflict, before lowering her eyes. She said, "There's a stream. And from the upstairs window, you can see the city, on a clear day. We're on a hill. I've seen the sea in the other direction. Daddy says it's not possible but I have. There's a big oak for climbing, next to the tower, and I went to the post office on my own, once."

"City got a name?" Reece said.

She gave a blank expression. Maybe didn't actually know.

"Australia, right?" Stomatt said. "With that accent. Not got many cities, do they?"

"Australia?" Leigh-Ann exclaimed. "Dammit, Sto, kid talks like Mary-fucking-Poppins. You ever even met someone that wasn't Arcadian?"

"I can't," Zip said. She cringed and closed her eyes. "He'll come, he'll come and we'll never be safe!" She was trembling, the emotion taking over her again, and Reece met Leigh-Ann's eyes with worry. Her responsibility somehow, now they were on the verge of making the kid bawl.

She put a hand on Zip's shoulder and said, "Enough for now, huh? How about you and me take a walk, Zip? See the goats."

Zip peeked, straightening up. "Goats?"

"You like that? And the sheep, cows. Might even spot a rabbit or two."

"I like rabbits!" The girl's eyes were bigger than ever.

Leigh-Ann guided her away from the others, all watching uncertainly. She mouthed at Reece, *Figure this out.*


Reece left the comms tower to head back to their room, with Caleb and Stomatt dogging his heels. He told them, "You might be right yet, Caleb – she might not belong back with her dad, but we got a responsibility to see that through. I do, anyway, I got us into all this. And you all seen what she can do. Won't necessarily come without reward, one way or another."

"You ain't got the feeling, though," Caleb said carefully, "we might not wanna cross these people?"

"We just took on Steer Trust," Reece smiled. "Who's gonna stop us now?"

Stomatt jumped to ruffle Caleb's hair, shoving his head. "Yeah, cheer up – we rich as all saints and you're crying cause some fairy with a sword got a beef!"

Caleb pushed back. "Get your dirty paws off me!"

"Go on and make me, you morose motherfucker." Stomatt lunged, trying to get him in a headlock. "Where's your muscle?"

Stomatt pushed too far and Caleb shoved him hard. "Said back the hell off, Sto!"

Reece skipped ahead, up the steps to the private little room. The instruments were laid out between their beds. La Belle Vérité chief among them. The matte black nickel and brass trumpet, his world in a twist of metal. As he picked it up and tested a note, Stomatt and Caleb tussled in behind him. Another note. Ran his fingers over the buttons for a little flourish. There was the sound. *That* was the truth, and it calmed the boys.

"Damn swords and gorillas," Reece said quietly. "And red eyes and psychic powers. Leave that to the breeze, we got this."

He gave it a blast as Caleb plugged in the electric bass and Stomatt squatted for a tom tom. The big trombone lay between them, a violin to one side – ready for later. Reece picked up a tune, blended it into the Stilt Town Serenade, that little light number he produced just for this place. Community looking out for each other, like the gang did. Except he'd seen Gray was unsettled and Zip was even more so. Didn't like those odds.

As they relaxed into the music, letting all that go, he let the truth run through him.

Sure enough, their journey didn't end here.


Come the calls for dinner, the gang joined the packed mess hall. Gray sat at the centre, with Noah and the same few hulking guards, watching as Reece made small talk with his people. Leigh-Ann watched the old man herself. A man capable of drawing all these people away from society, just for him. You couldn't trust that. Reece slowly led them over to him, and as they got close Leigh-Ann hung back with Zip.

"Heard the Serenade earlier, unless I'm mistaken," Gray said kindly, and regarded Zip. "And that dress is very becoming, young lady."

It looked like shit, Leigh-Ann didn't say. She'd get Zip back in the old clothes as soon as they dried. Zip mumbled thanks.

"Any more word from Fallon?" Reece asked. "Or on that other thing?"

"I had, you know I'd have come to you," Gray said. "Don't worry, Reece, it's all in hand. We've doubled the guard, got everyone recalled and the perimeter locked tight, but Fallon's not making a push. He'll back down once he accepts we're ready to fight back."

"Think that bullet in their window got them scared?" Caleb said.

"Plain as day Stilt Town's no pushover," Gray said. "Likely they'll wait till we're sleeping and try and sneak in. We're ready for it, long as everyone keeps their heads." He directed this at Stomatt, and Leigh-Ann too, for good measure. "Y'all just get yourselves some fine crayfish stew, bless us with sweet melodies, keep the faith."

"Always do," Reece winked, damn charmer. Leigh-Ann couldn't muster an ounce of that suck-up. And despite his and Gray's fronts there was something stifling in the air, with the Steers so close. Noah had an even harder face than usual, quietly eyeballing her around a fried chicken wing. Zip's continued tension didn't help – seeing the animals eased her a little, but the kid looked like she thought a ghost might jump out the ground. As they left Gray to head for the counter she squeezed Leigh-Ann's hand.

Leigh-Ann shifted closer to Reece and whispered, "Get the feeling Zip's right to be worried?"

Reece didn't play down the concerns, now. Something in his set said he'd been thinking along the same lines. He gave the commune's miller a quick how'd-ye-do before continuing towards the food, and waited until the rich aromas welcomed them forward before answering: "We'll get through dinner, think about our exit after."

# 18

When they disembarked at a rickety riverside town, Tasker found leaving the confined barge for the ominous forest a strange relief. Between the ups and downs of navigating Katryzna himself, he had spent days afraid he'd turn a corner and find someone with his throat slit for irking her. At least out here he needed only worry about himself and Henri, and Henri had sensibly backed off trying to flirt with her. He had discovered a new tactic for winning her friendship, by expressing wild shared enthusiasm for food. Katryzna was utterly oblivious to the bubble of tension she'd created, bouncing off the gangplank with an eager smile.

They took a small ferry across from Bokema to the southern riverbank and rode on motorbikes over narrow, bumpy tracks into the trees. Katryzna frequently peeled ahead, jumping the vehicle over bumps, either very skilled or enjoying the luck of the recklessly brave. When the mud-road and foliage became impassable, and they needed to walk the bikes, she swung her machete like a child's baton.

With her lost in that assault, Tasker quietly reiterated to Henri that they travel via the quietest route. At all costs, don't get noticed by the militia. Henri needed no persuasion there, never mind how much longer such diversions would take them. Then he swung the subject back to Katryzna and asked if Tasker had any luck with her on the boat. As if he could have escaped such details. Tasker didn't answer and Henri made his own conclusions, smiling happily. "She's softening, don't you see? You only need to treat a woman right – she'll give you her heart."

Tasker kept quiet, fairly sure no part of that was true.


Katryzna wasn't sure what had woken her, but she was out of her tent with her rifle in the pitch black before she'd stopped to think about it. In just her pants and top, she trod noisily through the undergrowth, expecting swarms of flies to descend. The way everyone talked about it, this forest was full of bugs ready to eat you alive or impregnate your flesh with worms, but she had seen little evidence so far. Made all their pills and repellent sprays seem a waste of time. But there was *something* out here, she knew that.

Between the trees, in the shadows.

Despite blinking hard, her sight wasn't improving; the darkness was absolute. She turned back to the tent and a tiny yawn drew her attention to the entrance, Rurik stretching as he exited. "What's going on?"

"Don't know. Pass me the torch."

He looked up, unamused, and she gave him a quick sneer before leaning past to get it herself. Never any help. She turned the high strength beam to the trees, casting jagged shapes all around. They had set up camp in a tight spot, three tents with no real perimeter. Katryzna scanned one way then another, tramping about. Could be anything out there.

Something, far off, made an ungodly noise. She spun to it. The sound came again, further away, moving. Had *that* come close enough to wake her? She turned back and went rigid, finger on the trigger.

Fifty metres away or more, a man was standing between the trees. The torchlight didn't quite illuminate him, even as Katryzna moved from side to side – obstructing trees cast heavy shadows over his features. He was just standing there.

"See that?" Katryzna asked Rurik, as he wandered up alongside her.

"No," he answered.

Hardly surprising considering the useless idiot didn't reach her ankle. Katryzna turned the torch away, checking around, then back to the man, still motionless. Then out to the side. There was another one. And another further back. She growled, picking out at least half a dozen silhouettes, staggered through the trees, all in shadow despite the torchlight. If she got closer, she sensed, they wouldn't be any clearer. Not the first time she'd seen spectres. Though they didn't usually haunt her in groups. She backed off, crunching twigs, and finally roused Tasker. He groaned sleepily, then saw the beam of torchlight and bolted upright.

"Katryzna – what is it?" he hissed, emerging in a half-crouch with a pistol. She gave him a bored look and checked the trees again. They were still there. Swinging the torch around – *all* still there – she realised they might not be in her imagination.

"Okay," she said. "Tell me if you see them, Sean."

Her nonchalance threw him for a second, then he stood, followed her torch beam and suddenly pulled her down into cover.

"What are you –"

"Henri, we got company!" Tasker shouted, moving in a crouch to the nearest tree. "Katryzna, stay down! You see who they are?"

Katryzna moved off to a different tree, clutching the rifle and giving him a scolding look for the stupid question. But he saw them. They were real. She hissed, "Why are they standing out there like ghosts?"

With Henri scrambling out of his tent, hurriedly preparing a rifle, Tasker slowly stood, and the edge of Katryzna's torchlight cast deep worry lines on his face. She stood for another look herself, aiming the torch at one of the creeps. Still not moving, a bunch of scarecrows, trying to freak them out?

"Who are you?" Katryzna shouted. "You can't see we're trying to sleep?"

Tasker made an upset sound, but waited for a response. None come. Henri was out now, his own torch ready and searching the trees. He said, "Matka's PFR shouldn't be out this far."

"Try your clicky tongue language or whatever," Katryzna suggested, and

Henri nodded. Except he called out in French. *She* could've done that. Still the men didn't move, ominously waiting for something, so Henri tried another language, one she didn't recognise. Still nothing.

"How about –" Katryzna started, and Rurik cut in.

"You can't just shoot random people!"

"Out here?" Katryzna told him, "I'm pretty sure I can."

On the other side of Rurik, still low, Tasker scowled. Didn't follow her chain of thought but didn't approve anyway.

She leant around the tree. "Last chance. Explain yourself or it's ba –"

The man in her torch beam ducked to the side, down into the thicket. Leaves moved around him as he crawled closer. Behind him, the other silhouettes dropped out of sight, quickly.

Katryzna fired. The shot was met by the cries of nearby birds and animals. Tasker shouted, but he saw the movement and backed off, raising his pistol. Torch clamped to the side of the rifle, Katryzna picked out one of the men and fired again. With an eruption of leaves, a black arm flapped up and fell down.

She swung the gun the other way, picking out another movement, but a sound drew her back to the first man. Shadows shifting where he'd fallen – not dead. She fired a burst, until he was still.

Tasker fired, too, at another approacher. Then Henri, on her other side, the pair accepting this was an attack. She glanced to the other shapes scrambling through the trees as the boys fired and tree trunks burst around them. Lots of shapes moving now, all coming from that general side of camp. She swung back to the sound of movement from her first victim. No, closer – her torch swung to light up the shredded face of a Congolese man on his belly, propelling himself out of the thicket on elbows, shattered teeth bared and bloody. Katryzna fired right between the eyes, bursting his head open. He flopped still, at last.

She stared. The earlier shots had torn through his torso. One had taken off half his jaw. And his clothes were already in tatters. As she stared, his fingers twitched, and she yelled and unloaded a half-dozen more shots into the back of his already-exploded head.

"Grab the stuff!" she shouted. "Whatever you can!"

"What?" Tasker turned as she skipped through the tents.

"I hit one, he keeps coming!" Henri shouted, reaching the same panicked conclusion as her.

Katryzna grabbed her boots and shouted over her shoulder as she hopped into them, "Stay if you want – I'm not!" The men stopped firing, to fall back and snatch their own gear. Their dark attackers were making horrible scuttling noises, circling closer. Katryzna fired a warning shot at one, knocking him back through the shadows. She jammed her clothes into the backpack and swung it over a shoulder, then pulled back, watching for where the strangers were. Picking a direction that looked quiet, she ran between the trees. A few paces in, it became a tangle of vines and leaves, and she angrily fumbled the rifle strap over a shoulder and pulled free the machete.

"Katryzna!" Tasker shouted from behind. Unclear if he was in trouble or wanted her to stop or just wanted to cry her name. No time to care; she hacked out a path through the weeds.

"On your left, on your left!" Henri said, bouncing up alongside her. He had his pack on, too, and a machete swinging much more efficiently.

She fell in behind him and held out her blade. "You cut, I'll cover!"

Without another word, Henri pressed on with a storm of two spinning machetes, while Katryzna kept pace moving backwards, aiming the torch and rifle. She fired, pulling up at the last second, as Tasker tumbled into their path. He raised a hand, the other down with his pistol. No pack on him. Tasker half-ran and half-tripped his way to join them as they kept moving. Katryzna watched the shadows, waiting for one of these things to jump at them. Her torchlight caught the peaks of the tents, far back now, and the shapes of men descending on them. Arms ripped into the clearing where they'd been moments before, material shredding.

# 19

Following dinner, Reece figured a performance was exactly what everyone gathered in Stilt Town needed, all still bustling in the mess hall, eating, talking and praying. They started out with the Ain't You Someone gambit. Stomatt's voice gradually rose as he loudly questioned Reece over exactly what music he played.

Ain't no bebop, dixieland or jive. Can't be swing nor big band with what you got. What do you call it? Show me. A few examples on the horn. Rougher than Creole, that some kind of street jazz? But we don't have streets in Cutjaw, LA. By this point Stomatt's up slapping hands against the table giving a back and forth tempo and they hit the high point together as Reece reels out something longer. The whole room can agree this is nothing less than raw, righteous Cutjaw Caravan Jazz.

Those that could keep up clapped along and all the rest smiled with daft glee.

While Caleb and Leigh-Ann slipped out unnoticed.

Reece could play all night. Feel the eyes of a hundred people loving every second, alive in it. The raw language of music brought them peace and calm – from the overworked kitchen staff down to little Zip, cheering and clapping along. She looked younger than she'd been since they first picked her up, like she hadn't heard real music before. A little more of this and she might even forget all the fears her daddy put in here. And Reece held everyone with his own kind of hypnosis, letting Leigh-Ann and Caleb do their thing. Making ready, just in case. No need to actually flee, no one harmed, no plans unsettled – just opening doors and making options.

With another tune down, Gray nodded along from across the way. Even Noah gave a concessionary shrug to say it wasn't half bad; by his standards that was practically an orgasm. Reece held up the horn for attention, turning on the spot. "Alright now, who's got a request?"

They started shouting out hymns – a bit of gospel would definitely stir this lot up.

"Go Down Moses?" Reece threw to Stomatt, who nodded and thumped up another beat. Give it a minute before bringing in the trumpet, work them up first. Stomatt started a throaty chant, and however much they hung on wanting the horn, they couldn't resist the words, some of them joining straight in.

Reece felt a little tug on his elbow and found Zip looking up. "Got a request, cher?"

"Reece," she said. Some of the joy went out of him. Hadn't taken long for her to regain her fear. "They're coming."

He frowned and scanned the room. Not a soul looked bothered about the dangers outside, right now. He leant close and whispered, "They're ready for it. Enjoy the music."

She glanced to the exit as Stomatt boomed: "Way down in Egypt's land!"

"They're not," Zip said restlessly. "They're not ready."

"Well," Reece said, lifting the trumpet. "We will be."

But he faltered before playing, seeing Noah's expression shifting. He looked unhappy now, as if stewing on similar concerns, of a sudden. Not a fan of the song? Stomatt belted, "Let my people go!"


Leigh-Ann rubbed her hands together to get some blood flowing, the temperature dropping fast now the sun was down. Her breath made clouds before her face as she watched Stilt Town's shadows. Outside the ruckus of the mess hall, the rest of camp was dark and she had some ominous feeling borrowed from Zip; guards were walking the perimeter wall and keeping watch in the towers, but Leigh-Ann couldn't help feeling it wasn't enough. And she didn't like getting stuck on lookout while Reece and Stomatt kept the party going.

"I can't get in," Caleb said in a hushed whisper, drawing her attention up. He leant out of a dark doorway, crouched so as not to be seen. "Need proper tools to crack the safe. And time."

"So what you got?" Leigh-Ann said. He held up a small packet.

"Might be five thousand, I reckon? Had it in a locker."

"Five thousand? We didn't go through all this for five fucking thousand."

"Didn't go through all this to steal from my uncle, neither, did we?"

"I told you this ain't *stealing* – he's got *our* cash, owed us." She took a breath to keep her voice down. "Sure you can't crack it?"

"You feel like tryin'?"

"Shit. So we come back for the rest another time. Once this all blows over."

Caleb crept down the stairs, every step creaking and making him wince. He whispered, "Maybe we shouldn't be doing this, Leigh? My uncle's done right by us. Even if we're square on the money, it don't feel right sneaking off."

"We're not sneaking off, Caleb," Leigh-Ann said. "Just giving ourselves the option to. Told Reece we shouldn't trust them with all that cash outright, should've kept our hands on it until we were sure to be safe here. Now we can't be sure of nothing, not even our money. You got a back door key at least?"

"Got that." Caleb patted a pocket. "But that's another thing – how far we gonna get on foot, going out the back?"

"Further than if we open the main gates and start up an engine. Fuck it, we're not making life easier yakking about it. Swing by the room and drop it off, I'll go back tell the others we're ready. And *don't worry* – it's only a precaution."

Caleb turned to leave. But he hesitated, looking into the dark. "Leigh, I ask you something? Being out here alone and all."

"You gonna propose in this romantic forest of building foundations?" Leigh-Ann joked. Then she couldn't hold down a laugh. "With a backdrop of holy wackos."

But Caleb's hurt expression stilled her amusement. "No. No, I wasn't gonna do that." He said it too seriously, leaving Leigh-Ann open-mouthed. Damn if he hadn't been thinking somewhere along those lines though. Just what she needed.

Leigh-Ann forced an awkward smile. "Joking, Caleb. Come on now, let's get moving." She went to punch his arm in a friendly way but he was too far off and the stretch made it more of a push. He frowned like this added to the insult. Turned away with a ponderous look, needing some time to think now.

She watched him amble off, then cursed under her breath and turned the other way. That boy with his notions, never getting the concept of I Don't Like You Like That. She was gonna have to have Reece play go-between again. Don't shit where you eat, dammit – how was the gang supposed to enjoy a carefree life on the road if she had to keep worrying about any of them getting hung up on her?

Those uncomfortable thoughts brought her back to the mess hall, but reaching the last gap before the yellow glow, she saw the way blocked. Two bulky guys standing before the door to the hall. Dammit, had to be Noah, with one of his cronies, and they'd seen her the same time she saw them, gospel jazz blaring behind them.

Neither moved. She put on a smile to approach the steps, saying, "No privacy in those latrines. And I *needed* my privacy."

That should've been enough to get Noah's usual look of disgust at her general existence, but he stared blankly. The guy next to him was no better, silent. Leigh-Ann stopped on the steps before them.

"Shouldn't be out here," Noah said. Something off with his voice. Hadn't Gray said no drinking?

"Didn't realise there was a curfew?" Leigh-Ann tried to laugh it off, going to pass him, but Noah stepped in the way. Here it was: calls of immodesty, no real lady, posturing because he couldn't get in her pants as easy as a Stilt Town girl's. Leigh-Ann waited. He said nothing, only looked a bit sweaty. "Well if you're not gonna give me shit, you wanna step aside?"

"Shouldn't be out here," he repeated, voice cracking.

"You on something? You guys –"

"Shouldn't be out here," his friend agreed, voice equally weird. She looked in their eyes. Wasn't booze – did they have something homegrown? The sort of thing might make them act on their general base misogyny.

Trying to keep cool, Leigh-Ann said, "I'm heading back inside, ain't I?" She tried to pass again, and this time Noah put a hand on her chest.

"Down," Noah instructed. He tilted his head the way she'd come.

"Yeah, no thanks –" Leigh-Ann started, but he pushed her, throwing her balance enough to send her skipping back onto the grass. She took a quick couple steps and balled her fists. "I ain't going nowhere with you."

"You're going." Noah quickly advanced. It took Leigh-Ann a second to react, surprised at his sudden approach. He didn't look angry, not crazed exactly – weirdly vacant. Leigh-Ann sidestepped but he matched her pace. With the mess hall's music rising, she'd need to scream loud to be heard. But Caleb would be back any moment. Noah took a quick step closer – Leigh-Ann shouted, "Hey, Ree –"

Noah suddenly had a hand on her mouth, and Leigh-Ann was dragged down as she kicked. Her arms were pinned by the goon, her shouts totally muffled. She was lifted, struggling – no use – and hustled under the nearest building, into deep shadow. She took a gutshot punch that pushed the wind out of her. Noah hissed, "Stop. Stop and be saved."

Wheezing to catch her breath, Leigh-Ann tried again to shout, but Noah clamped his hand tighter over her face. The men went rigid, watching something. Leigh-Ann searched the shadows – *Caleb!* He was jogging between the buildings looking one way and another, suspicious as a man could be. Leigh-Ann bit down hard on Noah's hand and he hardly reacted, giving her a lazy look. She screamed into the palm as he pushed harder on her mouth, totally muffling it. Caleb's eyes tracked their way. Ran right over them.

Didn't see. Didn't hear.

He kept on, briskly, up the steps and into the mess hall. The doors let out a second of hopeful light that swept over the surrounds, and Caleb gave one last look. Then he was gone. The doors closed behind him.

Noah squeezed Leigh-Ann's face and said, "Shouldn't be out here."


Reece took Caleb's return as an excuse for a break, putting down the trumpet and catching his breath. Sweaty from the fun. A couple people booed mock disappointment at the music pausing, but mostly they clapped and celebrated as he cut through the crowd, and Stomatt picked up another beat, encouraging Zip to join in. She was dancing, enjoying herself as if she had no worries left, finally. The kid did a twirl, eyes closed, lost in the moment.

Reece smiled as he took Caleb aside. "All good?"

"Not great," Caleb confided. "Got a small cut – real small, comparative – but got the key to the back. No signs of trouble, anyhow, might be that we can wait it out."

"Might be, only pays to be cautious." Reece met Caleb's eye, hit by a realisation. "Leigh-Ann not with you?" Caleb scanned the room. She should've been here first. Reece noticed another absence. "See Noah out there?"

"No. Could be checking on the guards?"

Rather than watching the band with general disapproval? This didn't feel right. Reece looked over to Stomatt and Zip, the pair drumming together now, with a little audience. Good. He moved away, out onto the steps, and checked the shadows. Quiet outside. Caleb caught up, with an urgent whisper bound to draw attention: "What you thinking?"

Reece narrowed his eyes at the dark. No way Leigh-Ann would linger out on her own in Stilt Town, not in the middle of the task she'd had. He said, "Thinking we'll spread out, find her fast."

"What's up?" someone called, the worry noticed inside.

"It Steers?" another man asked, and a mix of hushed questions and concerned silence swept the hall. Stomatt made a noise, shouldering his way through.

Zip came bouncing out with him and Reece fixed on her. "You sense something?"

She focused, all those fears flooding back in. And she definitely did sense it. "It's bad."

"Fuck." Reece jumped down the steps, scanning the shadows ahead. Shouldn't have sent Leigh-Ann out here. Of all people.

"What's going on, Reece?" Stomatt called from the top of the steps.

"Get the guns, Caleb. Keep Zip safe!" Reece cut away at a jog, crouching to see under the buildings. He could hear the crowd moving behind him, commotion building. No movement ahead, though. He ran faster, dodging between stilts, until he'd passed half the commune and reached an outer perimeter. A goat bleating made him slow down. Another. The worried cry of animals in distress. Sort of shit Zip kept hearing in her dreams. Scanning their low wooden pens, he couldn't see anything wrong. But the noises got louder.

Back through the buildings, Gray's people questioned, "What's got them spooked?"

"We got company? Report!"

"Steers still out on the road!" a guard shouted from high up. "Not moving. What's going on down there?"

The chickens were clucking, flapping their wings against the hutch, loud at some hundred yards off. Reece moved out from the buildings, watching the fields. He saw a silhouette of a man. A guard, halfway between the camp and the perimeter wall. Reece shouted, "You seen Noah or Leigh-Ann?" The man was motionless. Oddly stiff. Reece raised his voice: "You hear me?"

Wasn't some scarecrow, was it?

Voices were rising behind him, Stomatt's the loudest: "Leigh? The hell are you?"

"Hold up now, Steers on the move!" the elevated watchman shouted, and panic followed. Shouts for order, the thumping of feet up stairs and across walkways. Reece glanced back out to the man in the field and reached for his pistol. Wasn't there – left in the bunk – he only had his trumpet in hand, and tightened his grip on that.

"Reece where you at!" Stomatt boomed.

"They coming on the gate!" the watchman cried.

"Everyone keep calm now!" Gray's voice. Louder even than Stomatt. "We're prepared for this! They won't get in – but get to arms. Marie, you move along. Marie, you listening?"

Reece turned to the strange exchange and started back under a building.

"Get moving, Ruben, dammit!" another man shouted just ahead.

"Marie!" Someone else.

This wasn't about the Steers, this was weirder, Zip's domain. Picking up his pace, Reece threw a last look back to the field. He stopped. The guard was still standing there, and there was another shape now, further off. Another motionless man.

"The fuck is this?" Reece hissed, and a terrified woman matched his confusion with a shout of her own: "Why aren't you moving?"

Far across the camp, a gun went off. In the centre, Stomatt shouted, and near him Caleb joined in. Another gunshot followed, off in another direction, and the shouting and movement clamoured into a din. Reece spun, seeing people running between the stilts as more shots went off near the perimeter. But the chaos was *inside* the walls. Reece gave a final look to the field.

The silhouettes were finally moving.

Ambling towards him.

# 20

Following a long night of evasive movement, Henri finally guided Tasker and Katryzna into a village of wooden huts. He moved ahead while they waited in the trees, neither talking. No one had said much since the ambush, if that's what it was. In their flight, Tasker hadn't been able to make sense of it. Ghostly figures in the dark, watching them without striking. Not quite surrounding them, failing to catch up again, like they weren't within their wits. Definitely not the co-ordinated attack he'd expect from a militia. Were they even armed?

While they waited for Henri, who had dived into chatter with a stout villager as if they were old friends, Katryzna rested against a tree, staring at Tasker. He couldn't read her look. Weary in posture, but eyes bright, partly invigorated by the escape. If it could be called an escape. They had been driven further into the forest, and without half their gear. Tasker had proved their weakest link, failing to grab his bag in their flight. He couldn't even talk to the locals. Katryzna might've guessed his thoughts – she gave him a slight, knowing smile and a wink. Like she'd take care of him.

It didn't help.

Henri returned and explained, "This village has no love for the PFR and they have food. But they warn that five men went missing in the night – gone from their huts without a trace. Others have gone looking for them, but not returned. They are confused – there have been no rumours of militia activity near here, not for many weeks."

"Do they normally see them coming?" Katryzna asked.

"Rebels might strike quietly," Henri said, "but they are brash. They do not move unseen. And the men who are missing are not who you'd expect. Older, weaker. There are children here, untouched."

"Children," Tasker echoed. They might be abducted for soldiers, but who would take old men?

"There were six out there, around our camp," Katryzna said. "I think."

Tasker frowned, following her chain of thought. "Why would these villagers get up in the dead of night to stalk us?"

"A better question," Katryzna said, "is why they didn't stay down when I shot them."

"In that dark, with all that cover," Tasker said, "I'd say you missed."

"I do not miss," she snapped. "It's some kind of jungle mystics."

"There's no mystics here," Henri said, slowly. "These villagers are Kimbanguists."

"That *sounds* mystic?"

"Kimbanguist Christians," Henri explained. "They follow Christ, and the teachings of Simon Kimbangu, a Congolese man who they believe came down from Mount Zion –"

"Near Ikiri?"

"No," Henri got even slower, unsure if Katryzna was messing with him. Rather than face that head on, he said, "The point is they are puritans. They and the other villages nearby – they reject ideas of magic and witchcraft, even alcohol and dancing."

Now it was Katryzna's turn to regard Henri with a look of disbelief. She glanced from him over to the village, perhaps considering this muddy, low-tech village had at least some common ground with her. But she uttered, a little hurt, "They don't *dance*?"

"They're not our problem, are they?" Tasker said, hearing himself sound tired, irritable. "We're getting close to Ikiri, correct?"

"Closer. Mr Tasker, Ms Tkacz," Henri ventured, "if I may. We have lost our bikes. Much of our supplies. On foot, it will take us three days, at least, to reach Ikiri, moving safely. Not knowing what threats we face, I humbly suggest making a decision here."

"Can we retrace our steps?" Tasker said. "Get back to the camp?"

"I'm not sure it is worth the risk," Henri said. "But the villagers talk of a good road that will take us towards the river. Seeing as we are already in danger –"

"Turn back?" Katryzna said. "This weirdness proves we're on the right track."

Henri shifted anxiously, not a comforting sight from their muscle-bound escort. Tasker shared his concern, but Katryzna was right. He said, "If those were the people from this village, something or someone had control of them. None of us are in doubt they *would* have attacked us, right? In Laukstad, there wasn't anything to suggest outsiders, or other creatures – and here's some kind of answer to that. What if it was people from within their own community who were responsible? Something might've gripped them, too. We have to figure out what this is. We can't take bikes from the village?"

"They have none."

"And if we forget caution and take the better roads?"

"Yes," Henri said unhappily. "Taking better paths could halve the time to Ikiri."

"So what's the problem?" Katryzna said.

He gave her a grave look but didn't bother spelling it out. Tasker brushed right over it to say, "A day there and a day back, we can do that? Alone if necessary, as long as you can point us in the right direction. You've done your bit."

Henri stalled, wanting to take the offer, but couldn't. He said, "My bit ends with finding answers, the same as you."

Katryzna put a hand on his shoulder. "That's the spirit. We will not let zombies stop us." She beamed, and Henri managed to look even more uncomfortable.

*

The stout villager named Ade did his best to welcome the trio, and insisted they join him for an earthy tea and dried meats. He spoke in a local language which Henri translated, explaining the villagers were effectively hunter-gatherers with loose ties to three or four other settlements nearby. This village, Igota, was the closest anyone lived to General Solomon's territory, and the base of the Ikiri hills, as Henri referred to them. Igota used to trade with villages further east, but such contact was cut off after Duvcorp arrived, many years ago. The stories of that time had faded in detail, and the best man to ask, Mbu, was one who had gone missing in the night, but the broad strokes were local legend. The mercenaries had come through the rainforest with the brutal entitlement of an imperial expedition. For the most part, heavily armed, violent men, though their number included some who tried to befriend the locals, including a beautiful Congolese woman. Henri took this detail with sad hope: confirmation his sister had made it this far, practically to Ikiri.

The expedition had stayed in a neighbouring village before reaching Ikiri, where one of their number mutilated a local woman over some minor dispute. The Westerners fought amongst themselves over this – the man was ultimately taken away in restraints, to be punished by the Westerners themselves. There was violence in the forest shortly after – two other mercenaries were found dead from sword-wounds, and local trackers found evidence that another man had been chased through the trees. Perhaps the mutilator escaped from the group. Some in Igota still used his example to scare their children into behaving, Ade said. Watch out, or the outsider who roams the forest will get you . . .

After that, the Duvcorp expedition was never seen or heard from again. Contact was also lost with the closest eastern village; days later, Igota villagers travelled there and found the people savagely massacred. Not by men with guns but as if by animals. Brutal, horrifying scenes. The search party kept going, looking for answers, but retreated after hearing strange sounds at night. Since that time, as Henri first reported in Club Clash, many more villages in the area had similarly gone quiet – one as recently as a year ago.

Ikiri itself was now avoided like a graveyard, a site of some inexplicable evil. Not for the first time, Ade said: those hills had an old reputation. People had gone missing before Duvcorp's time, and no one lived directly on Ikiri. But after their arrival, the taboo area expanded. It all but confirmed Tasker's assumption that it wasn't Duvcorp's advance itself that was responsible for the deaths and disappearances, but something long concealed that they had unsettled. They weren't good people, no doubt, but their abuses up to this point were not unnatural, nor well hidden. The savage massacres, without explanation, happened *after* the mercenaries reached Ikiri.

The mystery was cemented by the arrival of Solomon a year or so later. His reputation had reached the surrounding territories, and the locals' superstitious habit of keeping clear of Ikiri now became a matter of survival. Villages were raided. People who ventured too close were hung from trees as warnings, to mark a perimeter. But Ade reflected the same doubts Smail had harboured: it was unclear *why* Solomon had settled in this area – there was nothing of value. Perhaps he merely desired land to call his own?

With the legends exhausted, and the trio rested, Ade and his friends offered supplies and wished them luck. The sort of luck offered to people you don't expect to make it.

On leaving, Tasker and Henri took a bag each, while Katryzna shouldered the canvas and poles of a makeshift tent. They followed a scrappy map and compass, wary that within an hour they would enter General Solomon's territory, where things might get even worse. The "good road" was ribbed uncomfortably by tyre tracks, and before long they had to veer off onto a path that required a lot of hacking. Katryzna volunteered – cathartic, she said, with a smile. Henri tried to share an appreciative look with Tasker, watching her push on ahead, but his prior enthusiasm had been sapped.

The ground grew steeper as they reached the base of the hills. Keep climbing up, that was the key. They discussed the previous day's events only once, when Katryzna asked, "Could the rebels have drugged those villagers? Turned them psycho?"

"Whatever happened to them," Tasker said, "its source is somewhere up here."

And on they walked.

By nightfall, the incline had become a climb, tiring but encouragingly mountain-like, even if Henri still insisted it was just a hill. What was the difference; it felt high. They kept going by torchlight, looking for a gap in the trees clear and flat enough to pitch a tent, which proved hard to find. The search took them an hour further than Tasker intended to walk, but it was progress. Finally, they raised the tent, and stood side by side studying their handiwork.

Katryzna burst out laughing.

"Oh, we're all far from home," Henri said, cheered slightly by their pitiful shelter.

Tasker merely smiled, too tired now to care. It was cover, at least. Just wide enough for all of them, though they were going to take shifts keeping watch. Katryzna insisted on going first, feigning energy, and as the men settled to sleep she began quietly chattering to her conscience. Tasker caught Henri's eyes alight in the dark, watching the tent opening. He had probably wanted to ask about her since the barge, but he kept quiet.

Outside, Rurik somehow made her laugh.

She was cut off by a faraway sound, the rolling cry of an animal. They were all silent for a long, chill moment, recalling the noises Ade claimed drove his people back, the rumours of horrors out here. Nothing more came. Finally, Katryzna whispered, "Do you get lions on mountains?" Tasker considered answering in the dark, but she continued, apparently replying to Rurik. "You know everything about how I should act, why shouldn't you know about African wildlife."

Her voice got quieter, the one-sided conversation dwindling. Tasker rolled over, expecting nervous energy would make sleep hard to come by. It did not.

Tasker blearily blinked his eyes open onto Katryzna's face. He reeled back with surprise, but froze at the weight of her leg pinning his. It was already stiflingly hot, and light was peeking through the canvas. Morning, and she'd crept in to practically sleep on top of him without waking him for his shift. On his other side, Henri snored. All packed in together – they could have been damn killed.

But they hadn't been.

Tasker pushed down his annoyance and disentangled himself. Katryzna stirred. Eyes half-open and groaning, she asked, "What time is it?"

"You didn't wake us."

"No? Thought I did. Rurik was keeping an eye out, anyway."

"Hm." Tasker climbed out of the tent and stretched, squinting against brighter sun than the day before. The trees were sparser here – the ledge they'd climbed gave something of a vantage point over treetops below. Wild, exotic and vast.

"You better not have tried anything funny at night," Katryzna warned, sleepily emerging behind him. Henri grumbled, slowly wakening. "Either of you."

"Back at you," Tasker said.

She looked out at the forest, too. "Did you hear those things out there? Your monsters."

"Gorillas, possibly," Henri said, not entirely convinced. "None came close?"

"Yeah, actually," Katryzna said. "We played cards while you slept." She looked to Tasker. "Is he serious? What are we *actually* dealing with out here?"

Not liking that doubt creeping in, Tasker said, "You said you could stop anything, didn't you?" Then he looked to Henri. "Besides, that was probably perfectly normal for a rainforest. Right?"

Henri offered a weak smile to say he hoped so. But doubted it.

Tasker turned, to where the slope rose and the trees became thick again. They had a day of hiking ahead, but they were close. He took out the map and checked it against the compass. If they left the camp and their belongings here, only took the weapons, they could reach the cut-off point by early afternoon. The last known signal from Duvcorp's team. Today they'd get an insight into exactly what they were chasing. Maybe get away before nightfall and whatever was out there came back.

With the burgeoning heat, a small breakfast and a lot of water were all they needed to keep going. Trekking higher, higher. The sun blazed even through the canopy, sapping anyone's desire to talk. Tasker checked the compass every few minutes, as the terrain got steeper. Roots climbed over jagged rock.

Then, with no clear difference in their surroundings, the compass needle started spinning uncontrollably. Tasker backtracked, down the slope, and it slowed down as he crossed some threshold – stopped turning entirely. Cursing, he continued back up the slope to where Katryzna and Henri were waiting. She had her arms folded in impatience, he looked exhausted. All three of them were wet with sweat.

"We're here," Tasker said. "Guess we follow a straight line and hope for the best."

"Fingers on triggers," Katryzna said. She already had her rifle ready, and Henri uneasily readied his. Maybe a bad idea; in Ministry work, combustible weapons were often more trouble than they were worth. Tasker was hot and tired, though, so he followed their lead. They walked on with tall steps, over rocks, scanning the trees, the earth, whatever they could. Katryzna said, "It doesn't *feel* special."

The forest answered with a feral cry, a long way away. It *did* almost sound like a lion. They exchanged uncertain glances but pressed on. This was only where the expedition lost the ability to communicate; the real danger lay ahead. It raised a question. The scientists must have realised their technology was failing them – why didn't they retreat to get a signal again? Tasker kept a hopeful eye out for discarded weapons or clothes, human technology of any kind. But the forest was thick and overgrown; no one had been here in years.

There were bigger gaps between the trees as they progressed, and larger rocks. And Tasker started to feel something. A wariness, chasing over his skin, hard to pin down. It was directional, pulling him towards something. He stopped and Katryzna stopped with him, shoulder brushing his back.

"What do you think it is?" she asked, no question that they were both feeling something unreal. Henri slowed down a few metres back and made an uncertain noise.

Tasker said, "I don't think it's in the right direction."

"How would you know? We could've got spun in a circle."

"But we've been going *up*. That way takes us down."

"So?" Katryzna didn't wait for an answer. "Doesn't matter. We're going to check it out, aren't we?"

"If it's not the destination?" Henri blurted out, all the nervousness of their night ambush and the animal sounds rattling him again. This weird feeling might break him. "Why should we investigate this – this thing – when we are so close?"

"If it scares you, don't come," Katryzna said, and pressed on, downhill, towards the strange feeling. Tasker followed, gesturing at Henri to join them. He jogged to catch up, afraid to be left behind. Katryzna moved faster as they got closer. She tore her way through some vines and skipped to a stop with a gasp. Surprise from her sounded as unnatural as this pull felt, making Tasker hurry. He froze at the sight of what she'd found.

A gnarled tree stood before them, at least two arm-spans wide. It rose into a dense, crooked canopy. At around head height was a woman's torso, hanging head-first out of the bark as though halfway swallowed by the tree, impossibly long hair draping down to the ground.

"What do you make of that?" Katryzna asked, as casually as if she'd noticed a light left on. Before she could answer, the woman lurched upwards, and Henri cried her name: "Sara!"

# 21

Noah's goon dragged Leigh-Ann through the double doors to the chapel as he punched the lights on. She kept kicking, for the little it was worth, as they heaved her between the pews, to the lectern. She tripped, pulling the goon down with her. The man kept his grip, kept a hand over her mouth. Noah grabbed a polished brass cross off the altar and growled, "Cleansed. Time you were cleansed."

The lights cast demonic shadows across his face, and Leigh-Ann saw mania in his eyes – worse than intoxicated. The man had snapped. Leigh-Ann screamed into his goon's fist, watching the hefty metal cross. Noah approached slowly, savouring what was coming. Then gunfire sounded. He looked up with confusion.

There was shouting. The others looking for her? Then more gunshots. Panicked cries. The goon slackened his grip at the sounds, and Leigh-Ann burst free. The man was too slow, this time, and she shot out of his reach to plough into the nearest pew. Noah took a desperate swing at her, missed and shattered an armrest with the cross. She was away, yelling, "In here boys – these motherfuckers want to kill me!"

Leigh-Ann skidded through the doors. In the darkness, people were running between buildings, under them, some fleeing and others chasing. All Gray's people, near as she could tell in their drab garbs. A man shrieked as he was struck from behind and rolled across the grass – another man on top of him, check shirt flapping as he brought both fists down on the guy's face.

Thumping footsteps drew Leigh-Ann's attention back – just in time to duck another swing from Noah, using the cross like a bat. It smashed into the chapel's doorframe, jarring him long enough for her to half-jump, half-fall down the steps. She landed on her knees and pushed up to keep running. A woman came screaming from under a nearby building. Aimed at *her*. Leigh-Ann dropped on instinct as the woman reached murderously over her – she shouldered her into the air with a cry, letting her own momentum fling her. Then Leigh-Ann was up and running, with glances one way and another. As chaotic as when that monster struck the farm. Only more people were shouting here, and firing off guns. *What the fuck was going on?*

"Reece!" Leigh-Ann shouted. "Where are you?"

"Leigh!" Not Reece – Caleb. He stumbled out between stilts, frightened for her, pistol in one hand, little Zip's hand in the other. "What's happening? Where you been?"

"Noah –" Leigh-Ann half-twisted back – the big guy was lumbering across the grass, waving the cross as he looked one way and another but was somehow unable to focus. His goon was just behind him. "Fuck, keep moving."

They moved into the shadow of another building, out of view. Caleb panted as he went, "Lost the others, looking for you." Another burst of gunfire. "Who's shooting? They're – hell, they're going at each other!"

"Someone spike the damn punch?" Leigh-Ann said, watching another pair of Gray's people grappling on the raised ledge of a building, one throttling the other.

"What punch?" Caleb asked desperately. "They were all normal a minute ago. We left the hall looking for you, all of us, and this started up behind us – you ain't seen Reece?"

A roar made them leap back as another pair of fighters rolled in front of them: Stomatt with one hand on a man's neck, the other punching his face. Zip shrieked and clung onto Leigh-Ann's leg as they tumbled across the grass. Caleb kicked Stomatt's attacker in the side and knocked him aside. He sprang onto hands and knees like a cat, eyes flashing in reflected light.

"Stay down, man, this –"

But the man jumped, baring his teeth, and Caleb fired. The chest-shot sent him rolling, wheezing. Likely fatal, but not right away. Leigh-Ann covered Zip's face with a hand, turning her away, as Caleb helped Stomatt to his feet. The big guy shouted, "Lost their fucking minds!"

"Breach!" the guard Teddy cried, somewhere on high, so shrill he was barely recognisable. "We've got a breach!"

"You think!"

"Come on," Leigh-Ann instructed. "Let's get eyes on whatever this is."

They ran for the nearest stairs, up onto a ledge. Kept going as more people grappled beneath them, up another set of steps to one of the town's second-storey tiers. Another gunshot met a flash of light in the field. Two men were backing towards the buildings, firing in the opposite direction, towards the walls. A dozen or more shapes were out there – hell, the Steers were through the entrance gate. A vehicle was wedged in the bars, but it'd created a gap and a gang of pricks were advancing, shooting. One of Gray's men in the field went down.

"The Lord is with us!" Gray yelled somewhere towards the centre of the compound. Gone mad like Noah? "Look to the light, stop turning on your brothers!" No, just his usual self.

"How they doing this," Caleb said, uncomprehending. The Steers were panning out into a line, shooting randomly at the buildings. But one twisted to shoot the other way – tore down his nearest friend with a burst of bullets. The others staggered and slowed, their confused yells echoing across the plain.

"Hell, it's got them, too," Leigh-Ann said. "Whatever *it* is."

She pressed on, dragging Zip by the hand, round the corner of the building. Stomatt let out a small laugh to say he was trying to enjoy this. Struggling. They ran over a short walkway. A woman made horrible violent noises, straddling someone on the ground.

"Juliette, no!" Gray roared, off to one side. He hobbled out with two large men and the three of them advanced on feral Juliette as Leigh-Ann kept running. Across the bridge and around another corner and there was Reece, sprinting across the grass below, armed only with his trumpet and trying to avoid someone grasping at him.

"Up here, Reece!" Leigh-Ann shouted.

He skipped but didn't stop, flashing them a glance then picking out a staircase ahead. He dodged through more scrambling people. They ran to the top of the stairs to meet him as the cries and gunshots grew unbearable.

"The fuck is going on," Caleb demanded again, almost whimpering it.

As Reece bounded for the steps, Noah and his goon leapt out the shadows to block the way. Noah swung the cross and missed by an inch as Reece bounced back and swung the horn. The trumpet's bell caught Noah on the jaw with a heavy clang, dropping him. He flapped about snarling, thrown but still coming, and Reece smacked him on the other side of the head, bending the instrument out of shape. The goon jumped over Noah to slam Reece to the ground, trumpet rolling off, and at the same time Stomatt shoved past Leigh-Ann and threw himself off their ledge, arms spread. The lunatic landed bodily on Reece's attacker and rained punches on him as the pair spun off to the side. Leigh-Ann cursed Stomatt's recklessness, barely better than the people gone mad, but damn he had his uses. In seconds, Stomatt had beat the man until he was motionless then backed off, panting. Leigh-Ann and Caleb ran down to reach Reece and pulled him up as Noah twitched on the grass.

"Back to our bunks," Reece said. "Get our shit and get out of here."

"What about the – what about –" Caleb stuttered, trying to make sense of it. What about the town. Gray's people, driven into murderous frenzy.

Leigh-Ann said what they were all thinking: "The hell can we do about it?"

"This way," Reece instructed. "I think."

Another shrieking attacker ran out of the shadows a short distance ahead and Reece pushed himself in front of the others, fists up – but a blade flashed along the madman's path. The scream was cut short and the man crumpled before a short, dark figure, arms and legs spread, long sword out to the side. Zip shrieked and squeezed into Leigh-Ann, again, both arms wrapped around her legs as Stomatt lurched in front of them.

"I got this little prick," Stomatt announced loudly. A head taller and twice as wide as this guy, he somehow managed to look feeble before the swordsman. Encased in shadow, Vile stepped to the side, big paces for a small man, a lion preparing to pounce.

"Leigh, take her – Caleb" – Reece gave them a push – "we'll catch you up."

Someone screamed a death-cry across the commune.

"Reece!" Gray again, coming into view with one man left. Their shirts were ripped, faces bloody. The old guy looked crushed, ready to collapse and leaning heavily on his cane, but his companion at least had a shotgun ready. Spotting Vile, Gray said, "What devilry have you brought upon us . . ."

An answer came from further afield, with a terrific scream of raw animal power that shook the buildings on their stilts. They all froze, under the swordsman's knowing watch. It had to be Giza, as alive as this bastard.

"Don't let them get me!" Zip cried, loud enough to move them all. Leigh-Ann shoved her ahead, running for a gap in the buildings. Caleb whipped up the kid and took the lead.

"Fuck this, go, Sto!" Reece shouted, following. Stomatt fell in too. "Shoot him!"

Leigh-Ann shot a look back over her shoulder as Vile gave chase, blade drawn to one side, and Gray's man fired. The blast clipped the swordsman, throwing him aside. The same time, there was another flurry of gunfire, higher up – Teddy or some other raised sentry? – cut off with an agonised scream and the crash of shattering wood. The ground shook with a heavy impact and another roar. Definitely the mutant gorilla.

The gang ran to the boys' bunk, where Caleb dropped Zip to leap up the steps. Leigh-Ann bolted after him and they snatched a bag each then jumped back down. Stomatt hauled Zip up onto his back, assuring her, "I got you," as Reece took his pistol and kept cover. Everyone ready, he pointed out over the dark field behind them. "Rear exit. Over there."

Caleb hurriedly tried to distribute weapons from the gun bag as they moved – a pistol for Stomatt, Leigh-Ann's Mac-10.

"Wait!" Gray wheezed, far behind them, hobbling to catch up while his guardian fearfully scanned all around. Vile had disappeared back into shadow. "What is this!"

A massive shape tore through one of the stilts beside him. The structure split apart around the huge emerging form of the beast Giza.

"Alban, run!" Reece yelled. He turned side on, one arm up in a marksman pose, and fired into the mass of darkness. Giza's long arms stretched out, propelling it in great leaps as Gray's man abandoned him and fled. Gray tripped over his own feet. One of Reece's shots knocked the beast off course – but not by much. With unreal agility for something so large, the gorilla rolled and kicked off another stilt to jump onto Gray. Leigh-Ann gagged as its huge fists beat Gray into the ground, the town leader barely able to scream. Reece pulled her away. "Nothing we can do!"

They ran on with all the energy they had left, Caleb and Stomatt already close to the perimeter wall. The guys pulled the rear bulkhead open, creaking on its hinges. They piled out into pitch dark on the other side, and went to heaving the door shut. Through the gap, Leigh-Ann saw the dual shapes of Vile and Giza stalking through the field. A casual pace – like the fuckers were toying with them.

Caleb got the bulkhead locked, for a second's breather, but none of them were fooling with the idea they were safe. Reece pushed on. "We make the river, lose them there!"

No fucking sense in it, Leigh-Ann knew, but didn't have the breath to say so – she was running too, all of them racing down a path they could barely see, between trees and weeds. Stilt Town's wall shuddered with a bang behind them. If that gorilla couldn't climb the thing, it'd smash its way through.

They ran on, Zip bouncing on Stomatt's back, big bags bouncing on Caleb and Leigh-Ann's. Bags of what? Leigh-Ann caught herself thinking. All that money was left behind – what'd they have now? Clothes and ammo? What now, what now. Minutes of mad running and none of them even knew what direction.

Sounds came through the trees, on both sides. Big thumping beats of the giant gorilla, crashing through the undergrowth. Flanking them on one side then going quiet. Reappearing on the other. Hounding them or herding them or something – not moving in for the kill. Leigh-Ann's heartbeat got hot and furious and unsustainable. Her foot hooked in something and she went down – Reece at her side a second later, arm through hers, hauling her up. The monster tore through the trees behind them, jagged teeth gnashing through shadow, and Leigh-Ann unloaded the Mac-10 with a defiant scream. With flash and fury the gun buried every bullet in the beast's bulk, sending it tumbling back into shadows with a whine, hurt but dammit how could it not be dead?

No time to consider it – the pair were up and running again, chasing the escaping sounds of the others up ahead. Giza roared, far off again, angrier than ever.

"Water, I see water!" Caleb shouted hopefully ahead. "Gonna be okay!"

They pushed for all they were worth, but as they caught up Stomatt shouted a curse. Reece and Leigh-Ann bowled into his back together, and the whole gang stopped before the stream. A motorboat was sitting there, ready to go. But a figure stood between them and it. Vile.

The parting clouds let some moonlight on his features. He was concealed head to toe in some kind of combat armour, like what special ops might wear, except tattered by age, ripped in places but revealing nothing but shadow underneath. Remnants of a balaclava covered his head, missing chunks as though it had been hacked at. The precious little flesh visible in the gaps was sickly pale, crossed with deep scarring, and his eyes stared reptilian from the mess. And down at his side, there was the long sword, flat along one edge, unadorned but unmistakably sleek, unblemished by the battle.

"Behind me," Reece whispered, stepping in front of the others, gun down at his side. He raised his voice. "The hell you want?"

Vile said nothing.

"You can't have her, hear me? One step closer, you're dirt."

The MAC-10 felt slick in Leigh-Ann's sweaty hand. Empty, she knew. Stomatt lowered Zip, flexing his fists, and Caleb stepped forward too. Vile merely waited. Cockily self-assured.

Reece took a breath. There was nothing he could say to this zombie-ninja motherfucker. He moved in a flash, gun up and firing in the same motion. He almost hit the bastard – but Vile moved impossibly fast, predicting the shot, down to the side. The swordsman spun across the ground, low, legs at spider-like angles. Caleb fired too, not even close, and the shadow spun between them. They dropped away as one, a flower of bodies falling to the sides, as Vile spiralled up in a shimmer of whispering steel. Reece rolled and fired again and Vile avoided the shots with unnatural speed, springing into the trees. Leigh-Ann scrambled to her feet, grabbing for terrified Zip, as Stomatt and Reece watched for the next attack.

Caleb stayed down, gasping.

A gash ran from his waist right up to his throat, blood seeping from every inch of it in thick black gushes. Leigh-Ann screamed, "Caleb!" as Reece stepped towards him – but the swordsman reappeared, sword raised.

"No!" Zip screeched, a pulse that shuddered through the trees. Leigh-Ann felt it pass through her bones, and flinched as Vile was thrown back. He hit a tree with a hard crack, and kept going, tossed into darkness. Zip kept screaming, marching between their group with her fists balled, rage directed into the shadows where Vile had fallen.

The gang froze as Zip went quiet. She breathed in heavy, tearful whimpers. Leigh-Ann looked down at Caleb; his blood had already stopped flowing, his eyes looking lifeless to the sky. Past her face. Reece grabbed at him uselessly, saying, "Caleb, no – no no –"

"You got him?" Stomatt asked Zip, fists raised as if to punch the swordsman.

Zip sniffed hard and admitted, "He'll be back. Soon."

Leigh-Ann searched the shadows. No sign of movement now. But the kid knew, didn't she? Reece was clutching at their friend. Stomatt turned and stared, impotent, waiting to be told what to do.

"We gotta go," Leigh-Ann said quietly. Too quietly, as Reece dipped into a low, anguished sound. "Reece, we gotta go!"

"I ain't leaving –" He turned to bite back, but Leigh-Ann grabbed him, pulled him up by the shoulder. Took one last look down at their friend. Sweet, gentle Caleb, dammit.

She gritted her teeth and shoved Reece. "Sto, get the kid – *Reece*, the boat – we gotta go!"

# 22

"*Pas plus*," the woman in the tree pleaded in broken fragments. She added something in one of the Congolese languages, then switched to English: "No more."

Her voice was raspy and unused, her face hollow. Her hair hung down to the ground in cordlike greasy black curls. Her faded clothes looked like the remnants of an eaten-away shirt, with many pockets, partly concealing a frail body. Her eyes were dark, too dark to see the irises. She lurched up, clawing at the air to try and drag herself free, towards them. Henri took quick, frightened steps towards her, hands raised but too shocked to get closer. There he froze, stunned.

At Tasker's side, Katryzna raised her rifle and said, "Stand clear, Henri –"

"Wait," Tasker said. "Just wait."

The woman slumped and sobbed. "No more . . . *sans elle*."

Tasker moved around Henri, studying the point where her body met the tree. She wasn't stuck, she was *fused* with it, bark growing into the bare skin where the shirt was torn. Henri whispered, hoarsely, "What's happened to her?"

Tasker twisted back. "Your sister?"

Henri struggled to pull himself out of the shock. He took another step towards her but backed off, repulsed. "We have to help her – how can she be here? Like that?"

"Let's pull her out?" Katryzna suggested.

The woman swung her way, bobbing like a bird. "*Non*! No more – *pas plus loin*."

Katryzna stared. "She's crazy."

Tasker couldn't blink either, no idea now what he'd imagined they'd find but sure he couldn't have predicted this. Were the others like her, somehow trapped by the rainforest itself? The tree-woman, Sara, *Henri's sister*, rasped again. "Henri, give her some water?"

Henri looked closer to bolting than helping her. But Sara swayed his way, focusing on him, and his deep, frightened breaths slowed. She whispered, "Henri. Henri." His arms drooped, face relaxing, as he looked sadly into her eyes. Then he hurriedly tore through his pack for the water. He approached and offered the bottle, offering rapid reassurances in French. He poured water that Sara lapped at thirstily. Then he took a step back, watching her. He spoke in French, the meaning clear: *how do we get you out?*

But when she stopped and looked him in the eye, he slumped back, muttering something in quiet resignation. Something had shifted in him, and it didn't look natural. Tasker checked with Katryzna to see if she saw it, too. Her brow was knotted and her hands tightened on her gun, so that was a yes.

"Is she . . ." Tasker began. But he didn't know what to ask, exactly.

Henri half-raised a hand to her, reaching for a connection. An understanding gripped him and he said, almost dreamily, "She cannot be moved . . ."

"*S'il vous plaît.*" Sara dragged the last word out at length. "*Please.*"

"We can end her misery," Katryzna said.

Henri met her eye, with an expression that said he didn't entirely disagree.

Sara hissed again, "No more. *Pas plus loin.* Without her."

"We can't continue," Henri somehow inferred. He was studying Sara as though reading her mind. "Not to where her team went. It's too dangerous. Not without . . . help."

"Help from who?" Tasker pressed, but Sara turned her gaze to him and he felt something swelling in him. A peace. Understanding of his own. She had drawn them here, generated that feeling that they followed. Saved them from continuing to certain death. He said, "We shouldn't continue."

Katryzna snapped: "I'm not letting some half-tree psycho tell me when to stop."

"Find her," Sara said, further trembling with emotion. "Katryzna."

Katryzna's face went taut. "How does this thing know my name?"

"You don't feel it?" Tasker said, calmly.

She glared at him – then Henri. Then around the clearing, as though checking the air itself. "Enough. You two need to focus, and this thing is –"

"Eyes loved you," Sara interrupted with an awe-filled realisation.

Katryzna fixed a deadly look on her. "What do you know about Eyes?"

It was a threat, not a question. Tasker stepped between them, slowly. "Don't." His voice came out mellow. "She's right. We can't go on. We need to find –"

Pain lanced through his face as he reeled from a slap, the crack of Katryzna's palm on his cheek echoing through the trees. Her face close to his, she clutched his shirt in a fist and said, "Get a grip – I'm not going on alone."

Tasker blinked, hard, and shook his head to refocus. She released him and he took quick steps away from the tree, holding up his hands. His senses came back sharper, the strangeness freshly apparent – a swaying woman hanging out of a tree, Henri standing in a trance. Sara looked surprised, even frightened, as Katryzna bore down on her. "What about Eyes? You tell me he's stuck like this, I will *scream.*"

The tree-woman pushed back into the tree, but laughed. "*C'est toi* – waited, I've waited –" Katryzna raised a fist but the woman slumped, laughter turning to tears. "Bring her. *Arrête ça.*"

"Yeah? I can stop it right now." Katryzna braced her gun but held back in the face of the woman's erratic nature. She glanced at Henri, the man vacant, not even seeming to watch. Tasker saw what he'd gone through himself – whatever Sara had become, she had entranced him and Henri. Subtly, merely to accept and believe her. Katryzna stepped to Henri and jammed a fist into his gut before he could react. He keeled over, wheezing, as Tasker opened his mouth to protest. But Rurik got there first, and Katryzna spun a circle, shouting, "What do you know? I'm the only one with any sense right now!"

"What – what –" Henri struggled to ask, on his hands and knees, tears in his eyes. He took in Sara again and fell to the side with a cry. "What's happening?"

"Stay down!" Katryzna ordered, then turned on Sara. "Explain or I put a hole through your skull."

Sara breathed deeply, gritting her teeth with the effort of holding her torso up. She hissed, "All are gone now. Only me. And . . . *it*."

"Sara," Tasker said. "That's your name? Sara –" He clicked at Henri.

"Ngoi," Henri said weakly.

"See your brother?" Tasker said. "We've come to help – talk to us – you remember coming here? Duvcorp?"

Sara nodded, heavy hair swaying. "Gone, all gone. *Pas sécurisé – hateful –*" She turned madly to Katryzna. "No further – *sans elle*."

"This again," Katryzna said. "Who is she talking about?"

She directed the question at Henri, but he was staring with teary eyes, at a loss.

"Find her," Sara's voice wavered. "*Tu*."

Letting out a little noise of deep frustration, Katryzna raised the rifle. "Make sense."

"She doesn't," a new voice advised. Low, thick Congolese accent with a French tint. "Your gun won't change that."

Sara cried shrilly as Tasker turned to find men in military fatigues dotted through the trees behind them. Around them, appeared as though ghosts. All armed with old assault rifles, many wearing dusty cloth masks. At their head was a man in a cap and aviator sunglasses, no weapon in hand. His face was just recognisable from the pictures Smail had shared, but gaunter, dark skin strangely ashen. General Solomon's once proud uniform was ragged, metal buttons hanging on loose threads, rank insignia peeling off his shoulder, his pistol holster cracked. They had the shabby collective appearance of soldiers who had dragged themselves out of a grave.

Henri raised his hands in surrender. "General Solomon – we mean no disrespect – this woman is my sister –"

"Save your breath," Katryzna said, eyeballing the soldiers. Hell, she was prepared to attack them. And given her reputation, she might survive, but Tasker and Henri certainly wouldn't. "You men want to die today?"

"No one needs die," Solomon said, with calm, measured authority, though his voice was dry. "The Popular Liberation Union welcome you. You are Katryzna, correct? I only ask you lower the gun."

"I'd rather not," Katryzna said. "People who know me are not normally friendly."

Solomon spread his hands to the sides. "We could have killed you before you saw us. And I only know your name" – he pointed at Sara, the tree-woman watching with horrified fascination – "through her."

Katryzna glowered from him to Sara. Wanting to bite back, but thrown again by the strangeness. She made an angry noise.

"We've been expecting you," Solomon said. "Though not your companions?"

"Agent Sean Tasker," Tasker said, quickly taking the opening for diplomacy. "UK government. And as he said, this is her brother. Henri."

Solomon regarded Henri with slow, sad curiosity. "Yes. I see it now. I invite you to talk, but not here. It is not safe out here. We have food, lodgings, at the camp."

"My sister –" Henri protested, half-rising.

"Has been there a long time," Solomon said. "And will remain there. *She* is safer than any of us. I wanted you to meet her, though. If you would please come."

"We're not done here," Katryzna said.

"Trust me, you have heard all she will say."

"Trust you," Katryzna echoed with a leer.

Tasker frowned at her. Sara had manipulated him and Henri, planting her message of danger, but that didn't make it untrue. The fact that she'd demonstrated such power fired all sorts of warnings. He said, "Katryzna, slow down. We don't know what we're dealing with."

"Isn't that why we are climbing this mountain?"

"I can tell you," Solomon said. "What lies up Ikiri will kill you if you continue. It would kill you now, if Sara wasn't protecting us. We will share all we know with you."

"Before or after you cut off our ears and boil our bones?" Katryzna shot back, only getting more agitated. "Thanks but I'll take my chances –"

"You asked her about the one called Eyes," Solomon said. Katryzna froze. "We know about him. We are not the monsters you might believe us. Our *curse* is not what we do, but what was done to us." She narrowed her eyes. "I guarantee your safety and your answers. If you wish to continue after we talk, I will take you on myself."

Katryzna gave Sara another look in her tree, and Tasker saw Henri doing the same, at pains to see what his sister had become. The woman was slumped forward again, chest moving with breaths but otherwise spent. If Solomon wanted to talk, this was their best hope. The man sounded tired, but vaguely hopeful. Katryzna met Tasker's eye, as close as she'd get to asking his opinion, and he tried to suggest consideration with his expression. She lowered her gun, unhappily. "Tell me about Eyes right now. Right here."

Solomon watched her, wearily, and said, "He was one of the named ones. The few people she has spoken of. He died to save her – so she has assured us. What more there is to tell, you'll have to come with me to hear."

# 23

As the gang sped down the river, the hazy dawn peeked through bald cypress trees either side of them. All they had in the world now was their dirtied suits, a big bag of guns and a pile of regrets heavy enough to sink the boat. Leigh-Ann sat on the middle bench beside Zip, thoughts racing. Caleb was gone. All he ever wanted was to do good by his family, including them. He *really* wanted that to include Leigh-Ann. Now he was dead? Just like that? Never gonna hear his goofy laugh again. For what?

Reece had his head down, at the front of the boat in a kind of misery coma. He'd taken them all out of the Cutjaw Shitheap for a better life, and where'd it got them? Stomatt sat at the back, manning the throaty outboard engine, tetchy. Not even space for his angry, irritable smile or malicious laugh now. Best friend dead. And Zip. Little Zip down at Leigh-Ann's side. Stiff as a board, hadn't even blinked since their escape. What *was* she? Did the kid even know?

No one had said much. All thinking the same shit.

Why Caleb, when all of them got to live. Plenty worse people deserved death more.

And what the hell, Stilt Town? People tearing each other's faces off – that monster gorilla – the swordsman that ignored fucking bullets? The kid who threw him through the air with a scream?

The last thing Leigh-Ann had said to Caleb was another *No*. He deserved better.

"What *are* you?" Stomatt finally broke their silence, addressing Zip. They all should've been comforting the kid but so far no one had the guts, and now this.

Zip flinched as he let up on the motor to lean closer. His suit, fresh before dinner, was now torn and bloodstained, as bad as the boiler suit had been. Reece looked up, in no better shape. One knee was torn, his jacket ripped near a tail.

"I'm serious," Stomatt said. "What *are* you?"

"Leave off, Sto," Leigh-Ann said, quietly.

"I been leaving off. She's been left plenty, and now Caleb's *dead*. Dead, Leigh, opened like a fucking piñata –"

"Sto –" Reece said, but Stomatt half-rose, not about to be told.

"You can fuck off all to hell. He died and we left him there all because of this kid." Stomatt laughed with nerves, throwing his hands up. Almost tripped out the boat, and scrambled for balance. "How we gonna leave him back there like that? When she coulda done that shit all along? Zap people with her *mind*. Oughta call you Zap, shouldn't we, not fucking Zip. Zap."

"Seriously Sto," Leigh-Ann growled. "You need to shut up before I gut you."

"Seriously? Caleb would be alive right now if it wasn't for this brat. Correct me if I'm wrong – I ain't wrong, am I?"

Reece half-rose, too, something fearsome stirring in his reddened eyes. "Caleb would've been the first of us wanting to help her – you think we had any damn choice?" His voice was cracking.

Stomatt shifted his weight and the boat rocked. Leigh-Ann snapped, "The pair of you stop before we all flip in the slosh!" The men held gazes. "We all loved him and we're all hurting but it ain't Zip's fault what happened – she's a damn victim too."

Leigh-Ann put an arm around the child, pulling her close. Zip remained hard with tension, worried eyes resting on Reece, not Stomatt. Shit, she saw it too. Reece had frozen back there and had to be a hair's breadth from snapping now. Their damn leader.

"Sit your ass down, Sto," Reece said tiredly, creakily lowering himself back onto the gunwale. Stomatt huffed but did as he was told, still angrily glaring at Zip.

"Question remains. What *are* you? Why didn't you do that with your mind before?"

"I'm just a girl," Zip whimpered. "I don't know – it only happened because – because Vile hurt him – I had to – I had to –"

"It's okay," Leigh-Ann said. "It was a good thing. You got us all out of there."

"This that power your daddy spoke of," Reece said, hoarsely. "Things you can do no one else can. Same power that makes Vile special?"

Zip nodded. Reece sniffed aggravation and rubbed his forearm. From weary to angry again. Thinking up a plan that wasn't gonna rest on logic, for sure.

"What else can you do?" Stomatt said. "Freeze time? We know you read minds."

"I can't do anything," Zip said. "It's *all* bad. Daddy said –"

"Daddy was scared," Leigh-Ann said. "And he obviously wasn't the only one. Vile and that beast back there didn't come at us head on, did they? They know about you? Scared of you?"

"Scared," Reece murmured, "like those farmers were scared."

Zip regarded him guiltily, fearful of his judgement.

"Not us," Leigh-Ann assured, eyeing Reece to support her here. "We ain't scared of nothing, Zip, and definitely not you. But we gotta know what's going on. You can sense feelings, danger? Put those Steers in a trance, threw Vile back. You got any idea how?"

"And what about them going psycho in Stilt Town," Stomatt said. "That wasn't the Steers. Gray's own people, biting each other up. That her, too? Spread some mind plague."

"No!" Zip cried. "It was *him* that made them act strange!"

"Vile?" Leigh-Ann said.

Zip didn't hear, racing on: "He makes people mad. Wants them to hurt each other!"

"But not us?" Leigh-Ann said. "How come not us? Gray? Half the camp –"

Zip shook her head quickly, the memories, the thoughts, mounting in her upset. "He can't – can't control everything, and especially not when you can notice it. When *I* can notice it." She frowned as though realising it herself. "That's why he does it when I'm sleeping."

Leigh-Ann tried to check in with Reece for that, and found him listening warily. More than bad dreams, wasn't it? Leigh-Ann ventured, "You weren't sleeping then, though."

"I was listening to the music," Zip whispered.

"Shit," Stomatt scoffed. "You want me to believe she protected us, rather than corrupted them?"

"Gave us a break, didn't she?" Leigh-Ann said. "You saw that monster – question to ask isn't what she is, it's what the hell is *he*. Like no one I've seen before, the way Vile moved – his skin. *That* bastard killed Caleb. Killed all those people, one way or another. Right, Reece?"

Reece's jaw was locked in grim acceptance. He nodded. "Damn right." His mind was going somewhere now.

"What you thinking?"

"What you think I'm thinking? This motherfucker came for her, cut down Caleb. Let him come again. Whatever tricks he's got, he's just a man. Next time we make ourselves ready."

"We can't!" Zip said, urgently. "Can't use my powers, signal them –"

"We're past that," Reece said. "They're coming, one way or another. Vile killed Caleb, Zip. And Leigh's right – he's gotta answer for everyone else. Everything Gray built, all *we* did – up in flames because of that bastard. But next time, when he comes – you do what you do, we'll do what we do. No more putting music first, we embrace who the hell we are and take him down."

He looked heavily up to Stomatt and Leigh-Ann. She said, "We ain't killers . . ."

"Good as." Reece shrugged.

"You ain't thinking straight, Reece," Stomatt said, for once not diving straight into a plan of reckless chaos. "Let me play devil's avocado and say it – those *things* were near on unstoppable. God rest Caleb and all those people but he wouldn't want us dying too. Can't tell me it's all on us, this thing."

"Then who's it on?" Reece spat back. "I didn't see anyone else out there about to stop them."

"We could drop her by a cop shop –"

"Cops? You hear yourself? When they ever done shit for us beside make things worse? You wanna crawl back in your hole in Cutjaw, Sto, no one's gonna hold it against you. But I ain't running off to hide after seeing my best friend *killed*. Can't bring him back but I can make that bastard pay."

"You can't," Zip said. Reece looked about ready to blow his top, but she sped on. "You can't stop him. He's not normal – not a real person –"

"Then what the hell is he?" Reece demanded.

"A monster," Zip insisted, more firmly. "The sort my daddy knows about. The sort my daddy knows how to *stop*." She was almost up out the seat, now, a fire in her almost as strong as his. "Only he knows how."

Reece kept staring, not needing to hear that, already feeling impotent, but told all the same. They'd all seen that maniac, all knew it was beyond them.

"You ready to tell us where Daddy is? Where's home?" Leigh-Ann came in, softly.

Zip relaxed again. "I already said. A mill, near a city. In England. I've never . . ." She went quiet again, shame weakening her resolve. "I've never been in the city. I don't *know* our address."

"Bullshit, she –" Stomatt started.

Reece cut him off, finding a new place to direct his fire: "We got another place to start. We pin down this Grithin in Memphis. He'll have answers, won't he?" He said it like he hoped not. Like going after this Grithin might give them someone else to hurt. And that's exactly what he intended to do.


A couple miles up Red River, the motor ran out of fuel. When it started struggling, the gang moored by a rickety riverside diner. A single-storey wooden shack whose stilts cut an unpleasant reminder of where they'd just been. Inside, it smelt of old fish and burnt fat. Three burly white men in swamp gear sat eating grits, watching them suspiciously. A big waitress wiped her hands on a greasy apron and asked if they were lost. The gang looked a sight, true enough, in their dishevelled suits, with a kid in a thick, formless dress. At least they'd washed off the blood in the river.

Reece tried to turn on his usual charm but it wasn't coming easy. His account of them being a band of travelling musicians, jumped nearby and lost their instruments, their ride and their money, sounded flat and empty. Leigh-Ann chipped in with colourful descriptions of fat, redneck assailants, right down to the boils on one guy's nose. Not happy being painted a victim, Stomatt said he'd knocked one of their teeth out. The pair of them gave a better account than Reece, claiming they were penniless and drifting with an aim to reach Memphis. A kid to feed between them. Why not – Zip was pretty enough, just the right shade if Reece and Leigh-Ann ever did bump uglies.

The waitress took it in with a dose of scepticism, but after lingering on Zip she insisted they have breakfast on the house. Offering up tin plates of dirty-smelling food, she explained they had a mighty long way to go just to get to the Mississippi, let alone Memphis. But might be she had some trucker friends who could help, if they waited round.

They settled into a corner, where Reece quietly took stock again. By now they should've been planning youthful retirement. Thinking of clubs they might play in New Orleans. Not mourning a friend, on the run. Shit, he'd shamed Stomatt with the idea but they *would* be better off heading back to Cutjaw.

Leigh-Ann ordered up a round of early-morning bourbon, which the waitress didn't blink at, and once the drinks arrived Reece stared into his glass in silence. They were waiting for him to say something. He cleared his throat. Best thing he could say now was that they oughta clear out.

Reece took his drink in hand and met the others' eyes. Leigh-Ann puffed her lips like she had things to say, too, but was waiting for him to go first. Stomatt, damn his eyes, gave his usual gummy smile. Gotta laugh, he'd say, now he was getting over the night's tension. Reece said, "Caleb was always with me. Long as I remember. We fought off the Howie twins together before we could even reach a cupboard door. Stuck by me for every hare-brained scheme I had – sold Harlan Jenson his own aluminium siding back, and took a whooping for that. Stuck by me when I lifted my first trumpet from that store in Leesville – swore on his life it couldn't have been me. Did all this because I wanted it. Loyal as a hound. Same as y'all. He never didn't do right by me, and now . . . now I gotta say –"

"It's time to do right by him," Leigh-Ann cut in, eyes warning Reece not to disagree. "You show us how, Reece. To Memphis and beyond. Cutjaw Kids gonna see justice done." She raised her glass and Reece did too, cautiously. "To Caleb."

"To Caleb," Stomatt agreed, "and to taking down the bastards that got him."

Reece hesitated. They'd go home if he said so, he knew it. Or into hiding, someplace better. But Leigh-Ann's expression said he better not dare. He forced a smile, at last. "To Caleb."

They clinked glasses and drank.

Stomatt let out a big breath as they thumped the glasses down. As if the panic and tension on the boat belonged to someone else entirely, long forgotten. That was how it had to be, wasn't it? Shit happened, you moved on . . .

As they finished their breakfasts, the waitress came and dropped a little metal dish in front of Reece. He expected a bill but instead saw a pile of cash. The waitress said with dreamy eyes that they needn't wait for the truckers. Folks down on their luck, with a kid in tow, deserved a hand. One of the boys there could take them to the interstate, where they could hop on a bus. Reece thanked her, but watched Zip. The way she avoided his eyes told him he was right to wonder. Hell. Their secret weapon and none of them knew how it worked. But they could figure that out on the way, Lord help them.

# 24

General Solomon led the trio down to a grass clearing populated by wooden shacks, decorated with macabre carved statues hanging off wires or standing on posts. Blocky, barely human forms sporting old blades and bullet shells like jewellery. Battle-scarred men lurked around the huts, wearing the same fatigues as their escort, carrying antique Soviet rifles or dirty, nicked blades, all harrowed and haunted. Tasker took note of one man leaning against a wall wearing a shirt long enough to be a tunic, a short axe on his thigh and heavy gold chains around his neck. His frame bulged, the best fed in camp.

Meat cooked in a bubbling pot over a central fire with a welcoming smoky scent. Solomon said, "Please, fill a bowl, rest your legs."

"What's in the stew? Human meat?" Katryzna said. She'd been eyeballing Solomon all through the journey, always a second away from knifing him.

"It's boar," Solomon said, plainly.

Katryzna sniffed at the broth. She dipped a finger in as Henri let out half a warning – she flicked the heat away and sampled it, all the while watching the general. She nodded satisfaction, then took up a tin bowl and started spooning chunky liquid in. "Suppose you save people for special occasions."

"There are no cannibals in this forest." Solomon paused. "Though, if you believe those rumours, there is the Blood Doctor, in Virguna."

Katryzna grunted dismissal, dropping onto an overturned barrel to start ravenously spooning stew into her mouth. Tasker and Henri took smaller, more cautious portions for themselves. It did smell good; robustly earthy. They joined Katryzna, Tasker perching on a crate, as Solomon sat on a fur-padded throne of a racing car seat supported by an old car wheel.

The general gestured to the man in gold chains, who peeled himself upright and ambled over. "I appreciate your concerns," Solomon said. "Ikiri is a dark place, and the last the world knew of us, we were bad people. We murdered and raided without cause. This is Jonah – he was my fiercest lieutenant, before we came here. Most feared him. Now, he is a priest of Ikiri. He understands Sara better than any of us." With that suspicious scowl, his axe and all that gold, Jonah looked like no priest. Following Tasker's thoughts, Solomon added, "A warrior priest. We are changed men, but must remain militant. Every day we survive here is a triumph. Sara's protection stretches only so far."

Henri cleared his throat, filled with concerns but too nervous to speak. Solomon waited, so he asked weakly, "How long has she been there?"

Solomon gave a sympathetic nod. "It must be unpleasant to see your sister so. She is no longer the person you knew. She cannot be saved – will not be saved."

"Does not need to be," Jonah added, in a deep, angry tone. "She has power."

"Jonah fears sharing that power," Solomon explained. "We all do, in truth. Ikiri is something to be protected, concealed and hidden. Its spread would damn others as it has damned us." Solomon arched his fingers together. "Though we do not fully understand it. Sara speaks to us only as she spoke to you. Not in sentences, sometimes not even in words. But she told us you would come, Katryzna. She repeated your name."

Katryzna paused, mouth full. She swallowed and said, "She knew Eyes, I guess he mentioned me."

"But she only used your name recently," Solomon replied. "Please, let me start from the beginning. I founded the Popular Liberation Union twenty years ago, and we were a *terrible* force. I killed my own uncle at the age of fifteen."

Katryzna made a noise to interrupt. "I killed *mine* at twelve."

Solomon raised his eyebrows. "Indeed? But look at us now." Tasker shared the feeling he saw reflected in Katryzna and Henri's slowly scanning eyes. Surrounding them like ashen scarecrows, the Cursed Union looked weathered, worn, and darkly frightening. Yet Solomon saw something else in them. "We came here to claim a fortune, but the mountain instead tried to claim *us*. We survive only through protecting one another – no man could stand here alone. This is Sara's influence. We are good people now – or we try to be. It is all we can do."

"The stories have it," Tasker came in carefully, not wanting to provoke the man but seeing there was room for a dialogue, "that you kill to keep Ikiri to yourselves."

"We warn off outsiders," Solomon said. "So they don't fall into the same trap as us. The outsiders themselves bring violence to us, when they are corrupted. And Ikiri has its own defences. The Westerners were gone long before we arrived. The nearby villages long dead or abandoned. But we found Sara Ngoi – trapped as she is today. Sustained by the tree itself. No longer truly human" – Henri winced, and Solomon's tone became consolatory – "but her mind is free – she feels the world. She knew my name, as she knew yours, Katryzna. She felt our natures and softened them. She tried to warn us about the darkness, but we touched it all the same."

"What –" Katryzna started, but spat food. Tasker could guess she might demand *what are you talking about?* She wiped her mouth and reconsidered. "Be specific."

"I will try," Solomon said. "But Ikiri is greater and stranger than anything of religion and false gods. The power itself is unclear – though its origin is clear. There is a chasm in the side of the mountain, large enough to walk into. It gave Sara the power she has now, long ago, though it trapped her. We cannot go inside ourselves. Two of my men tried. Only bits of them came out."

Katryzna snorted. "Bits – what kind of bits?"

"Blood, mostly," Solomon answered readily. "They were inside for three minutes, then an explosion of what *was* them came out."

"What's it look like, this place?" Tasker said. "How do you feel near it?"

"Jonah," Solomon said. "Describe it."

"A hole in the world," Jonah said, with gravity. "A gate to hell. To see it is to suffer."

"Be real," Katryzna said. "Is there a bear in there or something?"

"A bear?" Solomon said. "There are no *bears* –"

"A gorilla or a monkey or whatever," Katryzna said. "An *animal*. Or" – she clicked her fingers – "a trap! Duvcorp left mines, to stop anyone following them?"

"This was no mine. The mountain hums, there. The air shimmers. It feels *wrong*."

Tasker had encountered pockets of energy before. There was one beneath a lake in Russia that affected boat engines, but did little else. He couldn't recall any that made people explode. He said, "I'd still like to see it for myself."

"Getting close carries a risk of its own," Solomon said. "After we discovered it, we found we could not leave the area. If any of us travel beyond three miles of Ikiri, our minds decay. My men have turned on one another, as savage as the monsters in the hills."

This was it. The effect that had touched Igota. Laukstad. Not an outsider manipulating them or a monster they couldn't trace. They had attacked *each other*. Locked, somehow, in Ikiri's spreading darkness. He said, "It drives them mad?"

Solomon regarded him for a moment. "You know it, don't you? The corruption."

"We were attacked last night, before coming here, by men out of their minds."

"Who couldn't be killed," Katryzna added.

"I'm here because the same thing happened a long way away. In Norway."

The general was momentarily thrown. "Sara senses movement abroad. Could Ikiri reach that far?" He looked to Jonah for an answer, and the other man's grumpy expression suggested he had no idea. Solomon continued, "Ikiri is a jealous, violent power. And as we retreated, to here, we learnt our area of safety was only thanks to Sara's protection. She keeps the minds around her safe. But while we were safe from each other, the creatures began to emerge. You heard them, last night. Great, monstrous beasts stalk these hills. Almost impossible to kill. So. We are hunted by Ikiri for staying, yet unable to leave."

"Not much use to us, by the sounds of it," Katryzna said.

Solomon shared another look with Jonah, then said, "We have gathered some information that might interest you. About what became of Sara's companions."

"Everyone who came with her is gone," Jonah took over. "Four were buried in these hills. Five men have been named. Of the named ones, there was Moose, who died in Sarajevo –"

"In *Sarajevo*?" Katryzna cut in. "You seriously expect us to believe you know that?"

Jonah stared impassively, insulted by the question, so Solomon answered, "We have no reason not to believe Sara. She speaks, very rarely, of specific locations, very far away. You have come here, after all, talking of Norway – you know these links are possible." He addressed this more to Tasker, who had to agree, grim as it was to consider the implications. A force that could reach anywhere, as he had feared. "Jonah, go on."

Jonah grumbled but continued. "There is Fender, who *did not understand*. Shearjoy, who is to be feared – whose dangers Sara has identified in many places. And there is Eyes, who died to protect her. These are the lessons we have learnt." He puffed up his chest with importance and Katryzna stared with her mouth open.

"Where's his body?" she said. "What happened?"

"We don't know," Solomon answered. "This is what she has told us, and she cries for him. She connects him to a nameless *he*, a friend who left them behind. The rift between her, Eyes and this man, we believe, is what trapped her. It is also when we think the nameless girl was taken from here."

"The *she* Sara mentioned?" Tasker came in before Katryzna could heat up again.

"Yes," Jonah said. "*She* is our hope. One person who can calm Ikiri's dark heart. We could do nothing ourselves, to find her, trapped here, and so have waited, and waited, for help to come."

"Me?" Katryzna asked brightly, sitting back on her barrel.

"Not *you*," Jonah spat, taking offence. "*You* are a link. You can bring the girl to us. That is what Sara has promised us." He looked to Solomon as though he had doubts, now.

"You resisted Sara's influence," Solomon clarified. "I believe you could resist Ikiri's, too. If you can leave here and bring us this girl, we can end this curse. We know where the girl is – just over a week ago, the shroud that hid her was somehow lifted, and Sara saw her, at last. She has given us co-ordinates. If you can –"

"You discovered her location just now?" Katryzna said. "How brilliantly convenient."

"Around the time Laukstad got wiped out," Tasker said. Exactly as he had feared and Simon Parris must have suspected; something had changed with the threat out here. It was branching out, able to cause harm anywhere – and if they couldn't answer why Laukstad, they might as least answer why *then*. "There's a connection, isn't there? This power gets used, the girl comes out of hiding."

"Are you serious?" Katryzna said. "You believe this?"

"You saw Sara yourself, Katryzna. You felt her power –"

"I *felt* annoyed. As I do now. Annoyed and bored and thinking these guys are nuts." She made an irritated noise at a space down near the barrel, dismissing Rurik. "No, no – they don't know a thing and they're wasting our time."

Solomon was stony behind his dark glasses, some hint of his calm fading. However amiably he'd welcomed them, they were still in a rebel camp a long way from civilisation. Tasker quickly turned to Henri. "You know the expedition. Were those names familiar? Moose? Shearjoy?"

Henri startled, happy to have been dwelling in his own bubble. He stuttered a few non-words before making sense of what he'd heard, then nodded. "Yeah. Yes – Fender was the lead scientist. He was officially in charge. There was a man called Moose, too. Shearjoy, I'm not sure . . . maybe? As to the girl, I don't know. There was one female scientist, the rest were men. Certainly no children, if it's a girl –"

"It is a girl," Solomon said. "We're quite sure. And we believe she has been into Ikiri itself. It is possible that Ikiri only became corrupted because these people entered. The understanding we have is that Sara, Eyes and their allies fought to contain that corruption. Some survivors escaped to bring it back to your world."

Katryzna set her jaw and looked away, closing her fists tight. Tasker ran it back through his mind, trying to compare it to Ministry lore. Particularly combinations of anything that could warp a woman into a tree and control minds. There was a predator in Guatemala that could travel through shadows. Animals in Siberia that exerted a kind of hypnosis to distract prey. But there was usually a physical creature attached to energy manipulation. Not a doorway in a mountain.

"You are different," Solomon said, watching Katryzna. "Most feel Sara's pure heart in their own. Accept the truth as it is spoken."

"Most idiots?" Katryzna said. "Maybe you are just too scared to go in – too *explody*. So you make things up about people you don't know. You say Eyes is dead when you've got no idea. Sean, it's time we see for ourselves –"

"He is dead," Solomon insisted calmly. "Sara deeply regrets his loss. And you will die too, without the girl's help, if you don't bring her here. We will all fall to Ikiri. It is spreading, isn't it?"

"I'm not an international kid courier," Katryzna said, standing. "If Eyes was last seen entering some hole in the ground, that's where I'm going."

"Even after all I've told you?" Solomon said, flatly. "It was after discovering the power of Ikiri that we were trapped here. Once the force is aware of you, it will do all it can to destroy you. If you leave now, find the girl, there's hope."

Katryzna glowered with venom as if to say she wouldn't be so easily persuaded. But Tasker's mind ticked faster, seeing a fault in Solomon's thinking. He said, "The force is already aware of us. It took hold of nearby villagers – it already tried to kill us. It knows we're here. Just like Sara knew. But for whatever reason, it couldn't get directly at us." He looked from Katryzna to Solomon, both waiting for a conclusion that, while it made sense, he didn't really want to draw. "If it couldn't get us there, it won't make any difference now. I'm with Katryzna: I think we should see this place."

# 25

*Night, again, and people running, screaming.*

*This town perched on rocky outcrops, buildings flush with terrifying drops. Shadows moving between the houses, scurrying across sheer slopes like spiders, some fleeing while others chased. Men and women searching for knives and tools to fight the mad press of charging attackers.*

*A man slipped in his desperate attempt to draw a kitchen knife – a feverish woman snatched it off the cobbled floor. Jammed it deep into his side and screamed bloody fever in his ear.*

*A bell rang, men shouting from the top of a tower, calling for help – calling merely to be heard in their terror. Awful shrieks as people fell over the edge. Tripped, pushed, thrown into oblivion. At the town's periphery, a fire rose. No one to stop it. The bell rang more furiously, the screaming getting worse.*


Leigh-Ann perused her phone outside their motel room. Rest hadn't come easy, trying to sleep on the stiff bed with Zip twitching against bad dreams and Stomatt's snores shaking the dividing wall. At least the air was relatively fresh on the balcony, compared to the stale muskiness inside, parking lot fumes notwithstanding. A few miles south of Memphis, a little respite before honing in on this Grithin character.

The phone was a necessary distraction against Leigh-Ann's thoughts. Crazy fantasies about mutants and ghosts and psychic kids. Paranoia about what Zip might be capable of, stacked against what her dad and co might do. But the phone wasn't helping: Leigh-Ann's research said the phenomenon of creeps attacking each other with swords wasn't exactly uncommon.

Reece came strolling up and asked, "Couldn't sleep?"

"Got enough. You?"

He shrugged. "Save it for when I'm dead. I've been checking the news on their computer down there. No word about Stilt Town." His voice was dry, cheeks and eyes puffy, not in a good place. Leigh-Ann held in her sympathy. She didn't reckon they had the luxury to give in and cry quite yet. She held up her phone.

"Well, you wanna know how many results you get searching for sword attacks? Two days ago in Toronto, a week ago in Finland, one in the Big Easy itself just last month. There's people all over the world stabbing each other. Angry spouse, a psycho vet – two best buddies who fell out, just happened to like swords. Whole subculture of dudes solving problems with swords that no one knows about."

"One of many I bet," Reece said, distractedly leaning against the rail. "Probably the same for axe attacks. Rat poison. Socket wrenches, whatever."

"Yeah," Leigh-Ann said. "But I *did* get the report on this Memphis attack. Nothing new, except a photo of where it happened. Load of empty concrete." Reece nodded. "Something else up, Reece?"

Reece paused, which meant yes but he didn't want to say so. "I didn't find anything about the farm or Stilt Town."

"What, then?"

He took her phone and tapped in a search to show her.

There was a bad photo of Reece – his mugshot from five years back when he got picked up for fighting in Lake Charles. Bruised face, hair a mess, but still with a glint of mischief in his eye. Under it, a story. Reece Coburn, wanted in connection with a shooting in Waco, a crazed young thug out of Beauregard, LA, along with at least two friends. Call themselves the "Coburn gang" and are presumed armed and dangerous. No mention of Steer Trust, made it sound like a drugs turf war or something.

It was on a Louisiana state news site. Posted just this morning.

"Shit," Leigh-Ann said. "Fallon figured out who we are – widened the net without getting his own hands dirty?"

"Looks like," Reece said. "Either they found a trace of us in what was left of Stilt Town or someone survived to talk. On the positive, looks like it'll mean Fallon's handing us off to the authorities rather than come at us himself."

"After last night," Leigh-Ann said, "I guess he might. At least until someone slaps cuffs on us. Probably got his money back, even. Meaning all we managed to do was get our faces on a good old-fashioned Wanted poster while a ton of innocent people died." Reece nodded glum acknowledgement, like he needed telling. "Shit, Reece. It's not all on us – we stumbled in on something bigger than ourselves. Who knows how many others have been hurt because of this thing? But damned if I know what we do now. That's your area." Reece raised an eyebrow, so she prodded his chest. "I bring the cheer, motherfucker, you bring the plans." It made him smile at least.

"Just wish they could've got the name right at least," he said. "It's Cutjaw Kids, I *always* said that. Calling us a gang, putting my name up like it's all on me."

There was the old him coming out. The bit that cared most for how they carried themselves and everyone got due credit. She wanted to say welcome back – but a shriek rang out. Zip. They shared a quick look then both burst through Leigh-Ann's door. Leigh-Ann ran to Zip's side. The child sat upright in bed, sweating and panting, staring terror through the wall.

"Bad dream, sweetie, that's all –"

"No!" Zip locked fierce eyes on them. "It's real! I know it is! Svet. The bells!"

"Sweating bells?" Leigh-Ann joked, making Zip angrier.

"Svet's a town! The same happened to them – the same as in Stilt Town!"

That stilled Leigh-Ann, making her step back. Reece's face made it worse.

Hell, after the nightmare of last night, he believed it and she was having a hard time not. Reece said, "You saw it? This town, Svet?"

Zip nodded.

"Just like the other one? In the rainforest? You remember that?"

"Igota. And Villa Madero. There were more, before. Danvale. Laukstad. They're getting worse. It's *him*, I can feel it."

"Vile?" Reece asked. "How's he doing it?"

Zip shook her head, not privy to that. She continued quietly, "Poor . . . poor town. On a mountain. They had fur hats. They didn't want to hurt each other – they weren't thinking anymore." Zip screwed up her face. "Svet. Not in America, nowhere near here."

Leigh-Ann quickly started searching for the names on her phone. Igota? How did you even spell that? Random results about corporates or song lyrics, no use. Svet? A handful of different ideas, something in Prague, a resort in the Crimea. Not a mountain town. Villa Madero – that worked – a town in Mexico. News stories, in Spanish, with pictures. Leigh-Ann showed Reece.

"Hell," he said.

Bodies in the streets. What was left of bodies. Cheap homes ripped down. Viciously rent animal carcasses. Leigh-Ann said, "Reported yesterday." She hit the translate button. "Suspected drug gang? No witnesses. Doesn't look like they were shot to me." She turned to Zip. "What happened in Villa Madero?"

"Do you believe me?" Zip answered with fearful hope.

"We believe you. But what's going on, Zip? Why's this happening?"

"Because he *made* it happen, that's why."

"Got in their heads, the same way you did with those Steers?"

Zip swallowed. Shit, Stomatt was right. The kid herself might be capable of what they saw in Stilt Town.

"Why?" Reece pressed. "What's it to Vile, hurting these people – coming after you – our friends in Stilt Town –" He stopped as Zip's lip trembled. She didn't know any better than them, and all this was only getting her more scared. "Cher, you said your daddy hunted people. Did he . . . this sort of thing, is it familiar?"

"I told you," she said. "It's because I followed Daddy – I used my senses – that's why people are dying. But you can take me home, can't you? If we go back, it'll be safe again, he won't see us anymore. It'll stop!"

"Doesn't make any damn sense," Leigh-Ann whispered.

But Reece was firming up again. Seeing how big this really was, and the monster they were dealing with. Stilt Town was bad enough, losing Caleb a nightmare – but this went way beyond that. Getting his determination back, Reece said, "We're gonna make it add up, right?"


The gang reached the Memphis Harbor Town at mid-afternoon, on the trail of the men from the news story the boys in Stilt Town had turned up. Not hard, once you started asking around – they'd enjoyed having their names in the paper and were happy to talk up their part in the incident. A short, overweight slob and his younger, pock-marked colleague; Reece had Leigh-Ann lure them off the riverfront under the charade of another interview. They were all too happy to oblige, and even when they rejoined Reece they chose leering at Leigh-Ann over questioning the tatty suits or Reece's mad green hair.

Shorty pointed out over an empty stretch of asphalt. "Happened about here. We were on a break, middle of the night shift, sitting over there." Warehouses flanked them to one side, the river to the other, and the blue pyramid Zip spoke of was visible just over some rooftops to the north. "The guy came outta nowhere, you know? Appeared right next to us – Rudy damn near shit himself."

"He put a real fright on me," the other one, Rudy, admitted.

"Tall as Gus, he was, if not taller," Shorty continued. "And that's saying something – Gus is a *big* boy. Only this guy weren't as broad." Not Vile, then; hopefully Zip's father himself, Seph Mason. "He didn't say nothing, just stood there in this long coat, hood up, expecting Gus to recognise him. It was me, spoke first, wasn't it? Said, 'Can we help you, pal?' Then Gus got up growling."

"Always the quiet ones," Rudy said. "Came out of nowhere, didn't drink."

"Anyway," Shorty said, "this shady guy, he pulls out this sword from God-knows-where. Suddenly sticking out his sleeve. Must've been the length of my leg, what do you think?"

"*Your* leg, maybe. Length of a forearm at least."

"Watch it." Shorty forced a smile for Leigh-Ann. Probably took height jokes with less humour when there weren't ladies present. But the point stuck: a sword hid up his sleeve, that idea of Zip's, the *sword hand*. "Neither of them spoke – they just stared each other down. Then – BAM!" Shorty punched a hand into his opposite palm. "Gus whipped up this rebar from down there and they just start *going* at each other, springing about like Spiderman. By the time we got into cover it was over, they fought each other off into the shadows there. Disappeared. Then they were gone – all she wrote."

"Damn craziest thing I ever saw," Rudy said.

"The guy smelt funny too," Shorty added. "Hard kind of smell. I dunno how to describe it. Like something big. A bull. Interesting detail for your story?"

"Sure," Reece said, liking the sound of Seph Mason about as much as he liked Vile. "But we don't have a story if we can't pin these two down. Gus hasn't been back to work?"

"Nuh-uh. Dropped by his place a couple days ago. No answer at the door. You guys know what it was about?"

"The mystery's what's got us interested," Leigh-Ann said. "Got an address?"

"Certainly do." Shorty wrote it down on her phone, along with his number in case she needed anything else – anything at all. The pair had little else to share: Gus never spoke about his past, or plans for the future, or anything much else. He stared out into space a lot, they said, and must've been on the lam from something dark. One eye and an ugly scar over the other. Flinched at sudden sounds like a paranoid vet. That's what they figured him for – someone back from the wars, struggling with civilian life. Or a gangster thug or something? *Yakuza* specifically. Had to be, with those swords.

When Reece and Leigh-Ann parted from the men, he told her, "You watch over Zip and I'll take Sto to go knock on this guy's door."

"Forget that, let's go straight there," Leigh-Ann said. "I can handle myself."

"Don't doubt you can." He gave her a smile. "But there's no doubt Gus is really Grithin, right? Part of a whole community of nasty supercharged nuts? With all Zip's told us, and all we've seen, *I* might need more protection than you can give."

With that kind of cheek, and a mission to follow, yeah. He was on his way back, and Leigh-Ann gave him a punch on the shoulder to show she appreciated it.


Stomatt was busy changing TV channels every twenty to thirty seconds. Antiques show. Someone selling necklaces. Televised court case. News about a forest fire. The antiques show again. Vintage crime show. More news. Yadda ya. Better than looking the kid's way, with her weird eyes that searched inside him. Picking out the worst of him. No one needed that.

A cartoon came up, some moron cat chasing a bird, which Stomatt lingered on. Dumb cat ran into a plank, flattened his face, pretty funny. Stomatt clicked the changer, back to the crime show, and Zip sighed disappointment. He gave her a glance. "Liked that one, huh?"

Zip fixed her face blank. Didn't wanna talk.

Stomatt changed back to the cartoon. He sensed Zip smiling. The cat was propelling itself up off the ground with a hose now, like some kind of jet pack – but damn if he didn't miss the bird and fly head-first into a beehive. Zip laughed and Stomatt joined in. Stupid cat.

The kid shifted closer, then, watching properly. Stomatt took a tense breath, but got distracted as the cat started setting out bear traps. They laughed together as one snapped on his face. Funny music, too. He could lay out a beat like that, punctuate little animals chasing one another. Probably good money in it. One to throw Reece's way . . .

The cartoon ended with the cat trapped in a barrel, with another bird pecking at his head, and Zip swooned happily. Stomatt said, "Like seeing that nasty cat get whooped, huh?"

She looked uncertain. He'd made it an accusation, hadn't he? Shit. He tapped the changer, things getting awkward again. How was anyone supposed to deal with kids? Fuck, the others were straight with her, might as well go for it himself. "With your mind reading? How much you know?"

"I can't read minds."

"You know what people think, right? Knew about my mom. That's reading minds."

Zip shook her head. "Not in words. Like . . . I know feelings. They give me ideas. I know when you're unhappy?"

Stomatt paused. "I'm unhappy?"

"*You're* worried," she said. "You don't want anyone to know."

He straightened up. "I'm an open book, kid. Secrets are for cowards."

She didn't answer that, only looked a little ashamed. Yeah. What'd he have to hide? Always spoke his mind, always did what he wanted. Scared of a kid thinking him unhappy, pah. Stomatt flicked channels again. A news show had switched to game highlights.

"I keep secrets," Zip said, quietly.

"Like about where you live?" Stomatt huffed, making her flinch. Shit, she suddenly looked close to tears. "Ah. Look, everyone tells stuff to their friends, don't they? That's why we're upset about it – don't you think we're friends?" Zip sniffed. Stomatt put a big arm around her, gave her a squeeze. Anything better than risking bawling. Damn those two for leaving him babysitting. "And you *know* we'll find a place in the gang for you and those freaky powers." Something hit him, then. "Say. You ever played cards?"

The door clicked open and Stomatt half-jumped off the bed, reaching for the shotgun by the pillow. Reece froze in the doorway. "Hell, Sto, it's only us – and I definitely would've had the drop on you there. Everything cool?"

Stomatt found Zip nodding happily. Where was his mind a second ago? On the verge of a genius idea, wasn't he?

"Great. You and me are gonna knock on this Grithin's door."

# 26

Katryzna marched ahead of Tasker and Henri, behind Solomon and a couple of soldiers. She had little idea where they were now, having taken a truck part of the way up the hill, and the day's waning light wasn't helping. But so what – they weren't far off now. Eyes might be there. If that freak woman could live eight years in a tree, he could've survived in a cave. If anyone could, Eyes could.

He'd bring some normalcy to this whole thing, seeing as no one else was able to. They were all under some spell from that Sara woman, believing this crap about psychic energies and miracle children. Henri and Tasker were buying into it, she could hear them discussing it – Tasker asking if he was alright, Henri admitting that it was a shock, but he wanted to help. To end her suffering. *It wasn't her, was it?* he mumbled, regretful. *But what about her new skills?* Really buying into this mystic crap.

Rurik suggested, from Katryzna's shoulder, "You can't deny there's something wrong with this place. It gives me the creeps."

"You do not get to have creeps," Katryzna said, getting a backwards glance from the soldier ahead. She showed him her teeth and he looked ahead again. She turned to Henri. "If any of this *was* real, why didn't your sister send you psychic brainwaves already?"

"How?" Henri frowned. He turned to Tasker. "Could she have – somehow – what if she *did* contact me, and I never knew?"

"Her mind is elsewhere," Tasker said. "Locked in resolving whatever mess they created. Surely you feel it's not right up here, Katryzna?"

"What's *right*?" she shot back. "Doesn't feel right locked in prison or jumping out an airplane, but I don't blame that on living mountains or whatever. Sean. In your expert opinion, isn't this nonsense?"

"In my expert opinion," Tasker echoed, "it's not like anything I've come across. They've talked about things that sound like teleportation, but a naturally occurring displacement device wouldn't explain the massacres or how Sara works. And psychic energy wouldn't explain how she got in that tree – or how anyone got out of this place alive, unseen. Or why Duvcorp would kill to cover it up, but never came back here."

"They didn't know there were survivors," Henri said. "Or if they knew, Miguel didn't. He would never have hid my sister's survival, I'm sure."

"None of it makes sense," Katryzna grumbled. "Including your willingness to believe any of this." She stomped on ahead in disdain.

Rurik urged her, softly, "Give it a chance. *Try* and feel it."

She growled but resisted the urge to attack. Fine. She studied her feelings and felt nothing but the growing cold. Besides, who *wouldn't* get uneasy on some darkening mountainside about a million miles from the nearest telephone? She shook that idea off.

A sound whistled through the trees. The screech of some horrendous bird.

They all slowed down to listen for it, but it didn't come again. Katryzna said, "Why's Africa so *weird*."

"That's not a call I recognise," Henri said, worriedly.

"Now you are an expert?"

"We should move quicker," Solomon said. "It's not far now."

They continued at speed, without talking, until the soldiers stopped ahead, waving hands and calling for stillness. Clear of the trees was a great rock-face veined with roots and vines. At its centre, a jagged crack, filled with darkness. Katryzna stared wide-eyed. *Now* she felt something. This was exactly where it all led. This was where Eyes had gone. She took a tentative step closer, past Solomon, and the feeling strengthened in her. Air thick as water. She tensed and asked of the world, "What is this?"

Tasker shuddered behind her, with an involuntary noise. She shot him a look and saw Henri was edging fearfully towards a tree, for cover. The soldiers didn't look much better – all these tough guys glaring with thinly hidden worry. Solomon said, "You don't deny it now?"

"Don't tell me what I feel." Katryzna turned back to the dark hole. She gritted her teeth and took another step closer. Something pushed back. Like it was blowing out air, resisting her. Even if the air was still, the forest quiet.

"You can't go in there," Rurik said, full of fear.

"I can do what I want," Katryzna replied, strained. She took another step forward, and it got harder.

"Don't!" Rurik cried. More emotion than she'd ever heard from him, shouting into her ear. She swatted him off her shoulder and he fell shouting. Another step. The resistance came with noise now, a throb of unformed sound repelling her.

"Katryzna, that's enough!" Tasker called, from far away.

Then another sound – something like that monster from the night before. Closer than Tasker. Katryzna blinked against it, ignoring whatever comment Solomon made. She could do anything. Face anything. A dark crack of rock wasn't going to stop her. Another step and her vision blurred. Foot on the threshold of the entrance, hand on the rock to support her. Struggling to take that final step – feelings flooded into her. Pain, happiness, laughter, fear – visions, a thousand faces at once, fires burning and waves crashing – she heard her own sound of defiance rising up against the flood. Pressing slowly into the shadow, vision growing brighter, stranger – a cacophony of human sounds –

She was pulled back, suddenly, with panicked shouts surrounding her. She tried to break free but her arms were weak, mind unfocused as the faces and voices dispersed from her unclear vision. Tasker's voice in one ear: "Move – it's coming!" Henri's voice in the other: "My God what is it?"

And another animal scream, drawing closer.

Katryzna pushed them both off her, steadying herself to find her feet as they stumbled into the tree line. Her senses were returning, the world refocusing, and she heard a new savage noise. She was breathing heavily. There were tears on her cheeks. She hated it but she knew it then, that they were right. This place was unnatural and deadly. They could not stay. It had killed Eyes and it would kill them all, too.

"Hurry, hurry!" Solomon shouted, pushing them on. They were running through the trees, dodging branches, watching footfalls, as the animals closed in, sounding at once right near them and also very far away. One of the soldiers started shooting, but Katryzna couldn't see what at. The men were shouting in their native tongue now, panicked, firing at shadows. When Katryzna tried to slow and join in, she was pushed on by Henri, urging her not to stop.

Suddenly they broke out onto the truck, piling in. The wild sounds pressed ever closer, soldiers firing at them as someone started the engine. Then, with final panicked shouts, they were all in and driving away.

Katryzna rested her head back against a window, recovering her breath, trying to understand what she'd felt. Tasker and Henri were both watching her, terrified, confused, but looking to her for something. Hoping that she'd reflect the same belief they'd already got from that tree freak. Katryzna closed her eyes, listening to the sounds of the unholy beasts, just audible now behind the truck engine. She said, quietly, "If this thing killed Eyes, I will burn it all down." She opened her eyes, and found the guys looked no less worried. "We will get this child."


Tasker barely slept, hearing the noises of the monsters of Ikiri hunting for them. During the evening, Katryzna had retreated into the same miserable quiet that caught her in the hotel, revisiting the truth that Eyes was dead over and over, not knowing what to do with it. Once they'd settled into a private hut, she barely reacted to the sounds outside or Tasker's attempts to spark conversation. Henri, too, had lost his carefree manner after their previous night's encounter, seeing his sister, and now this. He wasn't all there. Leaving Tasker alone to consider the possibilities: that Ikiri's corrupted power was capable of lashing out to cause such harm as he'd seen in Laukstad. That the people thought to have gone missing here might still be out there, guarding this secret. Somehow, deep down, he knew that this child Sara spoke of, this girl, was necessary. And with the possibility of Ikiri striking anywhere, at any time, they had to cure this haunted land as quickly as possible.

The wretched things never got close, but those sounds had all the screeching, death-hungry hallmarks of the preternatural creatures the Ministry investigated. The likes of which were culled in most places but carefully contained around such cities as Guidalezam in Mexico, Istanbul in Turkey. Under Ordshaw in England. He couldn't imagine the lives of Solomon and his men, evading such creatures every night.

Thankfully, the gentle dawn saw the creatures silenced, and Solomon roused a beanpole soldier to drive them to the edge of his territory, as eager to see them on their way as they were. He said they could take the Jeep further themselves, as his man would use a bike to ride back. He wished them the best of luck, and warned, "If you start to feel strange, come back."

Henri lingered at the edge of the camp, looking up towards the slopes of the hills as though he could see his sister stuck there. Sadness and shock behind his eyes, at a loss. Tasker asked if he wanted to say goodbye, but he shook his head.

"There's no hope," Henri said, "until we do what she asks."

He turned away, arms folded, rather than discuss it further.

Katryzna, on the other hand, approached the Jeep with something like disinterest, calling, "Are we going or what?"

Despite having accepted Ikiri had some illicit power, she scorned the idea of the PLU's curse, and insisted they wouldn't lose their minds because *she* wasn't a coward. Tasker sensed there was some truth in it, given they had been safe from whatever gripped those men from Igota, but it was no comfort for their driver, who watched the forest with mounting fear as he drove. He kept an AK-47 across his lap, impractical but inseparable from him. After a little over an hour of bumpy travel, he pulled the Jeep up where the dirt track split in two, disembarked with the bike and pointed down the left fork. "Two miles to Igota, then join the road to the river."

He rode away as quick as he could, almost falling off the bike in his urgency. Katryzna looked ready to mock his fear but held off, for some reason regarding whatever Rurik said with more generosity this morning. However cool she played it, Tasker had seen her fear before that cave. As they drove on, though, apparently now outside Sara's influence, Tasker started to feel more at ease himself. The further they got from Ikiri the better, as far as he was concerned.

When they came upon Igota, Henri pulled the Jeep to a stop with a worried sound. He stood from his seat to get a better view over the dirtied window. "Oh no. No no."

Tasker leant out to see. The village was destroyed. The closest hut had collapsed like something had been driven through it. There were bodies on the ground, limbs twisted at impossible angles, dry earth and wooden walls painted with blood. Near the entrance to the village sat stout Ade, their kind host, too much gore on his flesh to identify a single wound, lifeless eyes open with terror. There would be more, worse, if they looked closer. More children, brutally killed.

"Henri," Tasker said. "We should go."

"These people . . ." Henri said. "They were good people, they helped us."

"There's nothing we can do."

"At least we don't have to worry about those freaks' intentions the other night," Katryzna said, lightly. It didn't help Henri's trance, as he started to make a low keening noise.

Tasker leaned forward to tap him. "Let's go." Henri snapped out of it and nodded, dropping back into his seat. He started the engine again. Movement flashed out of the trees – more from between the huts – people, suddenly emerging. Tasker twisted in his seat. "Hell."

"Survivors?" Henri said with empty hope, quickly looking around them.

"Drive," Katryzna advised. "Straight through them."

Three people shuffled into the path ahead, standing at crooked angles as though held up by some force other than their own. All focused on the Jeep.

"Drive!" Katryzna shouted, loud enough to force Henri's foot down on the pedal. They surged forward, Henri shouting, and the villagers screamed and charged.

# 27

By the time they reached Grithin's address, Reece had heard Stomatt's rambling assessment of Zip's prowess a dozen times over. It essentially amounted to "the kid's alright" and "we should take her to a casino". Never mind casinos didn't let children in – he repeated the sentiments each time sounding like he'd just come up with the idea. It was the conversational equivalent of fitful, irritating scat music, with a predictable refrain, teasing progression then looping right back . . .

But then they were at the apartment: a two-storey red-brick block opposite a pair of desolate parking lots. It had big square windows and a set of steps that led up to a black-iron entrance gate. They worked out which were the windows for Grithin's place – ground floor, to the left of the entrance, curtains drawn, no sign of life. Stomatt leant heavily on the buzzer, but no one answered. Reece went back out to the street, checking their options: a balcony stuck out of the landing above with no way to climb up. Round the side, the block went back a way – different apartments forming the rear side. Reece came back to find Stomatt had his hands on the window, the lower sill about chest height, looking in.

"Can probably get onto the super," Reece suggested. "Say we're friends."

"Thin glass," Stomatt said, scanning the road. There were another couple of small blocks in sight, but this was a dead little pocket of squalor with few cars and no pedestrians. "We can be in and out real quick."

"Depending on what's inside," Reece said. "If anything."

"Your call, boss."

Reece bit his lip. Every second they wasted, that ninja freak and his gorilla were likely getting closer. "Fuck it." He drew his pistol and bunched up his jacket under it, gave the street one last glance and tapped the handle hard into the base of the window. The pane cracked straight across with a sound that split across the street. Reece gave it another tap and the lower pane split out, four or five segments falling inside and crashing with tinkles. He winced. But still no sign of movement on the street.

"This place is dead, man," Stomatt assured. "We're good."

"Keep watch," Reece said. He reached under the dangling sharp blade of the upper pane and unhooked the window, then pulled the sash up. With Stomatt's help, he wriggled inside. Glass crunched underfoot as he steadied himself in a dark living room. Not much to see bar a moth-eaten sofa and an old TV. Lot of dust.

Pistol in hand, Reece moved through darkness, curling his nose at a stagnant, heady smell. He passed through a corridor, checking a kitchen yellowed with age before coming to a bedroom-cum-office. A rickety wooden desk flanked a sunken camp bed which bowed under the weight of a man too tall to fit on it. Ripped with muscle, lean, he would've been in great shape if not for the gash running up his side, and the other crossing from his left ear down to his sternum. Both had been partly cleaned but were almost black from dried blood – he hadn't lasted long enough to properly dress them. Bandages and needles scattered the floor next to him. Reece took a step closer, covering his nose – Grithin, and the one eye hidden by scarring confirmed it was him, had been dead a while. He was in work overalls, likely came back here after that fight and hadn't done much more. Besides those two big cuts, his clothes were ripped in a half-dozen other places.

Reece checked the desk to the side, madly strewn with papers, some spread across the floor. Someone had gone through Grithin's files in a hapless way. And there were a *lot* of files.

Hell.

Newspaper clippings, photos of faces, police reports, all with big, frantic writing scrawled over them. Reece shifted closer, pushing a couple printed maps aside to reveal a set of photos. Men's faces. Some had been circled then crossed out, with big feverish markings. Hard-looking men, some in uniform, sitting next to news articles with daunting headlines: *Maniac Swordsmen Slays Ten. Unexplained Murders in Albuquerque. CEO of Fenk Co. Found Dismembered.* Reece turned over one of the photos, a shovel-faced man, and found a word written on the back. *Ruin.* He turned over a couple more: Mad Moose, Shearjoy, Flay. "Scorecard" looked the least offensive, with a skinny, bespectacled mathematician look. Shit, these were guys with abstract monikers fitting to Vile. Many dead, going by the crosses. No sign of Vile himself, though.

Then, another one caught Reece's attention. Headhunter.

A square-headed, cold son of a bitch – this one with a smaller photo attached by a paper clip. Half the age she was now, but recognisable all the same, with the name jaggedly scrawled on the back. Zipporah. Underlined multiple times, like it'd been repeated excitedly. So Grithin was a hunter just like her father. It wasn't one man against the monsters – they considered each other monsters?

Reece noticed the stains on some of the papers on the floor, then. Finger smears of blood. A big boot print on one, next to something that'd been screwed up. Reece crouched to pick it up and unfolded another map – an area he didn't immediately recognise, with a bunch of towns named and an X marking a spot. A conclusion had been written in big triumphant letters: *Mason.* Reece looked from the map over to Grithin's body. Well, hell, the guy had located the Headhunter. Might've been just about to pay him a visit when Zip's dad caught up to him first.


The news came up on the TV half an hour after the boys left. Leigh-Ann's instinct was to tell Zip to look away, but, hell, the kid had been there. Close shots, aerial shots, body bags, gathered law enforcement vehicles – none of that looked as bad as it had on the ground, with lunatics ripping each other's throats out. It was the idea of becoming a celebrity that troubled Leigh-Ann more. Her face was on CNN – *her* rough-freckled features looking ugly out the TV like some kind of reprobate. National news. Could be international, even, couldn't it?

The unexplained massacre of almost a hundred people, that was something likely to spread everywhere. There were no survivors, they said, bar a handful of Gray's followers who'd been out of town at the time. The dead Steer Trust employees raised questions, with about two dozen found, but the reports chased that fact with Dustin Fallon sat sombre at a desk insisting his men were assisting with the pursuit of the Coburn gang, who Gray was harbouring. They were victims themselves, Fallon told the cameras – the Coburn gang *must* be stopped. Cue more flattering mugshots of the four of them. No mention of the fact that Caleb had bought it, like they hadn't even found his body yet.

The FBI were launching a manhunt, with the anchors warning everyone to be on the lookout, as if these psychos might creep in your bedroom window and cut your throat for no damn reason. Journalists would be swarming on Cutjaw to get dirt from families and friends. There'd be double-barrelled shotguns waved from porches.

If they got caught and avoided a deadly shootout, Leigh-Ann considered, she might get a book deal or go on a reality TV show. One of the Coburn gang, straight out of jail to eat bugs in the jungle for Saturday night thrills? It'd be a living.

When Reece got back with Stomatt, she showed them the news and Stomatt whistled and laughed. "They gonna make a movie outta us?"

"I know, right?" Leigh-Ann said. "Assuming we're not murdered by vigilantes."

"Whole of the South's gonna be gunning for us," Reece said. "And we got no story to tell that'll turn them off, short of 'track down this one's dad and let him explain'. Hell, we wanna be gone yesterday."

"No luck with Grithin?"

"Dead as roadkill," Reece said. "But not a total bust." He turned from the TV to Zip. "Got a thought, cher. The way you made them Steers look the other way, out on the highway? Just how well can you do that?"

"Um." Zip considered it. "It's not safe –"

"Never mind safe, nothing we're doing is safe. If you can get people to look the other way, that's all we can hope for. You flew here, didn't you? Got a plane all on your own? That's some amazing ingenuity and I'm sorry I didn't proper respect it sooner. Especially sorry your daddy's never respected it." He crouched in front of her, smiling. "Think you could do that again? Maybe walk us all right out of the States."

"Like through an airport?" Leigh-Ann said. "We'll walk right into cuffs."

"He's fixing on us going to England," Stomatt said.

"England?" Leigh-Ann exclaimed. "Just the other side of the damn pond, slide on over for a tea and cake? You serious, Reece? You think we can get on a plane now –"

"Not much further than DC, is it?" Stomatt said, defensively. "I had a friend flew Charleston to there, took him a couple hours. Bus from Cutjaw to Alexandria's four hours – ten, twenty dollars on the bus."

Leigh-Ann gawked. "Think England's an island just off Savannah or what?"

"No, 'course not, just saying it's not like trying to get into China or something."

"It might as well be! You got any idea how an airport works? Reece. Come on – we don't even know for sure Zip's *from* England."

Reece took a piece of crumpled paper from his pocket and held it up for her. A map, with the name "Mason" scrawled by a cross. Leigh-Ann checked the printed place names near it, one bigger than the others. "Ordshaw? What is . . ." She slowed down and looked to Zip. The child had been watching them all in chill silence. "That your home, sweetie?"

Zip swallowed, and admitted quietly, "Maybe."

Leigh-Ann bit her lip. "All right. So what, no one's gonna notice us prancing onto flights with stolen cash and no passports?"

"That's the dream." Reece winked, the cocky bastard, and locked on Zip again. "But I wanna test the waters first. Zip – this is for all our sakes. To get justice for them people in Stilt Town and Caleb – and to make sure all that never happens to no one else. Least of all *us*. I gotta say I'm scared of your daddy too, okay, and he must've had some reason for keeping you sheltered – but he's the best hope we got, and he wouldn't want you out here stranded when using your powers might help, don't you think? So how about we start small. See what you've got?"

Zip quickly nodded.

"Right. Let's start by looking the part."

Reece had them all undress and put Zip to the test by taking her with him down to the motel's cleaning service. Wrapped in a bedsheet, Leigh-Ann shared an unpleasantly tense twenty minutes with Stomatt waiting on Reece's return, or for police sirens or whatever, before he burst back in elated: even with their faces shining up on the news in the foyer, and that *unmistakable* ridiculous green hair, the receptionist hadn't given him a second look, only took the clothes and told him they'd be dropped by later.

For the next test, while they were lingering in their underwear, Reece got on the phone to a travel agency and coupled his chatty charm with Zip listening in, focusing hard, to swindle flight tickets to Ordshaw. The woman on the line agreed to every damn thing Reece asked – business class tickets, payment deferred, no question of names or passport numbers – just pick them up at the counter. Intensely staring at something they couldn't see, Zip warped that admin's mind at a distance of God-knows-how-far. Forget celebrity TV, there were a million and one scams they could run with this. Leigh-Ann said, "What if we put in a call to Quantico or some shit? Tell the FBI to back off."

"After those TV broadcasts?" Reece said, seeing Zip's rising panic at the suggestion. "We'd have to get a hell of a lot of folks to forget."

"But she's got something there, don't she?" Stomatt chipped in, lingering by the door. He kept checking out the window, past the curtains, as if he'd wrestle any coming threat to the ground in just his vest and trunks. "FBI says we're off the hook, everyone else can damn accept it."

"But *they* will notice," Zip insisted. "They're everywhere."

"What *they*?"

Reece sniffed at that, his easy smile fading. "The rest of them. The others like Vile." For Leigh-Ann, he said, "There were pictures at Grithin's. A whole heap of these bastards out there. No, Zip's right, we can't put up any flags that'd point them our way. Hell, even now, Vile's likely to pick up on what we've done, isn't he?"

Zip nodded guiltily.

"It's fine." Reece rubbed her head. "Soon as we're suited, we'll jump across town, hunker down by the airport. Then hope Vile can't fly." It came out like a joke, but after his smile lasted a second, he looked to Zip for confirmation.

She said, "Um. I don't know how he travels. Fast."

"Screw it, that creepy son of a bitch *better* keep following us," Stomatt said. "Can't wait to punch his damn teeth out."

"I'd pay to see that," Leigh-Ann said, picturing joy at the end of this road. Some madman hero waiting on Zip to come home, able to stand up to this bastard and explain away what happened in Stilt Town. Maybe a bigger book deal out of it – idiot fools playing their part in resolving a mass-murder plot. Provided Zip's daddy wasn't just as bad as Vile. He had a kid, though, didn't he? Stirring at that thought, Leigh-Ann asked, "Zip. Can you get our guns on that flight, too?"

# 28

The Jeep was making unhealthy noises all the way through the forest, and Henri was leaning into the dash as though he could push it on himself. One of the bodies had gone under the wheels, making the vehicle jump, and another had bashed its head against the windscreen, obscuring visibility with a web of cracks. Tasker suspected a couple of enraged people jumping out of the trees might've jammed something in the right rear tyre, but they were still bouncing along so he didn't raise the doubt. No way they were stopping to check any time soon.

It'd been the familiar, previously friendly villagers who were driven to mindless rage, hurling themselves towards a moving vehicle, bloody teeth bared. If Tasker had any doubts left over the Laukstad connection, they were gone. This is what had cost those fishermen their lives. Some inexplicable mania, apparently generated by Ikiri itself. The Ministry would throw resources at this, at last, but he couldn't tell all yet. Still couldn't be sure who to trust, or where the people wanting to silence this had got to; did they *want* this force to get worse? Better to keep a low profile until they secured the girl.

When they reached the next village, Henri sped up rather than slowed down, in case the people there were corrupted, too. They came upon a patrol post shortly after, though, and had to stop. Another Jeep, and three armed men – too late to turn back by the time Henri saw them. Besides, there were no other roads to choose from.

As Henri pulled up, Katryzna reached for her rifle, hidden under their bags in the foot well. Tasker shook his head – she didn't look impressed. The men levelled guns at Henri, regarding the bloodstained vehicle. Tasker rolled down his window and leant out, hoping a white face would be enough to warrant consideration. He gave the briefest introduction, using one of his many covers – Preston Pullwick, imports and exports – and asked who they worked for. The men sneered him off, speaking rapidly in unimpressed French. Henri answered in a forced happy tone. They looked from the driver back to Tasker, sceptically, as Tasker tried to interpret. Katryzna picked up something herself and laughed when the guards did. The way they looked back at Tasker, the joke was on him. The soldiers nodded satisfaction and invited Henri on with smiles. They went back to their vehicle and pulled out ahead.

"What'd you say?" Tasker asked, as Henri drove behind them.

"They're from the rebel force that controls the area the rest of the way to the river –Matka's men," Henri explained. "I told them you're lost. Basically."

"Just me?" Tasker said.

"The way he said it was funnier," Katryzna said. "And saved their lives. Well *done*, Henri."

Henri's smile turned more uncomfortable. "Well. They'll take us all the way to the river. You'll wire them whatever money they ask for. Don't worry, their ambitions won't run too high." He was finally relaxing, now they had an escort and a clear path out of the rainforest. Even if they were armed rebels, the mere fact that the men weren't out of their minds was a blessing. After a few minutes of driving, Henri said, "We are free of Ikiri's influence, aren't we? This is proof – people we can reason with – our minds safe."

"Sure," Tasker replied. All bets were off there, though. Whatever warped those villagers had also hit a village in the Arctic circle. He looked to Katryzna, expecting her take, but she was back to looking out the window, in her own grim thoughts.

By dusk they reached the river and crossed to Bokema, where the soldiers hammered on a squat hut for a moustached man in glasses. He had computers inside, satellite dishes up top, and evidently ran some kind of electronic wire service. Under the rebels' eye, he set up a satellite phone link so Tasker could call through to London. He arranged for Caffery to wire the rebels' asking fee of £3,000 to their chosen account, apparently making the three men the happiest people in the DRC and Tasker's new best friends. It wasn't insignificant – Caffery would complain about this for months – but the gift kept giving, as the rebels insisted on arranging a private boat to leave that evening to take them back to Kinshasa. The barge, after all, wouldn't be back for days. It meant Tasker could also arrange for Caffery to set up his flights as soon as possible. His handler demanded answers, of course, but had to settle for Tasker hedging with a promise that he'd have some real results soon.

Tasker settled with relief onto the boat, once they were cruising into the night, the well-compensated captain and his second not the sort to fraternise. The vessel was just big enough to give their trio a private compartment below deck, with a corner of thinly-cushioned benches. Henri brought down a bottle of clear liquid which he handed to Tasker. It smelt flammable; Tasker gave it a sip and gasped at the fiery pain. He said, hoarsely, "That'll do," and absently held the bottle across the small space to Katryzna.

She curled her nose and folded her arms. "Do you actually want me to hurt you?"

"Huh?"

She scoffed at her conscience, apparently down on the bench by her knee: "Shut up, *he*'s the rude one."

"Sorry," Tasker said. "I figure it's always polite to ask." He took the bottle back and drank deeper. Hell, he hadn't realised how tense he'd been, venturing into the interior. He almost wanted to laugh, at the relief of getting away. But Katryzna's past words came back to him, *the mind is a terrible thing to waste*, and he stayed his hand on the bottle. She was staring at him as though to see what he'd do next. He passed it back to Henri, saying, "Your mind, in particular, Katryzna, might've saved us. Able to resist Ikiri, apparently. Henri and me were jelly before Sara, without you. And we got clear of Solomon's supposed curse. How about you, Henri, did you feel anything in that village?"

"Like I could've died there," Henri said. When Tasker's gaze rested more steadily on him he gave it proper thought. "Yes. I felt lost. Or that I was getting lost. I've been . . . dizzy. Since we found Sara." He forced a smile, shaking his head at himself. "I have fought ferocious men, three on one, with weapons. I do *not* scare easily. But that – I was afraid. I was losing control."

"But you didn't," Tasker said. "And neither did I. Possibly because you" – he pointed to Katryzna – "never would have."

"Hear that?" Katryzna laughed at the space on the seat near her knee. "Yes – oh, jump in a toilet." She looked up. "Rurik says I shouldn't take credit. Apparently I am too *mad* to be manipulated." Her eyes rested on Tasker like she knew that was where his mind was going.

"I don't think you're mad," Tasker said. "Besides your imaginary friend, you've proved pretty sane to me. I do think you're special, though. Your openness, perhaps –"

"Open?" Katryzna laughed, harshly. "Idiot. Look at carefree Katryzna, best friend until she cuts your throat out." She grinned wickedly, challenging. "Exciting until she crawls into a hole, too sad to move. You know what I did after Eyes disappeared? Why I came here *now*? I was about to –" she dragged a finger across her throat – "finish a job, and then I just could not do it. I *broke*. Ended up in a jail. It was two years before I got out, and most of that time I didn't feel any better."

"Broke?"

"*Cried*," Katryzna spat. "Sat on the floor in darkness. I am miserable, Sean. What'd you think I was doing in the hotel, masturbating?" She looked away, disgusted at herself. "Were you paying attention? It was a year before Solomon came to Ikiri. There was infighting, there was a child, some of these people got away – Eyes might have been *alive* some of that time. I could have helped. Instead, I was stewing in a cell feeling sorry for myself."

Her words hung heavy in the air. Henri quietly said, "How? If you were imprisoned, how could you do anything?"

Katryzna's expression darkened. "I could've found a way. I live a *charmed* life, Eyes told me. Not the only person to say so." Hadn't Smail used a similar word? "I'm everything that shouldn't work in this world, an anomaly like those men Lopaz hired." She swung an arm. "Violent, horrible people, who somehow survived Ikiri the same as me. People that the world throws up to disrupt things – just as it threw us together. Look at you, partnering with someone crazy enough to get you out of there. They spoke about Ikiri like some terrible force of nature – well, so am *I*. My kind, we live to do damage. Systems glitch and set us free – ultra-powerful men decide we're too useful to let die. We're kept alive and we're kept from cages, and I could've used that to *save him*."

Her voice had become manic, almost desperate. Wanting to confess, to be believed and forgiven. She stared madly into Tasker's eyes and he stared back, at a loss. The very things she was beating herself up over, he realised, might be the very inconsistencies that kept her alive. He said, weakly, "Well, you weren't there then, but you're here now. And I'm thankful you're able to help get to the bottom of this."

"Don't you listen?" she hissed through gritted teeth, leaning closer. "Eyes trusted me and he died in a crack in a rock. I'm not a witch, I'm not supernatural, okay, Sean? I *am* mad."

Henri came in, softly, "Ms Tkacz, if I may?"

She gave him a sideways look.

"Your friend Eyes – I don't believe he was waiting on anyone to help him. If that's true, about people the world preserves – well, none of those men would rely on friends. It was not your responsibility." It calmed her, momentarily. Well done Henri. But he moved on, some of his past smile creeping back in: "And I agree with Agent Tasker that you are definitely *not* mad. He might be too stuffy to make his proposal directly, but I will. I would like to invite you to dinner when we get back to Kinshasa. No funny business."

She stared with momentary disbelief, then barked a mean laugh. "Inviting me to dinner *is* funny business. You've paid less attention than Sean."

"You like to eat, don't you?"

"We can't go back to the city," Tasker came in, then. They both gave him questioning looks. "At least, not us two. We might be the first people in years to get away from Ikiri alive – there's a dozen survivors from the expedition that might be watching. They were a step behind Parris, letting him talk – probably a step behind us when we got to Africa. But they'll have caught up now, I'd bet. We'll get off the boat early, head straight to the airport."

"Did you get Henri a plane ticket too?" Katryzna asked with sudden concern.

Henri shook his head. "I am not coming with you, no, I'm sorry. This thing affects my world too. If they mean to silence people, they might come for my family, my friends. I have to make sure they're safe."

"So I can return to find you dead too?" Katryzna's eyes burned.

Henri tried to smile. "I will be fine, this is where I belong. And I'll make preparations for when you come back with the child."

Katryzna didn't look happy, but Tasker saw the spark of something in her that he needed. She'd become protective, looking for ways to make right on whatever ills she was piling on herself from the past. He said, "We'll be back quick as we can. With a way to end this."

She nodded and exhaled loudly to get past this tension. A clear goal obviously helped. "Yeah. I am going to make it right, isn't it? Once we kidnap a child."

# 29

As the gang walked through Memphis International Airport, they kept scanning every face around them. But Zip's trick was working. They existed in a bubble where no one looked at them, no one spoke to them. The woman at check-in entered their details and smiled at Reece but asked no questions, merely wished them a good day. No one asked for their bags and when they got to the security checks, a guard gestured for them to go right on through with a friendly wink to Zip. Three guns in their single holdall bag, no x-rays.

Reece hummed a tune as they waited at the gate. That new composition growing stronger in his mind. Dramatic like theatre, not club music. He tapped it on the armrest, watching people not watching them. Eerie as those Steers at the gas stop, no one noticing these finely suited criminals and a kid in a burlap sack of a dress. Reece wished he had his trumpet, to make more of a scene. Lead the terminal in a parade of music. He hummed a little louder and caught Leigh-Ann watching him. Her expression was blank, nowhere near as relaxed, so he shot her a smile. She scarcely returned it. Then they were called to board, and the gang went on to the front of the line, welcomed through without a second glance. Caleb would've got a kick out of this.

"This what you did before?" Leigh-Ann asked quietly, checking over her shoulder as they walked onto the plane. "Just waltz on through and catch a flight?"

Zip nodded, innocently.

Imagine that. This kid was something else.

Leigh-Ann set about picking something to watch with Zip while Stomatt squeezed hard into his chair, jaw clenched against the idea of them flying. Reece said it'd be okay, safer than riding a bull, which the big guy had done a couple of times. That didn't help. Then the engines were whirring and they were rolling out for lift-off, and Stomatt bucked like he might freak out and hit someone. Zip took his hand. Stomatt regarded it like an alien gesture, then softened like he'd been drugged. Breathed out his worries. They banked up, Reece grinning, Leigh-Ann staring wide-eyed out the window, and once they cleared the clouds Stomatt shouted for a whisky. Soon, he was loudly annotating the crap on the entertainment service, and Reece had to tell him to keep it down. But the other passengers still didn't notice a thing. Just gave them dumb, creepily pleasant looks.

It was dark in England when they touched down, so they made their way to another hotel, all delighted by the accent of their chatty taxi driver. He noticed them better than anyone else had in the previous two days: asked if they were some kind of jazz band. He insisted he'd come see them play, but never asked where or when he could. At the hotel, Reece tried to sit up and keep vigil when the others hunkered down for the night, but weariness got the better of him and he had to turn in himself.

Come dawn, Leigh-Ann stirred him, looking rested herself. Wearing something of her old smile. She said, "Gonna sleep all day or you ready to grill this psycho father?"

After a hearty breakfast with sausages that touched Stomatt between wonder and disgust, they got a rental car and followed Grithin's map. Zip started to recognise the territory, excited that they were definitely going home. To her place on a hill, looking down on the city, where on a good day you saw the sea. As they got closer, Zip sat forward excitedly, guiding them. Pointing, as the crow flew, in the direction they needed. Reece drove along narrow, winding roads, past greenery lighter than Louisiana's. Up hills, through what passed for a small town – a single row of tiny, moss-swept stone houses settled in like they'd been there forever. Stomatt and Leigh-Ann pressed themselves to the windows to take it all in. Fairytale landscape, didn't look big enough for full-sized people.

Out of the village, the road curved again and again, gradually climbing, till they reached an old mill, stood at the hill's peak. Dark windows dotted the curved walls, and a ruined annexe flanked the right side of the building. The mill itself could've been abandoned, if not for the car out front. Zip was itching to burst out, announcing this was it, they were home! Leigh-Ann held her back, asking, "That your daddy's car?"

As Reece pulled up, the kid's brow knitted, searching whatever psychic wavelengths she could. She said, "Yes. He's there. Daddy's inside."

But in a second, he was outside.

The mill door was open and filled by a man with a massive frame, half-cloaked by a draping duster coat. He stepped into daylight, revealing his hard-worn face, features deep-set, angularly rugged and humourless. A blade stuck out of his right sleeve instead of a hand, and the set of his shoulders said he was ready to fight.

"You took a wrong –" Mason began, voice booming. He stopped abruptly. Noticing Zip. Her face lit up, as he said with deep, surprised, relief, "Zipporah."

"Daddy!" Zip cried, going for the door. "I'm so –"

"Release the child," Mason ordered, raising his blade-arm. The sleeve fell back, showing not a hand holding the weapon but a brass contraption; the "sword hand" was a metal box with cog mechanics around it, fused with his forearm.

Stomatt said, "The hell is that thing?"

"We're friends!" Reece called out, raising a hand out the window. "Bringing her back to you!"

"Here, Zipporah," Mason said, ignoring him. He stood as a pillar of defiance, even as he lowered his arm. Something whirred within the sleeve and the blade extended, two foot long, dark and nicked, like something salvaged from wreckage. He rolled his head to one side, upper lip curled back.

"Jesus," Leigh-Ann said. "He ain't happy to see us."

"They're my friends!" Zip cried, voice high with tension. She scooted back into hugging Leigh-Ann, demonstrating, which only make Dad madder.

"You should have killed her when you had the chance!" Mason took a step closer. His bone-shaking voice didn't sound capable of an ordinary tone. Hard to imagine a conversation where his every other word didn't make you flinch. And that accent was rough – nothing like Zip's educated tone.

Leigh-Ann opened the holdall on the backseat, picking through their guns as she muttered curses, but Reece said, "Hold up, give me a chance."

"Can't you mind-trick him or something?" Stomatt suggested, but Zip looked ready to wet herself. As shit-scared of her father as everyone else. Hell, they did *not* think this through properly.

"We rescued her," Reece hurried to explain, "and kept *Vile* off her back. Lost a friend doing it. You know who I'm talking about, right?"

The name made Mason stop. "Impossible."

"Yeah, we had the same idea seeing him in action. Look, I'm getting out, let's have ourselves a little talk, okay?" Reece slowly opened the door and stood, hands up. He felt a million miles from his pistol sitting on Leigh-Ann's lap, and half his usual height before Mason. The guy had to be pushing seven feet, broad as a doorway. Something told Reece he could clear their ten-metre gap in an instant.

"Who are you with?" Mason demanded. "Shearjoy? Ruin?"

Reece flashed a smile. "We're with you, if you'll let us talk. I'm telling you little Zip here was being chased by Vile –"

"Vile is dead," Mason cut in.

Reece laughed, light as he could muster. "He didn't look mighty healthy, but I promise you he's running around stabbing people. We come all the way from Louisiana to be here, my friend. To help her – and you."

Mason's madly trembling eyes ran from Reece to the car again, fixing on Zip. "Louisiana. You foolish child. Do you have any idea –" He pushed the frustration back. "Get inside. We will talk once I deal with these people."

"No!" Zip jumped out, past Leigh-Ann's snatching arms. She balled her fists at her side and said, "They're *good*! We need their help!"

Mason glared at her audacity. "I taught you better than this. Get inside."

"No!"

Stomatt rose slowly from the other side, as Leigh-Ann hurried after Zip. He looked the least comfortable with a pistol that Reece had ever seen him. Spotting the gun, Mason slid a foot back and his coat fell away to the side, revealing plates of dirty hammered metal over his chest and exposed leg – the duster covering fragments of armour. His blade-arm was cocked down at the side, ready to strike. "Get *inside*."

Reece raised his hands higher. "You want us gone, we'll go. But Vile is coming for her and we've seen how he moves. Figure it might take all of us to stop him, don't you?"

"Whatever trickery you're attempting –"

"It's not a trick!" Zip cried. "I'm sorry, Daddy, but I didn't know – Vile came from nowhere –"

"Stop saying that name! Vile is dead!" Mason roared so loudly that the trees themselves rustled nearby. So loud, in fact, he gave himself pause, unable to deny the height of his emotions. He reconsidered Zip, hesitant, but continued. "I broke his skull myself. A long time ago and a long way away."

"Well," Reece replied very carefully, "I shot him, more than once, and that didn't work. And given he killed my best friend and was after your daughter, I'd say we have a common interest. Less you think you're better off alone?"

There was the smallest shift in Mason's posture. Zip stared with silent pleading. Slowly, he lowered his arm and the brass contraption whirred, the blade retreating. He looked past them, seeming to scent the air. "Come inside."

# 30

For the two days they drifted along the river, making only brief stops to refuel and restock, Katryzna was pleased to find everyone basically pretended they hadn't talked to a tree-woman and been chased by zombies. Tasker and Henri started to get a little more chatty, asking about her past, but she threw them off with dismissive remarks. What else was there to tell, anyway? She was content instead to watch the trees glide past, the high rocky banks, the snout of an alligator. Henri blabbered at her about what was out there but she barely listened. Didn't bother to jump off with the others when the captain made his pit stops, either, just waited things out. Not despairing, not miserable. Content.

The boys were right. She might've failed Eyes, but this was a way to make good. She was better suited than anyone to bringing all this down.

Kinshasa came into view as a procession of low, miserable buildings gradually blossoming into the dirty dense metropolis. Tasker had the captain stop before the city proper, and he chose a jetty as rickety as those out in the forest, before a cluster of little huts and people busying themselves with nets. It would've been an unremarkable stop, except as they came to a halt a white man came ambling out onto the boards.

Smail was smiling, like they were supposed to be expecting him. The boat captain was already off the side, tying the boat in place, and he steadied himself as though expecting this encounter. Traitorous scum. Katryzna unzipped her bag on the deck, going for the rifle, but Tasker put a hand on hers. "Wait. He's British government, for Christ's sake."

"And he's not supposed to be here," she snarled back.

Smail strolled closer, hands in his pockets, jacket barely concealing his shoulder holster. He hadn't felt the need to wear that around them before. "Tasker! Delighted you made it back. All of you?"

Henri's footsteps sounded on the steps up from the cabin, and Tasker tilted a low hand to indicate he stay hidden. As Henri discreetly moved back into cover, Tasker put on one of his false smiles. "Surprised to see you here, Charles."

"Indeed? The river does talk, and I thought you'd appreciate a friendly face." He definitely didn't look friendly; the judgement on his face screamed *you were going to cut me out?* "We've a secure ride waiting, back to the hotel. Can I take your bag, Ms Tkacz?"

"You may not," Katryzna said, holding the bag closer. British government, who cared? He'd bleed like anyone else. Rurik hissed from her shoulder, "Yes, you moron, and his blood will be on all of you."

"So?" Katryzna said.

Tasker said, "We're going straight to the airport."

"Without so much as a goodbye?" Smail sounded strangely sure of himself. Up the jetty, the fishermen had cleared out already, and the huts beyond were still, everyone getting the hint and shifting off to shelter. Save two big Africans loitering at the bank, probably with pistols stuffed in their belts. "What did you find out there? Won't you come for a drink and share?"

Tasker followed Katryzna's assessment of the jetty, to the boat captain off the bow and back to his second, on the deck, behind Katryzna. The boatman had a hand behind a barrel, *definitely* hiding a pistol, scared about using it. Tasker said, "How'd you –"

Katryzna didn't care for the explanations – she dropped the bag, holding onto the rifle, and spun to the boatman. He whipped up his pistol and the captain fumbled aside, drawing a pistol of his own. Tasker shouted but she pulled the trigger. The gun clicked empty. She pulled again, same – and the boatman ordered, "Don't move – don't!"

The pigs had emptied their guns at some point? That's where a complacent journey got you, dammit. Had the boatmen been bought before they left Bokema, or on one of the stops? Didn't matter. Katryzna weighed up her rifle, considering simply clubbing the man down.

"I got him!" the captain announced, his pistol aimed at Tasker, who had his hands out to his sides. Up the jetty, the two locals covering them as well. One had a pistol, but the other had a miniature machine gun of some sort. He'd probably kill everyone by accident if he started spraying.

Smail stood proud as the pair moved down past him. "Very well, this is where we are. I can't simply let you leave without a report."

"I'll report on what I find in your guts," Katryzna promised.

"One more, below," the captain told Smail.

It didn't surprise the spy. "Outside, Henri, or we hurt them!"

"I think you hurt them anyway!" Henri shouted from below. "No, thank you." Good on him, Katryzna would have done the same.

"Get him for God's sake." Smail gestured to the boatman covering her. The captain shifted his aim to her as the man moved. "Tasker, didn't I warn you people lose perspective around this woman. Or was it the secrets of Mount Ikiri that inspired this subterfuge?"

"You knew we'd be on this nothing wharf," Tasker said. "You don't already know everything else?"

Smail smiled modestly. The captain shifted uneasily as the boatman reached the cabin steps, both of them super cautious. Neither was quite close enough for Katryzna to jump on, and with this soggy deck she might slip anyway, but they were definitely both dead men. Rurik whispered, "He's willing to talk, you don't –"

"Shut. Up."

The steps creaked as the boatman entered the cabin and warned Henri in French.

"There is something out there, isn't there?" Smail continued, addressing Tasker. "Share freely, and I'll make this painless. Otherwise . . ."

"You want those answers, have SIS run their own investigation," Tasker replied.

Below deck, there was a shout and a crash. The boat swayed, a gun went off – the captain was distracted and Katryzna pounced. Her boot skidded over the slick deck and she cartwheeled over the side as the captain fired up – the bullet going where her chest would've been. She flapped her arms, lost her grip on the rifle, and hit the jetty hard. But didn't stop. She swept her foot as she rolled, kicking the captain's leg from under him. Before he hit the deck, she had her hunting knife out and stuck it in him. Two quick jabs in the neck, before she rolled off, ripping his pistol from limp fingers and firing without aiming, flat on the boards.

Smail ran like a terrified penguin, his two goons covering him with shots peppering the boat. Katryzna clipped the nearest man with a shot to the arm, spiralling him off onto the muddy verge, and the other dived for cover as he let the little machine gun rip. Too rattled to aim properly, his spray went high and messy. Both he and Smail ducked around the huts as Katryzna kept firing until the pistol ran empty. She screamed an animal noise and tossed the useless thing in their direction, then pushed herself up and jumped in the boat, down into cover.

"Tasker!" Smail cried shrilly. "See sense! Finish her and I'll let you walk!"

"Come aboard and we'll talk about it," Tasker shouted back. He was crouched by the low wall himself. Watching the cabin, unsure if it was safe.

Katryzna called, "Henri, are you okay?" By way of answer, Henri poked his head up the steps, keeping quiet. He raised a hand for attention, then slid the boatman's pistol out, over to Katryzna. Quieter, she instructed, "Start the engine. Let them think we're leaving."

Keeping low, Henri moved for the controls. There was movement by the huts, Smail or the other guy rushing to another position. Smail fired a hopeful shot, nowhere near.

"Tasker!" Smail tried again. "There's nowhere to go!"

"There's a whole river, idiot!" Katryzna yelled back, then started to quickly slide across to the back of the boat.

"Who are you doing this for?" Tasker shouted. "Sloppy as hell for SIS!" Smail was quiet. "Someone else got you keeping watch? Duvcorp, since Lopaz lost his edge?"

"Duvcorp are nothing, Tasker," Smail called out. "The smartest thing they did was give up on Ikiri. Lopaz's a loose end no one bothered to trim, that's all."

The boat engine coughed, then spluttered, then settled on a noisy hum. Katryzna peered into the river. Even close to the bank it was as welcoming as a thick rotten soup. Probably full of snapping jaws and tetanus or whatever.

"You're moored, you fools!" Smail reminded them, almost amused. "Tasker. There's no running from this. You have no idea what you're dealing with."

"No? I'm guessing it's the ones that got away," Tasker shouted. "What leverage have they got? Money, threats? How'd they get you onside?"

"Leverage? You saw Ikiri, didn't you? You tell me about their leverage."

Katryzna twisted herself with great care over the side of the boat, to Tasker's alarmed look from the opposite side. He mouthed something that Rurik mimicked: "Be careful!"

"What *did* you see?" Smail pressed, voice giving Katryzna pause.

She smiled and mouthed to Tasker, "He doesn't know."

Tasker considered it as she lowered herself down, then shouted, "You'd cross your own government to figure this out?"

"Please," Smail snorted, oblivious to Katryzna half in the water. "To keep this quiet, and keep *them* happy, I would cross anyone. To figure it out? I'd keep you alive a little longer."

Katryzna let go and sank into chill water. The flow immediately pushed her on. Dark, thick water. She powered down, underwater breast-stroke towards the nearby edge, moving faster than she'd expected. Crap, bad idea. But she drove on for all she was worth – hit the bank and surfaced suppressing a splutter. She snatched at land, tearing up clumps of grass and mud to stop the river's push, then pulled herself up, out, and rolled with a breath of relief. Suddenly expecting gunfire, she jumped into a crouch – but found herself hidden by tall grass.

A way upriver, the two men were still shouting. Perfect.

Katryzna stalked through the grass, drawing the pistol from her belt and flicking it aside to clear the water. She ran in a half-crouch onto a dusty road, where any remaining civilians had already run for cover at the sound of shooting. Smail's irritating voice came clearer: "– powerful enough to resist governments!"

She panned along the closest hut wall and peered out, putting the jetty back in view. The chump with the little machine gun was the next building over, pressed to a wall, almost by the boat. Katryzna stepped out and fired twice, throwing the man into the wall and down to the ground. Smail shut up. She paced quickly the other way, out into the road, as the spy moved away from his own wall, pistol in two hands by his waist. His mouth formed a surprised O, but she fired too fast for him to lift the gun – a bullet right through the face threw him back into a door.

Katryzna ran past him, scanning the area. There was a little drinking stall across the road, where a couple of men were cowering behind barrels and a counter. No one else about. She jogged onto the jetty, shouting, "All clear, boys, time to go!"

Tasker and Henri hesitantly rose from cover. Henri looked impressed, relieved, but Tasker wasn't so happy. "You killed him?"

"Yeah. He tell you who sent him?"

"No."

"We'll figure it out next time they catch up to us." Katryzna beamed. How could he resist that smile? He tried to, unhappy that nonsense conversation had been cut short, as he slowly climbed down from the boat.

"It was never Duvcorp," he said, looking from the dead captain up towards the hut where Smail's legs poked out into the road. "The survivors from Ikiri have a hold over some powerful people. Smail was working for them and he didn't even know *why*."

As Henri jumped down, Katryzna gave him a friendly, appreciative pat, before turning back to Tasker. "It's not just tree-woman who can bend people to her will, is it?"

Tasker nodded agreement, eyes still on Smail. Rurik interpreted, "He's upset you killed the British spy, Katryzna."

"In case I did not notice," she snorted. Tasker frowned, so she moved on: "Let's find his car and get out of here. Henri – I owe you one. Next time we're in town I'll get you a lemonade or something."

He regarded the bodies. Surely, finally, not interested in going on a date now. But he said, "I pray the rest of your journey is safer than this, and Godspeed to you both. Indeed, Ms Tkacz, when you come back, and we have saved the world, I will let you take *me* out."

# 31

Mason dropped heavily into an old armchair that barely took his weight. Zip ran to his side for a hug that he ignored, staring dead at the gang as they entered more slowly. The mill was as dilapidated on the inside as out, a dark open-plan space with a chipped wooden table covered with scrappy paper, dirty dishes piled in a sink and – one simple marvel – a rickety old piano tucked behind a rotten central staircase leading up to, presumably, the bedrooms.

As the others hovered near the entrance, Zip rattled out apologies, saying she'd never leave home again, she was sorry, so sorry. Mason scarcely seemed to listen, staring at Reece. The man seemed intent on killing him with his eyes. Zip hurriedly explained she had followed him to America, then been chased by Vile, captured on the farm, rescued – attacked again! Giza! Then there were Steers on the road, and – wow, Stilt Town! – before the madness and poor Caleb. Poor Caleb. Zip slowed, sniffing. Mason continued watching Reece with nothing less than accusation.

"It's okay now, though, isn't it?" Zip said. "We're back and you can stop Vile, can't you?"

"It's not okay," Mason grunted. He finally looked at her, neck-deep in disappointment, and she shrank under his gaze. "You left the circle of my protection, Zipporah. They will all come, now." He breathed a deep, angry breath. "But perhaps it is time. I am ready." He looked at Reece again. "You have my gratitude for returning her."

"As shown by the joyous reunion," Leigh-Ann whispered. Not really quiet enough.

"You claim you fought Vile yourselves?" he continued, ignoring her.

"That's right," Reece said. "Short, dressed all in black, carried a sword. Looked like he'd crawled out a grave."

Mason considered Zip as she stared, imploring him to believe. "Very well. I shall see the truth of it myself. You may go now. Forget any of this happened." He nodded to the door. Zip flicked the gang a concerned look.

"Yeah," Reece replied slowly. "I don't think so."

Mason paused, with genuine surprise that they were still there. "I said you may go. Why are you . . ." He went quiet. Expecting something to happen? Then back to Zip. "You foolish child, what have you been doing?"

"I . . . I told you," she answered meekly. Her father huffed loudly and kicked up from the seat, back to his full height. Looming – he was a sure loomer. He scanned each of the gang in turn, face folding with aggravation. Leigh-Ann caught Reece's eye, to ask what was going on.

Reece said it for them all: "He's fixing to mess with our minds the same way Zip can. But he can't. Zip's shielding us, ain't she?"

"Not knowingly," Mason said. "Then we do this the old-fashioned way. I suppose it would break her heart for me to harm you. So how much do you want, to go away and speak nothing of this?"

Reece checked quickly with Leigh-Ann and Stomatt – both looked as thrown by the suggestion of monetary reward as he was. "We don't want your *money*. You remember our damn friend was killed?"

"So. You wish to stay and fight?"

"You gotta appreciate you need help. Holing up in here leaving a kid all on her own while you go on murder rampages, you ain't exactly well equipped for this."

Mason stared hard. "Is that so. Well, perhaps you can slow them down. There are spare rooms in the annexe. Until we see if any of you survives, further talk would be wasted breath."

Damn but he had mastered the art of speaking down to people. Could've been an English Lord if not for this ruinous shack of a home. Zip avoided looking at any of them, cowed. Leigh-Ann said, "Can we at least discuss her powers? Seeing as we might need them."

Mason answered, harshly, "This will *not* involve Zipporah."

"No one wants to involve her," Reece said, "but you got to admit –"

"The plan is established," Mason cut in, as if he'd just laid out some masterstroke of strategy. "You may rest. Make yourselves ready."

"It'd make us a hell of a lot readier," Stomatt said, "if you told us what's going on. You all freaks out a lab? Magicians? What is it?"

"There are powers in this world that you cannot understand," Mason rumbled, his hostility simmering back up. "Powers people cannot be *allowed* to understand. I am the shield, I am the sword that keeps this world safe. You will leave us. Wait. Prove yourselves when they come, *then* we can talk."

"When *who* comes, dammit?" Leigh-Ann said.

"The Legion of Ikiri," Mason replied as though it were obvious. "Whoever's left to find us. Now go."

Reece tensed, about ready to smack this guy, arm made of sword or not. Zip quickly shook her head at him and said, "Please. Rest. It's comfortable out there."

Leigh-Ann touched his elbow and quietly added, "Yeah, another minute with Chuckles here and I'm gonna flip." He gave her a sideways look, and she nodded to the side door. Back to Mason. The man looked ready to go to war. Reece raised his hands in submission and turned away. Hell, at least they were close to the answers, even if this brute wasn't talking.

As they made their way out, Mason lowered his gaze to his daughter and studied her. Zip said, "I missed you, Daddy." He stiffened, and it took all Reece's will not to scream at the bastard.

The side door led out to a stone corridor as dimly lit and run-down as the mill, with three doorways off to the left. The first opened onto a bedroom that barely looked liveable, with crates stacked to one side and a single bed lying under a mountain of dust. A small window let in the barest daylight. Reece tossed their bag into Room One and continued on.

"Don't like him?" Leigh-Ann said.

"Not much less than I expected to," Reece said, checking the second bedroom, then continuing to the third door. He stopped before a cluttered office space, a central desk covered with scattered papers, photos and maps plastering one wall and a rack of swords and bludgeoning weapons on another.

At his shoulder, Leigh-Ann gasped, "Holy serial killer mess."

"Grithin times fifty," Reece said. He walked in to scan the photo wall. Some of the same faces he'd seen in Memphis, some new ones. He checked back over a shoulder in case Mason was coming after them. The man must've known they'd snoop – didn't care what they pieced together for themselves?

No. He expected them to die when the trouble caught up to them . . .

"Here." Leigh-Ann pointed to a group shot in the middle of the wall; tons of mean-looking men in combat fatigues, with the sort of guns you could use to suppress armies. Mason was at the centre, the most miserable of a pretty miserable bunch. About half of the faces had been crossed out.

"That's Grithin," Reece pointed. The big bald guy had two eyes, back then. Running his eyes over the others, Reece picked out the shortest of the group, also crossed out, standing apart, with a little ratty face that said he knew he wasn't popular. "From the size, I'd venture that was Vile."

"Right?" Leigh-Ann said. "With the cross suggesting *deceased* again?"

"Guess they were mistaken," Reece said. The photo's background offered no convenient landmarks, just a cracked wall. He studied the other pictures: tons of faces, more than Grithin had collected, along with CCTV shots and other clippings that picked them out around the world. That ratty-faced man didn't feature in any of them. "He's not here. Vile. He wasn't in Grithin's collection, either. But there's more here than he had. Basilisk. Loan. Look, these are younger." He checked the main photo again. "They weren't part of the original crew. Shit . . ."

"They're people that got recruited or figured something out later?" Leigh-Ann voiced his rising concern. "Meaning we hang around and keep asking questions, we get up there too?"

Interrupting that thought, Stomatt said, "What's with the medieval weaponry?"

He was running a hand over the rack of tools. Swords, axes, hammers suited for breaking things. Up-close-and-dirty tools, nicked and grimy from frequent use.

"Along with that armour he's wearing," Leigh-Ann said, "this is only getting weirder."

"Yeah." Reece looked over some of the papers on the desk.

There wasn't much to indicate the group's origins, only where they'd dispersed to after whatever happened. Rap-sheets of dates and locations accompanied some of the names, where Mason had traced the men over the years. Some had past job roles, ex-military and security companies. And even after a quick scan Reece noticed a pattern in the dates. Almost all showed no professional positions in 2009 and randomly dispersed locations afterwards. These men had done something together in 2009, and Mason had spent the eight years since tracing them. Paris, 2014, Makassar, 2016, Santa Marta, 2017. Grithin was seen in Croatia, Russia and Colombia. "Ruin" was shown in news-clippings of violence in Cairo. "Shearjoy" had his name over a list of companies and names: Raystaten, Warlowe, Duvcorp, DGSE, Audrey Flan. The connected companies, men and women had profiles of their own, with addresses. Some names were crossed out.

For it all, nothing jumped out about Louisiana – no sign of Fallon, the Steers or Stilt Town. This was a world apart: a plague that'd spread everywhere but didn't need to hit them. But it had, and it might just as well have been Caleb up on one of those lists. Damn all these people – Reece would be ready when Mason's trouble came.

After his frosty welcome and wall-like conversational prowess, Mason provided hospitality in the form of crusty towels for cold showers and, a little later, a dinner of baked beans in steel bowls. While Reece occasionally tried to engage him, Leigh-Ann tried to reconnect with Zip, smiling at the child and asking if she'd rested and commenting on how *interesting* her home was. Interesting like a broken toilet.

Zip smiled back but had lost her tongue in Mason's presence. Leigh-Ann felt awkward talking near him, too, and it was a wonder to see Stomatt all but silent as he struggled to keep up his defiant leering smile. The place had an aura like a graveyard.

But once Mason finished his meal, he leant back on his bench and finally opened up: "When she was not here, and I could not feel her, I believed Zip dead. One of the others must have blocked me, knowing that we were separated. But I have meditated, carefully, and understand we are easily found, now. Grithin located us. Others must have, too. At least four are on their way."

It silenced the room.

"You, uh," Leigh-Ann ventured, "saying you guys can sense each other?"

Mason's unblinking eyes told her that was surely obvious.

"Like ants?" Stomatt suggested. "They share a hive mind and that, don't they?"

"Okay," Reece moved on, "four *what* are on their way? Because Vile, he wasn't natural – and that ape –"

"Giza," Zip put in.

"Yeah that. Where'd *that* come from?"

"Ikiri," Mason said. "And yes, I admit that those coming are not what I expected. They are not of the Legion's ranks; someone has unleashed them from Ikiri itself. I was a fool to think such a thing could be contained. Shearjoy, at least, should've been watching. Though it's possible he himself unleashed this horror."

"He's another one like you?" Reece said.

"With a dumbass name," Stomatt offered.

"He is one of the Legion, yes," Mason said. "You've seen photos of the others." The gang averted guilty gazes, but he sounded like he'd expected them to study the office. "Zipporah's powers are both a threat and a beacon to them. I kept her hidden, all this time, to face them on my own terms. But when she left . . . she was exposed. Now, they will not stop coming." He looked up as though contemplating what else to share, then decided merely on immediate plans: "Tonight, we will run two watches. Four-hour intervals."

"Fine," Reece said. "We've got guns, bit of ammo. Got any yourself?"

Mason snorted at his apparent ignorance.

"Got something against guns?" Reece said. "We saw your stock. Vile's running around with a sword, you've got that arm of yours – what's with the blades?"

"Bullets are too uncertain," Mason said.

That hung there for a second before Stomatt guffawed. "Typical fucking Brit, you don't *get* guns here, do you?"

Mason's glare silenced him. Given the photos of these soldiers, he definitely got guns. "When I kill one of the Legion, I want to be sure of it. If Vile has truly returned, I will take his head off, close and personal enough to remove any doubt."

Leigh-Ann choked on the comment. "Jesus, pal – there's a kid here."

"She understands," Mason replied coldly. Zip's little face was down-turned as she stirred her beans. Used to this mountain of weirdness. "All you need worry about is slowing them down. I don't care how."

"Best method we seen," Stomatt said, fork pointed down the table, "was when Zip zapped the motherfucker with her mind."

Mason arched an eyebrow, then turned on his daughter. Zip cringed.

Stomatt blundered on, "Can you all do that? What's the deal?"

"No," Mason said, not removing his gaze from Zip. "Ikiri granted heightened senses, powers of distraction, but not . . . that."

That word again. Leigh-Ann said, "What the hell is this Ikiri? How'd she get mixed up in it? Any of you?" That got her a healthy dose of mind-your-own-business from Mason's scowl. With a side order of we're-done-discussing-this silence. She tried to smile it off, and added, "We all think she's real special. Be nice to know exactly why."

Without explaining further, Mason got up and threw his bowl in the already-full sink, then stomped across to the central stairs, with thumps like the steps might break. No goodbye. Leigh-Ann exchanged a *seriously?* look with the boys, and they both mugged. This guy was intense.


If his general demeanour, tone and room of dungeon weapons weren't indicators enough, a night of split-shifts outside the murder-mill gave Leigh-Ann all the confirmation she needed that Mason was a creep-ass of the lowest degree. The cold English night was bad enough, which required a mountain of blankets to fight off, but worse was watching the sinister shadows of the mill with its irregular edges. It could've been haunted, but nothing supernatural could be grimmer than the hulking master of the house dragging his blade-arm about. What kind of psycho replaces a missing hand with an extending knife? And who raises a child here? To that point, how'd Zip turn out so *normal*?

The sun crept up after hours of Leigh-Ann jumping at shadows and generally reassuring herself she was never complaining about her trailer in Cutjaw again. A different impression came in daylight. The mill stood high on its hill, the fields below twinkling with the glitter of wet dawn. The blocks of a city were just visible in the distant haze. She hadn't appreciated where they sat, the evening before. Made England look soft. Safe.

Maybe that's what did it – Zip being exposed to this beautiful nature. This view and that cute village they'd driven through on the way up might've kept her sane.

Mason interrupted Leigh-Ann's thoughts, appearing a foot from her shoulder. "Go in, there's food."

"Jesus!" Leigh-Ann barked. "You can't –" She stopped. He actually *could*, with his size, that face and hands that could crush bricks. She swallowed and went inside, leaving him standing glaring at the hills like they personally offended him. Where she saw soft, he no doubt saw *weak*.

In the kitchen area, Zip was up on a stool stirring a pot, sweet cinnamon filling the room. Leigh-Ann grinned. "Whatever that is, I *love* it."

Zip wrinkled her nose. "It's only porridge."

But it was the best damn breakfast Leigh-Ann ever tasted, coming off a night like that. And it helped that Reece joined them in good spirits, throwing Zip compliments and getting smiles from her. Stomatt was starting to relax, too, getting brave enough to insult Mason's upholstery. When the swordsman was out of earshot. The morning was theirs and they were gonna enjoy it, scarcely tensing again when Mason rejoined them to skulk in a shady nook.

"I got designs on that." Reece pointed at the piano.

"You'll need a hammer and nails," Leigh-Ann said. "It's ready to collapse."

"I'm game." Reece beamed, standing and flexing his fingers. "If Mr Mason approves?"

Mason was nursing his murder-stump with the other hand, like stroking a pet. He grunted wordless assent and Reece bounced over to the piano. He knocked out a few bum notes – the thing worked, but not well. He opened it up and tweaked a few strings – who knew he had that talent – then he sat back and produced something that was, well, not great, passable. Then, after a little warm-up, he dropped into something he'd apparently been planning a while. Heavy chords and a steady descent. Simple, but powerful. He played a few bars and shot a look over his shoulder for approval. Leigh-Ann gave a thumbs up. It was borderline classical. Then he let rip, skipping over faulty notes to throw in improvised riffs, teasing out the tune. Back where he belonged, only sounding darker. Leigh-Ann breathed it in. Music the opposite of light and smooth. Powerful. Damn if it wasn't powerful. Even Mason was listening, absorbed.

Reece sat back, smiling his most honest grin. "How'd you like that?"

"Fresh, my man!" Stomatt answered loudly. "Damn fresh sound."

Zip looked excitedly to her father for approval. Mason dragged a hand over his face as though pulling himself from a daze, and his general disapproval sank back in. He said, "Exactly the sort of distraction we don't need. Can't sense them if your head's elsewhere."

"Can't – what?" Reece could scarcely believe it. "Morale mean nothing to you?"

"Can't *sense* them," Mason snapped, stomping over to the stairs. Angry enough that it was clear it wasn't *their* distraction he was worried about. Gritting his teeth, he shook his head and clambered noisily up. Stomatt caught Leigh-Ann's eye and mouthed, "The fuck's his problem?"

She had an idea that the answer was long and complicated and painful.

# 32

The overnight flight out of Kinshasa was a world apart from the journey in, with Tasker on the phone trying to shore up provisions for once they touched down. All he needed, really, was a car and maybe a hotel, but Caffery kept pressing for answers – what had he seen? How were they justifying the spend out there? What had happened in the forest? What was back in England? Tasker batted off one question after another. Finally, the threat that was bound to come: "We can't keep writing you blank cheques. You'll have to report in in London."

"I don't need your cheques," Tasker replied hotly. "Not now. When I touch down, I'll make my own arrangements."

He turned off his phone and reflected it might be a good thing to stay out of touch. If the leak that had got Parris killed originated with the Ministry, the less he said the better. He still balked at reporting that they'd killed a British spy – with luck, whoever was running Smail would at least temporarily assume he had succeeded in stopping them. Bigger things weighed on his mind, though, such as how grim it felt to be right about this. With the girl back in England, the threat was right on his doorstep. He avoided calling home to keep it from becoming too real.

After landing, Tasker ushered Katryzna through the airport, while looking out for threats. She got distracted by a gift shop, fixing on a postcard of a sketched dog, and he hissed, "Not now."

She batted him off with happy smiles, the gunfight on the jetty having lightened her mood back to increasing irresponsibility. She was used to being chased by the most powerful men in the world, she confided; it was the opportunities she got to defend herself that made it fun. Tasker urged her on, through customs, out to a car rental office, where he had to wait an impossibly long time for someone to process the papers. The news cycled silently on a flat-screen behind the rental counter, something about an earthquake in India. Tasker leant back against the counter and studied Katryzna again. She'd slumped back into a plastic chair, yawning far too broadly.

"Shall we take a day?" Tasker suggested. "Get a hotel room, continue tomorrow."

Katryzna narrowed her eyes. "You scared?"

"Cautious. You got any idea what we might come up against?"

"Ah. Like that?" She pointed a finger over his shoulder. Tasker frowned before looking, as if it might be a trick. She was pointing at the news, though; the story had changed. An aerial shot of a field filled with cabins, surrounded by police and medics. The headline ran: CONFIRMED NINETY-THREE DEAD

IN GRAYSTOWN. It cut to a closer image: investigators mulling over body bags. Lots of body bags.

"What is this?" Tasker said. The young man behind the counter looked up.

"You didn't see? Some religious cult in America, went nuts and killed each other."

A sinking feeling that this personally affected him was confirmed as Tasker found Katryzna's eyebrows raised in agreement. Tasker took out his phone but hesitated. Wait until they were on the road. He hurried the rental guy on. With the keys in hand, he whisked Katryzna out to their car and pulled onto the motorway. Forty-minute drive, soon pulling into country lanes. After ten minutes he found a news broadcast on the radio and got more details of Graystown. Almost a hundred people brutally murdered by *each other*. A handful of roaming criminals who'd been in the area were now unaccounted for. But who'd believe a handful of criminals could pull off this madness?

It had the same bloody hallmarks of Laukstad.

He pulled up in a lay-by canopied by trees, short of their destination by a half mile. Katryzna trotted off to piss, while Tasker turned his phone back on. Multiple missed calls from Caffery and, oddly, Deputy Director Sam Ward. Well, they were here now, he might as well face the music. He returned Ward's call.

"Agent Tasker, you're back in town?"

"They told you?" he replied, imagining Caffery trying to head him off in frustration.

"Yes," Ward said. "About an hour ago, I was asked to look out for you. I wanted to talk anyway –"

"About Graystown? I just saw it on the news."

"Then we're on the same page. They've kept some of the details from the reports, but it's the same, isn't it? Halfway across the world, on a much bigger scale."

"You found a connection between them? Laukstad and Graystown?"

"Not yet, but our American friends were running novisan scans in the area, this time. There was a big surge. But if Duvcorp have scans for Graystown, too –"

"I don't think they're behind it," Tasker said. "They pulled out of the Congo. It was the people they left behind that are the problem. Parris must've been moonlighting on it all this time; I'm guessing his superiors were pressured into dropping it, but he never did himself. The people who stuck at this, who were still killing to protect it, they might have people in Duvcorp but . . . well, they definitely have influence in the government."

Ward was quiet for another moment. "I was afraid you might say that."

"What?" Tasker frowned. Katryzna came bounding back out of the trees, sighing with loud satisfaction. He waved a hand for quiet, and she stuck her tongue out. "Why'd you say that, Deputy Director Ward?"

"I've found – that is, my people have found – three other massacres that fit the same pattern as Laukstad. Following the numbers on Parris's list. There was mass hysteria, unexplained deaths, *savage* murders, all with no discernible connection. A small Canadian town called Danvale, two weeks ago – a village in Argentina a month ago. All bite marks and other wounds seemingly coming from people, but no sign of anyone new in town. These weren't ever flagged by Ministry Support, despite their unexplained nature. I'm worried they've been *purposefully* ignored. And again, the angles all point in the same direction. What did you find in the Congo, Agent Tasker?"

Tasker could've predicted it but it made it no easier to hear. As Solomon suggested, the corruption was spreading. Ikiri was lashing out across the world – with no clear indication how or why, only that the threat originated in that cave and it was getting worse. It'd been paranoia before; now he knew how easily those corpses *could* be people he knew. He said, "If I tell you, I'm pretty sure it'll make you a target. But I'm honing in on some answers. Once I'm done, we can talk. But can you do me a favour, Deputy Director? If anyone comes looking for me, friend or not, throw them off, for now."

Ward hesitated. "I'll do what I can. Agent."

"Thanks." He hung up, and found Katryzna staring expectantly. He said, "There's a chance this is even bigger than we feared."

"Oh, that," Katryzna replied, blandly. "I mean. I hope so?"

Tasker looked up through the trees. Hard to believe beyond this thicket there might be a child that could help them make sense of this. He said, "Let me go first. Try not to do anything rash."

"Only what's necessary," Katryzna replied brightly, enjoying this.

He tried to ignore it, tense enough already. He moved as quietly as possible, off the road through the woods and up a steep bank of grass, with her ambling more casually behind. The track took them onto the road's end, where it expanded onto the plot of a rotten mill, exactly where Solomon's maps said it would be. Two cars outside.

Tasker signalled Katryzna to wait, and moved closer to listen at the oaken front entrance. Piano music came from inside. He crept under one of the high windows and peered in. A group of people – a murky green-haired guy in a fancy suit at the piano, a big man and a woman at a table in similar suits, and an even bigger guy by the wall in a duster. And at the table – there was a young girl, and in the instant of seeing her Tasker knew she was the one. Though she was lighter-skinned than her mother, he saw some of Sara in her. Innocent face focused happily on the music. She was the key. But – shit – the pianist rolled his head to the side and Tasker ducked with alarm. The man from the news report. The fucker they were looking for in America. Graystown, sure enough, was part of this, and the kid was with those responsible.

Crunching gravel announced Katryzna sauntering up with her pistol ready, other hand resting on the hilt of her sheathed knife. He waved for her to stop and whispered, "Back to the car."

"Is the kid there?" she asked, callously loud. Tasker checked the mill for movement, but the music had everyone's full attention.

Tasker said, "There's at least four people in there."

Katryzna shrugged. "Four is nothing."

"We have no idea what they're capable of."

"And what? You want to *ask*?"

"I want to act smart," Tasker insisted. He had flashes of the reckless Clash Club and Smail gunned down. The mess they might make if Katryzna waded in. "We'll lay low, wait for nightfall. Make a move when they're asleep." Katryzna considered it, then continued, past him. He hissed, "You hear me? We're not just walking in there."

"I can look, can't I?" she answered with irritation, then went to the window and looked in. She whispered to her shoulder, "Yes, he already made that clear." She turned back with a heavy frown. Another glance to the window said she wanted to go in right away and confront whatever concerned her. But she shook her head with a sharp Polish word to her conscience, then moved away again, still frowning.

"What is it?" Tasker said.

She raised a finger for quiet, deep in thought, and continued past him. He hurried after her, back into the trees, heading towards the car. Pulling slightly ahead, she muttered to her shoulder.

"It's not the odds, is it?" Tasker asked, drawing up next to her.

She sniffed at that, something beneath her consideration. "No. That kid."

"What about her?"

Katryzna stopped, frown intensifying, unable to quite figure out a puzzle. Her face had been similar after seeing that messed-up cave. "There is something about her . . ."

"That's the idea, after everything."

"Not that. Something . . ." She trailed off. Unable to put it together in her thoughts, much less to say it. She fought it down, at last, and laughed at herself. "Sean. I think I know how you felt now. Around that tree-woman. You think it's the kid's doing?"

Tasker looked from her back to the mill, dread mounting. Hadn't even considered the sort of defences the kid might have. Had she had some impact on him, too, which he hadn't even realised?

"I think she's even messed with Rurik." Katryzna laughed. "He tells me don't hurt them, any of them. I mean, he always says that, but he says they are her people. They should not be hurt either." She scowled at her shoulder, but couldn't keep up the disdain. "I have a similar feeling. I do not trust it."

"Are you up to this?" Tasker asked.

Katryzna locked eyes with him, face steeling serious again. "Am I —"

There was a slap of sound in the branches above and Tasker tensed as they looked up. The leaves rustled, a patter building through the trees, and he relaxed as large raindrops started breaking through. Only rain. Getting heavier, quickly. Might be a good thing, for extra cover; Tasker was starting to feel they were going to need all the help they could get.

# 33

"I knew this place was rainy," Stomatt said, watching through the kitchenette window, "but thought it was supposed to be dreary, pathetic rain?"

Reece watched through another window. The deluge had made the already gloomy mill even darker, with Mason's weak lamps doing little to help. Lightning struck and thunder followed seconds after, dangerously close with them in the only building at the top of this hill. He said, "Often get storms like this up here?"

"Sometimes," Zip replied, standing on a chair to watch too, Leigh-Ann behind her. It was a simple pleasure, and if Mason stayed out of their way meditating upstairs, or whatever, they could enjoy it all night. But Zip yawned broadly, and someone had to be responsible here. Reece said, "How about you turn in, Zip? Leigh can read you a story."

"Leigh can *read*?" Stomatt jumped in quick as the lightning.

"Comes easy to some of us," Leigh-Ann shot back just as quick. But patted Zip's back, rolling with the idea. "Shall we?" The child gave Reece a hug, eyes drooping.

"I'll set us up some cards," Reece told Leigh-Ann as she passed. "Seeing as music's not welcome." She nodded and took the kid up the stairs.

Stomatt pulled himself away from rain-watching to join Reece at the big table, and Reece dealt them in for a game of Cutjaw Slam. Falling into weak banter, tired themselves. Stomatt asked, "You think that bastard's tugging himself off up there?"

Reece winced at the thought, and was about to joke back when a crash made them jerk their heads to the door to the annexe. Rain howled in somewhere – the rear door blown open? Reece shot up, whipped his pistol off the table and moved to the doorway. Stomatt fumbled, catching himself on the bench and cursing loudly. Reece leant into the annexe as wind blew streams of rain through the corridor, the rear door knocking against the wall. Nothing there. He threw a look back – no sounds of movement above. Mason and the others must not have heard it. Stomatt hung back in the mill door, clutching his own pistol in two hands. Reece nodded for him to stay put as he moved into the corridor. Carefully, he passed the first bedroom – no movement there. Not in the next one either. He pushed the outer door closed against the wind and rain and reset the latch. Then he hit the light switch for the office, aiming in.

Nothing there.

He turned back to Stomatt. "Just the damn storm –"

Lightning flashed with a crack of thunder and the lights cut out. Another crash came from back in the mill, the front door swinging open. Stomatt spun back into the room with a shout and Reece ran. Stomatt fired and moved out of sight as a dark shape flashed across the doorway. "Sto!"

The shape flashed again, skirted right past the opening – Reece got off a useless shot before bowling out of the annexe – just in time to see Stomatt thrown back against a wall, yelling as he grabbed his gut and slumped down. Somewhere above, Mason roared and Zip shrieked. Reece shot as the shadowy intruder sprang across the middle of the room, blade flashing to the side, and the bullet hit stairs between them. The attacker slid down past the piano and Reece panned out into the room. Mason jumped onto the stairs, steps cracking under his furious weight. The dark attacker flashed out of cover again. The blade hissed behind the stairs, catching Mason as he came down. The big man fell, snapping the banister in two and booming like an injured beast as he swung his blade-arm out to one side. Reece fell back, towards the wall, to Stomatt's side, as Mason smashed into the floor. The intruder launched out of darkness for the kill. Mason rolled and Reece fired, the big guy looking up as his assassin was thrown back by the shot. Clenching down his pain, Mason jumped upright and swung the blade-arm out to one side, fully extended.

Lightning struck again – a flash illuminating Mason hulking towards the table, the intruder in a half-crouch on the other side of it. Mason heaved the table out the way, but it was too big and caught on the ceiling, tumbling past him. The attacker shot down behind it for cover and Mason grunted with the effort of following. He tripped on the fallen table and the intruder kept going, straight outside as Reece fired another shot, clipping the entrance. Mason kicked through the table with blind rage. The smaller attacker was leading him into the rain. Reece shouted, "Wait!"

But Mason stepped into the trap of the doorway as the mill entrance exploded in. Brick and wood splintered around him, the big man tossed like nothing through the air, into the table. Huge punching arms reached through the shadows towards him, too big to be human, but the massive beast jammed into the doorway – couldn't squeeze in even as it tore chunks of building off around it and flung rainwater across the room. Reece unloaded every bullet he had into the struggling shape of Giza, pacing into the centre of the room. His gun clicked, and the gorilla was still raging violently, roaring and spitting, teeth flashing white in the darkness. Reece dropped his clip and slipped another out of his pocket as Mason groaned weakly up out of the wrecked table.

A smash in the annexe drew Reece's attention again – the door broken open once more. Lightning struck to cast the shadow of a man in the corridor; Vile had circled round to flank them for the kill.


Leigh-Ann just had Zip down when the crash made her sit upright. "Just thunder –"

"They're here," Zip gasped.

The rain was still beating down, lightning struck – no way of knowing what was near or far. But the kid was too sure to be wrong, and Leigh-Ann went for the door. "Wait here. I'll check, okay?"

She started down the stairs, hearing the floor creaking in Mason's room, next storey down. The big guy loomed massive out of his doorway, eyes accusing the very shadows. He fixed on Leigh-Ann, blaming her for disturbing him, before another crash drew their attention back downstairs. The entrance smashed open, definitely the entrance. Movement inside – Stomatt shouting – a gunshot.

"They're here!" Zip came running down the stairs.

Mason reeled on her monstrously and said, "Stay."

"Zip can help, you –" Leigh-Ann started, but he shoved her chest, a simple movement that slammed her into the wall and did for all the wind she had in her.

Zip came running to her side. "Leigh!"

"You will not interfere!" Mason boomed, voice filling the tight space like an explosion as Zip screamed surprise. Then he was away, launching himself down the stairs, into more gunfire below. Leigh-Ann pushed herself up on her hands and knees, impossible a little shove could hurt so bad – she couldn't breathe – gasped – looked over to Zip.

The child had backed right off again, shivering with fear. Leigh-Ann wheezed, trying to say her name at least, held out a weak hand her way. But Zip was terrified, as the crashing continued downstairs. "Zip . . ."

Leigh-Ann keeled forward, coughing, struggling just to inhale. Some tremendous force hit the building, shaking them all, and the noises below got worse. She pushed herself back up, slowly, weakly recovering. Christ. She said, barely audible, "Zip, you can help –"

But Zip only screwed her eyes closed and squeezed her arms tight around herself, dropping into frightened sobs. Damn her fucking father. Leigh-Ann turned from her to the stairs and listed over to them. The moment she reached the top step, Reece shouted, "Stay there, Leigh! Hold back and shoot all hell out of anything that comes up!" He twisted on the spot, near the middle of the room, and shot towards the entrance. Down to the side, Leigh-Ann saw a figure step into the annexe doorway. Vile.

Leigh-Ann took a quick breath and shrieked, "Throw me a gun, Reece!"

But Reece backed off towards the kitchenette, met on two sides with that monster Giza pulling back then pushing again with another hard smash – it'd take down half the building in a second. Vile was staring in, motionless, savouring the challenge ahead.

"Come on you bastard son of a bitch," Reece said, masked in shadow himself but unable to hide the fear in his voice. "You're not getting past me."

Leigh-Ann threw another look back to Zip, saying, "Kid – sweetie –"

But she was shaking her head quickly, balled up against the world. Leigh-Ann could only watch as Vile stepped in and the bricks cracked around Giza. Reece swung the pistol up to fire. The room lit up brilliantly with another flash of light and the walls exploded in.


Katryzna was staring at the gun in her hands, imagining that she'd be killing a fair number of people again and ignoring Rurik's comments that she should care more, when she noticed the big shadow move through the rain. She looked to

Tasker to see if he'd noticed, but he was busy staring into la la land, hung up on his own insecurities. Without a word, Katryzna got out and moved to quickly pick out what had passed them. Too dark, too much water in her face. But there was something – going up the hill towards the mill. As quick as she picked it out, it was gone again, off over a hump in the ground.

Tasker's door slammed behind her and she shouted, "You didn't see that?"

"What?" He had a hand flat over his glasses, for all the good it did against the rain.

"Think it's time to go," she said, rather than bother explaining.

He nodded, grim-faced.

"Whatever happens up there –" Rurik started from Katryzna's shoulder.

She grabbed him in a fist and said, "Do not interfere." She shoved him in a pocket as Tasker gave her a worried look, but he said nothing. Then they started off, under the trees for limited cover. Lightning flashed, thunder right after. Katryzna picked up her pace, water soaking through to the bone. Tasker stalked ahead, gun low as he broke from the trees to race over the grass – another thunder crack. No lightning this time. Another crack. Tasker slowed down, turning Katryzna a look of concern. "Gunshots?"

"Yeah."

They ran together, sliding on the mud and almost falling, until they reached the mill in time for another shot, light flashing through the mill windows, and the great shape of something hunched before them, between the cars. Its torso heaved slow breaths as it perched like an immense gargoyle, its back to them, waiting. There was shouting inside, something happening.

"Piss," Tasker summarised.

"Get the car," Katryzna suggested. He gave her a look, but got it a second later. Whatever was happening, a quick escape was going to trump discretion, now. As Tasker turned, the shadowy monster lurched forward with a familiar animal roar. Something like the terrible sounds they'd heard around Ikiri. How did it get *here*? Tasker froze to watch as a man shot out of the mill entrance and the gorilla flew through the air into the door. Katryzna repeated, *"The car."*

Tasker nodded and retreated back down the slope, half sliding. The man who'd escaped straightened up, ignoring the monster that was trying to smash its way into the building. He strode quickly towards the building annexe, a blade down by his side. Someone new in the equation – an assassin here to thwart them? Katryzna flicked rain off her face and moved after him, little need for caution for all the noise the beast was making. The short man kicked through the annexe door and entered, and she hurried after him, keeping low. Another gunshot inside and the gorilla thing screamed all sorts of anger.

Katryzna slowed on entering the annexe, seeing the little swordsman was taking his time, calmly approaching the connecting door. He wanted to be seen. She crept in behind him, but paused at the sound of the engine. Tasker had moved quicker than she would've credited him. As the swordsman entered the mill, Katryzna checked out the window to see the headlights approaching, bouncing through the rain. He wasn't slowing down.

Oh hell yes – he skidded towards the building. Deliberately, she hoped. And as he got closer, and someone shouted inside, she ran forward. With a tremendous crash, the car slammed into the gorilla from behind and the building shook like it might collapse. The swordsman staggered, and she came out of the corridor with her pistol raised. Surprise!

He sensed it – moved as the gun went off. A fraction too slow, the bullet tore through his cheek and made him twist and reel with a scream that wasn't quite human. He dropped through the shadows with unreal speed, sword flashing again, and Katryzna followed him into the room, firing.

The mill was lit by a single car headlight – the other smashed and buried in rubble. The gorilla was pinned between the crumpled mess of Tasker's car and the wall that had collapsed around it. It was still moving, one arm free and flapping dangerously. The bottom of the wooden stairs towards the room's centre had been caught by flying chunks of wall and shredded; a kitchenette was strewn as though hit by a bomb, and a man was coughing on dust, a pistol in the hand covering his mouth as he pushed himself to his feet. Another man was shaking off debris, the big guy in a now shredded long coat; he flicked an arm to one side, blade sticking out of it. Both guys saw the swordsman come in and reacted at the same time, as Katryzna sidestepped the wrecked stairs to get a better angle.

The guy with the pistol dropped, firing as the swordsman jumped over him, blade missing his face by an inch. Katryzna fired, their bullets slamming into the little ninja and throwing him off course. He crashed into the sink and rolled, somehow able to kick off again, blade out and swinging for a kill-shot.

It connected with a metal clang as the big guy blocked, and the swordsman rolled again, swinging the blade for another stroke. The big guy's weapon, sticking out of his forearm, flashed in quick movements to deflect the dark guy's rapid blows, but the smaller man was driving him back, wearing him down. The gunman kicked clear of the mess around him, and another shot caught the maniac's chest and threw him off – enough of an opening for the big guy to punch the guy's gut. But even as the swordsman folded forward he brought his blade up, clinking off the big guy's weapon and slipping through his defences to hit him with a slice that made him grunt and fall back. Momentarily stunned, the big guy was down and the ninja had an opening, spinning to bring up his sword for a death-stroke.

The perfect distraction for Katryzna, now mere feet away, to fire right into the swordsman's dark-clad face.

The shot threw him into the kitchen cupboards, then down to the floor. He was still for a second – then twitched, sword arm wanting to come up. Katryzna cocked her head to one side. Stepped forward and fired again. Again. Another twitch and she kept firing, each bullet jolting the dark figure, until the slide clunked back on the gun, empty. She stood over him, watching for more movement, half his head spread across the counter. But it was done.

Another gunshot made her flinch the other way, Tasker standing on the chaotic ruin of his car, over the gorilla. The beast twitched under him and he had to fire again. Only two bullets to finish that one.

They met each other's gaze with a shared conclusion: these things did not die the way things should. Tasker was caked in dust, one lens of his glasses cracked, and blood down the side of his face. Better than they could say for the others. Katryzna picked out the big guy, down on one knee, heaving. He watched her with unreasonable hate considering she'd saved his life. He was cut bad; a great gash down from his right shoulder across his chest, having parted a plate of metal that should've protected him. Probably had more wounds she couldn't see. And the guy with the pistol, he was down on his arse, staring at her with a different kind of alarm, breathless.

"Don't, don't!" Rurik started up shouting from somewhere.

Katryzna regarded her gun again. Couldn't simply clear up the stragglers with no bullets, anyway, so she tossed it aside and held out a hand, flashing a smile. "Hello. I'm Katryzna. I would like to meet the child."

The man stared dumbstruck up at her for the briefest, silent second, before the building creaked around them. Rather than settle, the groan got louder, and something massive started splitting. Tasker jumped down from the car and shouted, "It's going to collapse. Where is she?"

"Fucking Christ, who are you people?" a woman cried from high up, a thick Southern American accent. Katryzna spotted the thin Black lady with big hair halfway down the wrecked stairs. A small shape shied behind her. The walls shuddered, the light from the car flickering as broken brick fell around it.

"Throw her down, we've got to go!" Katryzna demanded, holding up a single hand to catch the child.

The man at her feet pushed himself up and backed off, wary of them. Rather than figure it out, he moved for the stairs. "Quick – Leigh – the mill's coming down."

Tasker moved quickly to the other side of the broken stairs, holding his hands up, too. The woman, Leigh, edged down, taking the child by the hand, and helped her into their arms. Tasker hurried her towards the annexe door as the man helped Leigh. Katryzna checked the others: the swordsman practically decapitated, he definitely wasn't going anywhere, and the gorilla a sure broken mess. But the big guy was struggling to his feet. And she spotted another man, down near the entrance rubble, watching her with pale-faced worry.

"Help him!" the pistol guy shouted. "We have to move!"

"Now!" Rurik frantically joined in.

Katryzna rolled her eyes as she rushed to the fallen man's side. He was heavy to lift, and a mess all around his middle. They slipped on his blood as she got under his arm, but she hauled him up, and as the building quaked she limped with him to the doorway. Leigh ran to help, while the pistol guy raced for the big guy. In a slipping, staggering mob, they charged through into the annexe, as the mill creaked its last and the walls crumbled heavily in. Katryzna was thrown forward in a cloud of dust and an avalanche of bodies, tumbling against the walls and down to the floor with the building collapsing behind them.

The ground kept shaking for a moment longer, as people started coughing in the dusty dark. Katryzna shifted on bodies beneath her and twisted to find her face right next to Leigh's. She grinned into wide, frightened eyes. "And who are *you*?"

# 34

Time passed in a blur of necessity with no room for Reece to stop and ask questions. Leigh-Ann found an electric lantern in one of the bedrooms while he and the suited Brit tossed files off the office desk to lay Stomatt on. No room for Mason, so he slunk against a wall. Zip found a kit of medical supplies and ran around in circles, somehow everywhere and not getting in the way at the same time. There was arguing, shouting, as Mason refused to let anyone help him tie off the gashes across his chest and legs with steely determination. Something he had done before, from the looks of it. Reece and the Brit cleaned and bound Stomatt's middle, though the savagery of the wound demanded a hell of a lot more than a bit of gauze.

They spoke quickly as they worked together, Reece saying, "So who are y'all?"

"Agent Sean Tasker, Ministry of Environmental Energy. And you're the gang out of Graystown."

"Gang?" Reece kept the pressure tight as Tasker tied the bandaging. "We ain't whatever they been saying. Didn't get rated in *Two Shoots Magazine* to be called no gang. That bastard back there" – he huffed, the pair of them rotating Stomatt to finish the job – "he's the one got everyone killed. Coming after her."

Tasker glanced to Zip, standing by with Leigh-Ann by the door, then focused on finishing the job. They stepped off from Stomatt, regarding their handiwork. The bleeding was contained. Didn't mean he was gonna make it.

"We gotta get him proper help this time," Leigh-Ann said, hand rubbing Zip's shoulder. The child herself was eyeing the tatty woman with the shaved head. Outside, the rain kept beating down, hammering on the roof.

"I can get an ambulance," Tasker said, adjusting his broken glasses, "discreetly."

Mason tried to move, but his injuries held him in place. Clenching his teeth, he said, "No authorities. No calls."

"Think we want to?" Leigh-Ann said. "Sto's gonna die!"

"They'll bring trouble," Mason growled, eyeballing Tasker, then the woman. "If he's Ministry, he belongs to Shearjoy."

"I belong to no one," Tasker said. He turned to Reece. "We're not part of this – only interested in the child, to help."

Mason released a caustic laugh. "So much as touch Zipporah."

"We'll take better care of her than you," the woman said. Tasker as a government agent, Reece might buy, but she made no sense. Appeared as much a violent shadow as Vile, behind him, with a gun. That massive knife hanging from her belt. She moved with the same callous efficiency as the madman. These two were surely the others Mason warned were coming. And Reece's gun was down by Stomatt's head. Arm's reach away, not something he could subtly ready. Had to at least give talking a chance.

"You're not with them." Reece indicated the faces on the walls. "Then who are you?"

The woman mugged confusion, and pointed out the door. "Katryzna. We met back there?"

Tasker started checking the photos himself. "This is them – the ones who went out to Ikiri?" It made Katryzna look, too, and she suddenly leapt to the pictures, frightening Zip closer to Leigh-Ann.

"This Ikiri again," Reece asked. "About time someone explained exactly what it is. Some place they all went, you're saying? And *they*, meaning not you?"

"Yes it's a place," Tasker said. "It's dangerous, we're not sure exactly how yet. We've been tracking these people –"

"Is he here?" Katryzna interrupted, flitting along the wall like a bird and finding the group photo. "Where is he?"

"Vile's there," Leigh-Ann said. "But they figured him dead."

"Vile?" Katryzna said. "What Vile? Where's *Eyes*?" Mason shifted with recognition, and she spun on him with such tension that his blade-arm came up. Bent and chipped but still a savage hunk of metal. She had her knife out, unafraid. "You know what happened to him?"

Mason regarded her flatly. "How do you know Eyes?"

"How the hell do you think?" Katryzna spat, inching towards him.

"Oh." Mason lowered his blade. "It's *you*." He spoke with disbelief and disgust. "His . . . friend?"

"Share it with the rest of the room?" Leigh-Ann said.

"Legion or not," Mason said, "if she was close to Eyes, she's a killer. He was our civilian security expert. The deadliest man on the team. Why are you here?"

"To do right by him" – Katryzna pointed her knife to Zip – "by taking that child."

Reece flashed his hand out and whipped the pistol off the table. Katryzna's wide-eyed surprise turned to delight at seeing the gun aimed her way. He said, "Say that again. Slower."

"All right, hero," Katryzna said, rolling her shoulder as though she might jump him anyway, knife against a gun. "I am here for her. To make sense of what killed my friend."

Reece stepped back, towards Zip and Leigh – this woman might've saved them in there, but Mason was right to be worried.

"Stop, stop." Tasker held up a hand. "Can we talk before we gut each other? You two are clearly too young to be connected to Ikiri." He tapped the wall of photos next to him, then looked at Mason. "Their *Legion*? You've got mixed up in something you shouldn't have? She's not your kid, is she?"

"Might as well be," Leigh-Ann said. "God knows she's got no one else rooting for her in this international murder cult. But no – we just found her in need in help."

"We're not part of this either," Tasker insisted. "Katryzna, please lower the knife. Listen – you lived through Graystown, you've seen what's at stake – but she holds answers. You're special, aren't you honey?"

"Don't," Mason warned.

"You ain't having her," Leigh-Ann said. "Wanna strap her to a table with needles or what? Fuck off."

"No, we will take her to Ikiri," Katryzna replied factually. "In the Congo."

"The Congo? *Africa*? You out of your minds? Reece –"

"Bear with us," Tasker said, before she could appeal to flee. "What happened in Graystown, that wasn't the first time. There's been a half-dozen similar cases, at least – entire villages, towns driven mad, killing each other for no reason. And it's coming out of a power they uncovered. No one needs to take anyone anywhere quite yet – we just have it on some authority that she's the key."

"No," Reece said quickly, "you're wrong. It was Vile, in there, that did it. Corrupted people as he went. And he's dead now. It's over. Right, Zip?"

Zip choked on an answer. She collected herself and whispered, "Maybe?"

Reece lowered his gun to his hip, still ready. He asked Mason, "What do you say? You believe it was Vile now? Does this end with him?"

Mason sneered. "Not even close. See for yourselves how many more of the Legion remain. But they aren't driving towns mad – yes, there is power in Ikiri, but not like that. Not for *us* and definitely not for Vile. I killed him myself – he never even made it to Ikiri."

"But that *was* him?" Reece pushed, and Mason didn't deny it.

Tasker frowned. "He was the traitor? Who hurt those Congolese villagers and escaped? Killed two of your men?"

Mason almost looked impressed, but covered it quickly. "He was a liability. He almost escaped us, but we punished him."

"So this half-dead freak," Reece spit-balled, "made it to this place – Ikiri – after all. Came back to get revenge on your daughter? Maybe picked up powers you didn't appreciate."

"A man could not do that," Mason rumbled. "Not alone. And he was *not* in control. What you fought in there, that was nothing like the powers of the Legion. An automaton at best; monsters sent out of Ikiri. And *I* will find whoever's responsible. These are exactly the abuses I work to prevent."

"Christ, that's all this is to you, ain't it?" Leigh-Ann said. "Bunch of boys got hold of some power they don't want anyone else to have. Thinking you know best and ain't no one else can get a handle on it? That's why you've kept Zip so repressed? In case she could do shit like that with her mind?"

"Leave Zipporah out of this."

"No, I'd say it's time we brought her right in" – Leigh-Ann got hotter – "seeing as she could've helped us back there!" She turned this to Tasker and Katryzna. "You know she's special? What she can do?"

Tasker started to reply, but Mason boomed over him, "No! She is *not* to touch Ikiri."

In the quiet left by his outburst, Katryzna cleared her throat. "Well. *Sara* claims this girl is the only one that can end Ikiri's corruption. And she lives in a tree out there – she should know. Sounds to me like this handless oaf is scared of the kid."

Without entirely knowing what all that meant, Reece flashed on an idea. "Could Zip take away your power? Nullify it, the same way she protected us from going nuts like the rest of Stilt Town? That scares you?"

"She could cause untold destruction," Mason snarled.

"Or she could *stop* it. That's why not everyone was losing it in Graystown, isn't it? It's how we resisted Vile while other folks all fell apart. She can protect against this here shit, she just doesn't know how because you never let her!"

Zip peeled away from Leigh-Ann's thigh with some similar realisations creeping in. She asked, hoarsely: "Could I have helped? In Stilt Town? Or Villa Madero? Svet, Danvale, Igota, Laukstad?"

Tasker startled. "You know everywhere it's struck?"

"I was there," Zip answered, emotionally. "I *was* there." To Leigh-Ann: "It *wasn't* a dream. I could've done *something*!"

"Not safely," Mason said, his own voice cracking slightly, finally accepting he might have done wrong by her. "Not safely. To use your powers at all would signal them. To effect *that* kind of change, you'd have to be –" He swallowed. "Have to use Ikiri itself. And if you touched that place, there's no telling the damage." He lowered his gaze. "I had to take her away."

"Away?" Reece frowned. "She's *from* there?"

Mason went quiet, deciding he'd said too much.

"You're saying the place itself is capable of this power," Tasker processed this. "That's where we're coming from. She can stop it if she's there. Because that's where she started out?" He paused. "How old is she? You had a year before Solomon came. Was she born there, is that why . . . ? Is she *Sara's* child? My God." Tasker turned to Reece, to share his rising shock. "They left her mother there. In the forest. Trapped by Ikiri. She's *still* there."

"And Eyes?" Katryzna said. "What did you do to him? Was he protecting Sara from you?"

"Absolutely not," Mason fired back, taking this one personally. "We were working together. Doing what we had to. It was the *boy* that was the problem. Her *twin*."

That shook the room quiet, and the rain itself pattered to a stop outside. Mason took a breath, and continued, "Yes, they were Sara's, born of Ikiri. We stayed to stop the others from getting out – or returning. The children's power was immediately apparent. They had to be separated – from each other and from Ikiri. Eyes took the boy, I took the girl. But he made a mistake. He hesitated. Even at that young age, the boy resisted. I wasn't there but I sensed it all. Eyes was wounded, mortally. Near the mouth of Ikiri. Sara tried to drag him in, as if that would help. He died and she was damned. But the threat was contained."

"You contained the threat," Leigh-Ann said, weakly, "of two newborn kids? You're saying you people *murdered* –"

"They were more than children!" Mason cut in.

"They weren't even that!" Reece said. "You're talking about *babies*!"

"I have a brother?" A tiny whimper came from Zip. She was clutching closer to Leigh-Ann, more scared of her father now than ever. With good reason.

"No," Mason replied without apology. "You do not. It was necessary – the boy had power *far* beyond ours. He was capable of –"

"Destroying whole towns?" Tasker suggested. Simple as that. He shook his head, accepting a reluctant truth. "You never contained the threat. You're afraid of what she's capable of but it's already happening. The boy survived. *He* is in there – he's what corrupted Ikiri. These people going mad, this man and his monster coming after the child – they're coming from him, aren't they?"

"Impossible," Mason said. "I would have sensed his presence."

"You sure about that? You hid Zip and her powers, you think he couldn't have done the same? All these years, preparing for something."

"Waiting for his sister to come out of hiding first?" Reece suggested.

Mason's face was stone frozen. Something he'd never dared consider, but from the reaction, something that was very possibly true.

"God damn," Leigh-Ann whispered. "You're the worst father ever."

"So you're saying there's another one like her" – Katryzna pointed at Zip, working this through – "back there? We should have rolled a grenade in there."

"No!" Zip cried, pulling away from them. "He's my brother!"

"Cher –" Reece raised an impotent hand, but she wasn't running. She backed into the wall and screwed her eyes closed. Focusing, hard.

"Zipporah, don't –" Mason began, but Leigh-Ann snapped: "You don't tell her what to do no more!"

"It's true!" Zip flustered, finding it somewhere in her mind. "He is out there! I know it! He was in Svet – Madero – Igota! He didn't want me to know – did it while I was sleeping because –" She bit it down, shaking all over. "He's angry. He's really angry and he wants to hurt people. Everyone."

"We can stop this, can't we?" Tasker demanded.

"I'm happy to drag her back to that cave and make this boy pay," Katryzna said.

It took Mason a moment, staring grimly at his daughter, but he slowly shook his head. "No. If the boy survives, you won't be able to stop him. Don't you see? If he is truly corrupting people, it's because he knows he can find Zipporah. Vile and that monster, they're nothing against what may still come. To say nothing of what the Legion will do to stop you."

Zip regarded him with fearful pleading, willing it not to be true.

"Don't pay him no mind," Reece assured her. "Look at me, Zip. Caleb died for this, Sto's in no good shape either – that's never being for nothing. We're here for you. We'll do whatever it takes, find a way. Tap into those gifts of yours."

"She can't –" Mason started.

"I *can*," Zip snapped, then screwed her eyes closed again. "I can send thoughts to him – I can connect – we don't need to go anywhere. Daddy, I can do what you do, I can –" Zip gasped, suddenly, opening her eyes. "He knows. He knows I know – he knows I –" She winced, gritted her teeth and suddenly looked terrified. "No – oh no –"

"Easy, Zip –" Leigh-Ann started, but froze. "You hear that?"

Reece listened himself. Distant, but unmistakably a scream.

## 35

Reece ran out onto the drive, gun up and searching the dark. The rain had stopped, the gravel and nearby trees left glistening. All silent for a second, before another shout came, off to the left, past the trees. Reece threw a look back, finding the others hurrying out after him, Leigh-Ann with her hands on Zip, the child full of guilty fear. She'd triggered something, searching her mind for her brother?

"It's the village," Leigh-Ann said. "Down the road. How many people live there?"

"No," Zip said, breaking away across the drive. "No, not again!"

More screams came, closer. A sound of something big smashing.

"The evil is upon us," Mason rumbled, leaning up against the doorframe by Tasker and Katryzna. The British agent looked particularly pale at the thought – disbelieving the madness had caught up to them here. "She *brought* this. We must leave."

"No!" Zip reeled on him, fists balled at her sides. "Not this time!" She screwed her eyes closed again, fighting to focus her energy. She let out a pained sound.

"Zipporah!" Mason shouted, straightening up to his full height. "Can't you see you've done enough? *You* are the threat here –"

"I can stop it!" Zip cried.

"You're not to!" Mason roared, making Tasker and Katryzna step away from him. Zip's eyes shot open, old fear coming in. "That power is *never* to be touched."

Except this guy didn't know, did he? Thought Vile was dead, and that the boy was dead, and spent all Zip's life keeping her in the dark. Now they had more trouble coming, and she might be the only one of them with some clue towards fixing it. Reece said, "What I say, Zip? Don't listen to him. You better off without a father like that. You think you can do something? I wanna see you try."

The screams were rising, down the hill, more people joining in. Another crash. Still uncertain, Zip checked one face after another. Leigh-Ann put on an encouraging smile, using all her willpower not to freak out, and said, "Try, Zip."

"She's a weapon, you morons," Mason growled. "A bomb waiting to explode."

"Respectfully, sir" – Reece stood square to him with the pistol down at his side – "I disagree."

New screams echoed up the hill. Louder, nearer than before. Katryzna jumped onto the balls of her feet. Not frightened but readying herself. Grinning. "Do something fast if you're going to, or I'm taking over."

"She's already done too much," Mason said. "If she tries *anything* else, I will cut all of you down." His metal murder-stump whirred an unhealthy sound and the blade extended, just a tiny bit longer. "Zipporah, come here." He absolutely would try and attack four people carrying guns and knives. Given Vile's efforts, he might even succeed. Reece flexed his fingers on the pistol regardless. Surely he could get a bullet in this maniac before he cleared the distance.

Tasker slid a wary foot back, too, hand hovering towards his holster. He gave one lame attempt at final diplomacy: "Gentlemen . . ."

Zip stared dead at her dad, the strength of the four of them there bolstering her. She took a deep breath and said, "I'm going to stop him." She screwed her eyes closed again, and Mason rumbled an animal growl. He sprang forward.

Katryzna was suddenly on him, knife at his neck, her other hand slamming his blade-arm back into the wall so hard the stone cracked. He moved the other arm up fast in his stumble, but she deflected the punch with her elbow as she dug the knife in. Mason froze at the cut, blood cresting over the blade. More than a head shorter than him, she had the big guy pinned.

"You've done enough," she told him, with soft menace. "And you'd be dead already if not for the *howling* whine of my conscience." She cringed at her shoulder. "You want to help, tell the kid to look away!"

Zip wasn't looking, though, eyes closed, keening slightly as she shook. The screams down the hill were coming. Not people attacked or afraid, but the mad, murderous sounds of feral beasts, out for blood.

"Reece," Leigh-Ann whispered. "Think we oughta move –"

"Hold on," he hissed back, seeing Zip straining. Doing the Lord knows what but *something*, and something her hard-ass dad didn't approve of, that had to be good. The thump of feet approached up the road, a good number of people charging, together.

Tasker suggested, "Let's get to a car –"

He stopped as the first silhouettes ran up out of the dark. Katryzna dropped away from Mason, turning to face them. Twenty metres down – three, four, more people, eyes madly wide, mouths open in attack. Leigh-Ann and Reece spun away, taking quick steps back – and Zip exhaled loudly, falling down. Reece dropped into a quick crouch to catch her. Her eyes flitted, breath shook, and the gnashing, pattering charge of the people staggered into an uneven stumble, aggressive shrieks turning to quivering gasps of confusion.

The approaching people stopped not ten metres off from the mill, arms out to steady themselves, slung into deep, silent confusion. Their mouths moved wordlessly – slowly regaining their senses. The world beyond was quiet again.

"Holy hell," Leigh-Ann whispered.

Zip blinked up at Reece. A faint smile appeared on her face. "I did it?"

"Looks like." Reece grinned. He helped her up, as one of the people asked what was going on, terrified. They looked completely lost, exchanging frightened looks, worrying over the odd collection of people before them.

Tasker moved carefully past the others, giving Zip only a brief, questioning look, before raising an authoritative hand, "Stay calm. We think there's been fumes released from the ground. You're alright now? You know where you are?" He was quick. Good. As the people checked themselves and shook their heads, he went on. "You're experiencing shock. Don't worry, I'm with the government."

"What happened *there*?" One of them noticed the wrecked mill.

A new shout came from further off in the dark. More confusion – something similar to that written on these people's faces. Tasker directed them back towards the road. "Looks like it took the whole village, huh? Let's see what's going on."

They uncertainly followed his calm direction, and Tasker led them away. He threw a look back to the others saying figure this out, follow on, and moved down the road. Leigh-Ann uttered, "She did it. Stopped them dead in their tracks just like that. Didn't she?"

"Zip," Katryzna said, suddenly at their side. Her grin had spread in mad awe. "That was . . . *wild*. I would like to formally invite you to the Congo." Zip looked up uncertainly at the woman who would surely fit *wild* better than her, and Katryzna went right on, particularly focusing on Leigh-Ann: "You can come, too? We can have a whole party."

"Fools," Mason croaked, pushing off from the wall. He stared at Zip with new malice, like she'd utterly betrayed him. By peacefully damn resolving whatever hell had been about to descend on them. Even as the sounds down the hill quietened, Tasker swiftly getting ahead of it, Mason rumbled, "You'll all die."

Katryzna flipped back to an angry shout: "Last warning, handless – not another word like that about my friends!"

"If you're so sure of the danger," Reece said, coming in past Katryzna, "then join us. Do something right with your damn life, if you care one iota for Zip. Give her the best damn chance she can get."

Mason glared vehemently. Too proud to so much as consider it. He said, "You'll bring this world to ash. Her responsibility is yours now."

"You cold motherfu –" Leigh-Ann started.

Reece put a hand on her chest, holding her back. "Suits me just fine. She's a Cutjaw Kid now, and we take care of our own."

# EPILOGUE

Blood and shattered glass mingled with the rivulets of rain as people darted about trying to help one another. A cloud of general confusion hung over the village – distraught, injured people sat on low walls or helped one another clear away debris. Windows had been smashed, cars dented, pots and pans scattered across the road. Two people were seriously injured, another dead. Cuts and bruises all round, at the least. Tasker assured everyone this was a natural anomaly – trapped gases driving people from their senses, that old Ministry staple. They didn't all believe it, but what other choice was there?

As he surveyed the scene, he tried to cling onto the relief that a worse disaster had been averted. But this was everything he had feared; the horror of Laukstad on British soil. If it could take a whole village then what next? Cities? The country? Rebecca's safety was the very tip of it. Tasker held that in, though. He had the means, and the allies, to stop this spreading. He watched the criminal Reece supporting an old lady as she crossed the road, whispering encouragingly. The big-haired Leigh-Ann was with Zip, handing out plasters, and an ambulance was on its way to see to their other friend. With a little respite, at last, Tasker returned to the car where Katryzna was leaning, watching like it was a show. She said, "Will your Ministry come through with memory wipes or something?"

"No need," Tasker said. "Give it a few days and no one's going to seriously question the cause. But it's something I can really take to the Ministry now." He took out his phone, but weighed it in his hand. What was it Mason had said? *If he's Ministry, he belongs to Shearjoy.* Fully aware the MEE was at least partly compromised.

"Worried you'll get in trouble for this mess?" Katryzna asked.

"Worried I don't know how big this mess is. I haven't known who to trust for a while."

"That's *easy*," she grinned, pushing off from the car. She patted his cheek. "You trust me. No one else. Always worked for me."

He couldn't help but smile back. "And you're gonna get us safe passage to Ikiri?"

"I can." She shrugged. "I've got my ways. And I already convinced the Americans to come – they seem like fun. Want me to get us a private plane?"

He didn't doubt she could. It would likely involve people getting hurt and wouldn't keep them hidden. Her conscience apparently took the same view, as she irritably said, to the side, "It would be for a greater good! I cannot win with you!" She rolled her eyes back to Tasker. "Rurik might not get it, but you should, Sean; I can do whatever is necessary."

"Yeah." Tasker smiled, believing that, but equally happy he still had that invisible voice in her head to help him focus her dangerous potential. "Leave the plane to me." He'd call Ward. There was no keeping her away from the mess here, after all; they could talk in person and avoid a trail. Book on a few flights, straight from the airport to a private boat, and they'd be back in Ikiri before anyone knew it. Thwart the machinations of this wicked spirit living there, use Sara's help to identify and clear up whatever members of Mason's "Legion" remained. Save the world, as Henri had so blithely put it.

As Tasker pictured the end game, his phone buzzed. No caller ID. He answered.

"Agent Tasker," a man said, voice chocolate smooth with a nondescript accent. "Is the Headhunter there?"

Tasker said nothing for a moment, meeting Katryzna's eye again. As she sensed trouble, her hand hovered over her knife, like she could stab someone down the phone. Tasker finally replied, slowly, "Excuse me?"

"You know him as Mason, I suppose? He is alive, isn't he? And his loving daughter?"

"Who is this?"

"A friend, if you want one. Or an enemy, if you choose that path. Either way, this is a courtesy call, Agent Tasker, to let you know I'll be seeing you soon." He could practically hear the man smiling down the phone. "Oh, and one other thing. If you happen to kill the child before I get there? Then I'll let your daughter live."

Tasker went silent, his heart dropping through his stomach.

"Think about it," the man said brightly. "And do tell everyone Shearjoy says hi."

# GIVEN TO DARKNESS

# 1

"Hell you think's up with him?" Leigh-Ann asked, distractedly, as she guided an old man towards a little cottage.

Reece Coburn, walking the other side of her, followed her gaze to Agent Sean Tasker. Evening was dragging into night, and they'd all come out of their battle at the mill worse for wear; Reece and Leigh-Ann's suits were torn ragged and Reece could imagine her complaining about the dirt in her curly hair for days. Tasker's suit was similarly thick with wet dust and one lens of his glasses was cracked, but he'd taken charge after the fight like it came naturally. Told the villagers a gas leak had made them all lose their minds for a minute. Now this quaint cluster of English cottages had glass all over the village street and doors broken off their hinges, and people were bleeding and crying, but things were under control as Tasker marched about making important calls. Exactly what form of government his Ministry of Environmental Energy represented, Reece didn't know, but since the spook had swept into their lives trying to put down the same monsters that'd been hounding Reece's crewe, he chose to trust him for the second.

"Looks like he's handling things to me," Reece told Leigh-Ann.

"That a good thing?" she replied. "Him being with the Feds and having that feral woman for company and all? Maybe we need to bounce, Reece."

Katryzna, Tasker's knife-wielding Eastern European companion, stood near him, with her arms folded. Her khakis and once-pale shirt were filthy from the confrontation in the mill – where she'd swept in and saved all their lives, moving like a woman built for killing. She'd shot dead the unstoppable swordsman, Vile, and even helped drag Stomatt from the collapsing building. Where Leigh-Ann saw a liability, Reece figured Katryzna's presence proved Tasker could work with an honest bunch of outlaws like them. He said, "We ain't bouncing with Stomatt needing help and no idea where to go next."

"And where in America did you say you young folk are from?" The little voice of the old man interrupted their exchange. Reece and Leigh-Ann turned as one to find that the small guy with beady eyes, wearing an excessively loose biege shirt, had sat down on the wall. He was one of many locals they were trying to shift back into their homes, so they could return to Max Stomatt, left injured in what remained of the mill.

"Why you sat down when we're trying to get y'all back indoors?" Leigh-Ann said, not bothered he'd been listening. The villagers had their own problems, having momentarily lost their minds and tried to kill each other, making them unlikely to care if these two helpful Americans had been on the news for crimes in Louisiana. Which was as well, because they definitely didn't fit young forBlack, lithe and pretty under her huge mess of curly hair – as far local as a girl could look around here.

"Give me a break," the old man said, "reach my age and see how far your ankles take *you*."

"We're from the finest plot of land west of the Mississippi," Reece answered his question. "Cutjaw, a town not much bigger than your own. And when we got a crisis like this, you know what we do? Them that can help, help, and them that can't help get on out the way." He said this with a pointed look to Leigh-Ann, driving home exactly why they weren't running yet.

The old boy nodded like that was perfectly reasonable. "And what brings you here?"

Reece gave him a grin, holding off on admitting the truth: not like they could admit to having smuggled themselves across the ocean to return a kidnapped girl to her father, on the run from a swordsman and a gorilla who moved too fast to shoot.

"Helping *you*, if that ain't clear," Leigh-Ann answered. "Y'all had quite a night."

"Strangest of my life." The man's little eyes surveyed the carnage.

"Here's hoping."

"I wasn't myself," he continued. "Wasn't thinking straight. Angry like I've never been." He locked eyes with Reece. "I don't believe those terrible things I thought. I'm a good man; always tried my best."

"All any of us can do," Reece said. "You heard Agent Tasker, right? It was some kind of gas high – wasn't *you*. Not any of you. Like being drugged up or half-asleep."

"Hell," Leigh-Ann said, "anything can happen when you're half-asleep. We got sleep doctors for that, out in Calcasieu."

The man looked confused, which was a good thing. They couldn't have him dwelling on the grim reality. At least one of his neighbours had died here.

A big engine approached and blue lights flashed over the village. Tasker had moved further away, to show an ambulance where to go. As Leigh-Ann led the old man on, Reece waited for the ambulance to pull up next to him. The driver called in a Scottish accent, "You Coburn?" He was big with a wiry red beard, like a pirate in uniform. He had a younger, sharp-nosed skinny guy in the passenger seat, hunched over a phone like a bored teenager. "You've got a friend needs help?"

Reece pointed. "He's up a ways. I'll hop in and show you. You good, Leigh?"

Leigh-Ann looked up, from him back over to Tasker and Katryzna, then back to their car – where Zipporah was just visible in the dark, politely waiting. That brave little kid, seven years old with unnatural powers and unnatural people wanting her dead, was watching through the window, keeping herself out of the way. They'd only wanted to bring her home safely.

A lot of people had died along the way, and her home hadn't proved safe at all – not least because her father was a psycho. Now the mill was gone and her father had run off after threatening them, leaving them little option left but to see this through to whatever end it brought. Vile and his gorilla were dead, but the force behind them wasn't. Reece and Leigh-Ann were going to need all the help they could get to figure it out before it caught up to them again.

They had to trust in Tasker and his killer colleague. Reece assured Leigh-Ann, "You'll be fine here with them. I'll be back quick as I can."


"Where are you?" Agent Sean Tasker asked into the phone. "Why weren't you answering?"

"Home," Helen Tasker replied. "We've just started watching an animation about Vikings. What's wrong?"

Tasker ran a hand through his hair. They were okay. Home, safe. His mounting panic crashed against the sound of his wife's voice, but the sick feeling wasn't gone. He wasn't sure how much time had passed since he'd received the call threatening his family; it couldn't have been more than 20 minutes, but it felt painfully long. That slick, arrogant voice had told him to kill the child Zipporah or his daughter would die. He could practically hear the smile in Shearjoy's threat, when the man had said he'd see them all soon. Tasker had wanted to shout, punch something, anything to rail against the bastard. Helen's current safety didn't remove the threat, nor that feeling.

"Sean?" Helen said, when he hadn't answered.

"Yeah, it's nothing," Tasker replied, on automatic. "Was just calling out of . . . I was just calling."

"I see," Helen said. She wouldn't ask more, knowing the nature of his job. She was unflappable; he could tell her to get the gun from the safe, board up the doors and brace for impact, and she would do it without question. But that could alert Shearjoy. Who knew how the man operated? Tasker worked for the Ministry of Environmental Energy – his family's identity were protected, likewise his phone number, yet Shearjoy had got that information. He had powerful connections, Tasker knew that already. He might have more unnatural powers, too; others involved in this mess could move fast, heal quickly, even use psychic gifts. He gave a quick glance to Zipporah, a silhouette sitting quietly in the car. Not knowing exactly how he might be monitored, Tasker had to make it seem as though he was at least considering Shearjoy's offer. He needed time.

"I've had a tough week," Tasker said. "It's that tension seeping through, that's all."

"Mm." Helen was unconvinced, but didn't press. What else could he tell her anyway? That an ex-mercenary called Shearjoy, murderously intent on keeping his past secret, might want them dead if he didn't commit murder himself?

"I'm . . ." Tasker looked back past the broken glass and disorientated locals, elderly folk hovering outside cottages. "I'm actually in England. Outside Ordshaw."

"Ordshaw?" Helen exclaimed, and her surprised delight quickly shifted. "Are you coming home?"

He hesitated long enough for her to draw her own conclusion.

"Just remember you promised to be back for Rebecca's play."

"I remember," Tasker lied. How long since they had last spoken? A week or two, when he called from the hotel before he headed up the Congo River to Ikiri. When was the play? Would they even survive long enough for it to go ahead? He missed what Helen said next, and asked, "What's that?"

"Your partner? How is she working out for you?" Helen asked.

"Good," Tasker said, picking out Katryzna down the road. The bloodstained assassin had wandered away and was running a hand over her shaved head as she tried to engage the slender American with big hair, Leigh-Ann. She was making Leigh-Ann uncomfortable, with her manic smile and that big hunting knife hanging off her hip. The American didn't know the half of it: Katryzna was violently erratic and frequently argued with her imaginary conscience, Rurik. She was the most unstable person Tasker had ever worked with. But she had joined forces with him, trekking into the Congo and fearlessly facing down killers, to honour a friend who had disappeared out there. Tasker told Helen, "Her heart's in the right place."

"That's loaded praise, Sean. Listen, do you want me to get Rebecca, or . . ." That *or* carried weight. *Or not let her know he was this close and couldn't visit.*

"Not right now, I think," he said, quietly. What were his options? There'd already been leaks from the Ministry about this case, so it was a risk to send agents to keep an eye on the house. If he tried to go there himself, to get them clear, the Legion – Shearjoy's men – might see him coming. They had his phone number, so he had to assume they had some idea where he was.

Yet however dangerous they were, there was a bigger picture to deal with. There was a threat in the Congo, that place Ikiri, which stretched beyond his current understanding. Just an hour ago, the people in this English village had been ready to tear each other apart – the same way villagers in the African forest had come clawing for him at night. The same way the people of Laukstad, a Norwegian fishing village, had murdered each other a few weeks back He had seen horrors there to last a lifetime, not least a dead child in the snow. Throats torn out with human teeth. The villagers right here would've done the same, if Zipporah hadn't intervened. With her mind alone, she had stopped it.

Even with his family threatened, Tasker's instincts had kept him tackling what had happened here. Between his unanswered calls home, he had called the Ordshaw MEE's Deputy Director, Sam Ward, with instructions to give this village the standard Ministry treatment: have an agent cement the gas leak narrative, let the local authorities deal with the rest. Now, Tasker needed to search the mill, or what was left of it. Zipporah's father, Mason, had been researching Shearjoy and the others like him – the Legion. His work might tip

Tasker off as to exactly how far their influence stretched and how to stop them.

"Sean?" Helen's voice came in again, and again he hadn't heard what she was saying. "Rebecca is itching to see these Vikings."

"Yes, that's good." Tasker smiled despite everything. "Give her a kiss from me. I love you both so much."

Helen's pause said that sounded more serious than he intended. "Come home as soon as you can."

With that, she was gone, and Tasker wondered if he should race right home after all. Put his family first and leave Zip in the care of an assassin and two thieves – he glanced to Leigh-Ann, trying to help an elderly lady right a large plant pot, with Katryzna dogging her heels. Once again, he picked out Zip in a car window, up the road, face just about visible in the shadow. That small girl might be the only thing stopping Ikiri's madness. There was no question that Tasker could risk her life for the sake of his daughter's. Whatever Shearjoy threatened, he *couldn't* hurt Zip.

Zip noticed him staring and waved, happily. But her hand hung in the air and her expression darkened. She knew something was wrong. Of course she did; on top of everything else, the child had some ability to read minds.

Tasker took a step towards her, but a car pulled up in front of him. Deputy Director Sam Ward in her old Honda Civic, her face bright and alert and ready to get stuck in. A small beacon of hope. Where the rest of the Ministry had proved cautious about Tasker's investigation, Sam Ward had thrown herself into resolving this mess, under the radar, appreciating his concerns about their superiors.

Tasker looked up the road after the ambulance, then back towards Zip, the child still watching him. Piss, the fact he was even considering Shearjoy's threats had thrown his focus. Whatever else they did, he needed to get all of them moving. He went to the Honda's passenger side, telling Ward, "Can you continue up the road, ma'am? To the mill."

"How bad is it?" Ward asked as he got in. She was young for a director, barely thirty, if that, though her sharp suit, neat bob of hair and workhorse attitude showed maturity beyond her years.

"Under control," Tasker said. "Some bad injuries, but mostly it's a lot of confusion and broken crockery."

Ward drove at a crawling pace, taking in the damage. They passed Leigh-Ann coming out of a doorway. "Who's that?"

"One of the Coburn Gang," Tasker said, referring to the moniker the international news had given the criminals. "There's another two with your medics. How'd you get here so fast?"

"Um." A guilty note said Ward had been tracking him herself. He couldn't be too upset, seeing as her keenness had brought him this far.

"Does anyone else know we're here?" Tasker asked.

"Not from my people. Only my tech, back in the office – he doesn't know the details. Sorry, I only thought you might need backup. Was it the same as Laukstad?"

"No," Tasker said. "This time we stopped it."

"How?"

The road turned, towards the mill, and Ward cursed and went quiet. Seph Mason's home was a wreckage, with rubble piled on top of a car – the car Tasker had rented – and a massive creature's half-buried corpse. The rear of the car stuck out; Tasker could retrieve his spare suit and glasses, at least. Dim electric light came from a small annex, the only part of the building still standing.

"Can we save the debrief for later?" Tasker said. "We need to go off grid, fast."

"Absolutely," Ward said. "And your phone – I'll have my tech watch it, in case anyone else tries to track you."

"Thanks. Come with me." Tasker got out and led her into the building, to the operations room where the two paramedics were working fast to help Max Stomatt, the big criminal prone on a table. Reece leant against a wall, arms folded with concern for his friend. Mad writing, weapons and photos of hard men decorated the walls, painted with sprayed blood. The faces of the mercenary Legion scowled from the dark, like they disapproved of the men treating Stomatt. Mason had once been one of their number; if he was anything to go by, these men would scoff at injury as weakness.

"Reece Coburn, meet Deputy Director Ward," Tasker said.

"A pleasure, ma'am," Reece said, straightening up and holding out a grubby hand. He looked like he'd crawled out of a swamp, skin dark with dirt, suit torn, and his hair an erratic green mess, murky in the weak light. "Long as you're not here to take us in?"

"No," Ward said, taking the hand uncertainly. "That is – I didn't expect to find you here. Agent Tasker?"

"They came to get answers over Graystown," Tasker said, taking papers off the wall. That was another massacre to add to the list; Tasker had thankfully not seen the full details there, but from Reece's cringe at the name, the Americans had. It probably made Laukstad look tame. Over a hundred had died in that Louisiana commune, all part of whatever force was chasing Zip.

But Tasker's focus shifted as he spotted Shearjoy's name on a paper pinned high above eye level. He grabbed it. "This research covers the men Duvcorp left behind in the Congo, the team they sent to investigate energy readings. The survivors were mostly mercenaries, ex-soldiers rather than scientists."

"Working theory being," Reece put in, "these guys got some powers out in Africa, like ten years ago, which made them lose their minds and they gave up everything to go hunting one another. Right, Agent Tasker?"

"Close enough," Tasker said. "It was eight years ago, 2009."

"So they've turned on each other?" Ward said, regarding the room warily. "Has Duvcorp been sponsoring some to silence the others?"

"Duvcorp are out of the picture," Tasker said, gathering more papers, "as near as I'm aware. Not sure what I already told you? Some of these mercenaries banded together in a group calling themselves the Legion, and they've got influence with some powerful people. Presumably they're working together to stop anyone else getting the same powers Ikiri gave them. While those that aren't working with them want all the power for themselves, if Seph Mason was anything to go by. He's the man who owns this place."

"Went renegade on all of them, Reece put in. "Said he was the only one could be trusted with what he knew."

"And where is he now?" Ward asked, concerned the man who'd compiled this serial-killer mess of information might jump from the shadows.

"Long gone," Reece said. "Ditched us around the same time we figured on trying to prevent a massacre. And good riddance to him; the guy's been hunting people down like a game of international murder tag. Got his daughter Zip mixed up in it. We aim to unmix her."

"Help me gather this," Tasker said, grabbing another paper and stuffing it into a nearby duffel bag. "We're not staying."

"Aye, he needs more help than we can give him here," the bearded paramedic said.

"Can't go to no hospital," Reece said. "We're wanted men." He quickly added for Ward, "Innocent, though."

"Agreed, we need to keep a low profile," Tasker said. "Deputy Director Ward, you have private facilities?"

"AGa-21, will that do?" Ward addressed the paramedic. "I can have Dr Hertz meet us there."

The paramedic nodded. "Should do."

"Go on ahead," Tasker said. "We'll follow. Reece, Deputy Director – I'm especially interested in the one called Shearjoy."

"How's that?" Reece said.

"Mason said it himself, didn't he?" Tasker said. "Shearjoy's got a hand in the Ministry. If we're going to make it back to Ikiri, we have to deal with his Legion first. And we *have* to get back to Ikiri. That place itself is responsible for hundreds dead already, in Laukstad, Graystown, very nearly here. Unless we can stop it, as quickly as possible, a lot more people are going to die."

# 2

How the hell Leigh-Ann ended up stuck in a car with the lunatic killer, she did not know. They were bringing up the rear of a three-vehicle convoy, led by the government folks, with Zip in back, and Katryzna had been badly hiding small attempts to sneak looks at Leigh-Ann. She also kept starting to speak then baulking. Reminded Leigh-Ann of Brady Fontwell, down Melancony's Bar'n'Grill. One of countless guys so afraid to talk to a girl that he stewed on it forever rather than risk a quick rejection and the chance to move on. Except this vagrant-looking attack dog of a woman had taken on the mute sword-freak Vile and stood down Mason, so her fear over making conversation was especially weird.

Leigh-Ann just hoped wherever in hell these suits were leading them, it'd have a bed and maybe some booze. Bed *rooms*, at that – with a wall between her and Katryzna. The woman whispered something to herself, and then nodded, steeling herself to speak up. Leigh-Ann looked in the mirror to Zip and quickly spoke before Katryzna could: "How you holding up, sweetie?"

Zip looked up with surprise. She forced a tired smile. "I'm okay."

"Way past your bedtime, huh?"

"I don't think I should sleep."

"Oh, you should *always* sleep," Katryzna told her, twisting in her seat. "Being rested is a weapon." She turned this sagely to Leigh-Ann. Trying hard.

"Ain't none of us need to be told sleep's good," Leigh-Ann said. "But we just about established bad things happen when *Zip* does it."

"It's when my brother feels safest," Zip explained. Leigh-Ann frowned. How could Zip be so certain when she'd only learnt she had a brother that evening? Another kid with powers, going by what they'd pieced together from Zip's father and Agent Tasker. Seemed like the boy was stuck out in Africa, somehow making people go crazy while he tried to kill Zip. Presumably also responsible for sicking Vile and the gorilla on them. Zip said, "If I sleep, he'll do bad things. Make people attack each other."

"We were in this place, Stilt Town, where a bunch of people lost their minds," Leigh-Ann added for Katryzna's benefit. "People we knew from way back. Killed each other, damn near every last one of them. Killed one of the best guys I know and all."

"Ah," Katryzna said. "It happened to me in the forest. The villagers attacked us at night."

Leigh-Ann gave her a sideways glance. Suspecting that might've happened anyway. But Katryzna had been out there, hadn't she? To this Ikiri in the Congo, with its disruptive magic. Leigh-Ann said, "You lost a friend to this too, right?"

"Eyes," Katryzna said. "He cared about me. Not many people do." She gave Leigh-Ann a suddenly sharp look. "But he was *not* one of Mason's soldiers. He worked for the company. A problem solver. Like me. Well. Better than me." Her brow knitted. "I want to make it okay. I do not know exactly what happened to him. It was a long time ago and all we found there was Sara in a tree and she was mad."

"Sara being . . .?"

Katryzna glanced at her shoulder, distracted. She muttered in another language, Polish? Then she told Zip, "She *was* your mother. But she is stuck in a tree and it has made her insane." She quickly told Leigh-Ann, as Zip's face froze in shock. "They went in a cave – I didn't believe it until I saw it, but this cave was *not* somewhere you want to go. It killed some of them, gave others powers, and changed Sara into something else."

"A tree."

"Only half a tree." Katryzna moved her hands, as though gesturing could help explain it. "She hung out of it. Out of the middle of it."

"And you up and left her there?" Leigh-Ann raised an eyebrow.

Katryzna's eyes drifted, rerunning whatever she'd seen in Africa. "Sara did strange things with her mind. It made people behave how she wanted. If she wanted to get out of that tree, she could have made people help her. She is something else now. Not a mother, anyway. She hides people in the area. With her mind. She put Sean and Henri in a trance. I do not know, it is hard to explain. You will see when we go there."

The last sentence was almost a question. Leigh-Ann didn't rise to it. Zip looked troubled enough already. Her gaze drifted out of the window and her lips moved with silent calculations.

The little Honda ahead turned into a tight road flanked by houses. As they moved between vehicles parked either side, Leigh-Ann leant over the wheel to make sure she wasn't gonna smack the wing mirrors off. The Brits had no idea how to build streets with any elbow room.

As Zip hadn't said anything yet, Leigh-Ann thought out loud herself: "Sounds like Momma and you share some powers, maybe? Telling what people are feeling. Pulling the wool over people's eyes, like we ain't there. Sensing things from way off."

"Sara could do that!" Katryzna said. "She sensed *everything*. Places that had been attacked around the world – and exactly where to find Zippy."

"I don't know anything about my mum," Zip said, quietly. "Daddy never mentioned her. He only said she was gone. But I would like to – maybe I could reach out to her, the same way I did with my brother?" She paused. "I sensed him very strongly. He's angry, Leigh. *Really* really angry. And strong. He's also scared. He doesn't want to be seen. I don't know what he'll do when I sleep again."

"Well, see," Leigh-Ann said, "he's gotta sleep, too, right? And didn't you prove that whatever he's got, you can stop it? He does anything, you'll set it right, won't you?" In the mirror, she saw Zip's eyes shimmer with doubt. Yeah, no one had any damn idea if that was true. "Anyway, you're stronger than you think, and you got us backing you."

"*I* will take care of you," Katryzna insisted. "Protecting people is not much different to hunting people. I kill them before they kill us."

Leigh-Ann shot her a warning look. This woman should *not* be around kids. The look was enough to remove Katryzna's grin. Then she flashed forward, swiping a hand at the dashboard, trying to hit something that wasn't there. She snarled a short tirade in Polish. When she looked up again, trying to force another smile, Leigh-Ann said, "The hell?"

Katryzna cleared her throat, straightened up and spoke in a forced polite tone. "I apologise. Do not listen to Rurik." She paused, considering whether to explain, then said, "My conscience. But Zippy. Your brother is nothing to be scared of. None of these angry men are. They are cowards."

Leigh-Ann kept staring for a second, trying to figure it out: the woman was hearing a voice she called a conscience, but preferred to argue with it than heed it. Great. But she had a point, which Leigh-Ann latched onto: "Yeah, someone told me that anger and fear are the same thing, Zip. So if your brother's *really* angry, then he's *really* scared. After you stopped all his zombies, he's the one oughta be afraid to sleep."

"You think so?" Zip didn't sound convinced. Wanted to be, though.

"For sure," Leigh-Ann said.

The ambulance ahead pulled off the road, through a gate in a tall wall, and they followed, reaching their destination and interrupting the discussion. Leigh-Ann said, "The hell kind of safe house is this?"

The building before them was a huge, ugly mess of big square angles and white-framed windows, like someone had glued a half-dozen town houses together without considering where the parts went. Steps and ramps went up to at least three different entrances, all with safety bars and barriers around them. The biggest one had a glass reception area with a faded sign above it: *Barnfield House*. There were wheelchairs in the lobby.

The ambulance continued around the side of the property, and Leigh-Ann followed to some parking bays at the rear. Off to the left sat a cramped garden, a couple trees and bushes packed in between encircling walls, about what you'd expect from a country beset by tiny roads.

Leigh-Ann decided, "This country was designed for dwarfs."

The second Leigh-Ann parked, Katryzna jumped out. She rushed off with another echo of Brady Fontwell: too nervous to stay a second longer than necessary. She ran to the Honda, where a little lady in a pantsuit was getting out. The paramedics were already out with Stomatt, rolling his gurney through a wide fire escape. Alive, thank God. In good hands? But *oh*, the crazed killer jumped in for a hug that Businesswoman was *not* ready for, which made Leigh-Ann bark a laugh. Katryzna backed off smiling, talking like they were old friends, while the little woman didn't have a word to say back, just big frightened eyes. Sean Tasker didn't help, getting out the other side of the car – a square-shouldered, strapping gentleman who just upped and hefted a packed bag after the paramedics. Katryzna skipped after him.

"That woman," Leigh-Ann said to Zip. "You've got a gift. What do you think of her?"

"We can trust her," Zip said, confidently. "She's kind and honest and she wants to help. She's worried for her own town, and a bit scared of Katryzna."

Leigh-Ann frowned. "You're talking about the suit? I mean Katryzna herself. Should we be scared of her and all?"

"Oh," Zip said, and her brow furrowed. "She's different. Like . . . a ball of wool? Or spaghetti. Noisy. I don't know; some people are easy to understand, others hide it, like my daddy, but . . . she's confusing." Then Zip smiled. "But she likes you."

"Don't I know it. Shit."

Reece hooted for them as he reached the fire escape himself, which he held open for the Englishwoman. Leigh-Ann sighed and got out, beckoning Zip to come with her. "This a private hospital or something?" she called to him.

"Nursing home," Reece said, as they approached. "Apparently no one'll know we're here." Inside the door, there were stairs going up and the shiny metal doors of an elevator. The suited woman was waiting, averting her eyes like she was self-conscious about getting involved. Reece introduced her anyway. "Sam, Leigh. She's –"

"Yeah, can you give us a minute?" Leigh-Ann cut in. She pulled Reece away by the elbow, just clear of the door, leaving Zip with the suit. "We really wanna be jumping in bed with these people so quick?"

"Sam's all right," Reece replied. "I've been filling her in, and she seems like good people. Besides, we're buying time. Get some rest, get Sto good, then we figure out what's next."

"Easy as that? I just rode in with a girl says she kills people for a living," Leigh-Ann said, wanting to pick up right where Reece had brushed the issue off back in the village. "And these folks, they're the fucking man. Even the woman looks like the man."

Reece moved further from the door, throwing a look back like the suit might hear. "You see us having a choice? Might pay to have the man on our side for once, no?"

"We got Zip, remember," Leigh-Ann said. "We can do like we did to get here: make people look the other way while we hop on a couple planes. Go *home*."

"To where everyone knows to find us?" Reece said. "Zip's tired as all hell, Leigh. Already got the world on her shoulders. These might not be our people, but they got an interest in ending this. That's gotta work for us."

"Sure, but we don't know who they are, except for being stone killers with" – she threw a hand up – "secret nursing home hideouts? And they want us to go to Africa? Is that really what we're about?"

Reece followed her gesture, considering it for a second. "We'll have a sit down, okay? Get the full measure of them. As soon as Sto's good." He paused. "As to Africa, we gotta consider it." A smile teased his lips. "Always wanted to travel, didn't you?"

"Wanted to follow the Blues Highway and hit up clubs, not rumble in the jungle."

"Consider it an upgrade," Reece said.

Leigh-Ann tried to stay mad, but it was hard to keep up when he got that playful twinkle in his eye. A promise that nothing was serious as it seemed. She looked away and huffed, "You got us private rooms, at least?"

"Let's find out," Reece replied. He led the way in, to find the woman and Zip talking quietly.

Sam spoke in a prim British accent like she was right off the TV: "I think I can find a bear somewhere here."

"Okay," Zip said, through a little yawn.

"Y'all getting on?" Reece said.

Zip smiled and rubbed one eye with a balled-up fist, bless her. Reece was right: whatever else, the kid needed rest. Leigh-Ann crouched and said, "Sweetie, we'll find you somewhere to lay your head."

"Ms Ward said she would get me a teddy," Zip replied through another yawn. She blinked and tried to steel her face. "But I wanted to say something." She gave a sideways look to the British lady. "We *can* trust them, Leigh. Ms Ward is nice. Katryzna will help us, I think. But . . . I'm worried about Agent Tasker."

# 3

Tasker left Stomatt in the medical room with a stern-faced doctor in surgical dress. The Scottish paramedic assured him this whole wing was secure – they had a single corridor with a medical bay, two bedrooms and a common area. No connection to the rest of the building. It was a purpose-built safe house, piggy-backing on a care home, where no one would notice strange noises or medical staff and men in suits coming and going day and night.

Ignoring Katryzna, who was raiding cupboards and told him through a mouthful that she'd found chocolate, Tasker spread Mason's papers over a circular coffee table. As well as bullet-lists and photos, there were biographies and reports that Mason must have hired investigators to produce. Shearjoy's photo had his real name scrawled under it: Alfred Hawkins. A nondescript, round-headed man with rough skin and a black teardrop tattoo on one cheek. He didn't look like an Alfred. His C.V. described a background in the British Army, then jobs at security companies that handled former war zones. He was more than a typical grunt – Assistant Director at Torn Fang, Chief of Operations at Storm Shield. The jobs ended in 2009, the year Duvcorp sent the mercenaries to Ikiri, in the Congo, and from 2010 onward Mason had listed names and dates of the man's contacts, some with surveillance photos attached. Shearjoy had met with the CFO of Warlowe Ltd, one of the world's largest freight operators, and had lunch with Audrey Flan, the French vice president. Numerous Duvcorp employees – including the late Simon Parris, whose murder Katryzna had witnessed and described to him – were listed with question marks. There was also a page detailing the acquisition of a property, the Hall of Cainon, in the Carpathian Mountains.

"He's the one that called?" Katryzna asked, peering over Tasker's shoulder with a half-finished chocolate bar in one hand. She took the photo. "Looks feeble."

Tasker took no notice; he'd told her nothing of the specific threat, only that Shearjoy said he was coming. He sifted through the other papers, and spotted what he was really looking for: *Shearjoy +* ~~*Chief Operations Agent*~~ *Deputy Director Finway. Met 02/04/12; 13/08/15; 21/01/16. Presence near Theed Street: 06/13; 06/16.* Tasker knew Finway, the Ministry's chief for South London. Theed Street was their main office. The dates were a running tally of Shearjoy consolidating a relationship. Tasker thumbed through and found similar tallies next to Audrey Flan's name, and likewise for two American governors.

Katryzna snatched the first page off him. "Mason is a real stalker, isn't it?"

"Shearjoy is my concern. The Ministry sweeps otherworldly secrets under the rug. Duvcorp, Raystaten, companies like that" – he stabbed a finger into some of the names on the paper in front of him – "play their own games, hide their own truths. This man has access to the worst kind of people."

"People like me?" Katryzna said, cheerily.

"Pretty sure there's no one else like you." Tasker stood, brushing her off, though the reality was Shearjoy must have access to the same contract killers as the industry giants. Someone had murdered Simon Parris at the start of all this, after all – presumably a Legion grunt – when Parris had leaked information about Laukstad to the Ministry, undermining his own company, Duvcorp. Considering Duvcorp had supposedly given up their interest in Ikiri once the mercenaries had gone missing, the Legion most likely had a hand in the company. The Legion's main goal, after all, seemed to be keeping knowledge about Ikiri hidden, which went together with murdering each other to limit those in the know. Though that might've also indicated something more primal: Mason's crusade, and the way he'd reacted to mention of his son, a boy potentially more powerful than him, suggested an almost irrational aversion to competition. It had to be why Shearjoy wanted Zip dead – they were afraid of her power in the same way they feared each other.

But while Mason's hunt was small-scale and personal, the Legion had spread their claws wider than Duvcorp, to affect governments and even the Ministry itself. This research would help; if Tasker could figure out the Legion's set-up, he could create a strategy to avoid them or even confront them. Starting with figuring out what influence they had inside the Ministry.

Tasker turned to leave, and found Reece and Leigh-Ann in the doorway, Zip between them and Ward just behind. None of them looked happy. Reece's fingers were taut as though he should be holding a weapon. The handle of his ornate pistol stuck out of its shoulder holster.

"Whatever this is, it can wait," Tasker said.

"You keeping something from us?" Reece said.

Tasker looked down at Zip, the child clinging to Leigh-Ann's leg. She'd known when she looked at him in the village, across the street, and she knew now – wouldn't even meet his eyes. He asked, "What did you tell them?"

Zip shook her head quickly, not wanting to speak.

"Leave her be," Leigh-Ann said. "You're the one's got explaining to do, *Agent*."

"I'm going to plug the leak in the Ministry," Tasker replied flatly. "That's all."

"Sure," Leigh-Ann said, "and what's really going on?"

"Can I – shall we all go in?" Ward's head bobbed behind their shoulders.

Katryzna asked from behind him, "Is this about that call with Shearjoy?"

The Americans' icy looks got colder and Ward asked, "You had a call?"

"Sure, Shearjoy called Sean," Katryzna said, before he could explain. "He said they are coming, want to kill us, bla bla. Let them come, it will save us time."

"How would they get your number?" Ward asked.

"As we've established," Tasker said, "the Ministry isn't entirely secure. These papers show that Shearjoy met with Deputy Director Finway. Amongst others. I'll be gone a few hours, that's all."

"You want to do some shit alone, at a time like this?" Reece said.

Tasker held his gaze, waiting for everyone to calm.

"There's more," Zip whispered, afraid to say it. It wasn't a guess; she knew. But she hid her face up against Leigh-Ann's thigh.

"It's not something you need to worry about," Tasker said.

"Then how come I'm worrying?" Leigh-Ann said.

Katryzna cleared her throat, and Tasker braced for her to start trouble without knowing why. When he looked back, she was conferring with her right shoulder, taking notes from her invisible conscience, Rurik. "No, but thanks anyway."

The nonsensical response defused some of the tension, enough for Ward to timidly suggest, "There's protocols for this. We should sit down. I've got people –"

"He threatened my daughter." It came out hotter than Tasker intended. Apparently he wasn't in complete control. Tasker tried a smile but that didn't work, going by their concerned expressions. "I'm dealing with it."

"What you talking about?" Reece asked. "This Shearjoy clown said what?"

"He threatened my daughter," Tasker repeated. "And I am going to sort it out."

"Wow," Leigh-Ann said, then stepped aside with a flourish, rolling an arm. "*Excuse* us, didn't realise I was standing in the way of Liam Neeson right here. Reece, let him by, he's got skyscrapers to siege or some shit."

Tasker glowered.

"We have people –" Ward started again.

"No," Tasker said. That came out angry. He took a breath, tried again. "I don't want to draw any attention to this. My family are safe right now, and they will be as long as the Legion think I'm considering their offer. I'm going to chase up their connection with Finway, and I'll protect my family, quietly. None of you are getting involved."

"You don't get to decide that," Reece said. "They threaten you, they threaten all of us."

"Just keep Zip safe. I'll handle the rest."

"Fuck that," Reece went on. "We –"

"Hey," Katryzna cut in. Here it came – a violent contribution one way or the other. But with everyone watching her, she quietened her voice and muttered, "*Language.*"

It took a moment to grasp her concern. Leigh-Ann said, "Okay – sweet, but Zip's cool with swearing."

Katryzna's brow knitted. "And what?"

"Look," Reece came back in, "we became a damn team when we took down Vile together. And if they're gonna hold your family against you, they might go after ours, too. We already lost Stilt Town to this shi –" He caught himself, with a quick look at Katryzna. "This craziness. I lost my best friend. You tell me these guys wanna make those kinda threats, we're gonna do something about it."

"That's *exactly* why I need to go alone," Tasker said. "If they made you choose between helping my daughter and saving your own families? Or each other? I can keep a lid on this, contain it. Your job, all of you, is to get Zipporah safely to Ikiri."

"Yeah, we ain't fully sold on that either. You know she's just a kid, right?"

"A kid who came from an unnatural, dangerous place," Tasker said plainly. "The only person capable of going back. Ikiri needs a very special power to tackle it. She is that power. She's everything to this."

"According to her mother," Katryzna offered helpfully.

"Who lives in a tree?" Leigh-Ann said.

"This kind of weirdness is the reason we need to keep *all* our focus!" Reece said. "If this is a thing that's still got room to spread and get stranger, and worse, I don't want it hitting Cutjaw any more than it already has; that means we stop it falling on your doorstep before it falls on ours."

"Then trust *me* to do that –"

Katryzna snorted, unimpressed, shifting closer. She looked to her shoulder again and said, "Even Rurik thinks you are wrong, Sean. That is a low bar." Turning sideways, she snapped, "I agreed, don't ruin it!" Then quickly composed herself and turned back to Tasker. "You will get yourself and your family killed. If they scare you, you will make mistakes. That is what you are doing. Do you know how I survive?" She waited. With the state of her mind, and her appearance, her survival certainly came at a cost, so Tasker said nothing. Katryzna prodded his chest. "I do not scheme. I do not belong anywhere. No one sees me coming because no one saw me going. Yes?"

"Forgive me," Tasker replied, "but I think my idea of subtle might be more effective than yours. Especially where –"

"There is no *subtle* that works here," Katryzna said. "There is" – she held up a finger – "surprise, and there is" – another finger – "doing necessary things."

"I'm aware of that. Hence –"

"Hence shut up," Katryzna said. "They know you are here. In this area? With the child. And these two were on the TV. Do they know *I* am here?"

Tasker paused. Shearjoy had indicated knowledge of Zip and her father, and addressed a message to *everyone*. But he hadn't mentioned Katryzna. The Legion could deduce Reece's involvement from Graystown, but Tasker had been careful to keep Katryzna anonymous for their journey to Ikiri; in the Ministry, only Ward had known she was with him. The only possible link was the man she'd interrupted killing Parris, but that was before he and Katryzna joined forces. Still, Tasker said, "What difference does it make? The Ministry are my people, all I –"

Katryzna gripped his jaw and squeezed his cheeks, leaning in close to say, "The difference is who cares about the Ministry? I go to your family and make them safe. Quickly, unexpectedly. The rest is details."

Tasker's eyes were drawn to the chocolate staining her teeth.

"Trust me, Sean," Katryzna said. "I am a good friend to have."

She released him to step back with a bright look. Tasker rubbed his stubbly cheeks. Everyone stared at Katryzna like they didn't know what to make of her.

Zip's little voice came in: "I could find Shearjoy?" Tasker frowned as she shuffled under their combined gaze. "I think."

"Zip, don't —" Leigh-Ann started.

"I want to," the child said. "My daddy used his mind powers a lot, as much as regular research. I have my own power, don't I?"

"You use your powers," Reece said, "and that shows the bad guys exactly where we are, right? That's how Vile tracked us."

"My brother sent him," Zip said. "Shearjoy's men can't travel that fast."

"No," Tasker decided. "We're doing nothing to put a target on you, Zipporah."

"And we do not need to, because we have *me*," Katryzna said, giving Tasker another prod, unbalancing him. "If you go near your family or this Ministry person or even away from this child, Shearjoy's men could stab your daughter in the face. No. Give me your address, I will take them somewhere safe, then we can get moving." She thought for a second. "Yes. I can be back in a couple of hours."

"I haven't even told you —"

"Doesn't matter. And while I'm gone, you can do the hard work and read through that nonsense Mason left behind." She clicked her fingers and opened her hand. "Keys." Tasker stared, to make her recall their car was buried under the collapsed mill. She turned to Ward. "You? That little old car will be better, actually."

"Um," Ward said. Deputy Director or not, she wasn't used to dealing with field operations this frantic, demonstrated by how she'd mostly kept quiet here. "I can get you a Ministry vehicle in a short while. If we really think this is a good idea."

"I can *be* there in a short while," Katryzna replied. "I will take good care of it, I promise — I am an excellent driver."

Ward looked to Tasker, deferring to him to back the woman off. Could he possibly consider Katryzna's offer? Trust Rebecca's fate to her? But she was right. There was a possibility the Legion wouldn't expect her, and a high probability they would pick up on him going anywhere. It was just a question of how much safer it was to put his family in Katryzna's hands.

"I'll go with her, how about that?" Reece said carefully. "We can —"

Katryzna made an irritated noise. "I work best, and quickest, alone. And even if you were not on the news, you look like a sewer monster, people will notice you." She turned back to Tasker, oblivious to Reece's incredulous expression. "Companies pay me a lot of money to do these things. I will do it for you for free. Sean. I can help."

Tasker frowned. Charles Smail's words came back to him: in Kinshasa, where they'd first met, the British agent had confided to him that the SIS had a thick file on Katryzna Tkacz, full of things they suspected her of but hadn't proved, including crimes against multinationals and the Russian mafia. She had thwarted Smail's own attempt to kill the pair of them. And it *would* only take her a few hours to reach his family. She might be volatile, and dangerous, but she was right. That might be exactly what he needed against Shearjoy's sprawling conspiracy.

Tasker said, quietly, "Okay. Do it. Make sure my family are safe."

# 4

"Henri Ngoi?" a man asked, loudly, as Henri exited the store, a bag of food under one arm. He had come late at night, when the streets were empty, but here were two men, bulging with weight beneath their light coats. One leant against an old Toyota as the other moved towards Henri with a hand up, warning him not to move. "We need to ask you some questions."

Henri looked from the hand down to the lump at the man's hip, a gun under his jacket. Moving into Ngiri Ngiri, a neighbourhood close to central Kinshasa, clearly had not taken him far enough from trouble. But from the leaning man's cocky posture, and the closer one's triumphant smile, these men figured they had already caught him. Henri's eye went to the alleyway, five metres away? These men relied on their weight and guns. He was willing to bet they were not fast; Henri was tall, trained to fight and ate well – he probably had more actual muscle on his lean frame than both men put together.

"You want to talk?" Henri pointed past them. "I have a room just across the street."

When they instinctively turned to look, he tossed the shopping and ran. Didn't look back as they shouted at him to stop, just caught the shop's gutter pipe and swung around it to redirect. He sprinted up the alley and out onto another street of blocky concrete houses. He ran across the road as the men crashed into stacked boxes behind the shop, cursing one another.

"Shoot him!" one ordered, and Henri glanced back. The bigger one, already short of breath, shoved the other to keep going as he drew a large pistol from his belt. Henri kept running, stooping to make himself a smaller target, and the gun fired. He flinched as the bullet cracked concrete far above his head, and he dived for another alley. He ran into the darkness and skidded to a halt, finding his way blocked by a wall.

The man with the gun yelled at his companion to move faster, get him, and the other man's footsteps quickly approached along with his panting breaths. Henri took two quick steps back, then launched forward, kicked a foot into the building on the left and sprang off it, up, to kick off the house to the right. He just got hold of the top of the wall. He scrambled over it as the man entered the alley, shouting.

On the other side of the wall, Henri landed on a car, metal bending under his weight. A light came on in the next building, a man shouting inside. He did not stop to explain, but jumped to the ground and kept running, out onto the road where another row of irregular square buildings stretched ahead. He sprinted on, throwing occasional glances over his shoulder, and as he got to the end of the road he saw the men scrambling out, having found a way round. He had a good distance between them now, and sped down a side street, out of view.

Kept running.

Henri took another turning and glanced back – no sign of them – then turned again. He picked out a circuitous route, doubling back, and finally skidded to a stop at the corner of a building, spying the two men pushing each other in blame for losing him. They moved down another street, slow and huffing, ready to give up. He smiled. Amateurs; they had spotted him at the shop, but were not ready for trouble. From their frustration, it was clear they did not know where he was staying.

Carefully watching that they had not seen him, Henri trotted back to his hideout, where the sounds of television and families loudly chatting rose from the surrounding houses. He passed a small group cooking meat over a fire outside their home, gave them a smile and continued up the crumbling steps. He paused to check around him, finding no signs of trouble, no reaction to the gunshots a few blocks across. Far off, there were sounds of car horns and men shouting. Maybe a car accident, maybe the same men who had chased him, taking their anger out on someone else.

Henri breathed relief and stepped inside, to see Miguel Lopaz where he'd left him, reclining in a beat-up armchair with a bottle of Castel beer, three empties at his feet.

"Shop closed?" Miguel asked, and Henri paused, recalling why he had gone out. The supply run had primarily been for Miguel, his friend and mentor, the old Spaniard expat who had first come to Kinshasa to manage a Duvcorp expedition eight years ago. Miguel had only arranged the logistics, organising a mean team of mercenaries to escort Duvcorp researchers looking for a strange energy source in Ikiri, but in the years Henri had known him, he had periodically disappeared when he feared someone was following up on that mission. On this occasion, Henri knew someone actually *would* come for them; he had been to the interior himself, with the Englishman Agent Tasker, and seen both that Ikiri had dangerous powers and people would kill to keep it secret.

"There was trouble," Henri said, and moved through the room to grab his bag. They only had one holdall each, travelling light to keep moving. "Someone knows we're here, we should go."

"Knows we're *here*?" Miguel stood sharply, sloshing beer.

"In the area." Henri shouldered his bag and threw the other. Miguel caught it against his body, with a grunt, struggling to hold onto both the bag and the beer. "Two men with guns." Henri smiled to defuse the news. "Not as quick as me though, see?"

"White men?"

"No, locals, and cheap hires at that."

Miguel huffed, tossing the beer down. "Sure you lost them?"

"Yes, but it's not safe here, is it? I have another place we can go, over in Binza."

"Yeah, give me a second," Miguel said, struggling to unzip and search through the bag. "I'm not going unprepared."

"That ship's sailed," a man said, announcing his presence in the doorway. He was white and pear-shaped, especially big around the waist, with long dark hair hanging down over his shoulders. Thin on top. His loose beige slacks and crumpled linen shirt made him look like a drunk tourist. But Henri would have sensed his dangerousness even if he hadn't vaguely recognised him: one of the men that had been gone to Ikiri eight years ago. An ex-Duvcorp mercenary.

This one spoke with a strange accent. "It's been a long time, Lopaz. I'd ask how you've been, but I can see that pretty well from here."

"Flay." Miguel said the name with grim recognition, face tightening. It brought back a memory to Henri. When they'd been gathering in a warehouse before the expedition, his sister, Sara, had mentioned this man. She'd excitedly told Henri that she had never met a man with a Welsh accent before, and whispered, "Do you think Flay means the same thing in Wales?"

They had never looked it up, but having learnt some of the other colourful names the mercenaries went by, Henri was fairly confident it did.

"In the flesh," Flay said, taking satisfaction at being remembered. "Your boy there is very fast, you know that? Trained him well. Or did you pick up a few tricks out at Mount Ikiri, lad?"

Henri shook his head. "We turned back and saw nothing. If that is why you're here."

"I'm joking," Flay said, leaning slightly forward to show off a crooked-toothed smile. "Obviously I *know* you haven't been touched by Ikiri, because if you were you would've done a better job of getting away. Would've sensed me coming and all, isn't that right, Lopaz?"

"Got no idea what you're talking about," Miguel mumbled. "Whatever any of you went through, whatever you think I know – it's nothing. I'm living a different life now."

"Just went into hiding for the fun of it, that's right?"

"Had the British government poking their nose in, asking questions. I didn't want anything to do with it. Still don't, understand?"

Flay exhaled loudly. "But you talked, didn't you? Because they went there. To Ikiri. They even came back – that's what I hear. And your lad here, he rather proves it."

"It was the Englishman, not Miguel," Henri said. "Smail, he set it up, he sent me out there. He wanted to know about Ikiri himself, that was all. Miguel had nothing to do with it – you see my nose?" Henri turned side on, to show what was left of the scab from where Katryzna had hit him. "I got that trying to stop them."

"See," Flay said, "this is all mighty murky from where I'm standing. An SIS agent murdered along with two of his men, trying to apprehend a group who'd visited a place we strongly encourage no one to explore. A group including a known associate" – he indicated Henri with a finger – "of Miguel Lopaz. Who we hoped had nothing to do with said place. Making it difficult to lay all this at poor dead Smail's feet. He was a snake, and he should've reported them to us, but that doesn't mean you're not a snake, too. And frankly I don't care for the details. He was a liability, you're a liability. Shearjoy's been too soft on the lot of you for too long."

"So cut the bullshit." Miguel stiffened. He still had the bag held across his chest, one hand stuffed in where he'd been interrupted. "If you came to kill us, you would've led with that. What's it you want? You have some angle for us to make things right?"

"Henri, isn't it?" Flay asked, pointedly ignoring Miguel. "I remember you. Skinny thing, you were, hovering around the warehouse and the docks while we got everything in order. Wanted to tag along but big sister Sara wouldn't let you."

"*I* wouldn't let him," Miguel snarled. "Because I know how to fucking do my job and keep things professional."

"No, Lopaz," Flay replied darkly. "You have *no* idea. We're going to have a long talk about what happened out there, Henri. Everything you saw and learnt. Everything you discussed with the idiots who swept through. And if you don't want to talk, well, I can work with that, too."

"A talk," Miguel echoed. "That's all you want?"

"For now."

Miguel plainly didn't believe a word of it, and Flay was enjoying teasing them. The ex-Duvcorp mercenaries had stayed away from this country ever since they left. For one of them to come back now, it was serious. Smail, as their watchdog, had betrayed their trust and they wanted to tie up the loose ends. Henri and Miguel might survive a talk with this man, but not much more than that. The silence that stretched between them seemed to confirm it.

"Why don't you have a nice seat there, Lopaz?" Flay nodded to the armchair. "You can get us all another beer, Henri, what do you say? Has the beer improved since last I was here? Seem to recall it tasted like pi –"

The bottom of Miguel's bag burst open with a loud thump, the pistol inside muffled by clothing, and the shot skewed badly. It caught Flay in the leg, making him lurch into the door frame on his good leg. Miguel fired again, tearing through more of the bag as he drew the pistol out, but Flay was moving – he got to Miguel so quick the second shot went right over his shoulder. Miguel shouted, "Run, Henr –"

He cut off with a gag as Flay hit him, carried him across the room and slammed him into the wall hard enough to crack it. Flay drew back just as quickly, a long, thin knife in his hand. He stabbed twice, three times, lightning fast, and it was all Henri could do to break himself out of the shock before Flay turned to face him.

The pistol was down in the far corner, Miguel bleeding from the mouth and all over his chest, held up only by Flay's other arm, sad eyes imploring Henri to get away. There was no humour in Flay's face now, only the dead, savage stare of a predator. But as he stepped away and Miguel fell, Flay lurched, his leg wound almost bringing him down.

With one last look at Miguel, Henri ran.

# 5

When the Scottish paramedic told Reece that Stomatt was going to be okay, Leigh-Ann's expression distorted in mixed relief and disbelief. Reece knew what she was thinking, taking in their friend in a clinical room, bound up in bandages, skin paler than ever, the usually taut, teasing face slack. The same lunatic swordsman, with the same opportunity, had killed Caleb, a better man than all of them. Reece could hear Leigh-Ann's question without it being voiced: *Was Sto seriously just too asshole to die?*

"Ain't it said God watches out for drunks and fools?" Reece said. "Straight out the Bible."

"It's not in the Bible," the paramedic said, "but also not untrue."

A scholar as well as a field surgeon. The paramedic confided that they weren't totally out of the woods: there was discolouring around the wound that was unusual. They'd keep an eye on it and see how things developed, he said; just keep Stomatt off his legs and give him plenty of fluids in the meantime. He'd been really lucky.

Reece figured it wasn't just luck at work here; put aside the confusion about the wound, this UK Ministry had provided world-class care. They were something else. Tasker had put down that mutant gorilla without so much as a question and none of these guys had batted an eyelid at the destruction of the mill or the chaos in that village. Leigh-Ann was maybe right to be worried about them, but they had already proved a good ally to have. And whatever she said about Stomatt, the pair always rubbing each other the wrong way, he was a Cutjaw Kid, and he stood up for his friends without question. Same way they had to do now: stand up for Zip, make Caleb and Sto's sacrifices worth something.

Reece took a breath, giving Stomatt a parting look, then steered Leigh-Ann down the hall, to the common room. Time to settle exactly who and what it was they were dealing with.

Ward and Tasker were sitting in the low chairs, apart from one another, skimming through Mason's papers. Tasker looked tired and fed up, worse than before, even though he'd found himself a new pair of glasses and a clean shirt and jacket. Ward put on a pleasant smile, though. She hadn't doubted a word of what Reece had told her on the way over, about picking up Zip in the Texas farm, Vile and the gorilla, the madness in Stilt Town, Zip's ability to read minds and even influence them. He also covered Grithin, a former-mercenary who they'd found dead in Memphis – murdered by Mason as part of his quest to kill everyone who'd touched Ikiri. As far as they knew, Grithin wasn't one of the Legion, but he had similar research to Mason's, suggesting they were all at least partly caught up in this decade-long effort to stamp each other out. Some of them out on their own, some of them working together, with no guarantee what mix of crazy powers any of them had. Ward took it all in with sympathy and concern, and just a slightly unsettling hint that her people encountered such things regularly.

"Zip's down," Reece said, "and Sto's good. We got a lot to thank you for there. But before we turn in ourselves, seems we've got a few things to hammer out. Namely, what happens next – but first, who exactly *are* you?"

The pair regarded him with slightly different levels of caution; Ward looked almost worried, *wanting* to say something, but Tasker's face was neutral, well-trained in this. He took the lead: "The Ministry investigates unusual occurrences. Broadly speaking, things not covered by standard institutions."

"Paranormal shit?" Leigh-Ann prompted.

"In short," he said, "preternatural. Things that are yet to be explained."

"But you're like vampire hunters, that's what you're saying? You're hearing that, same as me, right, Reece?"

"Let them tell it," Reece suggested.

"We're not vampire hunters," Ward said, amused but in an awkward way that said however silly the suggestion was, it was close to the mark. "But I'm sorry, we're bound to certain confidentialities."

"Right," Reece said. "So once this is over, you gonna have us killed?"

"Absolutely not – I promise," Ward replied with shock. "There may be discussions over what can be shared publicly, but we are here to help and to protect people, never to hurt them."

"Guess we wouldn't be worth it anyway, would we?" Reece went on, watching for her response. "Not like anyone's gonna listen to some Cutjaw trailer trash on anything like this. Prefer to think we did it, or just say we're crazy." Ward held his gaze, firmer than he would've expected, but didn't rise to the comment. Just waited for him to go on. She was tougher than she seemed, and when it came to it, he had no doubt this Ministry had bigger teeth than she was making out. He said, "What you want from us, then?"

"What do we want from you?" Ward echoed with surprise. "We're here to help with *your* situation."

"No offence, but no one who looked comfortable in an office ever did shit for Cutjaw. Y'all are into something deeper, much deeper, that's plain enough. If you don't wanna share that, fine – but if you're planning on taking Zip away, doing anything with her, then it's through us. So I'll ask again. What's it you want?"

"You know what we want," Tasker said, plainly. "She needs to come to Ikiri. That's where we can put her power to good use. The more important question here is what *you* want, isn't it?"

Reece shifted, feeling Leigh-Ann's gaze boring into the side of his face. What they really wanted was to cut loose from all this, wasn't it? Now Zip had no home left to go to, she might as well ride free with them. Go to shows, pick up an instrument, leave this life behind. But the papers on the table were evidence enough that they were a long way from that reality. And her brother out in Ikiri wasn't leaving her be. Reece said, "We don't want her taken away. Don't want her used in any way she ain't happy with. Don't want to be separated from her, neither."

"Absolutely," Ward said.

"Want to know how all this works, too," Reece said. "Everything y'all know about it. Even if you need us signing something, say we'll never speak a word of it, or whatever. We can't go into this half-cocked, with only half the picture."

Tasker deferred to Ward, who held Reece's gaze. Weighing up exactly what to share. She said, "I can give you some broad strokes. Duvcorp – that is, the multinational with interests in just about everything – followed an energy pattern to Ikiri. We've studied the same energy, and its effects are still widely unknown. We've barely touched on exactly how to measure it. But it has been connected to creatures that might otherwise be considered . . . unnatural. It's possible this energy altered that beast at the mill from what it once was. We've seen evidence of it in unusual creatures before."

"Seen it bring people back from the dead?" Leigh-Ann put in, referring to Mason's claims that Vile, the Legion man with the sword, had been killed out in the Congo years before he appeared hunting them in Texas. Believable enough, considering how hard the swordsman was to stop.

"No. That's new."

"What about these psychic powers?" Reece asked.

Ward hesitated, so Tasker answered, "Those parts are all new to us, too. All we know is that this energy – novisan, it's called – plays *some* role in the way Ikiri and the Legion operate."

*Novisan.* So that was this magical power these people hid from the world.

"Honestly," Ward said, "I hoped over the course of your investigation you might bring back information we can use to develop our knowledge."

"Well shit," Leigh-Ann said, "anything else we can do for you while we're here? I hear global warming needs solving?"

"Alright," Reece said, trying to keep on track, "so what about this Legion? What do you know about them and their powers?"

"That information," Tasker said, holding up a sheaf of papers, "is mostly contained here. We've not encountered them before, but it appears Mason took careful notes. Mostly to do with physically fighting them. I've counted twelve men labelled as Legion so far, with another four labelled 'independent'."

"Sixteen guys?" Reece said. It wasn't many, considering how big a deal Mason made them out to be.

"Sixteen that Mason deemed noteworthy. Presumably the ones who could tap into Ikiri's powers; only eight of that total, I believe, were connected to the original expedition, so maybe the others were trained up later." Tasker through the papers, pointing at details. "Flay, favours knives. Lizard, independent, 'water assistance?' Two Canton Brothers, one's got a leg circled, 'metal foot'. *Ruin* – he's got more notes than most, seems this guy really pissed Mason off." Tasker pulled up photos of a building which he spun round for everyone to see. "And it's not just people. Mason mapped out an estate these men carved for themselves in the mountains, four years ago. There's more like this, two crossed out. They've been building strongholds. Mason had notes about the defences, how many men on guard duty."

"What was inside?" Reece asked.

"No idea. This is a mess, with little hint at the through-line, just notes on what makes these people dangerous and how to defeat them in combat. It all points to a particular single-mindedness. They might all be like this, plotting to kill one another."

"Like Grithin did," Reece recalled, grimly.

Tasker nodded. "It seems everything besides tracking and fighting was incidental to Mason. It's a power-struggle, and one that would see Zip, with her heightened abilities, as a particular target. Mason's notes show the Legion have greater resources, connections in government departments, law enforcement, tech companies. They've used their gifts to accure different kinds of influence, which might speak to more diverse goals, but the speed that Shearjoy threatened me after we caught up to Zip suggests this violence is still their priority. Only unlike Mason, they'd be capable of tracing phones, running facial recognition on cameras, everything."

"In addition to tracking the big psychic beacon in Zip's mind," Leigh-Ann added.

"In addition to that, yes."

"We have counter-technology," Ward said. "I'll have my people block attempts to trace your phones – that is, my person. I have a technician I trust. We're not sure about the wider Ministry, right now."

"I ain't *got* my phone," Leigh-Ann huffed. "That and all else we had was lost back in that mill, unless you got someone can go unbury it."

"Better we go without anyway, right?" Reece said. "Wouldn't risk phones going up against the Steer Trust back in Louisiana – why we wanna mess with that tech going up against spooks?"

"*We* are spooks," Tasker replied unashamedly. "I would welcome another call from Shearjoy, or an attempt to trace me. Then we'd be ready to counter-trace them."

"That our plan then?" Leigh-Ann said. "Wait for their heads to pop up then knock them down? Meanwhile trek to Africa?"

"It's not that simple," Tasker said. "However we go about this, we have to assume the Legion will be watching, and Ikiri is a long way to go with that threat hanging over us. At the least, we need to find out how to avoid them – but forming some sort of dialogue would be preferable."

"Meaning you wanna get hold of one of these pricks and shake the hell out of him," Reece said, to a cold look from Tasker.

"Can't y'all just get us a helicopter?" Leigh-Ann said. "Fly right from here into Ikiri in a couple hours so we can avoid this shit entirely?"

"No, we can't," Tasker said, "because such a helicopter doesn't exist. But even a private flight would be difficult to get into the Congo unchecked, in one leg. We're going to have to cover a lot of distance on ground and in the air. Go through airports. There are a lot of ways the Legion can get to us between here and Ikiri."

"So where do you even start with that?" Reece said.

"Exactly what I was talking about," Leigh-Ann scoffed. "Wanna rope us in on a big old conspiracy, bleed us for all we're worth."

"We don't need to bring them down," Tasker said. "But we do need leverage. Katryzna securing my family is the start, then we can knock back. Lean on the Legion's contacts, find a way to back them off. Failing that, we need to be able to predict where they're coming from and how to avoid them."

"Great," Reece said. "Nice and ambiguous. Listen, they got you rattled, pulling that stunt talking about your daughter, but no one's mentioning we got a bigger concern here. We even got time for this? Zip's brother's getting bolder and we're all agreed, I think, that he's able do his thing because he's in Africa? So we *have* to be there, too?"

"Whatever else it does," Tasker said, "I'm fairly sure Ikiri amplifies his powers, yes. I can't say exactly what it'll mean for Zipporah, but I'm convinced it will give her more power, too, to do good the same way it's given him the ability to do damage."

"Right, so all that considered, as long as Sto's taken care of, I'd be just as happy cutting out for the Congo yesterday. Just get us guns, ammo and a free pass to end these bastards, that's all we need."

"If you want to get yourselves and everyone else killed, sure," Tasker said. "How about you park your gusto for a second while we form a plan that will work?"

"I can get you those things," Ward came in, more diplomatically, before their tensions could rise. "I can arm you, arrange transport, whatever you need, but you need to work with us. Let Agent Tasker take the lead; he knows what he's doing and how to deal with people like this. Please. We have everyone's best interests at heart."

Reece paused, not liking where they'd ended up, but he was tired, and felt ratty enough that they might only argue if this went much further. Hell, Tasker had to be exhausted too; his eyes were dark and he had an extra emotional burden to carry. Reece exhaled and said, "Sure, we're in this together. Just wanna make sure it's done and we ain't caught up some place we shouldn't be, understand? At the end of all this, we're taking care of Zip."

"No one's saying otherwise," Ward spoke before Tasker could.

Reece eyed her, and said, "Hell. You get us ammo, passports, that stuff? Anything we want? You get your hands on a horn for me, too?"

"A what?" Ward said.

"A trumpet," Leigh-Ann said. "Like the pipes you find behind the can, but it makes music when you blow in it."

"What do you need a trumpet for?"

"To play *music*." Leigh-Ann rolled her eyes extravagantly.

"I busted mine on the way out of Stilt Town," Reece explained. He tried on a warm smile. If they were doing this, it'd at least be on his terms. "All for nothing if we can't carry music with us."

# 6

Katryzna made the two and a half hour journey to Bracknell in one and a half. Rurik complained annoyingly, but there weren't many cars on the road this late at night, and the flashing speed cameras would be Ward's problem. From the way the woman had driven to the safe house, Katryzna expected she could afford a few driving violations, and Katryzna could pay her back, besides. The bigger problem was finding the address: it was one thing to home in on a town, but this place was the residential equivalent of Sean's unremarkable suits: peaceful, ordinary, anonymous. After thirty minutes of driving through the town's square and soulless heart, Rurik needled. "Are you sure it wasn't Hill Gate Street?"

"Hill Gate *Road*," Katryzna insisted, slouched over the wheel, staring for street signs. "And we haven't seen a Hill Gate Street either so why are you talking?"

He wanted her to call Sean, or her job fixer Fosa, either of which would require shame and apology. But she diligently pressed on, and half an hour later, Katryzna finally turned onto Hill Gate Road. She drove past a big black Volvo on the corner and picked out Sean's house under the streetlights, a semi-detached clone as plain as the rest of the town; dull brick facade with white-framed windows and a white garage door, a patch of flowerless grass out front and a blue Peugeot in the drive. There were lights on in the windows, but thick curtains hid the interior. The building stood on a bend in the road, with hedges on the other side. The Volvo was parked just in sight. Men sitting inside.

Katryzna pulled up outside the house and rolled her neck.

From the dashboard, Rurik said, "They could be waiting for a friend?"

"Then they are waiting in the wrong place." Katryzna pulled her shirt over her gun and got out, as Rurik insisted she be careful. Careful, though, was making sure those men didn't tell anyone they'd seen her. From the shift in their silhouettes behind the windshield, they were already stirring, so she trotted towards them, throwing a friendly wave. Thick and thin: a big guy behind the wheel and a slim one in the passenger seat. The latter reached inside his coat, going for a phone or a weapon, didn't matter which. Katryzna drew her gun and shouted, "Not another move!"

She marched closer, picking out their faces in the red of her car's rear lights: a bearded slob at the wheel and the passenger sad-looking with loose sagging skin. Both a bit older than the average goon. She gestured for them to lower the window, and the driver reluctantly did so.

"Whatever you're thinking," he said, gruffly, "we're government agents."

"I am thinking," Katryzna said, "that government agents are not bulletproof." She scanned their shapes – various bulges in their clothes but no obvious guns. She said, "Turn on the light. Slow."

The driver hesitated, but did as he was told, reaching for the light above the mirror. It revealed sour expressions and crumpled, stained clothing. She could believe they were with the government now. If they had guns, they wouldn't be quick enough to use them.

Katryzna lowered her pistol. "You are here for Sean's family?"

"You're making –"

"Threaten me and I will hurt you. What are your names? You do not look like murderers – you would not be good at it. You are watching in case Sean comes back? To warn someone? What are your *names*?"

They both remained still, startled. The driver said, "Agent Bath."

"Agent Walters." The passenger spoke for the first time, voice raspy.

Katryzna wrinkled her nose. "Bath and Waters? Is this a joke?"

"Walters," the passenger repeated. "We're with the Ministry of Environmental Energy. We have orders –"

"Try again. You are working for Shearjoy."

"Never heard of him," Bath said. "Just who in hell are –"

He went quiet as she tapped her pistol against the window frame, pointing it in. She met Walters' eye and said, "You seem smart, Walter. If you are helpful, it will save you pain and I will not have to hear Rurik whining." She threw a look back to her car, where she could imagine the little conscience preparing a miserable scolding.

"Don't know what you want," Walters mumbled through his nose. "We're on official –"

"You are hiding in the dark – do I look like an idiot? Do not answer that, I haven't had a chance to shower. Okay, new game: first one to explain keeps his kneecaps."

It took them a second to process, so she reached the gun in towards Bath's leg. Walters cried out in protest, pressing back into his seat, the panic finally getting him – but his partner saw an opportunity and grabbed for her arm. She whipped the gun back so he snatched at nothing, while she grabbed the back of his head with the other hand. She slammed his face into the steering wheel with a sharp honk of the horn, pulled him back for a quick breath then smashed his face in harder, holding it there. The horn sounded louder as she moved the gun to his temple and he squirmed with complaints. Walters shouted at her to stop, they'd talk, as he threw worried looks up the road.

She let go, took a step back, and the horn cut off. A quick glance saw no lights coming on in Sean's neighbour's house, but there was a flutter of the curtains in Sean's. A shape there and quickly gone again, worried about being seen? Bath slumped, coughing on his complaints as Walters wheezed fearful noises.

"Talk!" Katryzna demanded.

"Don't know," Bath snorted. "Don't know any Shearjoy or what this is about. We get paid to be discreet, okay? Deputy Director ordered we watch the house, let him know if anyone came. Follow the occupants if they leave."

Katryzna scratched the fuzz on her head, looking back to the house. Whoever had braved the window had disappeared. Staying out of this. Rurik whispered, "As it should be. Do you understand what they're saying?"

"How do you always catch up?" Katryzna said, spotting him on the wing mirror.

"These are Sean's people," her conscience went on. "The Ministry. They are already keeping watch. Director Ward must have sent them!"

"She would not." Katryzna frowned and turned back to Bath. The man looked alarmed. "Deputy Director Ward sent you?"

Bath and Walters shared a look, the name not familiar. Bath said, "Finway. South London office. Listen, if you know the MEE, then you know –"

"I do not care," Katryzna sighed, straightening up. This was a problem. Even if they were doing the Legion's work, she could hardly kill the agents; it would create complications for everyone. If she left them here, they would report seeing her. She pointed the gun again and both men flinched. "Give me your wallets." They hesitated. "Quickly." They did so, fumbling, and she took out their cards. "This is where you live, *Jim*? Your wife? I am keeping these. Report that you have not seen anyone and I will leave your wife alone, okay?"

"You fucking –" Bath found a little courage again.

"I said she will be safe, pay attention. Unless you annoy me. Anything happens to Sean's family, worse will happen to yours. And later you. Trust me, I bear grudges."

"It's nothing do with us!" Walters piped up. "We're just doing our job!"

"Then you and your family have nothing to worry about, isn't it?"


Tasker jolted awake and leapt on his phone as it rang.

Katryzna said, "Sean?"

"Yeah." Tasker did not dare move or hope for what she might share. He blinked rapidly, inwardly cursing himself for falling asleep. He'd been going through Mason's files alone, over and over. Cross-checking names, dates, locations, looking for any chink that might tell him where to find the sixteen men or their associates. But for all the details, and broad indicators of the countries and companies Tasker couldn't outright trust, they were all hints at places the Legion had been, not where they were to be found. Which he supposed was the point: where their time wasn't spent hunting each other, it was spent evading each other.

"Your wife and child are home," Katryzna said, "and these two Ministry agents claim that someone called Finway told them to keep watch."

"Bloody hell." Tasker slumped, tension flooding out of him. But – "They sent our own people?"

"Looks like it. I have already persuaded them not to betray me. But do you want me to kill them and take your family somewhere else?"

"No!" Tasker said, almost rising from his seat. There was no reason for Finway or anyone else from the MEE to be involved here, except with Shearjoy's interference. And if there were corrupt agents keeping watch, there was no telling what other contingencies the Legion had in place. Helen and Rebecca couldn't stay at the house. Nor risk coming to him. "No to hurting the Ministry agents, but . . . I'll call Helen and let her know to go with you."

"Okay," Katryzna said, "but do you want them to come to meet Finway?"

"What? What do you mean, meet him?"

"He will know how to find Shearjoy, yes? Your family can wait in the car?"

"Katryzna, stop," Tasker said quickly. "No. We'll find a safe house for them."

"Oh yes, that works too. My people can find somewhere."

"Your people?" Tasker said. "What people?"

"Fosa. I will ask him when he gets Finway's location. We have lots of safe places in London. It will be fine."

"Slow down. Who's Fosa?"

"My assistant. You know, the one who got me Simon Parris's address?"

"I didn't know . . ." Tasker paused. Of course she had people of her own. He had never considered it, somehow. But she had a whole life before this that he'd barely touched the surface of understanding. "Katryzna. I don't want my family to meet anyone – I don't want anyone to see them. Can you do that?"

"That is what a safe house is for, Sean."

"Okay. And I need you to wait, so I can catch up to you."

"It is late, Sean, and everyone is tired," Katryzna replied, impatiently. "Just trust me. Go on and warn your wife I am here."

"No, you –" Tasker started, but she hung up. He stared at the phone. Had he replaced Shearjoy's threat of danger with the threat of Katryzna? He tried to call her back, but it rang with no answer. The number was blurry on his phone, his thoughts foggy, and he realised how numb he felt. He rubbed his eyes, took a breath, and called Helen. The moment she picked up, with the loud sounds of a movie in the background, he said, "There's someone coming to get you. I don't want you to worry, but it's important you do as she asks. I'll need you to lay low for a couple of days."

"Sean?" Helen said. Rebecca immediately piped up "Daddy?" as his wife continued, "You sound unwell, Sean, are you –"

"I'm just tired. She'll be there any minute," Tasker continued quickly. "Please, grab a few things and go with her – you can trust her, no matter how she looks. Or what she says. Just. Try not to engage too much."

"Is this what was going on outsi –" The bell rang and Helen gasped. "What's happening?"

"I'm sorry, Helen. Everything will be okay, I promise."

The bell rang again, and Helen audibly rose from the sofa, muttering. Rebecca asked to talk to him and the phone was handed over. "Daddy, you're missing a really good film, the girl wanted to fight and –"

"Sweet mercy," Helen's voice came from far off.

"Who is it, Mummy?"

"She's a friend," Tasker said. "Don't be scared, Rebecca. You just need to go on a little trip. It won't be for long." He couldn't hear what was being said at the door, but Katryzna sounded cheerful in contrast to Helen's measured dryness.

"Daddy, she looks strange," Rebecca whispered, fearfully.

"She is," Tasker said. "But she's a friend."

"Sorry, honey," Helen's voice came back. "We've got to go."

"Are we going to see Daddy?"

"Oh, what are you watching?" Katryzna asked abruptly. "Your house is *nice*. You decorated it, I think, not Sean."

"Can you wait by the door, please?" Helen replied calmly. "And – are you alright?"

"Yes, of course. Oh. This is not my blood. There was a man with a sword. It was – what?" She apparently fell into discussion with Rurik. "Well, I don't know, they are Sean's family, so – that's what I'm trying to do!"

"Daddy?" Rebecca whimpered.

"She's a friend," Tasker repeated, weaker this time. What the hell had he done? He pictured his living room, with the three-piece Chesterfield suite, its framed family photos from Germany, Canada, Thorpe Park, intruded upon by the inexplicable horror of Katryzna. But better this than leave them unprotected from the merciless Legion. Surely, better this.

Tasker stayed on the line, promising he would see them soon, while Helen reassured Rebecca and gave instructions. He asked Rebecca about her play, school, anything to keep her mind off what was happening. Helen didn't ask questions, just whipped up their travelling bags, responding to Katryzna with the briefest of remarks. When they finally left, Katryzna said, "Give the nice men a wave."

Tasker finally heard his wife crack as she realised the house was being watched: "Jesus."

Katryzna's car engine started and Helen asked for the phone back. Tasker pre-empted Helen's question: "Those are Ministry agents. I trust Katryzna more, right now."

"But are *you* safe?" Helen asked.

"Now that you're clear of this?" Tasker said. "Definitely."

He signed off and just held the phone. No idea where they were going and not wanting to know, to be sure he couldn't betray them. His eyes strayed down to Mason's notes and he realised he needed a more permanent solution. When Katryzna called again, he would arrange to meet her in London. They could track down Finway together, and start there. For a moment he burned to leave right away. But his energy was drained, physically and emotionally. He drooped in the chair and took in a shuddering breath. Restrain yourself, he thought. Recover your energy, take on the world tomorrow.

# 7

"Fuck am I?" A bassy shout woke Reece, and he almost fell out of bed as the shout turned to a groan of pain. He darted for the door as Zip sat up in her bed and Leigh-Ann stirred opposite, complaining, "That motherfucker trying to put us on a map?"

Out in the corridor, Tasker was approaching the medical bay with his pistol out like he might shoot Stomatt for being so damn loud, but he paused on seeing Reece. Their eyes locked in silent acknowledgement that they were both red-eyed and just woken, neither wanting trouble. Reece flashed a smile and went into the room. Stomatt was wincing over his abdomen, drip cables jangling as he moved, electronic monitor having a beeping fit. Reece pushed him down flat, saying, "You're good, Sto, take it easy. Wanna rip out your stitches?"

"Who in *fuck* gave me stitches?" Stomatt spat. "The hell are we – we get caught?"

"Sure, Sto," Reece said. "Got caught in a place without locks or guards. Think any prison hospital would've left you in anything less than shackles?"

Stomatt breathed heavily into his pain, as his mad eyes checked his surroundings. It was a sterile room, windowless and plain aside from shiny, expensive-looking equipment. Tasker watched through the doorway, out of Stomatt's sight. "So what happened? Fucking sword-freak got me."

"And the mill fell down, remember that?"

Stomatt frowned. "Yeah, kinda. Some filthy boy pulled me out – I dream that?"

"No, but thank your stars she ain't around to hear you put it like that. Shit, Sto, it's good to see you awake. Wasn't sure we'd get to talk before we left."

"Left for where?"

"Someplace you can't come with your weak-ass intestines," Leigh-Ann said, sliding into the room with Zip just behind her. They, at least, looked better for the night's sleep, in the baggy, clean t-shirts they'd found in the hideout's cupboards.

"Ain't nothing wrong with my intestines," Stomatt snorted. "Come here say that to my face, I'll show you what a weak intestine gonna do." He made a show of pulling up the hospital gown, to show off his swollen gut, but he winced again, and fell deeper into his pillow, eyes rolling back. "Hurts like a motherfucker."

"Figure you got Grade A narcotics pumping into you right now," Leigh-Ann said, moving closer to look accusingly at the drip. "But it ain't easy accounting for your weight."

"Shit," Stomatt huffed.

Reece was more concerned with the exposed bit of belly he'd seen; some still showed, between the shirt and the dressing. Dark veins snaked away from the wound. He said, "That's some damn peculiar kind of bruising."

He felt Zip's hand take his and looked down at her with a frown. She gave a slight shake of her head, warning him not to mention it, spare the big guy the shock. Reece nodded, and Zip said, almost experimenting, "Max. You're going to be okay."

"Well," he croaked, "since *you* say so." But he pushed down the pain to give her a big grin. "Ah, little Zip, we got you out, huh?"

"Yeah, and we're gonna send you home," Reece said. "Once you're good to go."

"Home? Where we're Most Wanted?" Stomatt tried to push himself up again, onto his elbows, and roared.

"You stubborn ass, stay down!" Leigh-Ann slapped his shoulder. They'd all gathered closer, like a glove of family. He settled, breathing slower, deeper.

"How's it I'm always the one ends up injured?" he said. "Y'all look right as rain."

"Lucky, I guess," Reece said.

"But you telling me home's safe? We all going back?" He met their faces in turn, even Zip's. "What happened while I was out? Telling me it's over?"

Reece took a breath. "Yeah, man. For you it is." He looked over his shoulder, no telling what this day would bring the rest of them. Tasker gave away nothing in his steely gaze, and instead nodded that he would leave them to it, before moving away.

"But not for you?" Stomatt said. "Don't give me that, Reece. We got unfinished business? Ain't that Vile fucker toast?"

"One down," Reece said. "But a few more to go. You focus on recovering, Sto. We gonna get you young nurses and the best drugs, don't you worry." Stomatt started to protest, but no amount of defiance was getting him out of bed. There was a bang in the hallway, and quiet cursing, drawing Reece's attention away.

"This some bullshit," Stomatt murmured, blinking heavily. "Can't even exactly see right. What they got me on?"

"Best drugs available, from what we seen," Leigh-Ann said. "We made some new friends while you were out."

"I'll let Leigh tell you all about it," Reece said, giving Stomatt a pat. He left them to investigate the noise in the hallway. Sam Ward was fumbling her way out from the elevator, struggling with some big shopping bags. He rushed to help her, setting the shopping down. "You just getting back in? Tell me you ain't been up all night."

Ward smiled, skin dark around her eyes. "There was a lot to take care of. Back at the village and for going forward." She nodded to the closest bag, stuffed with clothes, labels poking out. "Sorry they're just from George; Asda was the only shop open. But I got various sizes."

"Trust me, if it ain't bloodstained or torn, it's fine," Reece told her, picking through for a quick idea of what she'd got. This George guy made shapeless shirts and loose-threaded slacks, a one-style-fits-all medley, but Ward had at least chosen vivid colours and a navy blue jacket that could almost work, in a dollar store kind of way. He said, "The way things been going, I just hope it's all disposable."

"I brought food, too," Ward said. "Have you spoken to Agent Tasker? He wants to follow up a lead in London. You can stay here while we plan the next move."

"Ah hell, don't bench me. I'd love to see London; sure Leigh would, too. Not far, is it? Whole of England's just a few hours apart, right?"

"It's not the distance that's the problem. It's safe to be moving everyone around. You know, this shouldn't be in your hands. If you want –"

"No better hands for it," Reece cut in lightly.

"I'm serious," Ward said. "This is our job. Agent Tasker's family are safe now, your friend is stable, no one knows we're here. You can rest."

"While you take up the slack? No offence, but where I'm from we don't let pretty ladies fight our battles for us."

She raised a sceptical eyebrow. "What about ugly ones?"

Reece paused and offered a sheepish smile, running a hand back through his murky green hair. "Sorry, that was cheap, huh? I just woke and none of us are used to getting outside help, let alone from a –" He gestured a hand broadly at Ward, to encompass all she represented, but her expression only got less impressed. Reece leant slightly closer to clarify: "A kind and plainly *upstanding* pillar of society."

"Thanks," she replied, and he could see she was holding back a smile. Definitely a part of her enjoying this, under the polite exterior. To be a director at her age – not too many years older than them – he figured she probably didn't get to have fun often.

"We ain't layabouts, though," he said. "You know we took on the Steer Trust before all this kicked off? Four-piece band outta Cutjaw handed a big-shot business mogul his ass. Not good enough? We also won a Battle of the Bands down Melancony's, when all of us were no more than fourteen. Got a write up in *Two Shoots Magazine*, and all."

"I'm not sure those skills are transferable to the current situation."

"That's because you haven't heard me carry a tune yet. Played piano for Seph Mason and threw him right off, sure enough."

"The elusive Seph Mason. Is that why he left you?"

Reece smirked. "Actually, it was Katryzna putting a knife to his neck. That and Zip going against his orders. Y'all got people on his trail though, right? You know he's gonna pop up again."

"I do," Ward said, "and there's no sign of him. Where do you think he was heading?"

Reece recalled the last time they'd seen the one-handed brute, in a fix between anger at Zip using her powers and upset at the idea that his son was still alive. He said, slowly, "At a guess, I'd say he's either gone looking for his boy or slunk off to sulk in private. Considering he didn't even know Zip had travelled Stateside, I'd be inclined towards the latter. But shit, we were talking *music*, and speaking of which –" Reece gestured to the bags – "I don't see a horn."

"Sorry." Ward reached into a jacket pocket. "I did get this. It's not much." She held up a harmonica, shining chrome, extra long.

He took it and turned it over. "24-hole Suzuki. You picked that up at a supermarket?"

"I took it from home," she admitted. "A gift from an ex."

Reece raised an eyebrow. "You play?"

"He did. At least, he was learning. We weren't together long. I never got into it."

"You don't play and weren't together long and he gave you *this*?" Reece laughed. "Was he kind of an asshole?" That got an actual smile. "Ah but you're missing out. Thing like this gives some complex sounds." He gave the harmonica a test, ran up and down the holes, bent a few notes. Nodding, he got into it. Down the hall, Stomatt shouted appreciation, and Zip appeared in the door, eyes wide. As Reece finished up, he met Ward's impressed gaze. "Boyfriend never played it like that, huh?"

"He did not."

"See," Reece said, "Cutjaw Kids surprise you at every turn. And you know we're monster hunters now? All you gotta do is fold us into the action."

But while he felt Ward was softening, some of her amusement left her. She looked away and said, "I suppose you're in it already, so I'm not going to stop you doing whatever you feel the need to. But this might get a lot worse before it gets any better. There's an awful lot I'm unclear on in this entire situation, with all these dangerous people still out there running around. And" – she lowered her voice – "there's something unusual about your friend's wound."

"Yeah?" Reece said, tensing. He'd seen it himself, the discolouration. Ward's expression said whatever he was thinking was probably right, and that his guess was as good as hers. "Well, you're the one knows at least some of this territory. What are we gonna do about it?"

Ward shook her head. "There's little precedent for the particulars here. But I suspect all the answers lie in the same place."

"Alright then." Reece stepped aside and spread his arm invitingly up the hall. "After you, ma'am. Dying to know how you see us resolving all this together."

# 8

Katryzna approached an odd apartment complex with a lightness in her step. Helen and Rebecca Tasker had liked her, she decided, despite their general reluctance to talk. She had delivered them to, in her opinion, a pleasant terraced house in a London suburb, where the surfaces were mostly clean and there were lots of blankets. Fosa (once she had evaded his initial barrage of questions as to what on earth she had been up to) had insisted it had not been in use for many months. The dusty smell confirmed that. Sean's family did not complain, anyway, and they had time to, while Katryzna caught a nap on the sofa. She even asked on the way out, "It is an okay place, isn't it?"

Helen gave her a slightly unpleasant look, mostly because she had been woken up by Katryzna rummaging in the cupboards. She nodded, though.

Now, with the sun dawning, Katryzna told Rurik, perched on her shoulder, "This is going well. You can say it, you know. After so many years complaining, now I am doing good, you can say something nice."

"That woman and child," Rurik said, "were terrified of you. And that apartment had mould. And Sean told you to wait – you shouldn't *be* here. You didn't even apologise to Fosa for not keeping him updated. So forgive me if I hold off on the praise."

"There you go again," Katryzna huffed.

She stopped to take in their destination. Deputy Director Finway was evidently important, given the expensive building where he lived. Just around the corner from the busy King's Cross Station, the apartment units looked like giant silos that had been converted to glass, with the metal skeletons of their former selves rising around them in a strange hug. Sleek interiors shone out in pockets of glowing light. The name above the entrance read: Gasholders.

Katryzna said, "There is a joke there. Hot air and wind, you know?"

"Hilarious," Rurik replied wearily.

"At least I am trying."

Katryzna entered and looked up at ringed walkways climbing towards the ceiling, framing the big circular lobby with its palm-tree planters. Shaking her head at the clash of tropical and industrial, she continued up a curving staircase. When she reached the second floor, a sour-looking woman in a dress came out of an apartment. Katryzna waved. The woman stared with alarm and slowly, uncertainly, held up a hand in return. Almost a wave. Satisfied, Katryzna continued to the next floor.

"She's probably going to call the police," Rurik hissed in her ear.

"You worry too much."

The address Fosa had given her took her to an oak door on Level 8. She knocked loudly and waited, peering back over the wall into the central space, a long drop to the lobby. No one answered, so she banged louder, and louder, until the door suddenly opened a crack and a short man glowered out. He demanded, "Who the hell are you?"

"Katryzna," she replied with a bright smile, innocent enough that he opened the door in confusion. He had a wide head with ears that stuck out at odd angles, a mess of thinning hair and skin dotted with blemishes. Standing only as high as her chin, he was more goblin than man, only he wore a fancy soft jumper with a shirt collar sticking out.

"Am I supposed to know you?" he asked, resuming hostilities, voice high and shrill. "Well, what are you doing here?"

"At least check he's the right person," Rurik said, as Katryzna's fingers curled into a fist.

"Oh. Yes. Are you Finway?"

The man straightened up importantly. "Right, you got the address, fuck knows how, given the state of you. This some kind of joke? Bulson put you up to it, sent around some –"

"Shut up," Katryzna told him. "I am here about the Legion."

The word worked like magic: Finway froze to regard her anew. Fear crept over his arrogance, then he swallowed and tried to recover. "Okay. That makes sense, I suppose. And what? I have everything under control, don't I?"

"Define everything."

"Are you serious? Pissing hell, you can go back and tell him he's got a right nerve. Sending anyone to my home, looking like *this*, talking like I'm some fucking –"

Finway coughed as he folded over Katryzna's fist and fell into her shoulder. She shunted him back into the apartment and kicked the door shut behind her. Finway knocked over a small table and a vase smashed on the hardwood floor. He rolled onto his hands and knees and tried to push himself up, gasping for breath, but Katryzna rested her knife against his neck.

"Can we skip this?" she asked. "You are small and pathetic, you have no excuse to underestimate me."

But he couldn't help it, and spat, "You're fucking dead."

Katryzna grabbed his neck and swung him into the wall. He tried to spin and kick with untrained, panicking limbs, but he only collapsed to the floor. She jumped on him and pinned him with her knees, then brought the knife between his eyes. He went still. "First rule. Stop swearing."

"What the fuck –"

She nicked his brow and he shrieked and tried to the blink the blood out of his eye. That made it worse, so he squeezed the eye shut and glared with the other one. Realising he was in actual trouble. He said, "What's this about? I've done all I was asked – if there's a problem he could've called."

"Who?" Katryzna asked. "Shearjoy?"

"Oh fuck." A new level of alarm gripped him. "Fuck off –"

Katryzna bounced his head off the floor, hard. "I said. Watch. Your. Language."

"Stop – okay!" Finway groaned. "Jesus, what's wrong with you? Can I say Jesus? Hell."

Katryzna gritted her teeth, waiting for the next curse. Rurik said, "You kill him for how he speaks and we won't get any answers."

"We won't anyway, if he cannot control his tongue."

Finway stared with the incomprehension Katryzna was used to. He said, "You're one of the others, aren't you? Listen, I've got money, I've got contacts – I can be a powerful ally."

"That is better," Katryzna said. "Now we have an understanding, here is what I need. You are not going to help Shearjoy anymore, yes? You are not going to go near Agent Sean Tasker or his family and you are not going to tell the Legion about this. You are also going to tell me where to find him."

"Tasker?" Finway frowned.

"Shearjoy."

It took a second, then Finway laughed. He took another look at her, then laughed again, hysterically. "Oh that's rich. You idiot. You fucking moron –"

Katryzna poked the tip of the blade into his nostril and he went still. But he struggled to keep down more chuckles, tears mixing with the blood in his eyes.

"Right, the language, sorry," Finway said. "But you really are a *fucking* dead woman."

She tore the blade to one side and he screamed as blood flicked across the floor. Rurik shouted at her to stop as Katryzna braced the knife to stab in his stupid mouth. But his scream turned to babbling, begging. "Stop, stop! I'm talking, aren't I? But it's the truth! You probably signed my death warrant just being here. Tell you where Shearjoy is? You've got zero idea what you're doing!"

"I know how to make you hurt. A lot."

Finway tried to pull his head at least a little way from the knife, twitching with pain, but she squeezed her knees tighter onto him and he grunted. "All right. Yeah, I believe you, but so what? You wanna torture a civil servant in his home, no one's giving you a gold star for that. Different ball game thinking you can cross the Legion, especially if you think *I'm* the one's gonna give them up."

"Yes, yes" – Katryzna rolled her free hand – "and now I cut another piece off you and we reconsider how tough you are, while Rurik screams at me to stop."

"No, you're not listening. I only met that smug git a couple of times, years ago. Ever since, it's been untraceable phone calls and deposits in the bank. Believe me, I tried to track him myself – we've got a few tricks at the Ministry after all – you think I want these corrupt fucks hanging over my head? There's always *one more thing* they want. And now? Going after one of our own? Fucking disgusting."

Katryzna swallowed her irritation as Rurik yelled at her to stay focused.

The man's swearing was not the issue, her conscience insisted. She asked, "What are they hanging over your head?"

"What do you think?" Finway laughed again, without humour. "Look at this damn place. Look at me."

Katryzna looked from the blood-streaked little man to the lavish apartment. A marble kitchen counter was visible down the hall. Abstract paintings and small sculptures littered the place. Like a bad museum for people pretending to be cultured.

"I did things for them when I was climbing the ladder," Finway said. "They helped *make* me. Problem is that when they make you, they can always break you."

"That is sad," Katryzna said, standing.

Finway rolled aside to squeeze a hand over his nose as she walked into his living room and considered the scale of the apartment; a spiral staircase went up, another staircase went down. Apartments were not supposed to work like this.

"*Millions*, if that's what you're thinking," Finway said, climbing to his feet, voice muffled by the hand on his nose. "This place is worth fucking *millions*. Not rock star money – bloody oligarch money. I couldn't afford a place like this in twenty lifetimes. I have to pretend I inherited it or some shit. Got lucky investing. Reality is, it's probably tied me to blood money in China or the Eastern European slave trade, I don't even know."

"You should sell it," Katryzna advised.

He laughed, then shook his head, seeing she was serious. "Like I said. You've got no idea."

"I know that everyone leaves a trail. And if you hate them, you will help me find it. You have contact details for the Legion?"

"They call me. Or, mostly, they don't, I just get a job come through that I know is their handiwork. Nonsensical projects that I give a stamp to authorise, that sort of thing. Cargo ship needing clearance, warehouse that needs to be ignored, you know."

"They have cargo ships and warehouses?"

"And building projects that make this place look cheap – aren't you listening?" Finway gestured to the apartment. "This was a *gift*. They are minted up the fucking arse."

Katryzna rubbed her temple, fighting the urge to hurt him.

"Who even *are* you?" Finway asked, coming closer. "You bust in here to cut me up and can't stomach purple language? You raised in one of those Lithuanian murder convents or some shit?"

"I have no idea what you are talking about," Katryzna said.

"Yeah? That's one thing I *did* trace. The Legion run training camps for psychos. Except by the time I got a bead on that one, they'd shut it down. Maybe you tell me something – what's it they're all up to, they need to be training killers?"

"They are killing people," Katryzna said. "Obviously. You have done work for them. You must know something useful, and you need to give it to me before I get bored."

Finway paused. "Why? Tell me where you're coming from, maybe I figure a way to help."

Katryzna stared, with no interest in sharing, but Rurik whispered, "He's got no love for the Legion, can't you see that? He wants you to stop them."

"Or he's pretending," she replied, then told Finway, "I do not have many friends. These Legion people have crossed the ones I do have."

"Right," Finway said. "So you're not even connected to this? A layman like me?"

"I do not lie with men, no," Katryzna said, unsure how that fit in.

"I mean you got none of their –" Finway paused over the right wording. "Freaky nature. I've seen them. I can give you that for free: they're not natural."

"That is not a problem," Katryzna said. "You threatening Sean's family is a problem."

"Uh-huh. Well, you might tell Agent Tasker I'm the least of his worries. If it wasn't me keeping an eye on his family, they'd have someone else. Probably do have someone else. Lady, I work with the Ministry, high up – we're dodgy as fuck. These guys make what we do look like child's play."

"Details!" Katryzna raised her voice, with a step back towards him and a swing of the knife. "Give me something important to them."

Finway considered it, reading her face.

"You think they will come for you," she said. "Because of me. But if you help me, I will stop them."

"You get top marks for crazy, at least," Finway said, slowly. He shook his head and sniffed. "What difference's it make now, I guess. Best I can give you is the last place I know they were into. About a year back, they contacted me to grease some wheels with the ONF. French environmental agents. Got them to stop looking into activity in a location in the French Alps. They were building something out there. If it's anything like that murder convent, chances are they're gone already. That's all I've got."

"A location in the French Alps," Katryzna echoed. "That's it? You expect me to say *oh that's nice* and go on your word?"

"Piss off," Finway snorted. "Give me some credit, I keep records. I'll show you the files. Why the hell not – you go gunning for these people, you're dead anyway."


As Katryzna ended their call, Tasker buried his frustration at her moving without him to quickly move on – he immediately called Helen to check that she was okay. She answered tiredly, saying yes, the journey had been fine, and they were now alone in a house that, while filthy, was stocked with food and, presumably, secure. She asked if Katryzna was coming back, in a tone that suggested it might be best if she didn't. Tasker assured her they were safe now and no, with any luck they'd be left alone until this was over. He hung up and tried to dwell on the positives. Katryzna had a lead, his family were clear of it, and she had claimed to have left Finway more or less on side. Tasker tried to ignore her cryptic comments about him bleeding. He gathered Reece, Leigh-Ann and Ward in the common room to summarise Katryzna's call: the Legion had a location in the Alps, dubbed the Hall of Enoch, a secluded, derelict property which they had acquired last year, requiring a lot of blind eyes towards planning permissions and the movements of machinery.

"There was a Hall of Cainon in Mason's notes, in the Carpathian Mountains," Tasker told the group, "so it fits the pattern."

"What's with the Bible names?" Leigh-Ann asked.

"Beats me," Tasker said. "Goes with the Legion, though. Maybe they just wanted an easy source of inspiration."

"Zipporah is from the Bible," Zip said. She sat on a small stool in the corner, keeping out of the way while the grown ups talked. They could've been a family, Tasker thought: Reece, Leigh-Ann and the kid were in bright-coloured shirts and trousers out of the same set, washed and at least partly presentable. Except Reece's hair was still a muddy-green mess and Leigh-Ann's was in a big black tangle – and Zip's eyes shone brighter red than they had in the night. The child continued, "My daddy told me that my mother chose it."

"Yeah? He mention the Legion making references like this?" Reece asked. "Might help us get in these guy's heads."

Zip shook her head. "But I've been thinking." She paused, with the clear worry that her ideas would complicate their lives. "I could ask my mum."

It was barely audible. A whisper.

"Zip," Leigh-Ann said, carefully, "we established your mom's trapped out in Africa? Right, Agent Tasker?"

Tasker nodded, not taking his eyes from the child as he waited for more.

"My mum has power," Zip said. "Katryzna said so. If she has power, like me and my brother, and if I was able to touch *his* mind, then I can touch hers. She asked me to come back, and she knew where I was, so she can help, can't she? She would know about the Legion, maybe."

"We discussed this," Reece said. "Ain't no one asking you to put yourself on the map again. No using them powers unless absolutely necessary, Zip."

"But we'll be moving soon, won't we?" Zip said, picking up speed. She'd given this thought. "If we go somewhere where we are ready to leave, quickly, then I could create a connection, and we could leave straight away, before anyone catches up. We need to move quickly anyway, don't we?"

"No," Reece said. "I don't like it. Now the Taskers are in the clear, we can cut a straight line to Ikiri, there's no –"

"Nothing's changed," Tasker came in. He lowered his gaze to the mess of Mason's files. "I hate to say it but that's the truth. Just because my family are safe right now, it doesn't mean the Legion won't still come after them. The same for yours, as you said yourself, Reece. Look at all this; Mason was on the back foot with the Legion. He hid himself away for eight years trying to pinpoint them. But we've got two things he didn't: a location not in his research and a willingness to use –" Tasker paused, careful in his wording.

"A willingness to *listen* to Zipporah. Is this what you want, Zip? To try and touch base with your mother?"

Zip nodded.

"Even knowing your gifts might create a signal?"

"Yes," she said. "I could have done more before, if my daddy let me. It's not just for me – I really think it would help."

Rather than force the decision himself, Tasker met Reece's eye, inviting his input. Uncomfortable, the American looked to Leigh-Ann. She shrugged and said, "I'll be the first to admit she knows what's up better than us. Real question is, where we gonna go in the meantime?" She in turn looked to Ward. "You guys seriously don't have any helicopters?"

"I can arrange a plane," Ward said. "Just tell me where to."

"All right then," Tasker said, "I guess we give this a try."

# 9

Henri gave himself time to mourn only after half a day spent moving from one part of the city to another, watchful for anyone following. He collapsed at the bank of the Bumbu river, as private a spot as he could find in a stretch flanked by sheet-metal shacks with log supports. With his long, thick arms draped over his knees, Henri finally cried, releasing the pressing, burning strain that gripped his chest.

Miguel was dead, and he had led the killer to him. Miguel, the cranky old man who saw threats in every shadow because the threats were *real*. Henri alone had known Miguel's background, remembering the people who had taken his sister away, but he had also seen Miguel change, leaving the mercenary life behind to start a new life in Kinshasa. He'd been lost, at first. Angry and afraid. But he stood up for the young men, taught them what he knew, helped keep Club Clash running. He let them be angry, in the ring. He let them be violent and headstrong and furious at the world – always in the ring. And they left it there. That in turn let them be decent people outside.

Henri had followed Miguel without question, without any other choice, after Sara had never come back. She had gone into the forest with those mercenaries believing the Lord would guide her. That He would help her guide them, even. Henri admired her ambition, and when she didn't return, her drive to do better lived on through him, not only keeping him from falling apart but keeping Miguel from collapse, too. With backing from the great Duvcorp, Miguel drew in enough money for both of them, and Henri ensured he survived. They worked well together. For many years.

And now Miguel was dead and Sara . . . suddenly she wasn't, but was breathing the spirit of Ikiri, not her own. The mercenaries were back and the never-ending cycle of white men staking a bloody, tortuous claim in the Congo continued.

Dragging a forearm over his wet eyes, Henri wished that Katryzna were there. She and Tasker could stop these people. They understood these people, and where they were coming from. All he knew how to do was stay out of the way. Except Flay was coming for *him*. They knew he had been to Ikiri, so he could not be allowed to live – and they would hurt others he cared about before this was over.

Henri rose, sniffing back the last tears. No, there was no more staying out of trouble. He had known this would be the case the moment he ignored Miguel's concerns and agreed to join up with Agent Tasker. He still had a part to play. He would lay low, yes, but he could fight.

Steeling himself, Henri walked down the bank to a food stall, a grimy plastic sheet propped up over rusty-legged tables and stools. He ordered *maboké*, spiced catfish cooked in banana leaves, and his stomach rumbled at the aromas. He had gone the whole day without food, hadn't he? It had taken all his focus to keep moving.

He took his first bite and the flavour flooded his senses. Then murmurs swept through the other patrons as something caught their attention behind him. An old man quickly finished his mug of wine, folded his newspaper and left. Henri slowly turned. Of course, it was a white man, descending the slope from the road behind the stall.

Well, so be it. Henri took another mouthful of food. He would not fight hungry, at least. The man moved with slow deliberation. Not Flay, but taller, in a long, dusty overcoat with only one hand showing; the right sleeve bulged at the cuff, with nothing coming out. Henri shovelled in another quick mouthful of food as the man ducked under the roof of the food shelter, and stopped, stooping, letting Henri take him in. His face was familiar: the man who had been in charge of Duvcorp's mercenaries. Sara had laughed with him before they left, even touched his arm. She had said, when Henri worried, that it did no harm to disarm such men. Back then, this man had smiled too, as much as his English restraint allowed. But he had aged badly, with his face deep-lined and scarred, and it looked like he might not have smiled since.

"You need to come with me," the man said, voice rusty and hard.

"I am eating," Henri replied, and took another mouthful.

"Bring it with you."

"No thank you," Henri said around the food. "You want to fight, we can do so here." He quickly took more of the spiced fish, along with a big chunk of leaf, filling his mouth as distraction from his rising fear. He had mastered his nerves for fighting in the ring, but it was never the same in the real world. The stakes were always kill or be killed, out here. And just like Flay, the man had dead eyes like a shark's. The last patrons were gathering their food and moving away as the stall proprietor peered from under the counter, hiding. Most likely there was a weapon behind the bar, but he was unlikely to use it on a white man.

The man waited until Henri finished his next mouthful. Henri took a breath and asked, "How did you find me?"

"The same way the Legion will. Everyone leaves a trail."

Henri hadn't – not in any easily discernible way. He had never been to this place before, nor planned his route, merely fled through the city. But he understood. His sister in Ikiri could locate people at a distance. Why shouldn't the other survivors do the same? Henri paused, though, and said, "The *Legion* will? You're not with the others?"

"I work alone. Usually. I have need of you."

"I'm not –" Henri swallowed. "I'm not looking for work."

"Are you looking to survive?" He made it sound like an opportunity, instead of a threat. Henri met his eye, trying to keep up some defiance, and the man continued, "My name is Seph Mason. We were close, Sara and me.

You are her brother, aren't you? I didn't know she had survived. At least, I convinced myself she hadn't. But you were with them, weren't you? You saw her again."

The image of Sara trapped in the tree came back to Henri; the horror of finding her not in her mind, barely in her body. She was hanging half-submerged in the trunk of a tree, weighed down by uncut feral hair, talking in unfinished sentences, eyes wild. The freak result of a power Henri could not understand. He said, "If you care about her, I'm not sure you want to see her now."

"All the more reason, if she is suffering."

"Not suffering, but . . ." Henri paused. "You know what it's like out there."

"I thought I did," Mason said. "Considering the Legion are here, hunting you, they have doubts, too. Ordinarily, I would wait for them to come for you while you weep. But they are a lesser concern right now."

"Weep?" Henri replied hotly. "Miguel was my friend – my mentor. How are –"

"I will provide transport," Mason interrupted without feeling. "I merely need a guide to be sure I reach Ikiri as quickly and with as few complications from the locals as possible. In return, I will make the Legion go away. For good. Yes or no?"

Henri stared, uneasily. General Solomon had explained some of what had happened to the mercenaries who touched Ikiri, and the conclusion was that none of them came back good. "Why should I believe you're any better than them?"

"Better for what?" Mason said. "I do not wish to kill you, that should be enough. But I will stop this. Ikiri's power does not belong in the hands of man." He paused. "And I wish to keep my child out of this. Your niece."

Henri's eyes shot open. "My – the one they're –" He rose to his feet, caution shattered by hope. "Did you meet Katryzna – Agent Tasker? Did they send you?"

Mason stiffened. "We spoke. They are not with me."

"What? Why not? Surely they explained what Sara told us? The child –"

"Does not belong here. Quite the opposite. This is my task to complete."

Henri hesitated. "But you did meet them?"

"Yes, and they are likely to follow. I intend to remove the need. That's why I need your assistance."

"If I say no?" Henri asked.

"It will slow me down, but I will get there. You, on the other hand, will be on your own." Mason held his gaze with unblinking eyes. Fully confident.

Henri looked at the fish again and swallowed. It wasn't much of a choice.


Mason drove a sputtering truck through Kinshasa, heading towards the Congo River, and Henri flinched as he saw the man's right-hand sleeve slip back, revealing a chunky metal contraption where his hand should be. A damaged shard of metal stuck out, which he hooked loosely onto the steering wheel. Equally strange, Mason focused more on the city around them than on the road ahead. He drove fast, through gaps that looked scarcely wide enough, and he never consulted a map or looked for landmarks. It was like the truck was driving itself, while Mason watched for threats. But early-evening Kinshasa was its usual self, with people cooking and sharing drinks, loud vehicles clogging the roads, and occasional soldiers loitering with cigarettes or negotiating deals with street vendors.

They pulled into N'Dolo Airport, where Mason steered past a gate in the fencing with a wave to the watching guards. They seemed to not even notice them. Henri turned in the seat, asking, "Do they know you? How long have you been in the city?"

Mason didn't answer. It made as much sense that the airport staff ignored them as it did that he had been able to swerve through Kinshasa so competently, or that he had been able to track Henri down at all. More eeriness on top of what Henri had already seen: Sara in the tree, the dead walking in the forest, the sounds of unnatural creatures. All part of the same thing. The old superstitions he and Sara had put aside when they moved into the city, manifest in ways that even the village spiritualists would doubt.

Mason left the truck by a hangar and strode past staff preparing planes for flight. A technician rushed over and handed him some keys, and he led the way to a light aircraft, red and white striped with a single propeller. It looked barely big enough for two. Henri said, "Where do you plan to fly to?"

"To the airstrip in Bumba," Mason said, prepping the equipment. He took the radio and relayed details, saying he was ready for takeoff.

"You, personally, want to fly?" Henri said. "My friend, do you know Ikiri is in dangerous territory? If we take a plane over –"

"Get in," Mason ordered.

Henri looked from the cockpit out to the hangar and the staff, hoping someone might at least acknowledge the strangeness of this. Mason hooked the metal contraption that replaced his hand onto the steering column.

"You are not serious." Henri laughed. "Mr Mason, come on, we will find a real pilot – or I can find us a fast boat. I see now why you needed my help."

Mason met his eye, absent of humour. "Get in."

Henri stared back. This was as sure a way to die as any. But the man was serious. He raised his hands in surrender and climbed into the cramped passenger seat. Mason gave sharp instructions for Henri to secure himself and the door, then they were rolling down the runway. Henri could only laugh again as they accelerated and the plane shuddered. He cried out, "You are a crazy person! We are going to die!"

"Not here," Mason promised. "Not yet."

They took off and the plane rattled and bounced between air pockets, but it steadied, and the lights of Kinshasa stretched out beneath them. Henri marvelled at the headlights moving up and down the veins of the streets. His beautiful city, crawling with the life of an anthill. He was leaving it behind again, twice in so many weeks, for a place he knew to dread. Left behind, too, was Miguel and whoever was after him. A tragedy he could put off for now.

"You are a good pilot," Henri told Mason, only because it had to be true, if they were to live. Mason grunted confirmation. "What happens when we reach Bumba?"

"I'll find a chopper."

"A helicopter?" Henri exclaimed. "Never mind the militias, do you know that Ikiri interferes with electronic equipment? We could fall out of the sky. There was a reason you didn't fly there before, yes?"

"I'm willing to take that risk now."

"Maybe I am not."

"You're welcome to leave at any time," Mason said, in the flat tone of a man who knew Henri had no choice. Was he like this before? He tried to remember over the distance of eight years. Was this truly a man that Sara had cared for?

"Can you tell me about my sister's daughter?" Henri asked.

Mason made a noise like the subject was ugly to him. "She is healthy. Smart."

Henri waited for more, but Mason was done. "She does well in school? With many friends?"

"No. I have kept her safe, and will continue to do so. Once this is resolved."

The way he spoke invited Henri to be quiet, and stirred uncomfortable thoughts that this was not all as well as he would have liked. How could this man have a child? Where was she? Katryzna and Agent Tasker should have come back. Had Henri made a big mistake, putting any trust in Mason?

# 10

With the seed of Zip's idea sown, the group quickly got going. While Reece and the others packed up supplies, Tasker picked out an airstrip where Katryzna could meet them. Stomatt was out again and didn't respond when Reece cleared his throat to get him to stir so they could say goodbye. It seemed he'd used up all his energy in his earlier waking belligerence. But he wasn't in danger, as far as they knew.

Reece tried not to consider the weirdness around his wound.

"Best leave him to it," Leigh-Ann said. "Needs all the beauty sleep he can get."

"I'll keep you posted on his condition," Ward promised, and Reece gave her a smile. They were leaving her behind, too, which Reece wasn't happy about either, but she insisted she'd support them from here. She also suggested he stow his gun in the bag; best not draw any more attention than necessary. That, with a wry look at his wacko dye job. He'd tried to wash some more of the colour out that morning, without much success.

Tasker advised Katryzna to stay put until they were nearby, rather than give her the details of the meeting point outright, clearly not trusting her to keep things quiet. Then he took the wheel of the rental car. Reece left him to all the organising; as their future likely included more authority figures, years of experience said anyone from Cutjaw was on the back foot there. Reece could take the wheel back later.

The promise of a tough morning kept them all quiet for a journey up through the hills, with the winter sun peaking over the horizon. In the late morning dark, the heavy rain of the night had left the air crisp, fresh. Cold in a way that sent shivers through your bones. Just as well Ward's care package came with puffy coats that just about kept out the chill.

They all got out at a parking lot by a country lane, wide enough for only a handful of vehicles, flanked by trees and serenaded by the buzz of a nearby road. Two other cars were there, with no sign of their owners. Cages in back suggested dog-walkers.

Tasker explained, "We're by the A387; five minutes and we're on a fast road to almost anywhere in the UK. Anyone that knows we were here won't have much to go on."

"So we're gonna light a fuse and run?" Leigh-Ann summarised.

"Yeah." His eyes fell on Zip, his voice measured, calm. "As soon as you're ready."

"I'm ready," Zip said. Tasker nodded for her to go ahead, but she waited, looking to Reece, and he gave the nod she actually wanted. She stared into whatever was in her mind. The sounds around them seemed to disappear in her bubble of concentration – was Reece being drawn into her focus with her? It only lasted a second before the buzz of the road burst back on them and Zip let out a short gasp. She looked up at Tasker, fully alert again. "She's out there. She is. I can feel it."

"But?" Leigh-Ann picked up on her discomfort.

"It's not just her." Zip bit her lip and screwed her eyes closed to try again. The sounds dimmed again, this time for longer. Her eyelids twitched as though dreaming. Her lips quivered as she spoke in her mind. Words came out: "He's not –" Then she gasped again and drew back. A car engine roared past them, but when Reece spun he saw no movement. Their road was empty, it couldn't have been anywhere near.

"The fuck . . ." Leigh-Ann muttered.

"I can't do it," Zip said, pacing a little towards them, then away. "It's not safe. She is there, but it's not safe – when I go there, I can feel too much. He can feel it, too. My brother, she says, beware him. Ezekiel. He has a name." Zip shook that off. "She said to come, that's all. Have to come. To be there. But I asked – I told her it's not easy, and about the Legion – she said they're *his* problem. *Him.*"

"Ezekiel's?" Tasker suggested but Zip shook her head.

Without warning, she went into that state again, hurrying to figure something out, and got out the barest bleat of a warning before she brought the world back again. This time sounds of traffic invaded their space along with snippets of music and a radio host talking. Leigh-Ann jumped as Tasker turned on the spot.

"You're drawing us into this," Reece said. "Those sounds –"

"Just the road," Zip said, as though it was nothing. "Down the hill. It's hard to focus. Sorry. I had to look, but he's not here. My daddy is gone. A long way gone. But" – she focused gravely on Tasker – "they're not far away. At least, compared to Ikiri."

"What's that even mean?" Leigh-Ann said, unsettled.

"The Legion," Zip replied with a little stomp of frustration that they didn't all immediately get it. "There's one coming for us. I felt him and he felt me."

"Shearjoy?" Tasker said.

"I don't know. I don't know – I don't –"

"Slow down," Reece said, crouching by her before she could freak out. "We got this, cher, you know that? We're ready to go. We only need to know where's best."

Zip swallowed with deep uncertainty. She shook her head, no idea.

"What've we ended up with, then?" Leigh-Ann demanded. "We know the Legion's gunning for us and Mason ain't nearby, but Zip's momma still wants her in Africa. How we any better off than before?"

Reece's vision went suddenly black. The world muted for a moment, and when he tried to voice his surprise, no sound came. He turned, finding himself in an abyss, then he took a step forward and was knocked back by the chords of some painfully loud pop song. As he cringed, the parking lot came back and he found he'd moved away from Zip, almost in the trees. Turning with surprise, he found Tasker and Leigh-Ann looking equally unsettled, likewise distanced from each other and about to fall over.

"I'm sorry!" Zip cried. "I'm trying – I wanted to –" She took quick breaths, processing whatever was going on in her mind, as Reece exchanged concerned looks with the others.

"Think we oughta stop this," he suggested. "We'll hit the road, Zip. You can –"

"It's Ruin," Zip said, abruptly.

"Come again?"

"He knows where we are. And I can –" She cringed, hit by something inside her, and started quickly shaking her head. "He's close, he was ready, he's coming."

"Who?" Leigh-Ann demanded.

"Ruin!" Zip shouted like it was obvious, and the branches above them shook, birds taking flight. They all froze, to give her a second to calm before she exploded. She breathed quickly and said, "I wanted to find them. I wanted to know what to do, so I just . . . I just asked. Tried to find out" – she met Tasker's eyes – "what's in the mountains."

"In Ikiri?" Tasker said.

"In France," she said. "It's not the only one. Just the latest. It *is* important to them. And – and one of them is there. I'm sure. One of the Legion is there."

"Only one?"

Reece saw the agent's mind ticking and said, "This ain't the time, is it? My money's on us getting out of Dodge right now. We can plot a course on the way."

"Agreed," Tasker said. "Everyone, in –"

Zip winced, doubling over with her arms tight around her belly. Her little cry made Reece and Leigh-Ann drop to her sides. She looked into Reece's face with passing pain. He asked, "That them?"

She shook her head, eyes filling with fear.

"Your brother?" A nod. Reece leant closer. "We gonna be long gone in a minute, he won't have a prayer of catching up."

"He sees me," she whispered. "And something is coming. Something terrible."

Reece fought to keep his own face calm, but her fear was infectious. He said, "We got you, Zip. You know that?"

"I don't *know*," Zip said, screwing her eyes closed. "He can create *evil*, and –"

"And we're gonna stop him," Reece said, firm enough that she had no choice but to rally. "Let's all of us get in the car and move."

*

Katryzna had not travelled far from Finway's grandiose apartment. Anyone looking for her would expect she'd leave the area, so instead she'd parked under the closest moderately-sized bridge she could find. After enjoying a little more sleep in Ward's car (wondering if the seat's slightly floral smell had rubbed off the little Deputy Director herself?), she walked the streets of London looking for something to eat. She saw a big bullet train billboard promising Paris in ninety minutes for £29. And here she was waiting forever for Tasker to give her directions.

She could probably get to this Hall of Enoch and get answers quicker than they could get their nonsense together in Ordshaw. But Tasker had insisted they do this together. It would make a change: she could agree with Rurik on that. It was good to have company.

Katryzna spotted some pastries through the window of a tiny coffee shop, already full of people in smart clothing, waiting sullenly in line, and she fondly recalled Eyes, when they had shared breakfast in Madrid. When she had insisted they eat before finishing a job, the sulky assassin treated her to all the strange little pastries she could fit in her gut. He looked appalled, then fascinated, asking where all the food went.

"This is nice," she had told him. He smirked in faint agreement. Behind him, locals glanced her way, less amused. Turning their noses up at her. She gave them a mean expression and they looked away, but Eyes followed her gaze and became less amused.

"We shouldn't stay long," he said. Meaning, not long enough to cause trouble. Not long enough to be noticed together, for sure. She'd said that, testily.

Eyes never raised his voice, or moved dramatically, but when she shouted at him he gave her a look that made you shrivel. She had been threatened by Uncle Nikita as a child (not her real uncle and definitely not a friend), and his daughters had tried their best to bully her, but she had never been afraid in the way Eyes made her feel. It was worse than a promise of danger. She did not want to disappoint him. She liked Eyes. He sat and listened to her. He did not say things to judge her. She'd wanted to stretch out that breakfast, to do *more* with him, let him buy her lunch, safe in the knowledge he didn't want anything more than friendship. To look out for her, to smile fondly as she bucked against the system and bit off more than she could chew, literally, figuratively, whatever.

But he said they had to go. He had his own image to maintain, and he quietly, calmly told her they should leave the city separately. She swallowed her frustrations. If another man had spurned her like that, she would have cut him. But she would not have cared, if it was another man. She never cared about men – that's what made it so strange.

The Londoners in the queue ahead of Katryzna eyed her the same way those Spaniards had in Madrid, questioning what on earth she was doing there, amongst *them*. Did Sean and Reece look at her the same way? Sean's message had carried the same tone: *Lay low. Wait to hear from me, we'll meet at an airfield.*

As in, stay away from us. Not wanted, not welcome. The darkness crept in at the edges. Didn't Leigh look at her uncomfortably, too? Beautiful Leigh, of course *she* wouldn't want anything to do with Katryzna. With a little more time alone, maybe Leigh would see Katryzna differently, though. If the men weren't too busy pushing her away.

No. Katryzna knew she was an idiot. She had said she could protect people because she killed people. Leigh probably hated her. And even Sean was turning against her. Katryzna considered out loud, "Why did he not ask me to wait at the airfield?"

"You know why," Rurik said. "You'd probably set it on fire."

"I would not," Katryzna said.

The man in line glanced over his shoulder, then looked suddenly ahead, afraid she might mistake him for caring. Katryzna's shoulders sank.

"Do they even want me to come?" Katryzna whispered.

"Would *you*?" Rurik countered.

"I can be useful. I have been useful. No, no. They will be in touch."

A woman further up the line cleared her throat to suggest disapproval without actually saying it. Katryzna stared fire at her. Didn't that stuffy fool know she had a gun under her shirt?

"No, because no one carries a gun in London," Rurik said. "And you're wondering why Sean's keeping you at arm's length. He has better help now. People who don't consider murdering strangers over nothing."

"Shut *up*," Katryzna snapped, and everyone who'd been avoiding looking her way gave her glances. She hung her head, covered her face with an arm by pretending to scratch at her hair, then continued in a hushed snarl, "You shut up – they haven't left me, I just need to wait."

"Yes, quite," Rurik sighed. "If we're all lucky, you'll wait until it's over."

Katryzna snatched at him angrily and he jumped off her shoulder, just avoiding her grip. She froze with both fists clenched, avoiding eye contact with the queueing people. The two clerks had stopped serving to stare. She should just get her pastries, calm down. Then she could help, her own way.

She could get to Paris in ninety minutes. Fosa could get her the directions. The others couldn't fly that fast, could they? Even if they had reached an airfield without her, which they probably hadn't. Yes. She would move fast. Prove herself before they got a chance to reject her. She lunged forward, snatched a croissant and darted out of the shop, knocking a man down, before anyone had a chance to stop her. A few people shouted but no one followed. They might have all hated her, but at least they were afraid.

# 11

Tasker tried to plan as he drove. They'd made it to the motorway, where the steady traffic felt like a comfortable, unobtrusive buffer, giving him time to zone out and think. From the airfield, they could get to France and investigate the Hall of Enoch on the way to Ikiri. Or they could go straight on to Ikiri and take their chances with the Legion. He was erring on the side of caution, though; plainly enough, Ikiri's power was much more complex than mind-control. Zip's abilities went beyond whatever had been evident of Sara. The child was picking up on things hundreds or thousands of miles away, and even pushing her senses onto them just by being in close proximity. Which was just as well, as children were a minefield where the Ministry was concerned. Field agents were frequently reminded of the infamous Dundreggan case, where a dozen MEE agents were caught in a five-month search for a river creature that turned out to be entirely invented by a child. In this case, Tasker was sure they'd all experienced some kind of afterglow of Zip's perceptions, even if it was hazy, local noise. She could not be underestimated.

There would be time to tease out the details as they travelled, whatever route they took. Shaken as she'd been, Zip was resting again, drained. Leigh-Ann, in the back seat with her, was leaning against the window looking out, searching the countryside for some solace she couldn't find in the car. Reece, in the passenger seat, sat tightly self-conscious. Not liking sitting still. Tasker asked quietly, "Have you experienced anything like that before?"

Reece shook his head. "We only used her gifts to get by customs. She blasted Vile with her mind, one time, and she saw them coming before they struck, but we ain't tested any of this. Guess she hasn't either."

Tasker hummed understanding.

"Bad things happened right after she sensed them before, though," Reece said. "I oughta have my gun ready."

"Do you know how to use it?" Tasker asked. It came out more accusatory than he intended, and Reece looked at him sideways.

"I'm quicker than most. Whatever's up the end of this road, Agent Tasker, I'm ready to put it down." He paused. "You're thinking, shiny gun like that, must be for show? But it was crafted by Blanc Tweedman, best gunsmith in all the South. Perfectly weighted, shoots straight as a flagpole. Had a trumpet to go with it, but we lost La Belle Vérité out in Stilt Town." Reece grinned. "I ain't some kinda clown, Agent Tasker, however I might look right now."

"I don't doubt you're serious," Tasker replied, "I'm only thinking we're not in an everyday kind of situation. Drawing a gun on a person's different to shooting cans."

It gave the American pause. "Well, I know which I'd rather do, but I assure you I got more than enough experience in both by now."

Tasker made a noncommittal noise of acceptance.

"Tell me something, though –" Reece started, but Zip screamed, so hard and sudden it made Tasker jerk the wheel, and a driver behind leant hard on their horn.

The kid clamped her hands over her ears and shrieked, "He's trying now – he's trying it – *stop!*"

Tasker checked his mirrors quickly to swing across towards the hard shoulder. Leigh-Ann struggled over Zip, trying to grab her shoulders as she bucked against something unseen. Tasker caught her face in the mirror, staring through the world. He made it to the slow lane, cars whipping past, and asked, "We okay?"

"Oh no," Zip gasped, eyes widening anew. Tasker followed her gaze, out to a lorry ahead of them, logos hidden by filth. An expensive car in the fast lane shot past a couple of dawdlers in the middle. The child shrieked again, and all the vehicles in view jerked as though struck by her shockwave. The closest car swerved sideways, into the wheels of the truck, and the sports car swerved the other way, into the central reservation and over it. Airborne. The lorry jack-knifed across the lanes, and in the mirrors Tasker saw more cars twisting one way or the other – knee-jerk reactions – and in a horrific second the chaotic mess crashed together. Tasker stomped on the accelerator and pulled onto the hard shoulder, the car banking as a minivan swung behind them, missing by a hair. They bounced over the lane markers, everyone twisting about trying to see what was happening.

Every vehicle in view was out of control, crashing into each other, rolling, crumpling. Zip yelled as Tasker veered around a skidding car and on, past the carnage. Brakes screamed up and down the road and Tasker steered in frantic, instinctive movements. A car screeched to a stop just in front of him, and he swerved to avoid it, wheels squealing as he stopped, surrounded by metal carnage.

Tasker whipped his head around, finding they were packed into a slalom of tangled cars and trucks, quickly filling with smoke. In the car ahead, a balding man was clutching the wheel, pale and petrified. A passenger was slumped against the rear window – blood oozed down the glass. The back of the vehicle was crumpled, bumper hanging off. To the right, the car that had struck it was folded to one side, blocking two lanes. No room to drive around to the left either, where the bank angled steeply up through hedges. Tasker glanced in the mirrors and back over his shoulder. Leigh-Ann was whispering comfort to Zip, while Reece rubbed his shoulder where the belt had dug in.

"The *hell* just happened?" Leigh-Ann demanded, pulling off her belt to try and get a look through the darkening surroundings. The sounds of settling metal were replaced by pained groans, then cries. Somewhere in the distance, a woman screamed, again and again, each sound outdoing the last.

Tasker put the car in reverse, pulled back a few feet and stopped.

"What you doing?" Reece called.

It was no use; the gap between the truck behind them and the next broken car was too narrow to get through. They were penned in.

"Hey!" Reece slapped Tasker's shoulder. "You wanna take a second?"

"Out," Tasker decided, opening his door. "Everyone move, fast."

"What are you –" Leigh-Ann started.

"This was for us," Tasker said quickly. "We need to get clear. We'll take a car from up front."

"What about helping these people?" Zip croaked, eyes wet with tears.

"There's no time."

"All these people –" Zip started.

"Are in more danger if we stay, aren't they?" Tasker asked.

Zip considered it, and maybe tapped into a little piece of her power to check. Either way, she drew a conclusion that made her nod with mounting fear. Reece looked to Leigh-Ann and she put on a brave face.

"Stick close to me," Tasker said, and stepped out into the smoke.


Reece kept a tight hold on his bag, pulling Zip along with the other hand. He wanted to abandon the bag for just the gun inside, but hadn't had time to stop and it wouldn't help to run around swinging a pistol. The destruction echoed what he'd seen in Stilt Town, back home. It was hard to see where the damage of the crashes stopped and the damage done by violence began, but plainly there had been violence – some cars' windows were cracked from the inside, people bloodied and slumped. Like the occupants had lost control, attacked each other in their own vehicles. Except it had all stopped now. No one was attacking each other, and the screams were of pain or sorrow, not madness. Some people were shouting instructions, trying to help each other.

The smoke was a blessing, however it made them cough and squint, as it hid the full extent of the bloodshed, if not all of it. Reece covered Zip's eyes as they passed a car with its windows shattered, a man draped over the hood like he'd collapsed there drunk. Except with pieces missing.

"Don't look," Reece said. "Weren't because of you."

"My brother," she said, weakly. Not the first time.

"Just think, he can do all this bad from where he is, you'll do twice the good once we get you there," Reece said, not thinking where that came from.

Tasker told them Ward would take care of this. She'd send the best emergency responders, and keep it quiet even if it reached the national news in minutes. The agent was justifying the fact they were fleeing, not stopping to help. "Through here," he said, taking them past a woman face down on the asphalt.

Finally, they pulled clear of the smoke, hurrying into the open road – their side of the freeway, three lanes ahead was empty bar a handful of dormant cars, doors open where the owners had run back to try and help. The other side of the road was nose-to-nose traffic, people standing from their vehicles, shouting, holding up camera phones, or just staring in horror.

Tasker rushed towards a car left open. No one inside, probably belonging to one of the men shouting in the smoke, "On my count, pull – one, two –"

Reece fought all his instincts to go back, to do *something*. But he had Zip to get clear, and he followed Tasker at a trot. Food wrappers and old soda cans lay crumpled in the footwells of the car. Reece was just about to get in when a screech of metal drew his attention to the traffic on the other side, a way down the freeway. A van was punching through the metal divider. People shouted complaints as the metal snapped around its bumper, and the van bounced over the reservation with a spark. It turned towards the wreckage rather than away from it, like it could drive through.

The van accelerated towards them, and Reece and Leigh-Ann straightened up. She said, "This guy's got some place to be?"

Zip got the edge on them by just a second, gasping right before it was possible to make out the driver's face: "It's him."

The van stopped a dozen yards away, and the driver leaned over to grab something from the passenger seat. Leigh-Ann asked, "*Which* him?"

Tasker was already standing, pistol in hand, as Reece hurried to unzip his bag.

"Gun!" someone yelled from the other side of the central reservation. The road was thrown into new panic, people shouting, running, diving into vehicles for cover. Engines started up, brakes squeaked as cars tried to find some gap to escape. In the seconds of distraction, the man jumped down from the van and started towards them.

"Take her, take her!" Reece said, pushing Zip towards Leigh-Ann, fumbling for his gun.

Tasker shouted: "Stop!"

Leigh-Ann pulled Zip down behind the car as the kid yelped, "Reece!"

The newcomer was short, but square with muscle, padded with body-armour. He had a humourless, battle-worn face, nose flattened, flesh pocked with scars. Stains of tattoos rose up his neck, and he had a crude, chunky machete hanging from one hand. His boots thumped against the road, like he carried more mass than was natural, and he grunted before speaking.

"Where's Headhunter? And the Russian?" An English accent, rough and ugly. He pointed the blade at Reece, to stop him opening the bag. "Don't test me."

"You're Ruin?" Tasker said.

The thug, evidently Ruin, gave him a slightly surprised look. He scanned the car for Zip, then settled back on Tasker. "Give me the girl and walk away, Agent *Tasker*." He made the name a threat.

"You ain't taking a step closer," Reece said. "She's a kid!"

Ruin glared. "Hardly." He rolled his shoulders in readiness for a fight. It made no sense; he was fifteen paces away and had to know both Tasker and Reece had guns. He said, "I don't need to hurt all of you, but I won't ask again."

"Your threats are no good here," Tasker said. "My family are clear of this –

you can tell Shearjoy we're not rolling over."

"Idiot," Ruin said. "You bought them a day? Two? No one *ever* gets clear of this. But I only came here for her." He pointed the machete towards where Zip was hiding. "She's a bomb that'll get everyone killed. Step aside and you can all live."

"Like I said," Reece said, "you ain't –"

Ruin didn't let him finish, but moved in a flash to the side. Reece fumbled to draw his gun. Tasker fired but cursed at the same time, a miss. The man was gone. Six feet to the side already, so fast it was like he disappeared for a second. Reece twisted and ducked; he pulled the gun clear but stopped, as Ruin ran before the sea of cars, packed with people. Tasker got off another shot, causing screams, then Ruin was on them with a thump that rattled the car – Tasker was hit and went down, gun clattering across the road. Reece dropped down past the car door, pistol ready, but Ruin was too close and kicked down, catching his chest. Reece rolled and fired into the sky before Ruin booted the gun out of his hand. The machete twirled as Ruin swept it up, all so quick Reece could barely keep up.

Zip screamed, "Stop!"

The whole world obeyed.

For just a second, Ruin was a statue, machete over his head, and even the drifting smoke seemed to hang motionless above him. Then he collapsed backwards, and the machete dropped and twanged across the road. The man gasped with deep terror, as Reece pushed himself up onto his elbows. Ruin clutched at his chest, veins bulging on his neck; something wasn't working, like a dead engine spluttering as it tried to get going. Some kind of freak heart attack? His eyes went furiously to Zip, as she peeked from cover behind the car, just a second before he crumpled completely flat. Reece grabbed his pistol from by Leigh-Ann's foot and hurriedly stood, spun back on the man. Tasker was leaning on the car door, his gun retrieved, too, but his grip was limp from the blow he'd taken.

Ruin twitched, eyes wide, locked with angry disbelief.

Zip pushed between Reece and Leigh-Ann, pleading, "No – I didn't –" Ruin flinched back. He tried to raise a hand but didn't have the strength. He blinked, once, and went still, eyes glassily open. Zip stared with her mouth open. Silence reigned for a moment, then the sound of a helicopter chopped through the sky. A short way off, quickly getting closer.

"Get in," Tasker told them hoarsely. "Quickly."

Reece stared without understanding. Was Ruin dead? Didn't that make them safe? But Tasker had the haggard look of a man who knew they weren't, his new glasses bent out of shape and his jacket torn at the shoulder. "You're hurt?" Reece asked him.

"Just winded." Tasker shook his shoulder as if to shake off the wound. His mouth twisted with pain. "Come on." He dropped into the driver's seat and started the engine.

The helicopter was getting louder. People were talking across the freeway. This was all too much and too mad. Reece shook himself out of the confusion and huddled Leigh-Ann and Zip into the car, pushing the kid when she resisted, rooted by the horror of Ruin's body. Reece whispered, "It's okay, cher, you did good, you did good."

"That's not good!" she cried, tears in her eyes. From world-class pile-up to psychic murder in ten seconds, couldn't even begin to unpack it. Reece gave Ruin one last look himself. Not sure what was worse, the speed and ferocity of his attack, or the sheer simplicity of Zip's defence. He looked away. More people were emerging from wrecked cars, sharing his shocked questions. Tasker was right: the only thing that made sense right then was that they had to get away.

# 12

Tasker hid the pain lancing up his right side. It was nothing, really – Ruin had caught him a hard blow to his ribs. It'd leave a nasty bruise, maybe, but considering how the man had moved he'd got off lightly. Ruin hadn't wanted to kill him. He was either wary of murdering a government agent or genuinely only wanted to take out Zip, the one person he considered a real threat. The latter thought rested uneasily; if Ruin actively avoided collateral damage, and the Legion actually had some kind of moral code, what did it say about their fear of Zip? To them, she was the monster.

He didn't voice his concerns, focusing on the relatively empty road ahead. Zip was shuddering as she tried to hold in tears. Leigh-Ann put an arm around her and whispered that she should let it out, don't be afraid to feel. Except from the tone of her voice and the way Reece sat rigid in front, it was clear *they* were afraid of her emotions. No one was saying it – it didn't need saying – but while Ezekiel might've just made six lanes of traffic implode, Zip had made a man's heart stop by wanting it hard enough.

Nothing in the Ministry canon compared to those kinds of mind-powers. There had been various government programmes to develop psychic soldiers over the years, most extensively realised with the experiments conducted by the CIA half a century ago, and there was zero evidence that anyone could so much as read a mind, let alone move objects or cause harm. Any doubt Tasker had that Zip's powers had been exaggerated were gone. His new doubt was whether the Legion had good reason to be worried about her – especially given that they could only assume going to Ikiri would make her *more* powerful.

"That was a bad man," Leigh-Ann assured. "He would've killed all of us. You saw how fast he moved?"

Zip nodded, with a big sniff. "Like my daddy. I wish he was here. Where *is* he? He could help. He would –"

"He would've held you back," Leigh-Ann said, and shifted to squeeze Zip tighter. "Your pop's way of doing things is what got us where we at. Wherever he went, as long as it's far from us, I'm personally okay with that."

"For all we know," Reece said, "it was his mad crusade got animals like Ruin gunning for you in the first place."

Tasker grunted affirmation at that; he wasn't the only one who saw it.

"But he protected me from them," Zip said quietly. "And from myself. He didn't want me to do that."

"Didn't want you to take care of yourself, you mean?" Leigh-Ann said.

"Hell, sweetie, you had a *shitty* pop, but that means you get to join the club. Caleb's pa ran out on him, and my mom's drunk by sunrise. Sto's ma beat him. Remember, Zip? You read that right outta Sto's mind, the sorta woman she was. Big bad wolf, she whaled on Sto so loud people called the sheriff. But you know what? Reece went in with a bat and knocked her so hard she crashed through the wall."

"You hit a woman with a bat?" Tasker asked, distracted by the chatter.

Reece replied modestly, "I was eight years old, and she weren't exactly ladylike."

"See, same age as you now." Leigh-Ann nudged Zip. "You following in Reece's footsteps and you didn't even know it. Both of y'all heroes."

"But I'm *seven*," Zip said. She took a bracing breath. "And that man is *dead*."

"See what he did to Agent Tasker?" Reece said. "And I was about to get skewered. Gave us no choice. Right, Agent?"

"Definitely," Tasker said. "Sometimes we need to do unpleasant things to make the world a better place, Zip."

Zip pulled out from Leigh-Ann's grip to scoot towards the car door, a serious look on her face. "I don't want to do it again. To hurt anyone. Ever. I *won't* do it to my brother."

Leigh-Ann looked into the mirror to implore more from Tasker. Usually, it was enough to tell children he had things under control. They tended to respect a man in a suit. But Zip saw through that, he knew well enough, and in the time it took him to think what to say, Reece took over:

"Only way you get to avoid hurting anyone," Reece said, "is if you never have nothing to do with no one. World's a difficult place. Best we can do is keep trying."

"But when I hurt people –"

"You *had* to. And you didn't know you could, right? Now you know, that means you know how *not* to. You don't have to do it again."

Zip bit her lip. "I don't?"

"Absolutely not, cher. You make the rules. And when we get to Ikiri, we'll put all this to rest, like Agent Tasker says. He works with the government, you gotta trust what he says, right?"

"That's right," Tasker said, more thankful than ever for the Americans. He was usually better at this, he told himself. Shearjoy's phone call had thrown him, that blow had thrown him. He needed to recoup.

A passing sign told him they'd covered a good distance. Hell, he hadn't even contacted Katryzna yet, with everything else going on. Nor had they discussed exactly where they were going. He pulled off the motorway, saying it was time to take a break and take stock. They went down a country lane to a small petrol station opposite an empty field. Tasker took out his phone and tried to call Katryzna. It beeped, disconnected. Had she turned off the phone? Run out of battery?

Reece said, "Phone get busted in the fight?"

"I don't think so," Tasker said. He brought up Ward's number instead.

She answered after two rings: "Thank heavens, Agent Tasker – are you alright?"

"We are," Tasker said; she must have already put together what had happened on the motorway. "Are you locking it down?"

"Not me," Ward said. "The London office have sent people; they picked up a spike in novisan. Are you on site?"

"No, we're still aiming for Farnborough. But I can't get hold of Katryzna. If I send you her number, can you trace it?"

"Absolutely."

Tasker did so, then asked, "What are they saying, the London office? How're they reporting the man with the machete?"

"A man with a machete?" Ward echoed with surprise. "What happened?"

So London were keeping a lid on it. "There was one of the Legion on the scene; he was already tracking us at the time of the incident. Dead, now. I discharged my firearm across the motorway." That confession just rolled out, and he wasn't sure why.

"Oh my," Ward said. "No, none of that's come out – but there were witnesses?"

"Lots."

"I'll see if I can get involved."

"Best not," Tasker said. "They might realise you're in touch with us. I only wanted to check in, Deputy Director. If you can get hold of Katryzna –"

"Yes, definitely," Ward said quickly. "I'll get you a trace, just a minute."

"You've lost the wild woman?" Leigh-Ann asked from the back.

"She's not in trouble, too, is she?" Zip looked up with alarm.

"Why would you think that?" Tasker frowned. "That was your brother back there, wasn't it? He got in those other drivers' heads and made them crash?"

"Yes," Zip said quietly. She made a face to demonstrate concentration. "When I realised he was attacking, I pushed it away. Made it stop. But it was too late – he did it there on purpose. Because we were driving fast and there were lots of cars. *Because* we were close to Ruin. He knew all that – he must have. What if he knows Katryzna is helping us, too?"

Tasker didn't have an answer: didn't want to consider it.

"What's next?" Leigh-Ann said. "Stampeding animals? Falling planes?"

Ward's voice came back on the phone, cautiously, as she'd clearly heard all that: "I don't think she's in trouble, I think she's on the move. The last recorded location we could ping was half an hour ago. Folkestone, Kent."

"Kent?" Tasker replied with surprise. "She was supposed to be waiting in bloody London."

"Yes. But the obvious link between London and Folkestone is the Channel Tunnel," Ward pointed out.

Tasker swore. "She's gone ahead of us."

"Ahead where?" Reece asked.

"France."

"Secret-murder-camp-in-the-mountains France?" Leigh-Ann said. "As in, gunning for the Legion herself?"

"But they have someone there!" Zip cried. "Another one like Ruin! I felt him – I told you I felt it there, it's dangerous, she can't –"

"I know that," Tasker replied. "But she doesn't." Telling Katryzna to sit tight seemed like a big mistake now. The Hall of Enoch was a red flag to her bullish ways. "I guess she got an idea to handle this herself. Again."

"I can keep trying to reach her on the phone," Ward said. "And we have agents in France, someone could intercept her."

"She wouldn't take kindly to that." Tasker tapped his hands against the wheel. If Katryzna was in motion, she might not even look at her phone until she got to where she was going. She'd ride right into the Legion's stronghold, not even appreciating what men like Ruin were capable of.

"We're heading for the plane right now, right?" Reece said. "We can get there faster, cut her off."

"Assuming we'd have any clue where to cut her off," Tasker said. "We'd need to go to the Hall itself." Tempting as the Hall of Enoch was, with its promise of more answers about the Legion, it was a dangerous diversion that they hadn't agreed on. Ezekiel was growing bolder, but Ruin's abilities, and attitude, raised more questions that warranted answering. Not to mention the fact that Katryzna had liberated Tasker's family from this, and delivered them to a safe house; he couldn't leave her in the lurch. Her innate survival skills were as inexplicable as Zip's gifts, but there had to be a limit to her luck. Tasker thought out loud, "I can intercept Katryzna and get you three on a flight bound for the Congo. We can catch up later."

"Except what the hell are you gonna do against another Ruin?" Reece said.

Tasker gave him a look, then considered Zip again. The child was motionless, distracted from what she'd already done by the darkness that lay ahead. He said, "You were able to reach out to your mother, Zipporah. Do you think you could reach Katryzna?"

She looked startled for a second, but swallowed and said, "Maybe."

"You don't have to," Reece quickly said. "Remember that, Zip – anything you don't want to do –"

"I want to," Zip told him. "I do." Without warning, she squinted her eyes in that focused way of hers. Searching the world. Only for a second, this time, before she gasped. "No – he's watching. He's laughing. He wants me to try, he wants to – he said –" She took quick breaths and slowed down. "There's more coming. If he can keep sensing me, he can keep throwing things at us."

"That little shit," Leigh-Ann snarled. "Swear we can't get to Ikiri quick enough."

"We gotta make that pit stop ourselves, don't we?" Reece asked. "Agent?"

Tasker was still, awash in this rapidly moving, unmanageable mess. The threat and question of the Legion would hound them if they didn't take the initiative. Katryzna knew it, or at least had acted on it. They had to, too. He said, "Doesn't seem we have a choice. If we haven't got hold of her by the time we reach Farnborough, we'll head for the Hall of Enoch."

# 13

In Mason's company, Henri had moved faster through the forest than he ever thought possible. The helicopter ride was mercifully short, showing that Mason *did* have some sense in him, stopping way before the Ikiri borders. They abandoned the vehicle in a small clearing in favour of bikes, and Mason pushed on without restraint. The man had as unnatural a sense for the terrain as he had for driving through Kinshasa, taking the paths between trees faster even than Katryzna had done. But where she was reckless, Mason was precise, showing no hesitation in navigating obstacles. It was a marvel to see this large white man hunched over a motorbike with his metal stump on one handlebar, moving with speed and grace, but always grim and serious.

After riding through the night, with Henri trailing Mason as best he could, offering frequent prayers that he not fall off or hit a tree, they reached a wider road, safe enough to move quicker into the interior. They stopped frequently for Henri to muddle over maps and confer with locals to ensure they were going the right way, and gradually they drew towards Ikiri proper. They pulled off the better roads as they got close, to avoid rebel soldiers. Despite having left General Solomon's PLU, the militia controlling Ikiri, on good terms, Henri suspected they might shoot first and ask questions later when it came to Mason.

Mason never tired, scowling at Henri when he suggested they slow down or take a break. Henri's body protested, with dawn light creeping through the trees, and in a moment of dulled concentration he lost control of the bike, one wheel skidding as he jolted back awake. He almost rode off the track. Mason stopped and threw a nasty look back, full of condemnation. Henri tried to play it down with an apologetic smile: "It has been such a long ride – I've rarely ridden so long without coffee, at least."

Mason continued to stare hard, and Henri feared he might simply leave him behind. But the white man huffed and said they could rest at the next opportunity. It took another half an hour, and Henri struggled to keep his eyes open the full way. He was considering simply pulling over when they finally found a handful of wooden shacks lining one side of the road. The buildings were empty, with no food stored outside or clothes hanging from the lines strung between walls and posts.

Mason paced around, suspicious scowl ever-present, and came back to the bikes to say, "There are mats in the second hut. If you must, lie down for twenty minutes."

The suggestion came with an edge that Henri should really consider, very carefully, if it was necessary. He was barely standing now, so no amount of scowling could change his mind. "I think I must."

"But we are close. We are on the edge of Ikiri's influence." It was not a question, so Henri gave it a questioning look of his own. Mason explained simply, "I feel it."

Henri considered the empty homes as he lay down. It was likely the dwelling of a single family who had slipped away from a nearby village to take a small piece of land for themselves. Outcasts, loners, who knew. Any number of troubles could have befallen such a small community. But then, Henri recalled the village of Igota, where he had taken refuge with Katryzna and Tasker. Those people had not *gone*, but were changed. Igota, too, was just outside the border of Ikiri's influence. Between here and General Solomon's camp, beneath the slopes of Ikiri itself, there might be no safety.

With that in mind, Henri got only a weak and fitful rest, and he stirred sooner than was sensible. He found Mason outside, staring into the trees as though concentrating on something. Following his gaze, Henri could not make out what it was, and the one-handed man gave no explanation.

Henri's body protested as he got back on the bike, making him stagger. Mason glared again. Digging into one of the saddlebags, he drew out an energy pack, something like military rations. He tossed it over and Henri hungrily tore into it, sucking at a thick, chocolate liquid. It coursed through him and he exhaled appreciation. Resting his head in a hand, Henri said, "I am sorry. Just a moment."

"Good," Mason replied, with the full extent of his sympathy.

Henri eyed him, unsure what was wrong with the man. How was it possible this abrupt thug ever flirted with his sister? Sara, for sure, was better than this. Perhaps she had merely seen his strength? This was, after all, a very dangerous place. Henri said, "When you came here before, did you . . ." He wanted to ask if they'd seen the same things as he had. People driven to crazed bloodlust, or worse – the creatures that made those noises in the night. Such things could change a man.

"We went through a lot," Mason said, simply. He revved his engine again, to end the discussion.

After another hour, the track become impassable for the bikes. The terrain was vaguely familiar to Henri: there was an incline and it was becoming rockier, the trees wider apart. Mason's attitude shifted as they surely penetrated the bubble of Ikiri's influence. Leaving the bikes behind, he stalked through the trees, glaring into the distance, relying on some sense that Henri did not understand.

They climbed slopes, followed one trail after another, and wound around and around, up and down, with Mason only growing tenser as he sweated and snarled. Every time Henri tried to speak, the big man shut him down with a glower or a snapped word. Focusing, now, doing his part. But he was running about like a dog after rain. Trying to pick up the scents of eight years ago? Surely nothing would be familiar now.

Henri asked if it was the cave Mason was looking for, then told him about their visit. Katryzna had hoped to enter it herself, but thought better of it when they arrived. It was a dark and terrible place. Mason insisted he was different and he would gain access. But they had to find it first. As the light started to fade, Henri found his concerns rising, and he tried to make conversation to push the fears back: "We do not have to talk about Ikiri. We can talk about football? You look like a Chelsea fan, I'm thinking?"

Mason only marched harder up the slope.

Henri was sure they must have gone in circles, but nothing seemed familiar. He said, "Should we turn back? It's not safe here at night."

"It's not safe full stop," Mason sneered. He glared at the trees like they offended him. "I should be able to find it."

Henri resisted the urge to ask how, exactly.

"It's playing with us," Mason continued, frustration finally loosening his tongue. "There is a new shroud here. I cannot penetrate it." With a shout, he punched his metal wrist sideways and cracked the closest tree trunk. He shook the arm off, scattering wood. "You have been here recently. Why can't you find it?"

"I didn't find it before," Henri said. "The PLU took us there. And –"

"We haven't seen them, either," Mason said, accusingly.

No. They had seen no signs of Solomon's men, or the roads they used, and they had been walking for hours. Mason heaved a deep breath, seeming to decide Henri was useless, so Henri made a suggestion: "If we descend the hill, we will find a road. We can navigate downhill, can't we?"

Mason gave him a withering look, but shook his head in concession, and turned to make the decline. He moved no slower now, picking his way between rocks, pushing off trees, and Henri trotted to keep up. They broke out between some trees to a clearing, revealing a view of higher, tree-lined peaks. Henri looked up to check the darkening sky and slowed down as he spotted someone, far off – a tall, thin silhouette. The man was standing sentinel. Henri called out, "Mr Mason! I think I see one of –"

He stopped as the silhouette shifted, an arm extending to one side. Not carrying a gun and dressed, from the slim shape, in a fitted cloak unlike the bulky fatigues Solomon's men wore. The hand held out a long, thin weapon. A sword?

Mason clumped back into the clearing with a demanding expression. Henri looked to him and then back up to the peak. The figure was gone. He opened his mouth and found he wasn't sure what to say – had he imagined it?

Then the shrill note of an animal cut through the air, from where the man had been standing.

"You saw it?" Mason asked, without surprise.

Henri shook his head. "Something else. A man. With a sword."

Mason followed his gaze. He growled and said, "This place clouds my judgement. We need to get clear and rethink. Come on." He continued, as another animal sound came, far off. Henri picked up his pace and Mason started talking, this new threat waking up memories. "When we came before, disciplined, experienced men grew unruly. Stole. One forced himself on a woman. But when I faltered myself, Eyes kept my focus. Your sister intervened, too. When the civilians lost their bottle, Sara calmed them. She knew how to talk men down."

Henri threw a look over his shoulder at another screeching sound, then trotted to catch up with Mason. The man was not running, but moved at an impressive speed regardless. He practically punched the forest out of his way as he continued, "Despite Ikiri's effects, I was certain we could do the job. We *did* do the job – we got the researchers here safely, even when they wanted to turn back. With support from your sister and Eyes, we were unstoppable. And I have learnt much since then – I do not need them anymore. This place should *not* be able to control us."

He stopped abruptly, steeling himself. Something whined through the trees and he turned to it, roaring as a lion to a distant hyena. "Come to me, if you dare! Come to me!"

Henri froze at his side, sure now that this man would get them both killed. The creatures far off were silent, though – just the sound of the men's breath blowing through the trees. Mason waited, arms ready to receive whatever danger might come, and the moment stretched out painfully.

"Mr Mason . . ." Henri finally ventured.

"Do you believe in God?" Mason asked, without looking at him.

"I . . ." Memories of church flooded back. Sunday shirts and Sara wiping mud off Henri's cheek with a licked finger and a happy smile. He had not attended regularly since she left.

"Sara preached the Bible," Mason said. "Most of us saw it as entertainment. A storybook. The men egged her on. She played into it – any faith was good faith, she said. She laughed with them. Teaching them scripture without them realising it."

"As long as the Lord's word was heard," Henri joined in quietly. "That was what she wanted. But Mr Mason –"

Mason eyed him, not welcoming the input. "She likened this place to a fallen Babylon. A haunt for every impure spirit. As we all became; even the civilians shed their former lives to take up Ikiri's mantle. The only truth I *knew* was that this place and everything in it must be scourged. Everything that came out of it."

Movement in the trees seemed to stir at his words, something big, breathing heavily, coming closer. Henri itched to turn and run, without knowing where he could go, but his companion clearly intended to stay and fight.

"She called my fight righteous," Mason called. "After all, we had created pillars of wickedness that needed to be felled. Every man corrupted by Ikiri was another demon to be culled. Ikiri itself, a place that must stay hidden, lest it produce more of them. Stopping the spread became my job. They called me the Headhunter."

Henri studied the grave man's face and a sliver of inspiration came to him, something that might bring Mason back to his senses: "And what of my niece? I don't even know her name."

It drew a frown as Mason considered the child. The nearby beast moved again and he narrowed his eyes. "Zipporah. She was the lasting light."

"Sara believed she could make a difference, here," Henri reminded him. "For everyone else, this place is hell."

As Mason considered that, another animal howl sounded on the far side of a hill, bouncing over the trees.

"Move," he decided, and turned away from the sounds, to continue down the slope. Henri quickly peeled ahead as Mason threw looks back, in case the creatures came closer. They skipped down the slope, skidding and sliding between the trees, and Henri could not tell behind his own breath if the creatures were near.

He scrambled out of the trees onto an opening – a dirt road churned by tyres, and he skidded to a standstill to watch Mason emerge. Then he looked to the side, where a Jeep sat, a machine gun mounted on the rear with a soldier leaning over it, startled eyes fixed on them.

"You're with General Solomon?" Henri shouted, before the man could get up the sense to challenge them. "Take us to him!"

# 14

It took all day, but when Katryzna reached the Hall of Enoch she found she had cheered up. The novelty of taking a train underwater (even if you couldn't see it outside the dark windows) trumped her uncertainty over whether or not Sean or Reece or Leigh would be happy to see her again. At some point she had fallen asleep, ignoring a group of obnoxiously loud men in polo shirts, and only stirred at the movements of a whole carriage of people getting ready to depart. She pushed her way out to an exit, grabbing someone's dark green flight-style jacket on the way, then found a motorbike rank, where she rejected a fast-looking Kawasaki in favour of an old Honda with a simpler key socket. Katryzna rode out through the busy streets of Paris, wondering if she should have let Ward know where she had left the car. Especially as she had left her gun in it, rather than travel with it. She was not sure where it was herself, though, and considered she had better gift Ward this bike instead. The engine was too loud for her to hear Rurik's counter-arguments, so she decided yes, it was a good plan.

As she raced along the French highways, it gave her time to reconsider the negative feelings she'd had in the morning. She was putting her skills to good use, saving families, thwarting a secret society. Eyes would be proud of her. While operating in the top ranks of a corrupt world, he had confided that he would like to see his boss – Hank Duvalier, CEO of Duvcorp – struggling. It didn't matter what with: a jar of pickles, a knife-wound in his gut, whatever. Men like Duvalier never truly seemed to struggle.

"So why don't you stab him?" Katryzna had asked, and Eyes smiled even though she'd been serious. He puffed on his cigarette and gave her that same look he always did, like he was just happy she existed. It warmed her cheeks. She said, "I will do it for you."

"Don't," he replied, no longer amused. "You're worth more than that." He didn't explain that, and after another big drag he pointed his cigarette to the convoy they were waiting for. "Time to work."

Katryzna never got to ask what she *was* worth, but she always felt that Hank Duvalier should still get stabbed. It was something to do later. Like investigating Eyes' disappearance. Or buying new clothes. Time always slipped away. But now she was getting something done. Alfred Shearjoy and his horde of creeps definitely deserved stabbing, in their mountain lair. Normal people didn't lurk in mountain lairs, after all.

Maybe *this* was the more that she was worth? Helping people?

Katryzna followed tight, snaking roads up into the mountains, avoiding dark ice as the banks grew severe and the air got colder. The Hall finally came into view and she stopped at the gates, one foot stabilising her on the road. Wisps of snow turned in the bike's headlight beam, which bounced just enough light off the surrounding dusting of snow to light the structure ahead. Past a low brick wall topped with twenty-foot-high spiked bars sat a square mansion backed against rocky cliffs. It looked like someone had broken their way through the mountain just to create this nook. The building had narrow, two-storey-high windows criss-crossed with black iron. Square turrets stood at the corners, with peaked roofs given a lighter gleam with snow, and dead in the centre, behind a long driveway, sat a pair of double doors tall enough for a giant. This was definitely a place for evil conspiracies.

Only, there were no lights on, and the driveway's snow was untouched, with no vehicles anywhere in sight. Weeds climbed over the left side of the building. No sign there had been any visitors in a long time. The big double gate stood resolutely closed, with an expensive-looking electronic lock holding it in place. Katryzna got off the bike and rattled the bars, the sound echoing off the cliffs. Rurik climbed out of her jacket collar and said, "Do you want the whole mountain to know you're here?"

"Maybe," she replied. "We did not come to hide."

"But –" Rurik started, but she stepped back, making him stagger and complain, and she drove a hard kick into the gate.


Reece held on tight to the armrests as the little propeller-operated plane rattled into the clouds. Zip offered a pleasant smile to comfort him from the front. She was enjoying it, riding next to the moustached pilot while the rest of them were squeezed in back. Leigh-Ann's own nerves came out in comments that this was worse than a crop-duster, which the pilot took personally and said no farmer ever flew something this fancy.

Tasker went into some zen state, giving Leigh-Ann blank looks whenever she loudly blamed him for this shitty situation. Pushed against the window the other side of Reece, he was expert at betraying zero doubts. Part of his job to hide emotions, whether talking people down about monsters or riding a trembling bucket ten thousand feet high.

Reece wasn't sure if it was Zip's presence or Tasker's no-nonsense attitude that'd gotten them the flight, without anyone so much as asking for ID, but he was taking notes. He always told his Cutjaw Kids, confidence opens any door, and here was proof. But it probably helped if you looked important, didn't dye your hair funny colours, and didn't joke around. Tasker smiled in a cold, efficient way, friendly but restrained enough to say *don't mess with him*.

Reece wondered if he was thinking straight himself, or had his mind got warped along the way, between Tasker's charm and Zip's unknowing power? He hoped it was his own volition. His dad always told him the bottom line was to do the right thing. Cutjaw bred good people, no matter what Leigh-Ann said. Caleb's mom more than made up for his deadbeat dad, and Reece's own parents were saints. As Papa Coburn had it, whether working summers on a fishing trawler, late nights busking for nickels, or reaching for the stars, the measure of a man was in his *why*. Be sure whatever you're doing, it's because it's right. Taking on a global conspiracy of lightning-fast sword maniacs, facing down a psychotic murder child in Africa – that sounded right, no matter how Reece got mixed up in it. When Leigh-Ann asked how come he looked like he was trying to solve algebra, he said, "Thinking we're heroes, is all."

"Ain't we always," she said, unconvinced. "True now as when we lifted copper coils out Bo Nettle's yard, get him back for hustling Duke. And Duke got dog bit."

"Yeah," Reece said, remembering well. They'd made a tune out of it, Dog Chase; a dramatic, jaunty fan-favourite. Maybe there'd be something like that out of this, too. The March of Ikiri, picking up on that riff that came to him back in Louisiana. Hell, could be a whole album. Dark, brooding tunes, undercut with lively soul. He felt the harmonica Ward gave him, tight in his pocket, and figured once they set down he'd start testing some ideas.

But immediately on arrival at an airport near Lyon, it was all business again. Tasker got them a 4x4, smaller and much quieter than an American truck, and he asked Reece to drive while he navigated. They cut out through countryside and up slopes that got quickly steeper, before pulling through a town of peaked log cabins lightly sprinkled by snow, windows lit up warm yellow. This much snow had only hit Cutjaw maybe twice in Reece's life, and this was just the start of it, Tasker said. People were out in padded coats, against a backdrop of old lanterns and colourful shops. Nice place for a break, Reece imagined. Early evenings playing cosy jazz lounges, drinks round a fire pit overlooking white-tipped peaks. Could bring Ward and show her a good time, in thanks. Him and Leigh-Ann and the boys, too.

The dream faltered with the intrusive question of *which* boys.

Not Caleb. Not Stomatt right now. Duke scarcely left Beauregard, on account of nerves over such things as getting dog bit.

Reece refocused on the road as they left the town, pulling onto a darker, winding track. As the town came into view below, through the trees, Leigh-Ann commented that it looked like somewhere Santa could have a holiday home. Zip perked up, getting a bit of cheer back in her voice.

"You know about Santa?" Leigh-Ann feigned shock. "Figured your daddy would've banned that kinda talk." She put on a terrible British accent. "The only holiday to be celebrated in this house is Bladesgiving. Praise the sword!"

Zip's expression twisted as she said, "What's *Bladesgiving*?"

"The annual veneration of tools of sacrifice and murder?" Leigh-Ann said. "When men come together to grease and sharpen metals and howl to the moon. No? I was *sure* that was a European thing."

"We only had Christmas," Zip said. "My dad gave me books. I gave him a plant."

Leigh-Ann laughed. "Did he love it?"

Zip's pause contained a whole history of one-sided Christmas cheer. "I take care of it for him. Or, I did. I guess it's gone now. Do you get presents for Bladesgiving?"

"Hell, we gotta go faster," Reece said. "Arrive before Leigh drowns Zip in lies."

Zip's face screwed up in accusation. Leigh-Ann struggled to keep a straight face before bursting out laughing. "Ain't it the sort of shit these lunatics would worship?"

It drew a smile from Reece, but the track turned and the wheels hit something with a bang – a series of bangs. He pumped on the brakes as they skidded towards the verge, wheels sparking. He swung back and the girls shrieked as they finally stopped, askew.

Reece rested against the steering wheel as Tasker jumped out and ran down the road.

"The fuck," Leigh-Ann gasped. "What the fuck!"

"Something –" Reece breathed deeply. "Something in the road."

"Spikes," Tasker said, reappearing at his open door. "Got all four tyres."

"Hell," Reece said. "Shit. I'm sorry everyone – damn fool move."

"Not your fault," Tasker said. "No one would've seen them in this light. There's tyre tracks ahead, though. Maybe more than one vehicle. Either Katryzna avoided the spikes or got here before whoever laid them. If we're really lucky, she laid them herself."

"Admire your idea of luck," Leigh-Ann murmured anxiously, "being that she's even more dangerous than she seems."

"Ah hell," Reece said. "How close are we?"

"Halfway, at best. Another three or four miles to go," Tasker said.

"Three miles is walkable. Quicker than going back and boosting another car, right?"

"If we wanna drag an eight-year-old through thirty below?" Leigh-Ann said.

"I can walk," Zip offered. "I went to America on my own."

"You weren't walking into a trap, then," Tasker said. He stared into the darkness, trying to form a plan, once again betraying no clue that he was worried. "I can go on alone, it'll be quicker and safer for the rest of you."

"Hell with that," Reece said. "I'll go with you. Leigh, you run up behind with Zip; it's barely freezing, we can handle it."

"I'm all for not going to the murder mansion," Leigh-Ann said. "But you know all us separating is crazy. Pair of you gonna get stabbed in the dark or mind-warped into zombies."

"That being why," Reece said carefully, trying his best to sound as confident as Tasker, "y'all gonna be right behind us as backup. But we can't hang back, can we? We came to help Katryzna. No use turning up late."


The doors to the big mansion were locked more securely than the main gate, but the place had accessible glass windows. A few blows from the knife handle and a little wriggle-work to get between the iron bars, and Katryzna found herself in a barren parlour, just enough light from the night sky highlighting folding chairs stacked against one wall and a massive open fireplace in another. Otherwise it was empty.

"Anyone home?" Katryzna shouted, voice echoing, and Rurik hissed warnings from her shoulder. She rolled her eyes; clearly there was no one here.

She walked into the wide entrance hall, and through the opposite doorway saw an equally large and similarly sparse room. There was a stack of rolled material in a corner, possibly bedrolls? She continued up the hallway, which opened onto an enclosed courtyard, two storeys high. Skylights allowed weak moonlight to pick out big pot plants, benches, and arched doorways in each of the four walls. A viewing galley above was accessible by a big staircase to the right, and a pile of tools were scattered by the far wall. The handle of a shovel? A wheelbarrow? Katryzna's footsteps over the tiles rang loudly, and when she spoke her voice was magnified by the emptiness: "I give it fourteen for imagination."

"Out of what?" Rurik asked.

Katryzna shrugged. She passed the tools and opened the door to another corridor, this one pitching into complete darkness. She probed a hand along the wall for a light-switch, found one, flicked it and nothing happened. "Do you think Finway betrayed us?"

"Or he was mistaken," Rurik said. "He *did* say they abandon these projects quickly. Either way, perhaps we should go?"

Katryzna frowned, then sniffed. "You smell that?" Her conscience hummed ignorance. "Dirt?" She continued into the darkness, running a hand along the wall and tapping a foot ahead to avoid obstacles. This corridor seemed as empty as everywhere else, but the smell got stronger and the air was growing colder, icy. "They were digging back here."

"It could be anything," Rurik warned her. "It could have literally nothing to do with the Legion. Finway might have just given you a random location."

Katryzna's toe struck something. She crouched, blindly feeling ahead. Rocks. A wooden handle, round, attached to something heavy, a hammer or pick? She continued down low, probing more. Aha! The hard plastic of something electronic with, yes, buttons. She pressed one and a cold halogen light made her narrow her eyes. The lantern lit cracked walls either side of her, poured concrete with whitewash scratched and stained. There were doors on either wall, and light bulbs hung from high up, without shades. At the end of the corridor was a great hole in the wall, with rubble piled either side of it, another wheelbarrow, and a cable running into it. Inside the hole, a tunnel had been dug through rock.

"See," Katryzna said. "I told you." She held the lantern up to head height, revealing the tunnel's gradual slope down, with wooden supports either side and above. "Think they were digging for gold?"

"No." Rurik's voice had got quieter. "I think they were digging for something we don't need to see."

His concern wasn't completely baseless. The last time Katryzna had stood before an opening like this was the cave mouth in Ikiri, a place steeped in dark promise. There was nothing so sinister in the atmosphere of this hole, though. Without answering her conscience, she continued into it.

A short way into the tunnel, where the air was shivery cold, Katryzna passed a petrol generator, its cables disconnected. A little further still and she found a small vehicle, the size of a golf cart but sporting thick tyres, and a big scooper half-filled with broken rocks. Just beyond that, another generator and a discarded drill that looked like it would take three men to operate. It sat before a broken rock face.

Katryzna ran her free hand over her stubbly hair. "This is disappointing."

"You'd rather find monsters?" Rurik whispered.

"Obviously," she said, and turned back. She kicked a rock ahead of her as she went back up the slope, noting she had gone quite a distance into the mountain. For nothing? But if the Legion just wanted to carve a useless tunnel, what was the purpose of this grand house? There were enough chairs and bedrolls in those rooms for a lot of people. Surely not just miners, given the elaborate construction.

There had to be something else here. In the upper floors, in some big boss's office. At the very least, Katryzna suspected, there would be a larder that might remain partially stocked. She returned to the tunnel exit and trod carefully over the rubble, saying, "But see I was *right* not to wait. Sean should have just –"

Katryzna froze. Way back down the hallway, silhouetted against the dim light of the courtyard, stood a man almost as wide as the door, a pile of curves where the vague shape of torso and limbs had been overindulged and under-exercised. His legs were apart and shoulders set in a ready pose, and a hammer as long as his leg hung from his left hand. He said, in a nasal American accent, "Katryzna Tkacz? You're trespassing."

She replied, "Finally. Some action."

# 15

Tasker moved ahead of Reece, fast. It was probably a mistake, leaving Zip behind, but his instincts were taking over. Get to the hall, make Katryzna safe. Worry about the details when he got there.

"Colder than it has any right be out here," Reece said, stomping his feet and rubbing his hands together as he tried to keep up. Tasker gave him a backwards glance, noting the American's flashy pistol. Recalling what Reece had told him, he hoped the man did know how to use it. But to do that, they needed to beat the gradient and the cold.

Tasker said, "Move faster, you'll keep warmer."

He pressed on, thinking of Helen and Rebecca. If they all got out of this, he'd get home and take them to dinner. Hear about Rebecca's schoolwork and gossip from Helen's social circle. Smile, cuddle on the sofa over TV he barely cared to watch. For a while, forget this was his life.

"Gotta say, Agent," Reece huffed, "I admire what you do. Act like this is all in a day's work. Can't imagine the things you seen."

Tasker didn't reply, considering that no, there was no way the man could. But rarely had his MEE assignments put so much personally on the line.

"Ms Ward," Reece went on, "so we're clear – she's okay with us busting these motherfuckers down, right? Any means necessary?"

Tasker gave him a look. "You're worried about what she'd condone, right now?"

"Your boss, ain't she?" Reece shrugged, a little defensive.

"Not exactly," Tasker said. It was an issue he'd buried deep, himself. He usually answered to London, via his handler Caffery. But he hadn't spoken to Caffery since the Congo, leaving Ward his sole ally in the Ministry, right now.

"I'd like to keep her on side," Reece went on, "is all. What happened with Ruin, back on the road, I take it we're not getting blamed for that? And what we do up here?"

Tasker slowed down. Reece gave a cheeky smile. He was younger than he carried himself, green in his own way. "The Ministry is good at keeping things quiet. Let me worry about my people. You just focus on getting through this."

Reece nodded.

As they continued, Tasker recalled first seeing these Americans' faces, as criminals on the news. He said, "Before you caught up to Zip, you were in some big trouble?"

"Duelling Dustin Fallon," Reece confirmed. "Greedy bastard got an army of cowboys intimidating small businesses. Damn protection racket, what it is. We shot up one of their warehouses and people got hurt. We had to defend ourselves."

"All right," Tasker said. "I'll take it as a positive. Means you've got experience in exactly what we need. And I promise I'll do my best by you, Reece, now and once we're through."

Reece smiled. "Provided we survive."

"Provided we survive."

"And if I were to call Sam up without –" Reece stopped abruptly, pricking up his ears, and Tasker listened too. It was a long way off, but the sound rolled around the mountains unapologetically.

"That a scream?" Reece asked.

Tasker didn't answer, just started to run.


Katryzna had barely drawn her knife by the time the guy cleared the distance between them. His unnatural speed sparked her instincts; she jumped to the side and the big hammer swung through the space she'd been in, to smash into the wall behind her. She dropped, rolled and tried to slash at him, but a booted foot stamped on her hand and crunched her fingers. She released the blade to whip it up with the other hand, and sliced across his calf. The man was gone, suddenly not in the space he should've been, but he flinched, steadying himself, a yard back, with a hiss that said she'd nicked him. He was more dangerous than she'd expected.

Katryzna shot a look down the corridor, then back to him. No time to run, not going to show him her back, so rather than retreat she leapt with a wild roar. He moved fast but she spread her arms, almost as wide as the corridor, and caught him by the tips of her fingers. She wrapped one arm round his thick waist and punched the other hand in to stab – he twisted and was gone again, her knife stabbing air. Katryzna fell through the empty space and raised an arm just in time to deflect a backwards hammer blow. She dropped the knife and landed on her rear, then hurriedly kicked back across the floor. The freakishly graceful bastard slowed down, studying her. His bearded face was round like a meringue, lit from beneath by the lantern, beady eyes analytical. There was something familiar about him that she couldn't place.

"Here, Katryzna, the rocks!" Rurik cried, jumping up and down by the tunnel entrance. She glanced over: lots of good-sized rocks indeed, big enough to brain a man, but metres away. The knife was off on the other side of her enemy.

The man leaned his hammer against the wall beside him, showing her open hands. This moron was inviting her to a fair fight?

"All right, ugly," Katryzna huffed, pushing herself back to her feet. Her left arm hung slightly numb from the hammer blow, so she shook it to restore feeling. "You didn't have enough yet?"

"On the contrary," he replied, almost cheerful despite the dead look in his eyes, "I've been looking forward to testing you. Ever since I found out who you were." His voice was higher than his bulbous physique suggested. Everything about him was *weird*.

Katryzna glared. To hell with it. She screamed and ran at him and he suddenly slammed her back into the wall, both his fists striking her chest. As he stepped back, she almost fell again, but she brought up an arm and a knee at the same time. He blocked one but missed the other, and she kept coming at him, yelling, throwing all four limbs into it, swinging her head, biting when he came close. He swept away one punch, twisted around a kick, shoved her knee down, kept blocking her, avoiding hits or otherwise seeming to absorb them in surprisingly rocky flesh. But she didn't stop – kept yelling and gnashing, so ferocious he never got a chance to hit back. Until something struck the back of her neck and she dropped flat on her chest, chin banging the tiles. Over-extended, let him get an elbow into her spine?

She blinked and pushed up onto both hands. His boot struck her jaw with an explosion of pain, snapping her up and sending her rolling over the floor. Into the rocks. She flashed sideways and caught a rock in her hand as he charged her. She swung it hard into his ankle and he shouted in pain, but it barely slowed him: his boot caught her in the gut, and she curled over it, stunned.

Rurik yelled at her to look out, no use – a rough hand clamped the side of her head and hauled her up, and she kicked feebly, feet finding nothing to purchase, as she was pressed into the wall again. His hands twisted around her neck, dangling her above the floor, squeezing the air out of her. She gagged, energy sapped, and tried to drag a clawing hand over his face, but even as she felt flesh peel into her fingernails he only tensed harder, and pushed back, arms outstretched so she couldn't reach him again.

Couldn't make a sound. Arms and legs going lax. Barely even able to focus on his emotionless eyes watching her die. Katryzna dug deep – searched for the one thing she had left, and hocked up phlegm. She spat right in his eye. His mouth twisted in distaste and he squeezed harder, her gob dripping down his nose. She forced a smile.

Small, final victory.


Leigh-Ann scuffed a foot through the undergrowth, kicking up twigs and a tiny bit of snow. There wasn't much of it, but Reece was crazy, thinking this was barely freezing. She could see her own breath and even with her hands firmly in pockets, arms tight to her sides, was shivering like nothing. Zip wasn't bothered, trotting alongside her. Leigh-Ann said, "How's it you ain't freezing when you've got barely any flesh on you?"

Zip shrugged with an innocent smile.

"Grew up on that nasty English hill, I guess, exposed to the elements."

The kid wasn't just ignoring the cold, though, she was all chipper for this mountain-climb of a walk. Leigh-Ann had had smoker's lungs from childhood, probably from her parents hot-boxing their trailer, and had trouble enough singing two or three songs in a row without a break. Wasn't enjoying the prospect of two more miles of this shit, and was gladder with each step that Reece and Tasker had run on ahead, not to see her like this.

"It was usually warm –" Zip started, then bowed forward with a pained gasp.

"What's that?" Leigh-Ann swept down to her side. Eyes darting to the shadows of trees either side of the road. "They here? Your brother trying something?"

"No" – Zip gasped again – "something else." Scared.

"Hey now listen – look at me, Zip. See my eyes? I'm right here with you, you hear my voice? Zip, you *got* this. Whatever you feeling, you know you got it. That's *your* power in there. Own it."

Zip pushed against the fear, concentrating. Her little brow knitted.

"That's the stuff. Show them, you the boss, right?"

"I'm the boss," she whispered, and closed her eyes, focusing. "It's the Legion man. He's – using his power. I can feel it."

"Up at the mansion?" Leigh-Ann said.

"I think so," Zip said. "He's powerful. And dangerous. And – and –" She closed her eyes, fighting her emotions. "Katryzna."

"She's gonna be okay," Leigh-Ann insisted, wanting to hear it herself.

"I could – I can –" Zip replied hurriedly, eyes darting from one side to another. Whatever idea she was trying to find, it was making her even more afraid.

"You feel him, you can get to him?" Leigh-Ann asked. "With your mind?"

Zip shook her head. "What if there are more nearby? What about my brother?"

"But you *can* do something? From here?"

"Yes. I think – I mean, I'm *sure* I can reach him."

"Katryzna's in trouble?"

Zip nodded with fear.

"Then do it!"

The kid squeezed her eyes closed at the urgency of the demand, bunched up her arms and shoulders, and grimaced at whatever happened in her head. Then she opened her eyes again, surprised as she looked around and saw the sky hadn't fallen.

"What happened?" Leigh-Ann asked. "You do it?"

"I don't know," Zip whispered. She got that focused look again, seeing something unique to her. "He's reaching for me." She shook her head, stood up more defiantly, fixed her expression. "No. *No.*" Little fists balled at her side, staring through the word, back down the road in the direction of that fairy tale town. She shouted, "No!" then took two deep breaths, and nodded stiffly, apparently satisfied.

"The fuck's going on, Zip?"

Zip gave her another uncertain look and Leigh-Ann suggested it herself: "You don't know?"

"No," Zip said. "I mean. Yes, I know. I did it, Leigh. I resisted my brother."

"Resisted how?"

"I felt him looking. Searching for something nearby. I pushed him back."

Leigh-Ann waited for more, but Zip merely stared, still muddling things through in her mind. "So what now?" With no more answer, Leigh-Ann looked up the road. "Guess we make double time and see exactly what's awaiting."


The man's concentration slipped. He glanced aside as though something was there and his hands went slack. Katryzna landed on her feet, gasping for air, as he took a step away, turning, making a confused noise. He snapped, "Get out!"

She fell to her knees, coughing, as he staggered too, and had to brace himself against a wall. He shouted, "Stop!", shook himself out of it, and turned back to Katryzna blinking hard. She snatched up the rock again and swung with all her weight. It caught his chin, somewhere in those folds of fat. He fell into the wall, and his hand came up much slower than before – halfway there when her second blow caught his temple. Not even a twitch before her third blow knocked him flat on the ground. Then she scrambled back, dropping the rock in favour of lunging for the hammer. Taking it in both hands she rose and spun back to him, bringing the heavy weapon high above her head.

"He's done!" Rurik cried, next to the felled man, waving both hands. "Katryzna – take him alive!"

She paused, and in that pause her last ounce of desperate strength escaped her. She could barely keep the hammer aloft. The man was a bloody heap, eyes rolling in their sockets, blood bubbling over his lips. She fell aside, letting the hammer go with a loud clang, and she crawled over to the knife. She spun back quickly, aiming it in case he had recovered. But he was lying still, wheezing, arms spread at his sides.

"Sean's family," Katryzna said. The words scratched her throat, so she coughed to clear it, which hurt even more. She tried again. "You people are going to leave Sean's family alone."

The man exhaled hard, fingers twitching, testing to be sure he was alive. He pushed onto his elbows with difficulty. Then back, to prop a shoulder against the wall, stopping him from sliding to the floor. His eyes were black shadows in a face streaked with blood. He replied with a rasped question, "Where's the girl?"

"Sean's family," Katryzna repeated. "Last chance."

"Not here," he said. "Nothing to do with me."

"I *know* they are not here," Katryzna said. "I am telling you to back off."

He eyed her, too thoughtfully for a man threatened with death. He breathed deeply, mustering energy. "The girl. How did she do it? She's not here."

"I hit you with a rock."

"She hit my mind. Impossible." He rolled back, looking upwards as he struggled to sit up. "Worse than we thought."

Katryzna sat against the opposite wall, knife resting on her knee.

The fight had gone out of him, replaced by troubled thoughtfulness. He said, "Didn't think the kid . . . Didn't think."

"No," she spat. "No one thinks properly. About me."

"About the kid . . ." He took another breath. "I know all about you. Eyes' girl."

"Eyes?" she echoed. "You knew him?"

He rolled his head to her again. "He was better than any of us." He wheezed out a high, resigned whistle. "Go on then. End it. I know . . . you can."

Katryzna rotated the knife. Sure, a cut throat didn't take a genius. But he almost sounded like he wanted it. Something in him yearned to be set free, waiting for a worthy escape. Eyes wasn't so different. "Talk, first," she said. "Is there any food here?"

# 16

Tasker ran past an old truck and a motorbike discarded by the open gates to the mansion, the lock smashed. He followed footprints through the snow to the entrance. The double doors had been left open, like the gates, but there were no lights on nor signs of movement inside. The agent readied his gun in both hands as Reece caught up. They slipped inside together, aiming down a long, dark hallway. A faint glow came under the far door, pushed to. Tasker continued along one wall, Reece along the other. A sound came from the other side, someone in there.

Reece put a hand on the door handle and nodded. He thrust the door open and Tasker entered, gun raised. The door's squeak drew the attention of a man sitting on the tiled floor of a large enclosed courtyard, propped against a wall. Dim electric light came from an open hallway. The man didn't move, regarding them curiously as they came closer, guns ready, checking for any other sign of movement. He was injured, breath coming out awkwardly, face swollen.

"Sean, Reece!" Katryzna's voice announced her presence above – voice throaty and dry. "You made it!" She was at the top of a staircase, coming quickly down with her arms full of supplies.

Immediately, Tasker saw in the little light that her face was also bloody and she was listing on her left side, masking injury. He asked, "You okay?"

"You know me, of course I am!" Katryzna said. "This is Scorecard. He tried to kill me."

"And he's just lying there?" Reece asked, protectively. "Oughta tie him up, at –"

"He's harmless," she said, walking over to the burly man. His expression suggested doubt at her assessment, but he didn't contradict her as she laid down her wares. A First Aid kit, packets of snacks and an elegant bottle of alcohol. She held the last up before him. "Purely for medicinal use."

"It's a Hine Antique brandy," Scorecard said, around what sounded like a mouthful of cotton. "Forgive me for this waste."

They watched as he opened the bottle and swigged heavily on it, before giving a relieved sigh. Satisfied with the care she'd given, Katryzna turned and bounced towards Tasker. "I'm glad you made it!" She raised her hands like she intended to hug him, but didn't finish and let them hang in the air as she grinned.

While Katryzna slowly dropped her arms, Tasker squinted at her captive, recalling Mason's files. He had put on weight and grown a beard, but it was there in the eyes. Scorecard, one of the least offensive-looking of the Legion. "Is he alone?"

Scorecard nodded, around another swig from the bottle, as Katryzna explained, "This place is empty. Except I found some food and that drink. Apparently they cleared out everything else a few weeks ago."

"Agent Tasker," Scorecard croaked, setting the brandy aside. "We have to talk."

"You wanna talk now?" Reece took a step forward. "After y'all threaten his family and attack our friend? Those spikes on the road could've sent us over the cliff."

Scorecard held his gaze with dark, unfeeling eyes, then nodded. "Mistakes have been made. But if you want your families safe, we'll talk."

Tasker moved closer himself, grip tightening on his pistol – to what? Strike the man? Shoot his leg, make him hurt – something, for even suggesting harming Rebecca and Helen.

"We didn't know for sure Zipporah was *alive* before two weeks ago," Scorecard said quickly, loudly, pushing through a wince of pain. He looked aside, took the brandy again and had another drink. After exhaling relief, he said, "She had a lot of people scared, myself included. With her and her father on the move, all of us at risk, do you blame us for being defensive? But Katryzna says you're not with Mason. This is plainly more complicated than we appreciated."

"You wanted to kill her," Tasker said, simplifying it.

"Before she could kill us," Scorecard said. Because there was the bottom line of their belief: if they didn't act fast, Zip would come for them? He huffed, "Where is the child?"

"None of your damn business," Reece said. "Think we gonna put her in a room with someone wants her dead?"

"Trust me." Scorecard stretched an ugly smile. "Bring Zipporah here, and I'll be the one at risk. Truthfully, I should've run. But I thought I could at least handle Katryzna on her own. Make a small difference. Now, it's up to you. Kill me if you want. It would be the usual way. But the Legion does not have to be your enemy. Without Mason steering you, you might find our interests align."

Tasker gave Katryzna a questioning look. She shrugged and said, "I was going to make him talk anyway."


Leigh-Ann pushed Zip down off the road, behind a tree, just shy of a sheer damn cliff, as headlights bounced towards them. She had her gun ready, pretty sure she could at least use it for a distraction while Zip did her thing. But Zip insisted, "It's safe. I *think*."

"Think ain't good enough," Leigh-Ann said, as the vehicle drew closer.

"It's Reece!" Zip cried, a moment before the truck appeared, two bobbing lights with a silhouette behind it. Leigh-Ann squinted, and as the vehicle passed she got a flash of his face. She jumped out shouting and waving. Looked like he wasn't gonna stop for a second, then he hit the brakes.

As Reece jumped out, Leigh-Ann shouted, "I'm guessing things ain't all bad?"

"Ain't all good," he said. Zip ran to give him a big hug. "Get in, you'll see."

He made a meal of turning in the tight road, lots of little adjustments to be sure he didn't fall off the cliff. Not the driver Caleb was. Then, Stomatt would've just driven off the edge, so this was a reasonable in-between. Reece explained as they drove: the big hall was abandoned but Katryzna, beat up, had a Legion brute captive and wanting to talk. Zip nodded like she knew exactly what he was talking about.

"Been tuning in, have you?" Reece asked.

"Did a little something back there," Leigh-Ann said. "We might not wanna hang around long."

"Anyone figures we're here, they'll have a time catching up," Reece said. "We've had a hell of a day. Hell of a week. Think we've earned a break."

"Think you just damn jinxed any chance we had," Leigh-Ann said. "Thanks."

They pulled up to the building and Leigh-Ann cooed at the scale of it. The looming mountain terrain and the dark of night made it ominous as a gate to hell. But inside, it was square, plain and mostly empty. Tasker and Katryzna had gathered folding chairs in a front room where their bearlike prisoner sat by a radiator, pipes groaning as the heating came to life. Katryzna (who had taken on a couple of new shades) almost attempted a hug but turned it to a wave. She introduced Scorecard, who had wanted to kill her, apparently, but got stopped by Zippy. Then she offered them a handful of protein bars.

Leigh-Ann took in the grand room. "This place, no offence, looks like a hotel got shut down because the caretaker murdered the tourists."

"It didn't work out," Scorecard said. His face was half-bandaged, with blood already soaking through, and his top was torn, but he looked oddly positive. Maybe thanks to that half-empty bottle of brandy by his feet. "But you are welcome. Now. If I had known you were travelling without Mason, I would've opened the doors to you. You are more special than we thought, Zipporah. Do you know what this place is?"

Zip looked around: nothing to recommend the room bar some fancy woodwork and a lot of headroom. But something drew her attention beyond the walls.

"They were digging a tunnel," Katryzna said. "Into the mountain."

"To find another Source," Zip said, uncomfortably. "But it's the wrong place."

Scorecard frowned. "What makes you say that?"

"Looks pretty abandoned," Leigh-Ann said. "Doesn't take a genius, lame-ass."

"No, I can feel it," Zip said. "There *is* something like Ikiri. Older, and almost gone. It's near, but not here."

"Interesting," Scorecard said. "I shut Enoch down, seeing as we had massacres in Norway and your emergence to deal with. I held some hope we might revive this project come the spring."

"There is a pull, in the mountains," Zip continued helpfully. "But it's very light, like an echo? You need to go more" – she pointed vaguely – "that way."

"Stop, Zip," Tasker said. "Not another word to help them. They're looking for another Ikiri? After the damage you caused, you want to open another wound here?"

"The opposite," Scorecard said, still watching Zip. "Ikiri fuels jealousy and hubris. Hate. We are locked in an obsessive game, with the power, with each other. The Legion's goal has always been to contain that. *My* goal has always been to make some sense of it. How better to quell the darkness than to understand its origins?"

"That's what you call running around killing innocent people?" Reece asked.

"Trying to take over the world?" Katryzna added.

"Hunting children?" Leigh-Ann finished. "That's quelling the darkness?"

"Defending ourselves," Scorecard said. "You've seen what Mason and his daughter can do? We need all the help we can get." His eyes settled on Leigh-Ann, for some reason picking her out as the reasonable one, the person to be convinced – maybe because she'd brought Zip in. "Mason told you we're evil, no doubt. Monsters. But we strike first only because to hesitate is to die. This work here has merit."

"Said every megalomaniac ever," Leigh-Ann offered, and it made him smile.

"Let me explain. We've been researching places of power. Agent Tasker is familiar with some, I'm sure: Varanasi, Istanbul, Ordshaw, Rostov, Hokkaido. Known areas pooling a certain type of energy. Cities grow –"

Katryzna made a noise that interrupted him, and when everyone looked her way she offered a shy smile, then whispered out the corner of her mouth, "Not now, he's talking."

Thrown, Scorecard looked to Tasker for an explanation, and the agent breezed past it to say, "Yeah you know about the work we do, congratulations. Ikiri's different, though. Novisan is directed there or altered from there. None of those places behave that way."

"No," Scorecard agreed. "And though they pool energy in similar ways, the results are quite individual. I imagined the same might be true of a place like Ikiri. We've studied the sort of energy readings Simon Parris passed on to you; our own powers connect back to Ikiri – as do certain phenomena across the world, which Hank Duvalier's research first identified. Ghost stories and the supposed supernatural with a peculiar flow of energy. Duvalier thought he was looking at a source of life, as though we were all universally connected to the one source. But Ikiri is *not* universal. Special, yes, and globally connected – but not the only place of its kind. I hoped that in the same way Varanasi and Rostov might –"

"Tsk, okay, okay! I'll ask," Katryzna said, irritably glancing at her shoulder. She met Leigh-Ann's eye in some shared joke, like *weren't voices in your head so annoying?* Leigh-Ann gave her an exasperated look back, but she smiled it off and asked, "Rostov-on-Don?"

"Yes," Scorecard replied slowly. "You're familiar with it."

Katryzna's eyes narrowed but she got self-conscious with everyone watching, and only gave a small bob of a nod. Without elaborating, she said, "Please. Continue."

Scorecard did so warily, and Leigh-Ann parked that as another thing to be worried about in Katryzna. Obviously she knew something about another weird place herself. "Well. I wondered if there were other hot spots like Ikiri, which could help us understand it. Through old myths, legends and rumours, I found an underwater trench in the Pacific Ocean; a valley of death in the Australian outback; and here, rumours of a subterranean labyrinth in the Alps. During the early Middle Ages they had colourful stories out here of the Antler King. A French industrialist built this site, you know, as a school for orphaned children. There were a dozen housed here when the town lost all contact with them. The bodies were never found. There was a village up this road, a hundred years ago, completely lost to landslides. One example of many obscure power sources, which even we, who are resistant, find hard to pinpoint. These are all places with the barest trace residues of what once was. Like Ikiri, they twist your senses as you get closer. But if we *could* get close, we might find an antidote to Ikiri."

"Find more power, you mean," Tasker said. "In my experience that's what drives people like you. You hunt it out, you guard it jealously."

"I would trade it all to be free of this," Scorecard spat back, his cool slipping. He took a breath, and again fixed on Leigh-Ann. "Look at my eyes. We all lost something in Ikiri. There's an emptiness in us, a base –" He choked with sudden emotion. "After Ikiri, we could tune in to energy and feelings, but could scarcely feel for ourselves. There's an emptiness inside that can't be filled." Leigh-Ann saw it then: a hollow depth to his gaze. Emptiness was right. Yet all around those eyes his injured face was wrinkled with apology and sorrow. "Just about the only decent thing any of us has achieved is preventing this curse from spreading."

"Except you've been training people," Tasker said, not done yet. "Hunting for more power sources, setting up camps – you seriously want us to believe this is some noble enterprise to make it stop?"

"There is nothing noble about it, no. But the alternative would be worse. The likes of Mason, unchecked. There's a man that would see himself as custodian of this world, trusting no one else to these secrets. Without even considering that there may be powers out there none of us can stop alone." Scorecard's eyes fell on Zip as he reconsidered. "You *were* at Graystown, weren't you? And you, Agent Tasker, you saw Laukstad?"

"Neither were her responsibility," Tasker said. "Or her father's."

Scorecard frowned and Zip whispered the explanation: "It's my brother. He's the problem."

"Your brother?" he replied. "Impossible."

"Fuck off with possible," Leigh-Ann said, and moved on before Katryzna could complain about the cuss. "Week ago I didn't believe in mutant gorillas and mind-reading. Zip says some little bastard in Africa's making people go nuts, you better believe her."

"And you thought Zippy couldn't hurt you from a distance," Katryzna reminded Scorecard, something they'd already covered.

"Yes," he said, slowly. "You're right, of course. We couldn't sense Zipporah all this time, after all. It's . . . the boy is still out there? The greatest trick the devil ever played. We thought Mason or one of our own was responsible for Laukstad. Graystown, at the least. But her *brother*?" He shook his head and winced. The pain of a whole heap of regrets was dragging him down. "I have to call Shearjoy."

"Excuse me?" Reece cut in. "You're wanting us to think your heart's in the right place, when you didn't even know what was causing the massacres you've been killing people to cover up?"

"I do not apologise for trying to avoid drawing *any* attention back to Ikiri," Scorecard replied calmly. "We could not risk a repeat at Ikiri or anywhere else. And we would've found the people responsible for the massacres eventually."

"And you would've had Zip killed in the meantime?" Tasker rumbled. "Because you all thought if her father wasn't responsible, she might be? You didn't even know. Shearjoy threatened my family, to get rid of her. Ruin came after us on the motorway, with a *machete*. You people saw her as nothing but a threat, when taking her back to Ikiri is the *only* way we can stop Ezekiel."

Scorecard narrowed his eyes. "Indeed, if it's true about the boy, we sincerely need to reconsider. But you were with Mason, what were we supposed to think? His mission was no more crude than our own. Where *is* the Headhunter?"

"We scared him off." Katryzna waved a dismissive hand.

"Scared Mason?" Scorecard said with disbelief. "No. He lives to kill for Ikiri. If he didn't hurt you just for knowing Zipporah was alive, then –" He paused, another idea forming. "But you convinced him her brother was alive, too? And Mason left the child in your care? If he knows Ezekiel's alive, he'll return to Ikiri, at last. He was always more vicious than any of us."

"You're lying," Zip said. "My daddy is *not* bad. He just doesn't understand."

"Please." Scorecard's voice turned suddenly bitter. "He's had plenty of chances. Hurt plenty of people who didn't deserve it. Lied to you your whole life, no doubt. Did he even tell you had a brother? Or that he had him killed? He didn't even do it himself –"

Zip shrieked, eyes closed, fists balled, and the light flickered. Everyone froze as though there'd been a quake, and Leigh-Ann half expected Zip to say her brother was striking again, or she sensed some new evil about to charge them. But Zip took quick breaths to recover and said, "You're lying. He is my dad, and he is good, and you don't know anything!"

Scorecard's stare softened as she panted with emotion, and Leigh-Ann found her hand squeezing Zip's shoulder for comfort. A little more of a push and all their hearts might stop, right? She whispered, "Maybe we oughta take five, what do you say?"

Zip looked up her, eyes teary. "He took care of me. He's my dad."

"Yeah, but," Leigh-Ann said, crouching. Fuck it, no sense skirting around a thing that Zip plainly needed to face. "You know he's hurt people, right?" The girl's red eyes were redder than ever, glowing with it, and Leigh-Ann couldn't help compare them back to Scorecard's. That thing they'd all lost, she realised, wasn't gone from Zip. The kid's eyes were more alive than anyone's. Leigh-Ann glanced to the others, who were watching her like she was the one gonna produce some pearl of wisdom and make this alright. She swallowed and said, "Important thing is *you're* different, Zip. Different to all these pricks."

"And you get to choose what we do next," Reece added.

Zip looked between the pair of them, uncertainty fading as she sniffed back a last tear and settled her mind. "I want him to tell his people we're going to Ikiri. All of us and all of them. We can explain to Shearjoy and we can work with my daddy. And we'll fix it. Together."

# 17

There was great commotion as the soldiers led Henri and Mason into the Cursed Union's camp, with every member of the militant community scrambling to watch. An audience of men, women and children, all wearing the PLU's uneven uniform of patchily repaired fatigues, climbing over huts and leaning around macabre totems of stick figures with bullet-jewellery. They penned the newcomers in, watching with whispers, as the group continued to the centre of the camp, where General Solomon waited on a throne of scrap metal, his robust shaman Jonah standing to one side in a shirt tunic and gold chains.

"We've been expecting you," Solomon said loudly, quietening the whispers. "The nameless *he*, the man who abandoned Sara to take the child."

"Took our hope," Jonah sneered, and murmurs of discontent ran through the camp. Keener, younger men rapped knuckles and gun-butts against metal and wood in a drum roll of agreement. The Union were trapped here because Mason had left Ikiri corrupted, after all. When he had taken away the child who could calm Ikiri's power – their only means of escape.

"Let him speak!" Solomon raised his hands for quiet.

Henri edged away from Mason, as the big white man only stood taller, inviting their attention and whatever trouble might come. The same attitude as when they'd heard those monsters out in the forest, which they had barely escaped. There was no fear nor apology in Mason's face as he said, "You want hope? Take me to Ikiri and I will end this."

Solomon ignored the request to address Henri: "We did not expect you, though. I am sorry you have returned, Henri Ngoi."

"He is not the only one who found me," Henri replied. "And I fear he's not the only one to have returned here."

"No," Mason said. "I am just the only one who can resolve this. You clearly can't."

This got a vocal response, dozens of irate soldiers stomping and shouting, curses in Congolese and French and English. Calmer heads held back the more agitated men. A particularly angry boy's high voice pierced above the others, "You fuck! You fuck!"

"Mr Mason," Henri whispered urgently, "they are not our enemy."

"That's to be seen," Mason said. "General Solomon. What's it to be?"

Solomon remained stoic, sunglasses hiding his feelings. The camp quietened again, though the audience had trouble staying still. They wanted blood, and Henri was sure if they took Mason's, they would want his too, by association. At last, the general leaned forward and said, "Did you know what you left behind?"

Mason stared, and Henri saw that the man was not ignorant of his legacy. Why should he be, when the survivors of Ikiri had more power than anyone had known? They'd had an English spy watching from Kinshasa, after all. Mason said, "I knew you were here. I knew Ikiri created a barrier around itself." He glanced to Henri. "I suspected Sara was not dead."

The audience started up again and this time Solomon stood to shout, "Quiet. Let him talk. You will talk, won't you? Explain yourself."

Mason considered the crowd, as likely to start an impossible fight as he was to talk. "What is there to say?"

"Convince me you are worth the air we breathe," Solomon demanded. "You left us trapped with creatures from hell and now you wish to make amends? You cannot return so easily."

"I have no desire to return," Mason said. "Only a duty. And if I had understood the true threat, I would've done it sooner." He stopped there, but Solomon kept staring, waiting. The moment could have stretched into an eternity, but the one-handed man lost patience and huffed. "We were all tainted by Ikiri, but that boy . . . it seeped off him. The animals emerged after his birth. We stayed as long as we could, trying to understand this power, but the boy drew too much darkness, even as the girl pushed the monsters away. Sara tried to argue, but we all understood what needed to be done. I proposed drawing lots, but Eyes volunteered. Insisted. He believed himself most capable. I believed that, too."

"And so you left them all there?" Henri mouthed. "You never knew for sure –"

"The creatures came. It was not safe for anyone, at that time. I felt what happened next. Eyes died. The child died. You cannot possibly understand. Ikiri allowed us to sense the world in ways that go beyond your imagination. It was changed by our presence, but it was *contained*. I knew it would not permit anyone to enter. Yet clearly the child was more powerful than I thought, even then. I *believed* him dead. If he is still there, though, I will resolve it."

"So you say," Solomon said. "Sara suggests you are not to be trusted."

"You put your faith in the wrong prophet," Mason growled.

"Who else?" Jonah said. "She spoke of many fallible men, but could not even bring herself to name you."

"Then who did she name? Who did she think worthy?" Mason turned, taking in his upset audience, and now he apparently itched to be heard. He boomed, "I was the *only* person fully committed to what was right. Fender wanted to abandon what he'd uncovered. Shearjoy built a greedy bloody empire. Scorecard schemed to spread the disease. Ruin, who I trusted, did *this*." Mason held up his metal-cased stump and shook it for all to see. He picked up speed. "Moose lost control, Grithin turned coward, Canon thought himself a god, Chops mutilated in the Legion's name. Eyes, even Eyes . . ." Mason slowed down. "I was sure he, of all of us, was reliable. Apparently not."

"How could he be?" Jonah said, unfazed by the outburst. "No one could resist Ikiri's power without the girl. You took her away. The only hope of stopping this, and you took her."

"I did what was necessary."

"Yes," Solomon said. "To protect yourself? The girl was a good luck charm. She guided you past the monsters and kept you from Ikiri's reach. You, alone."

Mason glowered, seeing no reason to justify himself.

"What became of her?" Henri asked.

"Nothing," Mason said. "She lives. She is well."

"Nothing?" Henri echoed. "Does she know about Ikiri? Her mother? Does she —"

"She is not involved," Mason snapped. "You haven't listened. I led them here, I seeded these children, I was responsible for everything. I have protected the world from this ever since. I have never hidden behind a child, and I have no need for her here. Do you want me to end this or must I add your blood to the bargain?" His voice had risen to a shout, and he had swollen up, seeming to grow as he spoke, forceful enough to still the entire camp.

Solomon and Jonah shared a look, even these leaders of men shaken by Mason's presence. The general rubbed his chin and started slowly nodding. "Why should we believe you came to stop this, and not to take from Ikiri, as you did before?"

"Eight years," Mason rumbled. "Eight years I have been pruning Ikiri's toxic limbs. How dare you think I would want *more* of this?"

Silence followed as Solomon considered his words and the audience shuffled impatiently. Henri wished he was far away, back in Kinshasa, back in time at a point where he could still tease Miguel for believing there was anyone left to cause trouble for them.

A creature howled in the far distance and a few in the crowd murmured worries. Solomon looked towards the sound and said, "They are out in force, lately. They know you're here."

"I am not afraid of them," Mason said.

"And yet *you* came to *us*."

Mason breathed out angrily, big shoulders rising and falling. "Do you have a path to Ikiri or not?"

"We can take you there," the general said, carefully. "But I am not inclined to. Definitely not until dawn, and not before we consult with Sara. Before *you* consult with her. Let her see you and let her cast judgement."

Mason held Solomon's gaze with unblinking malice. From the way he spoke of Sara, in the little he had said, Henri could only imagine that his fond memories were marred by the thought of what had come next. Whatever peace he had made was wrapped in darkness. Yet Mason overcame that with the same resolve Henri expected he would employ in a fight, and growled, "With pleasure."

# 18

Katryzna was quietly thankful that Zip's little outburst brought the talking to a close. Even with all that alcohol, Scorecard was struggling after she'd almost cracked his head like an egg. She was unsteady on her feet herself. Her arm was throbbing where it had been struck, and her head ached, and it was hard to ignore it all. And then there was the uneasy feeling Scorecard's mention of Rostov gave her. Of all the cities, he had to bring up the one where she first met Rurik. Probably a silly coincidence.

Sleep and lots of water would sort her out and everything would be good tomorrow. They had established that the Legion were missing information in their efforts to hoard Ikiri's power to themselves. Scorecard, at least, had seen they might be better off working together, and called some people to ensure the Legion were aware of it. He made arrangements to settle things with Shearjoy – not contacting the man himself, as they didn't work that way, but promising they would meet him in the Congo, where his people were already busy. Tasker wasn't too happy about that, but in Katryzna's experience it was always best to get close to people you didn't like, so you knew where they were. They could all continue to Ikiri together and finish up there. One way or another. A plane would be fuelled in Lyon airport and the Legion would stop attacking them.

A good day's work, Katryzna reflected, sitting with her back against the wall by the door. Scorecard drooped by the far wall, all but passed out, while Leigh-Ann and Zip set up bedrolls and blankets for themselves at the centre. Sean would sleep by the window, Reece was off rummaging somewhere else. All given it would be a nice slumber party.

Sean came over and said, "You eaten enough? Need anything?"

"I'm fine," Katryzna said.

He hesitated, and Rurik suggested, "He wants to tell you coming out here could have got you all killed."

"That's *why* I came alone," Katryzna replied quietly. Sean gave her an odd look.

"I appreciate it," he said. "However it all went down, it's worked out. And we can figure out the rest as we go. Long journey still ahead."

"Are you not mad at me?" Katryzna asked.

"Mad?" Tasker replied with surprise. "I'm in your debt. Thank you. For everything."

Katryzna squirmed, not expecting that. Rurik started to goad her for making assumptions and she scuffed a shoe his way. She mumbled, "It's nothing."

"It's not," Sean replied firmly. "Helen, Rebecca –"

"I did not touch them," Katryzna told him quickly. "They are probably enjoying a break right now, do you think? They are fine."

"I wasn't questioning that – I know they're fine, that's the point. They mean the world to me, Katryzna. What you did for us – it's a lot. Whatever else comes out of this, I promise I'll see you taken care of."

Katryzna fixed a bemused smile. "You think there is a way to take care of me?"

He didn't look amused and Rurik tutted at her. She wrinkled her nose at her conscience, as Sean said, "You've come from somewhere that's given you baggage. You're going places you don't need to. Whatever you need, I'll help."

He turned to go. Katryzna stared at his back, thrown. Did he know more than she thought? Did he know more than *she* knew? Where had she come from that mattered? She needed to say something more. She blurted out, "Sean?" He looked over a shoulder. She stalled, then said, "You have a very pretty wife. Well done."

He gave her an uncertain smile and a quiet thanks, then carried on.

Rurik said, "You are such a creep."

"What?" Katryzna whispered. "I was talking about his wife, not his daughter."

"Wow, you made it worse. It isn't good for anyone to catch your eye."

"I hate you so much." Katryzna exhaled largely, resting her head against the wall. She didn't have the energy to be mad at Rurik, and knew he wasn't entirely serious. They had had a tough evening and he needed to vent, too. "Do you want to talk about Rostov?" she asked.

"Why?" Rurik said. "We're never going back, what difference does it make."

Footsteps came down the hall and Katryzna rolled her head aside to find Reece returning from his sweep of the building. He looked down at her and asked, "You comfortable there?"

She shrugged.

"How you holding up?" She gave that a *go away* smile. No sense encouraging conversation; she'd only say something to upset him or he'd say something to upset her. But he persisted. "That's gotta hurt like a son of a bitch, you sure –"

"You sure you don't want to talk normally?" Katryzna cut in.

"How's that?" Reece frowned.

"Normally. Without replacing normal words with insults," she told him wearily. They never got it. "The mind is a terrible thing to waste."

"Give him a chance," Rurik said. "Here he is –"

"I *know* where he is," Katryzna hissed, and, at Reece's startled look, added, "Look. My English is not perfect, and I am not nice, but there is no need to add ugly language. Can we agree on that?" she asked Rurik. "Manners cost nothing."

"Manners," Reece echoed, sceptically. "No offence, Katryzna, but how's a bit of cussing trouble you, when cutting people up doesn't? Know which one I find more ugly."

Katryzna held his gaze, finding not scolding but mild humour in his eyes. His lips slightly upturned. She said, "Do you think I cut people too much? Be honest."

"Not my place to say. Guess we don't choose the trouble we get sucked into. People like us."

"You think you are like me?" Katryzna raised an eyebrow.

"In this same room, ain't we?" He was plainly lingering, after something.

It brought to mind when he'd arrived here, and Katryzna narrowed her eyes suspiciously. "You said I was a friend. Earlier."

"Yeah, well, like you said. Manners cost nothing." Reece winked. "You need anything? Painkillers, fresh Band-Aids, hot cocoa?"

"You have hot cocoa?"

Reece slowly shook his head. "Nah, but it couldn't hurt asking."

"Ah. You are teasing me? Flirting? To be clear, I appreciate the offer, but I will not sleep with you. It is not you – men are no use to me."

Reece looked like he'd been stabbed. "Okay. No. That's –" He forced another smile. "Doesn't mean I can't still be a gentleman, does it?"

"You will not get anything for it," she warned.

"Make you happy, keep you alive and well, that's not nothing."

Katryzna squinted at him, as Rurik whispered, "He may actually just be friendly?"

"You may *actually* suck," Katryzna replied out the side of her mouth, and rather than confuse Reece this time, it made him smile again.

He looked from her over across the room, to Scorecard, and it looked like his mind was going the same place as Sean's. Thanks, you did well, all of that. But he said, "You rest up, huh? I'm keeping watch."

"Not on me."

"For monsters, Katryzna," Reece told her, tapping his nose. "Though hopefully this place is secure." He backed away, crossing his fingers.

She watched him check on Leigh-Ann and Zip, whispering good nights. Katryzna wondered if they would cuddle for warmth, later, and what that would feel like. Leigh-Ann didn't look her way, and had only muttered thanks when Katryzna handed out some snacks before. That was fine. Katryzna was used to it, and they'd met eyes a few times, which was better than nothing. It was always easier to get men's attention. But as Sean said, they had a long way to go together, and if Reece wanted to be friends, that was a start. The important thing was this group had not entirely rejected her. Yet.

While the others slept, Reece sat at a window with a blanket and his pistol on his lap, looking out at the shadows and snow that separated them from the road. It had been a couple of hours since Zip had used her gifts on Scorecard, and for now it looked like nothing bad was coming for them. But that didn't put him much at ease.

His mind raced too hard to sleep, with thoughts coming from all directions over what they'd gotten themselves into, where everything seemed more complicated than he had accounted for. They were en route to a place that no one came out of good. Hell, Reece wasn't that good to begin with. He was a thief. Wasn't afraid of pulling a trigger. Led Caleb to his death and all. He suspected Agent Tasker wasn't a great deal better, morality-wise, and there was no doubt when it came to Katryzna. Though she, at least, had a kind of ignorant innocence about her. Didn't know better, that was the thing. All of them were living the lives they had, was all. Backwater musicians with guns, Polish assassins, Brits in suits, all in the muck together.

That drew him guiltily to Stomatt, laid out more or less forgotten in the UK. Hell. Was he healing up? Left with weird black track marks and a confused paramedic; might've taken a turn for the worse by now, for all they knew. Was he gonna walk again? Another life ruined because Reece had wild dreams of justice that spiralled way out of control.

Somewhere between those muddled thoughts, Reece jolted to a sound of crunching movement outside. He blinked rapidly. Dammit, there was a crest of blue light out there, morning creeping in – he'd sat the whole night already?

Another crunch and he shot up, knocking the chair over. Something moved off towards the rock face, quickly flashing out of sight. Reece pressed himself to the window to better see. The little dawn light wasn't enough. More rapid crunching drew his attention in the other direction. He shouted, "Wake up y'all, we got company!"

It gave them one second's warning before a feral screech came – the howl of something big and feline, behind the outer wall. Reece ran out the room, past Katryzna as she stirred, into the next room with its smashed window. He stuck his head out the broken pane, into the cold air. Just in time to see the tail end of a long, slithering creature disappear up the wall, moving round the far tower.

"The hell's going –" Leigh-Ann shouted, and was cut off by Zip screaming: "He got them!"

She sounded so stricken, Reece sprinted right back to the other room and skidded down on his knees next to her. Tasker was up by the window, pistol in hand, as Leigh-Ann struggled to get free of her sleeping bag. Scorecard, propped against the wall by the radiator, stared studiously as Katryzna grabbed her knife.

"Cher, cher, what is it?" Reece said, taking Zip's shoulders.

Her eyes were wide open and roaming. They picked Reece out of whatever else she'd seen. "He did it! I couldn't – I shouldn't have slept."

"Zip, there's no –"

A window smashed in the room above, and Reece stood, pistol ready, as something thumped into the building. It stopped above them, then gave another piercing howl. Reece met Katryzna's eye, opposite him, as she stood with her big hunting knife like that'd be enough to take on the world.

"I know that sound," Scorecard said, as the creature padded heavily over the floorboards, towards the courtyard. "How did it get here?"

"Truck's a hell of a distance now," Leigh-Ann announced, looking out the window.

"Block the door." Tasker pointed at the chairs stacked against the wall.

"No time," Reece said, "and I doubt it'd keep. Zip, you with us?" She looked pale. "Cher – we need you with us now."

"I can't," she said, eyes trembling. "They're not – I can't stop them."

"They?" Leigh-Ann shot back. "What *they*? There more than one?"

"Think I spotted two, at least," Reece said. "Not as big as that gorilla."

"Much faster," Zip whispered.

"What gorilla?" Scorecard asked. He was up and unwinding his muscles, flexing.

"We got hunted across America," Reece said. "Vile and a gorilla. Caught –"

"Vile?" Scorecard said incredulously. Something creaked far off, and wood snapped, drawing his attention. "How did you draw them out from Ikiri?"

"I don't know!" Zip cried back.

"Well, pass me my damn hammer!" He clicked a finger at Leigh-Ann – his weapon lay on the floor near her. "There's –"

"Down!" Tasker shouted, as he tackled Leigh-Ann and the window smashed right by her. A blur of dark movement rolled over them, into the centre of the room, kicking up blankets as it scrambled for footing. Tasker's pistol, knocked from his hand, went sliding over the floor. Reece swung Zip up under one arm and turned his back on the creature to shield her. He twisted the other arm back, gun raised, as the monster righted itself. Long as a car, but low to the ground, four limbs hinged up past its thin body, tail lashing behind it. Yellow eyes flashed Reece's way – *Zip's* way.

Katryzna fired, Tasker's gun in her hand: one shot ripped through the creature's shoulder, but the thing twisted fluidly around and slunk close to the floor, so fast that the next shot went over it. It leapt as Reece's own shot clipped its hind leg. It was momentarily airborne, launching at Katryzna – then it slammed into the floorboards so hard they broke. Scorecard was suddenly next to it, grimacing as he heaved his hammer out of the creature's cracked skull. The tool came loose with a squelch. Reece stared – how had Katryzna lasted two minutes against a man that quick? Scorecard breathed heavily, eyes wide with freshly kindled wildness. The creature twitched, so he brought the hammer down again with a nasty shout. Reece covered Zip's eyes.

"All right, you got it!" Leigh-Ann shouted as Scorecard drew back for a third strike. "Can we *go*?"

He looked at her with a hazy mania Reece recognised from when Stomatt had had too much to drink and would fight anyone who got close. A complete 180 from the sensible man they'd talked to last night.

"Focus," Reece shouted. "There's another one in the building and –" He paused, seeing Tasker was still down, holding his left shoulder. The creature had hit him as it came in. "Ah, hell."

"I'm fine," Tasker insisted, but he stumbled as he tried to stand. "Just clipped me." Leigh-Ann ducked to help him up, shooting Reece her *this-is-fucked* look. The agent's jacket was shredded and bloody around the top of his shoulder, and he gritted his teeth against the pain.

"Wait here," Scorecard instructed. He paced across the room, dragging his hammer, its gory head scratching up wood. "I'll handle these things."

"Reece, we got one of them," Leigh-Ann said. "We can make that truck now."

"I said *wait*," Scorecard snapped, but as he turned to her a second creature jumped in from the corridor, splintering a chunk of door frame, and slammed into his chest. Zip screamed at the flurry of fast-moving claws and biting teeth, tearing shreds from the man before anyone else could react. Scorecard was knocked flat, but his struggling limbs moved fast, fighting back, creating a ball of movement too chaotic for Reece to get a shot in. Katryzna fired into the wood by Scorecard's head, then again, catching the beast in the middle of its back. It reared up screeching and spraying blood. Her next shot hit an overlarge eye and threw the creature into the wall. She kept firing as it flopped down and Reece ran to grab Scorecard's collar with his gun hand. He dragged him clear as two more gunshots finally stilled the creature. Katryzna backed off, her heavy breathing filling the room. She turned to ask, "How is our secret weapon?"

Reece stood over Scorecard, holding Zip close to him as she sobbed into his shoulder, arms squeezed too tight to ever let go. The man's chest was torn open, a mess of shattered bone and ripped flesh, more of him on the outside than in. His dark eyes stared up through the ceiling, mouth open in a rigid death snarl.

"Shit," Leigh-Ann said. "Shit on *shit*."

"Nothing we can do," Reece said, a thousand fears rising up his throat. Had to carry Zip right out of there, the others with him. "You walk, agent?"

Tasker nodded, leaning on Leigh-Ann's shoulder, in too much pain to speak.

Reece felt in his pocket – still had Scorecard's truck keys from when he picked up Leigh-Ann the night before. "We're going for the truck, getting off this mountain. Katryzna, grab the meds."

"Rurik thinks we should take him," Katryzna said, standing over Scorecard.

"All due respect," Leigh-Ann snapped, "*fuck* Rurik, he ain't gotta deal with this!"

Katryzna looked up with absolute shock.

"Katryzna," Reece said. "There could be more of them, and she's right – there's nothing we can do." He shifted Zip's weight. "It's okay, cher, we gonna be good,"

She pushed back, locking teary eyes with him. "It's not about *us*! Lyon, Ezekiel got Lyon!"

"That a person, or –" Reece started.

"The city we flew into," Tasker said, with effort.

"What do you mean *got*?" Leigh-Ann asked.

Zip squirmed free of Reece's grip and landed on her feet, frustration boiling up. "Because I slept, he attacked again! He attacked *Lyon* and it's so big, so bad – I couldn't stop it!"

A crash somewhere in the building jerked them all to attention. Katryzna ran into the hallway and shouted, "I don't see it!"

"Fuck," Reece exhaled. "Explain on the way, okay?" Another howl sounded far back. "Y'all ready to run?"

# 19

As Leigh-Ann patted his wound, Tasker pressed into the seat, biting down with all his will against screaming from the pain. His jump made her flinch, too, her nerves overwrought as Reece drove fast down the mountain. They'd left behind at least two creatures scrambling through the Hall as they piled into Scorecard's truck, and there might easily be more on the road.

"Watch the spikes," Tasker warned and Reece swerved, barely slowing down. Wait, they'd moved them when their rental burst its tyres, hadn't they?

"Saved my damn life, idiot," Leigh-Ann said, as she aggressively dabbed at the big cut again, alternating between soaking up blood and trying to wash it out with rubbing alcohol. Tasker bucked and hissed in the seat, fighting against the agony. The vehicle was filled with harsh fumes, making Katryzna push up against the window the other side of Tasker, curling her nose. Leigh-Ann kept on, "Hell you thinking, jumping in front of a mutant jaguar."

"Wasn't," Tasker said, with another wince. He'd seen it launch at the window just in time to push her down, and hadn't appreciated how badly it had struck him until it was over. He had a four-inch gash from his collarbone down across his right pectoral. But they had bigger problems than his arm: he was struggling to focus on the phone in his hand.

Lyon was burning. Violence had erupted in the neighbourhood of La Guillotière, and spread through to the city centre. It had started half an hour earlier, and social media was already awash with images of trams overturned, shops burning, and ranks of soot-faced locals yelling in the streets. Zip said her brother had sparked it. She had stopped his influence as soon as she was able to, but she'd lost time while the creatures attacked. The violence had kept escalating regardless.

Her brother didn't need to keep attacking, evidently. Minute-by-minute, new fires were being started. Police were clashing with rioters on the Pont de la Feuillée and crowds were gathering in Place Bellecour. A seed of trouble had expanded to full-blown hysteria, which the government's panicked response had made worse. Sympathetic groups were riding the wave of the chaos: anti-government, anti-police, anti-whatever, it didn't matter. It was an opportunity to lash out.

Leigh-Ann finally tightened a bandage off, wrapping it up and over his shoulder. Tasker pushed her back by instinct, to relieve the pain. "Sorry. That's enough."

"Ain't nearly enough," Leigh-Ann said. "Needs stitching at the least."

"Once we're airborne."

"Airborne? You wanna jump on a plane with your arm falling off?"

"Plane ride will be smoother than this," Tasker said, with a strain. "You can stitch me there, I'll tell you how. This is our concern now." He held up his phone. "We need to be in Ikiri to stop it."

"Sure," Leigh-Ann snorted. "Go to Africa when shit's kicking off in France."

Tasker didn't respond, conserving his energy. It did feel like his arm was barely hanging on. But he couldn't afford to slack now. He called Ward and she quickly reacted to his voice: "Are you okay, Agent Tasker?"

"We had an incident," he said. "I'll be fine."

"An incident that almost killed him!" Leigh-Ann volunteered, exasperated.

"What's happening?" Ward asked. "We picked up a spike, but –"

"It was Ikiri that sparked it, but it's taken on a life of its own. Needs to be locked down, fast. Say there's something in the water, the moon, whatever. Make it clear the violence was *not* premeditated."

"I'm on it," Ward said, "for what it's worth. Where are you?"

"Moving," Tasker said. "We got a pass from the Legion. Headed to Ikiri."

"A pass?"

"Lyon needs to be locked down. Say there was something in the water, whatev –"

"Agent Tasker?" Ward interrupted.

He paused at the concern in her voice, realising he was repeating himself. Shit. His vision was blurring. Weak from blood loss and tension. Reece asked something – to take the phone? But Tasker said, "I'll call when we're further along," and hung up. "Someone pass me some water?"

"*Please*," Katryzna said, but she handed him a bottle. "Leigh's right, Sean. You need a doctor. I am not sure she can stitch that wound. Or any wound."

"I've patched up jeans before," Leigh-Ann said.

"You got people out here, surely?" Reece called from the front. "Someone can do you like they did Sto?"

There was the National Rangers, the ambiguous special branch of French security nestled in with France's ONF. Notoriously territorial and suspicious of the MEE, likely to conduct a full investigation into why Tasker had not requested permission to act on French soil. As for international Ministry agents, the closest would be in Lyon, and would definitely have their hands full. Besides which, involving anyone else would raise questions and take too long. Tasker said, "If we head straight for the Congo, I can have people waiting there."

Reece caught his eye in the rear-view mirror. Not believing it.

"Why can't I stop it?" Zip pleaded from the passenger seat. There was pain in her voice, Lyon weighing on her hard.

"Sweetie, you can't take that on," Leigh-Ann told her.

Tasker shifted out of the way, relieved that the focus was off him. However serious his wound, they'd already wasted a day because the Legion targeted him. Lyon was *his* fault, if anyone's; he couldn't delay them further. He looked at the phone again. Violence had erupted in Marseilles in support for the clashes in Lyon.

Leigh-Ann gave Tasker another look. "How come she can't stop it?"

"She did," Tasker said. "Her brother set it off, but now people are just being people."

"But if he can make people go mad, she should be able to calm them down! She can do anything, can't she?"

"Maybe," Tasker said. "From Ikiri. She'll be more powerful there."

"Hell." Leigh-Ann thumped back in her seat. "You getting us to this airport or what, Reece?"


The airport outside Lyon was full of people hypnotised by the news on the monitors or their phones. Staff spoke in whispers, out of respect. Against Tasker's protests, the group found a medical bay and a doctor dropped what she was doing to attend to Tasker. He was losing focus as they walked, but he was aware it wasn't natural, the way the people around them ignored their frantic, bloodstained group. Nor was it natural the way the doctor worked with glassy-eyed focus and no questions. Zip had done something, influencing people around them, maybe without even knowing it.

Tasker told the others to secure a plane while the doctor stitched him up, but Zip insisted they stay together, fearing she could not protect them if separated. All the tears had drained from her blotchy red eyes, and she was replacing her despair with new determination to get through this. She even kept Katryzna in place, as the woman volunteered to find croissants and Zip insisted *No*. She didn't know how far she could reach. Maybe she could secure the whole airport, maybe the district. Maybe just the room they were in.

Meanwhile, Ward's best efforts clearly weren't working: the media explained the widespread rioting as a response to a spate of police violence within an estate in Lyon. Protests were emerging in other cities across France, calling for justice for a young man named Fabrice Loup, who had been left comatose by a police beating two weeks earlier. A patrol vehicle had been set on fire in Marseilles and two officers were stabbed in Lyon. Eyes were turning to Paris as thousands gathered in the streets.

"Ain't no one tying this back to Stilt Town," Reece noted.

"Not exactly an obvious connection," Leigh-Ann said.

"True enough." Reece looked to Zip. "And they're saying dozens dead. *Only* dozens. In a whole city gone mad, those numbers could be a hell of a lot worse."

Zip didn't reply, not exactly pleased, and Tasker silently shared her sentiment. The numbers might have been better than Graystown, but between the motorway and Lyon it was becoming apparent that Ezekiel was rising towards an utterly devastating potential.

Once the doctor finished stitching, and handed over some strong painkillers, Tasker insisted they go immediately. No, he did not need to rest. They continued unseen through the airport, until they reached hangars housing private jets. There was no guessing which was the Legion's plane, if it was even there, and it would invite trouble turning up without Scorecard. Tasker prepared to commandeer a businessman's jet, instead. An expensive car sat by one, with uniformed staff loading luggage. Zip pulled ahead of Tasker, as he prepped what to say, and she addressed the uniformed man at the base of the jet's steps: "We need you to take us to Africa."

"Got it," the man replied with a smile. "We're almost ready. Chloe, tell M Patenaude there'll be a diversion. Let me tell the pilot."

"I'll tell the pilot," Zip said, and scurried up the steps.

The group were left dumbstruck. Katryzna said, "I *like* her."

Tasker watched Chloe as she picked out an upright, silver-haired man near the car, who did not look happy. Tasker straightened up as the man stormed towards them, shouting in French. Patenaude. Which companies had big interests in this region? There were –

"It's fine," Zip called, reappearing at the top of the stairs. Patenaude stopped. His face went from angry to understanding in a blink. "We just need your plane – it's important."

Then Patenaude smiled and answered gently, in French, "By all means. Good luck."

"Agent Tasker?" Zip said. "Are you coming?"

Tasker digested the man's change of heart and the crew racing to complete the preparations. It was group hypnosis on a level he couldn't conceive – and effortlessly done, with Zip galvanised by the morning's trauma. He recognised the trance-like obedience as that which had gripped him and Henri when they'd faced Sara Ngoi near Ikiri. But only a day ago Zip had shown zero confidence in what she was capable of. She was quickly adapting.

Tasker climbed the steps with the others, feeling his legs wobble as he did. He watched as Zip flitted in and out of the cockpit. Reece accompanied her, making friendly introductions, showing no surprise at what she was capable of. Leigh-Ann and Katryzna sank into the plush leather seats, part of a suite laid out like a lavish living room. Tasker took a chair opposite and oozed into the cushions, letting go.

They were soon taxiing and the pilot jovially explained over the intercom that they were clearing things with the tower. Then they were airborne, and Tasker found his last energy was gone. Reece asked vaguely if the painkillers were working. Tasker tried to put on a brave face, but he could see he wasn't fooling anyone. He rested his head back and closed his eyes.

He heard Reece trying to distract Zip: "Now for some serious business, cher. Long flight ahead, reckon we've got time for me to teach you how to play a harp?"

Katryzna made some disbelieving comment as Tasker slipped away.

He blinked awake to the sound of long, drawn-out notes bending up and down. The haunting music belonged more appropriately in a swamp or a cellar than in this jet's bright interior, but it was made all the stranger by being uniquely melodious. A harmonica could sound like that? Tasker held onto the sound for a minute, before slipping back into unconsciousness.

The next time he woke, it was to more tentative toots. Zip was testing the instrument with deep focus. The others talked quietly over it, as Reece said, "No crowds up here, no creatures."

"Hey Sean," Katryzna said, seeing his eyes were open. "Were there any flying creatures in Ikiri?" Tasker tried to respond, but his answer came out in a mumble.

"Are you okay?"

"He look okay to you?" Leigh-Ann asked. "Get you some water, Agent Tasker?"

He nodded. His shoulder was throbbing. The doctor said it was fine, didn't she? A deep cut, but hitting nothing vital. Were the creature's claws poisoned? Reece finished his point: "Well, even if there were some way to get us here, her brother's gotta be tired out from this morning, anyway."

"Assuming he *gets* tired," Leigh-Ann said.

"He does," Tasker murmured, struggling to stay awake. It had to cost Ezekiel something to lash out, or they wouldn't have had a moment's rest since this began. But Tasker had no energy to explain his thinking.

"Our bigger problem," Katryzna said, "is that the Legion are waiting for us. They will be unhappy that Scorecard was ripped open." She looked at an empty space on her armrest. "Well, it is true, isn't it?"

"He spoke to them, didn't he?" Leigh-Ann said. "We'll be all right."

Tasker closed his eyes as Katryzna replied, "If not, I will protect you from them."

"My hero," Leigh-Ann joked back.

Zip tested the harmonica again with a blunt squeak of a sound.

"Imagine you're closing your mouth on that one hole," Reece said. "Visualise that good, clean sound."

The noises faded as words turned around Tasker's mind. Visualise. Good. Hero.

When he opened his eyes again, Katryzna was asleep, head lolling gracelessly back with her mouth open. Leigh-Ann, next to her, stared with fascination. Seeing Tasker awake, she whispered, "Where did you find her?"

"She found me," Tasker muttered.

Reece had his head against the window, taking in the world below, whispering to Zip. Tasker looked out his own window, to an expanse of golden sand beneath them, split by big grey, rocky plains like the skin of an elephant.

"How you imagined Africa to be?" Leigh-Ann asked, quiet not to wake Katryzna.

"Harder than I expected," Reece said. "Figured there'd be more sand dunes."

Tasker closed his eyes again, and next time he opened them the land was green again. The pilot was talking through the speakers: "– fifteen minutes we'll be in Nairobi."

Grass and trees surrounded the modern glass and concrete complex of the airport in Nairobi. A quick stop for fuel where the others got out for fresh air.

Tasker watched them through the window, groggy from sleep or drugs, not sure which. He checked the news on his phone and found the French protests had spread further: people were demanding justice for Fabrice Loup in Berlin, Barcelona, London and more. Rapidly getting more out of hand, with no one curtailing the media's hysteria. In his haze, Tasker felt like he was slipping deeper into a nightmare.

He dipped in and out of consciousness for the final leg of the journey. The land grew increasingly varied, thick with green and rivers, contoured with hills and mountains. Zip's efforts on the harmonica quickly improved.

Katryzna perked up as they crossed into the Congo, telling them to expect a hotel with a nice pool, fantastic grilled meat on the boat, *such a fun boat*, and Henri, surely Henri would greet them – he owed her a lemonade and they'd like him. But Tasker heard Zip say that they weren't going to Kinshasa. They had another route. Was that her idea, or thanks to the pilot? No, hadn't they discussed it with Scorecard, the night before? Shearjoy was already in the Congo, somewhere closer to Ikiri.

Katryzna complained about missing the grilled meats and Leigh-Ann said, "Hell, bet it wasn't nothing on a Cutjaw grill."

"Do you have crocodiles in cages?" Katryzna said.

Tasker drifted again, picking up vague details as Leigh-Ann and Reece responded with tales of a man named Trent Friendly who kept a gator like a guard dog. Twelve-foot by her account, six by Reece's. Either way, it got loose.

"But ten gators roll through town every year," Leigh-Ann said. "While we sleep."

"You're thinking of them spiders you swallow," Reece said.

"You eat spiders, Leigh?" Katryzna asked, impressed.

"The general *you*, I mean," Reece said.

Good people, Tasker thought. Ordinary, decent people. They had come this far despite the odds and were getting on with Katryzna; maybe Reece could handle this. He was young but with the right kind of confidence to lead them. Tasker hoped they'd survive, as he slipped back into darkness.

Then the pilot announced their final descent, telling them the sun was setting on another warm day in Kisangani. Ground temperature 26 degrees. "That's pushing 80, for my American friends."

"Man," Reece said. "We're in Africa now. Maybe we make it all the way to Ikiri without complications, get a break for once."

"Maybe you keep your jinxing damn mouth shut for once?" Leigh-Ann snapped, but Tasker found himself smiling. Almost there. Just the forest and the devil child to contend with now.

They landed and someone helped him up, whispering assurances as they climbed down the jet's stairs. He swayed, but was regaining focus. The heat was pleasantly bearable outside, a cloudy dusk setting on a single paved airstrip before a paint-cracked two-storey building. Reece asked again if he was okay, and he lied, *yes*, though his shoulder hurt like hell and he wasn't thinking straight.

He became more aware, however, as they all stopped suddenly. Katryzna had a hand on her gun (his gun?) by the time Reece warned, "Wait, we're expected, right? I'm guessing this is Shearjoy's welcome committee."

A man and a woman stood before an old bus, both in crumpled shirts and light linen trousers, the only white people outside the terminal building. He was leaning on a cane, she was toying with a . . . hatchet? The man stepped away from the bus, with a bad limp, and held up a hand. He was fat, almost pear-shaped, with long dark hair hanging over his shoulders. Thin on top. As he smiled at them, Tasker tried to recall him from Mason's files. The woman, also familiar, made a stark contrast behind him. She had a jowly, dour face and hair tied in a tail that fell over one shoulder. The man boomed in a broad Welsh accent, "Where's Scorecard?"

Tasker blinked hard, trying to push down the agony of his shoulder and the distant disquiet that they were in trouble. It was hard enough to stay upright, though, and while he concentrated on that, Reece stepped forward. Thank hell.

Reece said, "Ain't nobody here but us chickens. But we're good to dance."

# 20

"We have somewhere to talk," the fat man said in that funny Welsh accent, a playful glimmer in his eyes. "Shearjoy's waiting."

Reece shot a glance to Tasker, but the agent was sweating and struggling to stand, propped against Leigh-Ann. Left it to Reece. He said, "Where you want us to go?"

"A hotel. Luxury transport provided gratis." The man turned and opened the door to the bus then climbed aboard, favouring his right leg and his cane. His companion lingered, watching them with less friendliness, then followed on.

"They are not good people," Katryzna said, considering doing something about it.

"They're Legion," Tasker said. "Flay. The other . . . I think she was a researcher."

"Glad you're still with us, Agent Tasker," Reece said. "Any other tips?"

"Hear them out," Tasker said, weakly. "If it goes wrong . . . let Katryzna handle it." He finished with a small groan, and Reece wasn't sure if he was joking. They shouldn't have travelled so quickly, with him in this state, and the idea of meeting with this Shearjoy card, however Scorecard might've dressed things up, still didn't sit right. But it was too late to go back.

Katryzna took Tasker's suggestion seriously: "Yes, I can do that."

"What else we gonna do," Leigh-Ann huffed, "hang around holding our dicks?"

"Death bus it is, then," Reece said.

They half-carried Tasker aboard, with Zip and Katryzna taking up the rear. The Welshman, Flay, slouching over the wheel, beamed as they passed. "What's up with him? Shellfish on the flight?"

"Something disagreed with him, true enough," Reece said.

"That right?" Flay's voice rose when he saw Zip: "Ah, welcome – you probably don't remember me, little one, but I was good friends with your old man, once upon a time."

"Like the rest of y'all, huh?" Leigh-Ann said.

"True enough," Flay replied, echoing Reece's words. "True enough."

Once they'd taken their seats, Flay drove out of the airport, past dark, overgrown fields. He called out, "You know, of course, Shearjoy won't be happy if something's happened to Scorecard."

"Then Shearjoy won't be happy," Reece said, more confident than he felt. "What happened to your leg?"

"Gunshot," Flay said. "A few days ago." He said it with a boastful leer that invited more, which Reece didn't rise to.

The woman leant over the arm of her seat beside Flay, staring. She had a slouched, fluid posture and predatory eyes that recalled those demonic creatures from the morning. Reece avoided looking at her. Katryzna was glaring at their hosts in a threatening matter, though. For Tasker, meanwhile, it was an effort to sit upright. No matter how many painkillers the agent had chugged, his jaw had barely relaxed since France. They'd be lucky to keep him awake to meet Shearjoy. Reece would have to negotiate safe passage to Ikiri himself, along with safety for Tasker's family and peace between their groups.

They pulled into a dusty, low-rise city, where motorbikes filled the gaps between slow-moving trucks and hawker stalls lined the edges of the main roads. Bushy palm trees rose overhead. Reece leant over the aisle. "Hey Katryzna. Thoughts on if these guys try anything?"

She looked at him sideways, suspicious of his attempt at conversation. Then she leant closer to him, their faces almost touching, and whispered, "Kill them before they kill us." He held her gaze until she nodded to say he was welcome, then she sat up to look forward again. She rolled her eyes the other way, to where her conscience stood on the back of the seat. "That was implied, isn't it?"

Reece sat back. Well, she had Plan B arranged.

He saw a grand building roll past, white-washed and pillared, lit by spotlights, behind tough metal fencing. Not far removed from a Deep South estate. As they continued towards what had to be the city centre, a river came into view, wide and black as coal. Squint and it wasn't a far sight from the Mississippi at night, only the boats here were low and narrow, weighed down with supplies.

Flay took them away from the river, to a five-storey hotel painted bright yellow with sharply peaked, tiled roofs and classical pillars lining the many balconies. Pink, yellow and blue letters rose over the entrance gate in a wavy line, like a circus sign, reading "Full Business Hotel".

They went through a lobby chilled by air conditioning, past a smiling, colourfully dressed receptionist, to a recreation area with square sofas, a massive TV, a dartboard and a mosaic-tiled bar. There was only one person there: a slim white guy with an unremarkable round face, bar a teardrop tattoo on one cheek. Shearjoy himself. He was leaning against the bar with a welcoming grin.

"Quite a place, isn't it?" Shearjoy said. His skin was youthfully smooth, with only slight wrinkles around his eyes to hint he was as old as Mason or the others. Dressed in combat trousers and a stretched blue t-shirt, he looked like a backstage sound engineer, not an international tyrant. His accent was unremarkable, British. "Sit where you like. Who's drinking? Yours is a whisky, Agent Tasker? A lemonade for the child? It's fresh. Don't worry, we have the place to ourselves. Though we seem to be one short?"

"Scorecard didn't make it," Flay said, closing the double doors. He folded his arms to settle in as doorman while the woman draped herself over an armchair. Katryzna drifted to the other side of the room, considering an old beer poster framed on the wall.

"A disagreement along the way?" Shearjoy asked. "That's a terrible shame." He was smooth and genial; not a sound engineer, no, more like the faux-friendly lawyer who had grilled Reece and Caleb as teenagers, charming until he accused Reece of holding up a liquor store in Dequincy. When he switched tunes, that man had preached their guilt like Gospel. Shearjoy was definitely capable of the same.

"Try monster cats invading your mountain getaway," Leigh-Ann said.

Shearjoy looked to Tasker as though he, the most respectable amongst them, might better explain. But the agent was unsteady and his formerly fine suit and shirt were ripped, revealing his bandages.

Reece whispered, "You want a seat, Agent? I'll do the talking."

"I'm fine." Tasker blinked to keep his eyes open, skin white in this light.

"Yeah." Reece raised his voice, to take over. "Cats, like Leigh said. Zip's brother got a nasty habit of sending monsters after us. Y'all probably know about that, though?"

Shearjoy studied him carefully, then said, "It's not something we'd expect in France. And the rest of you survived?"

"We had the sense to run," Leigh-Ann said.

"Well. This isn't a good start. Scorecard was –" Shearjoy paused, regarding Flay and the woman with doubt. He was fighting some emotion. "He was one of the few people who wasn't planning to try and kill me at some point."

Reece raised an eyebrow, but Shearjoy was already turning away, to prepare drinks from the bar. Scorecard had said, hadn't he, that none of them really got along. And of the three Legion in that room, he could see Shearjoy might have a tough time dealing with Big Bones and the mad woman. She was picking at her nails with the head of her axe.

"I want guarantees for my family," Tasker said abruptly, running the words together. "It's over with them, understand?"

"Is it?" Shearjoy said, pouring out a beer.

"Or this ends, right now," Tasker growled. The effort was making him sway.

Reece tried to meet his eye in warning and whispered, "Think you oughta sit down, Agent? Please."

Tasker returned the look uncertainly. His hostility was replaced with confusion, unable to keep focus. As if guiding a geriatric parent, Reece helped him into the closest armchair and the agent gave in. Reece avoided Leigh-Ann's eye as he felt her trying to catch his, concern all over her face.

"Your family are safe," Shearjoy said, approaching with a whisky tumbler in one hand and a glass of beer in the other. "I bring you peace of mind, as well as the finest whisky the Congo has to offer. Scorecard explained, and your willingness to bring the child here precludes any previous threat. And you're not in the best condition for us to be fighting anyway, Agent Tasker."

Tasker grunted, but wasn't up to any more response. Reece came in to save him the effort, "What about your attitude to Zip?"

"Likewise changed." Shearjoy smiled flatly. "The Legion is not *senselessly* violent. Unlike her father. Take the drink, please, I'm trying to be gracious." Reece accepted the proffered glasses and placed them on a table as Shearjoy returned to the bar. "I don't make a habit of unnecessary murder."

"But it's so rarely unnecessary," the axe woman said. Her accent was slow, thick and impossible to place.

"Do you sleep with that weapon?" Katryzna asked loudly.

"She *does*." Flay almost laughed. "Chops has been carrying it ever since Ikiri."

"What is wrong with you?" Katryzna asked. "Did no one teach you about guns?"

"Our fights are personal," Shearjoy said. He suddenly had another beer for Leigh-Ann and a smaller glass, a lemonade, for Zip. As Reece had done, they accepted the drinks just to get him to move away. Leigh-Ann immediately put hers down but Zip held hers in two tight hands. Shearjoy said, "It's safe, and very tasty. Something for you, Katryzna?"

"I will have two burgers," Katryzna said. "If we decide not to kill you."

Shearjoy nodded like that was perfectly reasonable. "To more properly answer, our powers remove any guarantees when it comes to killing at a distance. Hence we favour extensions of ourselves over projectiles." He indicated further down the bar, where Reece now saw a sword lay sheathed, some kind of old rapier. "But none of us travelled here to discuss Chops' penchant for skinning people, did we? Scorecard said the boy survives and the corruption of Ikiri is his doing. That's your claim?" He focused on Zip, and she shied from the attention.

"That's her claim," Reece said. "She's shown us enough that we trust it."

"I'm aware," Shearjoy said. "You hit Scorecard's mind from a distance? And stopped Ruin's heart? What else have you been up to?"

"Helped people regain they senses," Leigh-Ann said.

"Ah. And all on your own? Where's Daddy?"

"Out of the picture," Reece said. "Scorecard figured he might've come here."

"Might've," Shearjoy said. "Well, given these developments, I hope you'll accept my apologies. I'll be the first to admit when I've made a mistake, and if the boy lives and she believes she can get back into Ikiri, then obviously we have a mutual interest in seeing Zipporah returned home." He regarded Chops and Flay again. "My proposal is that we escort her, and you, and everyone connected to you, walks away."

"You want to take Zip –" Reece started.

"Ourselves, yes. The surviving founders of the Legion. I would trust no one else."

"And your second offer?" Reece said. "Seeing as you couldn't have a rat's hope of ever thinking we'd agree to that."

"It's for your own safety," Flay said.

"I have been to Ikiri," Katryzna said. "And I am not sure that *we* need *you*."

"Ikiri knows you are coming, now," Shearjoy said. "Or rather, the boy does, if we believe he lives. The region is already less stable than it was on your last visit. But we want the same as you: to remove that threat."

"No one's leaving this to you," Tasker slurred. He took a hard breath, biting his teeth together. "We've got an idea of how you operate."

"Please," Shearjoy said. "The MEE are hardly innocent. Your family would have known nothing of any danger if you hadn't alerted them yourself." He pointed to Katryzna. "Though well played. You have honestly had us confused, Katryzna."

"I am told I do that well," she said, factually.

"Indeed; you had Ruin running in circles looking for you. None of us predicted you'd sided with the Ministry all this time. But let me be clear, what lies ahead is not a question of any threat *we* pose. There's no coming back from Ikiri. You all still have the option to walk away and I strongly suggest you take it."

Zip cleared her throat, twice. "Mr Shearjoy," she cut in, quietly, "I don't think you know the truth. Not for sure." She pulled a little away from Reece and Leigh-Ann. "Things will be different when I go there. And these are my friends. We're Cutjaw Kids and that means we stick together. No one needs to fight. We can help each other. We have to. I don't think" – she hesitated over admitting it – "I can do it alone."

"Well, if *she* says so." Chops rolled her eyes.

"Actually, yeah," Reece said. "Zip knows more than you, from all I've seen. Like, how to actually deal with this instead of just whaling on each other. Whatever she says, that's what we're doing."

"How heart-warming," Shearjoy said, lightly. "Truthfully, Zipporah, I have no illusions about what you can do, and by all means, this is your show. If you want to put your friends at risk, that's absolutely up to you."

"I want them to come," Zip agreed, though less sure of herself.

"Even knowing it's likely to get them all killed?" Shearjoy pressed, and Zip looked from Reece to Leigh-Ann. "Even if you survive Ikiri, it will corrupt them. And if you come back changed in any way that might be considered a threat – well, the Legion stretches far. Their vigilance will outlast any of us."

"Last I checked," Reece said, "you ain't done a good job of putting us down."

Shearjoy gave a game smile, but waited for Zip to conclude.

"I'm sure," she insisted quietly. "We need to all go together, to have a chance."

"All right." Shearjoy took a big breath. "We'll *all* return to Ikiri. Where no one, really, should *ever* have had to go again. Agreed? Chops, Flay?"

Chops merely grunted and Flay said, "What we're here for, isn't it?"

"Uh-huh," Reece said. He looked to Leigh-Ann for her take, and found anything but enthusiasm there. But she gave him an unhappy shrug.

Sometimes you had to ride with the devil, no two ways about it. Reece said, "Y'all know we gotta move fast? Her brother strikes while Zip's resting, and we can't stay close to people for any period of time. We don't want to be sleeping in town."

"We can be ready in an hour or two," Shearjoy said. "In the meantime, I've arranged rooms for you." His grin was wide and trustworthy as a damn crocodile: enough to say this journey couldn't ever end well, and there wasn't a damn thing to do but smile and like it. "But won't any of you join me for a drink?"

# 21

Despite the haunting sounds of creatures at night, Henri slept soundly on the frail cot Solomon's people provided him with. So soundly that when daylight came and he stirred, stomach rumbling, he found he had missed the morning's action. Mason was no longer in the hut and he could not find Solomon or Jonah. One of the camp's elder women took pity on him and explained he must wait. They had apparently considered he didn't need to accompany them for their meeting Sara and braving Ikiri.

He accepted a hot broth and a cold drink for breakfast and sat by the central fire pit, near Solomon's racing-car-seat throne, unsure how he felt. He must go back to Sara, he knew. Help her somehow or at least talk to her. He had a duty owed to his sister, still so pure of heart, but he had to admit that some small part of him was relieved not to have gone that morning. He was not ready to see her again, not like that.

Henri was saved from those guilty thoughts by the return of a couple of young soldiers who had been on morning patrol and wanted to talk over coffee. They joked about how scary Mason was, but confessed great relief that Henri had come back. One said, "More creatures hunt and more outsiders attack, day by day. They do not like to say it, but we are running out of time."

Henri looked into his coffee. Was he partly to blame, having brought Mason here? Or Tasker before that? Had he fallen into the very trap that Sara herself did: believing the white men brought hope.

"I saw a thing with two heads," the other guard said. "Big as a gorilla, strong, but long like the cats. I swear, two heads."

"Breathing fire, too?" His comrade laughed, but it sounded forced.

"You said there are outsiders," Henri said. "People like Mr Mason?"

"Out here?" one guard said. "No. Just villagers gone bad. Sara's messages are less clear now, though; others may come. Before, all she spoke of was the child. Get the child. But now she herself keeps saying it, 'The time has grown short.'"

"It's the Bible again," the other guard put in. "Jonah told us. Corinthians, 'The present world is passing away.' This is coming to an end. Perhaps a good one, where we can finally leave?"

Henri wracked his mind for the passage, but he suspected the source material was scarcely relevant. After all, what was holy out here? It was just an echo from Sara's past. But he said, "If Mr Mason cannot help, then my friends Agent Tasker and Katryzna will; they have good hearts, and they will come back."

Immediately undermining him, a shout of commotion rose from the edge of camp, and Henri and the guards shot to their feet, spilling food and coffee. A crowd of men pushed between the huts, carrying someone, calling for aid. Henri was shoved out of the way as they gathered in the central clearing, and he caught flashes of blood between the bustle of people trying to help. The bloodstained soldiers who'd delivered the man stepped back to let the medicine women in. A momentary parting in the crowd revealed a gold chain and the beige cotton of a shirt. Jonah?

"Stand clear, please." One of Henri's coffee-companions guided him back as Solomon swept in, shouting orders. The guard cursed and hurried away, along with many others who ran to grab guns. Some sprinted into the trees and others took up defensive positions within camp. A couple of women worked quickly on Jonah with dressings and instruments. Solomon strode up next to Henri and watched. From the shade of Jonah's skin and the slackness of his body, it was plain he was already dead.

The surrounding camp was finally still, quieter than at rest, as guards kept watch.

Solomon shook his head with disgust. He was sweaty, his shirt crumpled, and he had a rifle held loose across his waist. He said, "That man should not have come."

"Mason?" Henri swallowed. "Where is he?"

Solomon indicated the forest. "Not far behind, I am sure."

"Did he do this?"

"Not directly." Solomon spat to the side. "The beasts came – during daylight. Drawn to him before we reached Sara. If we had any hope he might change things, he did not. Mason was routed like the rest of us." The general made an unpleasant noise, staring at Jonah's face, then met Henri's eyes. "You should have stayed in Kinshasa."

A woman wailed over Jonah. Crying to the sky, demanding *why*, in a desperate, distraught prayer Henri had heard too many times. He felt an echo of his pain at losing Miguel, the sight of him stabbed, bleeding. He said, "Kinshasa was not safe, either. Nowhere is."

More shouting came from the edge of camp. Solomon readied his gun, but as he looked through the crowd he ordered the men to stand down. "Bring him here!"

Two men trotted up with rifles, throwing looks back as Mason marched after them. There was blood on his shirt and his metal stump, and he looked angrier than ever.

"We need to go," Mason told Henri.

"Did you stop them?" Solomon asked.

"I survived," Mason said. "This entire land is tainted. There is nothing to be taken from Sara, there is no safe path."

"As we already knew," Solomon said. "You thought you were so different? And now you've brought this upon us, you wish to leave?"

"The taint was already here," Mason snapped. "You've cowered from the monsters for so long that the witch's shadow can no longer hide you, that's all."

The gathered soldiers bristled with complaints, but Solomon raised a hand. "If they come now, it's not because of us. You provoked them. I say again: now you wish to leave?"

"To return better equipped," Mason said. "Have our bikes been recovered?"

"Mr Mason," Henri said. "If this camp is truly in danger, we can help –"

"I know only one way to help," Mason said, "and I cannot do it here. Ikiri is blocked to me. For now."

"Then we should wait," Henri said. "If we can hold out for Agent Tasker and Katryzna, we can secure the camp –"

"No."

"No? What –"

"Do not waste your breath," Solomon said. "He is as selfish as he was when they first lit this fuse and ran."

"I have been handling it ever since," Mason snarled back. "As I must now."

"Handling it for who? Who gave a thought to *us*? Who gave a thought to anyone out here touched by this?" Solomon's voice trembled, only just in control – a hint of his darker side. "Go. Walk as fast as you can, you'll have no more help from us."

Henri rushed to intervene. "General, if it's truly our fault then we can at least draw the trouble away, as surely as it's been drawn here? Please, give us some supplies, help us move faster and we'll take the monsters with us."

Solomon eyed him sceptically.

"Bikes, food for a few days' travel. We need only reach the western road –"

"We're heading east," Mason interrupted.

"East?" Henri exclaimed.

"Roughly." He locked eyes with Solomon. "I *will* return. When I do, it would be for the best if you are not here."

"Is that a threat?"

"It is reality." Mason drew himself up somehow even taller, muscles tensing. "Listen to Henri. Flee this place, while the boy is at least distracted by me."

The general scoffed. "I will protect my people. As it has always been."

Mason grunted and turned to leave, only to find a wall of people blocking his path. He came breast to breast with the most fearless of Solomon's men. But Solomon gestured and they stood down, eyeing Mason as he passed. Henri hesitated, trying to apologise with his eyes. Solomon said, "You do not have to go with him."

Henri swallowed. His response came out weak, but he said, "As I said. If I help him away, it will surely help the camp."


Mason refused to talk as they travelled through the forest. A day passed on the bikes Solomon's people had reluctantly provided, then a night in an abandoned village, and Henri was gripped by doubts that he had made the wrong choice, and should have stayed. But it all moved so fast, and the horrible sounds escalated as they travelled. He only hoped Mason knew what he was doing. If they headed east far enough, most likely they would hit the river, as it bent back around. From there, they could get far away. But leaving was not Mason's intention, Henri was sure.

He had only become harder in his resolve, glaring into shadows, jaw set in some nameless, endless fury. On the journey towards Sara, and in the attack that left Jonah dead, Mason had been forced to admit the truth that had become evident the day before, while they could not find Ikiri. He could not do this alone – and the answer lay in this direction. Henri wanted to ask, but feared the man was on a hair-trigger and might snap at any moment. He had not wiped the blood from his metal stump.

The going was easier than on the way in, at least. Mason took frequent breaks, which at first Henri thought was for rest, before realising the man was meditating. Waiting for inspiration or searching for solace against what he had seen in the forest? Those creatures' screams alone could chill any man. Or had Mason reached Sara, after all, when the chaos started? That he spoke of her as a witch was a change, after all.

On their second night, having put enough distance between themselves and Ikiri that they were surely far enough from its foul influence, Henri determined to make the man talk again. Once they had eaten their dried meats, and Mason settled into a stiff, seated position on the ground, he searched for the right words. He cleared his throat, and as he did, Mason suddenly erupted, "Tonight is the night. Save your questions."

"The night for –" Henri started, but the big man's glare silenced him.

They fell into the same routine of Henri awkwardly trying to rest while Mason focused on some internal quest. At some late hour, Mason shot up and announced, "It's time."

He stalked through the trees and, after a stunned moment, Henri jumped up and followed, throwing a look back to their supplies and bikes. He made a couple of false starts trying to ask what Mason was doing, but the man moved too quickly; Henri needed all his focus to keep up without tripping. He was soon committed to following, at speed, by virtue of being too far from camp to safely find his way back. Mason was apparently fully aware of where he was going.

Then he slowed down, suddenly moving quietly. He waved a warning hand for Henri to do the same. They crept through the trees until Mason stopped and pointed. There were three tents in a rough arc, unlit, the campers out of sight and apparently asleep. All except one: a large man sat before the tents, one leg outstretched on the ground as he looked skyward. He had the same look Mason had when meditating. And even at a distance, in the dark, his bulbous shape was familiar to Henri, whose fists clenched with hostility. He hissed, "He killed Miguel."

"He's killed many," Mason replied, coldly.

"I came with you to get away from him –"

"And I wanted my daughter left out of this. Our needs changed." Mason shook out his right arm and with a shriek, a blade slid out of the metal contraption at the end. He inhaled deeply, preparing for battle, and Henri took a step back. No question, now, that he had chosen the wrong path.

# 22

Events blurred together in Tasker's mind, so minutes might have passed between England and the Congo; Scorecard's voice making arrangements, then the creatures bursting into the mountain hall; the flight back to the Congo, another hotel, another country; the claws lancing through his flesh. Helen's voice, concerned but not afraid, "We're absolutely fine; I'm only worried about you."

"Don't be, it's just a precaution," Tasker heard himself say. "It won't be for long."

"But this business in Lyon – it's got people on edge even here. They set a police car on fire in Tottenham."

"That's why I'm calling. Wanted to make sure you're well clear of it."

"We're staying put, just as your friend said. Sean. Who exactly was she?"

"Just that," Tasker said. "A friend. I'll see you soon."

There must have been more. He surely heard Rebecca's voice and gave her his love, in an echo of a thousand similar calls. Then it was over, and all he was really aware of was how worried everyone looked.

Katryzna's face loomed large as she asked, "Are you *dying?*"

Tasker shook his head, but that made the world slosh as though underwater. He struggled to focus. It wasn't just the drugs. He could clearly feel the pain in his shoulder, spreading down his arm. But he struggled to keep conscious. So close to the finish, how was he supposed to protect anyone now?

"Before you do," Katryzna continued, "I think we should talk. I'd like to know about Rostov."

"Mm," Tasker responded dreamily, "there are fairies there."

There were more questions, maybe laughter, who knows what else he said, it just drifted by. Then he was sitting on a bed, in a room with low light and a window onto a dusty balcony. Katryzna was outside, looking over the railing, with Reece just inside the door.

"We'll come right back," Reece promised, the middle of a conversation Tasker had lost the opening to. "It's a risk, but the bigger risk would be you going literally anywhere right now."

"What's the risk?" Tasker asked.

Reece stared as it sank in that Tasker hadn't followed whatever came before. "I'm talking about what happens if we split up. In theory, that Ikiri power can reach anyone, anywhere, but Ezekiel's not going to waste it on you, is he? Not like it'll help stop us. Another question entirely if the Legion can be trusted, though. Just gotta hope they got nothing left to gain from hurting you, right?"

Tasker closed his eyes, still trying to catch up. "You want me to stay here?"

"Not exactly a case of *want*," Reece said, crouching in front of Tasker to better get his attention. Tasker hazily met his eyes. "We're going into some jungle and you're in no state. If you recoup, a day or two, you might follow on, but better if you stay here, make sure it's safe for us to come back."

"Give me a day. I'll be up in the morning."

"We ain't waiting to morning. And a day might become two, three. Things got real bad real quick in France, Agent Tasker. And besides, you earned a break. It's not on you no more. Can't be."

Tasker repeated that in his head. Not on me. Can't be. He said, "There's no other support from the Ministry here."

"Since your people got us this far?" Reece smiled, but he couldn't keep it up. "Hell, I know that, and don't especially like it, but Shearjoy got a point. If Ikiri messed his folks up so much, the less people involved the better. I'd leave Leigh with you, even, if she'd let me."

"No," Tasker said, picturing that joking woman with big hair and this bluesy Cajun blundering into the forest. Their only hope. "I can't let you go in alone."

"Yes, yes," Katryzna said, entering the room. "I will be there. I will take care of everything."

Tasker blinked at her. "That's even worse."

"Your chest is turning black" – she moved closer – "and you can barely move your arm. You should have stayed in England."

"Is it –" Tasker closed his eyes against another pulse of pain. He opened them again to look at the dressing over his wound. It was clean, innocuous. "How bad is it?"

"Well, you're sitting up talking," Reece said. "But it ain't *good*. Reckon it's the travelling just exacerbated it. There's a doctor on the way, you'll be taken care of."

Tasker shook his head again, and braced, forcing himself to stand. Katryzna pushed him back down and Reece told her off as Tasker groaned at the renewed pain. He was useless. Would only get in the way. His eyes streamed as he breathed deeply.

"Better than him hurt himself!" Katryzna replied to Reece, or maybe her conscience? "He doesn't even know!"

"Agent Tasker, you still with us?" Reece said. "I've got this, you believe that, don't you?"

Tasker steeled himself and slowly nodded. He had to. "I believe it."

"And when we get back – you can still do your bit, okay –"

"All right. Go on, both of you. I'll do . . . what I can."

Reece backed off, ready to leave, but Katryzna leaned in, so her nose almost touched Tasker's, eyes studying his. He tensed under her scrutiny, trying not to breathe in her hot breath. Minty? She said, "Try to sleep. But just in case, keep this under the pillow and remember everything I taught you."

She backed off, nodding sagely, as he tried to muddle through what he could have learnt from her. He saw she'd squeezed his pistol into his grip.


Leigh-Ann exited the en suite feeling buoyant, finally fresh and clean like she hadn't felt in days – but when she saw Zip perched on the end of the bed, she froze, thrown back to the same scenario back in Stilt Town. That was the last time they were really comfortable and it'd felt like they were coming out the end of something, except Zip had been crying over her dreams, and the worst was yet to come. Almost certainly still true, as they lugged their idiot asses into the African wilderness.

But this time, Zip was staring out the window at the cloudy night sky.

"Feels weird to be home?" Leigh-Ann asked, towelling off her hair.

"I don't remember being here before," Zip confessed.

"Yeah but we all Africa." Leigh-Ann laughed. "I grew up with toothless pencil-dicks always telling me to go back home, and hey, we made it."

"It's not a good place," Zip said. "Not for us."

"Hey now." Leigh-Ann sat next to her. "That's Ikiri talking. I saw a lot of folks outside smiling."

Zip nodded. "Yes. It is Ikiri. I can feel it more now. Not far from here, like a dark place in my mind. It hurts people who get too close. They were greedy and ruined it and made it darker."

"Shearjoy's gang?"

The kid paused, still struggling with what had already dawned on her. "My daddy's people. He did this, more than anyone. Ikiri was dark before, but people brought more darkness. He brought darkness."

"Shit. You're getting intense, you know that?" Leigh-Ann said. "And you just know all this, do you? Scent it in the air like a stale fart?"

"Yeah." Zip gave her a worried look. "Am I a freak?"

Leigh-Ann grinned. "Hell yes, and you oughta wanna be. A freak, Zip, is someone special. You got gifts and the closer we get to ending this, the more you can get on and use them. You don't need to do this darkly brooding thing, talking cryptic about darkness. You got a light in you, don't you? Why don't you try it and see?"

"Try my gifts? Now?"

"The hell not? Like Agent Tasker said, your brother gotta be tired sometime. I gotta believe if he was ready to come for us again, he would've done it."

Zip paused, then straightened up to accept the challenge. She closed her eyes. Breathing slowly, calmer than when she tried before. Getting better at it. "There's power in this building. Shearjoy, Flay, Chops. And Katryzna, she's different."

"Noodle brain again," Leigh-Ann said.

"Yes." Zip took another breath. "There's something clouding Agent

Tasker but it's not something I can feel, exactly. An after-effect. He touched Ikiri, too, in a way."

Leigh-Ann shifted uncomfortably. It seemed the place was like a disease you could pick up, and if Tasker hadn't pushed her down, that might've been her in there, wading through muggy thoughts.

Zip went on, "The rest of the town is . . . moving. Alive. The forest is alive. The river is alive. The trees talk, the air breathes and there's . . . someone out there. Strong like the Legion. But hard to see. Things are so unclear –" Her eyes shot open.

"Your brother?" Leigh-Ann asked.

Zip nodded. "He's not . . ." A low, frightened noise rose from her.

"All right, Zip, this another case of why you shouldn't listen to Leigh –"

"No!" Zip pushed Leigh-Ann away and jumped up. "He's in the darkness." She stomped a foot and spoke more firmly, "*No.*"

Then suddenly she was back, eyes soft and childlike again, and Leigh-Ann was staring, once again the fool left managing something that made zero sense. Zip looked strangely thoughtful and said, "He's suffering. He's not doing anything now, he's confused and hurt himself. With the feelings and the darkness, trapped in Ikiri. He hurts a lot. If he was taken away – if I could connect with him – we can help him. Please, can we help him?"

Leigh-Ann forced a smile that had to be anything but convincing. "You tell me."


Reece leant against the wall in the corridor, waiting for Ward to pick up. They'd lifted her number off Tasker's phone and he was using Katryzna's now.

Watching with her arms folded, Katryzna asked, "Do you think she is avoiding me?"

Before Reece could ask if Ward even had her number, Ward came on, incredibly polite: "Deputy Director Sam Ward, how can I help?"

Despite their circumstances, Reece had to smile, and he echoed her politeness: "Deputy Director, ma'am, this is Reece. Reece Coburn. From Cutjaw."

"Oh, yes?" Ward said, then caught herself and tried to compensate with casualness. "Reece? How are you? I wasn't expecting you to call. Which isn't to say –"

"I got your number off Agent Tasker," Reece cut in, "because he's a little out of it. We had a doctor look at him saying it was superficial, not something to worry on, but I want to keep you updated. We're going in without him."

"Without him?" Ward said. "Into –"

"Ikiri, yeah. Thing is, the doctor *said* this was just a cut, and Tasker's been treated, but there's – well – it's kinda black. Like, in the veins."

"Like Max's wound," Ward said.

"Yeah. Is Sto up? Be good to hear his voice."

Ward paused. Not a good sign. "He's not been lively since you left. In fact, he's mostly been asleep, as he is now. Otherwise he was . . . well, rambling. Dr Hertz doesn't know what it is – they can't find any trace of septicaemia, for example, but the wound is warm and remains dark."

"Hell. Can you do something for him?"

"We've got him on an IV, he seems healthy, it's just . . . I think we have to wait and see. But how was Agent Tasker wounded? He didn't explain."

"Cut by something out in France," Reece said. "Thing like the hellspawn that hit us at the mill. Same sort of unnatural."

"He might lose his arm," Katryzna pointed out, listening in. "Or worse."

"Where exactly are you now?" Ward asked with concern.

"A jaunty hotel in Africa," Reece said. "But like I said, we got to move without Tasker. In case we're not back in touch, so you know, it's Hotel Fun Business or something. Tasker's in and out of consciousness."

"There must be something else I can do."

Reece paused. "Just keep an eye on Sto for me. Thanks." He hung up before she could argue. Better he hadn't called; now he had Stomatt back on his mind, too. Katryzna was staring, so he said, "Think we'll find an answer to these wounds out in Ikiri and all?"

"I think you will need to be tough like Sean," she said, "if you want to take his place."

"I don't want to," Reece said. "Just don't seem I got a choice. Hell, but we came into this on the back of raiding a business out in Waco, I'll give it all I've got."

"You came into this," Katryzna said, "to protect a child you did not know."

He paused. "I'll give you that, but even still, I got La Belle Riposte" – Reece tapped the gun holstered at his shoulder – "and a will to do what's needed. *If* it's needed. And had a positive turnaround with this Legion, already, didn't we?"

"For now," she said. "If they need to be killed –" She twitched to the side and snarled at her shoulder. Then her eyes came back to Reece, waiting as though she'd left a decision with him.

Reece said, "Your conscience doesn't approve?"

"Rurik doesn't approve of anything, He would rather I die." She rolled her eyes sideways. "Yes, and so would everyone else!"

"I'd rather you didn't. Reckon you're better suited to this than us."

She eyed him, still suspicious of his motives. Not used to compliments, or people wanting to engage with her. "Even with a voice in my head?"

"He really doing any harm?" Reece said. "Back where I'm from, people hear voices, the sensible ones, they put them to work. Madam Carmelau makes a fortune off tourists wanting advice on how to live they life. Sounds like your Rurik wants to keep you alive at least."

"Madam Caramel probably hears better voices," Katryzna said. "All Rurik does is tell me I'm wrong. Stop. *Don't.*" She gave an exasperated huff.

"Well. No one's right all the time, are they?"

"I do not want to be *right*. I want to survive." She paused, gave Reece another uncertain look and glanced back up the hall, towards where they'd left Tasker. Concerned, seeming to consider whether or not she should be bothered by something.

"He'll be all right," Reece said. "We're the ones in trouble."

"He said . . ." She hesitated, and looked to her shoulder as Rurik apparently egged her on. "When we finish things here, Sean was supposed to help me with something."

Reece waited for more, not sure if she was just venting concerns or suggesting he might help her instead. Her brow furrowed, and he guessed she wasn't sure herself. He said, "Well, I got no government clout or a half of his know-how, but if there's anything we can do, you've more than earned it."

"I am a bit different, in my head." Katryzna moved closer and whispered, secretively, "Scorecard said Rostov is a powerful place. What if I am already like them?"

"I don't know," Reece said, not quite connecting the dots. "You're talking about one of those places he mentioned? You been there, I guess?"

She nodded. "Tasker said something about fairies."

"Right, that was after he started losing his grip? Maybe park that idea. Those places Scorecard mentioned, he said they weren't like Ikiri, and they were cities, right? Millions of people in them, not all like the Legion. You ain't the same as them."

"Hmm." Katryzna looked away. She twitched, Rurik adding something, and she said quietly, "But I met Rurik in Rostov. It is not normal."

It was Reece's turn to pause. He was pretty sure little about her was normal, but they had different concerns right then. He said, "Something we can work out later, I guess. Agent Tasker's gonna be okay to help you, but if he's not we got other options."

"I am not sure if Sam likes me like she likes you."

"I'll put in a good word," Reece said, leaning a little closer, but it shifted Katryzna's mind to other concerns, as she looked down the hall towards Leigh's door.

"And I think Leigh really does not like me." It came out so innocent and hurt, Reece imagined a life of repressed emotion. She added, "She is not your girlfriend, is she?"

"We had a thing, briefly, a million years ago," Reece said. "Been friends too long now to ever revisit that. And she's not – I mean, she's got particular tastes."

Katryzna raised a hopeful eyebrow, like particular tastes might mean an unwashed murderess who heard voices.

"She's got a funny way of showing friendliness, too," Reece said, to put a better spin on it. "Sure she's got nothing against you. But tell you what, help us through this, and once we're through we can make sure you got all the people you need onside. How's that sound?"

"You want to teach me how to talk to girls?" Katryzna clarified.

Reece paused. "Sure, we can work on that, too. But in the meantime, and I mean this with the utmost respect – do I need to worry about you committing random acts of violence?"

"Probably," Katryzna answered honestly, not even thinking about it, then scowled at her conscience again. "Well it *is*." She rolled her eyes back to Reece. "But I can try not to."

"That'd be great. Now I ain't Tasker, I'll own that, but I can do my best to get us through this, you follow my lead. Deal?"

She paused, like she wasn't sure if that was something she really wanted. Then she nodded, spat in her hand and held it out. Reece stared with surprise and she drew it quickly back, muttering, "Sorry, that is disgusting, I have never done it before."

"No that's cool," he said. He spat in his own hand and held it out to her. She looked at it oddly, then smiled and shook with a strong grip.

A door squeaked, and they turned, hands together, to see Flay emerge from the stairwell down the hall. He leered and said, "Aw, how sweet. You lovebirds ready to roll? Shearjoy says it's time."

# 23

Leigh-Ann held Zip up so she could see over the side as they drifted out from shore. The boat was something between a freight barge and a ferry, a big, low-lying platform hosting their gang of oddballs, Ruin's old bus from the airport and a handful of little motorbikes before a small control tower. Shearjoy chatted with the boatmen, all smiles and laughs, a contrast to Reece's distinctive lack of cheer as he looked out over the slick abyss of the river. Wasn't liking leaving Tasker behind. Or the thought of what awaited them.

Once they'd gone halfway across the water, downstream through the city, Shearjoy clapped for attention. He was walking about with his old sword sheathed down at his waist, now, looking like a corporate pirate on holiday. "We'll alight beyond Kisangani, probably a bit over an hour. From there, the name of the game is to get clear of other people. The roads are good for a fair way into the forest, and once we've gone as far as the bus is able, the bikes will take us the rest of the way. We'll piggy-back, two to a bike, most experienced driving."

Another great time to be missing Caleb. No chance in hell Leigh-Ann planned to sit backseat to any Legion bastard, but she wasn't a biker herself and doubted Reece was a natural. Katryzna stepped up, though, announcing, "Well, I am the best driver, obviously. But Reece can take Zippy. He is excellent, too." Apparently she had more faith in him than Leigh-Ann, wherever that had come from. "So I will take Leigh?"

Leigh-Ann gave Reece a *hell no* look but his face said *don't make a fuss*. Couldn't trust the kid with the psycho, and better the psycho you kind of knew. But shit.

"Suit yourselves," Shearjoy said. As he went on, Leigh-Ann found Katryzna looking away – was she smirking? "We'll drive through the night, taking shifts while you sleep on the bus. Two days, barring any complications, and we'll reach the Ikiri territory."

"We got enough fuel to get out there and back?" Reece asked.

"Good question," Shearjoy said, pointing enthusiastically. Like a game show host. "No, we absolutely do not. Likewise, we're likely to burst our tyres more than a few times, too. There are stopping points along the way, and I'm counting on resupplying with your friends in the Cursed Union" – he addressed Katryzna – "at the end of the road."

"There's a cursed what now?" Leigh-Ann demanded.

"Oh yes," Katryzna said. "General Solomon liked us. But he does not like *your* kind, Teardrop."

"My kind" – Shearjoy spread his hands – "are adaptable."

He turned away, speech done, and left them to ponder what wasn't exactly an exhilarating plan. The other Legion members parted, too; Flay hovered around the bikes while Chops slumped over a barrier on the far side.

Leigh-Ann said, "No one said anything about a Cursed Union."

"Just soldiers," Katryzna said. "They got trapped and now they sit in huts cooking very interesting stews."

"Great," Leigh-Ann said. "I mean, who cares that they're cursed if they can put up a gumbo?"

She watched Flay unfasten one of the bikes. He got an arm around one side of it and hoisted it up like it weighed nothing. With one gammy leg, he hopped to the bus, then climbed the ladder at the back one-handed, the other holding the bike. Stronger and more agile than he looked. Leigh-Ann said, "Jesus. Would not have pegged that greasy son of a bitch for that kind of talent."

"I could handle him," Katryzna said, as though to impress her. "We can dump them in the river. Find their other people afterwards."

"Just like that?" Leigh-Ann said. "Click your fingers and they all go away?"

"It might take a few weeks . . ." Katryzna listened for her conscience, then said, "Yes, but it is what I am good at."

"Katryzna," Reece said, her name a warning, and for a second Leigh-Ann thought he might've just poked a bear. But Katryzna gave him a questioning glance then shrugged and went quiet.

"Maybe," Zip whispered, then paused. "Maybe they won't be so angry, or want to hurt each other, if Ikiri changes. Maybe."

Leigh-Ann touched her affectionately. Bless her optimism. "Here's hoping, huh?" But another thought crossed her mind, then, as she realised Zip's hope went beyond these guys. What about her father? They'd cross paths with him eventually, for sure, just like Scorecard promised. It might not be a happy reunion.

"Do you think we'll see my mummy out there?" Zip added, though, adding a whole new complication that made Leigh-Ann squirm. Reports of her mother did not sound pleasant.

"Better not," Katryzna warned. "She was not really a person anymore."

"But she's my mum," Zip said.

"She is half a tree," Katryzna said. "I would not want to see *my* mum like that." She paused, thoughtfully. "I did not like seeing her much anyway, though."

"Yeah, we'll see what we can do, Zip," Leigh-Ann cut in before this could get more tragic. "Once we're done with your brother, maybe?"

Zip nodded tiredly, satisfied with that. Katryzna mumbled dejectedly, something about a pantry, and Leigh-Ann deliberately didn't look her way. She shoved her hands in her pockets and wandered off, muttering in Polish.

Leigh-Ann frowned. Forget Zip's family, she had more immediate concerns. She said to Reece, "Tell you what, I got the seriously short straw if I gotta ride with her."

"Give her a break, she's trying," he said. "And she'll keep you safer than any of us. Keep you warm at night, too, if you let her."

"Asshole. Think it's so funny, you ride with her, I'll take Zip." Leigh-Ann huffed, well aware no one could take that suggestion seriously. She stared at the bus and its dusty bikes and the weirdo bouncing up that ladder by himself, then away to the run-down houses and dark river rolling by. She said, "We're in Africa, Reece. *Africa.* What the hell business we got being in Africa?"

"Saving the world, near as I can tell."

"What the hell business we got *saving the world*?"

Reece shrugged. "Didn't I promise you the Cutjaw Kids were made for big things?"

"Well, I'm not looking forward to this one bit."

He smiled, though, and she was drawn to it, same way she always was; made to question how anything could really be bad, when this happy fool was still smiling. He said, "You'll say I'm jinxing it if I say it, but –"

"Don't, Jesus, for once," Leigh-Ann said, almost laughing at how big an idiot he could be. "Shit you even *think* that this is all gonna be all right, you've done us in."

"It will be, though," Zip said, quietly, and cut off any more complaint Leigh-Ann might've made. Sounded too earnest, too thoughtful, to say a word against. "It might not be easy, but we can do it."


They rode the bus through a riverside village and into the trees. The unpaved track plunged into darkness with only the headlights for visibility. So rough and shaky, Reece had no idea how both Leigh-Ann and Katryzna managed to fall asleep. Something in common there, at least.

Reece worked at keeping Zip alert, asking what was her favourite colour, animal, if she'd ever been to the zoo? He asked her about the cities she'd seen – what did she think of Memphis? What did people do for fun in Ordshaw? She thought carefully over the answers, and replied with details that made Reece figure she was either a brilliant guesser or had unnatural intuition. *The centre of Ordshaw is really for people with suits. They had nice old trams in Memphis.* Reece didn't recall seeing any when they passed through.

Anyway, it kept her awake and kept his mind off what hell they were riding into, and what troubles they'd left behind. Might Stomatt and Tasker be dying? Might these Legion bastards just go after everyone they knew later?

Shearjoy came to join him up the back, talking softly so as not to wake Leigh-Ann or Katryzna. "How does it feel, being close to Ikiri?"

Zip looked to Reece to check if it was alright to answer. He nodded; might as well stay friendly. She said, "It's harder to sense things out there."

"Like a fog?" Shearjoy raised his head, like he was sniffing the air. "Out here, the energies flow together."

"I guess."

"I ask you something?" Reece said. "You seen someone take a wound like Agent Tasker before? Gradually losing energy over a cut."

"With infections," Shearjoy said. "Loss of blood, or –"

"I don't mean like that," Reece said. "Connected to Ikiri."

Shearjoy considered it for an age, then slowly shook his head. "There was nothing unnatural about the way our men died around Ikiri. Or since. Our gifts related more to senses. Some enjoy quick healing, but not anything that would make wounds worse. Then, we did not succumb to the beasts from Ikiri itself. Perhaps you know something more, Zipporah?"

Zip shook her head politely, not looking up.

"Do you feel your brother now, I wonder?"

Another head shake.

"Neither do I. None of us have, since we left. We were so sure there was nothing out here but the site itself. I suspected it was your father who was responsible for the recent massacres. You, yourself, even. He has, after all, silenced the other likely candidates – Moose was the last of them, Carniferous before him. But our inability to sense the truth, in a way, is a proof of its own, as far as your brother is concerned. Does that make sense to you?"

It didn't to Reece. These people were on another level of strange, and if he hadn't been through all he had, he might've written them all off as delusional. But Zip said, "But I *can* sense something out there. There's bad energy. Bad people and worse things."

"People?" Shearjoy said. "Who?"

Zip tried, for a second, then quickly shook her head, afraid. Reece leant across her, forming a barrier against Shearjoy, to say, "She's tired, been through a lot. We gotta get into this right now?"

"Sorry." Shearjoy smiled. It made Reece's skin crawl, this guy a presence all of his own. "I just hope we understand each other. I see a better world ahead. You've no idea the extent of the work we've done, trying to master what Ikiri left us with. It's as much poison as nectar. But with her help, the seeds I've sown could flourish. People with gifts like ours, understanding of the world, in positions where we can really make a difference. Without the distractions the power brought."

"Yeah, no offence," Reece said, forcing himself to draw a line, "but I don't buy the benevolent dictator angle. Thing I find people with power all tend to have in common, is y'all only want more of it. Someone else gotta pay for that. So we're gonna see this through, make sure it's all safe, but I'll ask you to kindly leave Zip the hell out of your plans."

Shearjoy raised an eyebrow, a little impressed by the outburst. He showed his palms in defeat and backed off, but said, "Indeed we have a difficult enough task ahead of us. Plenty of time to discuss the future when it comes."

He went back to the front of the bus, leaving Reece to exhale relief. Probably not a good idea provoking the murderers. But damn if he was gonna let them draw Zip into their schemes.

She seemed to sense his discomfort and shifted closer, into a hug. He smiled, but she was tense, too. Something on her mind. She whispered, "It's the creatures. I don't like to talk in front of . . . around him. But about Agent Tasker? And Max? I know they got something from Vile and Giza and those things in France. I'm sorry."

"Hey, that ain't your fault," Reece said.

Still, she met his eyes with deep apology. "It is, though. All this is because of me and my brother."

"Because your own dad didn't understand you and panicked, way back when," Reece told her. "That ain't the same thing as it being because of you. You wait till we get there, see if things don't add up better when you get a chance to see where you came from."

Zip swallowed, not entirely happy about it. "The creatures came from there, too."

"Yeah." Reece rubbed her shoulder. There would be more of them out there, wouldn't there? Not much to be done but face them, though. "Yeah, they did."

Zip yawned, eyelids heavy. "Could you play some music, Reece? I really like it."

"Ah, I don't think now's the time, hey?" He ruffled her hair. "But listen, I reckon your brother's left us alone for a while, maybe he'll leave off a while longer. How about you get some sleep? Got a feeling we all gonna need our energy."

She nodded again, too tired to argue, and drooped against him. He closed his eyes, and wished he could reassure himself, too. After all, they needed her to keep them safe, rather than the other way round.


Before Reece knew it, there was light coming through the trees. Chops was driving, now. Zip stretched and noted happily that her brother hadn't attacked while they slept. They stopped for a break and Shearjoy passed out foil-packed energy bars and pouches of thick drinks, in various chocolate, meat or fruit flavours. Leigh-Ann summarised the experience of a hotdog biscuit as, "One of the weirdest-ass things in a whole month of weird shit."

"But you like it?" Shearjoy said. "It'll satisfy you for a whole day."

Katryzna complained, through a messy mouthful, that the local food was better.

Shortly into the afternoon, they stopped at a junction; the road branched off to a narrowing track. Flay and Shearjoy unloaded the bikes from the roof, refusing Reece's offer to help. The pair moved with strength and finesse that he couldn't have matched. They made the bikes look much lighter than they were and Flay's bad leg didn't seem to get in the way at all.

For the rest of the day, they rode two to a bike over increasingly overgrown tracks. Reece bounced along with Zip clinging tight, at first startled at the quick ease with which he managed to speed over the rutted ground, then trusting he somehow had this. Maybe it was the kid's influence, as she pressed her face into his back, or just the boon of following the Legion boys' example.

Their little convoy passed two villages, full of staring people, and one military checkpoint. Shearjoy spoke to a cluster of young men with assault rifles that looked way too big for them and they were cheerily waved on, a hint that he might have the same persuasive gift as Zip.

Into the night, Shearjoy took them to a clearing where the ground was scattered with tree stumps and broken logs. As they unpacked tents, Reece reflected they were remote enough that Zip might rest soundly again. If her brother knew they were coming, hopefully he'd be conserving his energy anyway.

Flay got a fire going, Shearjoy handed out more astronaut-rations and they settled in for the night. Reece considered playing a little harp, but something about it felt dirty, playing in front of these guys. Instead, he let the Legion keep watch and settled into a small tent with Zip between him and Leigh-Ann, leaving Katryzna one to herself and whoever wasn't on watch sharing the last one. Reece slept from the second he closed his eyes, and it seemed only a moment had passed when Zip's hushed voice whispered, "Something's happening."

"Huh?" Reece pushed himself blearily upright.

Leigh-Ann groaned, stirring on Zip's other side. "Starting to think we ain't getting a good night's sleep ever again."

"Listen," Zip said.

It was silent out there. Reece was no stranger to the wilderness; Cutjaw was practically feral land, with woods and a river that descended into swampland. He'd camped and boated overnight. The wild wasn't ever quiet like this. They held their breath rather than interrupt the silence.

An animal sound came from far away. High and wild, like the cats at the Hall of Enoch. It came again as Reece scrambled out from his sleeping bag and grabbed for his pistol. Zip put a hand on his forearm. Her big eyes shone red in the dark. "He's coming."

"Here?" Reece asked with alarm. Well. This might be over sooner than expected. The animal's cry came again, a long way off, searching. A responding sound came from another direction.

"Shit, are those things hunting for us?" Leigh-Ann whispered urgently.

"No," Zip said, with deep focus. "Not us, him."

"What?" Reece shot back. "That don't make any –"

Zip jumped in surprise, a second before something crashed outside and a man grunted. Reece shouldered through the tent flaps, gun in hand. He stopped as he saw two shadowy figures moving in the space between their tents. He recognised Flay's build, the big man doubled over as he stumbled through the ash of their fire. The tall silhouette behind him brought an arm up fast. Longer than it should be – wielding a weapon. *No*, fused with one.

"Mason –" Reece said, but the arm came down quicker than he could act, and Flay collapsed to the ground. The same time, Chops burst out of her tent with a mad battle-cry. Torchlight shone out behind her as Shearjoy followed, picking out the one-handed man and the crazed woman as she swung her axe at him. The pair moved quicker than was natural, Mason back-stepping and flashing his blade-arm up in sparking defences, as Chops came at him from all angles like a wolverine.

Zip and Leigh-Ann pressed behind Reece but he pushed them back, warning, "Stay put!" No way he was getting in the middle of this, barely able to pick out either combatant. Katryzna came out the third tent with the same quandary, darting side to side with a knife in her hand.

Fast as Chops was, in the midst of her attack Mason found an opening and struck, sending her through the air with a grunt. She rolled and sprang onto all fours, ready to strike again. In the moment's break, Zip ducked under Reece's arm and shrieked, "Daddy, stop!"

Mason's eyes flashed, startled by her presence. Katryzna was about to pounce, when another man appeared behind her and grabbed her arm, shouting, "No, he'll kill you!"

Katryzna reeled to strike back but stopped with a surprised shout: "Henri?"

In the distraction, Chops leapt and Mason ducked under the swing of her axe.

"Stand down!" Shearjoy shouted. "All of you! Mason!"

The pair kept fighting, boots scuffing clouds of dust as axe and blade-arm clanged together again, again.

"I said *stop!*" Zip screamed, with a desperate, tearful strain – not quite the blast she'd used on Ruin, maybe holding back because of that memory. Neither attacker fell down, but they suddenly parted and squared off, panting. Zip was breathing quickly too, about to cry. "Daddy, why?"

Shearjoy ran the torch from the pair down to Flay, then back up to Mason. The full detail was hidden deep in shadows, but Reece saw enough to know Flay's head was halfway severed. Shearjoy said, calm as if Mason had just walked mud on a carpet, "You had to do that?"

"Why –" Zip whimpered again, and Leigh-Ann pulled her back with hushed whispers, "Don't look, sweetie. Fuck."

"Shearjoy," Mason sneered the name like a curse. "You actually came."

"I was always the responsible one."

"It's time, then. You and her together if you wish." He gestured at Chops. "We'll finish this now."

"*We* can't, can we?" Shearjoy almost laughed. "Dammit man, if we'd known the truth of what we left out here, we could've reached an accord a long time ago. If you hadn't *hidden* her, all these years, she might've told us. The Legion has always fought for a common good, Mason. You can't see that, even now?"

"Good?" Mason rumbled like an animal and pointed his bloodied blade at Flay. "This man murdered Loan. Burnt down a school. Cut the hands off villagers in Urmitan. And she" – he gestured to Chops – "skinned men alive in Bolivia. You have all *run* from me for too long. You –"

"Came to help," Reece interrupted, before he could reach boiling point. "That evil shit spewing out of Ikiri's gotta stop and they know it, same as you! Whatever your past, no one wants more senseless death. They listened to that message a damn sight better than you."

Mason offered his usual furious glare, and Reece felt he'd be added to that same hit list for talking back. But Chops drew his attention back with a sneer: "You crept in like a coward, Headhunter. Ever the snake."

"Crawl back in your hole," Mason snapped. "You goblin wretch."

"I'll say what I said to you in Shanghai." Shearjoy raised his voice. "We have a long way to go and would do better to work together. You've made one mistake this evening; don't make more."

"Our destinations are not the same."

"So you didn't come looking for your dear daughter? Did you get lost on the way back to Ikiri?"

"You know *nothing* –" Mason snarled.

"I know Ezekiel lives!" Shearjoy shouted, stepping towards him. Much smaller, thinner, but unafraid. "I know we can't even hope to find him without her help, let alone stop –"

A far-off nightmare creature interrupted his shout with a harsh carrion cry. Everyone looked up, as if something had passed across the sky.

"It's been getting worse," the man by Katryzna said, in a low Congolese accent. "The creatures have spread. Them and more."

"And what are you doing here?" Katryzna demanded. "With *him*?"

"More important," Leigh-Ann said, itching to move from the tent, "are those things coming for us?"

"They don't know where we are," Shearjoy said. "But that" – he pointed at Flay – "won't help. I don't want to fight you, Mason. I can overlook this, if you will, for once, just *listen*."

Mason was busy taking in the far-off sounds. He glanced Reece's way again, starting to appreciate the complexity of his situation. Whatever he'd intended, sneaking in to murder the Legion, this wasn't it. But he said, "Zipporah, you will come with me."

"The hell she will," Reece said.

"Zipporah," Mason repeated, more firmly.

Zip squirmed free as Leigh-Ann said, "You don't have to –"

"No, let me!" Zip said, and pushed past Reece, to stare her father down. She was tiny before the massive man. "If you love me, you'll stop this."

"This isn't a game," Mason growled.

"I know! You said you would protect me! And that you kept me safe! But you left my brother behind and you let him become dangerous! We're not safe, no one is, because of *you*!"

"You don't know what you're talking about. I –"

"*You* don't know!" Zip shouted. "He's trapped in Ikiri and he's hurting and he's taking it out on everyone. He shouldn't have that power or that pain. These people, *all* of these people, want to help. Why don't you?"

"That is exactly what I doing," Mason said, even more firmly. "You have no idea how bad these people –"

"You're bad!" Her voice rose to a piercing shriek, shaking birds from trees. "You are bad! Everyone says it! I know it's true! You are a bad man! You're selfish and violent and you don't even know what you're doing! You're all the same kind of bad!"

Mason's stony expression faltered at last. His look of hurt, made more eerie by the faint torchlight, looked entirely unnatural on that stern face.

"You're here," Zip continued, on the verge of tears. "You made it this far. You *do* care, I know it. Why don't you help us?"

Mason's shoulders slumped, just slightly, as he stared at her. Zip shot forwards and wrapped her arms around his legs and he stiffly let her. He looked up, taking in the people surrounding him, mute.

The animal noises came again, closer than before. From different directions, two if not three of them. It didn't break the moment, as Mason's resistance broke against his daughter's strength of will. Reece looked to Shearjoy, who wore a blank face. Chops had her axe down by her side, at least, and Katryzna had her knife ready. She raised a questioning eyebrow. Should she? Reece subtly shook his head. For better or worse, Zip had just claimed Mason for the troop.

An animal gave a closer cry. Much closer, and more shrill.

"We oughta get moving," Reece suggested, someone needing to say it.

"Agreed," Shearjoy said. "Touching as this is."

"Shearjoy," Mason said, that one word containing threat, and defiance, and a whole, deeper message to do with their long history. They exchanged a hard look, but Zip kept squeezing her dad, holding the darkness down.

"Yeah, I know," Shearjoy said. "Let's make it to daylight, shall we, before we decide what comes next?"

# 24

Henri tried to regain some cheer as the group walked through the night. Once the others had packed and he and Mason had recovered their own bikes, they all pushed the bikes down a trail, rather than ride in the low light, to avoid accidents or attracting the animals. The sounds got closer to camp as they hurried away, but though each screech or roar was chilling, the beasts could not track them. That was one positive. Seeing Katryzna again was another; this wonder of a woman brought a smile to Henri's face despite the difficulties. And while he had feared the size of the Legion camp, it turned out the young Americans were Katryzna's friends. They even looked different to the others, dressed in unusually ordinary clothes, though stained from a long journey – the man's hair was an odd shade of green and the woman's impressively big and curly, and both exuded an air of humour.

It had been vicious, seeing Mason sweep in to attack the man who killed Miguel, and Henri was unsure what to feel about it. The man had fought back violently, briefly, despite his injured leg, and had met a cruel end. Henri wanted to feel relieved or even thankful that justice had been done. But really, he'd wanted to see the man apologise. To make penance for Miguel's death.

There was no penance, though. No justice. Only more death.

Trying not to dwell on it, Henri brushed over the details when explaining what he had been through since Katryzna had left him. She was quietly angry at the news of Miguel's murder – another sign of her virtue, for she and Miguel had not got on, yet she understood he had not deserved to die. She blew air through her teeth, and the big-haired woman, Leigh-Ann, told her tiredly to leave it.

"I am not going to *do* anything," Katryzna said, in a tone that suggested she might.

She threw a look back to Reece to check, though. He seemed to have responsibility for both her and the child, which brought Henri back to an important question: "Where is Agent Tasker?"

"Back in the hotel," Katryzna said. "Decaying."

"Took a blow," Reece quickly clarified, "but he'll be good. Did more than his share already."

Zipporah walked with Reece, and she was a cause for celebration. With the creatures further back, quietening and screeching less frequently, Henri fell back in their chain to study the child more carefully. *His niece.* He gave her a fond smile. She was small and delicate, but he could immediately sense something about her that spoke to Sara's kindness, strength and charm. And despite her lighter skin and straighter hair, she looked so much like Sara, with the same small nose, the inquisitive eyes. She shied away under Henri's attention, and he said, "Please, do not be afraid. Do you know who I am?"

Zip shook her head but watched him as they walked. Concentrated. Then she stopped, and the sudden movement drew the others' attention. The woman with the axe, Chops, made an irritated noise from the back.

Just as he saw Sara in her, Zip sensed the connection in him, and launched forward for a hug. He laughed as Zip stepped back excitedly, explaining, "He's my family! We're the same!" She gave him a suddenly eager look. "How long have you been friends with my daddy? Why didn't he mention you?"

That took some of Henri's renewed cheer away. He redirected, "But look at you. She lives in you, like I cannot believe."

"My mummy?" Zip exclaimed. "Do you know where she is? Can I meet her?"

That sapped even more cheer. He couldn't imagine taking her before the strange vision that Sara had become. Henri said, "We'll see, huh? Anything might be possible now." He smiled at Katryzna. "And you found her! I knew you would do it."

"Fawn once we're safe," Chops snarled, before Katryzna could comment.

They were jostled into moving again and for a moment Henri thought Katryzna might bite back, but he continued, to avoid it. "Look at her, she's perfect. There's so much I want to know about you. So much for us to talk about."

"Then you might've let us sleep through the night before cutting people's heads off," Leigh-Ann said. "Right now we wanna be saving our energy and keeping quiet."

Zip looked guiltily away and Henri accepted that, yes, they still had the night to survive. But he was grinning, and couldn't take the rebuttal entirely seriously. Leigh-Ann had a charm of her own. He said, "Of course, my apologies. I am only happy things are finally turning around. Yes. I am *happy* this night."


Leigh-Ann had to admit that despite a shit night and a brutal murder, she was kind of happy, too. The creep Flay was gone and, while they'd gained another creep with Mason, they had taken on a Congolese guide who was more than pleasing on the eye. Granted, he had a scabbed nose and smelt like he hadn't washed in a week, but he wore as much soul in his smile as Reece, and somehow pulled off a thin moustache. He also laughed for Katryzna like she fascinated him, indicating either a heart of gold or a deep psychosis, and Leigh-Ann chose to believe it was the former.

When daylight came and they mounted the bikes again, she was half-tempted to suggest she ride with Henri, but he said she was lucky to ride with Katryzna, an *exceptional* rider, and the last thing they needed was to offend her. So they set out for another day of Leigh-Ann trying not to get too close to the woman that was sat in her lap while they bounced over hard mud.

The road widened halfway through the day, into a thoroughfare that might bring them back to people, but after another two hours there was still no sign of other vehicles, and finally their bike engines started complaining. They all slowed down, gunning the engines and finding them less responsive, until they had to stop. As they pulled up to the side of the road, Reece asked, "This weirdness something to do with Ikiri and all?"

Shearjoy and Mason hunched over, checking the bikes in a way that said this wasn't expected. Katryzna whispered in Leigh-Ann's ear, "He is not as smart as he pretends to be."

"No, clearly not," Shearjoy agreed. He was too far away to hear, but apparently that didn't stop him, and the surprise made Katryzna stiffen. "We were a lot closer than this when Ikiri affected our equipment before."

"We rode these bikes out of Ikiri yesterday," Mason said, and didn't elaborate to Shearjoy's questioning expression.

Henri said, "We came from General Solomon's camp."

Shearjoy digested that with a frown, then scanned the road like he didn't trust it anymore. The rules had changed overnight. But when he looked up again, he'd found a new grin, and announced, "Oh well, guess we're walking."

Zip took Leigh-Ann's hand and for a while they walked in companionable silence, before the kid whispered, "Ezekiel controls all this area. It feels like a" – she squinted – "like the difference when you jump into a swimming pool?"

"Like being underwater?" Leigh-Ann asked, wondering when Mason had ever taken her swimming. She couldn't imagine him in a public pool surrounded by screaming kids and their moms.

"No, like the *difference*. The world is different, when you are in the air, then when you are in the water. It's different here."

Leigh-Ann didn't have a response. Besides the bikes giving up, nothing felt much different to her. Though without the breeze on the bike, the heat was getting stifling. Her mind wandered. Did they have enough water? Could they get the bikes working again to go *back*? Was she starting to smell worse than Katryzna?

They stopped for a break at an abandoned village. Walls fallen in from disrepair, a rusted car overgrown with vines. Shearjoy and Mason separated for a search, the former watching Zip curiously and Mason in turn watching him. Shearjoy looked like he wanted to ask things, but also seemed to be completing calculations in his head. Chops, meanwhile, found a wooden post and started tossing small knives at it. Pulling them out, pacing away, throwing again. She watched Mason half the time, trying to goad him with ugly expressions, but he ignored her. Ignored everyone except Shearjoy – even his own daughter, when Zip left Leigh-Ann to go ask if he was okay. The man was a menace.

Leigh-Ann was damn thankful they never saw what was left of Flay in daylight, but for Mason to do him like that, and Shearjoy to so quickly move on, these people must all be touched in a special kind of way. They were only barely clinging to reality, and it warranted running from. But here they were. Sharing an empty village together, running out of supplies.

Henri took Zip's hand as her father glowered, and he offered to give her a tour of a real Congolese village. Leigh-Ann considered going with, but her feet screamed at her to just sit damn well down. She settled on a tree stump and looked up at Reece as he stood turning over Ward's harmonica. He was searching for distraction just like her. She tapped him with a foot and asked, "Gonna play or you just thinking about how that might've touched your little British playmate's lips?"

Reece gave her a knowing smirk. "Don't reckon I've had sex on my mind since before Waco. You?" He nodded to the huts, where Henri and Zip had gone. "Seems all right, don't he?"

"He is," Katryzna said, watching Mason and Chops from a few feet away. "He owes me a lemonade."

"Okay," Reece said.

"What else you thinking, then?" Leigh-Ann asked. "What wild thought you got, Reece, to make our day worse than being stranded in the jungle with three flavours of murderer?"

"Three?" Katryzna responded quietly, and Leigh-Ann avoided eye contact as the woman tried to figure if the random number included her.

"Oh, everything, is all," Reece said. "How we got here. Where we're going. How these guys are outta their minds, sick with murder hard-ons. This place we're going, what's the guarantee we don't all –" He waved a hand by his temple.

Well, there *was* a new and ugly thought. Leigh-Ann said, "Shit, Reece. But if we go nuts along the way, I guess we won't even know."

"Part of my concern," Reece said. "The way we got drawn into this. Our wanting to help Zip ever since. We might *already* have lost our minds."

"On account of *Zip*?" Leigh-Ann exclaimed, but he gave her a serious look and it made her think. The way Ruin, Scorecard, even her own dad, all treated the kid more like a bomb than a child. The hell of a coincidence they even happened upon Zip in the first place. But hell: "She's a good kid, and we're aiming to do a good thing. If we needed manipulating into that, it'd be a poor reflection on us, more than her."

Reece laughed. "That might just be the single most profound thing I ever heard leave your lips, Leigh."

"Yeah? Write it down and add it to the song of our adventures."

"Got a pen?"

"You should not worry," Katryzna interrupted, still watching Chops. "These people were bad to begin with. You are not."

"Respectfully," Leigh-Ann said, "we *have* done some shit in our time."

"Well," Katryzna straightened up, "you do not choose your words well. But they were killers before they came here. As Zippy said. All the same kind of bad." She reflected on that uncomfortably, surely thinking her friend Eyes and even herself were grouped in there. But she said, "You are not like us."

It wasn't much comfort, considering where it left her. Leigh-Ann looked to Reece for a positive response, but he raised his eyebrows to prompt her to take this one. Of all the times to delegate.

Leigh-Ann shifted on the stump. Probably gonna regret this. She said, "You ain't like them, either, Katryzna. We're lucky to have you along."

Katryzna turned to her with surprise, eyes widening. And thank fuck they were saved by the bell, as Zip came running up calling happily, "Reece! Leigh, we saw a pig!"

# 25

It was clear something was wrong at the militia's camp before the first huts came into view. By the way Henri described the area, someone should have greeted them sooner, to escort them or turn them away. When they saw the edge of camp at a bend in the road ahead, the reason was immediately apparent.

"Hold Zip, she doesn't need to see this," Reece said, as the group lined up in the road to take in the village.

"This," Katryzna said, "is why I cannot rely on people."

Reece shot her a look, but she only shrugged.

Henri was already moving ahead, staggering into the huts with fearful curses. The camp had been torn apart, walls smashed, bodies scattered. Some lay with hands on guns, others had been torn down from behind as though running. Some were only parts of bodies. Reece came forward with horror; just like Stilt Town, but this was daylight, with everything much more clearly on show.

There was also a big, fuzzy black shape towards the middle of camp, past a truck with a smashed cab. A massive dead animal, like the gorilla they'd killed back at Mason's mill. From the surrounding damage, more than one had come through here.

"We have to look for survivors!" Henri called over his shoulder.

"There are none," Mason declared coldly.

"Not human, anyway," Chops agreed.

Still, they moved in, splitting up to scan the carnage.

Henri darted from one body to another in disbelief, searchingly. He turned one over, and another, and when he struggled to shift a metal panel off a body, Reece snapped out of his own horror to hurry and join him. Together, they lifted the sheet and revealed a mangled mess. Reece stopped as Henri made a noise of despair.

"Look for the leaders," Katryzna said, "Solomon and his magician, they are the ones we want most."

"Magician?" Leigh-Ann gaped, up the road with Zip held close. "What in hell?"

"Jonah died before we left!" Henri shouted, his shock galvanising in anger. He pointed loosely to a body in a bright tunic, under broken totems and a tangle of torn rope, like he'd been buried in a net of fetishes. "There, you see! They had no time to bury him! We did this. This is our fault for coming here. For leaving them to this!"

"Not your fault," Reece said. He cleared his throat, to do better. "This is your world, man. You're not the one brought trouble here." His eyes ran to Mason, now standing over the dead animal.

The creature was a suitably unholy match to the sounds they had heard at night, partway between a gorilla and something that did not belong – a bear? But it was more massive than both, and its fur was patchy, with wrinkled bits of bald flesh showing between clumps.

"Ezekiel's pets," Mason said. "His creations."

"Get! Get!" Henri shouted, and another animal burst out between the huts before scurrying into the trees. It was small, a scavenger picking at the bodies. The flurry of activity lit a fire in Henri and he reeled on Mason. "You knew this was coming. Didn't you? You let me believe we could lead the creatures away but we didn't. We left these people to die."

"We got hit the same way out in Stilt Town," Reece told Henri. "If you'd been here, y'all could be on the ground here with them."

"No." Henri shook his head. "Not him. He could have helped."

Mason turned towards him, unimpressed. "Why?"

"Why?" Henri cried. He surged forward, to attack, and Reece jumped in front of him, putting up both hands. Henri was bigger than him, could definitely knock him down, but the man met Reece's eyes and paused. As much sorrow as anger there.

"It's not worth it," Reece said. "Not now."

Walking casually past, Katryzna pointed. "Is that Solomon?"

That deflated Henri. Through the dark carnage, there, down by the fire pit where these men had warmed food, was a man in uniform. He had fallen gracelessly onto his side, one arm draped up over the grill, sunglasses broken in two in the dirt along with a discarded rifle. Henri inhaled regret.

Katryzna hummed agreement. "He did not try to kill me, I respect him for that." She looked at her invisible conscience and said, "We have enough to deal with."

"Katryzna," Reece cautioned softly, and she looked like she would say more, explain at least, but caught herself.

"I am sorry, Henri," she said instead. "I suppose you were friends?"

Henri gave a noncommittal sound of his own. "These people fought to survive. All this time. How long they waited, and kept their faith. They were so close. Why did it . . . why?"

"I warned them," Mason said, dryly.

Before Henri could snap, Reece said, "Would you read the fucking room? These were people, families and women and fucking –" He stopped. This was an entire camp, their homes destroyed, but he hadn't seen any children.

"We did warn them," Henri said quietly, following his thoughts. "The children might have –"

"There is no one here," Mason said again. "And no one out there."

"You don't know!" Henri said. "You got lost, you are no expert, whatever you say!"

"He's right," Shearjoy said, walking in to join them like he was returning from a stroll. "You don't know, do you, Headhunter? I mean, I certainly don't, and I can't imagine our skills are *that* different. Ikiri is playing its usual tricks. There could be people out there, yet. There's definitely more to this than meets the eye."

"What difference does it make?" Mason said.

"Well, I could be mistaken" – Shearjoy studied Solomon's body for a second and went on – "but these creatures tore people apart. This man, though, has been left fairly well intact. Cut by a keen blade. Did you happen to invite anyone else back with you, Headhunter?"

Mason glared at him like he was playing games, but Reece followed Shearjoy's gesture to see that the camp leader's wounds were, indeed, more precise than the sort of damage done elsewhere. A quick glance at another body showed the difference – a man with a leg ripped off in a huge, ragged gash.

"It's not the Legion," Shearjoy said. "I would know."

"Vile," Mason said, reluctant to admit it, "came to my home. With a monster of Ikiri."

"Vile?" Shearjoy wore a disbelieving smile. "Now that's an interesting development." He scanned the village anew. "Sara kept alive in a tree, then the boy turns out to be alive. Now Vile, who was *definitely* deceased, is crossing seas on the hunt? And came back here on a lunch break?"

"No way Vile came back, after what we did to him in England," Reece said. Though how could he be sure, when he'd seen how many bullets that thing took, and how fast he moved? The man had looked dead before they even started fighting.

"I saw something," Henri said, hurrying it out like he didn't trust the memory of the silhouette in the dusk. "A swordsman was in the hills, I am sure. Two days ago. This man Vile, are you saying he was a ghost?"

"An echo of the man who died here," Mason said. "But real enough. The same way those creatures are echoes of what once lived here. Corruptions that should be dead."

"Vile wasn't the only one we left for dead out here," Shearjoy noted.

"Shit on shit," Reece said. "So we're talking more zombie swordsmen?"

"Who else died here?" Katryzna said, worried tone saying she already knew. "Who else *exactly* do you think was here?"

"Bruiser, Sawyer, Fender," Shearjoy said, "and Eyes."

"Eyes would not come back as a zombie," Katryzna snapped. "He was too smart for that." But she rolled into her own argument. "No, shut up. You wanted me to accept Eyes is gone, didn't you? All of you?" She bared angry teeth at Mason, then Reece. "Stop it. Stop trying to confuse me."

"He was gone," Mason said, "the same way Vile was. And if anyone else has come back, it will be the same way Vile did. Not as a man."

"You are not a man!" Katryzna cried nonsensically, then threw another look at Solomon's body and the undeniable blade wound. She kept shaking her head and looked up for support: found Reece. "Tell them. Tell them it's not him, no way."

Reece faltered, no idea what any of this was, in truth. Why shouldn't it be Eyes as much as Vile, or any of them, out here? But Mason had a point too, and Reece said, "If there is any trace of him left on this hill, it is not the man you knew."

"Those that leave Ikiri," Henri said, darkly, "are not the ones we once loved."

Katryzna looked away to something else. Rurik, perhaps, offering something more. She sniffed, then she rolled her neck. "We should find him, if we are going to do anything useful here. Eyes, whatever monsters are here. We should kill them properly."

"Right now," Shearjoy said, "I'd be more concerned about them finding us."


The sounds came much closer that night.

Reece sat outside his tent, gun at hand. There were long stretches of eerie quiet, the way he knew a forest had no right to be, then the hunting animals gave their cries and responses. Massive, feral beasts, lumbering between the trees, screeching and roaring. How could you recreate that sound? You could get a growl with a fluttering trombone, some kind of boom with a broken bass drum maybe, but add some strings, something screeching and slow. There were sounds mixed up together in there, it wasn't right.

Zip whispered from the dark of the tent, "They won't find us. Come in."

Somehow, Reece believed it. He let himself relax, but he stayed out to keep watch. The monsters weren't far off. They were sounding off in frustration at not finding them, but they were close. How hard would it be for them to stumble on the camp by accident? And Henri said the militia had been hidden all these years; something had changed there, so their own safety wasn't guaranteed. Once, Reece heard heavy footfalls moving between the trees, like someone had set a rhino loose nearby. It skirted them and thumped off with porcine huffs. He kept totally still.

Hearing those sounds out there, and with the new fear of another Vile on the loose, he could believe the need for their escort. But between Mason and that woman with the damn axe, he couldn't shake the feeling they already had a few Viles in their midst anyway. Chops didn't emerge while he watched her tent, that night. At one point he heard nasty whispers, indecipherable but like a mud witch casting a hoodoo spell. Shearjoy made a hushed comment that shut her up.

There was no other movement around the camp, but Reece got the feeling he wasn't the only one awake. Mason would be meditating in his tent, for sure. Katryzna would be thinking hard over whether or not it was her beau gonna come for them. Reece wished he could reassure her, but he didn't have much peace to pass on.

Hell, what little calm he had himself was likely thanks to Zip; he wasn't trying to deny it. Without her, they'd all be freaking out, for sure. Shearjoy watched them like he expected them to, the same way the Duvcorp expedition had. But Reece would take Zip into the heart of this beast, whatever it took. It was worth more than his life had ever been worth before, he knew that much. And he'd make music of it all, if he lived.

Violins and bass, and the scratching of metal. Running hard over a bent cymbal. Those noises out there could be contained. It'd make a haunting tune. They just needed to add a glorious coda.

# 26

Leigh-Ann climbed the forest hills with more energy than she had a right to, after the long journey, the horror of that massacred camp and another bad night's sleep. Must've been crack in those snacks Shearjoy was feeding them, couple of bites and you got the energy of a gazelle. She didn't exactly feel good about it, because she knew she *should* be exhausted, and she worried it wasn't just the energy bars.

They were getting closer to Ikiri, Zip promised, and as they were all counting on the kid, even Mason and the Legion, for directions, it made Leigh-Ann consider what was coming. She asked Shearjoy as they pushed through the trees, "When we getting our own superpowers?"

He gave her his usual smirk, which she could've wiped off his face with an empty beer bottle. "Being close to Ikiri is a hindrance," he said. "The positive stuff comes inside, if you can survive it."

Leigh-Ann left that cryptic bullshit to fall back alongside Reece. She said, "You're getting quieter and I don't like it."

"Funny, I was thinking the same about you. Can't imagine what Sto would say, the chance to see you silent."

"Oh *shit*, you think he'd be quiet out here, too?" Leigh-Ann tried to laugh. "Once we're through, we gotta come back with him, video that."

"Once we're through, I'm hoping this place won't work anymore."

"I'm down with that. But be real a second. Shearjoy's made big dick money out of this, doing his thing. Think it'll help us, too?"

Reece gave her an uncertain look.

"Humour me, Reece. We ain't got a future to look forward to, what we got?"

He nodded, gamely, and said, "Well, psychic powers might help us walk into Guillaume Fontaine's office in New Orleans and get him to sign us up on his label, no questions asked?"

"Provided we don't get stuck with shitty powers," Leigh-Ann mused. "Knowing our luck, we'd only be able to talk to leaves."

"Knowing our luck?" Reece laughed. "Leigh, we been alive and bucking against a shitty life longer than we had any right to be. Found me the best people in the world to rely on and I been blessed with talents and health to boot. Ain't no one come out of Cutjaw as well as us, believe that. Since when we been unlucky?"

Leigh-Ann couldn't help picking up his infectious smile, but lost it again as she said, "I guess it ain't been the same since everyone around us started dying."

It made Reece quiet again, and she regretted saying it, but it was the truth. Rather than respond, he touched her shoulder, to let her know that they were still here together. Had each other since childhood. He nodded to Zip, the child marching determinedly alongside Henri. "One thing I know: that kid oughta be more fucked up than any of us know. I dunno how she coped before, but *you've* pulled her through this far. She'd have a hell of a different attitude coming out here with her pop alone. So it ain't all been for nothing, whatever comes next."

Leigh-Ann lost her words, felt her cheeks reddening.

"And I don't know about you," Reece said, leaning in closer, "but I got no truck with this place turning me into an asshole like them."

She took that in with a fresh smile. Why the hell not believe that. Up, they pressed through the trees, sweating like bad ham, and yeah, she felt good enough about it. Superpowers or not, maybe they could handle Ikiri just by keeping damn positive.

The second that thought hit her, a roar shook the trees, rattling the leaves above. Everyone froze, looking between tree trunks. It wasn't the slightest bit clear what direction it came from.

"They're close," Mason announced from up front.

"You think?" Leigh-Ann demanded. "How many is *they*?"

"Does it matter?" Chops said. "One would be too many for you."

"Five," Zip said, suddenly in tune. "Two are close. Three more are getting closer."

"Anything else?" Shearjoy asked, meaning did she detect zombie swordsmen. Zip concentrated harder, as a different sound came: a whining pitch, similar to the animals at the Hall of Enoch.

"I thought these things only came out at night," Reece said, drawing his pistol. Shearjoy produced his long, thin rapier, Chops had her axe in one hand and a knife in the other, and Mason's mechanical stump came to life, extending the battered remnants of his blade.

"They know where we are," Zip announced suddenly, frightened.

"Is it him?" Katryzna asked, hurriedly drawing a pistol in one hand, knife in the other. Where'd she even got a gun from, picked it up back in the camp? Leigh-Ann wasn't moving, couldn't quite bring herself to touch a weapon and make this real herself. "Who's out there, Zippy?"

Zip met Katryzna's eyes with growing fear, an answer ready that she plainly didn't want to give. Katryzna made a move to make her talk, and Leigh-Ann's instincts put her in the woman's path. Katryzna eyed her unpleasantly, but another creature screeched in the distance. Birds erupted from the canopy with furious squawks. They flew overhead, hundreds of them, momentarily blotting out the sky with a thunder of wingbeats.

"Is he there?" Katryzna demanded, leaning around Leigh-Ann.

"This the time?" Leigh-Ann hissed back, and Katryzna squared up to her, knife damn notable down at her side. None of the awkward shyness in her now.

"If he's there, it is," she growled, but Reece stepped closer then, his own pistol vaguely levelled near her gut.

"Think we need to move," he said, but Zip cried out her answer abruptly, "Yes, he is! There are creatures but a – a person – or, he used to be!"

Katryzna turned as though she might see him.

"We should run," Shearjoy advised, as if fleeing for their lives was tantamount to jogging for a bus. "We don't have far to go – our best hope is to get there before they catch up to us."

"I'll help you, little one," Henri said, and swept Zip up onto his shoulders, as the others started moving. But Katryzna was rooted to the spot, glaring. Henri looked from her to Leigh-Ann, imploring, "Katryzna. We must go."

She snapped aside, signalling he go ahead. Reece put a hand on her forearm and the woman flinched, eyes mad.

"Whatever you're thinking," he said, "your man ain't out there."

"You don't know that. No one knew Eyes but me."

"But we all met Vile," Leigh-Ann said, "and he was nothing like a person."

Katryzna shook off Reece's hand, but looked between him and Leigh-Ann. Plainly, if they left now, she wouldn't follow. Reece said, "Reckon if you stay we all stay."

Zip's frightened voice cut back through the trees, pleading, realising they'd fallen behind. The others were moving ahead, not caring. The beasts rumbled, closer by the second. Leigh-Ann added, urgently, "Or we can figure it out at Ikiri. We just gotta get there, first."

"So go –"

A tree creaked loudly, something crashing through the undergrowth, and Leigh-Ann caught a flash of dark movement. Echoes of the gorilla Giza hunting them outside Stilt Town. Where Caleb died.

"Move!" Reece shouted.

Leigh-Ann grabbed Katryzna's arm and ran. The woman flapped like she might fight back, but Leigh-Ann moved so quick Katryzna had to fall into step, and it snapped her out of the trance. Then they were both running. Reece kept pace in parallel, bounding over rocks and roots. They breathed hard, slaloming through the trees at top pace.

Animal thumps sped up behind them, loud and fast as horse hooves, with the crash and snap of bark as it slammed through the trees. It made furious gnashing sounds and Katryzna risked a look while Leigh-Ann picked out Henri's back. She didn't dare take her eyes off him. They both ran faster.

A roar came from the right, another creature closing in, and Leigh-Ann shrugged out of her backpack, hopping over rocks and vines. As Henri pulled ahead, Zip bouncing and yelping on his shoulders, Leigh-Ann glimpsed Reece darting between trees to their side. Keep up with him, catch up to Henri, that was all. Her lungs were burning. Vision going white. Leigh-Ann staggered and heard herself wheeze. Cursed. A beast crashed into a tree that couldn't be more than ten yards back and she stumbled with a weak cry, no breath for more.

A gunshot made her flinch and brought her vaguely back. Katryzna's arm stretched over her head, firing again. Then Katryzna ducked and got a shoulder up under Leigh-Ann's arm and they were running together, slow and clumsy but moving; Leigh-Ann couldn't stop if she wanted, now, lungs be damned. An animal snarled to the side and Katryzna fired again, with a feral shout of her own. The creature whined, retreating.

"Up here, up here!" Reece yelled, and Leigh-Ann gave it her all, wishing and praying that one final slope was all it would take. Katryzna shoved her ahead as they climbed, the path narrow, and she rammed into Leigh-Ann's rear, pushing her up relentlessly. A harsh snap came just behind and Katryzna cried out but kept moving, kept pushing. Leigh-Ann scrambled up, barely seeing where she was going, hands scraping over mud and rocks until another hand caught her wrist and heaved. Reece shoved her past him and reached back to help Katryzna with one hand, the other firing his pistol down. The creatures were just beneath them, a tight snarling and lashing pack.

Leigh-Ann staggered upright and backed into a tree, seeing more of the same dense thicket here, elevated but not safe. The others were ahead, Henri and Shearjoy clambering over another tall rock, and snarls came from the left as Chops attacked something.

"Keep going, don't stop!" Reece shouted, dragging Katryzna to her feet. Both of them ran on, sweeping Leigh-Ann with them in a wave. Up they climbed, following Henri, hands and feet finding roots and cracks in the boulder. The animals got angrier below, smashing trees and stone, but they'd fallen behind. Couldn't use brute force to climb, the idiot beasts. By the time Leigh-Ann reached the top of the next rock, it sounded like the animals were struggling, giving her just enough time to catch a breath. Chops lumbered in from the side, blood on her face like war paint, eyes searching for another victim.

"This way," Shearjoy called from ahead. He slipped between trees, waving for them to follow, Henri and Zip just behind him. Leigh-Ann's heart thumped against her ribs, chest burning, and each breath seemed too shallow. Katryzna and Reece took an arm each and all but carried her on. No sign of Mason. Where the hell was Mason?

"Almost there!" Shearjoy announced, but Leigh-Ann could scarcely believe it. She'd used everything, but they wouldn't let her slow down. They chased after Henri as he shoved through branches after Shearjoy.

The beasts crashed into the forest close behind them, regaining their trail, but the woodland opened enough for the group to move faster. Leigh-Ann heard a voice cursing repeatedly and realised it was her own. Hell, if she had breath to swear, she had breath to run. She pushed off from Reece and Katryzna, who shouted encouragement. But Leigh-Ann's vision was going white again, and her arms were aching now, could barely feel her legs. Couldn't go much further.

Then the last trees thinned out to reveal a clearing where Henri had stopped by a big, impassable rock face. Shearjoy stood waiting, sword up. Leigh-Ann stumbled to a standstill herself, unblinking – they'd run into a dead end? But then she saw it, between the men. A gash in the rock, tall and wide enough to walk into. Dark as night. She staggered a final few steps closer, and was hit by a feeling as severe as the darkness, making her bite her teeth together.

"Why are you stopping?" Katryzna shouted as she and Reece sped into the clearing after Leigh-Ann. She spun back and shrieked. They did too: Reece, Katryzna and Chops turned shoulder to shoulder to face the tree line as the animals caught up, smashing through the trees. Dark shapes slashed viciously between the trees, filling the space with black bulging fur, yellow eyes, sharp teeth; hard to see where one shadow monster ended and another began, but they were all huge.

The monsters stopped, though, as if they were held back by the power of the cave. One crashed to the side – not enough space for all of them – and it tripped off the slope with a roar.

"They won't follow us," Shearjoy said, not sounding sure.

"This is the place?" Reece called over his shoulder. "We gonna be safe inside?"

"This is it," Shearjoy said. "But I wouldn't call it safe."

"Hell you say!" Reece shouted. "Sure as shit can't stay out here! Everyone here?"

"Where's my daddy?" Zip asked, voice shaking, as she moved away from Henri to stand in the cave mouth. She looked around, distraught. "He left us."

"His funeral," Shearjoy said.

Zip shot him a mean look but one of the creatures snapped forward, jaws clacking as it reached out from behind the trees. Katryzna fired into the writhing mass. The creatures retreated with a collective flinch, then resumed reaching between the trees, clawing the air only a few feet from them. A tree bent under their weight, leaning towards the rock face, and everyone backed off, pressing closer to the cave and its hot darkness.

Reece put his free hand on Katryzna's pistol, saying, "Maybe we don't provoke them, they stay back."

"They're getting courage," Henri said. "Zip – can we go in?"

Zip firmed up. "Yes. I can protect us."

The closest creature pushed around a tree, revealing a squashed, sharp-toothed face, higher than head height, poking out between huge, furry arms. Saliva dripped from its huge snarling mouth. Katryzna stepped around Reece and held her arm up to shoot it, but froze, something else catching her eye. She jumped back, into Reece, knocking them both down. Leigh-Ann saw him, then – a tall man amongst the creatures. Slender, wrapped in a shadowy cloak that hung in decayed strings, a big machete down at his side. It looked like half his face was gone.

"It is you," Katryzna said, pushing onto her knees, over Reece. "Eyes?"

The man watched them with predatory emptiness and the creatures loomed either side of him, dogs at his heel, waiting for a command.

"That's not him," Reece said, carefully disentangling himself, not to disturb the chill equilibrium. "Katryzna."

He tried to help her up but she pushed him off and jumped up, eyes fixed on the shadow man. She shouted, accusingly, "What is wrong with you?"

"That's not him!" Leigh-Ann shouted, desperately.

Henri called, "We need to go in!"

Then the man darted forwards and his machete slashed up towards Katryzna. Reece pulled her back, just in time. Chops came in from the side with a scream, and their weapons clashed – but the man locked hers against his and flung the axe away with a simple twist. She moved fast to bring up a knife while he spun and then it was over. Chops dropped to her knees, hands clutching her belly where he'd hacked her, looking up with hateful eyes, making savage, inhuman sounds of pain. He watched her with the same calm, unstoppable energy that Vile had, but he was taller, leaner, *darker*. In the light of the clearing, Leigh-Ann could see there was barely enough flesh to cover his skeletal face – not a man, not alive, definitely not Katryzna's Eyes.

The man pulled his machete free from Chops' gut and turned to them. Before she could collapse, one of the creatures snatched forwards and caught her with a claw. It dragged her, screaming, into the trees.

"Stop!" Zip shouted as the creatures retreated into the shadows with Chops' body, tearing at her. "I said stop!" Her powers weren't working on them.

The dead man took another step towards the group.

"Eyes, it's me!" Katryzna shouted tearfully, back down on the ground with Reece holding her protectively. Both had dropped their weapons.

"Can't you do something?" Leigh-Ann spun to find Shearjoy but he was gone.

"In!" Henri roared, pushing Zip ahead of him. The child cried out, reaching for Leigh-Ann's hand, but Henri moved too fast and they both tripped, stumbling into the shadow. Leigh-Ann reached for Zip herself, missing her hand and staggering herself. A couple of steps and she was there, the warm mouth of Ikiri engulfing her. She turned to see Reece dragging Katryzna after her. Katryzna was screaming and she kicked and cried out Eyes' name as the thin man walked closer, arm out to the side. But the whole scene was getting smaller, receding as Leigh-Ann was sucked in, deeper, like she was falling while standing, and then they and everything else was gone.

# 27

Tasker stirred from the bed. He wasn't sure how much time had passed between feverish dreams and paranoid thoughts, but his mind raced with the overwhelming sense that he needed to move to stop thinking, ignoring the heat radiating from his shoulder or the vague awareness that his skin and veins were showing black around the wound.

He had a vague recollection of a doctor visiting and expressing confusion over the wound. The man had redressed it and advised him to stay put. He couldn't, though. He sensed something calling him, and lying in bed only made his head spin with thoughts of the Legion, the amassing powers of Ikiri, and everyone he cared about suffering.

With his vision swaying, he made it out to the balcony. The view validated his mounting fears. Down in the forecourt, a white man stood near the hotel gates, leaning against the wall. He looked up at Tasker like he'd been waiting to see him. Couldn't have been there long, out in that heat, with that pale skin and overlarge bald head, but whether he'd been there five minutes or two hours, he was clearly expecting Tasker.

Breathing in the stuffy air, leaning on the rail, Tasker waited for his balance to return, and all the while the man kept staring. Tasker peeled his gaze away first, while he still had energy to go indoors without collapsing. He slumped into a chair and exhaled. Had a bad feeling, being here alone with strange people turning up. Something *out there* needed him. Dread crept up his body as he wondered how long Shearjoy's people would wait before deciding to silence him. Would they slip something in his food? Make it look like an accident? Could the doctor be trusted?

Tasker recalled Shearjoy's words well enough, distracted as he'd been at the time: the Legion and the Ministry weren't all that different. There was always a line past which it made more sense to remove problematic people than work around them. Simon Parris must have reached that level of problematic when he'd shared hints about Ikiri with the MEE. Since then, Tasker had proved himself to be even more of a threat than that. Katryzna more so.

He was sweating, aching all around his shoulder. But there was something else, a niggle at the back of his mind that had got him out of bed. His instincts told him it was Ikiri itself. Was he feeling some part of the sensations the Legion and Zip felt? A connection. An understanding. Was it the wound that affected him or something new – had they reached Ikiri and caused a shift?

They must be close, either way, and the presence of the Legion's people in the hotel proved the end was coming. Katryzna's parting words came back to Tasker: she *had* taught him one thing. The element of surprise counted against a meticulous planner like Shearjoy. She had disturbed Parris's clean murder and the abduction of Tasker's family through surprise. They wouldn't expect Tasker to act now, either.

Feeling his head start to turn in circles again, Tasker called Ward.

"Agent Tasker, please tell me you're feeling better?"

"Getting there," Tasker lied, failing to hide the strain in his voice.

"Oh thank God. Max Stomatt is stable, but he's not very responsive. Is there anything you can suggest, that helped you?"

Tasker frowned, not following. Max Stomatt was fine when they left, why should there be any connection between them? "Did we talk about this? My head's cloudy –"

"No, I spoke to Reece. I've been worried – it's been a few days, Agent Tasker, and I didn't dare send anyone to catch up to you, yet."

"Sensible," Tasker said. "Well, I'm sorry I've got nothing. Just . . . my head started to feel clearer. I'm wondering if they've done something, out there. Can you check for me? Have you had any indication of another power spike? Like Lyon, or . . .?"

"Not that I'm aware of yet," Ward said. "I'll have my people run fresh scans."

"Out here, specifically," Tasker advised.

"Okay. We have other problems, though. Finway's security cameras picked up Katryzna and he's got people looking for her. It's far outside my jurisdiction. London have also suggested a connection between Lyon, Laukstad and Graystown."

"But you haven't told them anything?"

"No. I want to be sure there isn't still someone there who can sweep it away. I want to send someone to assist you, though, Agent Tasker. A medical expert at least. We have a man in Nairobi, and I can get a review team, properly vetted –"

"No," Tasker said, more firmly than he intended. He forced his tone softer. "No, Deputy Director Ward. I'm not sure who'll come back from Ikiri or what state they'll be in; I need to assess it myself before we draw anyone else in."

"But if you're not fit –"

"I am," Tasker said, and the forcefulness of it made him wince. He corrected, "I will be. We're not going to leave the Congo without trouble, and our own people might add to it. But I'd like you to . . ." He hesitated. "I'd like you to see that there's no clear connection between anything that happens here and my family."

"Agent Tasker, please," Ward replied quietly.

"Make sure," he pressed. "I want the Legion to have no cause to go after them. If I don't come back, it has to end with us, out here."

"I would much prefer if we *stop* the Legion," Ward said.

Tasker gave a mean laugh. "At the risk of setting up the MEE in their place?"

"That's not for you to decide," Ward said. "I told you I have people I trust, I've dealt with Ministry corruption before – no matter how high it goes –"

"It's not going to get any of us home," Tasker said. "Do that for me, Sam? Insulate my family from this. The others', too."

Ward was quiet. Hating this call. Didn't often get in this spot watching manhole covers in Ordshaw, Tasker supposed. He waited, and finally she conceded. "Of course, I will do everything I can."

"Thank you," Tasker said. "There's one more thing. I need money. Lots of it."

Without asking much more, despite clearly wanting to, Ward agreed to Tasker's arrangements, and by the time they'd finished their call she said her people had found no sign of big novisan surges that morning. Not in the Congo or elsewhere. If it had happened, they could not monitor it, which Tasker suspected was fully possible for Ikiri. He ended the call and looked to the crumpled bedsheets, wet with sweat, and the dark lump of a gun that sat by the pillow. Time to get to work, he decided.

It helped quieten his clambering thoughts, having a physical goal, and he hazily dragged himself to the lift. He could talk with the staff at reception, get a feel for whether the hotel itself was compromised. With Ward's finances, he'd go down a Katryzna route. No sense calling in potentially-compromised Ministry agents. He'd recruit locals with only one focus: getting paid.

Then he was passing through the reception area, offering weak smiles, only vaguely aware of the staff watching him with concerned expressions. A woman rushed to take his elbow, offering to help him to the restaurant, or did he wish to go to the pool? Then he found himself in the rec room Shearjoy had commandeered and slumped on a sofa. The lady from reception shared words with the guy at the bar, both watching Tasker, and he caught the attention of two or three others sipping beer. In the far corner, on a high stool, sat the moon-faced white man, watching Tasker over a newspaper.

Shearjoy could have bought this whole hotel, everyone in it. He could have paid off every possible contact between here and the airport, leaving no chance of getting anywhere clear. The Legion had no need to act small. But Tasker suspected they wouldn't be so brazen. The fewer people involved the better, and from the way the hotel staff regarded him, he believed they were merely concerned, with no worse motivations. No, it was just the one man he had to worry about right now.

Tasker shifted uncomfortably, the pistol in his belt digging into his back. His skin felt warm all over, except his head, which throbbed icily with uncertainty or fever or what, he didn't know. He forced a smile when the receptionist returned, a big glass of water in one hand, a beer he'd apparently asked for in the other. She smiled back and watched him as she backed out of the room.

Two men in shirts, hunched over their drinks, resumed a conversation, pointedly not looking his way. The barman cleaned glasses. Another patron gathered up papers he'd been mulling over and left. Tasker watched them all, wanting them to know he was watching them, and the white man stared back, unflinching.

Minutes could have passed, or hours, Tasker couldn't tell, but eventually the other guests left, the rec room quietening for the afternoon. Had the Legion man warned them off? He hadn't seen any exchanges.

But then the barman was gone, too, and it was just Tasker and Shearjoy's man, still staring at one another across the full length of the room.

The double doors burst open and a second man hurried in. Another white man, unshaved. He frowned to see Tasker, before rushing to his companion and whispering something. The pair exchanged a heated discussion for a moment, and then the newcomer strode broadly back out the room, glaring Tasker's way. Tasker suspected whatever he himself might have sensed, and his effort to get down here and face them, might have rattled these men. Lost touch with Shearjoy, maybe? Picked up the disturbance themselves and knew things were bad?

The man tossed his paper aside and finally approached Tasker. Tasker sat up, to draw away from the back of the seat and make the gun accessible. The man said, accusingly, "Shouldn't you be resting?" Thick accent. Turkish? Or was Tasker not hearing clearly. He offered a questioning look in response and the man said, "Are you on medication? Should you be drinking?"

"What's it to you?" Tasker replied, his own voice unclear.

"I suggest you go back to bed."

"Have you heard from them?" Tasker asked. The man frowned, unsure about answering – should he admit to having anything to do with the Legion? "How long's it been? Two days?"

"In your condition? Better you go back to bed," the man kept on. "Yes, I think we talk to the hotel staff. Make sure you don't have unwelcome visitors or go wandering." He gestured to Tasker's shoulder. "We don't want you hurting yourself."

"Uh-huh." Tasker breathed in slowly. If the man was trained by the Legion, he might have picked up some of the original survivors' skills. He would be deadly, either way. But this was the time to lay their cards on the table. He said, "Maybe it's better I just shoot you here and now?"

The man stiffened, processed that and decided to laugh. Tasker pulled the gun out and laid it on the table. The man's smile vanished, the pistol making him freeze without Tasker needing to lift it. He wasn't sure if he would have had the strength to pull the trigger or the sense to shoot straight.

"You and your friend," Tasker said, "are going to leave this hotel in the next hour, and you're not coming back. That'll be how long my local agents take to set up a perimeter with a kill order."

"A kill order?" the man scoffed. "You are half dead. You are in no position –"

"All the more reason" – Tasker slid the gun closer as he leant forward – "for you to back the fuck off. I am taking no chances. Leave. Now."

The man stared, weighing up his options. Clearly his orders didn't include harming Tasker before it was necessary. Nor did his loyalty, apparently, stretch to putting himself in harm's way. Finally, he raised both hands and said, "Enjoy your drink."

He backed out of the room, like he believed Tasker still might shoot him.

Once in the lobby, he shouted something in Turkish, getting his friend moving. Tasker slumped onto the table. The barman reappeared, then, slipping in from a backroom, and Tasker met his eye. This would be somewhere to start. See if he had any friends who wanted to earn some quick cash. He'd set things in motion, at least, before the wound made him pass out again. The best he could do for the others, provided they could make it back from wherever they'd ended up.

# 28

Reece scraped his knees over rock and grazed his palms pushing up. He blinked into the darkness. There was no one else there, and as he probed through nothingness ahead with his arms, his footsteps echoed high, indicating a huge chamber. He called out, "Leigh? Zip? Where y'all at?"

The words bounced back at him and the sound of his footsteps changed, becoming metallic, *chiming*. Like the rocky ground hid metal cymbals. Looking back the way he'd come, or thought he'd come, he couldn't see a thing, but sensed it stretched a long way. Had he fallen? Down from the cave mouth into a sinkhole? He would've noticed, wouldn't he?

"Stay away," a voice called from high up. Reece spun to try and pick it out. "Stay. Away." A young boy, frightened.

"That you, Ezekiel?" Reece called back, echoes turning round his head. Then the crash of a cymbal. He looked down, couldn't see what he was standing on but it felt like solid ground. "Kid? You there?"

*There – there – there –* his voice faded into the black.

"Here!" Zip's voice, then, sharp and clear, off to the side. Reece called out to her, but only echoes answered. He jogged towards the voice, arms out in front of him.

"I hate you!" the boy cried.

"– only want to –" A fragment of Zip's response.

Reece chased the sounds, picking up speed as he found no obstacles in the way, almost running in the dark. The voices faded and his clanging footsteps got quieter, and suddenly he was moving through a silent abyss, even his own breath making no noise. He tested his voice and nothing came. He tried shouting. Mute. Clasped his hands over his ears, freezing at the deafness. He yelled silently into the void.

"All suffering . . ." The boy's voice came in a whisper just over his shoulder, and Reece spun, panic rising. He heard *that*, but nothing else. Fear swarmed on him – if he couldn't hear, what was he worth, what was *life* – and the weight of the thoughts pulled him down onto his knees, his groaning unheard.

"– can help –" Zip's voice slipped through, and sense flooded back. Reece heard his own breathing again and uttered a prayer. He listened for more, trying to pick out the children's distant argument.

A pinprick of light appeared. Reece stood again, blinking. Yes. An opening in the dark. He moved towards it and it grew larger as he approached. His footsteps got louder again, twanging with the abrupt, unreal notes of an immense piano. The chamber took an age to cross, but the opening got closer: a passage with a faint red glow. A silhouette stood there in the entrance. A man, his height, waiting and watching. Face unfamiliar.


Leigh-Ann walked through an overgrown tunnel of leaves and vines, bright with sunlight from an impossible source. White and pink flowers dotted the surroundings, beautifully fertile, alive. She wasn't sure how long she'd been walking, but it felt like a while, and her body had recovered, chest not hurting, lungs working like she hadn't spat them out running. Running where? How long ago? It didn't matter, she was in the most beautiful passage she'd ever seen, inhaling life.

"Little children suffer," a child's voice whimpered, and she froze.

"Hell was that?" Leigh-Ann asked the world.

"*Suffer,*" the voice repeated, more nasty, pointed. The leaves around her wilted, going quickly brown. Leigh-Ann backed up fast, the rot spreading like it might catch her. She turned and found the passage blocked not ten yards back, a tangle of broken logs and vines hanging across it. She turned again and found another passage, a new route that hadn't been there before. She jogged into it as the dying branches swept up behind her with a groan and a crackle, decay given voice.

Leigh-Ann picked up speed as the passage widened, and she remembered this fearful feeling. They'd been chased through the damn Congo, they were about to be killed when she fell into this place. Into a cave, which wasn't a damn cave, this was –

She skidded out of the passage to see a sweeping, glorious valley, wide as a field but curving up at the sides, like she was in an impossibly big bowl of plant life. Knee-high grass, stalks of flowers she'd never seen the likes of before, small trees whose winding roots promised ancient life. Greenery covered every inch of the place, snaking over rocks and rising up the curved walls which blended into sky, so that it was unclear where the plants ended and the brilliant blue expanse began. Leigh-Ann stared at it, trying to focus, but she couldn't make sense of it.

"– my friends!" Zip's voice came from somewhere up there, like a trumpet from Heaven.

Leigh-Ann shouted back, "Zip! Where are you?"

She moved into the valley, having to skip down the steep slope, gaze up, but the kid didn't answer. Another sound drew her attention forward again. Powerful running water. She moved closer to it, and picked out a grinding quality to the rush, like something was being broken up in rapids. The valley floor rose in a bank that she climbed, the sound becoming a torrent as she approached. She crested the slope and looked into the flow of a wide, glowing river of shimmering crystals, tumbling over each other, both fluid and solid at the same time.

"The fuck," Leigh-Ann whispered, transfixed. The waves of the crystal river warped hypnotically beneath her, sparkling with every colour and no colour at all.

"Don't belong here!" the boy's voice screeched suddenly behind her and Leigh-Ann spun with alarm, catching something in her eye. She lost her footing, or the ground fell away, or *something* – she was falling, and shrieked as the crystals engulfed her.


Henri knelt before an altar in a church that rose to impossible heights, crafted from winding tree trunks and thickly-leafed branches. The arches breathed and windows poured light on him; a living, natural church, celebrating all that was good. His heart grew as he stared, knowing this place to be pure, nothing like they had warned. A piece of him belonged here. A piece of everyone belonged here.

A shriek made Henri jump and spin round. It was gone as quickly as it came and he couldn't pinpoint the origin. Only now he realised he didn't remember coming here, and wasn't there something he should be doing? The church stretched a mile back, past pews of mossy stone, the air above twinkling starlight.

In the aisle stood his sister. Henri hurried down steps towards her, raising a hand, needing to touch her, to know she was real. He whispered her name: "Sara? You're here? You're alive?"

But as he got closer, her features faded, and his hand passed right through her. With a rush of air, she was gone, leaving behind only the faint memory of her smile. Henri stared at the empty space. She was here and she was real. She still had a presence, somewhere nearby, or all around him?

Words came to his mind and Henri muttered them aloud: "Whoever shall do the will of Heaven, the same is my brother, my sister, my mother."

"Heaven's will," a voice responded. Small, tremulous. Henri frowned, trying to see where it came from, but the walls of the church started to darken and fall away. Vines of wicked thorn crept in, reaching like tentacles, and Henri quickly backed up the aisle. The windows split with a web of cracks, the altar shook.

"Ezekiel, is that you?" Henri shouted. "I am your uncle – we're family!"

"Suffer!" the voice rose, impossibly loud, making Henri cry out. Through cracks in the ceiling, beams of shadow came down, decaying what they touched, draining colour. But a second voice responded, almost as loud, twice as desperate, "Speak to me!"

Little Zip, reaching out. Her voice cast beams of light that steamed through the shadow. Both shook the church, both dangerous in their own way, and more cracks spread. Henri continued back-pedalling, before turning on his heel and running.


Katryzna walked miserably down a tunnel, supporting herself with one hand on the stone, the other hanging limply at her side, dripping stupid blood. She had to hunch to fit in the cave, but it was big enough to walk in and somehow slightly light. The rocks had a kind of glow. But she had no idea where this tunnel was leading, or where everyone else had gone. What she did know was that this was not the same place General Solomon had led her to before. It was a cold and boring and empty cave, with none of the throbbing horror she'd felt last time.

Then, this still wasn't a nice place, and it was confusing, because she seemed to be deep within it and didn't remember walking all this way or separating from the others. And she heard occasional sounds like whispers, but it might have been the wind.

She had other things to worry about, anyway, like the fact that Eyes was not exactly dead. Or was he? Some nightmare version of his corpse had tried to cut her in half. His machete had nicked her cheek and caught her left bicep, and she had bled a lot, but she didn't intend to stop and worry about that. Her aim was to find the others, then get back outside and put Eyes to rest. She wondered if it was something she had always known she needed to do. Eyes was still out here, suffering. She had to help him move on.

"At least I can put my skills to good use," she commented. Rurik couldn't complain about that, could he? But her conscience was silent. Even more strange: he wasn't there. She was alone. Completely alone, and bleeding in a pointless cave. She thumped her fist into the rock and snarled. This was not how it was supposed to go.

She had friends now. Sean liked her. Reece liked her. Leigh was getting there. They all needed her and appreciated her and she was *not* supposed to die alone, lost in a cave. Frustration mounting, she shouted, "Where are you? Reece?"

Katryzna listened for an answer, but none came. Huffing, she continued, dragging her feet. But a few steps more and pain struck her, burning in her stomach. She bent forward, gasping. It took a moment to push it down, and she rested against the wall. What now? Food poisoning? Internal bleeding from an unnoticed blow?

It gripped her again, blind agony making her crease up, and she cried out.


The silhouetted stranger stepped back, as wary of Reece as he was of him. He had a soft-featured, uneven face, punctuated by a wart under his right eye. He was rotund around the belly but otherwise slim, and wore formless clothes a dull shade of accumulated filth, so old the stitching had come loose around one sleeve. Reece looked from his frightened eyes to the tunnel behind him, a shaft of strange-coloured rock. Clay? It went up in a long, straight line.

"Reece," the man said, tentatively.

"You one of them?" Reece asked. "Got left behind?"

The man shook his head. He wiped a thick-fingered hand on his grubby top and held it out. "Rurik."

Reece stared for a second. "You are not."

The man nodded nervously.

"Then you're not real," Reece decided. Which wasn't much of a surprise, considering his experience in the empty chamber. The voices overhead.

The alleged Rurik shrugged. "Maybe not. But I am here." He spoke with a Russian accent, thicker than Katryzna's. And he looked the right sort of scared for an imaginary friend finding itself visible to someone new.

Reece asked, "What the hell is going on?"

"I don't know," Rurik admitted. "Katryzna is close but I'm . . . a little disconnected."

"But you're not *real*," Reece insisted. "You're in her head – and you're supposed to be small!"

"I know!" Rurik shared the exasperation. He threw his hands up to indicate the walls. "This place is unnatural! My purpose is to question her, and without that I'm –" He spun around. "I can't be here."

"Christ," Reece said. Now he didn't just have an impossible location to deal with, but someone else's conscience with an identity crisis. Couldn't help feeling Mason or Shearjoy or *anyone* could've better prepared him for this.

"I need to find –" Rurik started, but was cut off by a boom. The walls shook and dust trickled from the ceiling as the boy's voice returned: "Seek death! Desire to die!"

"The fuck," Reece muttered, as the chamber rattled. Something cracked above, and he sprang back as a vast shape dropped through the darkness. It crashed into the ground with enormous weight, the tremor almost knocking him off his feet. Rurik caught him and Reece stared with alarm at a fallen hunk of ceiling. Not sure which part of all this was strangest. He said, "Let's move?"

"Agreed."

They headed quickly up the tunnel as the chamber continued to quake behind them, rocks cracking and tumbling. As they moved, the sounds quietened and the shaking stopped. This passage was somehow insulated from what they'd left behind.

"Did you come this way? Know what's up here?" Reece asked.

Rurik shook his head. "I don't –" He considered how best to word it. "Time and space do not work the same way for me as you."

"Because you're not real. So where did you come from?"

"We were outside," Rurik said. "With the monsters about to get us. You and Katryzna were together. Perhaps that's why I'm here to help you."

"Help me?" Reece frowned. "No offence, but if you're here to offer moral guidance, I'm good." Rurik shook his head, and pointed up the passage. Reece saw it was lighter in the distance, maybe another opening?

"I think I can lead you out."

Reece squinted and continued up the tunnel, the incline getting steeper, until he was stooped, using his hands to pull him up. The walls – stone sweating, wet – closed in, tighter, and he had to wriggle through, like the tunnel was shrinking the further he went. The rocks seemed to move around him. The light became blinding, as bright and brilliant as the previous chamber had been dark and empty.

Rurik encouraged him on: "Keep going! Almost there."

Then the ground fell away, and Reece was airborne, falling through brilliant white, before he landed hard on his rear and the light cut away to reveal a craggy cave. Katryzna stood over him, hands on her knees as she coughed and spluttered. She froze with alarm, then croaked, "How did you –"

Reece shook his head, no explanation.

Katryzna looked from side to side, distrusting the cave, as Reece got to his feet. He patted the rock to check it was real, and she asked, seriously, "Were you in my head?"

"No, I was in a . . ." Reece didn't have an explanation. This cave was completely different to wherever he'd been walking, with no sign of how he could've got here. "This place is messing with our minds, right?"

"It *wasn't*," Katryzna said. "I was doing fine until you fell out of my mouth. Reece. You are not allowed in there."

Reece frowned, trying to backtrack and somehow explain it. "I was lost in the dark, there were strange sounds – did you pull me out? Through Rurik?" Katryzna stared at him like he was crazy. He noticed her arm, then, slick with blood, and he stepped towards her. She flinched, to strike him, and he raised a hand.

"You're hurt," he said.

"I know."

"Let me help." He came closer and she lowered her fist, watching him warily. Her sleeve was cut already. He ripped it off and swallowed concern at the gash below. He tied the sleeve around the wound. Hissing, she raised the other hand to hit him again, but instead grabbed his shoulder, squeezing hard as he tightened the rag.

"Should slow the bleeding." Reece stepped back. "But we gotta do something more about it. And your face."

"Do something about *your* face," Katryzna said, and turned to start walking. "I'm not the one who appeared out of nowhere. Did you see any creatures down here?"

"No," he said, falling into step behind her. "I think we're safe from that at least. But I met someone claiming to be Rurik."

She stopped abruptly and gave him a scowl.

"Sounded Russian. Different accent to yours, right?" Her scowl softened, slipping halfway to confirming he might've actually met her conscience. Reece checked the cave again and some kind of explanation started creeping to mind. He said, "You been here all along? Someplace normal?"

"It is not normal."

"Better than where I was. Heard any voices?"

"Not even Rurik."

"I think you resisted it. This place. And maybe a part of you pulled me out of whatever mindscape I got stuck in. That's –"

A thin, frightened voice echoed down the cave, carried from a long way off. The pair shared a brief look, and Katryzna suggested, "Zippy?"

Leigh-Ann tumbled through the crystal water, drawn by a strong current. She grabbed about, trying to slow herself or at least get upright, but she couldn't figure up for down or left for right, and when she tried to shout or even breathe her mouth ballooned with water that felt packed with chunks of salt. It swept through her, kind of evaporated, so though she gagged she wasn't drowning fast. But she *was* drowning, getting pulled down into the terrible river. Dark, alone, forgotten, not even able to scream.

She lost momentum as she lost energy, unable to fight against the push, and her arms grew heavier, legs difficult to kick. Going limp, she gagged again, feeling life slipping away with her last air.

A steel grip caught her upper arm, and she was thrust up, out of the water, gasping for air. She spun, vision too bright to make out exactly what was around her, so she just bucked and struggled until thick arms wrapped over her and stilled her, a man's soft voice saying, "It's okay, you're okay."

He released her and she staggered two steps to the side, looking back with alarm. Henri raised his open hands. She glanced from him to the river. A trickle of a stream now, between rocks, no grass here, and the crystal light of the water was quickly fading. In seconds, it went still, shimmering like a pond, and it was all Leigh-Ann could do not to scream at how little fucking sense it made.

"You're okay," Henri repeated, locking onto her gaze, slowing his breathing. Demonstratively, she realised. Helping her to slow her own breath. She nodded back.

"I'm okay," she said, hoarsely, "but this place ain't." Her clothes, she noticed, were dry. Hair and skin too. But cut. Little scrapes all over, small cuts on her hands. Wasn't all imaginary, exactly.

Henri nodded. "But I think I've found a way through. Look." He pointed up, to the side, and Leigh-Ann saw they were in a cavern pointy with stalactites and jagged edges, barely lit by the glow of the water below and the exit Henri indicated above. A short climb up immense rocks that formed a natural staircase. Actually, scratch natural, they were neat and grand like steps laid for a giant.

"Seriously?" Leigh-Ann asked. Her voice was raggedy, she'd had enough.

"That's where the children are," Henri said, quietly. "Do you see her?"

Leigh-Ann looked again, squinting up the stairs. There was a silhouette there. A woman. Flickering in and out of existence like a candlelit shadow. As she stared, it disappeared entirely and the light faded, leaving only the open maw of a cave. Leigh-Ann said, "You explain any of this?"

"Not much," Henri said. "But there's part of my sister still here, in Ikiri. And Zipporah is working hard to keep us safe. We are lucky to have got this far."

"No shit." Leigh-Ann took a deep breath. Nothing left for it, she guessed, but to chase that shadow woman up the giant staircase. Not like the place could get much weirder. She gestured for Henri to lead the way, and he did so cautiously. The steps were too high to walk up, needing a bit of climbing, but they got there. Henri helped where it was steepest. Finally, they reached the opening, and Leigh-Ann uselessly patted some of the heaps of dust off her pants as they moved through to another chamber.

Leigh-Ann froze on the threshold and Henri went rigid next to her.

They looked down towards Zip and what had to be her brother, in what, for want of a better explanation, must've been the heart of Ikiri. Leigh-Ann summarised, weakly, "This place is fucked up."

# 29

Zip and Ezekiel were standing at the centre of a cavern that made Reece's first empty abyss seem small. It was an immense, near-perfect sphere, with faint ridges running around the full circumference like tiny ledges. The rock walls were interrupted occasionally by openings at various heights, holes into tunnels. The entrance Reece stood in with Katryzna was high in the upper hemisphere, making it impossible to climb down.

The children were on a plateau of rock in the middle, which rose maybe ten feet from the base and was toothed around the edges with rocky outcrops whose tips glowed faint blue. Similarly luminescent vines hung from the ceiling, giving the chamber an ethereal glow. Past the children, at the edge of the circle, was a cage of uneven rock pillars with someone hunched inside, penned in tight. Mason?

Reece took a good look at Ezekiel. He was the same height as Zip, hair longer, dark and sleek, and he was much skinnier. He faced his sister in a stand-off, hunched up and edgy as she raised her hands in a placating manner. Zip insisted, "I care about you! My friends care about you."

"Don't lie," the boy snapped. His clothes were so ragged they could've been old bandages, covering him in strands and trailing where they'd come loose.

"Look at the state of him," Reece said.

"He is a miniature mummy," Katryzna said. "No wonder this place is cursed." She made a surprised noise, and turned to her shoulder. "You have some explaining to do." Evidently Rurik had returned and Reece couldn't see him. Katryzna said, "He says this place was cursed before the boy got here."

Ezekiel barked nervously back at Zip, like a cornered animal, and with each sound the chamber crackled and the light flickered, tied to his mood. Zip tried again to soothe him: "Let me –"

"Nasty, brutish, selfish," Ezekiel hissed. "All over the world. Everyone hurts."

"*Sometimes*," Zip said desperately. "Everyone can be happy, too. Sometimes."

"You brought *him* here!" The boy pointed at Mason, who shifted in his cage with an angry, muffled sound, shoulders pressing against creaking rock. It looked like he'd outgrown an old cage that now totally squeezed him in. "He came to kill me. They all did. *You* brought them."

"No," Zip said. "They came to help me – we were never –"

"He says hi, by the way," Katryzna whispered, and Reece gave her a confused look. "Rurik. It was nice to finally meet."

"Later," he whispered, but she was already distracted.

"Look, Leigh!" Katryzna raised her voice. "Leigh! Over here! Henri!"

Reece cringed as her shout filled the cavern and Ezekiel screamed at the intrusion; the chamber lit up with thunderous bangs and electric sparks. Reece dropped back, pulling Katryzna with him as an arc of lightning exploded through the sphere and shot past them, lancing down the tunnel. It disappeared as quickly as it came.

Leigh-Ann shouted a curse and Reece rushed back into the tunnel mouth to see her and Henri in another opening, halfway down the other side of the sphere. Their opening was in the lower half of the sphere; they could slide down into the centre. But the room smelt like burning metal and steamed around the edges, hardly inviting.

The children were unaffected in the middle, though Ezekiel had retreated around a rock that half-hid him. Reece said, "Jesus, he's just a terrified kid."

"Who can throw lightning," Katryzna said.

Below, Zip was pleading, "No one wants to hurt you! We only want to help!"

"What use, the unrighteous witness!" Ezekiel cried madly.

"We need to get down there," Katryzna muttered. "Unless you have your gun?"

"I don't," Reece said. "Thankfully. We've gotta be careful."

"Yes? How do you want to handle it?"

Ezekiel was creeping back into the open, glowering at their position. He had jet black eyes, as dark and empty as Zip's were vibrant. However unnatural and powerful he might be, though, he was still a frail little shape. Reece said, "It's up to Zip. She's gotta talk him down."

"Ezekiel," Zip tried again, softly. "Ezekiel, please listen."

"Shouldn't be here," the boy replied. "None of you. Not *welcome*."

"We came to stop him, isn't it?" Katryzna said. "I only know one way, for sure."

"Might be time to learn another," Reece said. "He's a child, Katryzna."

"What, you have never killed a child before?"

He shot her a hard look, not on board for that joke, as the children batted each other's words back. But her face was serious. He said, "I'm not gonna let you do that."

"I do not need your permission –"

"He's a *child*," Reece repeated, frustration rising. Not just at her callousness, he realised, but at this whole fucked-up situation. Hadn't any of them taken a second to think about what would happen when they got here, faced with this? Only Zip, he realised. She'd said it herself. She didn't want to hurt her brother. But Mason had told them that was always the goal. Back when the children were born out here, he took Zip away while Eyes was left to deal with Ezekiel. Everyone was surprised Ezekiel was still alive; these maniacs had wanted him dead since he was born, they were so afraid of his power. And Katryzna had been Eyes' friend. Reece swallowed. "It didn't work out for the others, did it? For your friend?"

Katryzna's eyes narrowed. "All the more reason –"

"We're gonna find another way, okay?" Reece insisted. "I don't know how, but we've gotta. There must be another tunnel, we can get down there, help Zip. But we *have* to find another way. You wanna put Eyes to rest, not become him, don't you?"

She was impassive, as ready to strike him as accept that. But a part of her was reflecting on it, he could see that. She checked aside to the children, then back to their tunnel, and said, "Either way, we go down there."

"I know them," Ezekiel said, as he twitched from one side to another. Zip kept her distance. "I've felt every person and sorrow. Gods and abominations, sacrifice to devils."

"He's two crumbs short of a cracker," Leigh-Ann whispered to Henri as they peered back into the chamber.

Henri replied quietly, "There's bits of the Bible coming out of him. Sort of."

"How?" Leigh-Ann said. "How's he even know English, let alone the Bible?"

"Sara said it connects them to the world, Ikiri. All of life. And she was here with him, once. Stayed close."

"The sufferings of this time will be nothing," Ezekiel continued, tapping a finger into the opposite palm to help him recite something important. "Should be nothing. The glory will be revealed."

"Ezekiel." Zip shifted. "You don't have to do this. You don't have to stay here."

Her brother shrieked as she got too close. He stepped back and clutched his hair. "I want it to stop. You will stop it from stopping – you should *not* have come, you should not *be*. I know pain and misery. Only. But death ends suffering."

"I feel the bad, too," Zip insisted. "Maybe not like you, but I do. But can't you feel the good? People who'd do anything just to help?"

"No one helped me," Ezekiel said. "Not ever. My father –" He gestured erratically towards Mason's stone cage and sparks flew out of him. Leigh-Ann flinched as the chamber lit up and Mason shuddered in the tiny space. Henri moved to partly shield Leigh-Ann from whatever may come.

"Stop it!" Zip said, loudly. "Please! Let me show you the good!"

Ezekiel reeled on her. "Good? Christ came with peace and they killed him!"

It staggered Zip, his wild intensity. Seeing a way to help, Henri cleared his throat, but Leigh-Ann hissed, "Fuck's sake don't get his attention!"

Henri went ahead anyway, and called down, "Christ forgave."

Ezekiel scuttled to the side as though he'd been struck, moving into a spiderlike crouch. His eyes were wide, horrible holes. He mumbled rapidly to himself as he moved, the words getting louder, "He is family. Our blood –

another who left us –"

"Everyone thought you were dead," Zip told him. "No one knew –"

"Everyone *wanted* me dead!" Ezekiel screamed, and the stacks of rock lit up again. A lighter flutter of energy, only singeing the chamber. "I called darkness to defend me. I must, to make the world quiet. You are the danger, *people* are the plague, Ikiri is the cure. I've tried it, I know it."

"Shit, it's just like she said," Leigh-Ann said. "Kid's clueless, just a ball of mad emotions."

"You know it's not right," Zip was saying. "You haven't done all the terrible things you could because you *know* it's not right."

Ezekiel gave a scratchy, pitch-shifting cackle. "I thought you would stop me. I wasn't ready." He took quick steps back, raising his hands. "But can you? *Can you?*"

"If you help lower me," Henri said, "I think I can get down there."

"And get fried by electricity?" Leigh-Ann said.

Ezekiel lowered his arms and tried a smile. "You can help me, sister. We could do it together. Wash the world in blood and make it white."

"Like it ain't white enough," Leigh-Ann said, seeing Zip was rapt and this was only gonna get worse. She nudged Henri forward, agreeing to whatever hare-brained idea he had. He climbed over the tunnel lip, unnoticed by the children.

"You didn't choose his way," Ezekiel was saying, indicating Mason. "Now you can choose again. Do you choose me?"

Taking Henri's hand and a bit of his weight as he carefully slid down the steep slope, Leigh-Ann noticed shapes moving in another tunnel entrance, at the base of the sphere. Katryzna and Reece had found access, too.

"I do choose you," Zip insisted. "I choose to help you, and share my friends with you. The world is not all like Daddy. Or the dark things Ikiri shows you. I promise, there's laughter and animals and music and –"

"And the greedy tear it down," Ezekiel interrupted icily as Henri let go of Leigh-Ann and clumsily slid down. "You don't know. I can show you the world, Zipporah. I can show you Ikiri. Do you want to see what I see?"

Zip swallowed, then spread her arms. "Of course."

Ezekiel hesitantly spread his arms too, waiting for her to come to him instead. It excited Mason in his cage, making him rattle harder against the bars with angry sounds he couldn't quite get out. Gagged somehow. Zip stepped closer.

"This ain't good," Leigh-Ann told herself. Around the sphere, the others froze, watching.

Ezekiel folded Zip into a hug, then he squeezed and snarled, like he'd been waiting his whole life to spring this trap. Zip shrieked. Henri dived for the rocks and Leigh-Ann saw the briefest move from Katryzna before light burst from the children with another thunderous crack.

*

Katryzna jumped for cover, flattening Reece, as lightning arced overhead. It licked the walls around them, slapping stone with bangs. It crackled and spread.

"Up, move!" Reece shouted, pushing Katryzna off him. She pressed herself into the wall to avoid the blasting energy, the chamber too bright to see into, as Leigh-Ann yelled Zip's name. Reece swung an arm across Katryzna's chest, holding her back.

The lightning cut out and Katryzna went to move but Reece's arm stayed there. She bared her teeth as he looked her in the eye to say, "We gotta be careful."

It threw her momentarily. Was he trying to stop her or just trying to keep her safe? She didn't have time for this, but in her uncertainty she nodded rather than hit him, so he let go. Then she ran in. The central platform was vaguely smoking, and she could see the boy standing with a sickly smile.

"Sparky, get away from her!" Katryzna shouted, racing towards the rock wall. Ezekiel moved out of sight as she searched for handholds to pull herself up, and Reece ran to her side. He threaded his fingers to form a foothold and Katryzna frowned again, but he nodded urgently and she planted a shoe in his hands, letting him heave her up. She clambered over his shoulders and pushed his head to get a grip on the rock higher up, her cuts flaring with pain, then she swung over the edge of the platform and rolled to a stop. It struck her that this morning, Reece might have touched her more than most men ever had, and she had not hurt him. She *should* have hurt him, shouldn't have let him keep knocking her over or pulling her up. Except he had pulled her out of the way of blades and claws, and –

On her hands and knees, Katryzna paused, looking up to see Ezekiel was watching her. With his torn rags and dark hair and eyes, hands like claws and filthy skin, he was a wild animal, not as innocent as Reece said. He was half her height and would snap easily. Rurik told her, "He looks like you used to."

"Not *now*," she snapped.

Zip was down on all fours, stunned and hurt with a gentle steam rising off her, but alive. Mason pushed against the bars of his cage, which was cracked around the edges from the blast. Looking closer, Katryzna saw his mouth, then, messily stitched shut like a patchwork doll.

Ezekiel followed her gaze, hands restless at his sides. He made a weak, sorrowful noise, and said, "You don't understand. I didn't want you to come."

Reece's efforts to climb the wall behind Katryzna made her pause. She stood four or five paces from the boy, considering she did not have to kill him. She could just knock some sense into him. She took one step forward and Ezekiel gave a startled cry, throwing both hands up towards her. They lit up, like a double camera flash. But that was all. No boom, no lightning, and Ezekiel stared in horror at Katryzna. She stared back, no idea what just happened, except that it meant he could not stop her. His black eyes widened in fear. "How –"

"I won't," Zip said, with effort. She dropped back on her haunches, face slick with sweat. "I won't let you do any more."

"You *can't*," her brother hissed, and he raised his hands to her instead, but this time they merely fizzled. Zip winced, under strain, but she stared right back at him without fear.

"I understand it now," Zip said. "How it works. You won't hurt my friends."

With a scrape of rock, Reece huffed up onto the platform behind Katryzna. She looked down, unsure if she should help, as he clumsily finished the climb. The same time, Henri emerged from between the rocks on the other side, charred and dusty from rolling through the chamber.

Startled, Ezekiel turned on the spot. "You brought monsters here. To hurt *me*."

"No, Ezekiel," Henri said. "You know me, don't you? I swear if I had known I had a nephew, nothing would have stopped me from finding you. And these are my friends."

"Her?" Ezekiel sniffed a nasty laugh, pointing hard at Katryzna. "She was friends with Mr Eyes. The man who tried to murder a baby. *Me*." He swung the finger back to point at Mason. "Daddy's terrible friend. And Daddy is a terrible person." He leered at Zip. "You are, too!"

"No," Zip said.

"I am!" Ezekiel continued. "I need to be. My terrible things will make it stop. That's what you want, isn't it? Why won't you let me stop it all!" He spread his arms wide, towards the room, and again the room failed to spark. Thoughts came unbidden to Katryzna. This abandoned child was angry at the world. Friendless and left to burn in his own misery. Despite his frightened uncertainty, he kept going. "I can bring out people's true nature, you've seen it. I can make *everyone* see."

"Or you can find another way," Katryzna said, the words soft. The child eyed her fearfully, like he might scream if she moved any closer. A child, terrified despite his power, not just of her – of everything. She said, "If I am a monster, *przyganiał kocioł garnkowi*, tak?"

Ezekiel screwed up his eyes and she knew he understood; this place transcended language. They were the same. He said, weakly, "I have a plan, though."

"Hurt the world because it hurt you?" Katryzna said. "Because you have no one?" She scanned the others, Reece and Henri watching her warily, Zip exhausted, Leigh-Ann up in her tunnel. All were waiting, watching her, hanging on what she might do or say next. Hopeful, she realised, that she would do the right thing. Hopeful in a way no one ever was. She amused Eyes, didn't she? She entertained him. He never wanted her to change. She continued, quietly, "These are good people. Better than Eyes. All here for you. It is more than I ever had."

Ezekiel stared without responding, which was close enough to giving in. Those black eyes shimmered wet, emotions changing, and Katryzna gave Reece a quick questioning look. He nodded, just slightly, like she had done something right.

Zip shifted quietly forwards and held out a hand. Ezekiel stared at her, then back to the others, Reece, Henri, then Zip again. He whispered, "I've felt so much bad. Across the world. It hurts so much."

"We can help it," Zip replied. "We can do good together."

Ezekiel paused, just for a second, then sprang forward to embrace her. Katryzna tensed to jump but it was a genuine hug, free of thunder and electricity. The boy's shoulders shook as he sobbed.

Rurik murmured, "You see, you can –"

"Oh not *now*," Katryzna hissed and got a less favourable look from Reece.

Ezekiel blubbered, shuddering into his sister's shoulder. "I just – want it – to stop."

"Then let's stop it," Zip whispered, and as they squeezed each other, something passed between them. The room grew lighter, warmer, as though sunlight was pouring in. Katryzna watched the walls, where the rocks softened as she stared at them. Their texture changed – grass was sprouting.

"Do you see this?" she asked Rurik.

"We can –" Zip started, but there was a nasty crack in the rock, and a sudden, fast movement. As Zip shrieked, Katryzna looked back just in time to see Mason launching forward. The cage had weakened and he'd broken out to close the distance in one big, brutal stride.

The twins were separated as Mason ploughed through them, and Ezekiel was lifted skyward, folded over the big man's right fist. No, not a fist – the blade-hand stabbed out through the boy's back. Katryzna blinked as the boy's blood flicked over her and he dangled high above Mason's head. He regarded Ezekiel's twitching, gasping body without feeling, then swung his blade-arm aside so the boy flew off, over the edge of the platform. Zip, down on her back, screamed.

Mason tore the stitches from his lips, ripping his flesh, and shouted, "Finally! Well done, Zi –"

Katryzna was moving – the hope of moments before replaced with a need to kill. She yelled and Mason flashed to the side, so fast she barely saw it. Sharp pain swept up her right flank as she was slammed into the ground. She bounced, striking rock so hard it flipped her over to look up at him, his blade raised above a bloody grimace. Zip screamed again, loud and terrifying as all the beasts of the wild, and brilliant blinding energy burst through the room, throwing Katryzna right off the platform.

# 30

Reece was down on his knees, head ringing from the boom. The rocky walls came back into view as he started hearing groans. Not sure if the world was shaking or if it was just him. Limbs unsteady. It took him a few blinks to refocus. Still in the spherical chamber, but it was dotted with sparking lights. Cracks spread across the curved ceiling. Big chunks of rock were shifting. Hell, the chamber was coming apart. Behind the sparks and the snaps of emerging fissures, a wind was blowing. A powerful, loud push.

"We gotta go," he said loudly, to whoever might listen. He tried to stand and stumbled, braced himself against a wall. It was the base of the platform – he'd fallen off and was at the bottom of the sphere. He couldn't see who was still up there from this angle, but an unnatural bright light spread over its edges. There was someone else down on the ground, though – Henri, on his back, moaning as he slowly regained his senses. Reece staggered to him and repeated, "We gotta go!"

Reece pulled him up, the man heavy and not helping much, eyes lost. As Henri recovered, Reece looked one way and the other. There was a smaller body, around the curve of the platform base – Ezekiel. Reece ran to him but slowed, struck by the bloody mess of the child crumpled over the rocks. Ezekiel's black eyes were rolling and he was breathing, rasping through bloodied lips. Reece tried to pick out an exit: there was a tunnel mouth close by. "Hold on, kid, we're getting you outta here."

"Reece!" Leigh-Ann shrieked, and he looked up, seeing her in an opening above. She held onto the wall as the ground shook, then she looked over his head to the platform. "Oh shit, oh shit!"

"Leigh, you gotta get down here!" Reece shouted. "This place is coming down!"

"Do you see Zip?" Henri shouted.

Leigh-Ann nodded, transfixed, and said, "One of you get up there."

"You get Leigh, I'll handle the kids?" Reece hooked his arms under the child, taking care not to touch the chest wound, while Henri wordlessly rushed to start climbing the rocks.

"Zip, stop!" Leigh-Ann shouted. "You're bringing the place down!"

Reece straightened up with Ezekiel in his arms, the boy light as nothing. Had to get him clear, go back for Zip. He started for the nearest tunnel, but paused at the sound of Mason's cracking voice: "You see, you are the proof – *none* of you had my control!"

He was in pain, despite his words.

Reece tried to pick up his pace, but Ezekiel made a light, nasty little sound that made him pause. The dying boy was laughing, bloody face filled with malevolent glee. He coughed, though, staring up through the ceiling, and suddenly looked vulnerable again.

"That's enough, Zip – please!" Henri shouted. Reece threw a look back, saw Henri halfway up the slope, pausing in the act of trying to help Leigh-Ann down as he stared into the light. Across the other side of the shaking chamber, something snapped loose and fell – one of the hanging tendrils, which shattered against the ground.

"Stop," Ezekiel whispered. His black eyes fixed on Reece. "I have to stay."

Reece was locked still for a second. The cave was collapsing, and they needed medical aid. Except that blade had gone right the way through and there wasn't even a road out of this place, let alone a doctor within a hundred miles.

"You can't get out – not that way," Ezekiel said quietly. "Only with her."

Reece frowned, not following, but another look at the tunnel exit reminded him what they'd come through to get here. Ikiri wasn't natural, and that tunnel might as well lead into a pit of vipers or deeper underground as anywhere safe. The kids had some measure of control. There was no sense running.

"Okay," he said. "Okay, let's go."

He turned and carried Ezekiel quickly to the platform. He held him by the wall, trying to figure how he could climb with the boy. "You cling to my back –"

But Ezekiel suddenly writhed free from his grip and made his own unsteady way up over the lip of the platform. Reece hurried after him, slower as he struggled to find good places to hold. He froze halfway up as he saw Katryzna off to his left, spread out like a rag doll. Couldn't stop for her now; he heaved himself up and squinted into bright light as he picked out the silhouettes of Mason and Zip. Ezekiel hadn't got far, his burst of movement apparently over as he lay flat on his belly with blood smeared around him.

Zip stood in the middle of the platform with her arms spread to her sides, head forward. As Reece crept closer he saw the veins rising black all up her neck, like Stomatt and Tasker's wounds. Infected by Ikiri. Her eyes flared bright red. Mason was in front of her, hanging in the air like he'd been caught on a fishing hook, arms and legs twitching. He was bleeding from his nose and ears and out under his fingernails.

"Zip," Reece said, slowly standing. "What are you –"

Zip trembled from the strain of her focus as she held her father struggling in the air. More than held him, she was crushing him where he hung. The one-handed man gritted his teeth, eyes bulging, defiant to the end.

"Reece!" Leigh-Ann called from down below, a demand for a status report as she and Henri followed.

He shouted back, "Get Katryzna! Quick, Leigh!"

"I ain't going without –"

"We're right behind you!" Reece shouted, then turned forward. "Zip, you hear me?"

The room shook along with her, little stones crumbling out of cracks above, raining down. Reece sprang aside as one almost struck him.

"Give him to me," Ezekiel rasped and Zip's eyes finally shifted from Mason. Her father bobbed in the air, momentarily relieved. "Let me."

Zip suddenly came back to herself, his words cutting through, and her muscles relaxed all over. The glow cut out and Mason dropped heavily down, but the room didn't stop shaking and the cracks kept spreading. She regarded Ezekiel with horror. Forgetting her father, Zip ran to his side, crouched and took one of his hands. She scanned his wound as Ezekiel put on a strangely satisfied smile.

"I told you," he whispered, weakly. "I warned you."

"No," Zip said, tears filling her eyes. "We can save you! Take you away!"

"I cannot leave," Ezekiel replied, flatly. "Not ever. But I can take . . . that away." He indicated Mason with the barest nod.

"Please, Ezekiel, please," Zip cried, but his eyes were watching Mason as the one-handed man tried to rise from his knees. Reece stood over the children, not sure what he could do if the big man recovered enough to attack, but not moving either way. There was a huff and he glanced to find Henri climbing up beside him. Reece took his hand and hauled him up, and they both moved past the children, to block them from Mason. Henri warned the bigger man, "You stay down."

Mason looked up with an arrogant smile that invited the challenge, jaw bathed in blood from his torn stitches. The first sign of humour Reece had seen from him, and it was a vicious one. The room shuddered again and a great crack split along an upper edge.

"Help me," Ezekiel said. Couldn't quite sit up. Zip supported him with an arm around his shoulders as he dragged in painful breaths. "Purge . . . the evil."

Zip looked from him to Mason. Her father's amusement at Henri's threat shifted back to hate as he regarded his own children. But Zip had calmed from her own furious reaction, and her features softened as she stared back. She said, "I don't want to –"

Ezekiel clutched her hand and hissed. He looked older than before, a tired soul in a tiny, dying body. "I see your light, Zipporah. I wish I had it."

"You can!" she insisted. "You do!"

"Show me. One last time." He held his grubby hands up and Zip regarded them with worry. She looked to Reece and he had no words to help. Ezekiel had all the more reason to act on his grudges, now, to explode in whatever dark glory he still had left, annihilating his wicked father and all of them with him.

But Zip leant closer and whispered, "I will give you my light."

As they touched, the shaking calmed – only a little, with the walls still cracking, but there was a notable shift in the air. The children retreated slightly, looking into each other's eyes as though surprised at the charge that ran between them.

"You see?" Mason snorted a nasty laugh. Like his kids finally bonding was the biggest joke in the world. "You belong apart. You have *no idea* of the danger. You should've died out here. Better there never was an Ezekiel Mason."

The children's surprise shifted to fear, suddenly. He was right – they'd been playing before, acting on instinct, but now things were serious and they were afraid of themselves. Worse, they found a primal fear for their father, no matter what they could do.

Reece said, "That man don't own you, kids. All he's ever done is keep you down."

"And there never *was* an Ezekiel Mason," Henri said. "You are a Ngoi. Your mother was a beautiful and brilliant woman. She only wanted peace."

"And the darkness is *his*!" Zip added forcefully. "It's Ikiri! He left you. Trapped me!" She grabbed Ezekiel's hands tight in hers. "We can be whatever we want to be."

They disappeared into each other's eyes then, more passing between them as that combined energy rejoined, grew. It was thick in the air: an aura of Ezekiel's dark passion and Zip's noble light swam out around them, started to fill the room.

"Fools," Mason rumbled, finally shoving off the ground and regaining his feet. "They'll touch all life. They'll kill us all." He shook out his battered blade-arm, a reanimated mechanical monster standing tall before them. The children were far away, not seeing or feeling anything but each other's power, as the cave rattled harder, louder, and Mason readied himself. "Step away."

"I will not," Henri said, and Reece tensed alongside him. Between the two of them, against one man, it should've been good odds, but Mason wasn't normal and Reece couldn't see them buying much more than a second's time. Didn't matter. This was where they were and Mason was hesitating. He wanted them onside, not against him.

The walls shook more violently, the light brightening around the children. Mason said, "Can't you see what they're doing? Step *aside*."

Reece replied, "Fuck. You."

Mason stepped forward. Henri jumped at him without warning, swinging both arms around his waist and dragging the big man to the ground. Mason jammed an elbow up, injuries not slowing him as Henri was struck and rolled off him. Reece stepped in to swing a punch as Mason stood; he caught the man's jaw and felt like he'd hit a wall. Roaring, Mason kept rising, head cracking into Reece's nose and dropping him to the side. He rolled, pushed himself up, fighting through the daze, as Mason passed him. Henri sprang at him again, shouting defiance, and caught hold of Mason's leg. Before he could kick him off, Reece dived onto the other leg. Two grown men dragging at his ankles as Mason tried to shake them free. He drew his blade-arm up and Henri jerked sideways, pulling Mason's leg wide enough to stagger him. They fell down together in a messy heap, and while Mason kicked and tried to jam his arms back at them, Reece and Henri worked in unison to clamber over him, trying to pin him with their paired bulk.

They landed on an arm each, holding him down, and Reece looked up desperately to the kids, willing them to finish whatever they were building to. Mason bellowed as he bucked, his one arm throwing Reece off the ground – but Reece kept hold. Any second, Mason would break free, and they were within arm's reach of the kids. Henri threw a punch that snapped Mason's head back into the rock and Reece scuffed a knee into the guy's ribs. Then the big man burst upward with a volcano of force that threw them both back. He landed in a crouch, arm cocked back, bent blade ready to strike. A split second too late.

The children lit up like a flare and Mason screamed a base, pitiful noise as he was momentarily stunned by the brightness. Somewhere in the light, Reece sensed another presence: a woman, larger than life, bursting out in a wordless expression of peace. But the room made a violent rending sound like it was snapping in half, and Reece looked up to see a great hunk of the ceiling falling towards them. It crashed through the platform, with a force that threw Reece back. When he looked up, Mason was gone. Only a great hunk of stone and billowing dust where he'd been. The kids sat calmly together just clear of it, completely unscathed, glowing brighter.

Henri was at Reece's side then, pulling him up, saying, "Take the boy, I'll grab Zipporah! Before we're all crushed!"

Reece nodded numbly, both of them moving towards the ball of light that was the children. But as he reached out to touch them, the light flared brighter, and the world dropped away.


Leigh-Ann was stumbling through the cave, legs barely carrying her as she struggled with Katryzna weighing down her shoulder, trying to ignore the sounds of falling rocks and fighting that said nothing good was happening in the cavern behind them. Her one small mercy was that Katryzna wasn't dead or quite comatose, however bad she looked, and, after Leigh-Ann's weak-ass efforts at dragging her, the woman had stirred just enough to shift her feet and carry a mite of her own weight.

But the tunnel was shaking like the world was being pulled apart, and when Leigh-Ann tried to speed up she only tripped and dragged them both into the wall. Katryzna's eyes opened wider and her grip tightened, but she didn't get much sense back – only enough to mutter, "You are saving me?"

Leigh-Ann hoisted her up again, snapping, "Be better if you could save yourself!"

A quake almost shook her right off her feet again, and she looked back to see the tunnel filled with light like a train was speeding towards them. She didn't have time to yell as it struck and flooded her senses. She was suddenly weightless, losing the feeling for everything around her, even Katryzna.

And as she floated through the light, a strange peace grabbed her. Maybe this was Heaven? If this was death then at least it was painless.

The light started clearing, though, the world coming back into focus, and the scene ahead was at once familiar and a long way from paradise. The trees of the Congo stood before her, and spread between them were body parts and blood. The earth shook behind her, and the rocks crumbled with one last, groaning explosion of dust.

# 31

Reece waved a hand to clear the dust, which didn't help much. It was thick on his skin like a layer of salt. But though the dust twirled as it slowly cleared, the rest of the world was still. Quiet at last.

He carefully walked forward, checking in with his body as he touched the trunk of a tree. Outside again. Couple of scrapes and bruises, maybe, and one of his sleeves was hanging loose, but he'd made it out all right, all else considered. He could smell the grass and soil. Blue sky glinted through branches above.

Reece made his way slowly through tall grass, navigating gaps in the trees and roots with no path to speak of. Forest behind him and forest ahead. He used the ground's gentle incline to give him some sense of direction; if in doubt, going up seemed sensible. He'd get his bearings from higher ground. He felt a long way from the caves of Ikiri, though. One second he'd been bathed in light, the next out here in the open, and he wasn't sure how much of all they'd seen was even real. It felt dreamlike now, and there was absolutely no accounting for time or space in there. But they weren't questions he cared to answer yet. He needed to find the others, that was all.

Gradually, leaving the dust behind for familiar forest, Reece picked up a sense of a direction that felt right, and continued up one hill then down a slope. Without being able to explain it, he knew there was something ahead, and the closer he got the stronger that feeling became. Finally, the trees thinned and he made out a small grassy clearing. There were people there. Reece's heart lifted, but he slowed down at the edge of the trees when he made them out properly. Henri stood a little back from three smaller forms. Zip crouching next to her brother, little different to how they'd been on the cavern platform – and another body laid out on the grass.

Reece crept quietly out, with a grim idea he was about to find the children mourning their dead father. Little Ezekiel looked as innocent and vulnerable as Zip ever did, finally free of the cave and especially grubby and frail in the daylight. Both of them were coated in dirt that'd need hosing off. And beside them in the grass lay not Mason but a wild-looking woman in a threadbare slip of clothing, hair so long it stretched down her sides like an open shroud. She held the total peace of death, and somehow, without needing to make immediate sense of it, Reece got a feeling he knew her.

She'd been in there with them? She'd risen up, when the kids united.

The crunch of Reece's feet made Henri and the children look to him, their faces drawn down in sadness. Zip's cheeks glistened with tears. He wanted to ask if it was over, if they'd won, even what the hell had happened, but none of that could come out.

"Have you seen the others?" Henri asked, voice croaky.

"Not yet," Reece said. "Are y'all hurt?"

Henri shook his head. Zip stood, dusting her clothes down with careful attention and zero effect. She appeared decades more mature, her sad face too serious for such a small child. She reached up to take Henri's hand and turned square onto Reece, and he wondered at the change in her expression. It was in her eyes more than anywhere; those rich red eyes now looked deeper than before, tinged with shadow. Ezekiel stood, too, more hesitantly, his shy face turned down, his manic, frightened energy gone, along with, apparently, his wound. He'd changed too. His eyes were averted, but they were definitely different: lighter. Not far off the same shade as Zip's.

They had come together in there so powerfully, the pair had taken on some part of each other. And a piece of this woman down on the ground, too – she was their mother, wasn't she? The same time he realised all that, Reece sensed that Ikiri itself was gone. Some big part of it had been absorbed into the twins, but the rest of its power had exhaled in that great cloud of dust, as the earth crumbled on top of it.

"I don't understand *everything*," Zip said, evidently following his thoughts, "but we made things safer. Together, we touched everything before we closed the . . . door."

"You did?" Reece replied, wary of what that might mean, given Ezekiel's past.

"We drew the power back in," Ezekiel said, in a tiny, broken voice. "It's gone. At least from here, and those touched by it."

"Gone, like . . .?"

"The Legion will be weakened," Zip said. "The creatures stilled. The darkness passed."

Reece stirred, hearing more than he hoped to in that. He almost didn't dare ask, but said, "Stomatt and Tasker?"

Zip concentrated on that for a second, then said, reverting to the gentle modest kid he'd known, "I think they are okay. Thank you, Reece."

"Hell, all I did was stand there. Figure this young man gets the gratitude, dug himself out of a dark pit." Reece took a deep breath. "So what exactly *was* that place?"

Both children looked up at him, then, their wise eyes saying they knew but couldn't explain. A pocket of life, he figured. A pool of energy that could be warped in unnatural ways, and warped them just the same way.

There was a more important question, anyway, he guessed, and he asked, "It's over?"

"No," Ezekiel said, regretfully. "It's left problems behind." The tangled webs in Duvcorp and the Ministry and all over the world, for starters. The violence that had already been set in motion. "I didn't –"

"Know better," Reece got in quickly. "Shit. You didn't ever have a chance. All right. Are we . . ." He didn't especially want to ask, looking at the mother.

They didn't have tools to dig with and he wasn't sure he had the energy either. But she looked like she belonged there, a part of this land. Lived in a tree, they said. Sustained by Ikiri, the same way Vile and the monsters had been. When the children tore down that energy, she must've finally been put to rest.

"You go ahead," Henri said. "Find Leigh and Katryzna. I will see my sister is properly respected."


Some of the carnage ahead was what Leigh-Ann had seen happening, in flashes of panic as they'd fled from Ikiri's monsters. Bits of dark animals splattered about the place, blood up tree trunks and soaked into grass. But there was more now, she saw as she stood with Katryzna leaning against her. The remains of Chops, noticeable through shreds of clothing, and big hulking shapes of creatures that never should've been. The cave they'd entered was barely recognisable now, the wall of rock collapsed in on itself in a pile of huge, jagged slates, and in the blood-strewn clearing a man lay prostrate. Eyes, Katryzna's man, darkly wrapped in a long, draping coat, with only patches of sallow flesh, looking more a corpse than ever, that crude machete discarded at his side. He had a deep gash across his throat, which looked like it hadn't even bled. By all appearances, the man *had* been dead all these years, and was thankfully dead again.

But he'd left a different problem behind, as Shearjoy sat perched on one of the big boulders that'd fallen loose during the cave's collapse, idly twirling his rapier, tip resting between his feet. He looked cleaner than anyone had a right to be out here, no blood on him, and he gave her a cheery smile like she'd just arrived to his tea party. He asked, "I take it things went well?"

"The hell would I know," Leigh-Ann answered as she helped Katryzna down, to prop her against a rock. The woman was limp and pale with blood loss. Maybe exhausted or maybe she'd broken every bone in her body. Leigh-Ann said, "We survived, me and her. That's all I can say. You took care of all these by yourself?"

Shearjoy shrugged, then admitted, "Whatever happened in there hindered them. Then, ultimately, let them go." He titled his sword hilt towards Eyes' body. "Put them back to sleep."

"And you, what, sat hiding while we did the heavy lifting? That place was messed up."

"I warned you to stay away."

"Like we had a choice! Damn." Leigh-Ann checked the trees. So still and quiet now. But there was an ugly smell in the air, with all the blood and the bodies stewing in the heat of day. "You seen Reece? The others?"

"No," Shearjoy said. "But I'm dying to know what happened. The boy's gone, isn't he?"

"You tell me," Leigh-Ann said. He was watching her in a way she didn't like. Shouldn't be just her and this freak talking, out in the woods. And the cave behind her had collapsed – was there any hope the others had escaped?

She frowned. No, there had to be hope, because she was pretty sure she hadn't come out that way herself. Just kind of appeared here. None of that damn place made any sense. She said, "Maybe we oughta check the area – Reece can't be far off."

"Very sensible." Shearjoy jumped down from his rock and flexed his shoulders, gave his sword a little spin. She regretted stirring him into action, and looked down at Katryzna, wishing this woman would wake up. But Katryzna was awake – she was just staring at Eyes' body.

Shearjoy strode past it, towards them, saying, "How do you feel? We found the effects of Ikiri were immediate. Though it took many years to hone our talents."

"I feel like shit," Leigh-Ann said. "Pretty damn sure I didn't acquire no talents."

"Are you?" he replied. He'd already made up his mind, by the sound of it. No one came back from Ikiri unchanged, these bastards kept saying that. "If we'd known what was to come, back then, things would have been so much easier for everyone. It could've all ended before it started. Still, I like to believe there's no such thing as failure as long as you learn from your mistakes."

Leigh-Ann stiffened. "Lot of dead people who ain't coming back might disagree."

It made him smile. Not in a good way.

"Eyes," Katryzna finally spoke. She rubbed a hand over her face, then shakily stood, apparently still able to move. Ignoring Leigh-Ann and Shearjoy either side of her, she walked to Eyes, then sank down onto her knees. She frowned. "No. This is not him."

"Indeed," Shearjoy said. "He wasn't his usual cheery self."

Katryzna turned an unhappy look up, not appreciating what was apparently a joke. She said, "Was he cheery with you? Was he really good, at all?"

That made Shearjoy laugh. "I am quite sure you'd know better than me. But let's focus on the present. Will you tell me what happened in there?" He met Leigh-Ann's eye again, and she heard a promise in that question. Now Ikiri was over, as it must be, their only value was in offering that last piece of information.

"You want to know," she said, "maybe you shoulda come in." Katryzna hunched over Eyes, lost in her own thoughts, and Leigh-Ann raised her voice, hoping to alert her to their situation. "You're gonna want us silenced now, right?"

"Oh, you still have a use," Shearjoy said, happily. "I don't feel the children, as though they're gone, but we made that mistake before."

Leigh-Ann held his gaze while trying to assess her options in her peripheries. There was open ground either side of her, if she could weave between the trees. And avoid falling off a cliff. And she was certainly not quicker than him and would run out of breath in a second. Then there was Katryzna, distant and not up for running either. Best hope was for Reece to catch up. If he was even out here. Leigh-Ann had to draw this out, either way. She said, "All right. So, one minute I was in a valley, next drowning in a river, then we got a boy firing lightning bolts. Until Mason skewered his own damn kid."

Shearjoy's face lit up with wonder.

"Shit, child murder was exactly what you wanted for Christmas, huh?"

"And Zipporah?" Shearjoy said.

"You know, I didn't see what happened next," Leigh-Ann said. "What with everything falling apart. Last I saw, looked like she might pull her daddy apart with her mind. Which I reckon she'll do to you, too, if you hurt us."

"Possibly," Shearjoy said, and looked down to Katryzna. The woman hadn't moved. Seemed to be on another planet.

"Yeah, and you know Agent Tasker will be waiting on us," Leigh-Ann bowled on. Talking just to keep him from reaching murderous conclusions. "You know he's gonna be ready for you? Not gonna roll over on us going missing out here. You and your whole damn organisation, think you're all that? We got names and places, we got accounts – you ain't untouchable."

He replied with a smug smile, "On the contrary. Your best chance of getting to me is buried under that rubble." He pointed his blade to the fallen cave. "The world owes you gratitude, myself especially. The likelihood of ever finding worthy competition now is greatly –"

Katryzna moved quick as a cat, had the machete up and swinging faster than Shearjoy could react to. He dropped back with a face locked in alarm, one leg up and spurting blood from a severed ankle as his booted foot spun off in the other direction. He landed hard on his back and rolled to the side, reaching for the sword he'd dropped. Katryzna sprang forward and brought the machete down hard. Shearjoy's reaching hand came off, spinning past the sword, and he fell back with a scream as Katryzna pushed herself up. The second he turned, she jumped onto him with the machete in both hands pointed down, her full weight behind its hilt as it hit his chest.

Shearjoy made a startled sound, face locked in fear.

Not just scared, Leigh-Ann saw, as Katryzna leant hard on the blade, making sure he wasn't pulling it free. He couldn't move, let alone fight back, and he looked utterly confused. Never thought something like this was possible. All those lightning reflexes and psychic powers and government connections wasted. Blood oozed up over his chest, sprayed into Katryzna's face, and pumped weaker as the life in his eyes faded. She kept hold of his gaze the whole time. Finally, he was still, and she slumped back onto the grass.

Her attempts to catch her breath came quick, ragged, and Leigh-Ann realised she was crying. She crept closer, gingerly, and whispered, "Hey. You did it. You got that motherfucker."

Katryzna looked up at her, tears making streams of dirt and blood down her cheeks. She sniffed, hard, and said, "I do not care."

"I see that," Leigh-Ann replied.

"I do not care if he was bad," Katryzna expanded, shaking her head at Leigh-Ann's interpretation. She threw another look to Eyes. "He was my friend. My only friend."

"Sure he was," Leigh-Ann said. She put a hand cautiously on her shoulder, gave her a slight rub. "But you got us, too, now, right?"

Katryzna met her eyes again, uncertain.

"And we're gonna get out of here together, ain't we?" Leigh-Ann continued, realising she needed this – damn well needed this woman on side now, to help her out of here. "Can you walk?"

Katryzna scanned the clearing, unsure how she had got there. "Walk where?"

"Anywhere but here," Leigh-Ann urged. "I don't trust these things to stay dead."

She helped her up and the two stood there a second, looking at the bodies at their feet. Christ, Leigh-Ann really hoped the others got out alive.

Katryzna gave one more sniff and admitted, "Actually, I think I might collapse."

"Okay, but not here," Leigh-Ann insisted, and tried to move her. They shuffled in an awkward, sticky amble between the trees, onto a steep slope that made them skip down it. Leigh-Ann shouldered her way into trees so as not to fall over. Then she saw shapes moving ahead. People coming quickly through the trees. Hell, not more things from Ikiri? Shearjoy's back up?

She watched and waited, as Katryzna leant hard against her, catching her breath.

"Leigh!" Reece called out. "Leigh, tell me that's you!"

# 32

Henri carried Katryzna most of the way down the hill, with a quiet strength that Reece envied. He also guided them, somehow, back to Solomon's camp. It was a hard going, all of them low in energy, but they got there without incident – not even a hint of movement in the woods around them. There, they found a working Jeep and Henri took the wheel to drive them away. He was stonily focused for a long time, snatching glances at Katryzna, propped against the passenger door, then back to Leigh-Ann and Reece in back with the kids squeezed between them. Zip and Ezekiel huddled together for comfort, with her occasionally whispering reassurances and him nervously taking in the world like everything was new. His face was partially hidden behind that long hair. Reece resisted the urge to try and engage him, giving the kid space to adjust.

After a time, they reached some invisible threshold where Henri relaxed at the wheel. He said, "It's not there anymore. I don't know how I know it, but I'm sure." He twisted enthusiastically to the others in back. "Ikiri's border is gone. The point where madness grabbed people."

"It's all gone," Zip confirmed. "We took the power away."

Still toying with that feeling that the kids absorbed some of that, Reece wanted to ask where the rest of it had gone, but he wasn't sure he'd like the answer. Better no one knew, considering there might be more Legion-types who'd keep wanting to hunt such places down. Maybe it was just the cycle of things: a source of power like Ikiri bubbled up, swelled until it drove enough people out of their minds, then popped and reappeared elsewhere. Or maybe Scorecard had been dreaming, and there was only ever one Ikiri, which had burnt itself out, forever. Reece wasn't in the mood to talk about it, either way, and the conversation dropped.

They drove until dark, at which point Henri picked out a village where he managed to sweet-talk the villagers into putting them up for the night. They fed them and Ezekiel marvelled over the sensation of eating, and Zip giggled as she explained foods to him. A doctor gave Katryzna a look over; they surprised Reece with American medical supplies, a kit taken from a supply drop or something. She had a couple broken ribs, a big cut down her arm and side, and a possible concussion. Not life-threatening, all considered, but enough to leave her in a lot of pain. She'd retreated into herself, anyway. Leigh-Ann told Reece what happened after they got out, and he could appreciate where she was at. He'd lost people too, after all, and with things calming down, the time was coming to mourn them.

They set out again at first light, and soon hit a road that Reece told himself was familiar. A straight shot back to civilisation, for sure. His spirits lifted around the same time Katryzna stirred more, alert enough to make comments about how Leigh-Ann had saved her life. Leigh-Ann batted it off, saying Katryzna had done more than her fair share. The children laughed, starting to relax, too.

Reece took over the driving until dusk. They were close now, he guessed, so he offered to keep going through the night. Henri agreed, and they let the others sleep in back as they took shifts at the wheel. Finally, with dawn cresting through the trees, they pulled through the last villages and reached the river, where Henri arranged a ferry. He said they had to wait for a short while. Reece itched to keep going, to swim the river if necessary, to get back to Tasker and finally be done with this.

The group gathered around a scrappy bench by the pier, and he told them, "We'll be back in the hotel tonight. Rest up, be on the first plane out tomorrow, and settle everything. All of y'all welcome back in Cutjaw; it'll be a homecoming like you wouldn't believe."

"Because we won't be wanted felons no more?" Leigh-Ann said.

"Sam and Agent Tasker will sort something out." Reece waved that off. "Important thing is we'll all be away from here, and we can rest on the river or take in the sun on a trailer roof. Whatever we want. Road trip through the South, fire up a grill, jazz in the city, whatever. All y'all earned the good life and we'll sure as hell show it to you."

His eyes particularly lingered on Ezekiel, the dark child that had caused all this trouble. Not because he wanted to, Reece told himself. He'd had no sense over his own feelings, and there was a big bit of work left to set him on the right course now. He gave Reece a fleeting, uncertain look, and a thin smile, before looking away again.

Zip, meanwhile, slid off the bench and gave Reece a warm hug around his legs, before backing up. She looked sad, though, and he gave her a questioning look. She said, "I'm sorry, Reece. I want to stay with Henri. He will take us home."

"Come again?"

"Home," Zip said. "Our real home, it's here."

"Real home," Reece countered quickly, "is where your family at. And we family now, ain't we, Zip?" But he heard his own words. Henri was her actual family, and he stood behind the bench watching with Zip's same gently apologetic look. When had they even talked about this? Reece said, "You don't have to decide now."

"I do," Zip said. "I can't go back, I don't think."

"We ain't talking about going back," Reece said. "Cutjaw's not Stilt Town or that crusty British mill, there's a whole –"

"That's not what I mean," Zip said. "I don't want to talk to them. People like Agent Tasker or the Legion. I know he is good, but I'm –" She bit her lip, trying to come at this from another angle. "We have some gifts left. We can still do things, I can feel that, and I don't think they're things for . . . for *your* people. They wouldn't understand us. And Ezekiel needs time apart."

"Our people," Reece echoed, "are the same as yours. Living on the fringes."

"The fringes of something else," Zip said, with surprising clarity. "Through Ikiri, we felt *everything*, Reece. I can help here, I know it. I *want* to help here. There aren't as many —" She paused again, giving it thought. "It's better for me to help here."

"It's better for us," Ezekiel added meekly.

Reece took that in. Leigh-Ann looked sad as all hell but wasn't talking, and Katryzna was scarcely paying attention, face turned up to the night sky. He said, "Just like that? Gonna come on the ferry at least, right? Say bye to Agent Tasker?" Zip held his gaze to say no, and he bit his lip, shook his head. "Where y'all gonna go then? Not back in the woods."

"We'll follow the river back to Kinshasa," Henri said. "Maybe stop at my village on the way. I can show them where their mother grew up. They will be safe now. The Legion and the Ministry do not need to know they're still alive."

"Yeah," Reece said. "Yeah, I get that. But we'll know." He paused. Whatever Cutjaw was, it didn't exactly afford much more opportunity, and he was hardly a father-figure himself. He said, "That's what you wanna do, I trust you'll do it well. But you'll always have a home with us. All of you Cutjaw Kids, far as I'm concerned. You gotta write, be in touch. Promise me we ain't gonna be strangers."

"We have the internet," Henri said, with a smile. "Sometimes."

Reece held out a hand. Seemed the right time to do it, even if this wasn't quite goodbye. Henri shook, and he knew, without doubt, Zip and Ezekiel were going to be fine. Better than fine. They'd make their own land a better place. He took a breath and quickly patted his pockets. It was still there. He took out the harmonica and held it out to Zip. "You'll take care of this for me, then? Until we meet again."

Zip looked from the instrument up to him, and smiled then nodded, keenly. She took it, then launched forward into another hug. He hugged her back, keeping quiet, knowing if he said something more it was gonna come out teary.

"Well, *I* will visit Cutjaw," Katryzna interrupted, importantly. "Reece and me have unfinished business." She said that with a look to Leigh-Ann instead of him, and Leigh-Ann shot Reece a look of her own. Reece merely smiled back. One out of four wasn't bad.


Tasker had been sitting at the bar waiting for hours when a commotion finally alerted him to newcomers outside the hotel. He'd known something was coming, though he couldn't say what — he'd regained his senses more or less fully, and his wound had receded, hurting but not unnaturally, which meant something had changed. More than that, Ward had given him encouraging reports from France, and elsewhere, that suggested Ikiri's influence had calmed. But he couldn't be sure where that left him, or who was likely to come back from the forest.

The receptionist burst through the rec room doors with a worried expression, suggesting that question was about to be answered. He finished his whisky and took his pistol to go out to the lobby. Through the open entrance doors, he saw the armoured police vehicle, flanked by uniformed soldiers, now joined by a dusty Jeep. Two soldiers came inside, guns at their waists, calling orders over their shoulders. Just behind them, ushered by another couple of soldiers from behind, came Reece, Leigh-Ann, and finally Katryzna, who bared her teeth at the nearest soldier like she might bite him.

"Stand down." Tasker waved a hand, smiling broadly. The soldiers shifted to the sides, keeping careful watch. "They're friends."

The trio looked like they'd been rolling in dirt, and Katryzna in particular carried herself with pain, bandages visible through tears in her top – but their faces lit up to see him. Reece said, "Agent Tasker, you're up?"

"For the better part of a day," Tasker said. "And your friend in the UK is doing better too. I *hoped* you had something to do with that. Where's Zip? The others?"

Reece and Leigh-Ann exchanged a look like they hadn't settled on exactly what to tell him, but Katryzna said, "The others are all dead."

"No –" Tasker said, startled – that poor little child –

"Zip's not coming back," Reece clarified, to distinguish her from the *others*. "We met their uncle out there, Henri." He left it at that, with his eyes urging discretion. Tasker had to draw his own conclusion. Henri had got wrapped up in this again, but had made it away with Zip?

He picked up on another detail: "*Their* uncle?"

"Met Ezekiel," Leigh-Ann said. "And he's gone, too, before you ask."

"It's over," Reece said. "Near as we know, Ikiri's shut off. Nothing left. Found Mason out there, too, by the by. But him, Shearjoy, they're all done."

"Question remains," Leigh-Ann said, "if that actually makes us safe?"

Tasker took a moment to process the news. Even with those men dead, a massive network of threats remained – now without a leader. He said, "I took the liberty of securing this property. Shearjoy had two men here, but no more that I've been aware of. I think he intended to keep this expedition small, whereas a little Ministry funding proved persuasive with the locals. No promises what we'll find back home, though."

"If anyone tries anything, just tell them I cut Shearjoy to pieces," Katryzna said brightly. "That should make me the new boss, isn't it?" Rurik apparently scolded her as she snapped, "*I* think it's good news."

"You –" Tasker paused; better not to get into the details.

"What happened in Ikiri," Reece said, "I got a feeling it might've touched people that weren't even there. Maybe weakened the Legion all over, fingers crossed? Don't all make sense exactly, but what say we explain over dinner?"

"Sounds good to me," Tasker said. "Then I can see about getting you all home." He paused, and corrected, "*We'll* all be going home." His family were waiting, and, finally, he let himself believe they were safe.

He invited the group to freshen up in their rooms, and dismissed the soldiers, at least back to the perimeter. Reece shook his hand and winked on parting, and Leigh-Ann gave him a weary but satisfied smile. He had to marvel for a moment at the two unassuming musicians who'd come so far. They might be worth scouting, later, for future work. Then Tasker found he was left alone with Katryzna, as she lingered in the lobby.

With a hint of worry, she said, "Everyone gets to go home?"

Tasker considered her for a moment. Finway could be backed off now, surely, when they bit back against what remained of the Legion. But even if Katryzna walked free, the Ministry had been made aware of her, as well as whoever else might want to bring her down. He'd given it plenty of thought as his mind cleared – both her dark past and how she'd saved Helen and Rebecca – and he'd come to no useful conclusions, except to move on: "Name a destination. We'll see you there."

She looked up from under a heavy brow. "That is all?"

"What else do you want? I'm in your debt."

A slight smile crept onto her face, as she gave a sideways glance to her shoulder. "Rurik thinks I have corrupted you. He says you would have had no hesitation in bringing me to justice, before you met me."

"He's not wrong," Tasker said. "But my personal experience leads me to think you deserve better."

"He spoke with Reece, you know?" Katryzna recalled. "In the caves. That was strange, isn't it?"

"Yeah?" Tasker said. "What'd they talk about?"

"I forgot to ask. But I expect it was boring. Rurik is not a good conversationalist." She sneered at her shoulder. "You are *terrible*." But then she shook her head, mind wandering. "Maybe I will have a holiday, with Reece and –" She smiled, not bringing herself to name Leigh-Ann. Then she reconsidered. "I am bad, Sean. I *literally* chopped Shearjoy to pieces. And we all wanted to stop that child, but – who kills children? What is wrong with me?"

"Well," Tasker said, "from the fact you came back with them, I'm guessing you didn't do badly out there. And maybe you were dealt as bad a hand as him, starting out. Important thing is where we are now, and I have no complaints."

Katryzna turned her eyes away, momentarily abashed, then gave him another look. "Are you offering me a job?"

"What? I didn't –"

"Because important people *do* hire me. I am very expensive, I think. But I will not be like Eyes. If that strange little child could – if there's more ways for me to do what I am good at, but in a *clean* way? I can do what you do, can't I?"

Tasker's immediate thought, that it was unthinkable, was overshadowed by a question of *what if*. "We can have a long talk. About everything. There's no rush."

Katryzna nodded and said, "Okay. Talking is good. Rurik always says I should talk more. You can tell me about the Rostov fairies and everything."

Tasker froze and before he managed to put on a humouring smile he saw that she'd seen his shock. "I rambled when I was out of it?"

"About fairies," she confirmed. "You know something about Rostov."

"Yeah," he said, carefully. "Only what Scorecard already told you. It's a special city, and there are certain things there that people aren't used to. But they wouldn't change *you*, if that's your concern. You're special because of the way your mind works, if anything."

"What if I met fairies?"

Tasker hesitated. Everything in his training, and duty to the Ministry, said he couldn't touch this. But he did owe her a debt, and there were things about her he would like to know himself. He said, "That's for you to tell me, I suppose. Rurik's not real, is he? Doesn't have wings or touch things?"

"No," Katryzna said. "But what if he was when I first met him?"

"He had wings once? You met others like him?"

She shook her head.

Tasker kept a blank face, wondering himself. If she was an impressionable child, lost in the world herself, who was to say what she might have seen or done. Could she really have encountered a fairy, which left a lasting impression? Upset her mind enough to give her a resistance to Ikiri? Or something worse, less mundane? Then, what would it mean for her if she had? The Ministry would have questions. It was another reason for people to hunt her and cage her. Tasker finally settled for half-truths: "I wasn't thinking straight, Katryzna. If there's such a thing as fairies, I've never seen any, nor do I think anyone in the Ministry could help you there. Better we move, isn't it? Figure out what's next for you. Something good."

Katryzna watched his face for a moment, deciding whether or not to press for more, then she smiled, apparently satisfied. "I am glad you are not dead, Sean. But if you were, I want you to know, I would not wait years to avenge you, like I did with Eyes. I would not wait any time at all."

Tasker smiled back. In her way, he supposed, that was very high praise.

# Epilogue

**One Month Later**

Entering Melancony's Bar'n'Grill, Sam Ward silenced ten big drinkers who turned to her as one, letting the jukebox take over the hubbub with a twanging rock song. She could have had a big sign flashing over her head. Her navy suit was a far cry from the oil-stained shirts and caps worn by the hairy, burly patrons of the wood-panelled hall. Every surface looked sticky, from the floorboards to the thick bar to the walls papered with beer posters.

The stillness was supplanted by a man standing and saying, "Ms Ward, over here!"

Max Stomatt waved broadly, jostling empty beer bottles as his gut knocked the table. He grabbed at them clumsily, righting some and sending others rolling, then he gave up and stood to attention. Stomatt looked well, compared to last time she'd seen him; his skin had more colour, his patchily bleached hair had grown out to a more regular brown, and he was one of the best-dressed there, in a fine, long navy shirt.

"Max." Ward gingerly approached, wary that he was alone. "The doctor said you're okay without the cane?"

Stomatt grinned goofily, then frowned when she waited for an actual answer. "Why I wanna listen to a doctor? I know I'm fine." He pulled out a chair for her. "What you drinking? Beer?"

"Water would be fine. I'm driving."

"Who isn't?" Stomatt laughed. "Right, Clay?" The man he addressed, on a stool, groaned and slid down lower over the bar.

Another man said, loudly, "She the law, Sto? Looks like the law."

"Pretty lady wouldn't be talking to him otherwise," a moustached older gentleman in a bolo tie joked. Stomatt waved off a communal laugh and shouted an order for two beers. It was impressive, really, that a bar halfway between nowhere and a swamp was so busy this early in the afternoon.

Ward checked the empties on the table. "Sorry if I kept you waiting?"

"Nah," Stomatt said. "Would've been here anyway. But you come all this way and find Reece late? *That's* some bullshit. He oughta have picked you up from the airport."

"How've you been?" Ward asked. "No surprises with your wound?"

"No ma'am, no surprises." Stomatt laughed, though she wasn't sure why. "Everything's normal. Got a gig this evening, you know? Down Lake Charles. If Reece ain't put you on the list, I will." He paused as the bartender delivered two bottles of beer, eyeing Ward. Stomatt continued, "It's the third show since we got back, been on a roll. More people interested in the Kids since we got *note-or-iety* – few places in the Big Easy wanna book us, even. Shoulda gone monster-vigilante sooner."

"That's not what you're telling people, is it?" Ward asked with alarm.

"Pff, hell no, think we want to be called crazy? Only said a few things about finding a lost kid, returning her to her pop."

"And the situation with the Steer Trust?"

"Man, fuck them – they're under investigation themselves. They caused a stink while we were off in England, any angle they could find to intimidate Cutjaw. Some big-shot community lawyers took an interest, seeing as Steers turned up at Stilt Town with assault rifles. They –" Stomatt suddenly shot up, spilling his beer as Ward snatched hers to steady it. "There he is! You got a lady here waiting, the fuck's wrong with you?"

Ward twisted around to see Reece and Leigh-Ann entering the bar, him in tailored indigo trousers and a better-fitting shirt than Stomatt, her in stylishly torn jeans and a piped blazer. Like Stomatt's, Reece's hair was now a natural colour – dark brown – and neatly cut. They offered pleasantries and apologies, something to do with Trent Friendly tying them up in town, then Reece gave Ward a kiss on the cheek, ignoring her surprise and sitting.

"You're drinking Gilcrease?" Reece noted.

"Um." Ward looked at her untouched beer.

"Shit, you gotta be the classiest girl ever walked in here," Leigh-Ann said, "and two minutes with Sto, he drags you right down to his level."

"It's Gold Label, dammit Leigh," Stomatt said.

"It's fine," Ward said, as the bartender brought more beers for Reece and Leigh-Ann. They chinked bottles and Ward joined the toast with a sip herself. They watched for her reaction, then Leigh-Ann burst out laughing.

"Sorry, just this is the last thing I thought to see. Hunted by mutants and tripped in a river of crystals, but the director of the fantastic Ministry having a beer down Melancony's? That beats all."

"I'm only a regional director," Ward said, gamely, but Leigh-Ann bowled on.

"Bet that blue Chevy rental out there's yours, too? Probably had them laughing out they sides putting the little lady in the biggest car they could find."

"All right, bit of respect, Leigh, seeing she came all this way?" Reece said, though he was smiling himself. "But for sure we can show you a better time than this place, Sam. You'll hang around after the interview, right?"

"Excuse me?" Ward said.

"You didn't come a thousand miles just to talk shop?" Stomatt said, almost offended at the idea.

"More than a thousand miles from here to London, dumbass," Leigh-Ann said.

"Yeah, well she lives in Ordshaw, dumber-ass!"

"And she's starting to think even this meeting's too much," Reece said.

Ward smiled. She took her phone out and brought up the audio recorder, not that she was likely to record much of this discussion. She already had Tasker's reports for the details of what had happened, and didn't intend to expand on it officially, but she had her own ideas to explore. She said, "I actually spent the morning with the ILT in Alexandria – your version of the MEE."

"They got something to say about Stilt Town?" Reece asked.

"No, for the most part the investigation is closed; likewise the Ministry's investigations into other threads connecting to Ikiri."

"Until some other pricks decide they want a piece of that pie," Leigh-Ann said.

"It's unlikely. Novisan levels had reached an equilibrium out there; there's nothing left to investigate. But I have some good news – we've recovered, and relocated, about twenty people who formerly belonged to the PLU. General Solomon managed to get some of his people clear before the attack on his camp."

"We," Reece said, "meaning you sent agents out there?"

Ward paused. Tasker had disagreed with it, but she still felt justified, and said, "Just a clear-up operation. To get some ground readings and to be sure there was no sign of Zip." She gave Reece a look to invite more information there. Their accounts had been flippant about how Zip disappeared when the rest of them emerged from Ikiri, and the fact that Reece hadn't tirelessly searched for her suggested he wasn't too upset.

He took a sip of beer. "We all miss that kid more than you know."

"Especially as we got Christmas coming," Leigh-Ann sighed.

They weren't even hiding their casual attitudes: Ward was more sure than ever that Zip's unexplained disappearance was not the full story. "If Zip *did* come out of there, there are some very interesting issues we could discuss, that's all."

"Interesting to you," Leigh-Ann said. "I'd say the most interest to her would've been having a normal childhood, no? Don't see what right we got to expect anything more. Even if she's out there with her superpowers and all, what's it got to do with you? Bunch of interfering white boys fucked up that place first time around."

Ward gave the barrage a second to settle, then said, "Okay. As long as she's safe."

"You tell us," Reece said. "Any Legion psychos still hunting for her?"

"Well, it seems that Shearjoy's legacy has barely outlasted him. Deputy Director Finway has been cooperating, along with a few others from Mason's files. The individuals we've apprehended showed no unnatural resistance. And you haven't experienced anything unusual yourselves, since leaving Ikiri?"

"Still no superpowers," Leigh-Ann said. "But Brittany did bring my pan back, that was pretty unusual. Must've felt guilty having stole it, considering we coulda died."

"Like Caleb," Stomatt added, thoughtlessly, and Leigh-Ann gave him a nasty look as they hit a brief, uncomfortable silence.

"Had a nice funeral for him," Reece told Ward. "Got most of the town out. Had a big party for all of Stilt Town, too."

Ward nodded respectfully before continuing, "We really appreciate all you went through, of course. You have my deepest sympathies."

"Don't need sympathy," Leigh-Ann said, not unkindly. "Just some closure."

"Yes. My working theory is that those who were affected by Ikiri somehow relied on the existence of the site itself. So when it was . . . negated, it took some of that ability with it. Hence you were never touched quite the same way as the original expedition."

"Or we didn't pick anything up because Ezekiel was hoarding all the power," Reece said. "We'd have to find some survivors to be sure, wouldn't we?"

"If I'm honest, I'm not sure there are any left. Which is good and bad; we could have learnt a lot from them. The way they could locate each other, and sense certain things, it suggested a connection to novisan that would have helped our own research."

"As you try to map more weird shit?" Leigh-Ann said. "Shit's all wasted on you lot. Me, I was hoping on rapid-healing skills. Bet they do wonders for a hangover."

"Had big plans for Zip with her mind-reading, I did," Stomatt said. "Never even got the chance to hit the tables."

"Whatever they all had," Reece said, "chances are it wasn't all that. Mason and Flay hid their injuries, but they still got hurt bad. Still died. And Scorecard was amazed at how Zip could pinpoint a feeling at a distance; reckon the bulk of the Legion weren't up to much."

"Maybe," Ward agreed. "And as for Ikiri's specific powers – manipulating animals, resurrection, mass mind-control, some form of teleportation –"

"How'd they explain that gorilla appearing in England?" Stomatt blurted out. "Crept in on a boat?"

"They didn't," Ward said. "There were no traces of it outside ten miles from the mill. The same for the cats in France. They just appeared in the mountains."

"Same way we did," Reece said, "when we fell out of Ikiri. Got a theory on that?"

"Honestly, no. I'd hoped you might have *some* more clues."

"As in," Leigh-Ann said, "still hoped we'd have an in with Zip?"

Ward gave that a moment. She doubted there was much possibility there. "Actually, there's something else. Off the record. Have you heard from Katryzna at all?"

The trio went suspiciously quiet and Stomatt searched his beer bottle for distraction. Reece said, "She's Agent Tasker's girl, he's the one you wanna ask."

"He hasn't seen nor heard from her since she took him back to his family. She was an outlier, wasn't she? Ikiri had a different effect on her, or in some ways no effect. I've been digging into it and my feeling is that she can explain something about the nature of Ikiri."

"Hold up," Reece said, "you've been digging into it how? That girl's an enigma."

"Actually, if you ask the right people, her alleged crimes are quite well documented. She's just had powerful enough benefactors to avoid consequences. What's most interesting to me, though, is that you said *you* spoke to Rurik, Reece."

"Yeah. We all saw a lot in that place that didn't seem real."

"And there was mention that he came from Rostov. Was there anything else about him you remember? How he looked?"

"Wart on his face, I mention that?" Reece said, pointing to his own face.

"Anything else?" Ward asked.

Reece stared, more confused than trying to hide anything.

"Might help if you tell us your idea," Leigh-Ann said. "When we were discussing all the things we shouldn't tell you, we didn't figure you'd bring up an imaginary friend."

Ward gave a weak smile and said, "Katryzna spent time in a city called Rostov-von-Don in her youth, and it's known for energy fluctuations. Certain aspects about Rurik made me think . . ." She stopped. They had kept Ikiri secret well enough, but there was only so far she could go. "Maybe she was exposed to an unusual technology or substance that might have created a change in her."

"Unusual technology?" Leigh-Ann said. "Like they got aliens or something?"

"Radioactive crack?" Stomatt suggested.

"No, nothing like that –" Ward started.

"But a certain type of person from Rostov might indicate a connection," Reece summarised, astutely. "Sorry, but the guy was ordinary as they came. A normal height, too, not tiny like Katryzna said. But that place messed with our heads, what do I know, maybe I got small or it was all imagined. If I could tell you more I wouldn't trust it. You'd best be talking to her about that, more than any of us, I reckon?"

Ward didn't say it, letting her hopeful look give the answer.

Reece nodded lightly. "Well, that'd be assuming she'd have anything to do with us again, let alone want to talk to anyone official."

"I've kept much of this case close to my chest," Ward said. "Not just because of threats of Ministry corruption. I thought she might appreciate that."

"Sure, she might. Who can tell. Might be you'd be better off telling your bosses you're hunting for her, but just take the week off to sightsee. We got a concert tonight. Couple of concerts coming up. Maybe we can help you take the load off? Let your hair down, you never know who you might meet round here."

"Got room in my trailer if you need a place to crash," Leigh-Ann came in. "Show you Cutjaw ain't all bad. You know we got international appeal now, been on TV and all."

"On the news," Stomatt clarified, and Leigh-Ann snapped back, *that was the joke.*

As they insulted each other Ward held Reece's gaze, finding a clear invitation there. It should have been a quick refusal. She was not a field agent anymore and shouldn't strictly be here, with enough responsibilities waiting back in Ordshaw. But she knew they were more likely to talk to her than anyone else, and, intimidating as the woman's attention was, Katryzna would be too, if she was nearby. It could help explain some degree of novisan or even connect back to the tunnels under Ordshaw. Or it might just be a wasteful diversion with some people Ward had no more business being around.

A new tune came on the jukebox, something lively, opening right away with a flurry of brass instruments, and Stomatt excitedly cheered it, Leigh-Ann whooped. Some old favourite that finally united them. Their energy practically palpable, Ward relaxed back into her seat, hand teasing the cold, sweating beer glass, still looking into Reece's eyes. She cleared her throat and said, "Alright, I'll stay a while. Why the hell not?"

# A Note from the Author

This omnibus represents a story that I've spent half my life nailing down. While my original series following Katryzna, Reece Coburn and the Legion (the Brotherhood, back then) spanned half a dozen entries, I had never quite resolved Ikiri and Ezekiel until now. But here it is, a short journey compared to the background that went into it, and I hope you have enjoyed experiencing this world and these characters as much as I did. If it feels like there's questions left open, trust that it may be revisited in the future, though some is left for you to decide. After all, we cannot remove *all* the mystery from life.

From here, we're ending one journey and starting another – drawing the lessons of Ikiri into the wider world of Ordshaw. For the next thrilling entry in the series, check out *Dyer Street Punk Witches* today – or if you're yet to explore the series from the start, take a step back to where it began with *Under Ordshaw*. But if you have trouble parting with the Cutjaw Kids or Katryzna, they'll definitely be back for more. Difficult as this book was to pin down, two whole subplots were written and cut, including one focusing on an entirely new cast of characters – set in Cutjaw itself – so they'll find their way to light eventually. And I've still got those half dozen other novels from the past.

In the meantime, to help this book find more readers, please take a moment to leave a rating online; even just a few words can really help. You can review *The Ikiri Duology* online on your favourite store here and on Goodreads here.

**www.phil-williams.co.uk**

You can connect with me through:
Facebook: **www.facebook.com/philwilliamsauthor**
Twitter: **www.twitter.com/fantasticphil**
Email: **phil@phil-williams.co.uk**

# BOOK CLUB DISCUSSION QUESTIONS

The Ikiri Duology might seem like a mad, adventurous romp, but there's a lot going on in the background and between the two books. To help keep the fun going, you can enjoy discussing these questions with other readers or in your own ponderous head!

1.  This is a story of two halves, concerning a pair of opposed twins. What other examples of duality can you see in the story?
2.  If you were a Cutjaw Kid, what instrument would you play? And for more in-depth discussion, how does music fit into this tale of murderers and supernatural power?
3.  The story has an undercurrent of Christian language and imagery, and references to voodoo, yet none of the key characters are overtly religious. What role do you feel religion plays in the duology?
4.  Katryzna may not always be reliably connected to reality. What do you think her past life, and her relationship with Eyes, really looked like?
5.  There's no time for romance in a death-defying chase to save the world, but do you feel the many shifting relationships could've become something more?
6.  Ikiri itself is in the Congo, but the bulk of this story has a Western perspective. What does the story have to say about Imperialism and privilege?
7.  There are many powers connected to Ikiri, not all of which are fully explored. How do you interpret the way Ikiri worked?
8.  If you've read any other Ordshaw books, how do you feel Ikiri connects to them? If you haven't, can you predict where the story may go?

# ACKNOWLEDGEMENTS

*The Ikiri Duology* has a long history, and as such owes its current state to a lot of people who probably don't even know they were involved. Back when I first got access to the internet I pitched a lot of nonsense that would one day inform the evolution of the Legion of Ikiri, so first a big thanks to everyone that ever encountered that misguided alter-ego Zeke and the Brotherhood of EWW. My childhood friend Phil Rich, I believe, was involved when we first came up with that name. Something we might've put into a school newspaper, but the details escape me. Anyway, it's all part of it and thanks to everyone involved!

To more specific thanks, in the recent iterations, as always the biggest praise goes to Carrie O'Grady for editing this book and holding the ropey details to task. Any errors outstanding are my own. And many thanks to all those who helped me develop the cover design; in particular Stuart Bache and his SPF Cover Design community, who helped question the original design, and my fellow authors who are always supportive, Travis Riddle, Josh Erikson and Carol Park. Thanks to to my fellow authors who keep supporting me on my journey, Phil Parker, Jon Auerbach, Dave Woolliscroft, Kayleigh Nichol, Devin Madson, Richard Buxton and Steven McKinnon, and my always essential advance readers, Ami Agner, Adawia Asad, Sam Stokes, Heathyr Fields and the rest!

A growing group of book bloggers are also consistently pushing me on, some of whom offer me far more time than I deserve! Massive thanks to Justine Bergman of Whispers & Wonder, Lynn Williams of Lynn's Books, Jen and Timy on Rockstarlit Book Asylum, Mihir and the team on Fantasy Book Critic, Adam and Calvin and the Fantasy Book Review team, Maddalena of Space and Sorcery, and Sarah J. Higbee on Brainfluff. There are no doubt countless more that deserve thanks, and my humblest apologies to any I've missed out (but let me know, I'll get you next time . . . or edit it into a later edition and pretend it was here all along).

Finally, repeated thanks to my family. My siblings, Nick, Fran, Alex and Christen, who read my most pointless nonsense, and my parents for giving me the comfortable kind of life that let me slip away into this fancies. Above all, thanks to my wife, Marta, who makes it all make sense.

# About the Author

Phil Williams is the author of the Ordshaw, Estalia and Faergrowe series. Living in Sussex, UK with his wife, he also writes educational books and spends a great deal of time walking his impossibly fluffy dog, Herbert.

# Also by Phil Williams

**ORDSHAW SERIES**
*The Sunken City Trilogy*
UNDER ORDSHAW
BLUE ANGEL
THE VIOLENT FAE

THE CITY SCREAMS

*The Ikiri Duology*
KEPT FROM CAGES
GIVEN TO DARKNESS

THE ORDSHAW VIGNETTES VOL. 1

**ESTALIA SERIES**
WIXON'S DAY
BALFAIR'S CONFINEMENT
AFTAN WHISPERS

**FAERGROWE SERIES**
A MOST APOCALYPTIC CHRISTMAS

www.ingramcontent.com/pod-product-compliance
Lightning Source LLC
Chambersburg PA
CBHW030959190726
48285CB00004BB/1380